MARGARET ATWOOD

MARGARET ATWOOD

LIFE BEFORE MAN
CAT'S EYE

BLOOMSBURY

This edition first published 1993
Copyright © 1979 and 1988 by O. W. Toad Limited

The moral right of the author has been asserted

Bloomsbury Publishing Ltd, 2 Soho Square, London W1V 5DE

A CIP catalogue record for this book is available from the
British Library

ISBN 07475 1669-3

Typeset by Hewer Text Composition Services, Edinburgh
Printed in Great Britain by Clays Ltd, St Ives plc

LIFE BEFORE MAN

MARGARET ATWOOD

For G.

Acknowledgments

I would like to thank the following people who supplied comment, information, support, or other kinds of help: Carl Atwood, Lenore Mendelson Atwood, Ruth Atwood, Peter Boehm, Liz Calder, J. A. Donnan, Kate Godfrey Gibson, Jennifer Glossop, Beverley Hunter, Matla Kavin, Marie Kwas, Jay Macpherson, Marie Thompson, Fred J. Roberts, Rick Salutin, J. B. Salsberg, Savella Stchishin, Zenia Stchishin, Nan Talese, Mrs. Walpert, Jean Wachna, Mrs. Werblinsky.

I would also like to thank Donya Peroff, my tireless researcher for many years; Phoebe Larmore, my agent; and the many staff members of the Royal Ontario Museum and the Planetarium who gave me their time, especially Joanne Lindsay of Vertebrate Paleontology, who guided me through the Upper Cretaceous with a steady hand.

Note: *Lesje* is pronounced "Lashia".

Instead of a part of the organism itself, the fossil may be some kind of record of its presence, such as a fossilized track or burrow. . . . These fossils give us our only chance to see the extinct animals in action and to study their behaviour, though definite identification is only possible where the animal has dropped dead in its tracks and become fossilized on the spot.

— Björn Kurtén, *The Age of the Dinosaurs*

Look, I'm smiling at you, I'm smiling in you, I'm smiling through you. How can I be dead if I breathe in every quiver of your hand?

— Abram Tertz (Andrei Sinyavsky), *The Icicle*

Part One

Part One

ELIZABETH

I don't know how I should live. I don't know how anyone should live. All I know is how I do live. I live like a peeled snail. And that's no way to make money.

I want that shell back, it took me long enough to make. You've got it with you, wherever you are. You were good at removing. I want a shell like a sequined dress, made of silver nickels and dimes and dollars overlapping like the scales of an armadillo. Armored dildo. Impermeable; like a French raincoat.

I wish I didn't have to think about you. You wanted to impress me; well, I'm not impressed, I'm disgusted. That was a disgusting thing to do, childish and stupid. A tantrum, smashing a doll, but what you smashed was your own head, your own body. You wanted to make damn good and sure I'd never be able to turn over in bed again without feeling that body beside me, not there but tangible, like a leg that's been cut off. Gone but the place still hurts. You wanted me to cry, mourn, sit in a rocker with a black-edged handkerchief, bleeding from the eyes. But I'm not crying, I'm angry. I'm so angry I could kill you. If you hadn't already done that for yourself.

Elizabeth is lying on her back, clothes on and unrumpled, shoes placed side by side on the bedside rug, a braided oval bought at Nick Knack's four years ago when she was still interested in home furnishings, guaranteed genuine old lady twisted rags. Arms at her sides, feet together, eyes open. She can see part of the ceiling, that's all. A small crack runs across her field of vision, a smaller crack branching out from it. Nothing will happen, nothing will open, the crack will not widen and split and nothing will come through it. All it means is that the ceiling needs to be repainted, not this year but the next. Elizabeth tries to concentrate on the words "next year," finds she can't.

3

To the left there is a blur of light; if she turns her head she will see the window, hung with spider plants, the Chinese split-bamboo blind half rolled up. She called the office after lunch and told them she would not be in. She's been doing that too often; she needs her job.

She is not in. She's somewhere between her body, which is lying sedately on the bed, on top of the Indian print spread, tigers and flowers, wearing a black turtleneck pullover, a straight black skirt, a mauve slip, a beige brassiere with a front closing, and a pair of pantyhose, the kind that come in plastic eggs, and the ceiling with its hairline cracks. She can see herself there, a thickening of the air, like albumin. What comes out when you boil an egg and the shell cracks. She knows about the vacuum on the other side of the ceiling, which is not the same as the third floor where the tenants live. Distantly, like tiny thunder, their child is rolling marbles across the floor. Into the black vacuum the air is being sucked with a soft, barely audible whistle. She could be pulled up and into it like smoke.

She can't move her fingers. She thinks about her hands, lying at her sides, rubber gloves: she thinks about forcing the bones and flesh down into those shapes of hands, one finger at a time, like dough.

Through the door, which she's left open an inch out of habit, always on call like the emergency department of a hospital, listening even now for crashes, sounds of breakage, screams, comes the smell of scorching pumpkin. Her children have lighted their jack-o'-lanterns, even though there are still two days before Halloween. And it isn't even dark yet, though the light at the side of her head is fading. They love so much to dress up, to put on masks and costumes and run through the streets, through the dead leaves, to knock on the doors of strangers, holding out their paper bags. What hope. It used to touch her, that excitement, that fierce joy, the planning that would go on for weeks behind the closed door of their room. It used to twist something in her, some key. This year they are remote from her. The soundless glass panel of the hospital nursery where she would stand in her housecoat for each of them in turn, watching the pink mouths open and close, the faces contort.

4

She can see them, they can see her. They know something is wrong. Their politeness, their evasion, is chilling because it's so perfectly done.

They've been watching me. They've been watching us for years. Why wouldn't they know how to do it? They act as though everything is normal, and maybe for them it is normal. Soon they will want dinner and I will make it. I will lower myself down from this bed and make the dinner, and tomorrow I will see them off to school and then I will go to the office. That is the proper order.

Elizabeth used to cook, very well too. It was at the same time as her interest in rugs. She still cooks, she peels some things and heats others. Some things harden, others become softer; white turns to brown. It goes on. But when she thinks about food she doesn't see the bright colors, red, green, orange, featured in the *Gourmet Cookbook.* Instead she sees the food as illustrations from those magazine articles that show how much fat there is in your breakfast. Dead white eggs, white strips of bacon, white butter. Chickens, roasts and steaks modeled from bland lard. That's what all food tastes like to her now. Nevertheless she eats, she overeats, weighting herself down.

There's a small knock, a step. Elizabeth moves her eyes down. In the oak-framed oval mirror above the dressing table she can see the door opening, the darkness of the hall behind, Nate's face bobbing like a pale balloon. He comes into the room, breaking the invisible thread she habitually stretches across the threshold to keep him out, and she is able to turn her head. She smiles at him.

"How are you, love?" he says. "I've brought you some tea."

5

NATE

He doesn't know what "love" means between them any more, though they always say it. For the sake of the children. He can't remember when he started knocking at her door, or when he stopped considering it his door. When they moved the children into one room together and he took the vacant bed. The vacant bed, she called it then. Now she calls it the extra bed.

He sets the cup of tea down on the night table, beside the clock radio that wakes her every morning with cheerful breakfast news. There's an ashtray, no butts; why should there be? She doesn't smoke. Though Chris did.

When Nate slept in this room there were ashes, matches, ringed glasses, pennies from his pockets. They used to save them in a peanut butter jar and buy small gifts with them for each other. Mad money, she called it. Now he still empties the pennies out of his pockets every night; they accumulate like mouse droppings on top of the bureau in his room, his own room. Your own room, she calls it, as if to keep him in there.

She looks up at him, her face leached of color, eyes dark-circled, smile wan. She doesn't have to try; she always tries.

"Thanks, love," she says. "I'll get up in a minute."

"I'll make dinner tonight, if you like," Nate says, wanting to be helpful, and Elizabeth agrees listlessly. Her listlessness, her lack of encouragement, infuriates him, but he says nothing, turns and closes the door softly behind him. He made the gesture and she acts as if it means nothing.

Nate goes to the kitchen, opens the refrigerator and pokes through it. It's like rummaging through a drawer of jumbled clothes. Leftovers in jars, bean sprouts gone bad, spinach in a plastic bag starting to decay, giving off that smell of decomposing lawn. No use expecting Elizabeth to clean it. She used

6

to clean it. She will clean other things these days, but not the refrigerator. He'll tidy it up himself, tomorrow or the next day, when he gets around to it.

Meanwhile he'll have to improvise dinner. It's no large trial, he's often helped with the cooking, but in former times – he thinks of it as the olden days, like a bygone romantic era, like some Disneyland movie about knighthood – there were always supplies. He does most of the grocery shopping himself now, carting a bag or two home in the basket of his bicycle, but he forgets things and gaps are left in the day: no eggs, no toilet paper. Then he has to send the kids to the corner store, where everything is more expensive. Before, before he sold the car, it wasn't such a problem. He took Elizabeth once a week, on Saturdays, and helped her put the cans and frozen packages away when they got home.

Nate picks the dripping spinach out of the vegetable crisper and carries it to the garbage can; it oozes green liquid. He counts the eggs: not enough for omelettes. He'll have to make macaroni and cheese again, which is all right since the kids love it. Elizabeth will not love it but she will eat it, she'll wolf it down absently as if it's the last thing on her mind, smiling like a slowly grilling martyr, staring past him at the wall.

Nate stirs and grates, stirs and grates. An ash drops from his cigarette, missing the pot. It isn't his fault Chris blew his head off with a shotgun. A shotgun: this sums up the kind of extravagance, hysteria, he's always found distasteful in Chris. He himself would have used a pistol. If he were going to do it at all. What gets him is the look she gave him when the call came through: *At least he had the guts. At least he was serious.* She's never said it of course, but he's sure she compares them, judges him unfavorably because he's still alive. Chickenshit, to be still alive. No balls.

Yet at the same time, still without saying it, he knows she blames him, for the whole thing. If you had only been this or that, done this or that – he doesn't know what – it wouldn't have happened. I wouldn't have been driven, forced, compelled . . . that's her view, that he failed her, and this undefined failure of his turned her into a quivering mass of helpless flesh, ready to attach itself like a suction cup to the first crazy man who ambled along and said, You have nice tits. Or whatever it was Chris did

7

say to get her to open the Love Latch on her brassiere. Probably more like, You have nice ramifications. Chess-players are like that. Nate knows: he used to be one himself. Nate can never figure out why women find chess-playing sexy. Some women.

So for a week now, ever since that night, she's spent the afternoons in there lying on the bed that used to be his, half his, and he's been bringing her cups of tea, one each afternoon. She accepts them with that dying swan look of hers, the look he can't stand and can't resist. It's your fault, darling, but you may bring me cups of tea. Scant atonement. And an aspirin out of the bathroom and a glass of water. Thank you. Now go away somewhere and feel guilty. He's a sucker for it. *Like a good boy.*

And he was the one, not her, not Elizabeth, who had to go and identify the body. As her stricken eyes said, she could hardly be expected to. So dutifully he had gone. Standing in that apartment where he'd been only twice but where she had been at least once every week for the past two years, fighting nausea, nerving himself to look, he'd felt that she was there in the room with them, a curve in space, a watcher. More so than Chris. No head left at all, to speak of. The headless horseman. But recognizable. Chris's expression had never really been in that heavy flat face of his; not like most people's. It had been in his body. The head had been a troublemaker, which was probably why Chris had chosen to shoot at it instead of at some other part of himself. He wouldn't have wanted to mutilate his body.

A floor, a table, a chess set by the bed, a bed with what they called the trunk and limbs lying on it; Nate's other body, joined to him by that tenuous connection, that hole in space controlled by Elizabeth. Chris had put on a suit and tie, and a white shirt. Nate, thinking of that ceremony – the thick hands knotting the tie, straightening it in the mirror, God, his shoes were shined even – wanted to cry. He put his hands in his jacket pockets; his fingers closed on pennies, the house key.

"Any reason why he left your number on the table?" the second policeman said.

"No," Nate said. "We were friends of his, I guess."

"Both of you?" the first policeman said.

"Yes," said Nate.

* * *

Janet comes into the kitchen as he's sliding the casserole dish into the oven.

"What's for dinner?" she asks, adding "Dad," as if to remind him who he is.

Nate finds this question suddenly so mournful that for a moment he can't answer. It's a question from former times, the olden days. His eyes blur. He wants to drop the casserole on the floor and pick her up, hug her, but instead he closes the oven door gently.

"Macaroni and cheese," he says.

"Yum," she says, her voice remote, guarded, giving a careful imitation of pleasure. "With tomato sauce?"

"No," he says, "there wasn't any."

Janet runs her thumb across the kitchen table, squeaking it on the wood. She does this twice. "Is Mum resting?" she says.

"Yes," Nate says. Then, fatuously, "I took her a cup of tea." He puts one hand behind him, against the kitchen counter. They both know what to avoid.

"Well," Janet says in the voice of a small adult, "I'll be seeing you soon." She turns and goes back through the kitchen door.

Nate wants to do something, perform something, smash his hand through the kitchen window. But on the other side of the glass there's a screen. That would neutralize him. Whatever he does now will be absurd. What is smashing a window compared with blowing off your head? *Cornered.* If she'd planned it, she couldn't have done it better.

Friday, October 29, 1976

LESJE

Lesje is wandering in prehistory. Under a sun more orange than
her own has ever been, in the middle of a swampy plain lush with
thick-stalked plants and oversized ferns, a group of bony-plated
stegosaurs is grazing. Around the edges of this group, protected
by its presence but unrelated to it, are a few taller, more delicate
camptosaurs. Cautious, nervous, they lift their small heads from
time to time, raising themselves on their hind legs to sniff at the
air. If there is danger they will give the alarm first. Closer to
her, a flock of medium-sized pterosaurs glides from one giant
tree-fern to another. Lesje crouches in the topmost frond-cluster
of one of these trees, watching through binoculars, blissful,
uninvolved. None of the dinosaurs takes the slightest interest
in her. If they do happen to see or smell her, they will not notice
her. She is something so totally alien to them that they will not
be able to focus on her. When the aborigines sighted Captain
Cook's ships, they ignored them because they knew such things
could not exist. It's the next best thing to being invisible.

Lesje knows, when she thinks about it, that this is probably
not everyone's idea of a restful fantasy. Nevertheless it's hers;
especially since in it she allows herself to violate shamelessly
whatever official version of paleontological reality she chooses.
In general she is clear-eyed, objective, and doctrinaire enough
during business hours, which is all the more reason, she feels,
for her extravagance here in the Jurassic swamps. She mixes
eras, adds colors: why not a metallic blue Stegosaurus with red
and yellow dots instead of the dull greys and browns postulated
by the experts? Of which she, in a minor way, is one. Across
the flanks of the camptosaurs pastel flushes of color come and
go, reddish pink, purple, light pink, reflecting emotions like
the contracting and expanding chromatophores in the skins
of octopuses. Only when the camptosaurs are dead do they
turn grey.

10

After all it's not so fanciful; she's familiar with the coloration of some of the more exotic modern lizards, not to mention mammalian variations such as the rumps of mandrills. Those bizarre tendencies must have developed from somewhere.

Lesje knows she's regressing. She's been doing that a lot lately. This is a daydream left over from her childhood and early adolescence, shelved some time ago in favor of other speculations. Men replaced dinosaurs, true, in her head as in geological time; but thinking about men has become too unrewarding. Anyway, that part of her life is settled for the time being. Settled, as in: the fault settled. Right now *men* means William. William regards them both as settled. He sees no reason why anything should ever change. Neither does Lesje, when she considers it. Except that she can no longer daydream about William, even when she tries; nor can she remember what the daydreams were like when she did have them. A daydream about William is somehow a contradiction in terms. She doesn't attach much importance to this fact.

In prehistory there are no men, no other human beings, unless it's the occasional lone watcher like herself, tourist or refugee, hunched in his private fern with his binoculars, minding his own business.

The phone rings and Lesje jumps. Her eyes spring open, the hand holding her coffee mug flies into the air, fending off. She's one of those people unduly startled by sudden noises, she tells her friends. She sees herself as a timorous person, a herbivore. She jumps when people come up behind her and when the subway guard blows his whistle, even when she knows the people are there or the whistle will be blown. Some of her friends find this endearing but she's aware that others find it merely irritating.

But she doesn't like being irritating, so she tries to control herself even when nobody else is with her. She puts her coffee mug down on the table – she'll wipe the spill up later – and goes to answer the phone. She doesn't know who she expects it to be, who she wants it to be. She realizes that these are two different things.

* * *

11

By the time she picks up the phone the line is already open. The hum on the phone is the city's hum, reverberating outside the plate glass, amplified by the cement cliffs that face her and in which she herself lives. A cliff dweller, cliff hanger. The fourteenth level.

Lesje holds the phone for a minute, listening to the hum as if to a voice. Then she puts it down. Not William in any case. He's never phoned her without having something to say, some pragmatic message. I'm coming over. Meet me at. I can't make it at. Let's go to. And later, when they'd moved in together, I'll be back at. And lately, I won't be back until. Lesje considers it a sign of the maturity of the relationship that his absences do not disturb her. She knows he's working on an important project. Sewage disposal. She respects his work. They've always promised to give each other a lot of room.

This is the third time. Twice last week and now. This morning she mentioned it, just as a piece of conversation, to the girls at work, women at work, flashing her teeth in a quick smile to show she wasn't worried about it, then covering her mouth immediately with her hand. She thinks of her teeth as too large for her face: they make her look skeletal, hungry.

Elizabeth Schoenhof was there, in the cafeteria where they always went at ten-thirty if they weren't working too hard. She's from Special Projects. Lesje sees a fair amount of her because fossils are one of the more popular museum features and Elizabeth likes to work them in. This time she'd come over to their table to say she needed a little of Lesje's material for a display-case series. She wanted to juxtapose some of the small items from Canadiana with natural objects from the same geographical regions. *Artifact and Environment*, she was calling it. She could use some stuffed animals to go with the pioneer axes and traps, and a few fossil bones for atmosphere.

"This is an old country," she said. "We want people to see that."

Lesje is against this eclectic sort of promotion, though she sees the need for it. The general public. Still, it trivializes, and Lesje registered an inner objection when Elizabeth asked, in that competent maternal manner of hers, whether Lesje couldn't find

12

her some really interesting fossils. Weren't all fossils interesting? Lesje said politely that she would see what she could do.

Elizabeth, adept at cataloguing the reactions of others, for which Lesje holds her in some awe – she herself, she feels, cannot do this – explained carefully that she meant visually interesting. She really would appreciate it, she said.

Lesje, always responsive to appreciation, warmed. If Elizabeth wanted some outsize phalanges and a cranium or two she was welcome to them. Besides, Elizabeth looked terrible, white as a sheet, though everyone said she was coping marvelously. Lesje can't imagine herself in that situation, so she can't predict how she herself would cope. Of course everyone knew, it had been in the papers, and Elizabeth had not made much of an effort to hide the facts while it was going on.

They all scrupulously avoided mentioning Chris or anything relating to him in front of Elizabeth. Lesje caught herself blinking when Elizabeth said she wanted to use a flintlock in the display. She herself wouldn't have chosen guns. But perhaps these blind spots were necessary, were part of coping marvelously. Without them, how could you do it?

To change the subject she said brightly, "Guess what? I've been getting anonymous phone calls."

"Obscene?" Marianne asked.

Lesje said no. "Whoever it is just lets the phone ring and then when I answer he hangs up."

"Wrong number, probably," Marianne said, her interest flagging.

"How do you know it's a he?" Trish asked.

Elizabeth said, "Excuse me." She stood up, paused for a moment, then turned and walked steadily as a somnambulist across the floor towards the door.

"It's awful," Trish said. "She must feel terrible."

"Did I say something wrong?" Lesje asked. She hadn't meant to.

"Didn't you know?" Marianne said. "He used to phone her like that. At least once a night, for the last month. After he quit here. She told Philip Burroughs, oh, quite a while before it happened. You'd think she would've known it was building up to something."

Lesje blushed and brought her hand up to the side of her

face. There were always things she didn't know. Now Elizabeth would think she'd done that on purpose and would dislike her. She couldn't figure out how that particular piece of gossip had slipped by her. They'd probably talked about it right here at this table and she hadn't been paying attention.

Lesje goes back to the living room, sits down in the chair beside her spilled coffee, and lights a cigarette. When she smokes she doesn't inhale. Instead she holds her right hand in front of her mouth with the cigarette between the first two fingers, thumb along the jawbone. That way she can talk and laugh in safety, blinking through the smoke that rises into her eyes. Her eyes are her good point. She can see why they wore veils, half-veils, in those Middle Eastern countries. It had nothing to do with modesty. Sometimes when she's alone she holds one of her flowered pillowcases across the lower half of her face, over the bridge of her nose, that nose just a little too long, a little too curved for this country. Her eyes, dark, almost black, look back at her in the bathroom mirror, enigmatic above the blue and purple flowers.

ELIZABETH

Elizabeth sits on the grey sofa in the underwater light of her living room, hands folded in her lap sedately, as if waiting for a plane. The light here is never direct, since the room faces north; she finds this peaceful. The sofa is not really grey, not only grey; it has a soft mauve underfigure, a design like veining; a batik. She chose it because it didn't hurt her eyes.

On the mushroom-colored rug, near her left foot, there's a scrap of orange crêpe paper, a spillover from something the children are doing in their room. A scrap of flame, jarring. But she lets it lie. Ordinarily she would bend, pick it up, crumple it. She doesn't like anyone disturbing this room, the children or Nate with his trails of sawdust and spots of linseed oil. They can make as much mess as they like in their own rooms, where she doesn't have to cope with it. She once thought of having plants in this room as well as in her bedroom but decided against it. She doesn't want anything else she will have to take care of.

She closes her eyes. Chris is in the room with her, a weight, heavy, breathless, like the air before a thunderstorm. Sultry. Sultan. Sullen. But it isn't because he's dead, he was always like that. Backing her against the door, his arms clamping around her, shoulders massive when she tried to push him off, face heavily down on hers, force of gravity. Leaning on her. I won't let you go yet. She hates it when anyone has power over her. Nate doesn't have that kind of power, he never had. She married him easily, like trying on a shoe. She's in the room on Parliament Street, drinking wine, the slopped glasses making mulberry rings on the linoleum of his rented table, she can see the design on the oilcloth, tasteless wreaths of flowers, lime-green on yellow, as if it's been burnt into her eyes. They always whisper in that room, though there's no need to. Nate is several miles away from them and he knows where she is anyway, she leaves the number in case of an emergency. Their whispers and his eyes with their

15

flat hot surfaces, a glint like nailheads. Copperheads. Pennies on the eyes. Gripping her hand across the table as though, if he lets go, she will slide down past the edge of the table, the edge of some cliff or quicksand, and be lost forever. Or he will.

Listening, her eyes on the wrinkled surface of the table, the squat candle he bought from some street peddler, the deliberately tacky plastic flowers and the owl he'd stolen from work, not even mounted, eyeless, his macabre joke. The wreaths turning slowly on the surface of the table as on an oily sea, floating out; somewhere they did that as a blessing. Then rising, the violence in his hands held back, everything held back, falling, salt body stretching along her, dense as earth, on that bed she would never stay to sleep in, the sheets always a little damp, smoky, holding back until nothing could be held back. She has never seen that room by daylight. She refuses to imagine what it looks like now. The mattress bare. Someone would have come, cleaned the floor.

She opens her eyes. She must focus on something simple and clear. There are three bowls on the sideboard, pinkish mauve, porcelain, Kayo's, he's one of the best. She's confident in her taste, she knows enough to have earned that confidence. The sideboard is pine, she bought it before pine became fashionable, had it stripped down before having things stripped down became fashionable. She couldn't afford it now. It's a good piece, the bowls are good pieces. She wouldn't have anything in this room that was not a good piece. She lets her eyes slide over the bowls, over their subtle colors, their slightly asymmetrical curves, wonderful to have that sense, where to be off balance. There's nothing in them. What could you possibly put into such bowls? Not flowers or letters. They were meant to hold something else, they were meant for offerings. Right now they hold their own space, their own beautifully shaped absence.

There was your room and there was everything else outside, and that barrier between the two. You carried that room around with you like a smell, it was a smell like formaldehyde and the insides of old cupboards, mousy, secretive, like musk, dusky and

16

rich. Whenever I was with you I was in that room, even when we were outside, even when we were here. I'm in it now, only now you've locked the door, brown door with scaling paint, varnish, the brass-colored lock and the chain, two bullet holes through the wood where, you told me, they'd been shooting in the hallway the week before. It wasn't a safe neighborhood. I always took taxis, asked the driver to wait until I'd pressed the buzzer and was safe in the foyer with its gap-toothed mosaic floor. Safe, always a joke. The door's locked, not for the first time; you don't want me ever to get out. You always knew I wanted to get out. But at the same time we were conspirators, we knew things about each other no one else will ever know. In some ways I trust you more than I've ever trusted anyone.

I have to go now, she says. He's twisting a length of her hair, twisting and untwisting it. He runs his index finger between her lips, left-handed, across her teeth; she can taste wine and her own sweat, taste of herself, blood from a bitten lip, she no longer knows whose.

Why, he says.

I just have to. She doesn't want to say *the children* because it will make him angry. But she doesn't want them to wake up and not know where she is.

He doesn't answer; he keeps twisting and untwisting her hair, his own hair brushing her neck like feathers, his fingers sliding now over her chin and throat, as if he's deaf, as if he can no longer hear her.

17

LESJE

Lesje is walking beside William, hand in cool hand. There are no dinosaurs here; only similar walkers, on the prowl like themselves, an apparently aimless prowl through the lighted grid of the central city. In passing, Lesje glances into the windows of dress shops, department stores, appraising the cadaverous mannequins who stand with their pelvises thrust forward, hands angular on hips, legs apart, one knee bent. If these bodies were in motion they would be gyrating, jerking, a stripper's orgasmic finale. Since they are frozen plaster and wire, however, they are in good taste.

Lesje has been spending quite a lot of time lately in these same shops, on her way home from work. She flips through the racks, looking for something that might become her, something she might become. She almost never buys anything. The dresses she tries on are long, flowing, embroidered, very different from the denims and subdued classics she habitually wears. Some with full skirts; the peasant look. How her grandmother would laugh. That little sound, like a door creaking, that used to come from behind her tiny walnut-colored hands.

She's thought about getting her ears pierced. Sometimes, after checking through the dresses, she goes to the perfume counter and tries the testers on her wrists. William says he isn't interested in clothes. His one stipulation is that she must not cut her hair. This is all right, since she doesn't want to cut it. She's not betraying anything.

William asks her if she'd like something to drink. She says she wouldn't mind a coffee. They didn't come out to drink; they'd intended to go to a movie. But they spent too much time poring over the entertainment pages of the *Star*, trying to decide. Each wanted the other to take the responsibility. Lesje wanted to see a re-run of *King Kong* at the university film series. William finally confessed that he'd always wanted to see *Jaws*. Lesje didn't mind, she could see how well they'd done the shark, which was after all one of the more primitive life forms still extant. She asked William if he knew that sharks had floating stomachs and if you suspended one by its tail it would become paralyzed. William didn't know this. By the time they got to *Jaws* it was sold out and *King Kong* had started half an hour earlier. So they're walking instead.

Now they're sitting at a little white table on the second level of the Colonnade. William is having a Galliano, Lesje a Viennese coffee. Gravely she licks whipped cream from her spoon, while William, having forgiven her for causing him to miss *Jaws*, is explaining his latest problem, which has to do with whether more energy is lost in the long run by using the heat from incinerated garbage to run steam generators than by just letting the stuff go up in smoke. William is a specialist in environmental engineering, though the small raucous voice that occasionally makes itself heard behind Lesje's studiously attentive face refers to it as sewage disposal. However, Lesje admires William's job and agrees with him that it's more important to the survival of the human race than hers is. Which is true, they're all in danger of drowning in their own shit. William will save them. You can see it just by looking at him, his confidence, his enthusiasm. He orders another Galliano and expounds on his plans for generating methane gas from decomposing excrement. Lesje murmurs applause. Among other things, it would solve the oil crisis.

(The real question is: Does she care whether the human race survives or not? She doesn't know. The dinosaurs didn't survive and it wasn't the end of the world. In her bleaker moments, of which, she realizes, this is one, she feels the human race has it coming. Nature will think up something else. Or not, as the case may be.)

William is talking about dung beetles. He's a good man; why is she so unappreciative? Dung beetles were once of interest to her. The way in which Australia solved its pasturage problem – layers of dried sheep raisins and cow pads keeping the grass from growing – by a massive importation of giant African dung beetles, was once a beacon of hope. Like William, she saw it as elegant ecological problem-solving. But she's heard it before, and before. Finally it's William's optimism, his belief that every

19

catastrophe is merely a problem looking for a brilliant solution, that gets to her. She thinks of William's brain as pink-cheeked, hairless. William Wasp, she used to call him, fondly enough, before she realized that he found it a racial slur.

"I don't call you Lesje Latvian," he'd said, aggrieved.

"Lithuanian," she said. "Litvak." William had trouble with the Baltic states. "I wouldn't mind if you did." But she was lying. "Can I call you William Canadian?"

Billy Boy, charming Billy. Where have you been all the day. Shortly after this they had an argument about the Second World War. It's William's opinion that the British and, of course, the Canadians, including his father, who was a captain in the Navy, making William the world's authority, entered the war from superior moral principles, to save the Jews from being reduced to gas molecules and vest buttons. Lesje disputed this view. Saving a few Jews was a sideline, she said. Really it was grab and counter-grab. Hitler could have frizzled Jews to his heart's content if he hadn't snatched Poland and invaded the Netherlands. William found this point of view ungrateful. Lesje then produced the corpse of her Aunt Rachel, who hadn't been saved, whose anonymous gold teeth had plumped some Swiss bank account. What reply to this indignant ghost? William, routed, went into the bathroom to shave. Lesje felt a little cheap.

(Then there was her other grandmother, her mother's mother, who'd said: We welcomed Hitler at first. We thought he would be better than the Russians. You see what's happened now. Which was ironic, since her husband had been practically a Communist, back in the Ukraine. That's why they had to leave: the politics. He wouldn't go to church even, he wouldn't put a foot in a church. I spit on the church, he'd say. Long after his death Lesje's grandmother was still weeping about it.)

She's noticed recently that she's no longer waiting for William to propose to her. Once she thought it would follow as a matter of course. You lived with someone first, to try it out. Then you got married. That's what her friends from university were doing. But William, she now sees, finds her impossibly exotic. True, he loves her, in a way. He bites her on the neck when they make love. Lesje doesn't think he'd let himself go like that with a woman of, as she once caught him putting it, his own kind. They would make love like two salmon, remotely, William fertilizing the cool silvery eggs from a suitable distance. He'd think of his children as *issue*. His issue, uncontaminated.

This is the crux: William does not want to have a child by her. With her. Though she's hinted; though she could spring one on him unannounced. Guess what, William, I have a bun in the oven. Your bun. Well, he'd say, take it out.

Oh, very unfair to William. He admires her mind. He encourages her to use technical language in front of his friends. It gives him a hard-on when she says Pleistocene. He tells her she has beautiful hair. He gazes into her sloe eyes. He's proud of her as a trophy and as a testimony to his own wide-mindedness. But what would his family in London, Ontario, think?

Lesje pictures this family as numerous and pinkish blond. The members of it spend most of their time playing golf, between strenuous rounds of tennis. When they aren't doing this they gather on terraces – she sees them doing this even in the winter – and drink cocktails. They are polite to strangers but make remarks behind their backs, such as, "Fellow doesn't know who his own grandfather is." Lesje is confident about her grandfathers; it's the great-grandfathers that are the problem.

She knows William's family isn't really like this. But, like her parents, she grants extra rungs on the ladder to anyone with an authentic British name who doesn't noticeably live on a park bench. She knows she shouldn't do this. William's family probably doesn't have much more money than her own family does. They only have more pretensions.

Once she'd been afraid to meet them, fearing their verdict. Now she'd love to. She'd paint her teeth gold and come in jingling a tambourine and stamping her feet, her head covered with fringed shawls. Living up to their horrified expectations. Her grandmother clapping diminutive mole-paw hands together, creaking with laughter, cheering her on. Blood will tell. "We was talking to God when they was talking to pigs." As if age, in people as in cheese, was a plus.

"There were no dung beetles in the Neo-Devonian," Lesje says.

William is brought up short. "I don't follow you," he says.

"I was just wondering," she says. "About the parallel evolution of dung beetles and shit. For instance: which came first, man or venereal disease? I suppose hosts always have to precede

21

their parasites, but is that really true? Maybe man was invented by viruses, to give them a convenient place to live."

Wow, Margaret!

William decides she's joking. He laughs. "You're putting me on," he says. He thinks she has an offbeat sense of humor.

An Albertosaurus, or – the name Lesje prefers – a Gorgosaurus, pushes through the north wall of the Colonnade and stands there uncertainly, sniffing the unfamiliar smell of human flesh, balancing on its powerful hind legs, its dwarfed front legs with their razor claws held in close to its chest. In a minute William Wasp and Lesje Litvak will be two lumps of gristle. The Gorgosaurus wants, wants. It's a stomach on legs, it would swallow the world if it could. Lesje, who has brought it here, regards it with friendly objectivity.

Here's a problem for you, William, Lesje thinks. Solve this.

NATE

He hasn't worn a raincoat. The light drizzle beads his heavy sweater, his beard, collects on his forehead, begins to trickle. Since he has no raincoat, since he's wet and shivering, how can she refuse to let him in?

He parks his bike in the driveway, chaining it to the lilac bush, snapping the lock. As usual; but it isn't as usual. He hasn't seen her for a month. Four weeks. Tears from her, hangdog shrugs from him, and a lot of afternoon soap stuff from both of them, including *It's better this way.* She's phoned him a couple of times since, wanting him to come over, but he's avoided it. He doesn't like doing the same thing over again, he doesn't like predictability. This time, however, he phoned her.

She lives in an A, 32A, a flat in one of the big older houses east of Sherbourne. Main number at the front, the A entrance around at the side. When he rings she opens the door immediately. She's been waiting for him. No fresh-washed hair and velvet dressing gown though; just a pair of slacks and a slightly grubby light-green sweater. She has a glass, half-empty. A lemon peel floats in it, an ice cube. Fortification.

"Well," she says. "Happy Anniversary."

"Of what?" he says.

"Saturday was always our day." She's on the edge of being drunk, she's bitter. He can't blame her. Nate finds it hard to blame anyone for anything. He's been able to understand her bitterness, most of the time. He just hasn't been able to do much about it.

"Not that she ever stuck to it," Martha goes on. "Emergency this, emergency that. So sorry to interrupt, but one of the children's heads just fell off." Martha laughs.

Nate wants to take her by the shoulders and give her a good shake, throw her against the wall. But of course he can't. Instead he stands, dripping onto her hall floor, looking at her dumbly.

23

He feels his body sagging on his spine, the flesh drooping like warm taffy on a sucker stick. Butterscotch. Don't run with the stick in your mouth, he'd tell the kids, already seeing them fall, seeing the pointed stick skewering up through the roof of the mouth. Running, kneeling, lifting, a howl, his own voice. Oh my god.

"Could you keep the children out of it?" he says.

"Why?" Martha says. "They were in it, weren't they?" She turns from him and walks down the hall into her living room.

I should leave now, Nate thinks. But he follows her, slipping his wet shoes off first, feet padding along the old rug. The old rut.

Only one light on. She's arranged it, the lighting. She sits across the room from the light, in shadow, on the sofa. Plush-covered sofa where he first kissed her, unpinned her hair, stroking it down over her wide shoulders. Broad, capable hands. He'd thought he would be safe in those hands, between those knees.

"That was always her excuse," Martha says. She's wearing crocheted wool slippers. Elizabeth would never wear crocheted wool slippers.

"She never disliked you," Nate says. They've done this before.

"No," Martha says. "Why dislike the housemaid? I did the dirty work for her. She should've paid me."

Nate feels, not for the first time, that he has told this woman too many things. She's misinterpreting, she's using his own confidences against him. "That's unfair," he says. "She respects you. She never tried to interfere with anything. Why should she?" He doesn't reply to the crack about the dirty work. Is that how you felt about it? he wants to ask, but he's afraid of the answer. *Get your ashes hauled.* Casual talk at high-school lockers. He can smell himself, the wet socks, turpentine on his pants. She used to tease him, scrubbing his back as they sat in her claw-footed tub. *Your wife doesn't take care of you.* In more ways than one.

"Yeah," says Martha. "Why should she? She always wanted to have her cake and eat it too. That's you, Nate. Elizabeth's cake. You're a piece of cake."

Nate remembers that when he first saw her, behind her desk at Adams, Prewitt and Stein, she was furtively chewing gum, a habit she renounced when he hinted he didn't like it. "I understand why you're angry," he says. This is one of Elizabeth's tactics, understanding, and he feels sneaky using it. He knows he doesn't really understand. Elizabeth doesn't either, when she says that to him. But it always deflates him.

"I don't give a piss whether you do or not," Martha says belligerently. No sops of understanding for her. She's looking at him directly, though her eyes are in shadow.

"I didn't come over to talk about this," Nate says, not sure what exactly they've been talking about. He's never sure in conversations like this. The clear thing is that she feels he's wrong. He's wronged her. He's done her wrong. But he tried to be straightforward about it from the beginning, he didn't lie. Someone should give him credit for that.

"So why did you come?" Martha says. "Running away from mother? Wanted some other nice lady to give you a cookie and a tumble in the sack?"

Nate finds this brutal. He doesn't answer. This is, he realizes, what he had wanted, though he doesn't want it at the moment.

Martha wipes the back of her hand across her mouth and nose. She's dimmed the lights, Nate guesses now, not for romantic effect but because she expected to cry and didn't want him to be able to see too well. "You can't turn it off and on that easily," she says.

"I thought we could talk," Nate says.

"I'm listening," Martha says. "I'm real good at it." Nate doesn't think this is necessarily true. She's good at it when he talks about her, granted. All ears. *You have the best thighs in the world*. She does have nice thighs, but the best in the world? How would he know?

"I guess you've heard what happened," he says at last. Unable to say why Chris's death should make him want comfort. By popular wisdom he should be overjoyed, his horns gone, the stain on his honor wiped out by blood.

"You mean about Elizabeth," Martha says. "Everyone in this town always knows what happens to everybody else. They all came and told me, you can bet on it. They love it. They love to watch me when they drop your name. Both of your names. Elizabeth's lover dynamited his head. Some of them say

25

Elizabeth's *man*. So what? What'm I supposed to say? Tough tits? Serves her right? She finally got him?"

Nate has never known her to be so hard, even during their most violent arguments. What he liked about her at first was her vagueness, her lack of focus, an absence of edges that gave her a nebulous shimmer. Now it's as if she's been dropped on the sidewalk from a great height and has frozen there, all splayed angles and splinters.

"She hadn't seen him for a while," he says, taking Elizabeth's side as Martha ritually forces him to. "He wanted her to leave the children. She couldn't do that."

"Of course not," Martha says. She stares down at her empty glass, lets it fall to the rug between her feet. "Supermom could never leave the children." She starts to cry, making no effort now to hide her face. "Move in with me," she says. "Live with me. I just want us to have a chance."

Nate thinks, Maybe we already had one. They don't now. He begins to ease himself forward, out of the chair. She'll be on him in a minute, arms winding like seaweed around his neck, wet face on his chest, pelvis shoved against his groin while he stands there withered.

"How do you think it feels?" she says. "Like a backstairs romance with the kitchen help, only everyone knows, and you go back at night to your goddamned wife and your goddamned kids and I read murder mysteries till four in the morning just to keep myself sane."

Nate meditates on the kitchen help. Her choice of metaphor puzzles him. Who has back stairs any more? He remembers one evening, the two of them wrapped in a sheet, on the bed together drinking gin, watching *Upstairs, Downstairs* and laughing. The maid pregnant by the son and heir, being lectured by the ice-faced mother. That was early on, when they were having a good time. It wasn't a Saturday; it was before Elizabeth said, Let's be reasonable about this. We have to know we can depend on each other at certain times. She took Thursdays, he took Saturdays because it was the weekend and Martha wouldn't have to get up early the next morning. And that other evening, when Martha said, I think I'm pregnant. His first thought: Elizabeth won't put up with that.

If I console her, she'll say I'm a hypocrite, he thinks. If I

26

don't, I'm a prick. Out now while there's time. This was a bad mistake. Pick up my shoes in the front hall, shouldn't have locked the bike. "Maybe we can have lunch sometime," he says at the living-room door.

"Lunch?" Her voice follows him down the hall. "Lunch?" A retreating wail.

He pedals his bicycle through the rain, aiming deliberately for puddles, soaking his legs. Fool. There's something missing in him that other people have. He can never foresee the future, that's it, even when it's clear. It's a kind of deformity, like being tall. Other people walk through doorways, he hits his head. Once or twice and a rat would learn to stoop. How many times, how long will it take?

After half an hour he stops at the corner of Dupont and Spadina, where he knows there's a phone booth. He leans his bike against the side of the booth, goes in. Glass cubicle, light on, total exposure. Feeble-minded creep goes into booth, removes clothes, stands there waiting for Superman to take over his body while people stare from passing cars and some old lady calls the police.

He takes a dime from his pocket, holds it. His token, his talisman, his one hope of salvation. At the other end of the line a thin woman waits, her pale face framed by dark hair, her hand lifted, fingers upraised in blessing.

No answer.

ELIZABETH

Elizabeth sits in her kitchen, waiting to be surprised. She's always surprised at this time of the year; she's also surprised on her birthday, at Christmas and on Mother's Day, which the children insist on celebrating even though she tells them it's commercial and they don't have to. She's good at being surprised. She's glad she's put in a lot of practice: she'll be able to walk through it tonight with no slips, the exclamation, the pleased smile, the laugh. Her remoteness from them, the distance she has to travel even to hear what they're saying. She wants to be able to touch them, hold them, but she can't. Good-night kisses on her cheek, cold dewdrops; their mouths perfect pink flowers.

The smell of scorching pumpkin drifts down the hall: their two jack-o'-lanterns, displayed side by side in the living-room window, finally, the legitimate way on the legitimate night. Already admired sufficiently by her. Scooped out on spread newspapers in the kitchen, handfuls of white seeds in their network of viscous threads, some grotesque and radical form of brain surgery; two little girls crouching over the orange heads with spoons and paring knives. Little mad scientists. They were so intense about it, especially Nancy. She wanted hers to have horns. Finally Nate suggested carrots, and Nancy's pumpkin now has lopsided horns in addition to its scowl. Janet's is more sedate: a curved smile, half-moon eyes upturned. Serenity if you look at it from a certain angle, idiocy from another. Nancy's has a fearsome energy, a demonic glee.

They will burn this way all evening and then the festival will be over. Janet, reasonable child, will consign her pumpkin to the garbage, clearing the decks, ready for the next thing. Nancy, if last year is any indication, will protect hers, keeping it on her dresser until it sags and rots, unwilling to throw it away.

They've made her turn out the light and sit in darkness, with

28

only one candle; she wasn't able to explain to them why she doesn't want to do this. The light flickers on the walls, on the dirty dishes waiting to be scraped and put into the dishwasher, on the sign she herself tacked to the kitchen cupboard over a year ago:

CLEAN UP YOUR OWN MESS!

Sensible advice. It's still sensible advice, but the kitchen itself has changed. It's no longer familiar, it's no longer the kind of place in which sensible advice can be followed. Or at least not by her. On the refrigerator there's a painting, curling at the edges, Nancy's from last year; a girl smiles a red smile, the sun shines, bestowing spokes of yellow; the sky is blue, all is as it should be. A foreign country.

A dark shape jumps at her from the doorway. "Boo, Mum."

"Oh, darling," Elizabeth says. "Let me see."

"Am I really scary, Mum?" Nancy says, clawing her fingers menacingly.

"You're very scary, love," Elizabeth says. "Isn't that wonderful."

Nancy has made yet another variation of her favorite costume. She calls it a monster, every year. This time she's pinned orange paper scales to her black leotard; she's modified Janet's old cat's head mask by adding silver tinfoil horns and four red fangs, two upper, two lower. Her eyes gleam through the cat eyes. Her tail, Janet's former cat's tail, now has three red cardboard prongs. Elizabeth feels something other than rubber boots might have been more suitable, but knows it's fatal to criticize. Nancy is so excited she might start to cry.

"You didn't scream," Nancy says reproachfully, and Elizabeth realizes she's forgotten this. An error, a failure.

"That's because you took my breath away," she says. "I was too frightened to scream."

Nancy is satisfied with this. "They'll all be really scared," she says. "They won't know who I am. Your turn," she says into the hall, and Janet makes a prim entrance. Last year she was a ghost, the year before that she was a cat, both standard. She tends to play it safe; to be too original is to be laughed at, as Nancy sometimes is.

This year she wears no mask. Instead she's made her face up, red lips, arched black brows, rouged cheeks. It isn't Elizabeth's makeup, since Elizabeth doesn't as a rule use any. Certainly not red lipstick. She has on a shawl made from a gaudy flowered tablecloth someone gave them – Nate's mother? – and which Elizabeth promptly donated to the playbox. And underneath it a dress of Elizabeth's, hitched and rolled around the waist to shorten it, belted with a red bandana. She looks surprisingly old, like a woman shrunken by age to the size of a ten-year-old; or like a thirty-year-old dwarf. A disconcertingly whorish effect.

"Wonderful, darling," Elizabeth says.

"I'm supposed to be a gypsy," Janet says, knowing with her usual tact that Elizabeth can't be totally depended on to figure this out and wanting to save her the embarrassment of asking. When she was younger she explained her drawings this way. Nancy, on the other hand, was hurt if you didn't know.

"Do you tell fortunes?" Elizabeth asks.

Janet smiles shyly with her bright red lips. "Yes," she says; then, "Not really."

"Where did you get my dress?" Elizabeth asks carefully. They're supposed to ask before borrowing things, but she doesn't want to spoil the evening by making an issue of it.

"Dad said I could," Janet says politely. "He said you weren't wearing it any more."

It's a blue dress, dark blue; the last time she wore it was with Chris. His hands were the last hands to undo the hook at the back, since, when she put the dress on to go home, she didn't bother to do the hook back up again. It's upsetting to see her daughter wearing it, wearing that invitation, that sexual flag. Nate has no right to make a decision like this about something of hers. But it's true, she isn't wearing it any more.

"I wanted you to be surprised," Janet adds, sensing her dismay.

"That's all right, darling," Elizabeth says: the eternal magic words. It's somehow more important to them to surprise her than to surprise Nate. Occasionally they even consult him. "Has your dad seen you yet?" she asks.

"Yes," Janet says.

"He pinned on my tail," Nancy says, hopping on one foot. "He's going out."

Elizabeth goes to the front door to see them off, standing in the lighted oblong as they negotiate the porch steps, carefully because of Nancy's mask and tail. They're carrying shopping bags, the biggest ones they could find. She's been over the instructions: Only this block. Stay with Sarah because she's older. No crossing in the middle of the street, only at corners. Don't bother people if they don't want to answer the door. Some of the people around here may not understand, their customs are different. Home by nine.

Voices other than theirs are already calling: *Shell out. Shell out. The witches are out.* It's a revel, one of the many from which she once felt and still feels excluded. They weren't allowed to have pumpkins and they weren't allowed to dress up and shout in the streets like the others. They had to go to bed early and lie in the darkness, listening to the distant laughter. Her Auntie Muriel hadn't wanted them running up dentists' bills by eating a lot of candy.

NATE

First, Nate washes his hands carefully with the oatmeal soap Elizabeth favors these days. There's something harsh about it, Scottish, penitential. Once she'd indulged herself in sandalwood, cinnamon, musk, Arabian fragrances, pastel and lavish at the same time. That was when she was buying lotions with exotic names and the occasional bottle of perfume. She hadn't rubbed these lotions on him and it wasn't for his benefit she dabbed herself behind the ears, though he could dimly remember a time when she might have. He could remember it vividly, he knows, if he wanted to, but he doesn't want to think about it, those odors, that fragrant moth dance performed for him alone. Why tease those nerves? Everything is gone, the bottles are empty, things get used up.

So now it's oatmeal soap, with its hints of chapped skin and chilblains. And, for the hands, nothing fancier than glycerine and rosewater.

Nate applies some of this to his own hands. He doesn't usually dip into Elizabeth's cosmetics; only when, as now, his hands feel clumsy and raw, abraded by the Varsol he uses to get the paint and polyurethane off them. There's always a brown line left though, a half-moon around the base of each nail; and he can never quite rid himself of the paint smell. He welcomed this smell once. It said, *You exist.* Far from the abstractions of paper, torts and writs, the convolutions of a language deliberately dried so that it was empty of any sensuous values. That was in the days when physical objects were thought to have a magic, a mysterious aura superior to the fading power of, say, politics or law. He'd quit in his third year of practice. Take an ethical stance. Grow. Change. Realize your potential.

Elizabeth had approved of this move because it was the sort of thing that would infuriate her aunt. She'd even said they could live on her salary till he got started. Her indulgence

32

proved that she wasn't at all like Auntie Muriel. But as time went on and he did little more than break even, she'd been less and less approving. Supportive, as they said. This house, too small really, the tenants on the third floor, the workshop in the basement, were supposed to be temporary, she'd reminded him. Then stopped reminding.

It's partly her fault. Half of her wants a sensitive, impoverished artist, the other half demands a forceful, aggressive lawyer. It was the lawyer she married, then found too conventional. What is he supposed to do?

Occasionally, though by no means all the time, Nate thinks of himself as a lump of putty, helplessly molded by the relentless demands and flinty disapprovals of the women he can't help being involved with. Dutifully, he tries to make them happy. He fails not because of any intrinsic weakness or lack of will, but because their own desires are hopelessly divided. And there's more than one of them, these women. They abound, they swarm.

"Toys?" his mother said. "Is that useful?" Meaning: all over the world people are being tortured and imprisoned and shot, and you make toys. She'd wanted him to be a radical lawyer, defending the unjustly accused. How to tell her that, apart from the sterile monetary transactions, contracts, real estate, most of the people he'd had to deal with at Adams, Prewitt and Stein had in fact been accused justly? She would have said it was only training, an apprenticeship he had to undergo to make him ready for the big crusade.

The Amnesty International newsletter still arrives every month, his mother's copy, marked with asterisks to show him where to send his courteously worded letters of protest. Children tortured in front of their mothers. Sons disappearing, to surface months later, fingernails missing, skins covered with burns and abrasions, skulls crushed, tossed on roadsides. Old men in damp cells dying of kidney problems. Scientists drugged in Soviet lunatic asylums. South African blacks shot or kicked to death while "escaping." His mother has a map of the world taped to her kitchen wall, where she can contemplate it while drying the plates. She sticks little stars on it, red ones, the kind the teacher

33

used to dole out for second-best in printing. These innocent grade-school stars mark each new reported case of torture or mass murder; the world is now a haze of stars, constellation upon constellation.

Nevertheless his mother crusades, dauntless astronomer, charting new atrocities, sending out her communications, politely written and neatly typed, unaware of the futility of what she is doing. As far as Nate is concerned she may as well be sending these letters to Mars. She'd brought him up to believe that God is the good in people. Way to fight, God. Nate finds these newsletters of hers so overwhelmingly painful that he's no longer able to read them. As soon as they arrive, he slips them into the wastepaper basket, then goes to the cellar to pound and chisel. He consoles himself by thinking that his toys are the toys the tortured children would play with if they could. Every child should have toys. To remove all toys because some do not have them is not the answer. Without his toys, surely there would be nothing to fight for. So he will let his mother, worthy woman that she is, compose the letters; he will make the toys.

Tonight he's been finishing rocking horses; five of them, he finds it easier to do them in lots of five. He sanded them yesterday. Today he's been painting eyes. Round eyes, expressionless, the eyes of creatures made to be ridden for the pleasure of others. The black eyeliner of the girls on the Strip. This isn't how he intended the horses to look: he intended joy. But more and more, recently, the toys he makes have this blank look, as if they can't see him.

He no longer tells people he makes handmade wooden toys in his basement. He says he's in the toy business. This isn't because cottage industry has ceased to be viewed as charismatic or even cute. He never thought of it as charismatic or cute; he thought of it as something he might be able to do well. To do one thing well: this was what he wanted. Now he does it well enough. He has a monthly balance sheet. After supplies and the gouge the stores take are deducted, he has money left to pay half the mortgage interest and to buy groceries, cigarettes, enough liquor to coast on. Elizabeth isn't supporting him. She just acts as though she is.

Nate begins to shave. He lathers his throat, meaning only to trim around the edges of his beard, free his neck and the underside of his jaw of bristles; but he finds the razor moving upwards, circling the edges of his beard like a lawnmower circling a lawn. He's shaved his beard half off before he knows that it's his intention to destroy it. From behind the coarse dark hair his face emerges, the face he hasn't seen in five years, pallid, blood-speckled, dismayed at this exposure. His hands have decided it's time for him to be someone else.

He rinses his face. He doesn't have any after-shave – it's so long since he's used it – so he rubs some of Elizabeth's glycerine and rosewater over his new-mown skin. The face that looks back at him from the bathroom mirror is more vulnerable, but also younger and grimmer, the jaw clearly visible now, its furry wisdom gone. A man stroking his beard is one thing, a man stroking his jaw is another.

Before leaving the house he goes into his own room and scrabbles through the piles of coins on his bureau, looking for dimes. Then he changes his socks. He doesn't expect to be taking his socks off this evening; it's highly unlikely that he will. However. His feet are white and rootlike, the toenails greyish yellow from the cellar life they're forced to lead. He sees his feet for an instant, browned and running, on sand, on sun-warmed rock. Far from here.

LESJE

Lesje and William are having a game of cribbage. They sit at a card table, the same card table on which they eat meals when they eat together, beside their picture window, which has a breathtaking view of the picture window in the apartment building opposite theirs. This window is lighted, since it's dark, and two people are sitting behind it, eating what Lesje takes to be spaghetti. On the streets below, Lesje assumes, it's all happening. That was why she wanted to live here, at the crux, in the heart: because it would all be happening. "It" and "all" are words that have, however, retained their abstractness. She hasn't yet found either of them.

Lesje has stuck a paper jack-o'-lantern, purchased at Woolworth's, to the inside of their own picture window. Last year she bought some candy, hoping to be visited by a parade of little children in costumes; but no children, it appears, can penetrate to the fourteenth floor of this apartment building. The people who live here, whom she sees only in the elevators, appear to be young and either single or childless.

Lesje would like to be out roaming the streets herself, watching. But William has suggested cribbage, which relaxes his mind.

"Fifteen two, fifteen four, fifteen six and a pair is eight," says William. He moves his plastic toothpick. Lesje has a mere fifteen two in the crib, a pair of aces she put there herself. She shuffles and cuts, William deals. He picks up his cards and his lips purse. He's frowning, deciding what to set aside for himself.

Lesje's hand is so bad there's not much choice. She permits herself a walk by moonlight, along a path trampled by the giant but herbivorous iguanodons; she can see the three-toed prints of their hind feet in the mud. She follows their trail

36

until the trees thin and there, in the distance, is the lake, silvery, its surface broken here and there by a serpentine head, the curve of a plunging back. That she should be so privileged. How will she ever convince the others of what she has seen?

(The lake, of course, is Lake Gladys, marked clearly on the chart on page 202 of *The Lost World* by Sir Arthur Conan Doyle. Lesje read this book at the age of ten. It was filed in the school library under Geology, and she'd been doing a project on rocks. Rocks had been her big thing before dinosaurs. Her friends at school read Trixie Belden, Nancy Drew, Cherry Ames the stewardess. Lesje hadn't cared much for those stories. She didn't as a rule like stories that weren't factual. But *The Lost World* was different. They'd found a plateau in South America on which the life forms of the Upper Jurassic had continued to survive, along with other, more modern forms. She can't remember which came first, her passion for fossils or this book; she thinks it was the book. No matter that all those on the expedition had been men. She'd fallen in love, not with professor Challenger, the loud-mouthed assertive one, or even the young reporter or the sharpshooting English lord. It was the other one, the dry, skeptical one, the thin one; Professor Summerlee. How many times has she stood at the edge of this lake, his thin hand in hers, while together they've witnessed a plesiosaur and he's been overcome, converted at last?

She still has this book. She didn't exactly steal it, she just forgot several times to renew it and then was so embarrassed by the librarian's sarcasm that she lied. Lost, she said. *The Lost World* is lost.)

The lake glimmers in the moonlight. Far out, on a sandbar, a mysterious white shape flickers.

William has moved his toothpick again. She hasn't been paying attention, he's at least twenty points ahead of her. "Your go," he says. Satisfaction rosies his cheeks.

"Fifteen two," she says.

"It's your next crib," William says, consoling her, as he can well afford to.

The phone rings. Lesje jumps, dropping the jack of diamonds. "Could you get it, William?" she says. She suspects it's the wrong-number man; she's not in the mood for a monotone serenade.

"It's for you," William says, puzzled.

When she comes back, he says, "Who was it?"

"Elizabeth's husband," Lesje says.

"Who?"

"Exactly," says Lesje. "Elizabeth's husband Who. You've met him; at the Christmas party last year. You remember Elizabeth, sort of statuesque-looking; she's the one who . . ."

"Oh, right," says William. The sight of his own blood makes him queasy, so he didn't much appreciate hearing the story of Chris, though Lesje had to tell it to him, she'd been upset. "What did he want?"

"I'm not sure," says Lesje.

Sunday, October 31, 1976

NATE

Nate is running. His bicycle is behind him somewhere in the darkness, parked against a bench. The air is cool, strange against his new scraped face.

He runs for pleasure, taking it easy, jogging over dying grass grey in the street lights, through fallen leaves whose colors he can barely see but guesses: orange, yellow, brown. They collect the leaves in green garbage bags and truck them away now, but once they raked them into piles and burned them in the streets, the smoke rising wispy and sweetish from the centers of the mounds. He used to run with the others along the street, making sounds like a dive bomber, and then jump, clearing the mounds of leaves like hurdles. Forbidden, but if you missed it didn't matter, the leaves were only smouldering. Men shaking rakes, telling them to bugger off.

Who did he run with, twenty or was it twenty-five years ago? Someone called Bobby, Tom something. They're gone now, faceless; he gives them the nostalgia due to those who have died young. Casualties, though of nothing but his own memory. It's himself, his lace-up breeks with leather knee patches, those goddamn wool socks always falling down, mittens ice-beaded and soggy from bombarding the enemy, nose dripping over his upper lip, himself running he mourns.

And after that, no longer for pure fun, sprinting at high school and third man on the relay team, around the track with the stick he would pretend was dynamite, he had to pass it on before it exploded. He was too skinny for football then but he could run. They never won anything, though once they came second. *Mr. Clean*, they called him in the yearbook. His mother thought it was a compliment.

When he was at law school he used to come here to the same place, Queen's Park, an oval like a track. *Queens' park*. He remembers the jokes, the couples he really did see, in trenchcoats,

39

windbreakers, the casual intersections that aroused in him only a mild curiosity, a mild embarrassment. It was around that time his back started acting up and he stopped running; shortly after he met Elizabeth. An evolutionary mistake, the doctor said, meaning his height; men should have stopped at five feet. Now they were unbalanced. He told Nate that his right leg was infinitesimally shorter than his left, not uncommon in tall men, and he should wear a built-up heel. A piece of information about which Nate has done nothing. He refuses to join the ranks of the tin woodmen, those with false teeth, glass eyes, rubber breasts, orthopedic shoes. Not yet, not yet. Not before he has to.

He runs clockwise, against the traffic, the cars meeting and passing him owl-eyed, dark and sleek. Behind him are the Parliament Buildings, squat pinkish heart of a squat province. In the interior, red plush and plump as a cushion, seedy lucrative deals are no doubt being made, decisions about who will build what where, what will be torn down, who will profit. He recalls with more than discomfort, sheer disbelief, that he once thought he would go into politics. Municipal probably. *Pompous nit.* Stop the developers, save the people; from what, for what? He was once among those who felt the universe should be just and merciful and were prepared to help it achieve this state. That was his mother's doing. He recalls his convoluted pain, his sense of betrayal when he realized finally how impossible this was. Nineteen-seventy, civil rights abolished, a war with no invaders and no enemy and the newspapers applauding. It wasn't the arbitrary arrests, the intimidation, the wrecking of lives that had appalled him; that was no surprise. He'd always known such things happened elsewhere, and despite the prevailing smugness he'd never doubted they could happen here. It was the newspapers applauding. Editorials, letters to the editor. The voice of the people. If that was all they had to say he'd be damned if he'd be their megaphone.

His idealism and his disillusionment now bore him about equally. His youth bores him. He used to wear a suit and listen to conversations between older men about those in power, hoping to learn something. Remembering this, he cringes; it's like the string of love beads he wore once, briefly, when that fashion was on the wane.

Ahead of him, across the street to the left, is the Museum, illuminated now by garish orange floodlights. He used to lurk there by the doorway at closing time, hoping to catch Elizabeth on her way out. At first she'd been remote and a little condescending, as if he was some sort of perverted halfwit she was being kind to. It knocked him out; that, and the impression she gave of knowing exactly what she was doing. Lapping Queen's Park on Saturday mornings he would think of her inside the grey buildings, sitting like a Madonna in a shrine, shedding a quiet light. Though actually she never worked on Saturdays. He would think of himself running towards her as she receded in front of him, holding a lamp in her hand like Florence Nightingale. He's glad he never told her about this ludicrous vision. She would have laughed even then, behind his back, and brought it up later to taunt him. Chocolate box, she would have said. The lady with the lamp. Jesus Christ. The lady with the axe, more like it. Now it's a different figure he runs towards.

He passes the War Memorial at the apex of the park, a granite plinth featureless and without ornament, except for the Gothic wen at the top. No naked women carrying flowers, no angels, not even any skeletons. Just a signpost, a marker. SOUTH AFRICA, it says on the other side; he used to see that in the mornings, driving to work, before he sold the car. Before he quit. Which war? He's never thought much about it. The only real war took place in Europe, Churchill saying they would fight on the beaches, a hot trade in chewing gum and women's stockings, his father vanishing in a thunderclap somewhere over France. With gentle shame he recalls how he cashed in on that. *Cut it out, you guys, his dad was killed in the war*. One of the few uses for patriotism he still considers valid; and about the only use for the death of his father, whom he cannot at all remember.

He's running south, Victoria College and St. Mike's on his left. He's almost around. He slows; he can feel the effort now, in his calves, his chest, the blood thudding in his head. He hasn't breathed deeply like this for a long time. Too bad about the exhaust fumes. He should stop smoking, he should run like this every day. He should get up at six every morning, run for half an hour, cut down to a pack a day. A regular program and watch the eggs and butter. He's not forty yet, not nearly; possibly he isn't even thirty-five. He's thirty-four, or was that last year? He's always had trouble remembering the exact year of his birth. So has his mother. It's as if they both entered into a conspiracy some time ago to pretend he wasn't actually born, not like everyone else. Nathanael: Gift of God. His shameless mother takes care to point out this meaning. She pointed it out to Elizabeth soon after their marriage. Thanks a lot, God, Elizabeth said later, genially then. And later less genially.

He starts running harder again, sprinting towards the shadows where he's left his bicycle. Once around. He used to be able to do this twice, he worked up to three times almost. He could do that again. On sunny days he would run watching his shadow, on the right till the Memorial, on the left coming back; a habit that started when he was on the relay team. Beat your shadow, said the coach, a Scot who taught Grade Nine English when he wasn't teaching P.T. *The Thirty-nine Steps* by John Buchan. His shadow pacing him; even when there were clouds he could feel it still there. It's here with him now, odd in the street lights so much dimmer than the sun, stretching ahead of him as he passes each light, shrinking, headless, then multiplying and leaping ahead of him again.

He never used to run at night; he doesn't like it much. He should stop this and go home. The children will be back soon, perhaps are already back, waiting to show him their paper bags. But he keeps running, as if he must run; as if there's something he's running towards.

ELIZABETH

Elizabeth sits on her mild sofa, facing the bowls. Two disembodied heads burn behind her. The bowls are on the pine sideboard. Not her own bowls, she wouldn't let them use hers, but three bowls from the kitchen, a pyrex casserole, a white china mixing bowl, and another mixing bowl, stainless steel.

In two of the bowls are the packages the children wrapped in the afternoon, little bundles in wrinkled orange and black paper napkins, a witch and cat motif. Tied at the top with string. They wanted ribbon but there wasn't any. In each package are some candy kisses, a miniature box of Smarties, a box of raisins. They wanted her to make gingerbread cookies with jack-o'-lantern faces on them, the way she usually did, but she said she didn't have time this year. A lame excuse. They know how much time she spends lying in there on her bed.

The third bowl, the steel one, is full of pennies, for the UNICEF boxes the children carry around with them these days. Save the children. Adults, as usual, forcing the children to do the saving, knowing how incapable of it they are themselves.

Soon the doorbell will ring and she'll open the door. It will be a fairy or a Batman or a devil or an animal, her neighbors' children, her children's friends, in the shapes of their own desires or their parents' fears. She will smile at them and admire them and give them something from the bowls, and they will go away. She will close the door and sit down again and wait for the next ring. Meanwhile her own children are doing the same thing at the houses of her neighbors, up and down the front paths, across the lawns, grass for the newcomers like herself, withered tomato plants and faded cosmos flowers for the Italians and Portuguese whose district has so recently been perceived as quaint.

Her children are walking, running, lured by the orange lights in front windows. Later that night she will go through their loot while they sleep, looking for evidence of razor blades in

43

apples, poisoned candy. Although their joy cannot touch her, fear for them still can. She does not trust the world's intentions towards them. Nate used to laugh at her concerns, what he called her obsessions: sharp table corners when they were learning to walk, open wall plugs, lamp cords, ponds, streams and puddles (you can drown in two inches of water), moving vehicles, iron swings, porch railings, stairs; and more recently, strange men, cars that slow down, ravines. They had to learn, he'd say. As long as nothing serious happens she looks foolish. But if anything ever does, it will be no consolation to have been right.

It should be Nate sitting on this sofa, waiting for the doorbell to ring. It should be him this time, opening the door not knowing who it will be, handing out the candy. Elizabeth has always done it before but Nate should know she isn't up to it this year. If he used his head he would know.

But he's out; and he hasn't, this time, told her where he is going.

Chris came to the door once, not telling her, rang the bell. Standing on the porch, the overhead light turning his face to moon craters.

What are you doing here? She'd been angry: he shouldn't have done that, it was an invasion, the children's room was right overhead. Pulled her outside onto the porch, brought his face down to hers wordlessly, in the spotlight. Go away. I'll call you later but please go away. You know I can't do this. A whisper, a kiss, blackmail payment, hoping they wouldn't hear.

She wants to turn out the lights, extinguish the pumpkins, bolt the door. She can pretend she isn't home. But how will she explain the full bowls of candy, or, even if she throws the packages away, the questions of their friends? *We went to your house but there was no one home.* Nothing can be done.

The doorbell rings, rings again. Elizabeth fills her hands, negotiates the door. Easier to have put the bowls at the bottom of the stairs; she'll do that. It's a Chinaman, a Frankenstein Monster and a child in a rat suit. She pretends not to recognize them. She hands each a bundle and drops coins into their slotted tins. They twitter happily among themselves, thank her, and patter across the porch, not knowing, really, what night this is or what, with their small decorated bodies, they truly represent. All Souls. Not just friendly souls but all souls. They are souls, come back, crying at the door, hungry, mourning their lost lives. You give them food, money, anything to substitute for your love and blood, hoping it will be enough, waiting for them to go away.

Part Two

ELIZABETH

Elizabeth walks west, along the north side of the street, in the cold grey air that is an extension of the unbroken fish-grey sky. She doesn't glance into the store windows; she knows what she looks like and she doesn't indulge in fantasies of looking any other way. She doesn't need her own reflection or the reflections of other people's ideas of her or of themselves. Peach-yellow, applesauce-pink, raspberry, plum, hides, hooves, plumes, lips, claws, they are of no use to her. She wears a black coat. She's hard, a dense core, that dark point around which other colors swirl. She keeps her eyes straight, her shoulders level, her steps even. She marches.

On some of the lapels, breasts, approaching her there are still those reminders, red cloth petals of blood spattered out from the black felt hole in the chest, pinned at the center. Remembrance Day. A little pin in the heart. What is it they peddle for the mentally disabled? Seeds of Hope. In school they used to pause while someone read a verse from the Bible and they sang a hymn. Heads bowed, trying to look solemn, not knowing why they should. In the distance, or was it on the radio, guns.

> If ye break faith with us who die
> We shall not sleep, though poppies grow
> In Flanders fields.

A Canadian wrote that. *We are the Dead.* A morbid nation. In school they had to memorize it two years in a row, back when memorizing was still in fashion. She'd been chosen to recite it, once. She was good at memorizing; they called it being good at poetry. She was good at poetry, before she left school.

Elizabeth has bought a poppy but she hasn't worn it. It's in her pocket now, her thumb against the pin.

She can remember when this walk, any walk through this part of the city, would have excited her. Those windows with their

49

promises that are, finally, sexual, replacing earlier windows and earlier promises that offered merely safety. Tweeds. When did that happen, the switch to danger? Sometime in the past ten years the solid wool suits and Liberty scarves moved out in favor of exotica: Indian imports with slit skirts, satin underwear, silver talismans to dangle between the breasts like minnows on a hook. Bite here. And then the furniture, the *milieu*, the accessories. Lamps with colored shades, incense, whole shops devoted to soap or thick bath towels, candles, lotions. Enticements. And she was enticed. It once made her skin burn merely to walk along these streets, the windows offering themselves, not demanding anything, certainly not money. Just a word, Yes.

The goods are much the same now, although the prices have gone up and there are more stores, but that caressing scent is gone. These days it's all merchandise. You pay, you get, you get no more than you see. A lamp, a bottle. If she had a choice she would take the former, the other, but there's a small deadening voice in her now that cancels choice, that says merely: False.

She stops in front of a newspaper box, bending to look in through the square glass window. She should buy a paper, to have something to read in the waiting room. She doesn't want to be left with nothing she can concentrate on, and at the moment she can't bear the kinds of magazines they keep in such places. Full-color magazines, brighter than life, about health and motherhood and washing your hair in mayonnaise. She needs something in black and white. Bodies falling from tenth-floor balconies, explosions. Real life. But she doesn't want to read a paper either. They're full of the Québec election, which will happen in three days and in which she is not the least interested. She's no more interested in elections than she is in football games. Contests between men, both of them, in which she's expected to be at best a cheerleader. The candidates, collections of grey dots, opposing each other on the front pages, snorting silent though not wordless challenges. She doesn't care who wins, though Nate does; though Chris would have. There was always that unvoiced accusation, directed at her, as if who she was, the way she spoke, was a twist on his own arm, an intrusion. The language question, everyone said.

* * *

50

There's something wrong with my ears. I think I'm going deaf. From time to time, not all the time, I hear a high sound, like a hum, a ringing. And I know I've been having difficulty hearing what other people say to me. I'm always saying, pardon?

No, I haven't had a cold. No.

She rehearses the speech, then repeats it to the doctor and answers the doctor's questions, hands in her lap, feet side by side in their black shoes, purse beside her feet. A matron. The doctor is a round, sensible-looking woman in a white smock, with a light attached to her forehead. She questions Elizabeth kindly, making notes in the Egyptian hieroglyphs of doctors. Then, after they go through a door and Elizabeth sits down in a black leatherette chair, she looks into Elizabeth's mouth and then her ears, one after the other, using a light on the end of a probe. She asks her to hold her nose and blow, to see if there are any popping sounds.

"No obstructions," the doctor says cheerfully.

She fits a set of headphones onto Elizabeth's head. Elizabeth stares at the wall, on which hangs a picture done in painted plaster: a tree, a fairy-faced child gazing up at the branches, and a poem in scrolled script:

> I think that I shall never see
> A poem lovely as a Tree.
> A Tree whose hungry mouth is pressed
> Against the Earth's sweet flowing breast. . . .

Elizabeth reads this far, then stops. Even the idealized tree in the plaster oblong looks like a kind of squid, its roots intertwined like tentacles, sticking itself onto that rounded bulge of earth, sucking, voracious. Nancy started biting her in the sixth month, with the first tooth.

The doctor twiddles buttons on the machine attached by wires to Elizabeth's headphone, producing first high science-fiction sounds, then low vibrations, rumors.

"I can hear it," Elizabeth says each time the sound changes. She can tell what kinds of things this woman would have in her living room: chintz slipcovers, lamps with bases made of porcelain nymphs. Ceramic poodles on her mantelpiece, like Nate's mother. An ashtray with ladybird beetles on the rim, in natural colors. This whole room is a time warp.

The doctor removes Elizabeth's headphones and asks her to go back to the outer office. They both sit down. The doctor smiles benignly, indulgently, as if she's about to tell Elizabeth she has cancer of the ears.

"There's absolutely nothing wrong with your hearing," she says. "Your ears are clear and your range is normal. Perhaps you may have a very slight residual infection that causes plugging from time to time. When that happens, just hold your nose and blow, as you'd do in an airplane. The pressure will clear your ears."

("I think I'm going deaf," Elizabeth said.

"Maybe," said Nate, "there are just some things you don't want to hear.")

Elizabeth thinks the receptionist looks at her strangely when she says she won't be needing another appointment. "Nothing wrong with me," she says, explaining. She goes down in the elevator and walks through the archaic brass and marble lobby, still marching. By the time she reaches the outer door the humming has begun again, high-pitched, constant, like a mosquito or a child's tuneless song, or a power line in winter. Electricity somewhere. She remembers a story she read once, in *Reader's Digest*, while sitting in the dentist's waiting room, about an old woman who started hearing angel voices in her head and thought she was going mad. After a long time and several investigations they discovered she was picking up a local radio station through the metal in her bridgework. *Reader's Digest* repeated this story as a joke.

It's almost five, darkening; the sidewalk and road are slick with drizzle. Traffic packs the lanes. Elizabeth steps across the gutter and begins to walk diagonally across the street, in front of one stationary car, behind another. A green delivery truck jams to a stop in the moving lane, three feet from her. The driver leans on his horn, shouting.

"You idiot, you wanna get yourself killed?"

Elizabeth continues across the road, ignoring him, her pace steady, marching. Does she want to get herself killed. The hum in her right ear shuts off like a cut connection.

There's nothing wrong with her ears. The sound is coming from somewhere else. Angel voices.

LESJE

Lesje is having lunch with Elizabeth's husband, the husband belonging to Elizabeth. Possessive, or, in Latin, genitive. This man doesn't seem like Elizabeth's husband, or anyone else's for that matter. But especially not Elizabeth's. Elizabeth, for instance, would never have chosen the Varsity Restaurant. Either he has no money, which is possible considering the frayings and ravelings everywhere on his surface, patchy, like rock lichen; or he doesn't think she'll base her opinion of him on his choice of restaurants. It's a restaurant left over when others like it became classy, preserving its fifties furnishings, its grubby menus, its air of cheesy resignation.

Ordinarily Lesje would never eat here, partly because she associates the Varsity Restaurant with being a student and she's no longer that young. She isn't sure why she's having lunch with Elizabeth's husband at all, except that something in the way he asked her – the invitation had been a kind of outburst – made it impossible for her to say no.

The anger and desperation of others have always been her weak points. She's an appeaser and she knows it. Even in the women's group she went to in graduate school, mostly because her roommate shamed her into it, she'd been cautious, afraid of saying the wrong thing; of being accused. She'd listened with mounting horror to the recitals of the others, their revelations about their grievances, their sex lives, the callousness of their lovers, even their marriages, for some of them were married. The horror wasn't caused by the content but by Lesje's realization that they were expecting her to do the same thing. She knew she couldn't, she didn't know the language. It would be no good to say that she was just a scientist, she wasn't political. According to them, everything was political.

Already they were looking at her with calculation: her murmurs of assent had not been enough. Soon they would confront her. Panic-stricken, she searched her past for suitable offerings, but the only thing she could think of was so minor, so trivial, that she knew it would never be accepted. It was this: On the gold dome of the Museum's lobby, up at the top, it said: THAT ALL MEN MAY KNOW HIS WORK. It was only a quotation from the Bible, she'd checked on that, but it might keep them busy; they were very big on the piggishness of God. On the other hand, they might reject it completely. Come on, Lesje. Something *personal*.

She'd told her roommate, who was a social historian with tinted granny glasses, that she didn't really have time for the group, as her palynology course was heavier than she'd thought. Neither of them believed this, and shortly afterwards Lesje moved into a single apartment. She couldn't stand the constant attempts to engage her in meaningful dialogue while she was eating her corn flakes or drying her hair. At that time nuances had bothered her; she was much happier among concrete things. Now she feels it might have been useful to have listened more carefully.

Nate hasn't yet frightened her by asking her to tell him about herself, though he's been talking since they sat down. She ordered the cheapest thing on the menu, a grilled cheese sandwich and a glass of milk. She listens, eating in small bites, concealing her teeth. Nate has given no hint yet as to why he called her. At the time she thought it might be because she'd known Chris, she knew Elizabeth, and he needed to talk about it. She could understand that. But so far he hasn't mentioned either of them.

Lesje can't see how he can get through a conversation, even five minutes of one, without mentioning an event that to her would have loomed very large in the foreground. If it were her life, which it isn't. Until this lunch, this grilled cheese sandwich and – what is he eating? – a hot turkey sandwich on white bread, she thought about Nate, if at all, simply as the least interesting figure in that tragic triangle.

Elizabeth, who stalks about the Museum these days white-skinned, eyes black-shadowed, a little too plump to carry it off entirely but otherwise like some bereft queen out of a Shakespearean play, is of course the most interesting. Chris is interesting because he is dead. Lesje knew him, but not

54

very well. Some people at work found him remote, others too intense. He was rumored to have a ferocious temper, but Lesje never saw it. She worked on only one project with him: Smaller Mammals of the Mesozoic. It's finished now, installed in its glass case with push buttons wired for the voices. Lesje did the specifications and Chris built the models, using muskrat fur and rabbit and woodchuck, doctored, to cover the wooden forms. She used to visit him in that shadowy workroom, at one end of the corridor where they kept the stuffed owls and the other large birds. Specimens, two of each kind, in little pull-out metal drawers, like an animal morgue. She would bring coffee for both of them and drink hers while he worked, putting the shapes together with wood and Styrofoam. They guessed together about certain details: eyes, colors. It was odd, watching such a massive man concentrate himself on meticulous details. Chris wasn't unusually tall; he wasn't even overly muscular. But he gave an impression of mass, as though he would weigh more than anyone else the same size, as if his cells were closer together, squeezed inward by some irresistible gravitational force. Lesje never thought about whether she liked him or not. You don't like or dislike a boulder.

Now he's dead and therefore immediately more remote, more mysterious. His death baffles her: she can't imagine ever doing anything like that herself, and she can't imagine anyone she knows doing it. Chris seemed like the last person who would. To her at any rate. Though people aren't her field, so she's no judge.

But Nate; she hasn't thought much about Nate. He doesn't look like a betrayed husband. Right now he's talking about the election in Québec, which is taking place at this very moment. He bites into a piece of turkey, chews; gravy traces his chin. The Separatists, he feels, ought to win, because the other government is so corrupt. Also because of the notorious behavior of the Federal Government in 1970. Lesje vaguely remembers that some people were arrested, after the kidnappings. She was working very hard on her Invertebrates course at the time; fourth year, and every mark counted.

Does he think it would be a good thing in the long run? Lesje asks. That isn't the point, Nate says. The point is a moral one.

If William had said this Lesje would have found it pompous.

She doesn't find it pompous now. Nate's long face (surely he used to have a beard; she recalls a beard, at parties and when he'd come with his children to pick Elizabeth up after work; but the face is hairless, pale), his body hanging from his shoulders like a suit from a hanger, nonchalant, impresses her. He's older, he must know things, things she can only guess at; he must have accumulated wisdom. His body would be wrinkled, his face has bones. Unlike William's. William has put on weight since they've been living together; his bones are retreating back into his head, behind the soft barricades of his cheeks.

William is against the Parti Québécois because of their wish to flood James Bay and sell the electrical power.

"But the other side is doing that, too," Lesje said.

"If I lived there I wouldn't vote for either of them," William said purely.

Lesje herself doesn't know how she would vote. She thinks she would probably move, instead. Nationalism of any kind makes her uneasy. In her parents' house it was a forbidden subject. How could it be otherwise, with the grandmothers both lurking, questioning her separately, waiting to pounce? They'd never met. Both had refused to go to her parents' wedding, which had been a civil ceremony. But the grandmothers had focused their rage not on their offending children but on each other. As for her, they'd both loved her, she supposes; and both had mourned over her as if she were in some way dead. It was her damaged gene pool. Impure, impure. Each thought she should scrap half her chromosomes, repair herself, by some miracle. Her Ukrainian grandmother, standing in the kitchen behind Lesje while she sat in a chrome and plastic chair reading *The Young People's Book of Stalactites and Stalagmites*, brushing her hair, talking to her mother in a language she didn't understand. Brushing and weeping silently.

"Mum, what's she saying?"

"She says your hair is very black."

The Ukrainian grandmother bending to hug her, consoling her for a pain Lesje didn't yet know she had. She'd been given an egg once by the Ukrainian grandmother, one of the untouchable decorated eggs kept on the mantelpiece along with the family photos in silver-plated frames. The Jewish grandmother, finding it, had smashed the egg with her tiny boots, stamping up and down, a mouse's rage.

They're both old women, her mother said. They've had hard lives. You can't change anyone over fifty. Lesje wept over her handful of bright egg fragments while her little grandmother, repentant, stroked her with her brown paws. She bought Lesje another egg, somewhere; which must have cost her more than the money.

Both grandmothers spoke as if they personally had been through the war, had been gassed, raped, run through with bayonets, shot, starved, bombed and cremated, and had by a miracle survived; which wasn't true. The only one who had actually been there was Aunt Rachel, her father's sister, older by twenty years, already married and settled by the time the family left. Aunt Rachel was a photograph on her grandmother's mantelpiece, a plump dumpy-looking woman. She'd been comfortably off, and that was all the picture revealed: comfort. No foreknowledge; that was added much later, by Lesje, guiltily looking. Her father and mother did not discuss Aunt Rachel. What was there to discuss? No one knew what had happened to her. Lesje, although she has tried, cannot imagine her.

Lesje does not say any of this to Nate, who's explaining to her why the French feel the way they feel. Lesje doesn't really care why. She just wants to stay out of the way.

Nate has almost finished his turkey sandwich; he hasn't eaten any of his fries. He's gazing at the table to the left of Lesje's water glass, picking apart one of the Varsity Restaurant's white rolls. His place is scattered with crumbs. Things have to be viewed in a historical context, he says. He abandons the roll and lights a cigarette. Lesje doesn't like to ask for one – hers are gone, and it's the wrong time to get up for more – but after a minute he offers her one and even lights it for her, staring at her nose, she feels, which makes her nervous.

She wants to ask: Why am I here? You didn't really invite me to lunch in this third-rate restaurant to settle the future of the nation, did you? But he's already signaling for the bill. As they wait for it, he tells her he has two daughters. He says their names and ages, then repeats them, as though reminding himself or making sure she's got it straight. He'd like to bring them to the Museum some Saturday, he says.

They're very interested in dinosaurs. Could she perhaps show them around?

Lesje doesn't usually work on Saturdays, but how can she say no? Depriving his children of dinosaurs. She ought to be glad for the chance to spread the word, make converts, but she isn't: dinosaurs aren't a religion for her, only a preserve. Also she's oddly disappointed. There should have been more to it, after all that stuttering on the telephone, this assignation at a restaurant which, she suddenly realizes, Elizabeth can be depended on never to enter. Lesje says politely that she'd be more than delighted to walk Nate's children through the exhibits and answer any questions they might have. She starts to put on her coat.

Nate pays for the lunch, even though Lesje offers to pick up her half. She would rather pay for the whole lunch. He looks so broke. More importantly, it's still not at all clear to her what will be expected of her for this gift of a grilled cheese sandwich and a glass of milk; what she is being asked to do or give in return.

NATE

Nate sits in the Selby Hotel, drinking draft beer and watching television. TRANSIENT, PERMANENT, the sign in the entranceway reads, in big type, as if the two things are the same. Once it was an old man's bar, a bar for poor old men. He drinks at the Selby out of habit: Martha's place is only three blocks away, and he'd fallen into the pattern of dropping in for a few beers either before seeing her or, if it was still early enough, after leaving. He hasn't yet chosen a new bar.

He'll have to soon: the Selby, which when he started to drink there was full of anonymous faces, is beginning to clog with people he knows. They aren't friends exactly and he knows them only because they all drink here. Still, he's become a regular, and many of the old regulars are gone. Workers from Cabbagetown, frayed, silent for the most part, mutterers of dependably gloomy rote phrases. Now the place is being taken over by the same people who are taking over the mews flats and back alleys of Cabbagetown. Photographers, men who say they're writing a book. They talk too much, are too cheerful, invite him to sit at their tables when he doesn't want to. He has some standing among them, a woodcarver, worker with his hands, artisan, the man with the knife. He prefers bars where he's the first of his kind.

The bar he'll look for will be sober, quiet, devoid of pinball machines and jukeboxes and pimply eighteen-year-olds who drink too much and throw up in the can. He wants a bar half full of men in zip-front jackets and open-necked shirts with the T-shirt collar showing, slow and steady drinkers; serious television-watchers like himself. He likes to tune in on the national news and then get the sports scores.

He can hardly do this in his own house, as Elizabeth has long since exiled his ancient portable black and white set from the living room, where she said it was out of place, then from the

59

kitchen. She said she couldn't stand to have it blaring while she cooked and he could decide whether he wanted to watch television or eat, because if it was television she would go out for dinner and let him fend for himself. That was in the olden days, before Nate of necessity began to cook. He tried sneaking the set into the bedroom – he had visions of lying in bed watching the late movie, a Scotch and water in one hand, Elizabeth curled cosily beside him – but that didn't last a night.

The set ended up in Janet's room, where the children watch Saturday morning cartoons on it. When he moved into his own room he didn't have the heart to take it away from them again. Sometimes he watches it with them or sits in their room by himself during afternoon football games. But they're always asleep by the time the eleven o'clock news comes on. He could always watch it at his mother's, she never misses a night, but it's too far to go and she doesn't keep beer in the house. She wouldn't be too excited about this kind of thing anyway. Earthquakes, famines, that's different. Every time there's a famine on the news, Nate can predict his mother will be on the phone the next day, trying to bully him into adopting an orphan or selling Pieces for Peace to his toy retailers. Bits of colored wool made into gnomes, folded paper birds. "Christmas tree decorations aren't going to save the world," he tells her. Then she says she hopes the children are taking their cod liver oil pills every morning. She suspects Elizabeth of vitamin deficiencies.

Elizabeth, on the other hand, has no interest in watching any sort of news whatsoever. She hardly even reads the papers. Nate has never known anyone with as little interest in the news as Elizabeth.

Tonight, for instance, she went to bed at seven; she didn't even bother to stay up for the election results. Nate, watching everything fall apart up there on the screen, can't understand her indifference. This is an event of national and perhaps even international importance, and she's sleeping through it! The special crew of commentators can hardly contain themselves, one way or another. The Québeckers on the panel are trying hard to keep from grinning; they're supposed to be objective, but their faces twitch every time the computer flashes a new victory for the Parti Québécois. The English on the other hand are about to wet themselves. René Lévesque can hardly believe it; he looks as if someone has simultaneously kissed him and kneed him in the groin.

The cameras cut back and forth between the thin-lipped commentators and the crowds at P.Q. headquarters, where a wild celebration is going on. Dancing in the streets, jubilant outbursts of song. He tries to remember a similar kind of celebration on his side of the border, but the only thing he can think of is the first Russian-Canadian hockey series, when Paul Henderson scored the winning goal. Men hugged each other and the drunker ones cried. But this is no hockey game. Watching the discomfiture of the defeated Liberals, the stiff upper lips of the English newsmen, Nate grins. *Serves them fucking well right.* This is his own personal vengeance on all the writers of letters to the editors across the country. Repression begets revolution, he thinks, all you stockbrokers. *So eat shit.* Merely a quote from the Prime Minister, he'd say to the old ladies, if that was him up there on the screen.

Nevertheless, glancing around at the other drinkers, he's uneasy. His pleasure, he knows, is merely theoretical and quite possibly snobbish. No one here with him is much interested in theory. Not many of the book-writers out tonight, mostly zipfront jackets, and they aren't taking it well; they're grumpy and even downright surly, as if they're watching their next-door neighbors throwing a loud party to which they haven't been invited. "Fucking frogs," one of them mutters. "Shoulda kicked them out of the country a long time ago."

Someone else says it will mean the end of the economy: Who'll take the chance of investing? "What economy," his friend quips. "Anything's better than stagflation." A theme the commentators pick up, second-guessing the future between the songs and kisses.

Nate feels a surge of exhilaration shoot through him, up from the belly, almost sexual, out to the fingers where they hook around his glass. None of them knows, none of the bastards knows. The earth is shifting under their feet and they can't even feel it, anything can happen!

But instead of the wizened monkey-face of René Lévesque, who is thanking his supporters in the Paul Sauvé Arena up there on the screen, he sees Lesje, her eyes, her thin hands, floating across from him at the lunch table, veiled in smoke. He can't

61

remember anything she said; did she even say anything? He doesn't care, he doesn't care if she never says anything at all. He just wants to look at her, into her, into those dark eyes which are possibly brown, he can't remember that either. He remembers the shadow in them, like the cool shadow under a tree. Why did he wait so long, jittering in phone booths, spastic, unable to speak? At lunch he picked rolls apart and talked politics when what he should have done, he should have taken her in his arms, right there in the Varsity Restaurant. Then they would have been transported, they would have been somewhere else. How could he know where, since it would be somewhere he's never been before? Some place utterly unlike the country inside Elizabeth's blue dressing gown, or the planet of Martha, predictable, heavy and damp. Holding Lesje would be like holding some strange plant, smooth, thin, with sudden orange flowers. *Exotics*, the florists called them. The light would be odd, the ground underfoot littered with bones. Over which she would have power. She would stand before him, the bearer of healing wisdom, swathed in veils. He would fall to his knees, dissolve.

Nate, pushing back this image, places it in time: a Saturday matinée of *She*, seen when he was an impressionable twelve and masturbating nightly. His mother used to nag him about those matinées; I'm sure they're bad for you, she said. All that cowboys and shooting. A woman draped in cheesecloth, terrible actress, he'd shot paper clips and spitballs at her and jeered with the rest, he'd mooned over her for weeks. Nevertheless he wants to leap onto his bicycle and pedal like a maniac over to Lesje's apartment building, walk like Spiderman up the wall, swoop through the window. *Don't say anything*, he'd tell her. *Come with me*.

True, she's living with some man or other. Nate can remember him dimly, holding Lesje's elbow at last year's Museum Christmas party, a negligible pink smudge. He forgets about him almost immediately and returns to Lesje, his hand lighting her cigarette. Another inch and he'd have touched her. But it's too soon to touch her. He knows she gets up in the morning, eats breakfast, goes to work where she does incomprehensible things, disappears at intervals into the ladies' room, but he doesn't want to contemplate these details. He knows nothing about her actual life and he doesn't want to know anything. Not too much, not yet.

Saturday, November 20, 1976

ELIZABETH

They walk up the steps, bypassing the popcorn man with his candy apples and balloons and his noisemakers and plastic windmills, violent blue and red, a sound like dried birds still flapping. A family. When they come out again they will have to buy something for the children, because that is what families do.

Elizabeth said she would come with them because Nate was right, it's bad for the children that they never do anything as a family any more. The children were not fooled. They weren't overjoyed, merely surprised and a little apprehensive. "But you never come when Daddy takes us," Nancy said.

Now, in the vaulted rotunda with the Saturday river of children funneling through the turnstiles, she doesn't think she can take the pressure. This is where she works. It's also where Chris worked. It's all right for her to be here on weekdays, she has a good reason and a lot of memos to occupy her mind; but what is the point now? Why use her own free time to walk among empty suits and metal shells and bones discarded by their owners? Any more than she has to.

She'd taken care not to speak to him or even see him if possible during office hours. It wasn't that she cared who knew, though she didn't flaunt it, she didn't need to; in the Museum, by a process of discreet seepage, everybody ultimately knew everything. But she was paid to do a job, so many hours a day, and she took that seriously. She hadn't spent those hours on Chris.

Not since the first time, when they made love with most of their clothes on, lying on the floor of his workroom among scraps of fur, shavings of wood, beside the partly finished replica of an African ground squirrel. The glass eyes had not yet been inserted, the ragged sockets watched them. The whole Museum still smells of that day: preservative, sawdust, and the smell of Chris's hair, a molten smell, singed and rich. Burnt gold. His cold zipper which

63

pressed into the flesh of her inner thigh, the teeth rasping. She thought: I will never again settle for anything less than this. As if it was a bargain, which perhaps it was, though she'd never been able to see the invisible bargainer on the other side.

The children are in the gift shop, looking at the dolls, cloth lions from Singapore, clay babies from Mexico. Nate is fumbling with his wallet. It was his idea so he will pay, but she knows, knew when they left the house, that he wouldn't have enough money.

"Can you lend me five?" he says to her. "I'll pay you back Monday."

She hands him the money, which she has ready in her hand. It's always five. Sometimes he pays her back; when he doesn't it's because he forgets. She no longer reminds him, as she did in the days when she thought everything should be fair.

"I won't go in," she says. "I'll meet you on the steps at four-thirty. We can take the girls to Murray's for a sundae or something."

He seems relieved. "Right," he says.

"Tell the children to enjoy themselves."

She walks south towards the park, meaning to cross the road and stroll under the trees, perhaps sit on one of the benches and breathe in the smell of fallen leaves. The last smell of leaves she'll get before the snow. She stands on the curb, waiting for a chance to cross. A few tattered wreaths still on the cenotaph. SOUTH AFRICA, it says.

She turns and walks back towards the Museum. She'll go to the Planetarium; that will kill the time. Even though she helps with the posters and displays, she's never been in there. She works during the weekday matinées and she wouldn't ordinarily go to something like that in the evening, on her own time. But today she wants to go somewhere she's never been. The lobby is brick-lined. There's a motto on the curved wall:

THE HEAVENS ARE CALLING YOU AND WHEEL AROUND YOU
DISPLAYING TO YOU THEIR ETERNAL BEAUTIES
AND STILL YOUR EYE IS LOOKING ON THE GROUND
                            — DANTE

And below that: INFORMATION. ADVANCE TICKET SALES.

64

Elizabeth finds it reassuring that even eternal beauties cost money. The show is at three. She goes to the window to buy a ticket, though she supposes she could get in on her pass card.

"Cosmic Disasters, or the Laserium?" the girl says.

"Pardon?" Elizabeth says. Then she realizes that "Cosmic Disasters" must be the name of the current show. *Laserium*, however, suggests nothing to her but a leper colony.

"The Laserium isn't until four-fifteen," the girl says.

"Cosmic Disasters, then," Elizabeth says. The Laserium, whatever that is, would be too late.

She stands around in the lobby examining the covers of the books in the bookshop window. *The Stars Belong to Everyone. The Universe. Black Holes.* She's never felt much friendliness towards the stars.

The auditorium is a dome; it's like being inside a breast. Elizabeth knows it's supposed to represent the sky; nevertheless she feels a little stifled. She leans back in the plush seat, gazing at the ceiling, which is blank but glows with a faint light. The children around her wriggle and twitter until the lights dim. Then they hush.

It's sunset. All around is the Toronto skyline, its outlines and signs: the Park Plaza squat now compared to the Hyatt Regency beside it; BRITANNICA to the east; Sutton Place, the weather building, the CN Tower. This is earth.

A voice tells them that they're seeing the skyline as it would look if they were standing on top of the Planetarium. "Hey, that's neat," the boy next to her says. He radiates bubble gum. Elizabeth feels him beside her, a warm reassuring presence. Rubber sneaker soles.

The light on the western horizon fades and the stars begin to shine. The voice names the constellations: the Bears, the Dippers, Cassiopeia's Chair, Orion, the Pleiades. The voice says that the ancients used to believe people could become stars or constellations when they died, which was a poetic thought but of course not true. The stars are in fact much more wonderful and surprising than the ancients imagined. They are flaming balls of gas. The voice goes into a rhapsody of numbers and distances, during which Elizabeth tunes out.

The North Star: a small white arrow points to it. The voice speeds up time and the stars wheel around the pole. To see that you would have to stand for nights with your eyes glued open. The ancients thought that the stars really moved that way, but of course it's the earth that rotates.

The ancients had other beliefs as well. Ominous music. Today's show is about unusual stellar events, the voice says. The stars rotate backwards in time, to the year 1066. Picture of the Bayeux Tapestry, with William the Conqueror looking gleeful. The ancients believed that comets meant disruptions, war, pestilences, plagues, the birth of a great hero, the fall of a throne or the end of the world. The voice gives a dismissive laugh. Everyone knows better now.

Halley's Comet appears in the sky, faint at first, then brighter and brighter, its tail streaming out like blown cloud. The voice gives some information on the composition of this tail. The word "comet" comes from *cometes*, hairy. The ancients thought of comets as hairy stars.

Halley's Comet fades, then vanishes. It will return, the voice says, in 1985.

Stars begin to fall, a few at a time, then more and more. They aren't really stars, the voice explains, merely meteorites. Meteorites come in showers. They are probably debris left over from exploded stars. As the stars fall, slides of paintings – crowd scenes, Dances of Death, burning buildings – flash on the dome and the voice recites a few verses from Shakespeare. Then the voice produces some Northern Lights and begins to discuss their causes. Some people claim to have heard them, a high rustling noise, but this has never been recorded. Elizabeth feels a thin whisper close to her ear.

She's cold. She knows it's warm in the room and she can smell the children, coats, popcorn oil; but the Northern Lights are making her cold. She wants to get up and leave the auditorium. She looks around for the door, but she can't see it. She doesn't like the idea of groping around in the dark.

Now the voice is going to reveal something extraordinary. They've all heard about the Star of Bethlehem, haven't they? Yes. Well, maybe there really was a Star of Bethlehem. Above, the stars rotate back through centuries, two thousand years. See that?

The children breathe, *Oh*. A star is growing, bigger, brighter, till its light fills half the sky. Then, diminuendo. Like a firework, it's gone.

"That was a supernova," the voice says. "A dying star." When a star came to the end of its life, it might explode, burning up all its remaining energy in one spectacular burst. Someday our own sun would do that. But not for billions of years.

Then the remaining matter, lacking the energy to balance its own gravitational field, would collapse into itself, forming a neutron star. Or a black hole. The voice and its pointer locate a space in the sky where there is nothing. No one can see a black hole, says the voice; but because of their effects on objects around them they are known to exist. No light, for instance, shines through them. Nobody quite understands black holes yet, but they are thought to be stars collapsed to a density so great that no light can escape from them. They suck energy in instead of giving it out. If you fell into a black hole, you would disappear forever; though to anyone watching, you would appear to have been frozen for eternity on the black hole's event horizon.

The piece of blackness expands, perfectly round, lightless, until it fills the center of the dome. A man in a silver suit falls towards it, reaches it, stops.

The man hangs spread-eagled against the blackness while the voice explains that he has actually disappeared. He's an optical illusion. That would be a real cosmic disaster, the voice says. What if the earth, without knowing it, were approaching a black hole? The silver man vanishes and the stars twinkle again, while the voice explains that such a thing is not really very likely.

Elizabeth, shivering, stares up at the sky, which isn't really a sky but a complicated machine with tiny lights projected by slides and push-buttons. People do not become stars of any kind when they die. Comets do not really cause plagues. Really there is nobody in the sky. Really there is no round sphere of darkness, no black sun, no frozen silver man.

LESJE

Lesje feels awkward, as if the bones of her elbows and knees aren't really touching but are attached to one another with string. Gangling. Surely her teeth are larger than usual, her chest is flatter. She pulls her shoulders back. Nate's children aren't exactly unfriendly, but there's a withholding, a narrow-eyed evaluation. The new teacher. Prove to us that we should be here. Prove you're worth our attention. Who are you anyway and what are you getting us into? Nate said when he asked her to do this that they were very interested in dinosaurs, but at the moment she doesn't believe it.

The three of them are looking through glass at the effigy of the paleontologist, kneeling in his cubicle among simulated rocks. He has a hat on and he's chalky white, with clean-cut First World War air-ace features and well-trimmed hair. Silent Sam, they've nicknamed him. Quite unlike Professor Morgan, whiskered and unkempt leader of the only dig Lesje has been privileged to attend, as flunky and chief varnisher. He kept his pipe tobacco in his right pocket and emptied the old pipes into his left one. Several times he caught fire and they had to put him out. *Balderdash. Man doesn't know what he's talking about.* He thought Lesje was one of the biggest jokes he'd heard. *So you want to be a paleontologist. Better off learning to cook. Worst coffee I ever tasted.* Lesje cringing – because she respected his opinion, had read every one of his papers she could get her hands on, and his book on carnivorous dinosaurs of the Canadian plains – appeasing him with more and better cups of coffee, or tea, or Scotch, running her ass off like some dumb airline stewardess, trying to find ways to please him, until she discovered there weren't any. Luckily her current boss, Dr. Van Vleet, isn't anything like that, though he must be even older. On the other hand Lesje can't imagine him digging anything up. He specializes in the classification of teeth.

But the man in the glass case is a model. He's holding a fossil; presumably he's undergoing the ecstasy of scientific discovery, but his face isn't giving any of that away.

"What's he doing?" Nancy wants to know. Lesje suspects she doesn't really want to know, but it's part of this charade that the children must ask polite questions and Lesje must turn herself inside out trying to answer them.

"He's plaster-coating a bone," Lesje says. "He has to do it very carefully because it isn't real bone, it's a fossil. The softer parts of the bone decayed away and the shape of the bone has been filled up with minerals, so it's kind of like stone. It's very brittle."

"I know," Janet says. "Daddy told us."

"Is that your job?" Nancy says.

"Well, part of it," Lesje says.

"That's a funny job," Nancy says.

"Well, I do other things too," Lesje says, wondering why she's defending herself to a nine-year-old. Or is she eight? "Actually I've never done that much actual digging. I did a lot of bone preservation. Some of the fossils have to be preserved right away or they'll fall apart. We coat them with Gelva. That's a kind of resin."

The children stare through the glass at the rigid paleontologist, who the more you look resembles a corpse, Lesje thinks, with his pallor and fixed eyes. Janet's face is clamped as though she's caught an off smell, Nancy is curious but uninvolved. How can Lesje explain to them why she does this, why she loves doing this? The day they found the Albertosaurus, a thigh, a vertebra. Morgan: "What have we here?" Disappointed because it was a well-known species. But Lesje: *Live again*! she'd wanted to cry, like some Old Testament prophet, like God, throwing up her arms, willing thunderbolts; and the strange flesh would grow again, cover the bones, the badlands would moisten and flower.

But that can't happen, so the next best thing is these displays, with the admittedly plastic vegetation among which the bones, articulated and rearticulated after furious argument over which way the creatures had actually walked, rear their gigantic heads

69

and cavernous eye-sockets far above the craning necks of those who are, by the grace of their ancestors, still living.

In the Cretaceous twilight the children press buttons, watching the colored slides flip through their cycles while the Museum's automated voices drone. Lesje knows she's superfluous. Nate strolls up beside her, lounging, unconscious, and she wants to shake him. What is all this about, why has he put her through it? Made her sacrifice her free time (she could have been shopping! reading! copulating!) for this lack of an event? Is she being inspected, is it a test, has she failed? If he wants to make a pass at her – and she doesn't know what she would do if he did that, hasn't thought beyond that first pressure of his hand on some part of her body forbidden enough to be decisive – why doesn't he make it? (Not here and now, of course; not in front of the children. Who probably would not notice.)

But that doesn't seem to be the point.

NATE

The three of them, ahead of him, indistinct in the cavernous dark. Monsters loom over them, reptilian, skeletal, wired into poses of menace as in some gargantuan tunnel of horrors. Nate feels his bones eroding, stone filling the cavities. Trapped. Run Nancy, run Janet, or time will overtake you, you too will be caught and frozen. But Nancy, secure in the belief that he can't see her, is calmly picking her nose.

Lesje's silhouette bends towards the children. Elongated: Our Lady of the Bones. " 'Extinct' means there aren't any more of them," she says. Nate hopes she won't find his children ignorant or stupid. He's sure he's explained to them several times what "extinct" means. And they've visited this gallery often, though Nancy prefers the Egyptian mummies and Janet likes the armor, the lords and ladies. Are they playing up to Lesje to help him out, asking questions to counterfeit interest, are they already that perceptive, that sly? Is he that obvious?

"Why not?" Janet says. "Why are they all extinct?"

"No one really knows," Lesje says. "The world changed, and the new conditions weren't suitable for them." She pauses. "We've found quite a few eggs with baby dinosaurs in them. Towards the end, they didn't even hatch."

"It got too cold, you turkey," Nancy says to Janet. "It was the Ice Age."

"Well, not exactly," Lesje begins, but thinks better of it.

She turns back towards him, hesitating, waiting.

Nancy runs, tugs at his arm to make him bend down. She wants to see the mummies now, she whispers. Janet, his squeamish one, will protest, there will be a compromise, time will flow on; soon everyone will be one day older.

How could he desert them? Could he endure those pre-arranged Saturday outings? To see them only once a week, for that would be the price, the pound of flesh. How've you been, kids. Great, Dad. Stilted. No bedtime stories, impromptu chases along the hallway, voices at the cellar door. Unfair. But it will be that or some other unfairness, Lesje, as yet untouched, intact, weeping in a bedroom doorway somewhere in the future. Bright paint flaking from her, pieces of thin curved glass, a broken ornament. As for him, slivers in his murderous hands, sitting in the bar at the Selby Hotel, pondering the ethical life. Would he be any better off than he is now? He would watch hockey games with the other drinkers, echoing their raucous cheers. The ethical life. He'd been taught it was the only desirable goal. Now that he no longer believes it's possible, why does he keep on trying to lead it?

Limping home from school, purple and cut because his mother had forbidden him to fight. *Even when they hit me first?* Even when they hit you first. But he'd thought of a way around her. *They were beating up a smaller boy.* Not good enough. *Three against one.* Still not good enough. *They called him a kike.* Ah, that did it. Fire flashed from her eyes. In the name of tolerance, kill. My beamish boy. Nate, hypocrite at six and two inches taller than any of his tormentors, fought with fierce joy, inventing new injustices to account for his triumphant black eyes. Deeds Not Creeds, as the Unitarians said.

He can rehearse all the reasons for not acting, in this or any other situation; yet he knows his own past well enough to fear that nevertheless he will unaccountably act. Despite his scruples, and more desperately, more senselessly because of them. Because of his selfishness, as someone will be sure to point out. Not Elizabeth though. She claims she doesn't care what he does, who his ladyfriends are, as she puts it, as long as the children are protected. As she also puts it. She means her children. Nate is sure she's secretly convinced she conceived them through parthenogenesis, having conveniently forgotten the night of the bath towel and the other night, the many other nights. Laziness and habit. As for him, he'd like to think his children had sprung fully formed from his forehead. Then they would be entirely his.

As it is, Nate knows who would get the children. Though they've never discussed separating. Even during the worst times, she's never told him to leave, he's never threatened it. But it hangs between them in every conversation; it's the secret weapon, the final solution, the one unspeakable thing. He suspects they both think about it almost all the time: considering, rejecting.

Better to stop now. Instead of sweeping Lesje up from the carpeted floor of the Vertebrate Evolution Gallery and running up the stairs with her to the seclusion of Mammals and Insects, he'll thank her and shake her hand, touching her anyway that once, the long thin fingers cool in his palm. Then he'll visit the mummies and after that the suits of armor, and he'll try to avoid seeing any of these artifacts as images of himself. Outside, he'll comfort himself with popcorn and a cigarette, substitutes for the double Scotch he will by that time really need. They will wait on the stone steps of the Museum, a family, leaning against the plaque at the right-hand side of the door, THE ARTS OF MAN THROUGH ALL THE YEARS, until Elizabeth materializes from whatever limbo she's wandered off to, her stocky figure in the black coat proceeding evenly up the steps to claim them at the appointed time.

73

ELIZABETH

Elizabeth lies propped in the bathtub. Once she took baths for pleasure; now she takes them for the same reason she eats. She's servicing her body, like servicing a car, keeping it well cleaned, its moving parts in trim, ready for the time when she may be able to use it again, inhabit it. For pleasure. She's eating too much, she knows that, but better too much than too little. Too little is the danger. She's lost the capacity to judge, since she's never really hungry. No doubt she's taking too many baths as well.

She's careful to have the water at less than body heat, as she has a fear of falling asleep in the tub. You can drown in two inches of water. They say if the water is the same temperature as your blood your heart might stop, but only if there's something wrong with it. As far as she knows there is nothing wrong with her heart.

She's brought work home from the office. She's bringing work home a lot, since she seems unable to concentrate on it there. She can't concentrate on it at home either, but at least there's no one who might walk in on her and find her staring at the wall. She's always done most of her own typing; she's a crack typist, why not, she did nothing but that for years, but also she doesn't like to delegate her work. She made her way up to her present position by having a good telephone manner and by always knowing the details of the job above her a little better than the person actually doing it, so she has a natural distrust of secretaries. Now, however, the paper is piling up. She'll have to seize hold soon.

She frowns, trying to focus on the book in front of her, held up in one dry hand.

But it is hard for us to grasp these changes. It is hard for us to put ourselves in the place of people living in the old China (as millions still live in the Third World), toiling on

74

small plots of land, losing almost all they produce to the feudal landlords, at the mercy of floods and famine – who after a long war oust the landlord.

Elizabeth closes her eyes. It's a catalogue, a traveling show. Peasant paintings. It's in England right now and they can have it in a couple of years, if they want it. She's supposed to be looking at the catalogue and giving feedback. She's supposed to write a memo saying whether she thinks the show would be worthwhile and interesting to the Canadian public.

But she can't, she can't care. She can't care about the Canadian public, much less about this catalogue written by some armchair Marxist in England. From his point of view she's a landlord. She wonders about her tenants, with their sallow faces and their abnormally quiet child, dressed always a little too neatly, a little too well. They're foreigners of some kind, but Elizabeth doesn't know what and it would be rude to ask. Something from Eastern Europe, she thinks, escaped. They are unobtrusive and they pay their rent, nervously, always a day ahead. Are they fighting a long war to oust her? There are no signs of it. These paintings are from a place so utterly alien to her that it might as well be on the moon.

She skips the introduction, turns to the pictures. *New Village, New Spirit. Continue to Advance. The New Look of Our Piggery.* It's blatant propaganda, and the pictures are ugly. With their crude bright colors and clearly drawn smiling figures they're like the Sunday-school handouts she loathed so much as a child. *Jesus loves me.* She never believed that for a second. Jesus was God and God loved Auntie Muriel; Auntie Muriel was absolutely certain of that. As far as Elizabeth was concerned God could not love both her and Auntie Muriel at the same time.

They never went to church before they moved to Auntie Muriel's. Which Auntie Muriel might have known. Elizabeth won a prize for memorizing scripture verses. Caroline, on the other hand, made a spectacle of herself. It was Easter; they had on their new blue hats, with the elastic that cut into Elizabeth's chin, and the matching coats. Size ten and size seven but identical: Auntie Muriel loved dressing them like twins. The pulpit was banked with daffodils but the minister was not talking about the Resurrection. He preferred Judgment. *And the sun became*

black as sackcloth of hair, and the moon became as blood, and
the stars of heaven fell unto the earth, and the heaven departed
as a scroll when it is rolled together.

Elizabeth pleated and unpleated her picture of Christ coming out of the hole in the rock, his face translucent, two blue women kneeling before him. She folded his head back, then pulled the top of the paper, making him pop up again like a jack-in-the-box. The church smelled of perfume, too strong, waves of dusting powder from Auntie Muriel beige and upright beside her. She wanted to take off her coat. *Look, look*, said Caroline, standing up. She was pointing at the stained glass window, the center one where Christ in purple knocked at a door. She crouched, then tried to scramble across the pew in front, dislodging Mrs. Symon's mink hat. Elizabeth sat still, but Auntie Muriel reached across and jerked at the back of Caroline's coat. The minister frowned from his grape-draped pulpit and Caroline began to scream. Auntie Muriel took hold of her arm, but she broke free and pushed past the line of knees and ran down the aisle. They should have known, right then and there. Something wrong. She said afterwards that the purple was falling on her, but Auntie Muriel told everyone she'd just had an upset stomach. Excitable, they said; little girls often were. She should never have been brought to the main service.

Auntie Muriel decided it was the minister's fault and spearheaded the drive to get rid of him. They didn't have to listen to that sort of thing. More like a Baptist. Years later he'd been in the newspapers for doing an exorcism on a girl who really had a brain tumor and died anyway. You see? said Auntie Muriel. Crazy as a coot.

As for Caroline, when seven years later that scream took final shape and she made it totally, calamitously clear what she'd been trying to say, that was something else; that was a judgment. Or a lack of willpower, depending on how Auntie Muriel was feeling that day.

In the hospital, and afterwards in the institution, Caroline would not talk or even move. She would not eat by herself and she had to be diapered like a baby. She lay on her side with her knees curled up to her chest, eyes closed, hands fisted. Elizabeth sat beside her, breathing the sickly smell of inert flesh. Damn you, Caroline, she whispered. I know you're in there.

Three years after that, when Caroline was almost seventeen, an attendant was called away while she was in the bathtub. An emergency, they said. They were never supposed to leave patients like Caroline alone in a bathtub; those were the rules. They weren't supposed to put patients like Caroline into bathtubs at all, but someone had decided it would help her to relax, uncurl her; that was what they said at the inquest. So it happened and Caroline slipped down. She drowned rather than making the one small gesture, the turn of the head, that would have saved her life.

Sometimes Elizabeth has wondered whether Caroline did it on purpose, whether all along, inside that sealed body, she'd been conscious and waiting for the chance. She has wondered why. Sometimes, though, she's merely wondered why she herself has never done the same thing. At these times Caroline is clear, logical, pure; marble in contrast to her own slowly percolating flesh, the gasps of her decaying lungs and spongy, many-fingered heart.

In the room someone is singing. Not singing but a hum; Elizabeth realizes she's been hearing it for some time. She opens her eyes to locate the sound; the pipes, it must be, vibration of distant water. The wallpaper is too bright, morning-glories, and she knows she should be careful. No openings. She hadn't found those people in the sixties who'd torn their cats apart and jumped out of high-rise windows because they thought they were birds in the least glamorous: she'd found them stupid. Anyone who had ever heard those voices before or seen what they could do would have known what they were saying.

"Shut up," Elizabeth says. Even this much acknowledgment is bad. She'll concentrate on the text. *Criticizing Lin Piao and Confucius before the remains of an ancient slave-owner's war chariots*, she reads. The charioteers were buried alive. She peers into the picture, trying to see them, but all she can make out are the skeletons of the horses. Indignant peasants clamor around the grave.

Her hand holds the book, her body stretches away from her through the water, surrounded by white porcelain. On the ledge, far away, so far she is sure she could never reach them, are the toys the children still insist on floating in their baths, though they should be too old: an orange duck, a red and white boat with a wind-up paddle wheel, a blue penguin. Her breasts, flattened by gravity, her belly. Hourglass figure. Nancy's *Little Riddle Book*:

> Two bodies have I
> Though both joined in one,
> The stiller I stand
> The quicker I run.

On the next page over was a riddle about a coffin. Hardly suitable for children, she said that Christmas. Nate bought it, in a little boxed set.

Her knees jut from the blue water like mountains; clouds of bubble bath floating around them. *Bodykins*, imported. She bought it for Chris, for both of them, in some sybaritic dream; early, before she found out he didn't like having her look at his body except from half an inch away. He didn't like having her stand back from him, he wanted her to feel him but not see him. I'll get you where you live, he said, much later, much too late. Where does she live?

Sand runs through her glass body, from her head down to her feet. When it's all gone she'll be dead. Buried alive. Why wait?

LESJE

Lesje is out for lunch with Marianne. They've just had a sandwich at Murray's, which is near and cheap; now they're walking over to Yorkville and Cumberland to look in the store windows. It's no longer the place to shop, says Marianne, whom Lesje regards as an authority on such things; too overpriced. Queen Street West is the place now. But Queen Street West is too far away.

Marianne habitually has lunch with Trish, who's off with the flu. They've asked her along on these expeditions before but usually she says no. She's behind in her work, she says, she'll grab a sandwich downstairs. Surely they don't have much to offer her in addition to the gossip they provide at morning coffee. Marianne openly admits – or is it a joke? – that she went into Biology to meet medical students and marry a doctor. Lesje doesn't approve of such frivolity.

Now, however, gossip is what she wants. She craves gossip, she wants to know anything Marianne can tell her about Elizabeth and especially about Elizabeth's husband Nate, who has not phoned, written or appeared since he shook hands with her beside the EXIT sign at the dinosaur gallery. She isn't interested in him, really, but she's baffled. She wants to know whether he often does such things, makes such odd approaches. However, she isn't sure how to obtain this information from Marianne without telling her what has happened so far; which she doesn't want to do. But why not? Nothing has happened.

They stop at the corner of Bay and Yorkville to look at a bunchy blue velvet suit with gold braid trim and a blouse underneath, cuff ruffles and a Peter Pan collar.

"Too goyish," Marianne says, which is her word for tacky taste. Despite her blue eyes and blond hair and her madrigal name, Marianne is Jewish; what Lesje thinks of as pure Jewish, in contrast to her own hybrid state. Marianne's attitude towards Lesje is complicated. Sometimes she seems to include her among

79

the Jews; she'd hardly say *too goyish* in front of her if she thought of her as too goyish herself. Though, as one of Lesje's aunts explained to her, sweetly and maliciously, when she was nine, Lesje isn't really Jewish. She could be classified as truly Jewish only if it was her mother instead of her father. Apparently the gene is passed through the female, like hemophilia.

At other times, though, Marianne focuses on Lesje's Ukrainian name. It doesn't seem to bother her the way it would probably bother her parents; instead she finds it intriguing, though a little funny.

"Why should you worry? Ethnic is big these days. Change your last name and you'll get a Multiculturalism grant."

Lesje smiles at these jokes, but weakly. She's multicultural all right, but not in the way the grant-givers want. And her father's family has already changed its name at least once, though not to get a grant. They did it in the late thirties: who could tell, Hitler might invade, and even if he didn't there were enough anti-Semites in the country already. In those days, the aunts said, you didn't answer the door unless you knew who was knocking. Which is how Lesje has ended up with the unlikely name of Lesje Green; though she has to admit that Lesje Etlin wouldn't have been any more probable. For two years, when she was nine and ten, she told the teachers at school that her name was Alice. Lesje meant Alice, her mother said, and it was a perfectly good name, the name of a famous Ukrainian poet. Whose poems Lesje would never be able to read.

She changed it back, though, for the following reason. If she were to discover a country which had never been discovered before (and she fully intended to do this sometime), she would of course name it after herself. There already was a Greenland, which wasn't at all the sort of place she had in mind. Greenland was barren, icy, devoid of life, whereas the place Lesje intended to discover would be tropical, rich and crawling with wondrous life forms, all of them either archaic and thought extinct, or totally unknown even in fossil records. She made careful drawings of this land in her scrapbooks and labeled the flora and fauna.

But she couldn't call this place Aliceland; it wasn't right. One of her reservations about *The Lost World* concerned the names of the topographical features. Lake Gladys, for instance:

too goyish. And the whole primitive plateau was called Maple White Land, after the artist whose sketches of a Pterodactyl, found clutched in his delirious and dying hand, had first put Professor Challenger on the track. Lesje was sure – though it didn't say so in the book – that Maple White must have been a Canadian, of the pinkest and most frigid kind. With a name like that what else could he be?

Lesjeland, though. That sounded almost African. She could picture it on a map: seen that way, there was nothing ludicrous about it.

Once, after she was grown up, she'd gone to the Odessa Pavilion during the Caravan Festival. Usually she avoided Caravan. She distrusted the officially promoted goodwill, the costumes nobody wore any more. There were really no Poles like the ones in the Polish Pavilion, no Indians like the Indians, no yodeling Germans. She's not sure why she went, that time; perhaps she was hoping to find her roots. She'd eaten foods she remembered only vaguely from her grandmother's house and had never known the names for – *pirogi, medvynk* – and watched tall boys and auburn-braided girls in red boots leap about on a stage decorated with paper sunflowers, singing songs she couldn't sing, dancing dances she'd never been taught. According to the program, some of the dancers were named Doris and Joan and Bob, although others had names like hers: Natalia, Halyna, Vlad. At the end, with that element of self-mockery she recognized too in Marianne when she said *schwartze*, imitating her mother's views on cleaning ladies, they sang a song from Ukrainian summer camp:

> I'm not Russian, I'm not Polish,
> I am not Romanian,
> Kiss me once, kiss me twice,
> Kiss me, I'm Ukrainian.

Lesje admired the bright costumes, the agility, the music; but she was an outsider looking in. She felt as excluded as if she'd been surrounded by a crowd of her own cousins. On both sides. *Kiss me, I'm multicultural*.

She hadn't been sent to Ukrainian summer camp or to Jewish summer camp. She hadn't been allowed to go either to the golden church with its fairy-tale onion dome or to synagogue.

Her parents would have been happy to send her to both, if it would keep the peace, but the grandmothers wouldn't allow it.

Sometimes she thinks she was produced, not by her parents in the usual way, but by some unheard-of copulation between these two old ladies who never met. They'd existed in an odd parody of marriage, hating each other more than either hated the Germans, yet obsessed with each other; they'd even died within a year of each other, like an old devoted couple. They'd infested her parents' house in relays, fought over her as if she'd been a dress at a bargain. If one baby-sat for her the other must be given a turn or there would be histrionics: weeping from her Grandmother Smylski, rage from her Grandmother Etlin (who'd kept her name, who'd refused to scurry for cover with the rest of them). Neither of them had ever learned English very well, though Grandmother Etlin had picked up some scatological curses from the neighborhood children who hung around her store, which she'd used in garbled versions when she wanted to get her own way. "Jesus asshole, dog poop, I hope you die!" she would scream, stamping her black boots on the front doorstep. She knew the front doorstep was the best place to do this: Lesje's parents would do almost anything to get her inside, away from the observation of the street. *English people.* These bland clones of their imagination did not have tiny black-booted grandmothers who screamed, "I hope your bum falls off!" on the front doorstep; or anything remotely equivalent. Lesje knows better, now.

The strange thing about her grandmothers was how much alike they were. Both of their houses were small and dark and smelled of furniture polish and mothballs. They were both widows, they both had sad-eyed single male boarders stashed away in upstairs rooms, they both had fancy china and front rooms crowded with silver-framed family photos, they both drank tea in a glass.

Before she was old enough to go to school she'd spent half the week with each of them, since her mother had to work. She would sit on the kitchen floor, cutting pictures out of magazines and folders from the small travel agency where her mother worked, arranging them in piles – men in one pile, women in another, dogs in another, houses in another – while the grandmothers drank their tea and talked to the aunts (her father's sister, her mother's brothers' wives), in languages she couldn't understand and which her parents never spoke at home.

This should have made her trilingual. Instead she was considered bad at English, plodding, a poor speller, lacking in imagination. In Grade Five she'd been asked to write about "My Summer Holiday," and she'd written about her rock collection, with technical details of each rock. She'd been given a D and a lecture by the teacher. "You were supposed to write about something personal, something from your own life," the teacher said. "Not out of the encyclopedia. You must have done *something* else during your summer holidays."

Lesje didn't understand. She hadn't done anything else during her summer holidays, not anything she could remember, and the rock collection was something personal from her own life. But she could not explain this. She couldn't explain why her discovery that rocks were different from each other and had special names was so important. The names were a language; not many other people might know it, but if you found one who did, you would be able to talk together. Only about rocks, but that would be something. She would walk up and down the stairs murmuring these names, wondering if she was pronouncing them right. "Schist," she would say, "magma, igneous, malachite, pyrite, lignite." The names of the dinosaurs, when she found out about them, were even more satisfactory, more polysyllabic, soothing, mellifluous. Though she could not spell *receive* or *embarrass* or *career*, she spelled *Diplodocus* and *Archaeopteryx* from the beginning without a hitch.

Her parents thought she was becoming too wrapped up in these things and tried to give her dancing lessons to make her more sociable. Too late, she was not sociable. They blamed, silently of course, her Grandmother Etlin, who'd first taken her to the Museum, not because she had any interest in the things inside it but because it was cheap and out of the rain. Because her Grandmother Smylski had Mondays, Tuesdays and Wednesdays, Grandmother Etlin insisted on having three days as well, all in a row, even though it meant violating the Sabbath; which didn't bother Grandmother Etlin all that much. She kept kosher out of habit but was not in other ways visibly reverent. After Lesje started school they'd kept this Saturday custom.

Instead of synagogue Lesje attended the Museum, which at first did look to her a little like a church or a shrine, as if you were supposed to kneel. It was quiet and smelled mysterious, and was full of sacred objects: quartz, amethyst, basalt.

(When her grandmother died, Lesje felt she should be put into the Museum, in a glass case like the Egyptian mummies, with a label where you could read about her. An impossible idea; but this was the form her mourning took. She knew better than to say it though, at shiva, sitting in a corner of her aunt's huge pink and white living room while they all ate coffee cake. They'd finally let her into the synagogue, too, but it hadn't been mysterious at all. Neither the bright, clean-lined synagogue nor the pink living room seemed at all like her grandmother. A glass case in a shadowy corner, with her black boots standing at the bottom and her few pieces of gold jewelry and the amber beads spread out beside her.)

"Explain me," her grandmother would say, holding her hand tightly, for protection Lesje decided much later; and Lesje would read the labels to her. Her grandmother understood not at all, but nodded wisely, smiling; not because of the impressive rocks, as Lesje thought at the time, but because her granddaughter seemed able to negotiate with ease in this world she herself found so incomprehensible.

In the last year of her grandmother's life, when Lesje was twelve and they were both getting a little old for these mornings, they'd seen something at the Museum which upset her grandmother. She'd long ago got used to the mummies in the Egyptian gallery and she no longer said *Gevalt* every time they went into the dinosaur gallery, which was not at that time dark and equipped with voices. But this was something different. They'd seen an Indian woman, wearing a beautiful red sari with a gold band at the hem. Over the top of the sari was a white lab coat, and with the woman were two little girls, obviously her daughters, wearing Scottish kilts. They all disappeared through a door marked STAFF ONLY. "Gevalt," her grandmother said, frowning, but not with fear.

84

Lesje stared after them, entranced. This, then, was her own nationality.

"You'd look good in that," Marianne says. She sometimes gives Lesje advice on how she ought to dress, which Lesje ignores since she doesn't feel capable of following it. Marianne, who has to watch what she eats, thinks Lesje should be stately. She could be stately, Marianne says, if she wouldn't lope. They're looking at a long-skirted plum wool dress, subdued, exhorbitantly expensive.

"I'd never wear it," Lesje says; meaning, William never takes me anywhere I could wear it.

"Now here," says Marianne, moving to the next window, "you have your basic Elizabeth Schoenhof little black dress."

"Too goyish?" Lesje says, thinking Marianne is being derisive, and oddly delighted.

"Oh, no," Marianne says. "Look at the *cut*. Elizabeth Schoenhof isn't goyish, she's haute Wasp."

Lesje, deflated, asks what the difference is.

"Haute Wasp," says Marianne, "is when you don't have to give a piss. Haute Wasp is when you have this tatty carpet that looks like hell but cost a million bucks, and only a few people know it. Remember when the Queen picked up a chicken bone with her fingers and it was in all the papers, and suddenly it was *done*? That's haute Wasp."

Lesje feels she'll never be able to master nuances like these. William with his wines: full-bodied, bouquet. It all tastes like wine to her. Maybe Nate Schoenhof is haute Wasp, though somehow she doesn't think so. He's too hesitant, he talks too much, he looks around the room at the wrong moments. He probably doesn't even know what haute Wasp means.

Maybe Elizabeth doesn't either. Maybe this is part of being haute Wasp: you don't have to know.

"What about Chris?" she says. Surely the fact of Chris does not fit in with Marianne's definition.

"Chris?" says Marianne. "Chris was the chauffeur."

ELIZABETH

Yes, I know I've suffered an unusual shock. I'm quite aware of that, I can feel the waves. I realize it was an act directed ostensibly at me though not really at me, childhood imprintings being what they are, though I can't say I know of any in his case that would account for it. He had a bad childhood but who didn't? I also realize that my reactions are normal under the circumstances and that he intended me to feel guilty and that I am not really guilty. Of that. I'm not sure whether or not I do feel guilty. I feel angry, from time to time; otherwise I feel devoid. I feel as though energy is being constantly drained out of me, as though I'm leaking electricity. I know I'm not responsible and that there's little I could have done and that he might have killed me or Nate or the children instead of himself. I knew that at the time, and no, I did not phone the police or the mental hygiene authorities. They wouldn't have believed me. I know all these things.

I know I have to keep on living and I have no intention of doing otherwise. You don't have to worry about that. If I were going to take a carving knife to my wrists or do a swan dive off the Bloor Street Viaduct I'd have done it before now. I'm a mother if not exactly a wife and I take that seriously. I would never leave an image like that behind for my children. I've had that done to me and I didn't like it.

No, I don't want to discuss my mother, my father, my Auntie Muriel or my sister. I know quite a lot about them as well. I've already been down this particular yellow brick road a couple of times, and what I found out mostly was that there's no Wizard of Oz. My mother, my father, my aunt and my sister did not go away. Chris won't go away either.

I am an adult and I do not think I am merely the sum of my past. I can make choices and I suffer the consequences, though they aren't always the ones I foresaw. That doesn't mean I have to like it.

No thank you. I don't want pills to help me through. I don't wish to have my mood changed. I could describe this mood to you in detail but I'm not sure that would be of any benefit either to you or to myself.

Elizabeth sits on the grey bench in the Ossington subway station, black leather hands folded in her lap, feet in their boots placed neatly. Her tone, she knows, is slightly belligerent and she isn't sure why. The first time she ran through this conversation, sitting in her office that morning, she was totally calm. Having thus concluded that the psychiatrist Nate has so kindly decided she ought to see has nothing either to give her or to tell her, she phoned and canceled the appointment.

She's using the time she's freed to go home early. She will wrap Christmas presents, hiding the packages under the bed before the children get home from school. Already she knows the crackle of paper, the brightness of the ribbons, will be almost more than she can bear, those stars, blue and red and white, burning her eyes as if there's no atmosphere. It's the hope, the false promise of hope she can't tolerate. Everything is worse at Christmas; it always has been. But she'll get through it, she can depend on Nate to help in that, if in little else.

Perhaps this is what they're heading for: companionship, a thin arm extended, leaned on, two old people carefully descending from the front porch, one icy stair at a time. She'll make sure he takes his stomach pills and will monitor his intake of booze, he'll ask her to turn up her hearing aid and will read her amusing anecdotes from the daily papers. Military coups, massacres, that sort of thing. On weeknights they'll watch American sitcoms on television. They'll have photograph albums and when the children come over on Sundays with their own children these albums will be dredged out and they will all look at the photos, beaming; and seeing the picture of herself as she is today, this very instant, sitting here in the Ossington subway station waiting for the northbound bus, with the dim light filtering through the film of ash and oil on the plate-glass windows, she will sense again this chasm opening in herself. Then they will have a lunch of creamed salmon on toast, with eggs grated on top, a dish suited to their limited budget. Nate will play with the grandchildren and she will do the dishes by herself in the kitchenette, feeling Chris's breath as usual on the back of her neck.

Almost better to think of herself alone, in a small apartment, with her bowls and a few plants. No, that would be worse. If Nate were with her, at least there would be something moving. Keep moving, they said to those almost frozen, those who had taken too many pills, those in shock. U-Haul, An Adventure in Moving. I want to be moved. Move me. *We are the numb. Long years ago/We did this or that. And now we sit.*

The evening before, she knocked at the door of Nate's room, holding a pair of socks he'd dropped in the living room, presumably because they were wet. When he opened the door, he had no shirt on. Suddenly she, who hadn't wanted him to touch her for over two years, who'd found his long sparse body mildly repellant, who had chosen instead the thick, matted, richly veined flesh of Chris, who had rearranged time and space so that this torso she was now confronted with need never confront her, closeted as it was in an area clearly marked off from hers – she wanted him to wind his arms around her, string on bone but warm bone, press her, comfort and rock her. She wanted to say: Can anything be saved? Meaning this wreck. But he'd stepped back and she'd merely held out the socks, wearily, mutely, as usual.

Once she was always able to tell if he was in the house, whether she could actually hear him or not. Now she no longer can. He's absent more often now, and when he is there his presence is like light from a star that moved on thousands of light-years before: a phantom. He no longer, for instance, brings her cups of tea. They still give each other Christmas presents, though. The children would be disturbed if this ritual were omitted. She's finally bought him something for this year. It's a silver cigarette case. She thinks perversely of the contrast: the silver case emerging from his frayed pocket under the raveling sweater. Once he'd given her nightgowns, always a size too large, as if he thought her breasts were bigger than they were. Now it's books. On some neutral subject he assumes will interest her: antiques, pressed glass, quilts.

* * *

"Ready for Christmas?"

There's a man sitting beside Elizabeth. He's been sitting there for several minutes; she saw him as a brownish blur to the left, registered the shift as he crossed and recrossed his legs. Movement like rustlings in a hedge, furtive, almost not there. She turns her head, slightly, briefly, to look at him. He's wearing a brown topcoat, a little too small for him – it must pinch under the arms – and a brown hat. His eyes shine at her, brown also and small, like raisins. His hands, gloveless, dark hair on the knuckles, rest on the thick suitcase he holds across his lap.

She smiles. A long time ago she learned to smile easily, graciously, it takes no effort. "Not quite. No one ever is, are they?"

The man nudges closer to her, his buttocks inching along the bench. She feels a slight pressure at her side.

"You look as if you're waiting for someone," he says.

"No," she says, "I'm not waiting for anyone. Only the bus."

"I think we must be neighbors," he says. "I'm sure I've seen you on the street."

"I don't think so," Elizabeth says.

"I'm sure I have. I wouldn't forget." He lowers his voice. "A woman like you."

Elizabeth shifts away from the pressure against her thigh. Her other thigh is now against the arm of the bench. She can always stand up. But he begins immediately to talk about real estate values. This is harmless enough, and Elizabeth knows something about it. They both bought around the same time, it seems, both experienced the tortures of renovation, though he's done his living-room floor in cork tile, a choice Elizabeth herself would not have made. He tells a story about his contractor, the lies, the failures to show up, the deficient wiring. Elizabeth relaxes, leaning back against the bench. He's ordinary enough, but it's a relief to talk with someone practical, someone who can accomplish things. Simple competence, feet on the ground. *Bedrock*.

The man has children, he says, three of them, and a wife. They discuss the local school. He likes to read, he tells her, but only nonfiction. Books about history, famous crimes, the world wars. He asks her what she thinks about the results of the Québec election. "They'll never pull it off," he says. "Too much debt."

"Probably," says Elizabeth, whose attention is wandering now that there's no threat.

"We could have a drink sometime," he says abruptly.

Elizabeth sits up. "I don't think . . ." she says.

"You wouldn't regret it," he says, his eyes shining. He leans towards her confidentially. Sweet brandy on his breath. "I know," he says. "I know what you want. You might not think so to look at me, but I know."

"Right now I don't want anything," Elizabeth says, realizing at once that this is false. What she wants is to want something.

"All right," says the man. "If you change your mind, let me know." He hands her a little card, which she holds in her gloved hand without looking at it. "The office number," he says.

"I'll do that," Elizabeth says, laughing, turning it into a joke. She can taste the brandy in his mouth, blue flame flickering over her tongue. She looks at the card. There's a name, two numbers, nothing more.

"What do you do?" she asks, clutching at work, the objective world.

"Here," the man says, unsnapping the clasps of his suitcase. "Take your pick. Have a souvenir." He lifts the lid. The suitcase is full of women's bikini briefs, samples: red, black, white, pink, mauve, trimmed with lace, sheer, embroidered, some with – she can see – split crotches.

"I do a lot of traveling," the man says mournfully. "Pushing the line. Airports. They're big customers, airports." He lifts a pair of black briefs with the word STOP embroidered on a hexagonal scrap of red satin. "A very popular item," he says, his voice switching to a salesman's insinuating baritone. He sticks his finger through the split crotch, wiggles it.

Elizabeth stands up. "There's my bus," she says lightly. His hand, tented in black nylon, clothed like a puppet in some woman's empty groin, is absurdly and at last, at last, exciting to her.

For an instant only. The man fades almost at once, flattens, greys.

"Thank you for the conversation," she says, feeling she should thank him for something.

He withdraws his hand, looks up at her sadly. "Do you think I'd do this," he says, "if I didn't have to?"

90

NATE

When Nate is in the middle of his bath, soaping his long shankbones, Elizabeth opens the door and comes in without knocking. She closes the lid of the toilet and sits down on it, hunching forward, elbows on her dark-skirted knees. She wants to show him something she's bought as a Christmas present for Nancy. It's a small theatrical makeup kit; she got it at Malabar's, making a special trip. It has a few sticks of grease paint, some fake blood, and a couple of moustaches and pairs of eyebrows to match. Nancy will love it, Elizabeth says, and Nate knows she will. Elizabeth can always think up good presents for the children. He himself has to ask them what they want.

Elizabeth sitting on the toilet at right angles to his left shoulderblade makes him nervous. He has to turn his head to see her, whereas she can see most of him – naked, exposed – without making any effort. He's aware of the soap curds, the grey particles, the flecks of his own skin that litter the water. He scrubs his arms vigorously with the loofah, rough on the skin like a tiger's tongue. The loofah is his; he buys them at a little store on Bathurst that sells nothing but natural sponges; not one of those bath boutiques, but a grimy store, unadorned, that has the feel of raw materials. A small importer. Nate likes walking into this store, picking out his new sponge from the mounds of them that lie in heaps on the tiny counter. Himself, in aqua water, knife between his teeth, cutting the raw sponge loose from coral rocks, making it to the surface gasping for breath, heaving the sponge overarm into the moored boat. Eyeball-to-eyeball combat with a giant squid, one tentacle cut loose, then another. Nothing to think about but getting free. Clouds of ink obscuring the water, round welts on his legs. Plunging the knife right in between its eyes.

Elizabeth doesn't like his loofahs. She says that because he doesn't take the time to rinse and dry them between baths, they get moldy. This is true, they do get moldy. She doesn't understand that if each loofah were allowed to continue forever, he'd be deprived of the pleasure of going to the little store for a new one.

When she opened the door she let in a draft. Nate pulls the plug and clambers out of the tub, a towel clutched to his groin, feeling like a stick man.

Now that he's standing up in this room that is obviously too small for both of them, he expects her to leave. But she shifts her knees towards the wall and asks, "Where are you off to?"

"How do you know I'm off to anywhere?" he says.

She smiles. More like herself, her old self; the self that is, like his, getting old. "You're taking a bath." She leans her chin on her interlaced fingers, looks up at him. That nymph-on-a-lilypad pose. He wraps his abdomen, tucking the towel in.

"I'm going to a party," he says. "A Christmas party."

"At Martha's?"

"How did you know?" He hasn't wanted to tell her; not that he has anything to hide. It continues to amaze him, the way she's able to keep track of his activities without even seeming to be interested.

"She invited me."

"Oh," he says. He might have known Martha would consider it appropriate to invite Elizabeth. He folds his arms across his chest; ordinarily he would use her Arrid Extra Dry to roller his armpits, but he can't do that with her in the bathroom. He can feel his mouth sagging downwards.

"Don't look so devastated," she says. "I'm not going."

"That's all over, you know," he says, feeling he has no moral obligation to tell her, telling her anyway.

"I know," she says. "I've been hearing quite a lot about it. She phones me at the office."

This is something Nate has always resented: they talk to each other, about him, behind his back. It was Elizabeth who started it. She'd invited Martha to lunch early on; to explain, she'd said, to get things clear. Martha had complained to him first, but she'd gone. "Why not be friendly?" Elizabeth said. "It's not as though I'm the jealous wife. I hardly have the right to be." She laughed softly, that furred laugh that had at first entranced him. "We might as well behave like reasonable adults."

"What did you talk about?" Nate asked Martha afterwards.

"You," she said.

"What about me?"

"About who owns you," Martha said. "We figured it out that Elizabeth really owns you, but I get fucking privileges one night a week."

"I don't believe Elizabeth would say a thing like that," Nate said.

"No," Martha said. "You're right, she wouldn't. She's too goddamned discreet. Let's say she just *gave me to understand*. She might think it, but the only one who'd ever say it is me. Old garbage-mouth."

Nate wanted to tell Martha not to demean herself, but he knew she didn't really feel she was demeaning herself. She saw it as saying what she thought. She conceived of herself as down-to-earth and honest, and of Nate and Elizabeth as hypocrites who evaded the issues. But she only said what she thought to Nate; never to Elizabeth.

By this time Nate no longer wants to know what they say to each other during those office phone calls. He doesn't want to go to Martha's party either, but he feels he ought to. His presence is supposed to establish the fact that they can still be friends. This is what Martha said to him on the phone. He doesn't much want to be friends with her, but he thinks he should want to. He wants to be kind and as gentle as possible. He won't stay long, he'll just put in an appearance, make a gesture, cast his shadow on the wall.

"She sounded all right to me," Nate says, too defensively. "When she asked me."

"Don't fool yourself," Elizabeth says. It's one of her axioms that Nate is always fooling himself. She puts her hands behind her on the toilet seat and leans back, which throws her breasts up and out. Is this an invitation, can it be possible? Nate refuses to believe it. He turns his head quickly away, scowls at himself in the mirror.

"I'll be back around ten," he says.

93

"I expect you will," Elizabeth says. "You're not too popular in that quarter, you know."

You know. Always meaning that he doesn't. Both of them do that: the constant hints that there are things he doesn't know, important things he's missed and that they, with their finer perceptions, can pick up every time.

Elizabeth stands up, brushes past him, picks up his loofah from where he's left it lying in the bathtub, squeezes it out.

"Take care of yourself," she says. She walks out of the bathroom, carrying the box of false moustaches.

Martha has made a large bowl of eggnog. It sits on her dining-room table along with the bottles of Scotch and rye, the mixes, the ice in a bucket. A red paper accordion bell is suspended over the table. Nate bumps it with his head as he straightens up with his glass of Scotch. If he wants eggs he'll boil them. He always likes to know exactly what he's drinking.

Martha is wearing a long dress, some synthetic material, red, to match the bell. The neckline is too wide; it makes her shoulders look even broader than they are. Nate hasn't seen that dress before. One of her bare arms is hooked through the arm of the man standing beside her. She looks up into his face, talking, smiling. Apart from greeting him she's ignored Nate so far. The new man is pale blond, shorter than Nate, with a businessman's prim little paunch already beginning under the vest of his three-piece suit.

Nate knows a few of the people, leftovers from his earlier life. A couple of the receptionists and legal secretaries, two or three of the men who joined the firm around the same time he did. Someone slaps his shoulder.

"Nate. How's it going?" Paul Callaghan, one-time rival, now patronizing. "Still whittling away?"

"Pretty good," Nate says.

"You're probably smarter than all of us," Paul says. "Taking it easy. No heart attacks at forty for you." He floats past Nate, already smiling at someone else.

*   *   *

94

Nate is talking with a girl in a white dress. He's never seen her before, though she claims to have met him at one of Martha's parties, two years ago, she says. She's telling Nate about her job. She makes plastic models of Holstein cows which are sold to breeders and dealers. The cows have to be made exactly to scale, perfect in every detail. She's hoping to go into painted portraits of individual cows, for which she could get more money. She asks Nate what his sign is.

Nate knows he should leave the party. He's done his duty. But the girl seizes his hand and bends over his palm, squinting at his life line. He can see a short distance down the front of her dress. He watches this pinched landscape idly. He isn't very good at casual encounters.

Martha is there, right beside his ear. She wants to have a word with him, she says. She takes his other hand and he allows himself to be led from the living room, down the hall into the bedroom. Coats are piled on the bed.

"You're disgusting," Martha says. "You make me want to puke."

Nate blinks at her, bending his head towards her as if this will help him to understand. Martha punches him in the face, then begins kicking him in the shins. She's hampered by the long skirt of her dress, so she slugs him, aiming for the belly, hitting him in the rib cage. Nate catches her arms and holds her against him. Now she's crying. He could throw her onto the bed, roll her up in coats to hold her still, then try to find out what he's done.

"What did I do?" he says.

"Making up to her at my party, right in front of me. You always try to humiliate me," Martha says, her voice coming in spurts. "You know what? You succeed."

"I wasn't," Nate says, "We were talking about plastic cows."

"You just don't know how it feels to be left," Martha says. Nate loosens his grip. Martha steps back, snatches a Kleenex from the night table and blots her face. "Why don't you try feeling something for a change?"

The new man's head appears in the doorway, withdraws, reappears. "Am I interrupting something?" he says.

"Yes," Martha says rudely.

"I was just leaving," Nate says. He roots among the coats, fur and tweed, looking for his pea jacket.

"It's in the hall closet," Martha says. "I guess you know where that is."

Because of the snow, Nate hasn't brought his bicycle. It's five blocks to the subway station but he's glad, he wants to walk. His right eyebrow where Martha hit him is beginning to hurt. Is the skin cut? She was wearing a ring. What bothers him isn't the pain but the wise look Elizabeth will give him.

He's only gone half a block before he hears Martha behind him.

"Nate. Stop."

He turns. She's running, slipping towards him in her gold shoes, her long red dress, no coat. Smiling, gleeful, her eyes brilliant. "I just took all the pills in the bathroom cabinet," she says. "Sixty-two aspirin with codeine, twenty-four Valiums. I thought you might like to say good-bye."

"That was stupid, Martha," Nate says. "Did you really?"

"Wait and see," she says, laughing. "Wait till five in the morning when you get to inspect the body. Hell, you can cart me away to that cellar of yours. You can shellac me. I won't bother you with demands any more."

The man in the three-piece suit is picking his way down Martha's steps. "Martha," he calls, slightly peevish, as if calling a runaway cat.

"Martha says she took all the pills in the bathroom," Nate says to him.

"Well, she was just in there. Why would she do that?" the new man asks Nate.

"Stop discussing me as if I'm a *thing*," Martha says. She's swaying a little. Nate takes off his pea jacket and hands it to her. "Here," he says.

"I don't need that," Martha says. She begins to cry again.

"We'll have to take her down to the hospital," Nate says. He's familiar with the procedure, he's been through it with the kids. Mothballs, baby aspirins, Elizabeth's birth control pills.

"I'm not going," Martha sobs. "I want to die."

"We can take my car," the new man says. "It's in the driveway." Nate grips Martha under the arms. She goes limp. He begins to drag her towards the new man's car, which is new also, a dark blue Torino. One of her shoes comes off and the new man picks it up and carries it along behind them, like a trophy in some kind of sports parade or religious procession.

"Give me my goddamned shoe," Martha says when they're in the car. She buckles the shoe on, then checks her hair in the rear-view mirror. The new man is driving; Nate sits in the back with Martha, to keep her from, as the new man says, "doing anything." By the time they reach Emergency Admissions at the Toronto General she seems quite cheerful.

"You can't make me go in there," she says to Nate.

"You can walk in or be dragged in," he tells her. "Did you really take those pills?"

"Guess," she says. "You're so good at female psychology. You figure it out." But she walks in between them with no more protest.

She lets them tell the Admissions nurse all about the pills. Nate explains that they don't know whether she's really taken them or not.

"Did you check the bottles?" the nurse says. "Were they empty?"

They didn't think to look for bottles, Nate says. They were in too much of a hurry.

"Actually this is all a joke," Martha says. "They've been drinking. It's the Christmas spirit, they thought it would be fun to cart me down here and make me get my stomach pumped out."

The nurse hesitates, looking severely from Nate to the new man. "You can smell the liquor," Martha says. "They aren't like this except when they drink. See, they've been fighting."

The nurse squints at Nate's swelling eye. "Is this true?" she says.

"They used force," Martha says. "You can see the fingermarks on my arms. Do I seem to you like someone who's just swallowed a bottle of pills?" She stretches out her bare arms. "Would you like to see me walk a straight line?"

97

LESJE

Lesje joins the queue in front of the cashier at the liquor store. The time is past when they'd ask to see her birth certificate, but she still gets the same cold feeling. Whenever she has to present a document proving she is who she is, she's convinced they'll find something out of order or that it will have someone else's name stamped on it. The worst that ever happens is that they mispronounce her name, giving her the look that says, we thought you were one of us but now we can tell you aren't.

She's buying a bottle of wine to celebrate the return of William, which will take place this evening. William is in London, Ontario, celebrating Christmas with his family. Impossible, of course (Of course! She agrees!) for her to have gone with him. Last year this separation between them seemed like a conspiracy, both of them giggling over the puritanism, xenophobia and general dingy-mindedness of their respective families. This year it seems like a betrayal.

Not that she could have gone with him, even if invited. She was expected to go to her parents' house for Christmas dinner, and dutifully she'd gone, as she did every year. How can she deprive them of their only daughter, their only child, they who have deprived themselves of whole platoons of sisters, brothers, uncles, aunts, cousins and second cousins, all, it's understood, for her sake?

Her parents' house is neither far enough north to be impressive, like the aunts' houses, nor far enough south to be quaint, like the grandmothers'. Her mother's brothers did well in real estate, her father's sister married into a china shop. Her parents began the trek north but got stuck halfway up, on a nondescript street south of St. Clair. It was as if all their desire for transformation and change had gone into one act, their marriage to each other. They had none left over for two-car garages.

Her father doesn't possess that ferocious instinct for business, or is it survival, which is supposed to be Jewish; which had impelled her grandfather from door to door, buying castoffs; and which once gave her grandmother six stitches in the head, defending her front-parlor variety store against a young man with an iron bar. *Turn your back, they steal you blind. Not the Chinese kids though. Them you don't have to watch.* Lesje's father rolled to his present modest eminence of color television and a second-hand Chev on used fur coats, on bubble gum and jawbreakers, two for a penny and the pennies carefully saved. And was he grateful? No. Married a *shiksa*, and of the worst kind too. (Like Lesje.)

He owned a dress business, true, but reluctantly: his mother almost forced him into it after his father died. *Little Nell Dresses*, it's now called; once it was called *Tinker Bell*. Her grandfather once had a partner who got these names out of books he'd read. The dresses are for small girls; Lesje grew up wearing them and resenting them. For her, luxury was not the piqué and lace collars of the Little Nell line, but the jeans and T-shirts the other girls wore.

Little Nell neither expands nor collapses. It doesn't even make the dresses; they're made in Montreal. It merely distributes them. It's just there, like her father; and like him the methods of its existence are unknown to her.

She sat at the table covered with her mother's good linen cloth, watching her father with a certain sadness as he swallowed down the turkey and cranberry sauce, the mashed potatoes, the mince pie dictated by a religious holiday he would never have observed in the natural course of events and which her mother would have observed fourteen days later. At Christmas they always ate Canadian food. A capitulation, that turkey; or perhaps one more piece of neutral ground for both of them. Every year they chewed their way through this dinner, proving something or other. Elsewhere, one set of cousins was recovering from Hanukkah, another set was getting ready to sing the songs and dance the dances they'd learned at Ukrainian summer camp. Lesje's mother, in the kitchen putting hard sauce on the slabs of mince pie, sniffled with quiet stoicism. This too happened every year.

She could never ask William to this meal or even to this house. Don't irritate your father, her mother said. I know young people are different now but he still thinks of you as his little girl. You think he doesn't know you're living with someone? He knows. He just doesn't want to know.

"How's the bone business?" her father asked, the usual joke, his way of reconciling himself to her choice of job.

"Really great," she told him. He didn't see the attraction for a pretty girl, crawling around in the dirt, scratching for buried bones, like a dog. After first-year university, he'd asked her what she was going to be. A teacher, maybe?

"A paleontologist," she'd said.

A pause. "So what are you going to do for a living?"

Her Ukrainian grandmother had wanted her to be an airline stewardess. Her Jewish grandmother had wanted her to be a lawyer and also to marry, another lawyer if possible. Her father wanted her to make the most of herself. Her mother wanted her to be happy.

Lesje is uncertain about her choice of wine, since William fancies himself a connoisseur. He tends to condescend. He once sent back a bottle in a restaurant, and Lesje thought, He's been waiting a long time for the chance to do that. She dug out from the garbage the bottle they shared the night before he left and copied down the name on the label. He chose that one. If he sneers, she'll tell him. But this thought fails to cheer her.

She sees Nate Schoenhof in front of her in the line. Her breath jumps; suddenly her curiosity is with her again. For a month and a half he's been invisible, she hasn't even seen him waiting for Elizabeth at the Museum. For a time she felt, not rejected exactly, but disappointed, as if she'd been watching a movie and the projector had broken down partway through. Now she feels as if she has things to ask him. She says his name, but he doesn't hear her, and she can't step out of the line to touch his sleeve. But the man behind him notices and pokes him for her. He turns, sees her.

He waits for her at the door. "I'll walk you back," he says.

They set off, carrying their bottles. It's dark now and the snow is still falling, clumps of wet flakes drifting windlessly down, the

100

air moist, the sidewalk mushy underfoot. It isn't cold. Nate turns onto a side street and Lesje follows, even though she knows it's out of her way, this is east and she should be going south. Perhaps he's forgotten where she lives.

She asks him if he had a nice Christmas. Terrible, he says, how about hers?

"Pretty awful," she says. They laugh a little. It's hard for her to say how bad it was or why it was that bad. "I hate it," she says. "I always have."

"I didn't used to," he says. "When I was a kid I kept thinking something magic would happen; something I didn't expect."

"And did it?" she says.

"No," he says. He thinks for a minute. "Once I really wanted a machine gun. My mother absolutely refused. She said it was an immoral toy, why did I want to play at killing people, there was enough cruelty in the world and so on. But there it was on Christmas morning, under the tree."

"Wasn't that magic?"

"No," Nate says. "By then I didn't want it."

"Do your kids like it?" Lesje says.

Nate says he thinks so. They liked it better when they were too young to know what presents were, when they just crawled around in the paper.

Lesje notices that one of his eyes is puffy and dark, with what looks like a healing cut above it. She doesn't want to ask what's wrong with it – it seems too personal – but she does anyway.

He stops, looks at her mournfully. "Someone hit me," he says.

"I thought you were going to say you bumped into a door," Lesje says. "Were you in a fight?"

"Not as far as I was concerned," he says. "A woman hit me."

Lesje can't think of a good thing to say, so says nothing. Why would anyone want to hit such a man?

"It wasn't Elizabeth," Nate says. "She'd never hit anyone physically. It was someone else. I guess she had to."

He's letting her in, letting her listen in. She isn't sure she wants this. Nevertheless her hand moves up, drawn to his mysterious wound, touches his forehead. She sees her purple and white-striped mitten silhouetted against his skin.

101

He stops, looks down at her, blinking, as if he can't believe what she's just done. Is he about to cry? No. He's making a gift of himself, handing himself over to her, mutely. Here I am. You may be able to do something with me. She realizes that this is what she's been expecting from him, ever since his first phone call.

"It isn't fair," he says.

Lesje doesn't know what he's talking about. She opens her arms. One of his arms goes around her; in the other he holds his paper bag. Her wine bottle falls to the sidewalk, the sound muffled by the snow. As they're walking away she remembers it and turns, expecting to see it cracked, the snow around it red; it's too late to go back for another. But it's intact, and suddenly she feels very lucky.

Part Three

ELIZABETH

It's the third of January. Elizabeth is sitting on the slippery rose-colored chesterfield in her Auntie Muriel's parlor, which is truly a parlor and not a living room. It's a parlor because of the spider and the fly. It isn't a living room, because Auntie Muriel cannot be said to live.

Auntie Muriel is both the spider and the fly, the sucker-out of life juice and the empty husk. Once she was just the spider and Uncle Teddy was the fly, but ever since Uncle Teddy's death Auntie Muriel has taken over both roles. Elizabeth isn't even all that sure Uncle Teddy is really dead. Auntie Muriel probably has him in a trunk somewhere in the attic, webbed in old écru lace tablecloths, paralyzed but still alive. She goes up there for a little nip now and then. Auntie Muriel, so palpably not an auntie. Nothing diminutive about Auntie Muriel.

Elizabeth knows her view of Auntie Muriel is exaggerated and uncharitable. Such ogres don't exist. Nevertheless, there is Auntie Muriel, sitting opposite her, large as life, the solid bulk of her torso encased in two-way stretch elastic with plastic boning, the jersey of her mild blue beautifully tailored dress stretching across her soccer-player's thighs, her eyes, like two pieces of gravel, cold and unreflecting, directed at Elizabeth, taking in, Elizabeth knows, every disreputable detail of her own appearance. Her hair (too long, too loose), her sweater (should have been a dress), the absence of a lipstick-and-powder crust over her face, all, all are wrong. Auntie Muriel is gratified by this wrongness.

She's just a friendless old lady, Elizabeth thinks, trying out this excuse. But why? Why is she friendless? Elizabeth is aware of the way she ought to be thinking. She's read magazines and books, she knows the lines. Auntie Muriel was thwarted in youth. She had a domineering father who stunted her and wouldn't let her go to college because college was for boys. She was forced to

105

embroider (embroider! with those stumpy fingers!), a torture she later imposed on Elizabeth, who however turned out to be somewhat better at it and whose cutwork tea cloth with pink French knots still lies folded in a trunk in Elizabeth's closet, testament to her skill. Auntie Muriel had a strong personality and a good mind and she was not pretty, and patriarchal society punished her. These things are all true.

Nevertheless, Elizabeth can forgive Auntie Muriel only in theory. Given her own sufferings, why has Auntie Muriel chosen to transfer them, whenever possible, to others? Elizabeth can still see herself, at the age of twelve, writhing on her bed with her first menstrual cramps, nauseated with pain, Auntie Muriel standing over her holding the bottle of aspirin out of reach. *This is God's punishment.* She never said for what. In Elizabeth's view, no mere career would ever have satisfied Auntie Muriel's lust for slaughter. She should have been sent into the Army. Only in a tank, helmeted, gauntleted, her guns directed at something, anything at all, would she have been happy.

So why is Elizabeth here? More importantly: why has she brought the children? Exposed them to this malignancy. They sit beside her, subdued, wearing the white knee socks and Mary Janes they won't willingly put on for any other occasion, little mouths carefully shut, hair clipped back from their faces with tight barrettes, hands in their laps, goggling at Auntie Muriel as if she's a wonder, a mammoth or a mastodon, say, like the ones at the Museum, recently dug out of an iceberg.

In fact the children like to visit Auntie Muriel. They like her big house, the silence, the polished woodwork, the Persian carpets. They like the little crustless sandwiches Auntie Muriel sets out, even though they carefully take only one each; and the grand piano, though they aren't allowed to touch it. When Uncle Teddy was alive, he used to give them quarters. Not so Auntie Muriel. When Elizabeth's own mother had finally succeeded in frying herself to a crisp in that last tiny room on Shuter Street, setting fire to her mattress with a dropped cigarette and too drunk to know she was burning, Auntie Muriel drew up a list after the funeral. It contained all the items she'd ever lent, given or donated. *One light bulb, 60 watt, over the sink. One blue plastic shower curtain. One paisley Viyella housecoat. One Wedgwood sugar bowl*. Miserly gifts and chipped discards. Auntie Muriel wanted them back.

They smelled the smoke and broke the door down and got her out of there, but she already had third-degree burns on half her body. She lived for a week in hospital, lying on the mattress wet with drugs and the body's futile defenses, white cells leaking into the sheets. Who knows what she was remembering, whether she even knew who I was? She hadn't seen me for ten years, but she must have had some dim idea she'd once had daughters. She let me hold her hand, the left one that wasn't burned, and I thought: She looks like the moon, the half-moon. One side still shining.

Elizabeth has always considered Auntie Muriel responsible for this death. As for others, her sister's, for instance. Nevertheless, she is here. Partly because she's a snob, which she admits. She wants the children to see that she grew up in a house with a dinner gong and eight bedrooms, not in one like the diminutive row-house (though charming, and what a lot she's done with it) where they now live. Also, Auntie Muriel is their only close living relative. Elizabeth feels that this is because Auntie Muriel has either killed or driven away all the others, but never mind. She is their roots, their root, their twisted diseased old root. Other people, such as those in Buffalo, think that Toronto has changed, shaken off its blue-law ways, become chic and liberal, but Elizabeth knows it hasn't. At its core, where there should be a heart, there is only Auntie Muriel.

She has exiled Auntie Muriel from Christmas, having said no, finally, four years ago, to the dark table with six insertable leaves, the symmetrically arranged crystal dishes of pickle and cranberry sauce, the linen tablecloth, the silver napkin rings. Nate refused to come with her any more; that was why. He said he wanted to enjoy his children and his dinner and there was no point going to Auntie Muriel's if Elizabeth was going to collapse into bed with a headache as soon as they got home. Once, in 1971, she'd thrown up onto a snowbank on the way back: turkey, cranberry sauce, Auntie Muriel's selection of relishes, the works.

At first she'd resented Nate's refusal, interpreted it as a lack

107

of support. But he'd been right, he is right. She should not
be here.

Auntie Muriel is continuing her monologue, which is directed
ostensibly at the children but actually at Elizabeth. They should
never forget, she says, that their grandfather owned half of Galt.
Great-grandfather, Guelph, Elizabeth thinks. Perhaps Auntie
Muriel is going senile at last; or perhaps this family mythology
is only a mythology after all, and, like any oral history, its
details are undergoing mutation. Auntie Muriel does not correct
herself, though. She has never been known to correct herself.
She is now saying that Toronto is not what it was, and for
that matter neither is the entire country. The Pakis are taking
over the city and the French are taking over the government. A
shopgirl (implied: foreign, dark-skinned, accented, or all three)
was rude to her in Creeds just last Wednesday. And as for Creeds,
it has gone completely downhill. They used to put fur coats in
the windows and now they put belly dancers. She supposes that
Elizabeth, with her attitudes (implied: degenerate), thinks this is
all right, but she herself will never get used to it. She is old, she
remembers better things.

Elizabeth doesn't know which is worse, this conversation or
last year's, in which Auntie Muriel subjected the children to
an account of the trials and tribulations she'd undergone in
her attempt to gather the entire family together in one corner
of the Mount Pleasant Cemetery. In the story, she'd made no
distinction between the living and the dead, referring to her own
plot as though she herself were already in it and to the others as
if they were guests at a picnic she was throwing. Uncle Teddy
was already in the right place, of course, but Elizabeth's mother
and sister had to be moved from St. James and her grandfather
from the old Necropolis. As for Elizabeth's father, there was no
telling where he'd wandered off to.

Elizabeth could probably have interfered with these operations
if she wanted to, but she didn't have the strength. She knew what
Auntie Muriel was like when thwarted. If Auntie Muriel wanted
to play chess with her dead relatives, let her. Luckily they were all
in urns rather than coffins. They had no idea, Auntie Muriel said,
how cheeky certain lawyers and cemetery supervisors could be.

Of course these days a lot of them had foreign accents. She'd then described an intricate series of real-estate dealings that seemed to concern the trading-off of one plot in exchange for another. Her ultimate plan was to acquire a large block of holdings and then exchange it for a mausoleum. Elizabeth refrained from asking whether or not Auntie Muriel had reserved a spot for her.

Going home in the taxi, Nancy says, "She's funny."

This view of Auntie Muriel has never occurred to Elizabeth before. Funny in what way, she wants to know.

"She says funny things."

And Elizabeth realizes that, for them, this is all Auntie Muriel is: a curiosity. They like going to see her for the same reason they like going to the Museum. She cannot touch them or harm them, they are out of her reach. She can touch and harm only Elizabeth. Because Auntie Muriel once had all power over her, she will always have some. Elizabeth is an adult in much of her life, but when she's with Auntie Muriel she is still part child. Part prisoner, part orphan, part cripple, part insane; Auntie Muriel the implacable wardress.

She goes to visit her, then, out of defiance. Look, I've grown up. I walk on two legs, unsteadily maybe, but you haven't got me into one of those urns of yours, not yet. I live my life despite you and I will continue to live it. And see, these are my children. Look how beautiful, how intelligent, how normal they are. You never had children. You can't touch them. I won't let you.

LESJE

Lesje is doing something seedy. If someone, one of her friends, Marianne for instance, was doing the same thing and told her about it, she would think: seedy. Or even tacky. Very tacky, to be having an affair with a married man, a married man with two children. Married men with children are proverbially tacky, with their sad stories, their furtive lusts and petty evasions. Tackier still to be doing it in a hotel, of necessity a comparatively tacky hotel, since Nate is, as he says, a little broke. Lesje hasn't offered to pay the hotel bill herself. Once, long ago, her women's group might have sneered at this reluctance, but there is a limit.

Lesje doesn't feel tacky. She isn't sure whether Nate does or not. He's sitting in one of the chairs (there are two, both cheap Danish Modern with frayed corners, to match the blue frayed bedspread which is as yet undisturbed), telling her how terrible he feels that they have to be in this hotel instead of somewhere else. The somewhere his tone implies is not another, more acceptable hotel. It's a summer field, a deserted sun-warmed beach, a wooded knoll with breezes.

Lesje doesn't mind the hotel, even though the hum from the air conditioner is beginning to get to her. It's spewing out thick hot air which smells of upholstery and cigar butts, and they haven't been able to find the switch that turns it off. If this hotel had been a choice, she'd feel differently about it, but it's a necessity. They can't go to Lesje's apartment because of William, who was out when Lesje left but who may reappear at any moment, to find the note Lesje has thoughtfully propped on the card table: *Back at 6:00.* They can't go to Nate's, ever, unless Lesje takes time off work during the week. She works the same hours Elizabeth does, though Elizabeth probably has more flexibility. But today is Saturday and Elizabeth is at home. Not to mention the children. Nate hasn't mentioned the children, but even so he's managed to convey to Lesje that although he respects her, admires her and desires her, to his children she represents an evil from which he must protect them.

Hence this afternoon hotel. They've come to it by subway, since neither of them owns a car. This fact also rules out necking on side streets, which is what they should be doing at this preliminary stage, in Lesje's opinion. They have in fact necked on side streets, but it's been uncomfortable: feet freezing in slush, passing cars splattering them with brown sludge, arms hugging the bolster shapes of each others' winter coats. But no groping in the front seat.

Lesje considers groping in the front seat almost an essential. The only other affairs she's had have been with William, champion groper, and before him a geologist in fourth-year university who even then, in 1970, had a crew cut. Neither of these affairs was exactly romantic; both had been based on mutual interests, of a sort. It was hard for Lesje to find men who were as monomaniacal about their subjects as she was about hers. They existed, but they tended to go out with Home Economics types. After a day of pondering surds and pingoes they wanted to put their feet up and eat grated carrot and marshmallow salads. They didn't want to talk about Megalosaurus tibias or whether the pterosaurs had three-chambered or four-chambered hearts, which was what she wanted to talk about. The geologist had been fine; they could compromise on rock strata. They went on hikes with their little picks and kits, and chipped samples off cliffs; then they ate jelly sandwiches and copulated in a friendly way behind clumps of golden rod and thistles. She found this pleasurable but not extremely so. She still has a collection of rock chips left over from this relationship; looking at it does not fill her with bitterness. He was a nice boy but she wasn't in love with him. She is not exactly a paradigm of modish chic, she knows that, but she could never quite fall in love with a man who says "wow."

As for William, what they have in common is an interest in extinction. She confines it to dinosaurs, however. William applies it to everything. Except cockroaches; a cockroach has been found living in a nuclear reactor. The next age, according to William, will be the age of the insects. On most days he's quite cheerful about this.

Lesje isn't sure what she means by *in love*. Once she thought she was in love with William, since it upset her that he did not ask her to marry him. But recently she's begun to question this. At first she welcomed the relative simplicity, even the bareness, of their life together. They were both committed to their jobs, and they had, it seemed, easily met expectations and only minor areas of friction. But Nate has changed things, he has changed William. What was once a wholesome absence of complications is now an embarrassing lack of complexity. For instance, William would have lunged as soon as they were inside the door. Not so Nate.

They sit on either side of the large double bed which looms like fate in the center of the room, each with a cigarette, drinking out of the hotel glasses which contain Scotch from Nate's pocket flask mixed with tap water. Gazing across the bed as if it's a fathomless gulf, while Nate apologizes, Lesje listens, veiling her face with her hand, smoke making her squint. Nate doesn't want just an affair, he says. Lesje is touched by this; she doesn't think to ask what he does want. William has never been at such pains to explain himself.

Lesje feels that something momentous is about to take place. Her life is about to change: things will not be as they have been before. The walls of the hotel, patterned with greenish lozenges, are dissolving, she is moving through the open air, no longer snow-filled and tinged with exhaust fumes but clean and sunny; on the horizon there's the glimmer of water. Why then doesn't Nate stub out his cigarette, stand up, take her in his arms? Now that he has her in this tacky bedroom.

But instead he pours himself another drink and continues to explain. He wants everything to be clear at the beginning. He doesn't want Lesje to think she's breaking up a marriage. As she no doubt knows, Elizabeth has had other lovers, the most recent of whom was Chris. Elizabeth has never made any secret of that. She thinks of Nate as the father of her children but not as her husband. They haven't lived together, he means slept together, for several years, he isn't sure how many. They've stayed in the same house together because of the children. Neither of them can stand the thought of living apart from the children. So naturally Elizabeth will have no objection to his doing what Lesje wishes he would hurry up and do.

The mention of Elizabeth startles Lesje, who realizes that she hasn't been thinking about her at all. She ought to be thinking about her. You don't just stroll into another woman's life and take over her husband. Everyone in the women's group agreed, in theory at least, on the reprehensibility of such behavior, although they also agreed that married people should not be viewed as each other's property but as living, growing organisms. What it boiled down to was that man stealing was out but personal growth was commendable. You had to have the right attitude and be honest with yourself. These convolutions had discouraged Lesje; she hadn't understood why so much time was being spent on them. But at that point she'd never been in such a situation, and now she is.

She certainly doesn't want to play Other Woman in some conventional, boring triangle. She doesn't feel like an other woman; she isn't wheedling or devious, she doesn't wear negligées or paint her toenails. William may think she's exotic, but she isn't really; she's straightforward, narrow and unadorned, a scientist; not a web-spinner, expert at the entrapment of husbands. But Nate no longer seems like Elizabeth's husband. His family is surely external to him; in himself he's single, a free agent. And Elizabeth is therefore not the wife of Nate, she isn't a wife at all. Instead she's a widow, Chris's widow if anyone's, moving unpaired and grieving down an autumn avenue, leaves from the over-arching trees falling on her faintly disheveled hair. Lesje consigns her to this mournfully romantic picture, frames her, and then forgets about her.

William is another matter. William will mind; he will definitely mind in one way or another. But Lesje doesn't intend to tell him about this, at least not yet. Nate has implied that although Elizabeth would give the seal of approval to what he's doing and may even be pleased for him, since in a way they are good friends, now is not the right time to tell her. Elizabeth has been making an adjustment, not as quick an adjustment as he'd like to see but definitely an adjustment. He wants her to finish doing that before he gives her something new that she has to adjust to. It has something to do with the children.

So if Nate is going to protect Elizabeth and the children from Lesje, Lesje is entitled to protect William from Nate. She feels tender towards William when she considers his need for protection. He's never needed it before. But now she reflects upon the unconscious nape of his neck, the vulnerability of the hollow at the angle of his collarbone, his jugular veins, so

113

perilously close to the skin, his inability to tan instead of burn, the wax in his ears unseen by him, his childlike pomposity. She has no desire to hurt William.

Nate puts down his glass, grinds his cigarette into the hotel ashtray. He's come to the end of ethics. He negotiates the perimeter of the blue bed, walks to Lesje, kneels in front of her where she sits in her Danish Modern chair. He takes her hand away from her mouth, kisses her. She has never been touched with such gentleness. William's style has a lot of adolescent roughhouse, she now realizes, and the geologist was always in a hurry. Nate isn't in a hurry. They've been here two hours and she still has all her clothes on.

He picks her up, places her on the bed, lies down beside her. He kisses her again, tentatively, lingeringly. Then he asks what time it is. He himself has no watch. Lesje tells him it's five-thirty. He sits up. Lesje is beginning to feel slightly unattractive. Are her teeth too large, is that it?

"I have to phone home," he says. "I'm supposed to be taking the kids to dinner at my mother's."

He lifts the telephone from the table and dials. The cord trails across Lesje's chest. "Hello, love," he says, and Lesje knows it's Elizabeth. "Just checking in. I'll pick them up at six, okay?"

The words "home," "love," and "mother" have disturbed Lesje. A vacuum forms around her heart, spreads; it's as if she doesn't exist. When Nate puts down the phone, she begins to cry. He folds his arms around her, soothing her, smoothing her hair. "There's lots of time, love," he says. "Next time will be better."

Don't call me that, she wants to say. She sits on the bed, feet over the side, hands dangling from her wrists, while Nate gets their coats, puts his own on, holds hers out for her. She wants to be the one going to dinner with him. To his mother's. She doesn't want to stay here on the blue bed alone, or walk out into the street alone, or go back to her apartment where she will also be alone whether William is there or not. She wants to pull Nate back onto the bed with her. She doesn't believe there is lots of time. There is no time, surely she will never see him again. She doesn't understand why her heart is beating so painfully, gulping for oxygen in the blackness of this outer space. He's taking something away from her. If he loves her, why has she been exiled?

114

NATE

Jackass, Nate whispers. Ninny. Fraud. He's reading the editorial in *The Globe and Mail,* and he usually says such things while doing this, but right now he means himself. *Idiot.*

He sees himself hunched forward on the hotel room chair, raving about his scruples while Lesje sits across the room from him, unattainable, shining like a crescent moon. He doesn't know why he didn't want to, couldn't. He was afraid. He doesn't want to hurt her, that's it. But she was hurt anyway. Why did she cry?

His hands are still shaking. Luckily there's a drink left in his pocket flask. He slides it out from beneath his sweater, gulps quickly, then lights a cigarette to hide the smell. His mother, virtuous woman, does not drink. She doesn't smoke either, but Nate knows which is lower on her point system of moral crimes. Sometimes she buys beer for him but she draws the line at spirits. Poisoning the system.

The children are out in the tiny kitchen with her, sitting up on the counter, watching her mash the potatoes. She does this by hand; she doesn't have an electric mixer. She beats eggs by hand, whips cream by hand. One of his earliest memories of his mother is of her elbow, whirling around like a strange fleshy wind machine. Her television set is black and white and even more primitive than his. She wears aprons, printed ones with bibs.

From the cellar below him the pathos of his childhood rises to engulf him: down there are his baseball glove, the leather cracked, three pairs of outgrown running shoes, his skates, his goalie pads, carefully embalmed in trunks. Though she gives away almost everything else, his mother keeps these objects as if they're relics, as if he's already dead. In fairness Nate has to admit that if she hadn't, he might have kept them himself. The goalie pads, anyway.

115

He's read that goalies get ulcers; it figures. He wasn't heavy enough to play anything else, he didn't have the weight to check. He remembers the anxiety, everyone expecting him to hurl himself in front of a frozen rubber bullet traveling at the speed of light; the despair when he missed. But he loved it. It was pure: you won or you lost and it was obvious which. When he said this to Elizabeth she thought it was childish. Her own concepts of winning and losing are greyer and more snarled. Is this because she's female? But his children understand it, so far; Nancy, anyway.

He can see the children over the top of his *Globe and Mail*, their small heads framed by his mother's red-starred map of world-wide civil-rights violations. Beside it there's a new poster which reads: ONE FLASH AND YOU'RE ASH. His mother has added the abolition of nuclear energy to her long list of crusades. Oddly enough, it's not a trip she lays on the children. Nor does she tell them to eat up their dinners because of the starving children in Europe, or Asia, or India. (Himself, guiltily stuffing down bread crusts under his mother's blue benevolent gaze.) She doesn't ask if they are saving their allowances for the Bandage Campaign. She doesn't drag them through services at the Unitarian Church, with its noncommittal interior and its idealistic hymns about the Brotherhood of Man and its icon of a small black boy beside a trash can where most churches have God. The last time they had dinner with his mother, Nate almost choked on his turnips when Nancy began to tell a Newfie joke. But his mother actually laughed. She lets the children tell all kinds of jokes to her: moron jokes, Moby Dick jokes, and many more of dubious taste. "What's blue and covered with cookies and flies? A dead Girl Guide."

Nate would have been told it wasn't nice to make fun of morons or whales or Girl Guides: all were worthy. Much less Newfies. Is it because Nancy and Janet are girls and therefore not expected to reach the level of high seriousness that was and still is expected of him? Or is it merely because his mother is now a grandmother and these are her grandchildren? In any case, she spoils them rotten. She even gives them candy. Although he loves her for it, Nate finds himself resenting it. He can hear his mother laughing now, above the sound of the potato masher. He wishes she'd laughed more with him.

116

She smiled though. She was raised a Quaker, and Quakers, from what he'd seen of them, were smilers rather than laughers. Nate isn't sure why she switched to the Unitarians. He's heard Unitarianism called a featherbed for falling Christians, but his mother doesn't seem like a woman who has fallen anywhere. (Where is the featherbed for falling Unitarians? he wonders. Such as himself.)

He tries not to discuss theology with his mother. She still believes that goodness will win.

She's always used the war as an example, virtue triumphant, despite the fact that it killed his father. He can't remember whether it was before or after this death that she took up part-time nursing at the veterans' hospital where she still works, the legless and armless men that were young when she started there aging along with her, becoming, she tells him, more and more bitter, fading one by one, dying. She should leave such a depressing job, get something more cheerful; he's advised her to do that. But "Everyone else has forgotten them," she says, looking at him reproachfully. "Why should I?" For some reason her pious sacrifices infuriate him. Why shouldn't you, you're human, Nate has wanted to reply. But never has.

His father, no amputee but a simple dead man, smiles down at him now from the mantelpiece, a young face framed by the severe lines of a uniform. Violator of his mother's pacifist ideals, nevertheless a hero. It had taken Nate a long time to find out exactly how his father had died. "He was a hero," was all that his mother would say, leaving him with visions of rescues on the beach, his father wiping out enemy machine-gun nests single-handed or floating like a dark bat over some blacked-out town, his parachute billowing like a cape behind him.

Finally, on his sixteenth birthday, he'd asked again and this time – convinced perhaps that he was ready for the facts of life – she'd told him. His father had died in England, of hepatitis, without ever reaching the real war.

"I thought you said he was a hero," he'd said, disgusted.

His mother's eyes grew round and bluer. "But Nathanael. He *was*."

Still and all, he wishes he'd known sooner; he would have felt less overshadowed. It's hard to compete with any dead man, he knows, much less a hero.

117

"Dinner, Nate," his mother calls. She enters carrying the potatoes, the girls follow with knives and forks, and they all crowd around the diminutive oval table at one end of his mother's living room. Nate has asked earlier if there was anything he could do, but since he got married his mother has banished him to the living room during mealtime preparations. She won't even let him wash the dishes any more.

They're the same dishes, beige with orange nasturtiums, he used to wash so endlessly, grudgingly. They depress Elizabeth, which is one of the reasons she almost never participates in these visits. Elizabeth says his mother's things invariably look as if she ordered them out of a stamp catalogue, and there's some truth to this. Everything in his mother's house is serviceable and, he has to admit, rather ugly. Her table has a plastic finish, her chairs are wipable, her dishes garish, her glassware will bounce on the floor. She doesn't have the time for frills, she says, or the money either. Another thing that bothers her about the wooden toys he makes is the price. "Only rich people can afford them, Nate," she says accusingly.

They eat hamburger patties fried in leftover bacon fat, mashed potatoes, and canned beets with margarine, while Nate's mother asks the children about school and laughs gaily at their terrible jokes. Nate feels his stomach go cold; the canned beets sink, mix uneasily with his furtive Scotch. They are, all three of them, so unsuspecting, so innocent. It's as if he's looking at them through a lighted window: inside, peace and tranquil domesticity, this house, the tastes, the smells even, so familiar to him. Good, unassuming. And outside, darkness, thunder, the storm, himself a wolflike monster in tattered clothes, fingernails ragged, lurking red-eyed and envious, snout pressed to the glass. He alone knows the darkness of the human heart, the secrets of evil. *Kaboom.*

"Ninny," he whispers to himself.

"What did you say, dear?" his mother asks, turning her bright blue eyes full upon him. Older now, with crinkles behind spectacles, but the same eyes, shining, earnest, always on the verge of some emotion he cannot quite face: disappointment, joy. The perpetual spotlight in which he's always lived, alone on the stage, the star performer.

"I was talking to myself," he says.

118

"Oh," his mother laughs, "I do that all the time. You must have inherited it."

After dessert, which is canned peaches, the three of them wash the dishes and Nate is again exiled to the living room to do whatever it is that men are supposed to do after dinner. Nate wonders whether, if his father had lived, his mother would have gone in for Women's Liberation. As it is she doesn't have to. She does, of course, on the theoretical level, and she's fond of pointing out the almost innumerable ways in which women's basic human rights have been cropped, stunted, mutilated and destroyed by men. But if he had slippers she'd bring them for him.

He'll phone Lesje, see her again. He won't see her again. He's a horse's ass, he's made a mess of it, she won't want to see him again. He has to see her again. He's in love with her, with that cool thin body, the face turned in upon itself in statue-like contemplation. She sits behind a lighted window, draped in soft white, playing the spinet, her moving fingers luminous against the keys. Growling, he leaps through the glass.

Hahahaha Atwood's writ, at its best.

119

ELIZABETH

Elizabeth is sitting at the small desk in her bedroom (maple, *c.* 1875). It has a matching chair which she bought at the same auction. It's a wonder to her how the ladies of that time ever managed to get their great cabbagy padded buttocks onto the chairs made for that purpose. You were supposed to perch gracefully, skirts falling, fake ass billowing around your hidden real ass. No visible support. The apparition of a cloud.

In this desk Elizabeth keeps: her checkbook and canceled checks, her bills, her budget, her lists of things needing to be done around the house (one list for urgent, another for long-term), her personal letters, and the journal she started four years ago but has failed to keep up. This desk has not been opened since Chris's death.

She can now think: *Chris's death*. She almost never thinks *Chris's suicide*. This would imply that Chris's death was something he did to himself; she thinks of it, on the contrary, as something he did to her. He's not feeling the effects of it, whereas she still is. For instance, she has not opened the desk until now because in the upper left-hand pigeonhole, held together tidily by an elastic band, is the bundle of letters he was sending her in September and October; all on lined notebook paper in ballpoint pen, the handwriting becoming larger and more spidery until finally, on October 15, there had been just two words filling an entire page. She should not have kept these letters, she knows; she should throw them out now, immediately, without looking at them again. But she's always been a saver.

She avoids looking at the letters as she bends over her checkbook. Now that she's into it, she's even getting a certain amount of pleasure out of it. Order from chaos, all those unpaid bills cleared out of the way, entered into her book. Nate has paid a few things that had to be paid – the phone bill, the hydro – but everything else has been waiting for her, sometimes with two or

120

three politely outraged letters, requesting and then demanding. She likes to have her accounts settled, to owe nothing to anyone. She likes to know she has money in the bank. She intends always to have enough money for an emergency.

Unlike her mother, who'd sat crying for two days in the flowered chair by the window after their father was suddenly not there any more. "What am I supposed to do?" she asked the air, as if there was somebody listening who had a standard of behavior all ready for her. Her sister Caroline crawling up to her mother's lap, crying too, sliding off repeatedly, crawling back up her mother's slippery-skirted legs like some demented beetle.

Elizabeth had not wept or crawled. When it became obvious that their mother was not going to get up out of the chair and fix them dinner, she'd counted the quarters she'd been saving, the ones Uncle Teddy had been slipping down the front of her dress on their infrequent visits to Auntie Muriel's big house. She'd gone through her mother's purse, throwing the lipstick tubes and crumpled hankies onto the floor, finding nothing but a wrinkled two-dollar bill and some pennies. Then she'd let herself out of the apartment, using the keys from her mother's purse to lock the door behind her. She'd gone to the little grocery store three blocks away and bought some bread and cheese and marched back carrying the brown paper bag, stamping her rubber boots hard on the stairs as she climbed up. This was no great feat, she'd done similar things often enough before. "Eat this," she'd said to her mother, furious with her and with her sister. "Eat this and stop crying!"

It hadn't worked. Her mother had sniveled on, and Elizabeth had sat in the kitchen, chewing on her bread and cheese, in a white rage. She wasn't angry with her father. She'd always suspected he couldn't be depended on. She was angry with her mother for not having known it.

It was Auntie Muriel who had taught her how to keep a bank account, how to balance a checkbook, what *interest* was. Although Auntie Muriel regarded most books as frivolous trash and even schoolwork as of marginal value, she'd spent a good deal of time on this part of Elizabeth's education. For which Elizabeth is grateful. Money counts, Auntie Muriel used to say –

121

still says, when anyone will listen – and Elizabeth knows it's true. If only because Auntie Muriel enforced the lesson so strongly: she supported Elizabeth, paid for her well-made underwear and her blue tweed coats and her piano lessons, therefore she owned her.

Auntie Muriel's attitude towards Elizabeth was equivocal. Elizabeth's mother was no good, therefore Elizabeth herself was probably no good. But Elizabeth was Auntie Muriel's niece, so there must be something to her. Auntie Muriel worked at developing those parts of Elizabeth that most resembled Auntie Muriel and suppressing or punishing the other parts. Auntie Muriel admired backbone, and Elizabeth feels that, underneath everything, she herself now has the backbone of a rhinoceros.

Auntie Muriel is unambiguous about most things. Her few moments of hesitation have to do with the members of her own family. She isn't sure where they fit into the Great Chain of Being. She's quite certain of her own place, however. First comes God. Then comes Auntie Muriel and the Queen, with Auntie Muriel having a slight edge. Then come about five members of the Timothy Eaton Memorial Church, which Auntie Muriel attends. After this there is a large gap. Then white, non-Jewish Canadians, Englishmen, and white, non-Jewish Americans, in that order. Then there's another large gap, followed by all other human beings on a descending scale, graded according to skin color and religion. Then cockroaches, clothes moths, silverfish and germs, which are about the only forms of animal life with which Auntie Muriel has ever had any contact. Then all sexual organs, except those of flowers.

This is how Elizabeth puts it for the amusement of others when she's telling Auntie Muriel stories; notably to Philip Burroughs of Greek and Roman, whose aunt is Janie Burroughs, who travels in the same wee circle as Auntie Muriel. Unlike Nate, Philip can be depended on to know what she's talking about.

Auntie Muriel may be a droll story, but this doesn't affect her malignance. She's a purist as well as a puritan. There are no shades of grey for Auntie Muriel. Her only visible moral dilemma is that she thinks she ought to rank her family with the Timothy Eaton Church members, because of their relation to her; but she feels compelled to place them instead with the cockroaches and silverfish, because of their deplorable behavior.

Such as that of Elizabeth's mother, which even now Auntie

Muriel never fails to allude to. Elizabeth has never been sure why her mother vanished. Helplessness, perhaps; an inability to imagine what else to do. Auntie Muriel's version is that Elizabeth's mother deserted the family out of innate depravity – ran off with the son of her own father's lawyer, which Auntie Muriel saw as a kind of incest and which luckily didn't last long. She, Auntie Muriel, had rescued the deserted children and had begun immediately stuffing them with all the advantages.

Elizabeth, even as a child, did not fully accept this story. Now she thinks it may have been the other way around, that Auntie Muriel stole her and her sister away from their apartment while their mother was out on one of her expeditions, "looking for work," she told them. Then, once Auntie Muriel had the children safely barricaded into her own house, she'd probably told their mother she was unfit and it could be proved in court if necessary. This is more Auntie Muriel's style: self-righteous banditry.

She can remember the actual event but it tells her nothing. Playing movie-star cutouts with Caroline; then Auntie Muriel suddenly there, saying, "Get your coats on, children." Elizabeth had asked where they were going. "To the doctor," said Auntie Muriel, which seemed plausible. Caroline at the third-floor window. *That's Mother. Where?* Down below on the sidewalk, her face upturned in the streetlight, a sky-blue coat, Mayflies fluttering around her. Opening the window, smell of new leaves. Calling, *Mummy, Mummy,* both of them. Auntie Muriel's footsteps on the stairs, along the hall. What are you yelling about? That's not your mother. Now close the window or the whole neighborhood will hear. The woman turning, walking away, head sadly down. Caroline screaming through the closed window, Auntie Muriel prying her fingers from the ledge, the catch.

For months Elizabeth put herself to sleep with a scene from *The Wizard of Oz.* The book itself had been left behind, it was part of the old life before Auntie Muriel's, but she could remember it. It was the part where Dorothy throws a bucket of water over the Wicked Witch of the West and melts her. Auntie Muriel was the Witch, of course. Elizabeth's mother was Glinda the Good. One day she would reappear and kneel down to kiss Elizabeth on the forehead.

*   *   *

She leans back, closes her eyes. Dry eyes. Chris wanted her to quit her job, leave her home and her two children. For him. Throw herself on his mercy. His tender mercy. She'd have to be crazy, he'd have to be crazy to think she ever would. No visible support. He should have left things the way they were.

She sits up, reaches quickly for the bundle of letters, reads the one on the top. FUCK OFF. His last message. She'd been angry when she first read that.

She tucks the check stubs and paid bills and the duplicate rent receipts from the tenants upstairs into an envelope, marks it: *1976*. That finishes off the year. Now she can start another one. Time hasn't stood still while she's been away, as she now thinks of it. She's barely managed to hold things together at the office, but she has a lot to catch up on. The quilt exhibit, for instance, must be scheduled and promoted. The girls need new underwear and Nancy needs new snowboots: she's been coming home for days with a wet foot. And there's something wrong with Nate. Something is happening in his life; he hasn't told her about it. Perhaps he has a new ladyfriend, now that Martha has been used up. He's always told her before, though. She riffles back through the days, looking for clues; at the base of her skull the old chill begins, the old fear, of events, cataclysms preparing themselves without her, gathering like tidal waves at the other side of the world. Behind her back. Out of control.

She stands up, turns the key in her desk. She has backbone. She has money in the bank, not enough but some. She does not have to depend, she is not a dependant. She is self-supporting.

LESJE

Organisms adapt to their environments. Of necessity, most of the time. They also adapt to their own needs, often with a certain whimsy, you could almost say perversity. Take, for instance, the modified third claw on the hind foot of one of Lesje's favorite dinosaurs, the medium-sized but swift and deadly Deinonychus. This third claw does not, like the other two, touch the ground; therefore it was not used for walking or running. Ostrom, the noted authority and discoverer of Deinonychus, speculated from its position and its shape (sickle-curved, razor-sharp) that it was used for the sole purpose of disemboweling. Deinonychus's front legs, proportionately longer than those of Tyrannosaurus or Gorgosaurus, held the prey at a suitable distance; Deinonychus then stood on one foot while using the third claw of the other foot to slash open the stomach of the prey. A balancing act; also an eccentric way of coping with life, that is, the capturing and preparation of food. Nothing else even close to Deinonychus has yet been unearthed. It is this eccentricity, this uniqueness, this acrobatic gaiety, that appeals to Lesje. A kind of dance.

She has watched this innocent though bloody dance many times from the immunity of her treetop, which today happens to be a conifer. There is nothing in sight at the moment, though; not so much as a pterosaur. William has frightened everything away. He wanders below her among the bulbous-trunked cycad trees, ill at ease. Something is wrong; this isn't what he's used to. The sun is strange and there are odd smells. He hasn't yet realized he's in a different time.

Not realizing is his adaptation. Lesje is his environment, and his environment has changed.

William also sits at a card table, eating the Betty Crocker Noodles Romanoff Lesje has just dished out for him. She herself doesn't feel like eating right now. He's bombarding her with gloom: pollutants are pouring into the air, over three hundred of them, more than have yet been identified. Sulfuric acid and mercury are falling, metallic mist, acid rain, into the pure lakes of Muskoka and points north. Queasy fish rise, roll over, exposing bellies soon to bloat. If ten times more control is not implemented at once (at once!) the Great Lakes will die. A fifth of the fresh water in the world. And for what? Pantyhose, he says accusingly, fork dripping noodles. Rubber bands, cars, plastic buttons. Lesje nods; she knows, but she's helpless. He's doing it on purpose.

At this very moment, William continues relentlessly, birds are eating worms, and stable, unbreakable PCB's are concentrating in their fatty tissues. Lesje herself has probably been incapacitated for safe child-bearing due to the large quantity of DDT she has already stored in her own fatty tissues. Not to mention the radiation bombardment on her ovaries, which will almost certainly cause her to give birth to a two-headed child or to a lump of flesh the size of a grapefruit, containing hair and a fully developed set of teeth (William cites examples), or to a child with its eyes on one side of its face, like a flounder.

Lesje, who does not want to hear much more of this right now, truthful though it may be, counterattacks with the supernova theory *re*: the extinction of the dinosaurs. Eggshells grown so thin the young could not hatch, due to a dramatic increase of cosmic radiation. (This theory is not in good repute at the Museum, which favors a more gradual hypothesis; nevertheless, it gives William something to think about. It could happen here. Who can tell when a star may explode?) Lesje asks William if he'd like a cup of instant coffee.

William, glumly, says yes. It's this glumness of his, the disappearance of his customary buoyancy, that constitutes the adaptation. Like a dog sniffing the air, he senses the difference in Lesje; he knows, but he doesn't know what he knows. Hence his depression. When Lesje brings in the coffee he says, "You forgot I take cream." His voice is plaintive. Plaintiveness isn't something Lesje associates with William.

Lesje sits down in her easy chair. She wants to ruminate, but if she goes into the bedroom William will take it as an invitation, he'll follow her and want to make love. Lesje doesn't wish to do this right now. (Problem: copulation of Deinonychus. Role of the third claw, sickle-shaped, razor-sharp: how kept out of the way? Accidents?) Despite the fact that every cell in her body has grown heavier, is liquid, is massive, is glowing with watery energy, each nucleus throwing out its own light. Collectively she blinks like a firefly; she's a lantern, a musky signal. No wonder William hovers, priapic, anxious because she's twice locked the bathroom door while taking a shower and once told him she had a bad case of heartburn. Awkward William bumbles, June bug against the screen.

But how is it that Nate has failed to appear? He was supposed to phone on the seventeenth; he's two days late. She makes excuses to waft past the phone in case it rings, she stays in when she would otherwise go out, goes out when she can no longer stand it. She should have given him the phone number at work; but he could get her easily through the switchboard if he wanted to. Could it be that he's already phoned, that William has answered and, divining everything, has said something so vicious or threatening that Nate will never phone again? She doesn't dare ask. She doesn't dare phone Nate, either. If Elizabeth answers, he'll be displeased. If one of the children answers he'll also be displeased. If he himself answers he'll be displeased too because he'll know it could just as well have been one of the others.

Lesje takes refuge in work. Which was once the perfect escape.

Part of her job involves the education of the public on matters pertaining to vertebrate paleontology. Right now the Museum is developing a dinosaur media kit for schools, which will include film strips and taped commentary, as well as booklets, posters and guides to the Museum's exhibits. It's hoped that this kit will be as popular as the sale of the models of Diplodocus and Stegosaurus (grey plastic, made in Hong Kong) and of the dinosaur coloring book indicate it will. But how much to tell? What for instance, of the family lives of the dinosaurs? What about their methods of egg-laying and – delicate subject, but always of interest – fertilization? Should these be ignored? If not, will the various religious and moralistic parent-action groups now gaining strength object to this material and boycott the kits? Such questions would not normally have occurred to Lesje, but they have occurred to Dr. Van Vleet, who has asked her to look into them and to propose some solutions.

Lesje closes her eyes, sees before her the articulated skeletons of the Museum exhibits, wired into a grotesque semblance of life. Who could possibly object to a copulation that took place ninety million years ago? The love lives of stones, sex among the ossified. Yet she could see how such gargantuan passions, the earth actually moving, a single nostril filling the screen, sighs of lust like a full-blast factory whistle, might be upsetting to some. She remembers the Grade Four teacher who threw out the toad eggs she'd brought to school. She'd hoped to describe to the class how she'd seen them being laid, in a ditch, the huge female toad gripped by a male so small it looked like a different animal. The teacher listened to this recital *solo*, then said she didn't think the class really needed to know about things like that. As usual Lesje had accepted the adult verdict and watched mutely while the teacher carried her jar of precious toad eggs out of the room to flush them down the girls' toilet.

Why didn't they need to know about things like that? Lesje now wonders. What do they need to know about? Probably not much. Certainly not the questions that occur to her at times of free-ranging speculation. Did dinosaurs have penises, for instance? A good question. Their descendants the birds have cloacal openings, whereas some snakes have not only one penis but two. Did the male dinosaur hold the female dinosaur by the scruff of the neck, like a rooster? Did dinosaurs herd, did they mate for life like geese, did they have harems, did male dinosaurs fight each other at mating season? Perhaps that would help to explain the modified third claw on Deinonychus. Lesje decides not to raise these questions. Dinosaurs laid eggs, like turtles, and that will be that.

William says he's still hungry and is going into the kitchen to make himself a sandwich. This is an expression of dissatisfaction with Lesje's ability to meet his requirements: Lesje knows it but doesn't care. Ordinarily she would make the sandwich for him, since William has always claimed to be one big thumb in the kitchen. He will manage to break something out there or cut his finger on a sardine can (William, foe of cans, nevertheless has a periodic hankering for sardines that must be catered to). There will be wreckage and carnage, wounds, mutterings and curses; William will emerge with a tatty sandwich, blood-smeared uneven bread, sardine oil on his shirt. He will display himself, he'll wish to be appeased, and Lesje, she knows, will do this. In the absence of Nate, who has offered, when she comes to think of it, nothing at all. A wide plain. A risk.

The phone rings and William gets to it before Lesje is even out of her chair. "It's for you," he says.

Lesje, chest gripped by a fit of shallow breathing, seizes the phone.

"Hello," says a woman's voice. "This is Elizabeth Schoenhof."

Lesje's throat closes. She's been found out. Grandmothers converge on her, holding out her guilt, their grief.

But far from it. Elizabeth is merely inviting her to dinner. Her and William, of course. Nate and Elizabeth, says Elizabeth, would both be very happy if they could come.

Friday, January 21, 1977

ELIZABETH

Elizabeth is having lunch with Martha in the orange cafeteria of
the Museum. They're both eating sparingly: soup, fruit yogurt,
tea. Elizabeth has insisted on paying. Martha has not fought
her for half of the bill as she once would have. It's a sign of
her defeat.

So is the fact that they're eating here at all. The Museum
cafeteria is nothing special. Once, in the days of Martha's
ascendancy, when Elizabeth thought she might be a real threat,
she'd gone to considerable trouble to make sure they met for
these lunches in good restaurants, where Elizabeth could demonstrate her own knowledge of the superior menu and get Martha
slightly bombed on cocktails and wine. Martha doesn't hold her
liquor very well and Elizabeth has found this useful. She would
sip delicately at the edge of her own wine glass while Martha
downed the carafe, priming herself and finally spewing out
a lot more than she should have about Nate's activities and
imperfections. Every time Martha said something unflattering
about Nate, Elizabeth would nod and murmur agreement, even
though these criticisms irritated her, reflecting as they did on
her taste in husbands; and Martha's eyes would dampen with
gratitude. Not that Martha likes her. Neither of them has any
illusions about that. Soon she will not have to take Martha to
lunch at all; coffee will be sufficient. After that, she will have
dentist's appointments. Lots of them.

Elizabeth has removed the dishes from her tray and set them
out on an unfolded napkin, but Martha has no time today for
such niceties. She eats from the tray, slurping her soup, her
square face bunched into a scowl. Her dark hair is stringy,
pulled back and clamped to her scalp with a tortoise-shell
plastic clip. She looks brownish, pinched; hardly the confident
peasant, hearty and wide-chested, that Elizabeth had first found
herself having to deal with. She's here to complain about Nate,

130

as if Nate has broken a window with a baseball and Elizabeth is his mother.

"I hit him," Martha is saying, "right between the eyes. I guess I shouldn't have, but it felt good. He's a prick, you know. Underneath all that *understanding* stuff. I don't know how you can live with him."

Once Elizabeth would have agreed; now, however, she can allow herself a few luxuries. Poor Nate, she thinks. He's such an innocent. "He's a sensational father," she says. "You couldn't ask for a better one. The girls adore him."

"I wouldn't know," says Martha. She bites savagely into her cracker; brittle flakes sprinkle the tray. No class, Elizabeth thinks; she never did have any. Elizabeth has always known that sooner or later Martha would overplay her hand. She herself tries for understatement. She opens her peach yogurt and stirs the contents up from the bottom.

"I never understood at first why you were so nice to me," Martha says, with a little of her old belligerence. "Taking me out to lunch and so forth. I couldn't see it. I mean, if I was you I wouldn't have done that."

"I believe in being civilized about these things," Elizabeth says.

"But then I figured it out. You wanted to *supervise* us. Like some kind of playground organizer. Make sure it didn't go too far. Right? You can admit it now, it's all over."

Elizabeth frowns slightly. She doesn't like this interpretation of her motives, though it may be just slightly accurate. "I hardly think that's fair, Martha," she says. Behind Martha, something of more interest is taking place. Lesje Green has come in with the Curator of Vertebrate Paleontology, Dr. Van Vleet. They're going along the counter now, filling their trays. They often have lunch together; everyone knows there's nothing to it, since Dr. Van Vleet is about ninety and Lesje is known to be living with a young man who works at the Ministry of the Environment. They have lunch together presumably because they can't find anyone else to talk to about the old rocks and bones they're both so stuck on.

Elizabeth has always found Lesje hard to deal with: strange, sometimes pedantic, skittish. Too specialized. Today, however, she follows her with more than usual interest. The tipoff, now

131

that she's thought about it, was that visit to the Museum back in November. The children told her about the dinosaur lady who showed them around, but Nate hadn't mentioned her. He'd asked Elizabeth to go with them, which didn't fit; but Nate is such a bungler it's the kind of thing he would do. Increasingly he has that mooning look, he's rubbing against the furniture. She's almost certain she's right, and tomorrow evening she'll know.

"We were supposed to be having these heart-to-hearts," Martha is saying, "but we never did, really, did we? I mean, we'd both say a lot about *him*, but I never said what I thought about you and you never said what you thought about me. We were never really honest, isn't that right?"

Martha is itching for honesty right now, she'd like a shouting match, right here in the cafeteria. Elizabeth wishes Nate had picked a ladyfriend with more sense of style. But a legal secretary at a two-bit lawyer's office, what could you expect? Elizabeth herself has no time for honesty right now. She doesn't think it would serve any purpose to tell Martha her real opinions, and she already knows what Martha thinks about her.

But in any contest she knows she would win. Martha has only one vocabulary, the one she uses; but Elizabeth has two. The genteel chic she's acquired, which is a veneer but a useful one: insinuating, flexible, accommodating. And another language altogether, older, harder, left over from those streets and schoolyards on the far edge of gentility where she fought it out after each one of her parents' quick decampments.

These fast moves were done at night, to avoid witnesses and landlords. Elizabeth would fall asleep on a pile of her mother's unpacked dresses, beautiful frail dresses left over from some earlier time, and wake up knowing she would have to go out into the strange faces, the ritual tests. If anyone pushed her she pushed back twice as hard, and if anyone pushed Caroline she put her head down and charged, right in the pit of the stomach. She could get big kids that way, even boys. They never expected it from someone that short. Sometimes she lost, but not often. She lost when there were more than two against her.

"You're turning into a hooligan," her mother said in one of her spasms of self-pity, dabbing at blood. In those days Elizabeth was always bleeding. Not that there was anything her mother could do about it; or about much else. Elizabeth's grandfather helped out while he was alive, though he said her father was a bounder, but Auntie Muriel got hold of him in the last months of his life and he changed his will. That's what Elizabeth's mother said, after the funeral.

Then they moved again, to an even smaller apartment, and her mother wandered helplessly around the cramped living room carrying things, a teapot, a stocking, which she didn't know where to set down. "It's not what I'm used to," she said. She went to bed with a headache; this time there was a bed. Elizabeth's father came home with two other men and told her a joke: *What did the chickens say when their mother laid an orange? Look at the orange marmalade.*

No one put Elizabeth to bed, but no one usually did. Sometimes her father pretended to, but it was only an excuse to fall asleep across her bed with all his clothes on. Her mother got up again and they all sat around in the living room drinking. Elizabeth was used to this. In her nightgown she sat on one of the men's laps, his bristly skin against her cheek. He called her "baby." Her mother got up to go to the little girls' room, she said, and tripped over her father's foot. He put it there on purpose: he liked practical jokes. "Most beautiful woman in the world," he said, laughing, picking her up from the linoleum whose pattern of maroon and yellow tapestry flowers Elizabeth can see whenever she wants to. He gave her a loose kiss on the cheek, winking; the other men laughed. Elizabeth's mother started to cry, her thin hands covering the porcelain face.

"You're a turd," Elizabeth said to her father. The other men laughed even more at this.

"You don't mean it, your poor old dad," he said. He tickled her under the armpits. The next morning he was gone. It was after this that space became discontinuous.

Almost no one knows any of this about Elizabeth. They don't know she's a refugee, with a refugee's desperate habits. Nate knows a little of it. Chris knew it, finally. Martha doesn't, neither does Lesje, and this gives Elizabeth a large advantage. She knows there's nothing in her that will compel her to behave decently. She can speak from that other life if she has to. If pushed she'll stop

133

at nothing. Or, put another way: when she reaches nothing she will stop.

Two tables away, Lesje walks towards them, her tray listing badly, that otherworldly expression on her face which probably means she's thinking obscure thoughts but which reminds Elizabeth of someone having a minor epileptic fit. She sits down, almost knocking over her coffee cup with one of those gawky elbows. Elizabeth quickly appraises her clothes: jeans again. Lesje can get away with it, she's skinny enough. Also she's only a curatorial assistant. Elizabeth herself must dress more responsibly.

"Excuse me, Martha," she says. "There's someone I have to speak to." Martha, balked, rips the tinfoil top from her yogurt cup.

Elizabeth walks softly, puts her hand on Lesje's checkered shoulder, says "Lesje."

Lesje shrieks and drops her spoon on the table. "Oh," she says, turning.

"Can't come up behind her," says Dr. Van Vleet. "Learned that a long time ago. Trial and error."

"I'm so sorry," Elizabeth says. "I just wanted to say how pleased we both are that you'll be able to make it tomorrow."

Lesje nods, finally manages to say, "So am I, I mean, we both are." Elizabeth smiles graciously at Dr. Van Vleet and pauses beside Martha just long enough to say how pleasant it has been to see her again and she hopes they can get together soon; she's sorry, but she has to get back to the office now.

She feels very calm. She will manage.

She works in her office all afternoon, dictating memos and filling out request forms and typing a few special letters that need more thought. They've given a definite yes to the Chinese Peasant Art exhibit, which will now need some groundwork; but China is good copy these days and the show should be easy to promote.

Just before closing time she covers her typewriter and gathers her purse and coat. There's one more project she's promised herself she will take care of today.

She goes up the stairs, through the wooden door that keeps

out the public, along the corridor with the metal drawers on either side. Chris's workroom. Another man works here now. He looks up from the table as Elizabeth comes towards him. Small, balding, not at all like Chris.

"Can I help you?" he says.

"I'm Elizabeth Schoenhof," Elizabeth says. "I work in Special Projects. I was wondering if you had a few spare scraps of fur. Any kind will do. My children use them for dolls' dresses."

The man smiles and gets up to look. Elizabeth has been told his name but she's forgotten it: Nagle? She will look it up. It's part of her job to know the technicians in every department, in case she needs to use them for anything.

As he rummages among the clutter on the shelves behind his table, Elizabeth looks around. The room has changed, been rearranged. Time has not stood still, nothing here is frozen. Chris is definitely gone. She cannot bring him back, and for the first time she no longer wants to. He'll punish her for that thought later, no doubt, but at the moment she's clear of him.

She walks slowly down the marble stairs, fingering a handful of fur. Scraps. All that's left of Chris, whom she can no longer remember whole. At the door she stuffs the bundle into her purse, then takes the subway up to St. George and along to Castle Frank. She walks along the viaduct till she's roughly in the middle, over the snow-filled ravine and the rushing cars below. Like Auntie Muriel, she needs her burial rituals. She opens her purse and throws the fur scraps one by one into space.

LESJE

Lesje is sitting in Elizabeth's living room, balancing a small cup
of what she supposes is excellent coffee on her left knee. In her
right hand she's holding a liqueur glass half-full of Benedictine
and brandy. She doesn't know how she's ended up with two
containers of liquid and no place to put them. She's positive
she will very soon spill at least one and probably both of them
onto Elizabeth's mushroom-colored carpet. She's desperate to
get away.

But the others are all playing a game that substitutes the word
"moose" for any other word in the title of a Canadian novel. It
has to be Canadian. This apparently is part of the joke.

"As for Me and My Moose," Elizabeth says, and everyone
else in the room chuckles.

"A Jest of Moose," says the wife of the man from Greek and
Roman who works at the CBC.

"A Moose of God," replies the man, whose name is Philip.
Nobody calls him Phil. Elizabeth laughs and asks Lesje if she'll
have some more B & B.

"I'm fine," Lesje says, hoping she has murmured, fearing she's
blurted. She needs a cigarette but has no free hand. She doesn't
read novels and she hasn't recognized a single one of the titles the
others, even Nate, even, sometimes, William, have been batting
around so easily. *The Lost Moose*, she could say. But that isn't
Canadian.

The whole dinner has been like that. Just a couple of friends,
Elizabeth said. Casual. So Lesje wore pants with a long sweater-
coat, and the two other women are in dresses. Elizabeth for once
is not in black; she's wearing a loose grey chiffon number that
makes her look younger and thinner than she does at work. She
even has a necklace on, a chain with a silver fish. The other
woman is in flowing mauve. Lesje, in her perky, clean-cut
stripes, feels about twelve years old.

She's only been able to see Nate once before this evening. In desperation she called his house; one of the children answered.

"Just a minute." Abruptly; the slam of the phone hitting the floor. It must have tumbled from the table. A shout. "Dad, it's for you!"

They'd arranged to meet at the coffee shop in the indoor mall at the bottom of Lesje's building. Reckless: what if William?

"Why is she asking us to dinner?" Lesje wanted to know, by this time frantic. She couldn't back out now, it would look funny. To William as well. And if she'd said no at first it would have looked funny too.

Nate was cautiously holding her hand. "I don't know," he said. "I've given up wondering about her motives. I never know why she does anything."

"We aren't that friendly at work," Lesje said. "Does she know?"

"Probably," Nate said. "She didn't tell me beforehand she was asking you to dinner. I couldn't tell her not to. She often asks people to dinner; or anyway she used to."

"Did you tell her?" It was suddenly the kind of thing he would do.

"Not exactly," Nate said. "I guess I've mentioned you a few times. I'm thinking about you a lot. Maybe she picked up on that. She's pretty sharp."

"But even if she does know, why would she ask me to dinner?" This would be the last thing she herself would do. One of William's old girlfriends, a dental technician, is in the habit of suggesting they all three of them have lunch sometime. Lesje has consistently vetoed this.

"I guess she just wants to take a look at you," Nate said, "up close. Don't worry, it'll be all right. She won't *do* anything. You'll enjoy the dinner, she's a great cook when she feels like it."

Not that Lesje could tell. She was so paralyzed by apprehension that she could barely chew. The *boeuf bourguignon* could have been sand as far as she was concerned. Elizabeth graciously ignored the large amount left on Lesje's plate. During the first course she asked Lesje three well-informed questions about power-structures in Vertebrate Paleontology, a truthful answer to any of which might have cost Lesje her job if repeated in the

137

right quarters. Lesje hedged awkwardly, and Elizabeth switched the talk to CBC gossip, with the wife of the man from Greek and Roman supplying.

Elizabeth concentrated on William during dessert. She found his work with the Ministry of the Environment fascinating, and so worthwhile. She supposed she really should make the effort to cart all her old bottles and newspapers to those things, those bins. William, gratified, lectured her on the doom awaiting the world if she should fail to do this, and Elizabeth agreed meekly.

Nate, meanwhile, moved in the background, chain-smoking, drinking steadily but without visible effect, avoiding Lesje's eyes, helping with the plate-clearing and pouring out the wine. Elizabeth directed him unobtrusively: "Love, would you get me a slotted serving spoon?" "Love, could you just turn on the coffee while you're out there?" Lesje sat, nibbling the edges of her meringue, wishing the children were there. At least she would have someone she could talk to without blushing and mumbling and the certainty that at any minute she would open her mouth and some tactless clinker would roll out onto the linen tablecloth. Something about suicides or hotel rooms. But the children had been sent to spend the night with friends. Sometimes, Elizabeth said, much as one loved one's children, one wanted to spend a little free adult time. Nate didn't always agree, she said, directly to Lesje. He was such a doting father. He'd like to be with his children twenty-four hours a day. "Isn't that true, love?"

Don't call him *love*, Lesje felt like saying. You can't fool me. But she supposed it was a habit. After all, they've been married for ten years.

Which Elizabeth has taken care to emphasize. There have been references all evening to Nate's favorite foods and Nate's favorite wines and Nate's peculiarities of dress. Elizabeth wishes he would get the back of his hair trimmed more often; she used to do it herself with the nail scissors, but she can't get him to hold still long enough any more. Nate's behavior on their wedding day has been mentioned, though not explained; everyone in the room, including the Greek and Roman couple, seems to know this story. Except Lesje and, of course, William, who was in the bathroom at the time. Where Lesje herself at this moment fervently wishes she could be.

William has produced his pipe, an affectation he by and large reserves for company. "I know a better one," he says. "Ever played Star Trek?" But nobody has, and the rules, as William starts to expound them, are pronounced too complicated.

"Lifeboat," says the Greek and Roman woman.

Nate asks if anyone would like more B & B. He himself is going to pour himself a Scotch. Would anyone care to join him?

"Sensational," says Elizabeth. She explains that this game is very simple. "We are all in a lifeboat," she says, "and the food is running out. What you have to do is convince everyone else why you should be allowed to remain in the lifeboat instead of being thrown overboard." She says that this game is often very revealing psychologically.

"I sacrifice myself for the good of the group," Nate says promptly.

"Oh," Elizabeth says, giving a mock frown. "He always does that. It's his Quaker upbringing. Really it means he can't be bothered."

"Unitarian," says Nate. "I just think it's an unduly vicious game."

"That's why it's called Lifeboat," Elizabeth says lightly. "All right, Nate's overboard. The sharks have him. Who wants to begin?"

No one does, so Elizabeth tears up a paper napkin and they draw lots.

"Well," says the Greek and Roman man. "I know Morse code. I can help us get rescued. And I'm good with my hands. When we land on the desert island, I can build the shelter and so forth. I'm a pretty good plumber, too. A tool man." He smiles. "It's nice to have a man around the house."

Elizabeth and the CBC woman, laughing, agree that he should be allowed to stay on the boat.

Elizabeth is next. "I'm a sensational cook," she says. "But more than that, I have a very strong survival instinct. If you try to push me overboard, I'll take at least one of you down with me. How's that? I don't think we should be kicking people out of this boat anyway," she adds. "We should be saving them and eating them. Let's drag Nate back in."

"I'm already miles away," Nate says.

"Elizabeth's using threats," the CBC woman says. "Any of us

139

could use the same ploy; I don't think it should count. But if we're thinking of a long-term plan, I propose that I should be saved instead of Elizabeth. She's almost past child-bearing age and if we want to establish a colony, we'll need babies."

Elizabeth goes white. "I'm sure I could still squeeze a few out," she says.

"Not many," the CBC woman says brightly. "Come on, Liz, it's only a game."

"Lesje?" Elizabeth says. "You walk the plank next."

Lesje opens her mouth, then closes it. She can feel herself blushing. She knows this is not just a game, it's a challenge of some sort. But still, she can't think of a single reason why she should be permitted to remain alive. She isn't a good cook, and besides there's nothing much to cook. She can't build shelters. The CBC woman has used up the babies, and anyway Lesje has a narrow pelvis. What is she good for? None of the things she knows, knows well, is in any way necessary for survival.

They are all looking at her, embarrassed now by the length of time it's taking her, her obvious confusion. "If we find any bones," she says at last, "I'll be able to tell you whose they are." As if the history of bones matters, to anyone but her and a few other addicts. She's attempted a sort of joke, but it's hardly witty repartee. "Excuse me," she says, her voice a whisper. Carefully she sets down her cup, then her glass, on the beige rug. She stands up and turns, catching the cup with the side of her foot, and bolts from the room.

"I'll get a cloth," she hears Nate saying.

She locks herself into Elizabeth's bathroom and washes her hands with Elizabeth's peculiar brown soap. Then she sits, closes her eyes, elbows on her crossed knees, hands covering her mouth. The B & B must be getting to her. Is she really this graceless, this worthless? From her treetop she watches an Ornithomimus, large-eyed, birdlike, run through the scrub, chasing a small protomammal. How many years to learn to grow hair, to bear young alive, to nurture them? How many for the four-chambered heart? Surely these things are important, surely her knowledge should not perish with her. She must be allowed to continue her investigations, here in this forest of early conifers and pineapple-trunked cycad trees.

Everyone has a certain number of bones, she thinks, clutching for lucidity. Not their own but someone else's and the bones have to be named, you have to know what to call them, otherwise what are they, they're lost, cut adrift from their own meanings, they may as well not have been saved for you. You can't name them all, there are too many, the world is full of them, it's made of them, so you have to choose which ones. Everything that's gone before has left its bones for you and you'll leave yours in turn.

This is her knowledge, her field they call it. And it is like a field, you can walk through it and around it and say: These are the boundaries. She knows why the dinosaurs do many of the things they do, and about the rest she can deduce, make educated guesses. But north of the field history begins and the fog takes over. It's like being farsighted, the distant lake and its beaches and smooth-backed basking sauropods clear-edged in the moonlight, her own hand a blur. She does not know, for instance, why she is crying.

ELIZABETH

Elizabeth is lying in bed, arms at her sides, feet together. The weak light from the street lamps comes in stripes through the bamboo blind, falls in bars on the walls, broken by the shadow of the spider plants, curved fingers which do not hold or reach for anything. The window is open a little at the bottom, the wooden slat covering the three holes in the sash of the storm window is lifted, cold air sifts through. Elizabeth opened it before she went to bed, she needed air.

Elizabeth lies with her eyes open. In the kitchen below her, Nate moves dishes. She notes him, pushes him back. She can see up through the dark ceiling, through the joists and layers of plaster and the worn linoleum, blue squares, which she, slovenly landlady, should have replaced long ago, past the beds where the tenants lie asleep, a mother, a father, a child, a family, up through the pink ceiling of their room and out through the rafters and the patched and leaking roof to the air, the sky, the place where there is nothing between her and nothing. The stars in their envelopes of bright gas burn on. Space no longer frightens her. She knows it is uninhabited.

Where did you go? I know you aren't in that box. The Greeks collected all the pieces of the body; otherwise the soul could not get away from the upper earth. To the happy islands. Philip said that tonight, between the *boeuf bourguignon* and the meringue with chocolate ginger sauce. Then he changed the subject, he remembered and was embarrassed, he knew he shouldn't be talking about funerary customs. I smiled, I smiled. It was a closed coffin, naturally. They shipped him north in dry ice, rigid among the cold crystals, fog coming off him like a Dracula movie. Tonight I thought, they forgot something. Part of him has been left behind.

*　　*　　*

142

She could not move; nevertheless she had Nate take her to the train in a taxi, where she sat like a slab of rock all the way to Thunder Bay and then on the unspeakable bus. English River. Upsala on one side, Bonheur on the other, Osaquan up the road. He used to point out those names, and the irony, the indignity of having been born and forced to live in English River. "The English," they still said, Scots, French, Indians, what-have-you. The enemy, the despoilers. She was one of the English.

She sat in the back pew, kneeling when the others kneeled, standing when they stood, while Chris, surrounded by meager flowers, underwent the ceremony. Luckily it was in English, she could follow it. They even said the Lord's Prayer, a slightly different version. Forgive us our trespasses. When she was young she used to think that meant walking on other people's property. A thing she never did; therefore she did not need to be forgiven. As we forgive those who trespass against us. Get off the lawn, Auntie Muriel used to shout at the running children, opening the front door, then closing it like a mouth behind her voice. The old priest turned towards the people, raising the cup, mumbling, distaste on his face. The Latin was better, you could tell he thought that.

They didn't bury him at a crossroads with a stake, though. Death by misadventure. The shoulders were bowed, the heads bent, his mother in black in the front pew, with a real veil. The other children — Elizabeth supposed that was who they were — lined up beside her.

Afterwards there was coffee at the house. The neighbors brought cookies. One of those small northern bungalows, on a rock, pink and blue like a cake, dark spruce trees all around. Skidoo parked in the shed, the Eaton's Catalogue furniture, the worn store drapes four inches too short. Everything was the way she'd known it would be. The father's carefully learned English, the mother's dark face, baggy with grief and starch. We wanted him to have a chance. He was doing good. Always a smart boy. An education, finished his Grade Twelve, a steady job. Elizabeth thinking: Bullshit. You drove him out. Hit him when he wouldn't turn into you; right in that shed. We told each other a lot.

The mother: You a friend of his? From the city, eh? Then, as she'd feared, throwing back the veil, the bad teeth showing, pushing her dark face towards Elizabeth, her hair turning to snakes: *You killed him.*

But she could never have made it as far as the train, the taxi even. Chris disappeared without her help or connivance. As far as she knows, his parents, if they still exist, have never heard of her. And her images are all wrong, too. He let on to her at first, hinted, that he was part Indian and part French, Métis, that mythical hybrid; archaic, indigenous, authentic as she was not, his sense of grievance fully earned. He sneered at her, the whiteness of her skin and presumably her blood, made love as if exacting payment, and she'd let herself be bullied. As she would otherwise have not. Then one afternoon, lying depleted on his smoky bed, they'd gone past that into the land of perilous confidences, her scrounging childhood, hunger and unbrushed hair behind her mother's helpless pretensions. Never envy anyone, she'd said, until you know. Now tell me.

It was twilight, drawn curtains, he rubbed his hand over and over her bare shoulder, for the first time he would give her something, give something away, he could hardly do it. It made her wince, that effort, it was not what she wanted. Don't ever drop your defenses, she should have told him; they're there to defend you.

He was only a quarter French, and no Indian at all. The rest was Finnish and English; his mother's name was Robertson. They weren't even poor enough to be romantic, they ran the cigar store, the good one, not the other. No trapper he. The beatings were real enough, but less frequent than he'd said. Was that when her attention had begun to slip, was she that cruel, that snobbish? Probably. Despite this, she has not known what to answer to that mother's face looming like a moon, a moon seen close, cold and ravaged. No, she's said, more than once. It was malice, pride, it was his own damn fault. It wasn't me.

Now she finally wonders. What if? What if she'd left him alone. Foregone that jag, energy flowing into her. I wonder if you have some leftover fur scraps; my daughters make dolls' clothes out of them. To Chris, who had nothing left over, no reserves he could draw on, no free gifts to hand out. She'd known what she was doing. To be loved, to be hated also, to be the center. She had what he wanted, power over a certain part of the world: she knew how to behave, what fork to use, what

144

went with what. He wanted that power. He had two ties, one green, one purple. Neither of them would do. He looked better in a T-shirt, she told him; which she should not have done.

She had that power and she'd let him see it and touch it. She let him see he was deficient and she promised, what? A transformation, a touch on the shoulder, knighthood. Then she'd stepped back, showing him that he was after all only a vacation, a beautiful picture on a brochure, a man in a loincloth whacking the head off some nondescript coconut. A dime a dozen. Leaving him naked.

She thinks: I treated him the way men treat women. A lot of men, a lot of women; but never me, not on your goddamned life. He couldn't take it. Does she feel pity for him at last, or is it contempt?

Downstairs Nate rattles the silverware, rinsing it, she knows, before putting it into the plastic basket in the dishwasher. She's heard this sound often enough. She turns her eyes away from the stars, looks instead down through the floor. Nate shuffles, cigarette stub in his mouth, lost in some melancholy dream. Mooning, yearning. She watched him this evening, through the dinner which she did not in the least enjoy, the parlor games, she could see it all, he's in love with that giraffe. Coffee on the rug, a minor irritation, she'll have to get it steam-cleaned; also a satisfaction. Lesje is a clown. But is, despite her gawkiness and lack of poise, a younger woman, quite a lot younger than Elizabeth. Elizabeth finds this banal. Tedious, predictable. However, Nate has been what everyone would call *in love* before. She'll give him permission, express interest, be helpful, wait it out. She's been through this before, she can do it with one hand tied behind her back.

(But why bother, another voice says. Why not let him go? Why make the effort?)

There's something else, she remembers now, and it's dangerous. Before, he wanted to be protected. He wanted a woman to be a door he could go through and shut behind him. Everything was fine as long as she was willing to pretend she was a cage, Nate a mouse, her heart pure cheese. He is, she knows, a hopeless sentimentalist. Earthmother, Nate her mole, snouting

145

in darkness while she rocked him. I think that I shall never see a poem lovely as a tree. When she gave it up he found Martha, who could not do it nearly as well.

But this time he wants to protect. Looking down at the top of his head, the back of his neck, the way his hands move, deliberately, she knows it, even though he may not know it himself.

Elizabeth sits up in bed. Wires light in her legs and fingers, the walls with their shadows are in place again, the floor is there, the ceiling has healed over. Space is a cube around her, she is the center. There is something to be defended.

Stay in your place, Nate. I will not tolerate that void.

NATE

Sadly, Nate stacks plates. It's the rule that when Elizabeth cooks, Nate does the dishes. One of the many rules, subrules, codicils, addenda, errata. Living with Elizabeth involves a maze of such legalities, no easier to understand because some of them are unspoken. Like an unwary pedestrian, he only realizes he's violated one of these when the bumper hits him, the whistle blows, the big hand descends. Ignorance of the law is no excuse. He imagines Lesje to be without rules.

He sees himself bending to whisper at the bathroom keyhole: *I love you.* Irrevocable commitment, even though he isn't sure whether Lesje, barricaded behind the bathroom door where she'd been for the past half-hour, could really hear him. He isn't sure why she was upset. He'd seen her face as she headed out the door. The coffee stain spreading on the rug behind her; but it wasn't that.

He'd wanted to reach through the bathroom door, comfort her, he thought about knocking, decided against it. What if she opened the door? If he said that to her face, no wall between, he would have to take action. Even though he meant it. He would find himself in mid-air, hurtled into a future he could not yet imagine, Elizabeth left on the solid earth behind him, feet on the ground where she always claimed they were, a dark hummock, the children's faces two pale ovals beside her. Receding from him.

He thinks of them (riotously bouncing at this moment on their friend Sarah's spare bed, in the dark, stifling laughter) and sees, not their daily faces, but two little portraits. In silver frames, birthday-party dresses, the dead hues of a black and white photo tinted. He and Elizabeth do not own any such portraits. His children immobilized, stilled. Bronzed. He tries to remember what it was like before they were born, finds he can't. He can only go as far back as Elizabeth, trundling through the days and finally climbing ponderously from the car which he'd bought months before for this occasion, doubling over against the hood; himself solicitous and frightened. They wouldn't let fathers into the delivery room in those days. He walked her to the desk; the nurse looked at him disapprovingly. See what you've done. He installed her in a ward room, sat as she clenched and unclenched, watched as she vanished down the corridor in a wheelchair. It was a long labor. He slouched in a chair covered with green vinyl, reading back copies of *Sports Illustrated* and *Parents*, feeling his mouth fog up. He wanted a drink badly and all they had was coffee from a machine. Behind doors an earthquake was taking place, a flood, a tornado that could rip his life apart in minutes, and he was shut out from it.

Around him machines wheezed; he dozed. He was supposed to feel anxious and happy, he knew. Instead he found himself wondering: What if they both die? The bereaved young father stood at the graveside, clogged with grief, as the woman once so vibrant and sensuous, who'd smelled of crushed ferns, descended forever into the earth, cradling a stillborn baby the color of suet. He walked down a road, any road, thumbing, heading for some legendary steamer, pack on his back. A broken man.

When he'd finally been allowed in, the event was over. There was a baby where no baby had been. Elizabeth, depleted, was lying propped up in a white hospital gown, a plastic name on her wrist. She looked at him dully, as if he were a salesman or a census-taker.

"Is it all right?" he said, noticing immediately that he'd said "it" rather than "you" or "she." He hadn't even said, "Was it all right." It must have been; she was here, in front of him, she wasn't dead. They all overestimated it.

"They didn't give me the needle in time," Elizabeth said.

He looked down at the baby, wrapped like a sausage roll, held by one of Elizabeth's arms. He felt relieved and grateful, and cheated. She told him several times afterwards that he had no idea of what it was like, and she was right, he hadn't. But she acted also as if this was his fault.

He thinks they were closer before the birth of Janet, but he can't remember. He can't remember what *close* means, or rather what it would have meant once with Elizabeth. She used to make omelettes for him at night after he was finished studying and they would eat them together, sitting in the double bed. He remembers that time as good. Love food, she called it.

148

Nate scrapes leftover *boeuf bourguignon* into a bowl; later he will put it down the Garb-all. His lapses of memory are beginning to bother him. It's not only Elizabeth, the way (he deduces) she must have been, that's slipping away from him. He loved her, he wanted to marry her, they got married, and he can recall only fragments. Almost a year of law school is gone now; his adolescence is hazy. Martha, once so firm and tangible, is transparent, her face wobbles; soon she will dissolve completely.

And the children. What did they look like, when did they walk, what did they say, how did he feel? He knows events have taken place, important events of which he is now ignorant. What will happen to this day, to Elizabeth's disastrous dinner party, the remains of which are now being ground to shreds by the metal teeth under the sink?

Nate starts the dishwasher, wipes his hands on his pantlegs. He goes to the stairs, quietly before remembering: the children are away for the night. Lesje too is gone, fleeing almost directly from the bathroom, stopping only to snatch her coat, her young man in tow. The bun-faced young man whose name Nate can't at the moment recall.

Instead of going to his own cubicle, his cell, he pauses at the children's door, then walks into their room. He knows now that he will leave; it feels, instead, as though they have left him. Here are the dolls, the scattered paint sets, the scissors, the odd socks and rabbit-faced slippers they've forgotten in their haste to pack. Already they are on a train, a plane, headed for some unknown destination, being carried away from him at the speed of light.

He knows they will be back tomorrow morning in time for Sunday brunch, that tomorrow anyway everything will go on the same, that he will stand at the kitchen table dishing out scrambled eggs on toast for himself and the girls and for Elizabeth, who will be wrapped in her blue terry-cloth bathrobe, hair only half-brushed. He will dish out the scrambled eggs and Elizabeth will ask him to pour her a second cup of coffee, and it will seem even to him as though nothing is about to happen.

Yet he kneels; tears come to his eyes. He should have held on, he should have held on more tightly. He picks up one of Nancy's blue rabbit slippers, stroking the fur. It's his own eventual death he cradles. His lost, his kidnapped children, gone from him, kept hostage. Who has done this? How has he allowed it to happen?

149

LESJE

Lesje drifts along the street with the drifting snow. Cars in their chains jingle past her, their tires locked in ruts; slush clogs their fenders. In the night there's been a blizzard. She doesn't care that her feet are cold: she has no feet. The trees she passes are heavy with ice. Each twig glitters in the weak sunlight, lit from within; the world glows. Lesje stretches her arms out, feels the blood flow along them to explode in purple at each hand. She knows the blaze of light she sees is only a mitten. But it is a mitten transfigured, its acrylic fibers shining with their own atomic light. Dazzled, she squints her eyes. She's weightless, all pores, the universe accepts her finally, nothing bad can happen. Has she ever felt like this before?

It's only two o'clock. She left the office early, telling Dr. Van Vleet she felt she was coming down with something. Really it's Nate who is coming down with something: he phoned from his house, nasal, forlorn, he has to see her. Lesje walks to the rescue in her gum-soled snowboots, a nurse hurrying over frozen Siberia, driven on by love. She will put her hand on his forehead and miraculously he will revive. By the time she reaches his front steps and stamps her way up them her nose is running.

Nate opens the door, draws her inside quickly, shuts the door before enfolding her. Lesje is pressed against his brown wool dressing gown, which smells of old smoke and burnt toast. His mouth comes down on hers; sniffling, they kiss. He half-lifts her, then thinks better of it and sets her down.

"My boots will drip," she says, and bends to unzip them. She tugs at her boot heels, her eyes at the level of Nate's knees. He's wearing work socks, grey with red stripes around the top and white toes and heels. These socks, for some reason, fill her with tenderness and lust: her body is with her again.

In their stocking feet they tiptoe along the hall and up the stairs. Nate leads her by the hand.

150

"In here," he says. Although there is no one home, they whisper.

Nate folds back the Indian spread. Lesje can hardly see: the room is a blur around her, vision a shaft of light illuminating tigers, off-red tigers in a purplish jungle. Under the tigers there are flowered sheets. Wordlessly Nate undresses her, lifting her arms, bending her elbows as if he's undressing a doll or a child; Lesje stands still. He eases her sweater over her head, presses his cheek against her stomach while he kneels to slide down her jeans. Lesje raises one foot and then the other, stepping out, obedient. There's cold air, a draft somewhere in the room. Her skin contracts. Gently he pulls her onto the bed. She sinks into a hollow, petals flow over her.

He's on top of her, both of them impelled now by fear, the sun moving across the sky, the feet walking inexorably towards them, the sound of a door which has not yet opened, boots on the stairs.

Lesje is lying semipropped on two pillows. His head rests on her belly. The world is again the world, she can see detail, the luminous blur has faded. Nevertheless she's happy. She does not see this happiness as having any necessary result.

Nate moves, reaches for a Kleenex from the night table. "What time is it?" he says. They talk in normal voices now.

Lesje checks her watch. "I'd better leave," she says. She would rather not have Elizabeth or the children come back to find her naked in Nate's bed.

Nate rolls onto his side, rests on an elbow while she sits up, slides her legs over the side of the bed. With one hand she gropes for her underpants, lost somewhere in the flowers. She bends to look on the floor. Two shoes are there, on the oval braided rug, black ones, side by side.

"Nate," she says. "Whose room is this?"

He looks at her, he doesn't answer.

"This is Elizabeth's room," she says.

She stands up and begins to dress, covering herself as fast as she can. This is horrible, this is a violation. She feels grubby; it's almost like incest. Elizabeth's husband is one thing, Elizabeth's bed quite another.

151

Nate doesn't understand. He explains that his own bed is too narrow for both of them.

This is not the point. She thinks: The bed had no choice.

He helps her pull the tiger bedspread up and smooth the pillows. How can she tell him? She doesn't know why she is so upset. Perhaps it's the suggestion that it doesn't matter, that she and Elizabeth are interchangeable. Or his feeling that Elizabeth's bed is still in some sense his also, he can do whatever he wants in it. Lesje feels for the first time that she has wronged Elizabeth, that she has trespassed.

Lesje sits in the kitchen, elbows on the kitchen table, chin on her hands; Nate lights her cigarette for her. He's baffled. He offers her a Scotch, then a cup of tea. Smoke screens her face.

On the refrigerator there's a child's painting, held in place by a magnetic plastic tomato and a cob of corn. It's of a girl, hair a yellow blob, eyes fringed with enormous lashes, a manic red grin. The sky is a blue line at the top of the page, the sun a bursting lemon.

All the molecular materials now present in the earth and its atmosphere were present at the creation of the earth itself, whether that creation took place by the explosion of a larger body or by condensation of gaseous debris. These molecular materials have merely combined, disintegrated, recombined. Although a few molecules and atoms have escaped into space, nothing has been added.

Lesje contemplates this fact, which she finds soothing. She is only a pattern. She is not an immutable object. There are no immutable objects. Some day she will dissolve.

Nate strokes her hand. He is dismayed but she cannot comfort him.

"What are you thinking about, love?" he says.

NATE

Nate is down in the cellar. He's cutting out heads on the scroll saw, heads and necks for four-wheeled horses. Each horse will have a string on the front. When the string is pulled, the horse will roll along, head and tail moving in graceful rhythm. Or so he hopes.

As he works, he pauses to wipe sweat from his forehead. His beard is dank; altogether he feels like a mildewed mattress. It's a lot cooler down here than it is upstairs, though just as humid. Outside it must be ninety. In the morning the cicadas began their rasping songs well before eight.

"A scorcher," Nate remarked when he'd encountered Elizabeth in the kitchen. She was wearing a light blue dress with a smudge on the back, at the level of the rib cage. "Did you know you have smudge on your dress?" he asked. She liked to be told about such lapses: undone zippers, unhooked hooks, hairs on the shoulders, labels sticking out of necklines. "Oh, do I?" she said. "I'll change it." But she'd left for work in the same dress. Unlike her to forget.

Nate wants a cold beer. He switches off the saw and turns towards the stairway, and it's then that he sees the head, upside down in the square mud-pocked cellar window, staring in at him. It's Chris Beecham. He must be lying on the gravel outside, his neck twisted at right angles so he can get his head down into the window well. He smiles. Nate motions upstairs, hoping Chris will understand and go to the back door.

When Nate opens the door, Chris is already there. He's still smiling. "I was banging on the window," he says.

"I had the scroll saw on," Nate says. Chris gives no explanation of why he's here. Nate steps back to let him in, offers a beer. Chris accepts and walks behind him to the kitchen.

"I took this afternoon off," he says. "It's too hot to work. It's not like they have air conditioning."

This is only the fourth or fifth time Nate has ever seen Chris. The first time was when Elizabeth invited him to Christmas dinner. "He knows hardly anyone," she'd said. Elizabeth has a habit of doing that, inviting people to dinner who know hardly anyone. Sometimes these stray eggs for which Elizabeth plays hen are women, but more often they are men. Nate doesn't mind. He approves, more or less, even though this is the kind of thing his mother would do if she thought of it. As it is, she runs more to letters than to dinners. Elizabeth's waifs are usually nice enough, and the children like to have guests, especially around Christmas. Janet says it makes it more like a party.

Chris got a little drunk, Nate remembers. They'd had Christmas crackers, and Nate had found a prize eye in his, a plastic eye with a red iris.

"What is it?" Nancy asked.

"An eye," Nate said. Usually it was whistles or small mono-colored figures. This was the first year anyone had found an eye.

"What's it for?"

"I don't know," Nate said. He put it on the side of his plate. Somewhat later Chris reached across and took it and stuck it in the center of his forehead. He then began singing "The Streets of Laredo" in a lugubrious voice. The children thought he was funny.

Since then, Nate has come up from the cellar on several occasions to find Chris in his living room, having a drink with Elizabeth. They've been sitting at opposite sides of the room, not saying much. Nate has always poured himself a drink and joined them. He seldom turns down the chance for a sociable drink. One thing has puzzled Nate: although Elizabeth invites lame ducks for festive dinners, she rarely has people over for a drink unless their position at the Museum is either on a par with hers or higher. There's no way Chris fits either of these categories. As far as Nate can figure out, he's a taxidermist of some sort, a glorified custodian of dead owls. A technician, not an executive. Nate doesn't rule out the possibility that Elizabeth and Chris are lovers – Chris wouldn't be the first – but before this she's always told him. Sooner or later. He'll wait for that before believing. Things aren't particularly good between them, but they're still possible.

154

Nate opens two Carling's Red Caps and they sit at the kitchen table. He asks Chris if he wants a glass; Chris says no. What he wants, instead, is to have Nate drive over to his place with him for a game of chess. Nate is a little taken aback by this. He explains that he doesn't play chess very well, hasn't played much for years.

"Elizabeth says you're good," Chris says.

"That's because Elizabeth can't play at all," Nate says modestly.

But Chris insists. It will cheer him up, he says. He's been feeling down lately. Nate cannot resist this appeal to his Samaritan instincts. He goes upstairs to their room to put on a clean T-shirt. When he comes down, Chris is spinning one of the beer bottles on the kitchen table.

"Ever play spin the bottle?" he asks. As a matter of fact, Nate hasn't.

They take Chris's car, which is illegally parked across the street. It's an old Chevy convertible, once white, a '67 or '68 model. Nate's grip on car models is slipping. He himself no longer has a car, having sold it to finance his scroll saw, his bench saw, his belt-disc sander and other necessary machines.

Chris's car is missing a muffler. He exploits this aggressively, revving the engine like a thunder gun at each stoplight. They fart their way along Davenport, trailing clouds of noise pollution, gathering dirty looks. The top of the convertible is down and the sun, filtered through layers of spent exhaust, beats on their heads. By the time they reach Winchester and Parliament and Chris parks, again illegally, Nate is dizzy. He asks Chris, to make conversation, if there's much prostitution around here. He already knows there is. Chris gives him a look of undisguised dislike and says yes, there is. "I don't mind it though," he says. "They know I'm not in the market. We pass the time of day."

Nate wants to get out of this. He wants to say he has a headache, a backache, any sort of ache severe enough to spring him. He isn't feeling up to having a chess game in ninety-degree weather with a man he barely knows. But Chris is now brisk, almost businesslike. He marches them across the street and lets them into his apartment building, marches them across the stained mosaic-tile entryway and up the stairs, three flights. Nate, panting, lags behind. In the face of such certainty he hesitates to offer his dim excuses.

Chris unlocks his door and goes in. Nate, plunging, follows. The apartment is cooler; it's wood-paneled, must once have been intended for the semi-rich. Although it has two rooms, a wide arched doorway between them makes it seem like one. It smells of darkness: corners, dry-rot, a chemical smell. The chess table is already set up, in the room that also contains Chris's bed. There are two chairs, placed carefully on opposite sides of the chessboard. Nate realizes that this invitation was not a spur-of-the-moment whim.

"Want a drink?" Chris produces a mickey of Scotch from the glass-doored cupboard, pours some into a small tumbler decorated with tulips. Jelly jar, Nate thinks; he recognizes it from ten years ago. The Scotch is bad but Nate drinks; he doesn't wish to antagonize. Chris, it seems, will drink from the bottle. He sets it beside the chess table, gives Nate a peanut butter jar lid for his cigarette ashes, takes a white pawn and a black one from the table and shuffles them behind his back. He holds out his fists, huge, thick-knuckled.

"Left," Nate says.

"Tough luck," Chris says. They sit down to play. Chris opens with an insulting attempt at fool's mate, which Nate counters easily. Chris grins and pours Nate another drink. They settle down to play in earnest. Nate knows Chris will win, but out of pride he wants this victory to take a decent amount of time. He plays defensively, grouping his men in tight clumps, taking no chances.

Chris plays like a Cossack, swooping forward, picking at Nate's outposts, retreating to puzzling new positions. He jiggles one foot against the floor impatiently while Nate ponders his moves. They're both sweating. Nate's T-shirt sticks to his skin; he'd like an open window, a draft, but it's hotter outside than in here. Nate knows he's drinking more bad Scotch than he should, but the game is getting to him.

Finally he makes a good move. Chris will either have to take his Queen's Knight and lose his own knight, or he'll lose a rook. Now it's Nate's turn to sit back and stare intimidatingly while Chris worries his choices. Nate sits back, but instead of staring he tries to keep himself from wondering what he's doing here, which would be bad for his game.

He glances around the room. It's almost bare, yet manages to

156

give the impression of disorder. It isn't the objects in the room that do this, but their relation to each other. Nothing seems to be in the right place. The table beside the bed, for instance, is about a foot too far away from it.

And on the table, which is otherwise empty, is something he now knows he was meant to see. It's a little fish, silver, with blue enameled scales. He's last noticed it hanging on a chain around Elizabeth's neck.

Or one very like it. He can't be sure. He looks at Chris and Chris is gazing at him, the muscles of his face rigid, his eyes still. Fear shoots through Nate, the hairs on his arms rise, his scrotum contracts, the ends of his fingers tingle. He thinks: Chris is drunk. He finds himself wondering whether Chris really has Indian blood in him as Elizabeth implies, he's never been able to place that slight accent; then he's appalled at himself, falling into a cliché like that. Besides, Chris has hardly been drinking at all, it's he himself who's killed three-quarters of that poisonous mickey.

If he's right, if he's been brought here on (he now sees) the shabby pretext of a chess game, just to witness this object, this hostage which may or may not belong to Elizabeth, his options are limited. Chris knows he knows. Chris is expecting Nate to hit him. Then Chris will hit Nate and they'll have a fight. Smashing the chess table, rolling among the light puffs of dust that colonize Chris's floor.

Nate deplores this solution. The question is: Is Elizabeth a female dog or a human being? It's a matter of human dignity. Why fight over Elizabeth, who presumably can make her own choices? Has made them. Whoever wins, the fight would settle nothing.

Nate could pretend he hasn't seen the silver fish, but it's gone too far for that.

Or he could ignore it. Even to himself this would look like cowardice.

"Made your move?" Nate says.

Chris captures the Queen's Knight, stares at Nate, his chin out, tensed, ready. Any moment he may spring. Nate thinks: Maybe he's crazy. Maybe he's crazy enough to have bought another fish and planted it there. Maybe he's fucking insane!

Instead of taking the white knight, Nate tips over his own king.

157

"You win the game," he says. He stands up, scoops the fish off the table.

"I'll return this to Elizabeth for you, shall I?" he says, gently, affably.

He walks to the door, expecting at any moment to feel fists on his back, a boot in his kidneys. He takes a taxi back to the house; the driver waits outside while he gathers enough loose change from the surfaces of their room to pay him.

He places the silver fish carefully on the night table, beside his scattered pennies. She should have told him. It isn't friendly, the fact that she hasn't told him. The first time, she told him and they both cried, holding each other closely, consoling each other for some violation they felt as mutual. Then they discussed their problems, sitting up till four in the morning, whispering across the kitchen table. They promised reforms, repairs, reparations, whole new sequences of events, a new order. And the second and the third time. He isn't a monster, he's always stifled his outrage, he's forgiven her.

The fact that she hasn't told him this time means only one thing: she doesn't want to be forgiven. Or, put another way, she no longer cares whether he forgives her or not. Or, it occurs to him, she may have decided it isn't his right to forgive.

ELIZABETH

Elizabeth is sitting at the black-topped table in Fran's. Opposite her is William. In front of her is a waffle with a scoop of vanilla ice cream melting on it, and on top of the ice cream is a tentacled formation of partially congealed cinnamon-colored syrup. She watches the syrup run down and hopes the waitress won't comment on the untouched waffle when she brings the check.

Across the table from her William is eating a club sandwich and drinking draft beer. Eizabeth is only half-listening to the conversation, which consists of an account, by William, of recent research on carcinogenic substances to be found in smoked meats. She's more relaxed now. William doesn't seem to notice that they're in Fran's instead of some récherché little hideaway. The first two récherché little hideaways they tried had been full, and according to William they were the only ones in the area. An area Elizabeth no longer knows well.

Under ordinary circumstances she would have reserved in advance, but she needed to seem impromptu. She happened to be passing by the Ministry of the Environment on her way to do some shopping (false; she never shops at Yonge and St. Clair) and remembered their recent conversation (also false). She thought how fascinating it would be to pop in on William and hear a little more about the work he was doing (totally false), and if William wasn't busy for lunch, she'd love to have him join her (true, but not for the reasons William may have suspected).

William was even more flattered than she intended him to be. Even now he's swelling visibly, expounding with fervor on degenerate hams and the evil secret life of bacon. She prods at her waffle with her fork and wonders whether she should press his knee discreetly under the table, or is it too soon? She hasn't yet decided exactly how she'll go on from here. Either she will seduce William, to create some balance in the universe, a tit for a tat, or she'll tell him about Lesje and Nate; or perhaps both.

She cuts off a piece of waffle with her fork, lifts it. Then she puts it back on her plate. She remembers why this is something she can no longer eat.

It's May; Elizabeth is coming to life again. Two weeks ago her mother finally died, after smoldering in the hospital bed for longer than anyone could have expected. Elizabeth sat through that death, watching clear fluid drip from a bottle into her mother's good arm, holding the good hand, watching the good half of the face for any movement, any sign. For two days she didn't eat or sleep, despite Auntie Muriel and the doctor, who said that her mother would not regain consciousness, which was all for the best, and Elizabeth should save her strength. She walked through the funeral step by step, listened to the service, watched her mother float for the second time into the flames. She allowed her hand to be shaken and pressed by the friends of Auntie Muriel. Auntie Muriel planned the whole funeral down to the last detail as if it were an important tea party. She can't tell whether Auntie Muriel is mourning or gloating; there's a pleased fatalism about her. She has the flowers from the funeral around the house in vases – why waste them? – and the house stinks of death.

Auntie Muriel can't seem to stop talking about it. Elizabeth wants to stop talking about it. She wants to stop hearing about it, thinking about it. She never wants to think about her mother again. In two months, less than that, she'll be finished with high school and then she'll get out. Auntie Muriel wants her to go to Trinity College and continue living in the house; she says it will be better for Caroline, which Elizabeth sees as a ruse to trap her.

Elizabeth herself has no such ambitions. She wants only one thing: escape. She can't yet see what form this will take. She can see herself planning, finding a job through the *Star* want ads, hunting a furnished room, packing; making provisions. She can also see herself running out the front door in her nightgown and vanishing forever into a ravine. Both of these things are equally possible.

She can't bear to be inside Auntie Muriel's house with its greyish chrysanthemums, its festering gladioli. The room she

160

shares with Caroline is papered with small blue roses, their stems bunched into doilies, Auntie Muriel's version of girlhood; the furniture is painted white. On her bed Caroline keeps a blue fake-fur pyjama bag in the shape of a cat.

Elizabeth picks up a boy in a drugstore. It isn't the first time, but it's the first time since her mother's death; and in a drugstore. Before it's been street corners, the entranceways to movie houses. This is forbidden: Auntie Muriel allows only formal dances at private schools with the sons of her acquaintances. Elizabeth has no taste for these dances or for the pink-cheeked, short-haired boys who attend them. She prefers boys like this one. He has a ducktail and a red leather jacket with the collar turned up; his black eyebrows almost meet, his chin is cut where he's scraped it shaving. His shorter friend gets out of the car, muttering something to him and laughing, as Elizabeth gets in.

The car is festooned with plastic dice and feather kewpie dolls. Elizabeth likes such cars. There's danger in them but she knows she can control it. She enjoys the latent power of her own hands; she knows she can always stop in time. It excites and gratifies her to be able to do this, go to the edge and almost jump. (There's something else, too. The boys, any boys, any mouth and pair of arms, contain a possibility; some quality she can only guess at, some hope.)

They drive around for a while, then go to Fran's for a waffle. Food is always part of it. Elizabeth gobbles her waffle as if she's never seen one before; the boy smokes, watches her through narrowed eyes. His name is Fred or something and he goes to Jarvis. She tells him where she lives and he tries not to be impressed. Elizabeth feels she knows exactly what Auntie Muriel and her pretensions are worth. This doesn't stop her from displaying them. Auntie Muriel has her terrors, which are real enough to Elizabeth, but increasingly she also has her uses.

They drive around some more, park on a quiet side street. The smell of Old Spice shaving lotion fills the car. Elizabeth waits for the leather arm to arrive, across, over, down. She has no time right now for preliminaries, fumbling with hooks, inching around the rib cage; she does not want to dole herself out. She's filled with energy, she can't tell what it is, anger, fury, denial.

161

What she has in mind is more like a car crash, time squeezed together. Violence, metal on metal.

He's tangled in the steering wheel. Impatient, more reckless than he is, she opens the car door, pulls him down onto the wet grass. Somebody's front lawn. "Hey," he says. He's nervous, he glances up at the curtained windows.

She wants to shout, a huge raucous shout that will startle the darkness, bring the cold crab eyes in these stone houses hurrying to their windows; something that will unlock her throat. She wants to let go of the dead hand she's still holding.

She kisses this mouth that exists only now, does not stop or pull away when the hands move over her, twists to allow him. He groans, hesitates. Then for a minute she almost does scream: she expected pain, but not this kind or this much. Nevertheless she is grinning, teeth set; she exults. She hopes she's bleeding, a little anyway; blood would make this an event. When he goes limp she reaches down to see.

He doesn't understand, he's on his knees beside her, doing himself up, pulling down her skirt, apologizing! Awkwardly; he's really sorry, he couldn't help it, he didn't mean to. As if she's a foot he's stepped on, as if he's merely sneezed.

She gets out of the car a block from the house. It's later than she thought. The back of her coat is wet and she brushes at it ineffectually before getting out her key. She's convinced Auntie Muriel will be standing on the bottom step of the staircase in her powder blue dressing gown, accusing, malignant, triumphant. Elizabeth has fed her a story about evening choir practice, which, unbelievably, has worked several times before. But she's never stayed out so late. If Auntie Muriel is there, if she knows, Elizabeth can't imagine what she'll do. She can't imagine any actual punishment – rage, banishment, disinheritance – equal to her dread. When she's at a distance from Auntie Muriel she can think of derisive and vulgar things to say to her, but in her presence she knows she would be mute. If Auntie Muriel were roped to the stake she'd be the first to jeer; but who has the power to put her there? Auntie Muriel terrifies her because she doesn't know where to stop. Other people have lines they won't step over, but for Auntie Muriel such lines do not exist. Elizabeth's other fear is that these lines do not exist in herself, either.

But when she unlocks the door the hall is vacant. She walks

along the carpet and up the stairs, making it past the inlaid grandfather clock on the landing, past the Chinese vases on their spindly stands at the top of the stairs, pressing her thighs together, blood seeping gently in her clothes. She'll have to wash these clothes herself, privately, dry them in secret. She wants Auntie Muriel to know, wants her to see the evidence of this violation; at the same time she'll do everything to keep her from finding out.

She opens the door of the room she shares with Caroline. The overhead light is on. Caroline is lying on the floor between their beds. She's spread out the plaid mohair blanket from the foot of her bed and is lying on it, arms folded across her breasts, eyes open and fixed on the ceiling. Above her head and at her feet are the silver candelabra from the mahogany buffet downstairs. Beside her there's a bottle of lemon furniture polish. The candles in the candelabra have burned to stubs, gone out. She must have been like this for hours.

Elizabeth knows as soon as she sees her that she's been expecting this, or something like it. Caroline would not go to the hospital; she said she didn't want to see their mother. She refused to attend the funeral, and Auntie Muriel, strangely, did not force her. Elizabeth noticed all this, but only from the corner of her eye. Caroline had been so silent lately it was easy not to notice her.

Once, a long time ago, Elizabeth strode through the girl's half of a schoolyard at recess, her arms linked in a chain of other girls. *We don't stop for anybody.* That was the game: you couldn't stop for anybody. Elizabeth kept Caroline's arm gripped firmly under her own; she had to have Caroline with her in the chain so she wouldn't get run down. Caroline was younger, she had trouble keeping up. She was Elizabeth's responsibility. But Elizabeth has been concentrating all her energy, for years now, on saving herself. She hasn't had any left over for saving Caroline.

She drops to her knees, smooths Caroline's hair back from her forehead above the unblinking eyes. Then she moves one folded arm and puts her head on Caroline's chest. Caroline is still alive.

*   *   *

163

Once the ambulance and the stretcher had come and gone, but not until then, Elizabeth had knelt on the mosaic tiles of the second-floor bathroom beside the claw-footed tub and thrown up her Fran's Special, ice cream, cinnamon syrup and all. Her penance. About the only one she'd ever been able to make. If she'd been religious, one of the Catholics so detested by Auntie Muriel, she could have lit a candle for the repose of Caroline's soul. But Caroline seemed to have already taken care of that herself.

At the hospital they said she hadn't drunk any of the furniture polish. The open bottle was a sign, Caroline's last message; an indication of where she'd gone, since for all practical purposes she was no longer in her body.

Elizabeth watches while William finishes off his club sandwich and orders apple pie with cheese and a cup of coffee. She dislikes his tie. Someone with William's choirboy complexion should not wear beige and maroon. If Lesje lives with a man who has such poor taste in ties, she's hardly worth defeating.

William doesn't seem to have noticed that Elizabeth isn't eating; he's explaining why colored toilet paper is so much worse than white. Elizabeth knows she will take scant pleasure in sleeping with him or even in making the revelation she's come here to make. Perhaps she won't bother. She's amazed sometimes at the lengths to which people will go to distract themselves. She amazes herself.

LESJE

Lesje is cataloguing giant tortoises from the Upper Cretaceous. REPTILIA, she writes. *Chelonia, Neurankylidae.* GENUS & SPE-CIES, *Neurankylus baueri, Gilmore.* LOCALITY: Fruitland, New Mexico, U.S.A. GEOLOGY: Upper Cretaceous, Fruitland shale. MATERIAL: Carapace & plastron.

How ignominious to be dug up in Fruitland, Lesje thinks, after so many million years of peace. She's never been to Fruitland but she pictures little souvenir stands where plastic fruits are sold: grape lapel pins, magnetic tomatoes. Or probably, since it's the United States, college students dressed up as giant peaches and apples strolling among the crowds. Like Disneyland.

There's a number in black-ink figures on the slip of paper attached to the carapace, and she adds this number to the filing card. When she's finished with the larger specimens, she knows there's a whole tray of carapace fragments awaiting her. She'll cart it from the storage shelves up to her office, past the sandblasters and dentist's drills they use for cleaning fossils; when she's finished with it she'll cart it down again and slide it into the storage rack. After that she'll start on the fish earbones from the Miocene. There are hundreds of fish earbones, hundreds of tortoise fragments, hundreds of assorted vertebrae, knuckles, claws, hundreds of teeth. Thousands of pounds of rock, locked into the patterns of the once-living. Sometimes she wonders whether the world really needs more fish earbones from the Miocene. On days like this she wonders whether her job isn't, really, just glorified filing.

When she's settled in her cubbyhole of an office with the shell fragments and her clean cards, the phone rings. It's another school group, wanting a tour. Lesje slots them into her calendar. She no longer anticipates school tours with much pleasure. Once she thought she could teach them something. Now she knows there will be at least one child who will want to throw something at the dinosaurs – a bubble-gum wrapper, a pop-bottle top, a pebble – to show he isn't afraid. Mammal cubs, jeering their old enemies. Don't walk on the ledge, she will say. If you push all the buttons at once you won't be able to hear.

Should she make a cup of instant coffee in the wet lab, bring it back to her windowless cubicle, and stay late to finish the tray? Or should she, for once, leave on time?

She peers through the door of the large office adjoining the wet lab. Dr. Van Vleet has already gone, shoehorning his damp rubbers on over his scuffed black shoes and paddling off like a stooped tweed duck into the February slush. Lesje has always been compulsive about her job – she wants very much to do it well – but she's become irritable with it lately. No one, probably, will ever look at the Miocene fish earbones again, once she slots the tray into place. Except her, surreptitiously easing it back out some day to admire their symmetry and size and to imagine the gigantic fish with their bony sheathing, sliding like huge knees through the ancient oceans.

She completes one more card, then closes the filing-card box and goes for her coat. She slips her arms into it, bundles her head, checks her shoulder-bag for money. She'll stop at Ziggy's on the way back to the apartment and pick up something nice for dinner, something nice for William. Ever since she's come to suspect that she may eventually leave him, she's been very solicitous about William. She buys him surprises, tinned sardines, clams, things he likes. When he sniffles she gets him pills, lemons and boxes of Kleenex. It's as if she wants to make sure he's in good condition when she passes him on, trades him in. See, she'll say to him. Look how healthy you are. You don't need me.

She doesn't know how she'll tell him, though; or even when. Nate doesn't want to make any sudden moves, because of the children. He thinks he will rent an apartment or, better still, part of a house, so there will be room for his machines, and move into it a little at a time. He'll tell the children it's a workshop. He hasn't yet indicated when he would like Lesje to join him, just that he would. Eventually. When the children get adjusted. Sometimes they look at the want ads, trying to decide where he, or possibly they, will finally live.

Lesje looks forward to this time – it would be good to be with him in a neutral bed with no fear of opening doors – but doesn't exactly believe in it. She can't picture, for instance, actually moving. Folding sheets and towels, taking down her posters (from the Museum, mostly, stuck to the walls with masking tape), putting her few dishes and the frying pan her mother gave her when she left home into cardboard cartons. If she really is going to move, she ought to be able to picture it. (And where will William be? At the office? Standing by with arms folded to see that she doesn't take any of his books, or the shower curtains, which were his own purchases, or the *Organic Eating* cookbook they never use?)

Nate hasn't discussed this future move with Elizabeth, though he's discussed other things. Elizabeth knows about them. He and Elizabeth had quite a good talk about it one night while he was having a bath. It's a long-standing habit of Elizabeth's to talk to him while he's in the bathtub, Nate tells her. Though it bothers Lesje slightly to think of them having habits together, she asked, "Was she angry?"

"Not at all," Nate said. "She was very good about it. She's glad I've found someone congenial."

For some reason Elizabeth's approval annoys Lesje more than her anger would have.

"She does think, though," Nate said, "that you should tell William. She feel it's a little dishonest not to. She thinks it's only fair to her. She . . ."

"It's none of her business," Lesje said, surprising herself by her own abruptness. "Why should she care what I tell William?"

"They've become quite friendly," Nate said mildly. "They seem to have lunch together quite a lot. She says it puts her in a false position with William, that she knows and he doesn't."

Lesje hadn't heard about this friendship, these lunches. She felt left out. Why hadn't William mentioned anything about it? Though he rarely tells her who he has lunch with. But this may mean only what she thinks it means: that, like her, he seldom has lunch at all. She sees, too, the threat behind the message; for it was a message, Elizabeth the sender, Nate merely the unwitting deliverer. If she doesn't tell William soon, Elizabeth will tell him herself.

Yet she's been unable to say anything. There hasn't been

167

an opportunity, she tells herself. What's she supposed to do? Interrupt a cribbage game to say, "William, I'm having an affair"?

She swings along the street, head down, carrying the bag of potato salad and fried chicken she's bought at Ziggy's. William once told her she walks like an adolescent boy. But so does he, so they're even.

When she reaches the apartment, William is sitting at the card table. He has a solitaire game spread in front of him, but he's looking out the window.

"I got some stuff from Ziggy's," Lesje says cheerfully. William doesn't answer, which is nothing new. She walks through the kitchenette, leaving the bag on the counter, and goes into the bedroom.

She's sitting on the bed, pulling off her leather boots, when William appears in the doorway. He has a strange look on his face, as if his muscles are in spasm. He comes towards her, hulking.

"William, what's wrong?" she says; but he pushes her down on the bed, one arm across both shoulders, his elbow digging in beside her collarbone. His other hand rips at the zipper on her jeans.

William has always liked to tumble around a little. She starts to laugh, then stops. This is different. His arm is against her throat, cutting off her wind.

"William, that hurts," she says; then, "William, cut it *out!*"

He's got her jeans worked halfway down her thighs before it occurs to her that William is trying to rape her.

She's always thought of rape as something the Russians did to the Ukrainians, something the Germans did, more furtively, to the Jews; something blacks did in Detroit, in dark alleys. But not something William Wasp, from a good family in London, Ontario, would ever do to her. They're friends, they discuss extinction and pollution, they've known each other for years. They live together!

What can she do now? If she fights him off, kicks him in the nuts, he'll never speak to her again. She's almost certain she could: her knee's in the right position, he's crouching over her, fumbling at her nylon crotch. But if she lets him go ahead, there's a good chance she'll never speak to him again. It's absurd, and

William, huffing and puffing and grinding his teeth, is absurd too. But she knows if she laughs he'll hit her.

This is frightening; he's hurting her on purpose. Maybe he's always wanted to do this but never had the excuse. What is the excuse?

"William, stop," she says; but William tugs and rips, silently, relentlessly, forcing his torso between her knees. Finally she is angry herself. The least he could do is answer her. She clamps her legs together, tightens the muscles of her neck and shoulders, and lets William batter himself against her. He's pulling her hair now, digging his fingers into her arms. Finally he groans, oozes, unclenches.

"Finished?" she says coldly. He's a dead weight. She pries herself out from beneath him, buttons her shirt. She pulls off her jeans and underpants and mops her thighs with them. William, pink-eyed, watches her from the bed.

"I'm sorry," he says.

Lesje is afraid he's going to cry. Then she will have to forgive him. Without answering, she goes to the bathroom and stuffs her clothes into the laundry hamper. She wraps a towel around her waist. All she wants to do is have a shower.

She leans her forehead against the cool glass of the mirror. She can't stay here. Where will she go, what did she do? Her heart is racing, there are scratches on her arms and breasts, she's gasping for air. It's the sight of William turning into someone else that has shocked her. She doesn't know whose fault it is.

169

Wednesday, February 16, 1977

ELIZABETH

Elizabeth is having a bad dream. The children are lost. They are only babies, both of them, and through carelessness, a moment of inattention, she's misplaced them. Or they've been stolen. Their cribs are empty, she's hurrying through unfamiliar streets looking for them. The streets are deserted, the windows dark; there's no snow on the ground, no leaves on the hedges, the sky overhead would be full of stars if she could only look up. She would call, but she knows the children will not be able to answer her, even if they can hear her. They're inside one of the houses, wrapped up; even their mouths are covered by blankets.

She turns over, forces herself awake. She looks around the room, the looming bureau, the spider plants, the stripes of light through the blinds, making sure she is here. Her heart quiets, her eyes are dry. The dream is an old one, an old familiar. She began having it after Nancy was born. At that time she would wake crying convulsively, and Nate would comfort her. He would take her to the children's room so she could listen and see that they were all right. He'd thought she was dreaming about their own children, but even then she had known, though she hadn't told him, that the lost babies were her mother and Caroline. She's shut them out, both of them, as well as she could, but they come back anyway, using the forms that will most torment her.

She doesn't want to go back to sleep; she knows that if she does she'll probably have the same dream again. She gets out of bed, finds her slippers and dressing gown, and goes downstairs to make herself a warm milk and honey. As she passes the children's room she listens, then pushes open the door just to make sure. Pure habit. She will probably go on doing this for the rest of her life, even after they are really gone. She will go on having the dream. Nothing ever finishes.

170

Part Four

LESJE

Lesje's knife squeaks on china. They're having roast beef, which is a little tough. Her mother has never known how to cope with roast beef. Lesje cuts and chews; nobody says anything, which is not unusual. Around her is the sound she remembers from childhood, a hollow sound, like a cave where there might be an echo.

They didn't know she was coming until the last minute. Nevertheless her mother has set out the good plates, the ones with pink roses and gold rims that belonged to Lesje's grandmother. The other good plates have blue borders with silver rims and scenes of Scottish castles; they belonged to the other grandmother. The meat plates. Lesje's parents got them because, despite his transgressions, her father was the only son. Her aunt got the milk plates and has never ceased to resent it. There's a third set of dishes for everyday, which her parents bought themselves: oven-to-table stoneware. Lesje feels more comfortable with these, which are a neutral shade of brown.

Her mother offers her more Yorkshire pudding. Lesje accepts, which makes her mother smile; a placid, mournful smile. She has braids wound around her head only in old photographs, Lesje can't remember her with them, but she looks as though the braids are still there, shining through the matronly permanent she renews every two months. A rounded face, tidy features. Lesje's father too is round; which makes Lesje's height and stringiness a family mystery. When she was in her teens her mother kept telling her she would fill out when she got older, to console her for the lack of breasts. But she has not filled out.

Lesje's mother is pleased she's suddenly come to dinner; Lesje hasn't come to dinner that often lately. But she's also puzzled: she throws swift inquiring glances across the table at Lesje while Lesje wolfs her Yorkshire pudding, hoping for explanations, later, in the kitchen. But Lesje can't explain anything. Since

173

she's never told her parents in so many words that she was living with William (though her mother guessed), she can hardly say she's moved out and is now living with someone else. Marriage is an event, a fact, it can be discussed at the dinner table. So is divorce. They create a framework, a beginning, an ending. Without them everything is amorphous, an endless middle ground, stretching like a prairie on either side of each day. Though she's moved herself physically from one place to another Lesje has no clear sense of anything having ended or of anything else having begun.

She told her mother she'd moved. She also said she hadn't unpacked her own dishes, which is true and was her excuse for inviting herself so suddenly to dinner. But she gave the impression that the move had taken place that very day, whereas in fact it's been three weeks since she hired the U-Haul and bundled her possessions into cardboard boxes. She did it during the day, when William wasn't there, and with no prior announcement. To say she was moving would have demanded an explanation, and she was reluctant to get into that.

It's amazing how quickly her life with William was expelled from the drawers and torn from the walls and how little space it took up. She carried the boxes to the elevator herself, nothing was very heavy, and packed them into the U-Haul, which wasn't necessary at all, a station wagon would have done. Then she lifted them out and carted them up the rickety steps of the house she'd rented. It's a decaying row house on Beverly Street, not a very good one, but she'd only spent a day looking and she'd taken the first space available that was both cheap enough and big enough for Nate's machines. A developer owned it; he was going to turn it into a townhouse, so he was willing to give her a low rate as long as she didn't demand a lease.

She felt she had to get out before William apologized. If he'd apologized – as she'd been sure he would sooner or later – she would have been trapped.

The day after that thing happened – she doesn't know what to call it and has finally decided to think of it as *the incident* – William left early in the morning. Lesje had spent the night in the bathroom with the door locked, lying curled up on the bathmat covered with towels, but this had been overkill as he hadn't tried to get in.

It had pleased her slightly to think of him arriving at work unshowered, unshaven; squeaky cleanliness was one of his fetishes. When she heard the apartment door close she ventured out, changed into fresh clothes and went to work herself. She didn't know what to do or think. Was he violent, would he try it again? She resisted the desire to phone Nate and describe *the incident*. After all it wasn't that bad, she hadn't been hurt, she hadn't really been raped, not technically. Also, if she told Nate she would be putting pressure on him to do something; to move in with her immediately, for instance. She didn't want to do this. She wanted Nate to move in when he was ready, when he wanted to be with her, not because of something William had almost done.

After work she wandered around for a while, sitting in Murray's with a cup of coffee and a cigarette, walking along Bloor Street and looking at the store windows. In the end she went home, and William was sitting in the living room, pink-cheeked, cheerful, as if nothing at all had happened. He greeted her pleasantly and launched into a discussion of the caloric values produced by the controlled fermentation of liquid effluents.

This behavior of William's was more frightening than surliness or rage would have been. Had William forgotten all about the incident? Where had it come from, that burst of pure hate? She couldn't ask him, for fear of provoking it again. She stayed up late, reading a book on ichthyosaurs until after William had gone to bed. Then she slept on the living-room rug.

"More mashed potatoes, Lesje?" her mother says. Lesje nods. She's eating ravenously. This is the first real meal she's had in three weeks. She's been camping out in the almost empty house, sleeping on blankets unrolled on the bedroom floor, eating takeout food, bran muffins, hamburgers, fried chicken. She puts the bones and crusts in a green garbage bag; she has no garbage can yet. She has no stove and no fridge either and she hasn't got around to buying them, partly because she left a month's rent in an envelope for William, which has lowered her bank balance. But also she feels that major domestic appliances like these, even second-hand ones, should be shared by Nate. A stove is a serious commitment.

Lesje eats apple pie and wonders what Nate is doing. When her father says, "How's the bone business?" she smiles wanly at him. If you discovered a new kind of dinosaur, you could name it after yourself. *Aliceosaurus*, she used to write, practicing, Anglicizing her name. When she was fourteen this was her ambition, to discover a new kind of dinosaur and name it *Aliceosaurus*. She made the mistake of telling her father this; he thought it was very funny and teased her about it for months afterwards. She isn't sure what her ambition is now.

Lesje helps her mother stack the dishes and carry them out to the kitchen. "Is everything all right, Lesje?" her mother says, once they're out of her father's earshot. "You're looking thin."

"Yes," Lesje says. "I'm tired from moving, that's all."

Her mother seems satisfied with this. But everything is not all right. Nate comes to her new house in the evenings and they make love on her unrolled blankets, the hard boards jammed against her back. That's fine, but he hasn't yet said when he'll move in. She's beginning to wonder whether he ever will. Why should he? Why should he disarrange his life? He says he has to explain it gradually to the children; otherwise they might become disturbed. Lesje feels that she herself is disturbed already, but she can't tell this to Nate.

She doesn't seem able to tell it to anyone else either. Certainly not Trish or Marianne. She sits with them in the Museum coffee shop, smoking, tensed, always on the verge of blurting. But she can't. She's aware that from the outside William's behavior, the incident (which could be seen as an ignominious failure), her own flight and unconditional arrangement with Nate, might look naïve, gawky, laughable perhaps. *Gauche*, Marianne would think, though she wouldn't say it; or, a new English expression she's taken to lately: *thick*. She would give Lesje good counsel, as if she were planning a wardrobe for her. She'd advise bargaining, pressure, ruses, all things Lesje is not good at. You want him to live with you? Try locking him out. Why get a cow when milk's free? Lesje doesn't want to be the object of such amused, momentary concern. It occurs to her that she has no close friends.

She wonders whether she could talk to her mother, confide

176

in her. She doubts it. Her mother has cultivated serenity; she's had to. Juliet at fifty-five, Lesje thinks, though her mother was never Juliet; she'd been no spring chicken, as the aunts said. No balconies for her father, no elopements; they'd taken the streetcar to the City Hall. Lesje studied *Romeo and Juliet* in high school; the teacher thought it would appeal to them because it was about teen-agers and they were supposed to be teen-agers. Lesje hadn't felt like a teen-ager. She wanted to study alluvial plains and marl deposits and vertebrate anatomy, and hadn't paid much attention to the play except to fill its margins with drawings of giant ferns. But how would the Montagues and the Capulets have behaved if Romeo and Juliet had lived? A lot like her relatives, she suspects. Snubs at family gatherings, resentments, subjects that were not discussed, this or that grandmother weeping or raving in a corner. Juliet, like her mother, would have become impenetrable, compact, plump, would have drawn herself together into a sphere.

Lesje's mother wants Lesje to be happy, and if Lesje isn't happy she wants her to appear to be happy. Lesje's happiness is her mother's justification. Lesje has known this forever and is well practiced at appearing, if not happy, at least stolidly content. Busy, gainfully employed. But standing beside her mother, drying the dishes on the ageless dishtowel that says GLASS in blue down one side, she doesn't feel she has the strength to keep up this particular appearance. She wants instead to cry, and she wants her mother to put her arms around her and console her.

It's for William she wants to be consoled. The loss of William, familiar William, does hurt after all. Not because of William himself, but because she trusted him simply, uncaring, unthinking. She trusted him like a sidewalk, she trusted him to be what he seemed to be, and she will never be able to do that with anyone again. It isn't the violence but the betrayal of this innocent surface that is so painful; though possibly there was no innocence, possibly she made it up.

But her mother, encased as she is, would never be able to mourn with Lesje. She'd merely wait until Lesje had stopped crying and wiped her eyes on the dishtowel, and then she would point out all the things Lesje has pointed out to herself already: *No real harm done. You're better out of it. It was the only way. Everything turns out for the best.*

177

Her grandmothers would not have done this. They would have mourned with her, both of them; they had the talent for it. They would have wept, keened, wailed. They would have put their arms around her and rocked her, stroking her hair, crying extravagantly, ridiculously, as if she'd been damaged beyond repair. Perhaps she is.

NATE

In the cellar Nate, leaning against his workbench, fingers the handles of the brushes soaking in their coffee tin of Varsol. He's always meant to put in better lighting down here. Now there would be no point. In the dim yellowish light he feels like some huge insect, white and semi-sighted, groping its way by a touch that is also smell. Paint fumes and damp cement, his familiar atmosphere. He twists the screw on the small red vise, tightening it on a glued and drying sheep's head, part of a Mary Had a Little Lamb pull toy. He had no difficulty designing the sheep, but the Mary is causing trouble. He can never do faces. A sunbonnet, he thinks.

He's supposed to be packing. He meant to pack, he's been meaning to pack. He has pedaled a stack of cardboard boxes home from the supermarket and bought a roll of strong twine. He's collected newspapers for wrapping; they've been in a neat pile at the foot of the cellar stairs for two weeks. He's even taken some sandpaper and a box of mixed nails and screws to Lesje's and left it in the front room as a pledge of his good intentions. He's explained to her that he wants to proceed gradually. First he'll tell Elizabeth he's decided to move his workshop to a larger, brighter space. She'll be surprised he can afford it, but he can get through that. Then he'll tell the children the same thing. After they're no longer used to having him around all the time he will, by slow degrees, stop sleeping at one house and start sleeping at the other. He wants to make the actual break imperceptible to them, he's said.

He fully intends to implement this plan, but with a crucial difference he doesn't think he needs to discuss with Lesje: he wants to wait until Elizabeth asks him or even orders him to leave. It will save a lot of trouble later if he can give her the impression she's making the decision herself. He isn't yet sure how he is going to arrange this.

Meanwhile he has to cope with Lesje's obvious and growing depression. She hasn't been putting any pressure on him, any spoken pressure. Nevertheless he can scarcely breathe. For three weeks now he's been running up the cellar stairs when he hears the children come home from school so he can act cheerful and unconcerned and make them warm milk and peanut butter sandwiches. He tells them jokes, cooks them dinner, reads them longer and longer bedtime stories. Last night they said they were tired and would he please turn out the light. Wounded, Nate wanted to fling his arms wide, cry out: *I won't be with you much longer!* But surely the point is to avoid such histrionics. He darkened the room, kissed them good night, went to the bathroom to put a hot washcloth over his eyes. Already his reflection in the mirror was fading, the house was forgetting him, he was negligible. He blotted his eyes and went to hunt down Elizabeth.

This also is part of his scheme. He makes a point of trying to have an inconsequential chat with her at least every two days, giving her openings, chances. Perhaps during one of these chats she will dismiss him. They sit in the kitchen and talk about this and that while she drinks tea and he drinks Scotch. Once, not long ago, she would have avoided him in the evenings; she would have gone out or read in her room. It's been her contention that they have nothing of value left to say to each other. Now, for purposes of her own, she seems to welcome the chance to consult him on supplies, repairs, the children's progress at school. This fact alone makes him sweat. She's asked him a couple of times, with no particular emphasis, how things are going with his ladyfriend, and he's been noncommittal.

After these chats, during which he has to clench his teeth to avoid glancing at his watch, he leaps onto his bicycle and pedals feverishly down Ossington and along Dundas to catch Lesje before she goes to bed. Twice he's almost been hit by cars; once he ran into a hydro pole and arrived torn and bleeding. Lesje scrabbled through half-unpacked boxes, looking for Band-Aids, while he dripped onto the grimy linoleum. He knows these rides are dangerous but he also knows that if he doesn't get there in time Lesje will feel rejected and miserable. On several nights, too exhausted to make the trip, he's phoned instead. Her voice has been small, remote. He can't stand to hear her dwindle like that.

180

No matter how drained he is, he has to make love to her, or at least try to; otherwise she'll feel he's backing off. His knees are bruised from the floor, his bad disk is acting up. He wants to ask her to get a bed or at least a mattress, but he can hardly do that without paying half, and at the moment he doesn't have enough money.

After soothing Lesje he pedals home again. There he clatters dishes in the kitchen while frying a late-night snack of liver and onions. He sings sea shanties or puts on a record, an old Travelers or Harry Belafonte from the early sixties. He's kept these records, not because he's especially fond of the music as such, but because they recall for him a time when he was fond of it. Before his marriage, before everything; when all directions still seemed possible.

Elizabeth, he knows, can hear what goes on in the kitchen. She can't stand the Travelers or Harry Belafonte or noise at night in general, and the smell of liver makes her sick. He found this out early in their marriage and abstained, a compromise. She's big on the value of compromises. He's hoping now that his blatant failure to compromise will convince her she's had enough of him.

He doesn't really feel like singing, or eating either. By midnight he usually has a grinding headache. But he forces himself, tapping his knife against his plate and yelling along with Harry, his mouth full of partly chewed meat. "I see great big black TARANTULA," he bellows. Then, crooning, "Come back, Liza, come back, girl, Wipe de tear from yo' eye . . ." Once, during the era of Chris, he'd sung this song with ridiculous sentimentality. *Liza* was Elizabeth and he wanted her to come back.

He leaves his dishes in the sink, or if he's feeling especially daring, on the kitchen table itself, defying Elizabeth's handprinted sign:

CLEAN UP YOUR OWN MESS!

Then he staggers up the stairs, gulps four aspirin with codeine, and crashes into bed.

Ordinarily this behavior would produce quick results. A cold request, which, if not obeyed, would lead to a frontal attack, during which he would be accused in a chillingly level voice of everything from chauvinism to arrogant selfishness to sadism.

181

In the first years these arguments convinced him. His inability to complain, to complain skillfully and with feeling, put him at a disadvantage: when she challenged him to produce some habit of hers equally offensive to him, which she was of course prepared to give up on the spot, he couldn't come up with anything. He was used to thinking that everyone's rage and sense of oppression was justified; everyone's but his own. Anyway, he wasn't oppressed. At parties during the raucous sixties he'd been called a white pig, a male pig, even, because of his last name, a Fascist German pig. Instead of invoking his Unitarian past, his long-gone lapsed-Mennonite grandfather whose cheese-factory windows were smashed in 1914 because of his name, his father who'd died in the war, he found it less complicated to turn away and go out to the kitchen for another beer. Nor had he ever told Elizabeth the house was as much his as hers; he didn't really believe it. He stopped eating liver except in restaurants and played his Harry Belafonte records only when Elizabeth wasn't home. The children liked them.

This time Elizabeth hasn't responded to his transgressions. If he happens to see her the next morning, she's calm and smiling. She even asks him if he's slept well.

Nate knows he can't keep up his divided life much longer. He'll get an ulcer, he'll implode. An incoherent anger is growing in him, not only with Elizabeth but with the children: what right do they have to hook him, hold him back? Also with Lesje, who is forcing him to make painful decisions. His anger isn't fair, he knows it. He dislikes being unfair. He will take the first step today, now.

He kneels beside the pile of old newspapers. He'll wrap and box the small hand tools first and transport the boxes, one by one, roped onto the carrying rack of his bicycle. For the larger machines and unfinished toys he'll have to rent a truck. He shoves to the back of his mind the question of how he's going to pay for it.

He picks up a gouge, sliding his hand around the handle. In the early days of euphoria, after he quit his job, when he still believed he was returning somehow to dignity, the wisdom and simplicity of the craftsman, he spent a lot of time carving special handles for his hand tools. On some he incised his initials; on others he made decorative bands, flowers and leaves or geometrical motifs,

182

vaguely Indian. On this particular gouge he made a hand, carved as if the wooden fingers were holding the handle, so that every time he picked up the gouge there was another hand close within his own. It pleased him to use these tools of his, he felt secure, rooted, as if by carving them himself he'd made them already old. He kneels, holding the small wooden hand, trying to recall that pleasure. Holding, holding on. But the tools are floating away from him, diminished, like toys he once played with. The plastic machine gun, the man's hat he wore with the brim turned down, pretending it was a pith helmet.

He places the gouge on a sheet of newspaper, and rolls, starting at the bottom corner. Then, methodically, reading headlines as he goes, he rolls the chisels, the screwdrivers, the rasps, placing the wrapped tools side by side in the bottom of the first box. Old events flash past him, blacken his fingers: the Pakistani pushed onto the subway tracks, he remembers that. A broken leg. The child who strangled while being forced by her mother to stand on one foot with a rope around her neck as punishment. Gossip about Margaret Trudeau, for weeks. An exploding butcher's shop in Northern Ireland. Widening rift between English and French Canada. Murdered Portuguese shoeshine boy; cleanup of Toronto's Sin Strip. Québec language laws: Greek grocers in all-Greek districts forbidden to put up Coca-Cola signs in Greek. He flips through the papers, recalling his own reactions when he first read them.

Nate stops wrapping. He's crouching now on the cellar floor, absorbed in old stories, which come to him across time as one long blurred howl of rage and pain. And his own recognition: What else can be expected? Newspapers are distilled futility. Whenever his mother is being too irritating, too optimistic, he wants to say to her merely, Read the papers. Sheer delusion, the belief that anything can be done, ever. She does read the papers, of course. She even keeps a clipping file.

He's deep in an editorial warning against the creeping Balkanization of Canada when the cellar door swings open. He looks up: Elizabeth is standing at the top of the stairs, her face shadowed by the light behind her head. Nate scrambles to his feet. The chisel he's been holding, intending to wrap it, clanks against the floor.

"You're home early," he says. He feels as if he's been caught burying someone in the cellar.

183

Elizabeth has a cardigan over her shoulders. She draws it further around her; slowly and without speaking she descends the stairs. Nate backs against the workbench.

"You look as if you're packing," Elizabeth says. He can see now that she's smiling.

"Well, I was just sorting out some tools," Nate says. Now that it's time, he wants, wildly, irrationally, to deny everything. "To store them," he says.

Elizabeth stands at the bottom of the stairs and surveys the room, the dingy windows, the rags, the piles of sawdust and shavings he hasn't bothered to sweep up.

"How's business?" she asks. She stopped asking that a long time ago. She has no interest in it; she almost never comes down here. All she wants from it is his half of the rent.

"Great," he lies. " Just fine."

Elizabeth gazes back at him. "Isn't it time we stopped this?" she says.

184

ELIZABETH

Elizabeth tightens the cardigan, around her shoulders, across her back. Her arms are crossed, the wool she's holding bunched into fists. Straitjacket. She stands in the hall, watching the front door as if she expects someone to come through it. But she doesn't expect anyone to come through it. Doors are what people go out by, in their own ways. The doors close behind them and she's left looking at the place where they've just been. Conscious, semiconscious, semiconscience. Piss on them all.

Nate has just gone through the door, carrying a cardboard box. He set the box down on the porch so he could turn to close the door carefully, ever so carefully behind him. He's pedaling off to screw his stringy ladyfriend, as he's been doing for weeks, pretending otherwise. This time he's taking some rasps and chisels with him. Elizabeth hopes he will put them to good use.

In the ordinary course of things she wouldn't have minded this liaison. She doesn't feel she's a dog in the manger: if she doesn't want a particular bone, anyone else is welcome to it. As long as Nate does his share with the house and children, or what they've wearily agreed is his share, he can help himself to any diversions he chooses. Bowling, building model airplanes, fornication, it's all the same to her. But she resents being taken for a fool. Any ninny could have told he was packing; why did he bother to deny it? As for his moronic performance with the midnight fried liver and Harry Belafonte records, a two-year-old could see through it.

She turns away from the door and heads for the kitchen, her body dragging, suddenly heavy. She was calm, she's pleased with how calm she was, but now she feels as if she's swallowed a bottle of aspirin. Small holes glow red in her stomach, eating their way into her flesh. A bottle of stars. All she wanted was a straight confession, and she's accomplished that. He admitted he plans to move his workshop from their cellar to some unspecified place.

They both know where this is, but for the moment she's resisted the urge to press further.

She decides to make herself a cup of coffee, then changes her mind. She will eat no more acid this evening. Instead she pours boiling water on a chicken Oxo cube, and sits stirring methodically, waiting for it to dissolve.

She walks through the future, step by step. From this point it can go two ways. He will leave, gradually, without further prompting. Or she can speed up the process by telling him to go. There is no third way. He will not stay now, even if she begs him to.

So she will have to ask him, tell him to go. If she can't save anything else from the wreckage she will save face. They'll have a civilized discussion and they will both agree they are doing the best thing for the children. She will then be able to repeat this conversation to her friends, communicating her joy at this solution to all their problems, radiating quiet confidence and control.

Of course there are the children, the real ones, not the fantasy ones they will drag out as counters in the bargaining process. The real children will not think this is best for them. They will hate it, and Nate will have the advantage of being able to say, *Your mother asked me to leave.* But she will not be deserted, she refuses to be deserted against her will. She refuses to be pathetic. Her martyr mother, sniveling in a chair. She knows she's being manipulated into this position, by Nate – by Nate! – and she dislikes the thought intensely. It's like being beaten at an intricate and subtle game of chess by the world tiddlywinks champion. But she has no other choice.

She'll go on a diet, later, after he's actually gone. That's part of the ritual. She'll tart herself up, maybe get her hair done, and everyone will say how much better she's looking than she did before Nate left. She finds these tactics squalid and disapproves of them when she witnesses them in others. But what else is there? Trips to Europe she can't afford, religious conversion? She's already had a younger lover; she isn't in any hurry to do that again.

She rocks slightly in her chair, hugging her elbows. She's shivering. She wants Chris to come back. She wants anyone, just some arms that aren't hollow and knitted. The cracks

186

between the boards of the table are widening; grey light wells from them, cold. Dry ice, gas, she can hear it, a hushing sound, moving towards her face. It eats color. She pulls her hands back from the table, clamps them together in her lap. There's the grip of veins in her neck. Fingers twisting hair across her throat.

She's staked to this chair, she can't move, a chill moves up her back. Her eyes flicker, sweep the room for something that will save her. Familiar. The stove, pot on it, frying pan unwashed, the cutting board by the sink. The frayed and blackened oven glove, not that. CLEAN UP. The refrigerator. Nancy's drawing from Grade One stuck to it, a girl smiling, the sky, the sun. Joy, she thought when she placed it.

She stares at the picture, pressing her hands together, and for an instant the sun shines. But there's no friendly smile, malice is there in the yellow, in the hair. The blue of the sky too is an illusion, the sun is blackening, its tentacles curl like burning paper. Behind the blue sky is not white enamel but the dark of outer space, blackness shot with fiery bubbles. Somewhere out there the collapsed body floats, no bigger than a fist, tugging at her with immense gravity. Irresistible. She falls towards it, space filling her ears.

After a while she's in the kitchen. The house is ticking around her once more, the furnace hums, warm air sighs through the registers. From upstairs comes the chuckle of television; she can hear water singing in the pipes, one child or another running carelessly from the bathroom along the hall. So far she can always get back. Self-indulgence, Auntie Muriel would say. Make yourself useful. She concentrates on the yellow circle made by the top of the cup, willing her fingers to unclamp, move forward. She lifts the cup and warms her cold hands with it. Liquid slops onto her lap. She sips, filling time. When her hands are steady she makes a piece of toast and spreads it with peanut butter. She will take one step at a time. *Down to earth.*

She rummages for the felt pen she makes the grocery lists with and begins to jot down figures. In one column, the mortgage, the insurance, the electricity and heat, the monthly food bill. Children's clothes and school supplies. Dentists' bills: Janet will need an orthodontist. Cat food. They don't have a cat,

187

but she's bloody well going to get one and charge it to Nate. His replacement. Repairs. She'll have the roof fixed, finally, and the porch step.

In the other column she puts the rent from the tenants. She doesn't want to be unfair, just accurate, and she's willing to offset the tenants' rent against the mortgage.

Already she feels better. This is what she needs: small goals, projects, something to keep her busy. Other women knit. She can even sense a hint of that lightness of spirit she hopes to be able to describe, later, to her acquaintances. And really it may not be so bad. Freedom from that other set of rules, that constant pained look which is worse than nagging. Living with Nate has been like living with a huge mirror in which her flaws are magnified and distorted. Fly-eyes. She's been forced to see herself measured constantly beside his set of East York domestic standards, his pious nun-faced mother with her awful Melmac dishes and her faint smell of old wool and cod liver oil. She'll be free of that. It will mean she'll have to carry out the garbage bags herself on garbage day, but she thinks she can live with that.

LESJE

Lesje is having difficulty getting up in the mornings. In that prehistoric era during which she lived with William, she was able to depend on him. He liked being on time for work. He also liked getting up. He'd take a brisk shower, scrubbing himself with some kind of medieval flagellation instrument, and emerge pink as a rubber duck to ferret in the kitchen for Shreddies and milk, rubbing his head with a towel, making forays into the bedroom to prod Lesje and pull the covers off her legs.

But now, alone in the small chilly house, she has to force herself into the air, sticking her feet out one at a time from beneath the blankets, a lungfish ousted from its stagnant puddle. The house, with no furniture, nothing radiating back to her from the bare walls, absorbs what little energy she has. She feels she's losing weight and that the house is gaining it.

Sometimes, gulping instant coffee with artificial whitener, chewing a stale bran muffin, she goes to the living-room door to contemplate the small piles of sawdust Nate is now making. The living room, he says, is the only room in the house big enough for his machines. Though none of these machines has actually appeared yet, he's brought over some hand tools and a few unfinished hobby horses and has even spent a couple of hours in there, rasping and sanding. The piles of sawdust comfort her. They mean Nate is at least in theory moving into the house. Taking possession.

He has explained very carefully why he's still sleeping at what she thinks of as Elizabeth's house. Lesje listened, she tried to listen, but she does not understand. She feels she's blundered into something tangled and complex, tenuous, hopelessly snarled. She's out of her element. If she were in control of this, the moves would be concrete, straightforward. She herself has been straightforward. She loves Nate; therefore she's left William and gone to live with Nate. Why then has Nate not yet come to live with her?

He claims he has. He's even slept over a couple of nights, and after the second of these, watching him hobble around the kitchen in the morning, wincing every time he straightened up, she'd given in, squeezed her budget and bought a second-hand mattress. Which was a little like putting up a birdhouse: you couldn't make the bird move in.

"This is my real home," Nate says. And once, his head resting on her belly, "I want to have a child by you." He rapidly changed it to "with you," then said, "I want us to have a child together," but Lesje was so struck by the content she didn't notice the phrasing. She doesn't especially want to have a baby, not right at the moment; she doesn't know whether she's up to it; but she was touched by Nate's wish. He considered her not only desirable but acceptable. She sat up and lifted his head, hugging him gratefully.

What she can't explain is the gap between what he says he feels and what he actually does. She can't reconcile his proclamations of love – which she believes! – with the simple fact of his absence. His absence is evidence, it's empirical. It has hardened now to stone, a small tight lump she carries everywhere with her in the pit of her stomach.

She climbs the grey steps of the Museum, walks past the ticket-takers, hurries up the stairs to the Hall of Vertebrate Evolution, tracing again her daily path: the human skull, the saber-toothed cat in its tar pit, the illuminated scenes of under-sea life, with their hungry mosasaurs and doomed ammonites. The door that leads to her office is reached through this portion of the ancient sea floor. Most of the other offices in the Museum have ordinary doors; she's glad this one is camouflaged to look like rock. If she can't live in a cave, which is what she would prefer at the moment (meditation, bread and water, no complications), this is the next best thing.

Though she's been arriving late, she's also been staying later, sometimes till seven-thirty or eight, cataloguing steadily, squinting hunched over labels and cards, fixing her mind on tibiae, metatarsals, shards of the real world. She finds it restful, this contemplation of details; it stops that small noise in her mind, the worrying of something trapped behind the woodwork. Also she's putting off the return to her empty house.

If she's there alone in the evenings she prowls. She opens the cupboard in the tiny extra bedroom and stares at the four abandoned wire coat hangers, thinking she should do something about the chewed shreds of wallpaper and the mouse droppings on the floor. She tries to make herself do useful things, such as scraping the yellow mineral deposit off the back of the toilet bowl with a paring knife; but she's likely to find herself sitting half an hour later in the same place with nothing accomplished, gazing into space. She realizes now that her life with William, haphazard as it seemed, had at least its daily routines. Routines hold you in place. Without them she floats, weightless. She can never expect Nate till after ten.

She nods through the open door to Dr. Van Vleet, who nods back. He hasn't yet said a word about her lateness. She hopes that when he retires his replacement will be someone equally tolerant, in other ways as well.

When she steps through the doorway of her cubbyhole, Elizabeth Schoenhof is there.

Lesje isn't ready for this. She's been avoiding the cafeteria, the ladies' rooms Elizabeth is likely to use, any corner in which this encounter might take place, and she's assumed Elizabeth was also avoiding her. She doesn't feel guilty and she has nothing to hide. She just doesn't think they could possibly have anything to say to each other.

Now here is Elizabeth, sitting in Lesje's chair and smiling graciously, as if this is her office and Lesje is visiting it. Her purse is on the desk, resting on a tray of eel fragments, her sweater is draped across the chair back. She looks as if she's about to say, "Is there anything I can do for you?"

Instead she says, "I brought these requisition slips myself. The internal mail is so slow."

There's no other chair in the office; there's no room for one. Elizabeth seems to fill all the available space. Lesje backs against a wall chart, the geological ages marked in color blocks. Dinosaurs, a hundred and twenty million years of tawny yellow; man, a speck of red. She's a fleck, a molecule, an ion lost in time. But so is Elizabeth.

191

She glances over the sheet of paper Elizabeth has handed to her. They want something for the subway display case, preferably a leg and a foot. She'll have to discuss it with Dr. Van Vleet, choose the specimen, sign it out.

"Right," she says. Elizabeth must have turned up the heat. Lesje is broiling; she wants desperately to take off her coat, but feels that to turn away at this moment would lose her something. Besides, she needs the covering, the insulation between herself and Elizabeth.

"I felt we should discuss things," Elizabeth says, still smiling. "I think we should work together. It's in everyone's best interests, don't you think?"

Lesje knows she's talking about Nate, not about fossilized feet. But her tone of voice suggests a charitable project of some kind, a benefit concert, a rummage sale. Lesje doesn't think of Nate as a charitable project and she has no wish to discuss him. "Of course," she says.

"Nate and I have always tried to work together," Elizabeth says. "We've managed to stay good friends. I think it's always better that way, don't you? We often talk things over when he's in the bathtub." She gives a cosy laugh. She obviously wants Lesje to think that she herself is one of the chief topics of bathtub discussion.

Lesje knows for a fact that Elizabeth and Nate haven't talked about anything in such intimacy for months and months. Unless he's been lying. Would he lie? She realizes that she doesn't know him well enough to know.

When Elizabeth walks away fifteen minutes later, still smiling, Lesje cannot remember anything that has actually been said. She takes off her coat and hangs it up, then goes to the wet lab to make herself a cup of instant coffee. She isn't sure Elizabeth said anything at all, not clearly, not directly. But she's been left with two impressions. One is that Nate has been, or is about to be, fired for incompetence, and that she herself is therefore free to take him on. That is, if she wants to. The other is that she's just been hired for a job she hasn't applied for. Apparently she is going to be tried out as a kind of governess. Elizabeth, it seems, feels she deserves some time to herself. "It will be so good for the children," Elizabeth said, "to learn to relate to someone with unusual interests."

192

Lesje thinks she intended something more complicated, less neutral. Something like *foreigner*. Not dirty foreigner, exactly, as when in Grade Four the Irish-headed older girls gathered around her as she walked across the schoolyard. Pee-ew, they said, holding their noses, while Lesje smiled weakly, appeasingly. Wipe that smirk off your face or we'll wipe it for you. She could use a wash.

Elizabeth is too haute Wasp for that. More like *outlandish*, someone from out of the land. Interesting, mind you; as if she'll play the violin and do charming ethnic dances, like something from *Fiddler on the Roof*. To amuse the children.

Lesje sees she has been studying the wrong thing. Modern mammals, that would be of some use. Primate behavior. She recalls once having read something about apes' eyelids. The dominant ape stares, the others lower their eyes, flashing their colored lids. It avoids murders.

Tomorrow, when she's less depressed, she'll ask Marianne about this; Marianne is well up on primate behavior. Or Dr. Van Vleet, or anyone. Surely anyone at all will know more about such things than she does.

193

ELIZABETH

Elizabeth is lying in bed, the Indian bedspread pulled up to her chin. The window is open a little at the bottom, she left it that way when she set off for work this morning, and the room is chilly and damp. She's looking at the bedside clock, wondering whether it's worth the effort to get up, get dressed and go back to the office for an hour or so. Probably not.

Resting on her left arm is a head. William's head. William's head is on her arm because they've just made love. Before that they had lunch, a lingering, expensive lunch at the Courtyard Café, with cucumber soup and sweetbreads and undertones. And two bottles of white wine, which may have accounted for the undertones. William sighed a lot and shrugged several times, as if practicing subdued melancholy. He told her about a recent study on the effects of an uncooked all-meat diet as practiced by the Innuit, but his heart wasn't in it. Though they alluded to their shared problem, they didn't discuss it directly. Defection is painful.

Elizabeth said (but only once) that she was glad Nate finally seemed to be working out some of his conflicts and that she herself was finding it less of a strain to have him not so much, well, underfoot. This did not perk William up. During the chocolate mousse with Armagnac Elizabeth stroked his hand. They looked into each other's eyes, wryly: each was the other's consolation prize. It was logical; besides, Elizabeth felt she owed him one good fuck. It was partly because of her that Lesje walked out on him so suddenly. She didn't foresee the walkout. What she intended was a confrontation, then a reconciliation, and after the reconciliation Lesje would of course have been honor bound to renounce Nate. Elizabeth could then have been spending her time consoling Nate instead of William.

In the early days, this was how it had worked with Nate and herself, and she'd taken care never to divulge her lovers until she was ready to give them up. In theory at least. But neither William nor Lesje had behaved according to plan. She isn't exactly sure what happened. She went to lunch with William partly to find out, but William didn't want to discuss it.

Copulating with William was not unpleasant, she thinks, but neither was it memorable. It was like sleeping with a large and fairly active slab of Philadelphia cream cheese. Emulsified. It isn't that William is without mystery. He's probably as mysterious as any other object in the universe: a bottle, an apple. It's just that his mystery is not of the kind that usually intrigues Elizabeth. On second thought he isn't totally bland. Remembering the way he wielded his teeth, she's sure he has pockets of energy, even violence, hidden in him, like Mexican jumping beans in a box of cotton wool.

But she doesn't like boxes whose contents she can guess. Why open William? For her he contains no surprises. Chris had been a dangerous country, swarming with ambushes and guerrillas, the center of a whirlpool, a demon lover. Maybe for someone else William would be that: Elizabeth is old enough to know that one woman's demon lover is another's worn-out shoe. She doesn't begrudge Lesje the fascination Nate evidently holds for her, since she's never experienced it herself. What she envies is not the people involved but the fact. She wishes she could feel that again, for anyone at all.

William stirs, and Elizabeth worms her arm out from beneath his head.

"That was terrific," he says.

Elizabeth winces slightly. *Terrific.*

"Was it for you?" he asks anxiously.

"Of course," she says. "Couldn't you tell?"

William grins, reassured. "Hell," he says, "Lesje's not in the same class with you."

Elizabeth finds this remark in extremely bad taste. One does not compare one's lovers, not to their faces. Nevertheless she smiles. "I'd better hurry," she says. "I should put in an appearance at the office, I guess you should, too." Also: the children will be home from school in an hour. But she doesn't mention that.

She doesn't especially want William looking at her from behind, but there's nothing she can do to stop him. She gets

195

out of bed, hooks her brassiere, and pulls her magenta slip on over her head. She chose it in the morning thinking something like this might happen.

"You're damned sexy," William says a little too heartily; that tone might preface a slap on the rump. "Full-bodied."

Elizabeth shivers with irritation. Stupid; sometimes she's very stupid. *Get your goddamn jockey shorts on and get out of my bed*. She smiles at him graciously over her shoulder, and the doorbell rings.

Ordinarily Elizabeth wouldn't appear at the door half-dressed in the middle of the day. Neighbors talk, they talk to their children; someone may have seen William going in with her. But right now she wants to be out of the room.

"It's probably the meter reader," she says. She doesn't know whether this is likely to be true. Since he started working at home, Nate has always coped with such details. "I'll just be a second." She pulls on her blue dressing gown, ties the sash and heads down the stairs in her uncomfortably bare feet. The doorbell rings again as she unchains the door.

Auntie Muriel is standing on the front porch, looking with distaste at the peeling white rocker, the broken step, the neighbors' tiny front lawns with their withered remnants of last summer's gardens. She's wearing a white velour hat shaped like an inverted potty and white gloves, as if on her way to Easter church, and a mink stole Elizabeth remembers from twenty-five years ago. Auntie Muriel does not throw things out or give them away.

Auntie Muriel has never before come to visit Elizabeth. She's chosen to ignore the existence of Elizabeth's disreputable address, as if Elizabeth doesn't live in a house at all, but materializes in Auntie Muriel's front hall at every visit and dematerializes again when leaving. But just because Auntie Muriel has never before done something is no reason to expect she will never do it. Elizabeth knows she shouldn't be surprised – *who else?* – but she is. She feels her wind go, as if someone has rammed her in the solar plexus, and clutches the stomach of her dressing gown.

"I've come here," Auntie Muriel says, with a slight pause before *here*, "because I felt I ought to tell you what I think about what you've done. Not that it will make any difference

196

to you." She walks forward and Elizabeth of necessity has to step back. Auntie Muriel, breathing mothballs and Bluegrass dusting power, marches into her living room.

"You're sick," Auntie Muriel says, looking not at Elizabeth but at her perfectly arranged room, which shrinks, which fades, which exudes dust under her glance. Illness would be the only excuse for having your dressing gown on in the middle of the day, and a poor one at that. "You don't look well. I'm not surprised." Auntie Muriel herself does not look particularly radiant. Elizabeth wonders briefly if there's something wrong with her, then dismisses the thought. Nothing is ever wrong with Auntie Muriel. She clumps around the room, inspecting the chairs and the sofa.

"Won't you sit down?" Elizabeth says. She's decided how she will handle this. Sweetness and light, reveal nothing. *Don't let yourself be needled*. Auntie Muriel would like nothing better than to provoke her.

Auntie Muriel settles herself on the sofa but doesn't take off her stole or gloves. She wheezes, or perhaps it's a sigh, as if merely being in Elizabeth's house is too much for her. Elizabeth remains standing. *Dominate her through height*. Not a hope.

"In my opinion," Auntie Muriel says, "mothers of young children do not break up families for their own selfish gratification. I know a lot of people do it these days. But there is such a thing as immoral behavior and such a thing as common decency."

Elizabeth cannot and will not admit to Auntie Muriel that Nate's departure was not entirely her choice. Besides, if she says, "Nate left me," she'll hear that it was her fault. Husbands do not leave wives who behave properly. No doubt. "How did you hear about it?" she says.

"Janie Burroughs' nephew Philip works at the Museum," Auntie Muriel says. "Janie is an old friend of mine. We went to school together. I have my grandchildren to consider; I want them to have a decent home."

Philip's relationship to Janie Burroughs was something Elizabeth had forgotten during her witty, lighthearted resumé of her domestic situation at the lunch table last week. An incestuous city.

197

"Nate sees them on weekends," she says weakly, and knows at once that she's made a serious tactical blunder: she's admitted there is something, if not wrong, at least deficient, about fathers not living at home. "They do have a decent home," she says quickly.

"I doubt that," says Auntie Muriel. "I doubt that very much."

Elizabeth feels the ground sliding from beneath her feet. If she were only dressed, with no man in the bedroom, she'd be in a much better strategic position. She hopes William has the sense to stay put, but considering his general gormlessness she has no right to expect it. She thinks she can hear him splashing in the bathroom.

"I really feel," says Elizabeth with dignity, "that Nate's and my decisions are our own concern."

Auntie Muriel ignores this. "I never approved of him," she says. "You know that. But any father at all is better than none. You should understand that better than anyone."

"Nate isn't dead, you know," Elizabeth says. A fist of heat rises, hovers in her chest. "He's still very much alive and he adores the girls. But he happens to be living with another woman."

"People of your generation do not understand the meaning of sacrifice," Auntie Muriel says, but without vigor, as if the repetition of the thought has finally tired her. "I sacrificed myself for years." She doesn't say what for. It's obvious she hasn't heard a word Elizabeth has just said.

Elizabeth puts her hand against the pine sideboard to steady herself. She closes her eyes briefly; behind them is a network of elastic bands. With everyone else she can depend on some difference between surface and interior. Most people do imitations; she herself has been doing imitations for years. If there is some reason for it she can imitate a wife, a mother, an employee, a dutiful relative. The secret is to discover what the others are trying to imitate and then support them in their belief that they've done it well. Or the opposite: *I can see through you.* But Auntie Muriel doesn't do imitations; either that or she is so completely an imitation that she has become genuine. She is her surface. Elizabeth can't see through her because there is nothing and nowhere to see. She is opaque as a rock.

"I shall go to see Nathanael," Auntie Muriel says. She and Nate's mother are the only people who ever call him Nathanael.

Suddenly Elizabeth knows what Auntie Muriel has in mind. She's going to go to Nate and offer to pay him. She's willing to pay for an appearance of standard family life, even if it means misery. Which to her is standard family life; she's never pretended to be happy. She's going to pay him to come back, and Nate will think that Elizabeth has sent her.

Auntie Muriel, wearing a grey wool dress, is standing in the parlor beside the baby grand piano. Elizabeth, who is twelve, has just finished her piano lesson. The piano teacher, hopeless, pigeon-chested Miss MacTavish, is in the front hall struggling into her navy blue trenchcoat, as she's done every Tuesday for four years. Miss MacTavish is one of the advantages Auntie Muriel is always telling Elizabeth she's being given. Auntie Muriel listens for the front door to close, smiling at Elizabeth, a disquieting smile.

"Uncle Teddy and I," she says, "think that under the circumstances you and Caroline should call us something other than Auntie Muriel and Uncle Teddy." She leans over, fingering Elizabeth's sheet music. *Pictures at an Exhibition.*

Elizabeth is still sitting on the piano bench. She's supposed to practice for half an hour after each lesson. She folds her hands in her lap and stares up at Auntie Muriel, keeping her face expressionless. She doesn't know what's coming, but she's already learned that the best defense against Auntie Muriel is silence. She wears silence around her neck like garlic against vampires. *Sullen*, Auntie Muriel calls her.

"We have legally adopted you," Auntie Muriel goes on, "and we feel you should call us Mother and Father."

Elizabeth has no objection to calling Uncle Teddy Father. She can hardly remember her own father, and doesn't much like what she can remember. He sometimes told jokes, she can remember that. Caroline hoards his sporadic Christmas cards; Elizabeth throws hers out, no longer even bothering to check the postmarks to see where he's drifted to now. But Auntie Muriel? *Mother?* Her flesh recoils.

"I already have a mother," Elizabeth says politely.

199

"She signed the adoption papers," Auntie Muriel says, with unconcealed triumph. "She seemed glad of the chance to get rid of the responsibility. Of course we paid her something."

Elizabeth can't remember how she responded to the news that her real mother had sold her to Auntie Muriel. She thinks she tried to shut the piano on Auntie Muriel's hand; she's forgotten whether or not she succeeded. It was the last time she ever let herself be goaded that far.

"Get out of my house," Elizabeth finds herself saying, screaming. "Don't come back, don't come back!" With the release of her voice, blood surges through her head. "You moldy old bitch!" She longs to say *cunt*, she's thought it often enough, but superstition holds her back. If she pronounces that ultimate magic word, surely Auntie Muriel will change into something else; will swell, blacken, bubble like burnt sugar, giving off deadly fumes.

Auntie Muriel, face set, heaves herself erect, and Elizabeth picks up the object nearest to her and throws it at the repulsive white hat. She misses, and one of her beautiful porcelain bowls shatters against the wall. But at last, at last, she has frightened Auntie Muriel, who is scuttling down the hall. The door opens, closes: a bang, satisfying, final as gunshot.

Elizabeth stamps her bare feet, exultant. Revolution! Auntie Muriel is as good as dead; she will never have to see her again. She does a small victorious dance around her pressback pine chair, hugging herself. She feels savage, she could eat a heart.

But when William comes downstairs, fully dressed and with his hair brushed, he finds her curled unmoving on the sofa.

"Who was that?" he says. "I figured I'd better stay upstairs."

"Nobody really," Elizabeth says. "My aunt."

Nate would have comforted her, even now. William laughs, as if aunts are intrinsically funny. "It sounded like a bit of a fight," he says.

"I threw a bowl at her," Elizabeth says. "It was a good bowl."

"You could try Crazy Glue," William says practically. Elizabeth doesn't consider this worth answering. Kayo's bowl, which can never be duplicated. A bowlful of nothing.

LESJE

Lesje, in a grubbier than usual lab coat, sits in the downstairs lab beside the corridor of wooden storage racks. She's drinking a mug of instant coffee, which is all she intends to have for lunch. Ostensibly she's sorting and labeling a tray of teeth, small protomammal teeth from the Upper Cretaceous. She's using a magnifying glass and a chart, though she knows these particular teeth backwards and forwards: the Museum has published a monograph on them which she helped to edit. But she's having trouble concentrating. She's sitting here instead of in her office because she wants someone to talk to her.

There are two technicians in the room. Theo is over by the sandblasting machine, digging away with a dental pick at a semi-embedded jawbone. In Mammalogy, where the bones are real, they don't use dental picks. They have a freezer full of dead carcasses, camels, moose, bats, and when they're ready to assemble the skeleton they strip most of the meat off and put the bones into the Bug Room, where carnivorous insects eat the shreds of flesh remaining. The Bug Room smells of rotting meat. Outside the door, several pictures of naked women are Scotch-taped to filing cabinets. The technicians in that department work to rock and country music from the radio. Lesje wonders if solitary Theo would rather be there.

Gregor, the department's artist, is applying daubs of clay to a bone, some sort of ornithopod femur, it looks like. Though Gregor probably doesn't care that much what it is. His job is to make a mold of it, then take a plaster cast from the mold. Thus slowly and part by part, whole skeletons reproduce themselves. In the nineteenth century, Lesje knows, Andrew Carnegie cast and recast his own personal dinosaur, *Diplodocus carnegiei*, and presented the replicas to the crowned heads of Europe. No one can afford to do that any more; even if there were any crowned heads left.

201

Lesje tries to think of something to say to the technicians, not about *Diplodocus carnegiei*, that wouldn't do it; some way of opening a conversation. But she doesn't know what might interest them. They do their jobs and leave at five every night for their other lives, lives which she finds unfathomable. She knows though that the Museum is not essential to them the way it is to her. Gregor could just as easily be working in an art store, Theo could be cleaning cement from bricks or paint from old brass drawer handles. Perhaps they want to Scotchtape pictures of naked women up in here, too.

Nevertheless, she very much wants one of them, either of them, to say, "Come out for a beer." She would watch baseball games on television with them, eating potato chips and drinking from the bottle. She would hold their hands, roll on the carpet with them, make love as an afterthought, attaching no more meaning to that than to any other healthy exercise, a swim, a jog around the block. It would all be friendly and without any future. She wants actions, activities, with no significance and no hidden penalties.

She thinks with nostalgia of her life with William, which she sees now as having been simple-minded and joyously adolescent. The beauty of William was that she hadn't seriously cared what he thought about her. Once she wanted something less two-dimensional. Now she has it. It's true that she didn't love William, though she had no way of knowing this at the time. She loves Nate. She's no longer sure she's cut out for love.

Perhaps it wasn't even Nate himself that attracted her at first, but Elizabeth. Elizabeth and Chris. She'd looked at Elizabeth and seen an adult world where choices had consequences, significant, irreversible.

William never represented such a choice, William was open-ended. She must have thought she could live with William for a million years and nothing in her would really be changed. Obviously William hadn't felt like this. William, like a miser with a sock, had invested things when she wasn't looking, so that his outburst of violence had taken her by surprise. But she's beyond William now, even his rage. William was only momentarily painful.

Nate, on the other hand, is painful almost all the time. Holding her two hands he says, "You know how important you are to

202

me." When she wants him to say he would kill for her, die for her. If he would only say that, she would do anything for him. But *how important* invites measurement, the question: *How* important? For her Nate is absolute, but for him she exists on a scale of relatively important things. She can't tell exactly where on the scale she is; it fluctuates.

In the evenings she sits at their newly acquired table, beside the stove and the wheezy fridge she paid far too much for at the Goodwill store, and broods. When she lived with William he did most of the brooding.

"What is it, love?" Nate says. She does not know how to answer.

She prolongs her cup of coffee for as long as possible, but the technicians say nothing. Gregor whistles under his breath, Theo merely picks. Defeated, she carries her tray of teeth upstairs to the office. She has a school tour at four, once more into the dusky push-button Cretaceous, round and round the cycad trees with a thousand children, her voice unreeling. Then she will go back to the house.

She has to be there early, since this is the first weekend Nate's children are going to spend with them. She's been dreading it all week.

"But there's nowhere for them to sleep," she said.

"They can borrow sleeping bags from their friends," Nate said.

Lesje said they didn't have enough plates. Nate said the children would hardly expect a formal dinner. He would do all the cooking, he said, and the children would wash the dishes. She wouldn't have to do anything extra at all. Lesje then felt she was being excluded, but did not say so. Instead she counted the silverware and agonized over the baked-in grime on the floors. When she lived with William she would have hooted with scorn over such scruples. The truth was that she didn't want the children to go home and report to Elizabeth that she had no silverware and the floors were dirty. She hadn't cared what William thought of her, but she cares desperately how she will appear to two young children she doesn't even know and has no special reason to like. They have no special reason to like her, either. They probably think she's stolen Nate. They probably hate her. She feels condemned in advance, not for anything she's actually done, but for her ambiguous position in the universe.

On Thursday she went to Ziggy's and bought a bagful of delicacies: English shortbread in a tin, two kinds of cheese, chopped liver, fruit buns, chocolates. She almost never eats fruit buns or chocolates, but she'd snatched them off the shelves in desperation: surely this was what children liked. She realized she didn't have any idea of what children liked. Most of them liked dinosaurs, which was all she knew.

"That's not necessary, love," Nate said when she was disgorging the contents of her Ziggy's bag onto the kitchen table. "They'll be just as happy with peanut butter sandwiches."

Lesje ran upstairs, threw herself onto their mattress and cried silently, breathing in the smell of old cloth, old stuffing, mice. That was another thing: the children would see this mattress.

After a while Nate came in. He sat down and rubbed her back. "You know how important it is to me that you should all get along," he said. "If you had kids, you'd understand."

Lesje's belly clenched: she could feel it, a wall of muscle around a central hollow. He'd placed himself and the children, and Elizabeth too, in a tight verdant little oasis where such things as understanding were possible. In the desert without, isolated, single, childless and culpably young, she was made to stand in penance, watching a pantomime she could not decipher.

Nate had no idea he was being cruel. He thought he was being helpful. He stroked her back; she could imagine him looking at his watch to see if he'd done it for the required length of time.

Multituberculata, Lesje murmurs to herself. A soothing word. She wants to be soothed; she is not soothed. She dreads this evening. She dreads the thought of sitting at her own rickety table, with its inadequate silverware and cheap plates, feeling her jaws move, making awkward conversation or staring at her hands while two pairs of eyes watch her in judgment. Three pairs.

ELIZABETH

Elizabeth sits in the underground gloom of the Pilot Tavern, breathing in the smell of slightly stale French fries, watching the shadows. She spent several evenings with Chris here, once upon a time. It was a good place for them to go because they were unlikely to see anyone Elizabeth knew. She's chosen it now for the same reason.

The waiter has come for her order, but she said she was waiting for someone. Which is true. She has kissed her children good night, left out doughnuts and Coke for the baby-sitter, called a taxi and climbed into it, all so she can sit here in the Pilot Tavern and wait. Already she's regretting it. But she'd kept the card, that business card, tucked into the compartment of her purse where she stores her change and the folder for her identity cards. She knows she doesn't keep things like this unless she intends, sometime, to use them. An available body, stuck in the back of her mind.

She can still leave, but what then? She'd have to go back, pay off the baby-sitter, and lie down alone in the house that is empty but not empty, listening to the barely audible breathing of her children. When they're awake she can stand it. Though they're hardly great company. Nancy lies inert on her bed, listening to records or reading the same books over and over again: *The Hobbit, Prince Caspian*. Janet hangs around Elizabeth with offers of help: she will peel the carrots, she'll clear the table. She complains of stomach aches and isn't satisfied unless Elizabeth gives her some Gelusil or Phillips' Milk of Magnesia, from Nate's abandoned bottles. Nancy, on the other hand, slips from Elizabeth's arms, avoiding hugs and good-night kisses. Sometimes Elizabeth thinks the children are acting guilty rather than sad.

What's she supposed to say? Daddy hasn't exactly left, he's just left. Mummy and Daddy both love you. Nothing is your fault.

You know he phones you every night, when he remembers. And you've seen him on weekends, several times. But she and Nate have agreed she won't discuss the separation with the children until he himself has a chance to have a talk with them, a talk he's so far postponed. Which hardly matters. The children aren't fools, they know what's going on. They know it so well they aren't even asking questions.

The man in the brown suit is hanging over the table; he's bigger than she remembers, and he's no longer wearing a brown suit. His suit is light grey and he has on a tie with large white lozenges on it that seem to glow in the dark. He's become more prosperous.

"See you got here," he says. He lowers himself into the chair opposite her, sighs, turns his head for the waiter.

When she called, he hadn't remembered who she was. She had to remind him about their meeting in the subway station, their conversation about real estate. Then he'd been too effusive: "Of course! Of course!" She found this lapse of his humiliating. And then his laugh, thick as gravy, as if he knew what she wanted.

He cannot really know. All she wants is oblivion. Temporary but complete: a night with no stars, a road running straight to a cliff edge. A termination. *Terminal*. Before calling him, she was sure he could offer this. Perhaps he can. His hands are on the table, blunt, dark-haired, practical.

"I've been on the trail," he says. " Just got back the day before yesterday." The waiter comes and he orders himself a rum and Coke, then asks Elizabeth what she'll have. "A Scotch and soda for the lady." He explains how exhausted he is. The only thing that breaks the monotony of the long drives he has to make is his CB radio. You can get quite a few good conversations going on that. Playfully, he asks Elizabeth to guess what his handle is. Elizabeth demurs. "The Hulk," he says, smiling a little shyly.

Elizabeth seems to remember that, earlier, he had flown rather than driven. Either way, a traveling salesman. Someone has to sell things, she supposes; nevertheless she's well on her way to becoming part of an outworn joke. Surely she can do better than this. But she doesn't want to. Better than this is Philip Burroughs, the friends of friends, the husbands of friends, well

206

tailored, predictable. This man has a suitcase full of crotchless underpants, a halo of sleazy joy. *Carnival.* No circumspection for him, he won't take off his watch first and prop it on the night table, fold his undershirt, smell of peppermint, the tablets he's chewed for his ulcer. He's confident, he leans back, he breathes unspoken promises. For someone else he would be predictable, but not for her; not yet.

The drinks come and Elizabeth gulps hers like medicine, hoping to feel lust bloom like a desert flower between her thighs. The man in the grey suit leans across the table and tells her in a confidential voice that he's thinking of selling his house. His wife has a new one in mind, something farther north, a little larger. Maybe she knows someone who might be interested? The house he's selling has all-new copper wiring and he's had the floors wall-to-walled. He feels he can afford the move; he's added a new line. Notions.

"Notions?" Elizabeth says. Her body sits on the plastic-cushioned bench like a sandbag; heavy, dry, inanimate.

"For birthday parties," he says. Miniature helicopters, whistles, soft plastic skulls, monsters, toy wristwatches. That sort of thing. He asks her how her children are.

"Actually my husband and I have separated," she says. Perhaps this news will arouse in him the predatory responses that the words *separated* and *divorced* are supposed to bring out in married men. But it seems only to make him nervous. He glances around, ostensibly to look for the waiter. It strikes Elizabeth that he's no more eager to be seen with her than she is to be seen with him. Could he possibly think she's after him, wants him for domestic use? Preposterous. But it would be insulting to tell him so.

She wonders if she could try being honest with him. *All I'm interested in is a one-night stand. One hour if possible, and you don't have to talk to me. No strings, no lines, no hooks, I don't want to add to the clutter. I don't want you in my life; that's why I called you.*

But he begins telling her about an operation he had two months ago, for plantar warts. A lot more painful than you might think. It's no use, she might as well cut her losses. The time for this is over: pickups in the park, fumbling in the movies. She's forgotten the knack, the trick. How to want.

207

"I think it's time for me to go," she says politely. "Thank you so much for the drink. It's been a pleasure seeing you again." She slides her sweater-coat around her shoulders and stands up, easing herself out from behind the table.

He looks dismayed. "The night's young," he says. "Have another."

When Elizabeth declines, he scrambles to his feet. "I'll give you a lift home, anyhow."

Elizabeth hesitates, then accepts. Why pay a taxi? They walk to the parking lot through the warm air. He puts his hand on her elbow, a strangely old-fashioned gesture. Perhaps they could fox-trot, under the parking-lot lights. Her night on the town.

In his car, Elizabeth doesn't strain herself to make conversation. She tells him where she lives and gives semi-attentive murmurs while he complains about the poor quality of hotel food, especially in Thunder Bay. She's stone cold sober. Stone cold. There's some compensation: she's out of it cleanly, no harm done. He must realize she isn't interested. He stops talking and switches on his CB radio, twiddling the dial. Staccato voices crackle and fade.

But before he reaches her street, he turns the car into a dead end and stops it abruptly. The headlights rest on a checkerboard, a black arrow; beyond, a high wire fence. A factory of some sort.

"This isn't my street," Elizabeth says. At the beginning of the evening she would have welcomed this move.

"Don't play dumb," he says. "We both know what you're here for." He reaches down and unhooks the microphone from his radio. "We'll give them a thrill," he says. "Ten-four, ten-four, gimme a break."

Elizabeth fumbles for the push button on the seat belt, but before she can unlatch it he falls on her. Elizabeth, head forced back by the weight of his mouth, gasps for air. One knee is between her thighs, shoving her skirt up; his rump is squeezed against the glove compartment. There's something cold and metallic pressing against her throat and she realizes it's the microphone.

He thrashes, moans; his elbow flails the window. Elizabeth fights suffocation. *He's having a heart attack.* She'll be stuck here, under the body, until they hear her screams over the microphone and come to dig her out.

208

But in less than a minute his face collapses against her neck and he lies inert. Elizabeth works her left arm up, forcing an air hole.

"Wow," he says, pushing himself off her. "Great stuff."

Elizabeth pulls her skirt down over her knees. "I'll walk home," she says. She can hear her voice shaking, though she doesn't think she's frightened. Idiot, to have expected more.

"Hey, don't you want your turn?" the man says. His hand scampers like a spider up her thigh. "I'm good," he says. "Take a break and enjoy yourself." His left hand holds the microphone, as if he's expecting her to sing.

"Get your hand off my crotch," Elizabeth says. She feels as if she's opened a serious-looking package and a wind-up snake has jumped out. She's never appreciated practical jokes.

"Hell, I was just trying to be friendly," he says, withdrawing. He hooks his microphone back on the set. "Everyone likes a bit of fun."

"Get off the channel, Mac," says the voice on the radio. "Piss or get off the pot."

"I'll walk home," Elizabeth says again.

"I can't let you do that," the man says. "Not around here." He sits with his hands on his knees, his head bowed; he's looking at the steering wheel. "I've got a nip in the glove compartment," he says. "Live a little, have one on me. Let's both have one." His voice is listless.

"No thanks, really," Elizabeth says, forced back into politeness. She unlatches the seat belt; this time he makes no move to stop her. Sadness radiates from him like heat, she can see that now, it always has. When she leaves he will probably cry. In some odd, shrunken way he wanted to please her. Whose failure is it that she is not pleased?

Outside there are trees, the wind, then houses. She walks to the first intersection, looking for street names. Behind her she can hear the motor running, but he doesn't turn, doesn't pass her. Who is laughing? Something stuck in her throat. Nobody really.

NATE

Nate is out on the front porch, rocking gently in the rocking chair Elizabeth bought for fifteen dollars five years ago at a farm auction near Lloydtown. Before he sold the car. She'd had him paint it white to cover up the split back, wired together through small holes drilled inexpertly in each half. It would do for the front porch, she said. The same rocker, undamaged and stripped, would have been at least fifty dollars, she told him. Now after five years of weather the chair needs sanding and a fresh coat of paint. But if he does it, Elizabeth will ignore it. She's no longer interested in the furniture.

He holds his mind still and avoids looking along the street to where Elizabeth will soon appear in the late afternoon sunlight, walking through the fallen leaves on her way home from the bus stop. He's waiting for her, he actually wants to see her. This is a sensation so long forgotten that it's almost like a new one. His body in the chair feels angular as the chair, his spine tight. Something is about to happen, some beginning, things are about to change, and he isn't sure he's ready.

Six days ago she said she wanted to have a little chat with him. He expected a lecture on some procedure: the dishes, the laundry, who washed what of whose, who folded what, how objects on the floor were supposed to transfer themselves to the proper shelf. That's what her little chats usually amount to. *Pulling his weight.* He had his defense already prepared: when he does do things she doesn't notice he's done them, so how does she know whether he's pulling his weight or not? He'd delayed, pouring himself a drink, searching for his cigarettes, before sitting down reluctantly opposite her at the kitchen table.

But instead she told him bluntly that she'd stopped seeing Chris. Under the rules they'd agreed on, it was no longer any of his business who she saw. He wanted to remind her of this, of her side of the agreement. "Do what you like," he'd say. Why was she bothering him about it?

"I want you to do me a favor," she said before he could speak. Though she demanded justice Elizabeth did not often request favors, not from him, not lately. "If Chris should come around, I don't want you to let him into the house."

Nate stared at her. She'd never said anything like this before, presumably because she hadn't needed to. Her way of disposing of her lovers was usually terminal. He didn't know what she told them, but when she'd had enough of them they dropped from sight as rapidly, as completely, as if she'd roped a cement block to their legs and heaved them into the harbor. He suspected her of wanting to do the same thing with him – certainly she was fed up with him – but the children prevented her.

He wanted to ask what was wrong: Was Chris likely to come to the house? Why? But she would only say again that her life was her life. Once it had been theirs.

This is what he wants, wants back. This image, of a shared harmonious life, left over from some Christmas card of the forties, a log fire, knitting in a basket, glued-on snow, had been discarded so long ago by both of them that he'd forgotten about it. Now it was here again, a possibility in the present tense. Perhaps Elizabeth wanted it too, perhaps she was willing to try again. He felt he had to act decisively. She'd often accused him of being unable to act decisively. So he asked Martha out to lunch.

Martha was delighted. At a corner table in the Café Jurgens, her choice, she held his hand and told him how wonderful it was to be able to see him like this, spontaneously, outside the allotted hours. He watched her unhappily while she ate a grilled lobster sandwich and drank two whiskey sours. Behind her was a blown-up photograph of, was it Venice?

"You're silent today," Martha said. "Cat got your tongue?"

Nate managed a smile. He was about to tell her he couldn't see her any more, and he wanted to do it gracefully and calmly. He didn't even want to do it, exactly, although things had reached an impasse with them lately. But the fact was that with Chris gone there was an imbalance. Martha, too, would have to be

211

jettisoned; otherwise he might end up living with her. Which he didn't want. It would be much better for everyone if he could fix it up with Elizabeth; better for the children. He felt dismal about this but it was in a good cause. He would try for a clean break. He hoped she wouldn't scream at him. Vitality, he'd once called it.

But she didn't scream. She let go of his hand and lowered her head, staring at the crusts of her sandwich. He thought he saw a tear fall into the mayonnaise.

"You need something more," Nate said, hurriedly debasing himself. "Someone who can . . ."

"That bitch," Martha said. "She finally did it, didn't she? She's been working at it long enough."

"What do you mean?" Nate said. "Really, this has nothing to do with Elizabeth, I just think . . ."

"When are you going to get your own bellybutton back, Nate?" Martha said, almost in a whisper. She raised her eyes, looking him straight in the face. "I bet she even ties your goddamned shoelaces for you."

To the left there's a sudden roar, almost like an explosion. Nate's eyes jerk up. There in front of him, where he hasn't seen it for over a year ("Do what you like," he'd told her, " just don't make me watch") is Chris's old white convertible, this time with the top up. Nate expects to see Elizabeth get out of it and come breezing up the walk, over-affable as she always is when she's got something she wants but he doesn't. He doesn't really believe Chris has been banished, not permanently; he's gone on too long, she's been too intent on him for that. They'll be back to square one, where they've probably been all the time.

But Chris gets out alone. He comes up the front steps, stumbling a little on the one Nate has been meaning to fix, and Nate is dismayed to see how bludgeoned he looks. He has dark horizontal welts under his eyes, as if he's been slugged across the face with a belt. His hair straggles, his hands dangle heavily from the sleeves of his crumpled corduroy jacket. He stares down at Nate, the hopeless challenging stare of a drunk about to ask for a handout.

"Hi," Nate says weakly. He moves to stand up, so they'll be on

212

the same level, but Chris squats, resting on his heels. He smells of whiskey bottles, used socks, faintly rotting meat.

"You've got to help me," he says.

"Did you lose your job?" Nate asks. A fatuous question perhaps, but what is he supposed to say to his wife's castoff lover? He certainly can't order him self-righteously from the porch, now that he's actually here. He looks so beaten; surely Elizabeth alone could not account for such wreckage.

Chris laughs a little. "I quit," he says. "I couldn't stand it, being in the same building with her. I haven't slept. She won't even see me."

"What can I do?" Nate says. Meaning: *What do you expect me to do?* But he genuinely wants to help, anyone witnessing such misery would want to help, though his own knee-jerk sympathy dismays him. The bloody Unitarians again. He should hand Chris over to his mother; she would lecture him on how he should think about the positive things in life instead of dwelling on the gloomy ones. Then she'd put his name on a list, and several weeks later he'd get a parcel in the mail – soap ends extracted from motels, a dozen pairs of children's socks, a knitted chest protector.

"Make her listen," Chris says. "She hangs up on me. She won't even listen."

Nate remembers now the distant ringing of the phone in the middle of the night, two or three A.M., Elizabeth's half-moon eyes in the mornings. A month at least it's been going on.

"I can't make Elizabeth do anything," Nate says.

"She respects you," Chris says. "She'll listen to you." He looks down at the porch floor, then up at Nate with sudden hatred. "She doesn't respect me."

It's a revelation to Nate that Elizabeth respects him. He doesn't believe it anyway; it's a ploy used by Elizabeth against Chris, who is too dim to see through it.

"Tell her," Chris says belligerently. "She's got to live with me. I want to marry her. Tell her she has to."

Warped, Nate thinks. This is very warped. Does Chris really expect him to order his own wife to run off with another man? "You look as though you need a drink," he says. He wants one himself. "Come on in."

Halfway down the hall, Chris following him, he remembers

213

Elizabeth's plea. Don't let him into the house. It was a plea, he sees now, not a cool request. She hasn't renounced Chris; she's fled because she's afraid of him. It would take quite a lot to make Elizabeth afraid for her own safety. She must think he'll attack her, beat her up. The image of Elizabeth in that grip, white flesh buckling under those fists, powerless, whimpering, is only momentarily erotic.

The back of Nate's neck tingles. He's been heading for the kitchen, with its knives and skewers, but turns instead into the living room, wheeling too abruptly.

"Scotch?" he says.

Chris says nothing. He's leaning in the doorway, smiling: a rat smile, lip lifted back over yellowed teeth. Nate doesn't feel like turning his back on him to go to the kitchen for glasses, but he can hardly walk backwards. Late-movie scenarios unreel: himself conked with a brass candlestick or one of Elizabeth's heavy bowls, left unconscious in the hallway; the children kidnapped, held hostage, barricaded and terrified in Chris's two-roomed hideaway while Chris hunches over his chessboard like the Phantom of the Opera and the police megaphone from doorways; Elizabeth dumped bruised and naked in a culvert, bedsheet knotted round her neck. Preventable, all of it, and his fault; if only he hadn't . . .

Even as his own guilt flashes before him, Nate wants to give Chris something, some food, what? A bus ticket somewhere, Mexico, Venezuela, that's what he himself has often wanted. He wants to reach out, touch Chris on the arm; he searches for some maxim, trite but magical, some parable of hope that will restore Chris in an instant, send him out square-shouldered to face life. At the same time he knows that if Chris makes a move, just one move toward the staircase that leads to the closed door behind which the children were playing, half an hour earlier, an intense game of Admirals, he'll jump him and pound his head against the banister. He'll kill him. He'll kill him with no regrets.

There are footsteps on the porch, resolute, even; the click of the front door. Elizabeth. Now it will explode, Chris will charge her like a moose in heat, Nate will have to protect her. Otherwise she'll disappear down the front walk, ass first, slung over Chris's shoulder, pencils and keys tumbling from her purse. Maybe she would like that, Nate thinks. She used to imply that he himself was not forceful enough.

But "Get out" is all she says. She's behind Chris, in the hall; from the living room Nate can't see her. Chris has turned, his face folding, pleating itself like water hit by a rock. When Nate reaches the hall he's gone. There is only Elizabeth, her mouth set in that tight line of displeasure, pulling her leather gloves off finger by finger.

Watching her, thinking of Chris slinking across the street like a straggler from a defeated army, he knows that at some vague place in the future he himself will need to leave her.

215

LESJE

Lesje, balancing her tray, steers towards an empty table surrounded by other empty tables. She no longer finds it easy to come down for coffee with Marianne and Trish or to join them for lunch. They're still friendly enough, but they're careful. She can remember this feeling and sympathize with it: those in the midst of crisis are bad luck. They're curiosities and you talk about them when they aren't there, but when they are there they silence you. For Marianne and Trish, she's like static electricity.

Dr. Van Vleet is away; he gets rose fever every year, for which he takes herbal remedies prepared by his wife. Lesje wonders whether she will live long enough with Nate to learn herbal remedies and dose him with them. Or with anyone else. She tries to visualize Nate in an old man's V-necked cardigan, dozing in the sun, and fails. Dr. Van Vleet often says "in my day." Lesje wonders if he knew it was his day at the time. She herself does not feel that the time through which she's presently living is particularly hers.

She wants Dr. Van Vleet to be here. He never listens to gossip, he's heard nothing about her so-called private life. He's the only person she knows who is willing to treat her with amused paternal indulgence, which at the moment she feels very much in need of. He corrects her pronunciation, she laughs at his epigrams. If he were here now, opposite her at the table, she could ask him about something, some technical point, and then she wouldn't have to think about anything else. The feeding and breeding habits of the Pteranodon, for instance. If a glider rather than a flapper, how did it become airborne? Did it simply wait for a slight breeze to lift it by its twelve-foot wings? Some speculate that because of its incredibly delicate bone structure it would have been unable to touch down anywhere, on water or on land. If so, how did it reproduce? For a moment Lesje glimpses warm tranquil seas, gentle winds, the immense fur-covered pteranodons soaring like wisps of white cotton high overhead. Such visions are still possible, but they don't last long. Inevitably she sees a later phase: the stench of dying seas, dead fish on the mud-covered shores, the huge flocks dwindling, stranded, their time done. All of a sudden, Utah.

She sits down, facing away from the room. Elizabeth is there; Lesje spotted her as soon as she came in. A few months ago she would have gone out again, but there's no longer any point to that. Elizabeth, like gamma rays, will continue to exist whether Lesje can see her or not. There's a dark, somewhat hefty woman with her. They both look at Lesje as she walks by, not smiling but not hostile either. As if they are sightseers and she is a sight.

Lesje knows that when Nate moved completely in, or as completely as he's going to, Elizabeth should have felt deserted and betrayed and she herself should have felt, if not victorious, at least conventionally smug. Instead it seems to be the other way around. Lesje wishes that Elizabeth would vanish into some remote corner of the past and stay there forever, but she knows her wishes are not likely to have much effect on Elizabeth.

She peels the foil top from her yogurt and sticks the straw into her carton of milk. At least she's been eating better since Nate moved in. Nate is making her eat better. He brought some cooking pots with him and he usually cooks dinner; then he supervises while she eats. It disturbs him if she doesn't finish. The food he cooks is probably quite good, certainly better than she could do, and she's ashamed to admit that she lusts at least once in a while for a package of Betty Crocker Noodles Romanoff. She's been living for so long on convenience food, take-outs, heat n' serve, she's sure her capacities for appreciation have been blunted. In this way, as in many others, she cannot seem to avoid being inappropriate.

Her reactions, for instance. *Reactions* is Nate's word. He finds these reactions of hers, not disappointing exactly, but surprising, as if only a barbarian or an illiterate could have the reactions she does. He doesn't even get angry. He merely explains, again and again; he assumes that if she can understand what he's saying she will of necessity agree with it.

For instance. Elizabeth, when she telephones, as she does fairly often, to ask if the children have left their socks or their rubber boots or their toothbrushes or their underpants behind at Lesje's

217

house, is always polite. Of what then can Lesje complain? The truth is that she doesn't want Elizabeth to phone her at all. Especially not at the office. She doesn't want to be disturbed in the middle of the Cretaceous by Elizabeth, wondering if Lesje has happened to see a red and white mitten. It upsets her, and finally, awkwardly, she has managed to blurt this out.

But the children forgot things, Nate said. Elizabeth had to know where these things were. There were not unlimited supplies of such items.

Perhaps, Lesje ventured, the children could stop forgetting things.

Nate said they were children.

"Maybe you could phone her," Lesje said, "or she could phone you. Instead of me."

Nate pointed out that he had never been very good at keeping track of toothbrushes and rubber boots, even his own. It just wasn't one of his talents.

"Mine either," said Lesje. Or hadn't he noticed? On Sunday evenings, when the children were packing for their return, the house looked like a train station after a bomb attack. She did try, but since she didn't know what the children had brought with them, how could she be sure they'd taken the right numbers of things away again?

Nate said that since neither of them was proficient at this and Elizabeth was, having had long practice, it made good sense for Elizabeth to phone when any of the said items disappeared. Lesje could only agree.

Sometimes the children would be there for Friday dinner when Lesje was expecting to come home from the Museum and find nobody there but Nate. "Could you ask her not to spring them on us?" she said after the fourth time.

"What do you mean?" Nate asked sadly.

"I mean, isn't Friday a little late to tell you?"

"She told me on Tuesday."

"No one told *me*," Lesje said.

Nate admitted it had slipped his mind; even so there were better ways of phrasing things. *Spring them* he found rather blunt, even abrasive. "And I cooked dinner," he concluded reasonably. "It didn't inconvenience you, did it?"

"No," Lesje said. She felt at a disadvantage: she'd had no

practice at this sort of dialogue. Her parents, at least in her hearing, had never discussed each others' behavior and motives, and her grandmothers had never discussed anything. They'd limited themselves to monologues, wistful reveries from her Ukrainian grandmother, raucous commentaries from her Jewish one. Her conversations with William had centered on an exchange of facts, and even their rare disputes had been more like the squabblings of children: *I want. You did so.* She wasn't used to saying what she felt, or why, or why someone else ought to behave differently. She knew she was not subtle, that she often sounded rude when she meant only to be accurate. Invariably she came out of these conversations feeling like a mean-minded ogre. It wasn't that she resented or disliked the children as such, she wanted to say. She just wanted to be consulted.

But she couldn't say that; if she did, he might bring up that other conversation.

"I want to feel I'm living with you," she said. "Not with you and your wife and children."

"I'll try to keep them out of your way as much as possible," Nate said, with such dejection that she'd retracted immediately.

"I don't mean they can't come *over*," she said generously.

"I want them to feel that this is their house, too," Nate said.

Lesje isn't sure any longer whose house it is. She wouldn't be surprised to get a gracious phone call from Elizabeth saying that she and the children would be moving in the next day and could she please get the spare room ready and make sure all the stray socks and boots had been gathered together? Nate wouldn't protest. He feels they should both try to make things easier for Elizabeth, which as far as Lesje can see means doing everything she wants. He often says he thinks Elizabeth is being very civilized. He also feels he is being civilized. He didn't seem to think that Lesje should have to make any special effort to be civilized as well. She isn't directly involved.

"We have each other," he says. Lesje has to agree that this is true. They do have each other, whatever *have* means.

Lesje sucks up the last of her milk and puts the empty carton on the tray. She stubs out her cigarette and is bending to gather up her shoulder bag when a penetrating voice says, "Excuse me."

Lesje looks up. The dark-haired woman who's been having lunch with Elizabeth is standing beside her.

"You're living with Nate Schoenhof, aren't you?" she says.

Lesje is too startled to say anything. "Mind if I sit down?" the woman says. She's wearing a red wool suit with lipstick to match.

"I almost did, myself," she says neutrally, as if discussing a job she didn't get. "I'm the one before you. But he kept saying he could never leave his family." She laughs as if enjoying a slightly witless joke.

Lesje can't think of anything at all to say. This must be Martha, whom Nate has mentioned in passing. She sounded ineffectual. Lesje expected her to be about five feet tall and mousy. The real Martha does not seem ineffectual, and Lesje now wonders if she herself may at some future date be reduced to an equally pallid shadow. Of course Nate would not have mentioned Martha's large breasts and striking mouth, not to her.

"Having any trouble with *her*," Martha says, jerking her head.

"Who?" Lesje says.

"Don't worry, she just went out. Queen Elizabeth."

Lesje wishes to avoid being drawn into a conspiracy. To say anything against Elizabeth to this particular person would be disloyal to Nate. "She's being very civilized," she says. No one could object to that.

"I can see he's brainwashed *you*," Martha says with another laugh. "God, the two of them love that word." She grins at Lesje, a red gypsy grin. Suddenly Lesje likes her enormously. She smiles faintly back.

"Don't let them do a job on you," Martha says. "Let them start and they'll turn your head to mush. Fight back. Give 'em hell." She stands up.

"Thank you," Lesje says. She's grateful that anyone, anyone at all, has given her this much sympathetic thought.

"Any time," Martha says. "There's not much I'm an expert on but believe you me, I'm the world's living authority on *them*."

For at least fifteen minutes Lesje is elated. She's been vindicated; her own perceptions, which she has increasingly begun to distrust and even to disown, are possibly valid. Back in her office

220

though, replaying the conversation, it occurs to her that Martha may have had one or two ulterior motives.

Also: Martha didn't say what she's supposed to fight back against, or how. Martha obviously fought back herself. But it's to be noted – a hard fact – that Martha is not currently living with Nate.

NATE

Nate is going to his house; his former house. He can't believe he no longer lives there. Up Shaw Street, past Yarmouth, past Dupont, the railway tracks, the factory where they make some product he's never bothered to identify. Steel girders, something like that, something for which he has no use. It's a hot day, muggy, as they say; the air warm porridge.

He's spent the morning going from shop to shop where his toys are placed, Yorkville, Cumberland, lower Bayview Avenue, the boutique districts, hoping something had sold and he could collect, at least enough to keep him going. One Mary Had a Little Lamb. His share, ten bucks. He wonders if any of the owners was holding out on him; they must be able to tell he's desperate, and desperation, he knows, induces contempt. Waiting in the cute stores with their gingham aprons and patchwork chair covers, their tea cosies in the shape of hens, egg cosies in the shape of chickens, the bayberry soap from the States, all the country pretences, he felt a little of his mother's dismay. People spent money on this stuff, a lot of money. People spent money on his toys. Wasn't there anything better? It's a living, he thought. Wrong again, it isn't. He threw away a promising career, everyone said it was promising though they didn't say what it promised. He wanted to make honest things, he wanted his life to be honest, and all he has now is the taste of sawdust in his mouth.

But he's glad enough to have the ten. He's supposed to meet the kids at his old house. They'll walk the three long blocks up to St. Clair, Nancy walking ahead of them as if she does not belong with them, Janet keeping close but not deigning to hold his hand; lately she's decided she's too old for hand-holding. These are the ways they demonstrate their anger with him, which otherwise they conceal. Atoning, he'll buy them each an ice cream bar, and then they'll go to the Italian baker's to pick up the cake for Elizabeth. He'll pay for it and that will be the ten. Though he'll still have change from the five he borrowed from Lesje.

He can't connect the acts of carving the lamb, of painting and

222

varnishing, with their consequence: Elizabeth's birthday cake. He can't connect any act he can think of with any consequence he can imagine. The trees he's passing, leaves limp in the heat, the houses with their patchy lawns or gardens crammed with tomato plants, look segmented, a collection of units, not really attached. The leaves aren't attached to the trees, the roofs aren't attached to the houses; blow and it would all fall down, a Lego town. His body feels the same. There's a toy he once made, a favorite several years back, lathe work, a wooden man built of rings which slipped over a central post. The head screwed on, holding the man together. A clown's smile he used. This is his body, stiff fragments held together by his spine and his screwtop head. Segmented man. Maybe he needs a salt tablet.

He thought that by moving to Lesje's he could rid himself of the need to be in two places at once. But he's still spending almost as much time at his old house as at the new one. Lesje isn't supposed to know this, but she behaves as if she does anyway. He should have two sets of clothes, two identities, one for each house; it's the lack of this extra costume or body that is cracking him apart. He knew in advance, in theory, that separation is painful; he did not know it would also be literal. He has been separated; he is separate. Dismembered. He is no longer a member. His own house rebukes him, fills with ravens: *Nevermore*. It's this pain of his, sentimental, unbearable, that Lesje resents and Elizabeth ignores.

Elizabeth is being very civilized, up to a point. Deliberately, ponderously polite. Whenever he comes to pick up the kids she invites him in and offers him some tea or, depending on the time of day, an *apéritif:* Cinzano, Dubonnet. She knows he never drinks these things but she's rubbing his nose in it, treating him like a guest in his own house. Which is not his own house. He's willing to bet there are some bottles or ends of bottles left in his kitchen cupboard or in the bottom of the pine sideboard – Elizabeth isn't much of a drinker, she won't have finished them – but he can't violate this game by asking. So he perches on the edge of one of his former chairs, sipping a drink he doesn't like but can't refuse, while Elizabeth fills him in on the children – their marks, their latest interests – as if he hasn't talked to them for a year. As if he's an uncle, a new school principal. *I'm their father!* he wants to shout. *I haven't forgotten that,* she'd say. *But sometimes you do*. It's one of her assumptions, so deeply rooted she never bothers to discuss it, that he neglects his children.

He knows he should be getting a birthday present for Elizabeth, he always has before. Even if she herself doesn't expect it the children will. But Lesje would guess, partly because he'd have to borrow the money from her, and then there would be trouble. He doesn't want trouble, he doesn't need any more trouble of that sort. Lesje can't manage to see Elizabeth as a factor, a condition, something to be endured, like a snowstorm; morally neutral. Which is how Nate feels Elizabeth ought to be viewed. Instead she insists on regarding her as – what? her own private troll, a combination of the Dragon Lady and a vacuum cleaner. Nate himself tries to be objective. There's more excuse for his own failure in this respect than for Lesje's.

He wants to tell her she's taking everything too seriously; but how can he do this when among the things she takes so seriously is himself? Elizabeth ceased to do this some time ago, and he isn't even sure he can still do it. But Lesje can, she can do nothing else. He can't remember ever having been listened to so attentively; even his banalities, his random comments. Almost as if he's speaking a foreign language, one with which she is only slightly familiar. She thinks he knows things it would benefit her to learn; she thinks of him as older. Which flatters but alarms him: he can't risk total exposure, bare his confusion or his carefully guarded despair. He's never told her how he jittered in phone booths night after night, dialing her number, hanging up when she answered. Cowardice, failure of nerve.

In the bedroom he's beginning to think of as theirs, she glimmers like a thin white moon for him alone. By seeing how beautiful she is he's made her beautiful. But what if she discovers the truth? What he suspects is the truth. That he's patchwork, a tin man, his heart stuffed with sawdust.

He thinks of her waiting for him, somewhere else, an island, subtropical, not muggy, her long hair waving in the sea breeze, a red hibiscus tucked behind one ear. If he's lucky she'll wait till that happens, till he can get there to be with her.

(Though on the shore, at a discreet distance and despite his best efforts, there's always another hut. He tries to shut it out but it too is indigenous. For the children and, of course, for Elizabeth. Who else would take care of them?)

ELIZABETH

Elizabeth has taken off her shoes and is brushing her hair, standing in front of the bureau with its oak-framed mirror. The air is humid and unmoving, though the window is wide open. The soles of her feet feel tender and swollen. She hopes she will never get varicose veins.

In the glass oval, behind her own face, rigid and it seems to her puffy in the muted light, she can trace the shadow of her face as it will be in twenty years. Twenty years ago she was nineteen. In another twenty years she will be fifty-nine.

Today is her birthday. Cancer. In the Scorpio decanate, as some pretentious little fraud at the last Museum Christmas party told her. Someone from Textiles, floral prints and herbal teas. Since yesterday the earth has turned once on its axis, and now she is thirty-nine. Jack Benny's age, the joke age. If someone asks her her age and she tells it, they'll automatically assume she's being funny as well as lying. Jack Benny, of course, is dead. Not only that, her children don't even know who he was. Before this birthday her age has never bothered her.

She half-empties her glass. She's drinking sherry, has been drinking it for some time. A stupid thing to be doing, a stupid thing to be drinking; but since Nate left, the liquor cabinet is never very well stocked. She doesn't drink steadily the way Nate does and she forgets to replace things. She finished off a heel of Scotch earlier in the day. Another of his leavings.

The children insisted on throwing a birthday party for her, though she tried to head them off. When Nate lived here they'd celebrated her birthday in the morning, simply, with presents only. Parties were for children, she'd told them, and Nate had backed her up. But this year they went the whole hog. They seemed to think it would cheer her up. It was supposed to be a surprise, but she knew what was coming as soon as Nancy, elaborately and casually, suggested after lunch that she take an afternoon nap.

"But I'm not tired, darling," she said.

"Yes, you are. You've got big bags under your eyes."

"Please, Mother," Janet said. Janet has lately begun to call her "Mother" instead of "Mum." Elizabeth wonders if that tone of weary, superior exasperation has been copied from her.

She climbed the stairs to her room, where she lay on the bed drinking Scotch and reading *English Tapestry Through the Ages*. If they were preparing a surprise, she would have to be surprised.

At five Janet brought her a cup of undrinkably bitter tea and ordered her to come downstairs when she heard three whistles. She tiptoed to the bathroom to pour out the tea; returning, she could hear them arguing in the kitchen. She creamed her face and put on a black cotton blouse and the pearl pin she knew Janet considered elegant. When she heard Nancy's feeble whistles, she tightened the corners of her mouth, widened her eyes, and negotiated the stairs, holding on to the banister. Nude descending the staircase, in cunning fragments. Stewed, descending the staircase. But she wasn't really drunk. Tiddly, said Uncle Teddy.

They'd lit candles in the kitchen and looped pink and blue streamers with teddybears on them around the walls. "Happy Birthday, Mum," Nancy shrieked. "This is a surprise!"

Janet stood beside the cake, hands decorously folded. The cake was on the table. It had three candles on one corner and nine on the opposite one, "Because if we put thirty-nine on we couldn't get them all on," said Nancy. The writing, in impeccable baker's script surrounded with bridal wreaths of pink sugar roses, said "Happy Birthday Mother."

Elizabeth, who hadn't expected to be moved, sat down on one of the kitchen chairs and locked her smile into place. *Lockjaw.* This was the shadow of all the birthday parties she'd never been given. Her own mother had either forgotten or found her birth no cause for celebration, though there would be presents, remorsefully, days after the event. Auntie Muriel, on the other hand, had always remembered, but had made it the occasion for a solemn presentation of some large or costly item, something that radiated guilt in advance, that cried out to be scratched, lost, stolen. A bicycle, a watch. Not wrapped.

"Thank you, love," she said, hugging each of the children in turn. "This is the most wonderful birthday I've ever had." She blew out the candles and opened her presents, exclaiming over the lily-of-the-valley talcum powder from Janet and the puzzle from Nancy that required to have its three white balls and three black balls jiggled into their respective holes. Nancy is good at such puzzles.

"Where's your present from Dad?" Nancy asked. "He said he was giving you one."

"I guess he just forgot this year, darling," Elizabeth said. "I'm sure he'll remember it later."

"I don't understand that," Janet said reflectively. "He gave us the money for the cake."

Nancy burst into tears. "We weren't supposed to tell!" She ran from the room; Elizabeth heard her wailing up the stairs.

"She's been under a strain lately," Janet said in that adult voice Elizabeth finds so hard to bear. She followed sedately, leaving Elizabeth alone with an uneaten cake and a small pile of crumpled wrapping paper.

She cut the cake and filled two plates, then carried them upstairs, prepared to stroke and comfort. She entered the children's room and sat, rubbing Nancy's damp back as she lay face down on her bed. It was far too hot. She could feel sweat condensing on her upper lip, in the hollows at the backs of her knees.

"She's just showing off," Janet said. She was sitting on the other twin bed, nibbling a sugar rose. "There's nothing wrong with her really."

Elizabeth put her head down to Nancy's when the choking noises had subsided.

"What is it, love?"

"You and Dad don't love each other any more."

Oh hell, Elizabeth thought. He set this up. I should let him cope with it. Just stick them in a taxi and send them over. "I know it makes you unhappy that your father doesn't live here with us any more," she said carefully, correctly. "We felt it would be better for all of us if we lived apart for a while. Your father loves you both very much. Your father and I will always

227

love each other too, because both of us are your parents and we both love you. Now sit up and eat your lovely cake, like a good girl."

Nancy sat up. "Mummy," she said, "are you going to die?"

"Sometime, darling," Elizabeth said. "But not right now."

Janet came to sit on the other side of Elizabeth. She wanted to be hugged, so Elizabeth hugged her.

Mummy. A dried corpse in a gilded case. *Mum*, silent. *Mama*, short for mammary gland. A tree whose hungry mouth is pressed. If you didn't want trees sucking at your sweet flowing breast why did you have children? Already they're preparing for flight, betrayal, they will leave her, she will become their background. They will discuss her as they lie in bed with their lovers, they will use her as an explanation for everything they find idiosyncratic or painful about themselves. If she makes them feel guilty enough they'll come and visit her on weekends. Her shoulders will sag, she will have difficulty with shopping bags, she will become *My Mother*, pronounced with a sigh. She will make them cups of tea and without meaning to but unable to stop will pry, pry like a small knife into their lives.

She doesn't mean to now; she does now. Those careful questions about the other house: What were they given for dinner? How late did they stay up? Did they have a good time? And the equally careful answers. They can sense it's a trap. If they say they like the other house, household, she'll be hurt; if not, she will be angry. "It was all right," they say, avoiding her eyes, and she despises herself for placing them there, making them shift and evade. She wants them to be happy. At the same time she wants to hear of injuries, atrocities, so she can virtuously rage.

She brushes her hair, her face in the mirror a flat plaque. Leaden. She's making it too easy for him, he has it too easy. He isn't the one who has to wipe the noses and wake up in the middle of the night because his children are screaming in their sleep. If she even told him about that, he'd think she was using emotional blackmail. She tips back her glass; reddish brown slides down her throat.

It isn't Lesje she resents. Let him screw whatever he likes, why should she care? It's his freedom she can't take. Free as a goddamned bird, while she's locked in this house, locked into this house while the roof leaks and the foundation crumbles and the earth revolves and leaves fall from the calendars like snow. In the centers of her bones dark metal smolders.

She sits down on the edge of her bed, staring at her crossed wrists, the blue veins where they branch and river. Every second a pulsebeat, countdown. She could lie down with candles at her head and feet. Thirty-nine of them. She could stop time. *Wristwatch*.

With an effort she turns her hand over. It's eleven-thirty.

She checks the children's room. They're both asleep, breathing evenly. She goes back along the hall, intending to go to bed; but instead she finds herself putting on her shoes. She doesn't know what she is going to do.

Elizabeth stands in the hot night outside Nate's new house, Nate's old house, which she's never seen before. Although of course she's had the address and the telephone number. In case of emergencies. Perhaps this is an emergency. The house is dark except for a dim light in the upper window. The bedroom.

She'd wanted to see it, that's all. Make it enter her head so she can believe in its existence. (A dump, a slum; probably cockroaches. This tattiness pleases her; the house is much worse than her own.) But she goes quietly up the front steps and tries the door. She isn't sure what she'll do if it's open. Creep up the stairs, fling open the bedroom door as in some antique melodrama? But the front door is securely locked.

They've locked her out. They're ignoring her, giggling in the bedroom while she stands down here in the night, discarded, invisible. She will make a mark: a brick through the window, her initials on the door? She has nothing to write with. Should she kick over the garbage can, litter trash on the porch, scream? Look at me, I'm here, you can't get rid of me that easily.

But she can't scream; her voice has been stolen. The only power she has left is negative.

Suddenly she thinks: What if they look out the window and see me standing down here? Her face is flushed, the skin under her blouse is wet and prickling; her hair sticks to her neck. Disheveled, a disheveled cliché. They will laugh. She turns quickly away from the house and begins to walk north, sober now, annoyed with herself for having allowed herself to be led to this ignominious, this vacant street.

And worse: where are the children? Locked in the house, alone. *Ladybird, ladybird*. She's never left them alone like this before. She thinks of fires, of murderous climbers, silhouetted against their open window. Gross negligence. But if the children die it will be in a way Nate's fault. On her birthday; an obscure revenge.

Even to think this terrifies her. She thinks instead of the cake, the candles. *Little Nancy Etticoat, in a white petticoat and a red nose.* And Nancy, looking at the picture of the melting woman in the *Little Riddle Book*, said, *Is that me?* Pleased to be in a book. She was much younger then.

"If you blow out all the candles at once," Nancy said, "you'll get your wish." Nancy doesn't yet know about wishes, their danger. *The longer she lives, the shorter she grows.*

Part Five

NATE

This is it. Nate has spent several months avoiding this. He would rather be doing anything else at all. He has a brief vision of himself on a balsa raft, floating down the Amazon with malarial steam rising around him. A crocodile, or would it be an alligator, raises its head from the murky green water, stinking like a dead snake, hissing, lunging for him. Deftly he inserts a stick between its open jaws, twists and it's helpless, it falls astern and he floats serenely on, sunburned and emaciated but not done yet, not by a long shot. He wishes he hadn't lost his pith helmet in that skirmish. He's on his way to discover something, or perhaps he's already discovered it. A lost civilization. In his back pocket is a creased and water-stained map, which will be the only clue if the poisoned arrows get him. Delirious, he'll be. If he can only reach Lima. He tries vainly to remember which side of South America Lima is really on. A miracle of endurance, they will say.

But the pressure, the unavoidable vortex has him at last and he's being swept along, out of control, toward some chasm he can dimly perceive. He tries not to panic, though he can feel his eyes jerking, making the room flicker like an old film. He concentrates on his Adam's apple. He refuses to gulp, she'd spot that in a flash. He uncrosses his legs and crosses them again, left over right, the first step in a Boy Scout reef knot. There's nothing to drink but bloody tea, there isn't even a beer, and he knows for absolute goddamn certain that this is deliberate on Elizabeth's part. She thought it would unsettle him and she's right, right, right.

It's the mention of lawyers that's confused him. At the first words, "my lawyer," she said, and "your lawyer," he started shallow breathing. He knows, he used to be a lawyer himself. Who should know better than he does that there's no mystery, no occult power? It's all paper and verbiage. But fake though the structure is, it could wreck his life.

"Couldn't we do it without lawyers?" he asks, and Elizabeth smiles.

She's placed herself on the sofa, where she's curled with every show of comfort. He, on the other hand, is sitting on a pine pressback chair, from which, he notes, the cushion has been removed since the last time he was here. His ass hurts, bone against wood, his spine hurts, this chair was always too low for him.

"You can't have a divorce without lawyers," she says.

Nate begins to explain that there is in fact a way of doing it, but she stops him. "That would hardly be fair," she says. "You know the law, I don't. I feel I need protection."

Nate is hurt. Protection from him? It's a question of support for the children. She ought to know he will do anything he can.

She has a piece of paper, which she passes over to him. She hopes he will realize she's tried to be more than fair. She talks about dentists' bills while Nate focuses with an effort on the black marks in front of him. The children are upstairs watching television in their room, where Elizabeth has sent them. For several weeks she hasn't let him come into the house when he's arrived to pick them up for the weekend. He's had to lurk outside, once in the rain, like some pervert or magazine salesman, waiting for them to emerge from the front door with their pathetic little overnight cases. It was part of her campaign, part of the squeeze to get him into this corner where he now crouches. When he walked through the door today, Nancy thought at first that he was moving in again. *Home.*

He must make it clear to Elizabeth that he will not tolerate having the children used as weapons against him. (*Make it clear,* a joke. What power does he have, how does he know what she says to them when he isn't there?)

"Mummy says single-parent families have to work harder and pull together," Nancy told him last week.

"You aren't a single-parent family," Nate said. Elizabeth was behaving as if he were dead. But he wasn't dead yet and he wasn't going to die to oblige her. Unlike Chris. In the past few weeks he's felt a growing kinship with Chris, with that fatal desperation. "You have two parents and you always will have."

234

"Not if Mummy dies," Nancy said. Nate wants to talk to Elizabeth about this, this theme which has come up more than once. Has she been taking pills, has she been slashing her wrists where the children can see? Nate doesn't think so, doesn't think she'd go that far to spite him. She isn't looking well, she's puffy and white but she's neatly dressed and, though he looks, he can see no bandages or scars.

He knows what will happen if he tries to discuss the children's state of mind. He can foresee the scorn: What right does he have to comment? He's opted out. She acts as if he's gone off to loll in flowers and roll around on carpets of naked women, when the fact is he spends most of his life scrabbling for money. The recession hasn't ended. Maybe, he thinks, peering at Elizabeth's neatly typed list, he should point this out. For the first few years of it people believed it would, but now they've buckled themselves in for the long siege. They're no longer willing to pay eighty dollars for Jerome Giraffe and Horace Horse, no matter how lovingly hand-crafted. As for naked women, Lesje is hardly speaking to him. She claims he's deliberately trying to postpone the divorce.

"It's just a formality," he told her. "It doesn't mean anything."

"It may not mean anything to you," she said, "but Elizabeth thinks she's still married to you. Which she is."

"Only on paper," Nate said.

"If it doesn't mean anything to you, why not do it and get it over with?" Lesje said. Nate feels she is unhealthily obsessed with this question. A minor question, he tells her. He's tried to explain to her several times that relationships of ten years' standing (eleven? twelve?) don't just come to a dead stop. Elizabeth is the mother of his children. It's true she asked him to come over and help hang the new curtains in the children's room and it's also true he went; perhaps he shouldn't have. But that was a month and a half ago; he doesn't see why Lesje keeps bringing it up. They love each other, he tells her; who cares what's on file in the Registry Office? But Lesje turns away from him in bed, curling in on herself. Or she stays late at the Museum, or she brings home thick books filled with diagrams of fossil teeth and reads them at the kitchen table until she thinks he'll be asleep.

235

"Dinosaurs are dead," he said to her one day, trying to lighten things up. "But I'm still alive."

"Are you sure?" she said, with one of those ball-shriveling looks. As if he was a teeny little dog turd.

It's this, this desert, this growing fiasco, that has driven him finally into Elizabeth's mushroom-colored parlor. Her net.

He has a swift desire to stand up, lean over her, put his hands around her neck and squeeze. There would be some satisfaction in that. His mother has taken to saying that men should be protective of the rights of women; Nate can see this in the abstract. He knows about seamstresses, cookie workers, female university teachers, rape. But in concrete cases like his he sees no need for it. He is the one, surely it's obvious, who needs protection.

He resorts to an amusement of his high-school days, when he would practice silent metamorphoses on his teachers. *Hocus pocus*, and Elizabeth is a giant white sponge. *Presto change-o*, she's a big vanilla pudding. *Abracadabra*, a set of mammoth false teeth. *Kapow*, and she has bubonic plague. The mother of his children gasps, turns mottled and purpled, swells and bursts. He'll have the carpet cleaned, her carpet, and that will be that.

"Don't you agree?" Elizabeth says.

His eyes jerk from the page; he forces himself to look at her. Eye contact with the jury, so they were taught, always a good thing. He knows it will be dangerous to say, "Of course," so he'll have to admit he hasn't been listening.

"About the dentists' bills?" he asks hopefully.

Elizabeth gives him again her tolerant smile. "No," she says. "About the co-respondents. I was saying it would be better if I divorce you rather than the other way around, since it wouldn't be very good to use Chris as a co-respondent."

Nate wants to ask why not, since Chris is unlikely to be bothered by it. Whereas he can foresee certain difficulties with Lesje. But he knows this would be a tactless question. Also, the point in law is dubious. Though Elizabeth could swear she committed adultery, there's nothing but hearsay to back her up.

She says it would be bad for the children to drag the whole thing up again. She's right, of course she's right; everything these days, it seems, is bad for the children.

"I don't know," Nate says slowly. "Maybe we shouldn't use those grounds at all. Maybe we should go for marriage breakdown. That's a little more accurate, wouldn't you say?"

"Well, if you want to wait three years . . ." Elizabeth shrugs. "It's all the same to me, as long as I get the support payments." She says something about postdated checks and Nate nods vaguely. He's caught in a vise, the handle is turning, slowly, inexorably. What will squirt out of him? Turkey juice, nickels and dimes. No matter what he does he's screwed. Opt for a quick adultery case and Lesje will resent being dragged into it. "I didn't break up your marriage, remember?" she's said at least once too often. But wait three years and she'll resent that, too.

Nate fervently wishes he lived in California, Nevada, anywhere but this tight-assed churchified country. It's all the fault of Québec. Marriage, which ought to be a sieve, is a lobster trap, baited with flesh. How did he get into it? He can't remember. He scrabbles vainly, groping for a way out.

Can he, might he, ask Elizabeth whether she's slept with anyone else recently? Anyone, as it were, still alive? How to phrase it? He can't, he doesn't dare.

ELIZABETH

Elizabeth is sitting with her legs tucked under her, her flowered skirt (new, mauve tones, bought on impulse on a day of malaise) spread around her. She felt this position would create an effect of casual ease. She wishes to appear tranquil, serene, like her favorite stone Buddha in the Oriental collection. It will give her an advantage.

Not only does she wish to appear serene, she wishes to be serene. Sometimes she thinks she has achieved this; at other times she thinks it may only be immobility. Is the statue a Buddha or a chunk of stone? For instance: she does not appear, for the moment, to be interested in men. She still tries, examining strangers in the subway, picturing various members of the Museum staff in exotic postures, but nothing flickers. She's stopped accepting invitations to dinner: she's no longer willing to be that bored simply to eat. If she wants to devour the ground-up livers of deceased geese, the plucked carcasses of birds, wild or domestic, the pancreases of young cows, she can buy them herself.

She didn't used to get bored. She used to guess what the next move would be and then try to manipulate it. But now she knows the moves and can't be bothered going through the crude flatteries that will get her what, by popular consent, she is supposed to want. It takes two to tango and nobody waltzes any more. Rather than a parody, knee-squeezing at the Courtyard Café, she'd prefer a greaser, someone with no vocabulary at all, a leather shadow, a direct question in a back alley. Yes or no.

(Like Chris. Yes or no. Yes, she said, and then, after a long time, no. It was the pause that got him. The real reason she doesn't want Chris mentioned in the divorce proceedings has nothing to do with the law, with Nate or even with the children. She doesn't want him involved. To have his name uttered in that ritual way might cause him to materialize in the witness box, pale and accusing or – worse – fragmented, his head watching her with a Cheshire grin, his body still contorted in agony. She's got him safely buried, she wants no resurrection.)

She would like to sit here undisturbed in this quiet room, nibbling the biscuit that lies so far untouched on her saucer, thinking peaceful thoughts and letting events arrange themselves. Which isn't so easy. Elizabeth knows, from long experience, that events need help. Also her effortless pose is cutting off the circulation in her legs. But she doesn't want to change position, she doesn't want to move. It might suggest to Nate the idea that he too can move, that he is free to get up and walk out at any time. She knows – who better? – that there is always that freedom, that exit. One way or another. Nate, on the contrary, has never discovered it.

They've begun to talk about money, to discuss the details of her list. Item by item she leads him down the page. She has left this till the end, till she's certain he can see quite clearly that her cards are on the table. Her aces. If he wants a quickie, she'll dictate the terms. If he wants to wait the three years, it will give her time to maneuver, and she can always change her mind about contesting and make him wait five. The main point for him to grasp is that she doesn't care what he decides. In a way she really doesn't. It's not as though she's in any hurry to dash off and marry someone else.

He's telling her that, as she knows, he doesn't have very much money, hardly any in fact, but that he'll do everything possible. She indicates that his lack of money is no concern of hers. Whether he has a million dollars or ten, the children will continue to eat, wear clothes, go to the dentist, play with toys. They need allowances and lessons. Janet wishes to take dancing, Nancy has been skating for a year and Elizabeth doesn't see why she should give it up.

"Of course I could support them entirely on my own salary," she says. "Realistically I could do that, though we would have to cut down on certain things." She thinks of saying, We'd have to send the cat to the Humane Society, but decides this would be going too far. For one thing the cat, although promised, has not yet been acquired, and a cat in the bush is no hostage. And if they already had it the children would never forgive her for disposing of it. Nate or no Nate. She'll send him the bill, though, when it has to be fixed. "But I thought we'd agreed that you were going to participate as much as possible. The children need to know that both of their parents love them."

Nate is angry. "You really think that because I don't have any goddamned money I don't love my kids?" he says. "That's pretty crass."

"The children will hear you," Elizabeth says softly. "Maybe I'm a crass person. I guess I believe that if you really love someone you're prepared to make certain sacrifices." *Sacrifices*. This is straight out of the doctrine according to Auntie Muriel. She shifts her legs. She doesn't like to hear herself using Auntie Muriel's phrases, even when she believes in them. Though Auntie Muriel would have left out the word *love*.

She realizes the sentence is ambiguous: she could have meant the children or herself. Does she want Nate to love her and make sacrifices for her? Probably she does. It's hard to renounce tribute from those who once willingly paid it; hard not to exact. She lies on a bed, not her own in any real sense then, while Nate strokes his hands over her, shoulders, breasts, belly, the stretch marks from the children, he likes to finger those, any trace of mutilation, thighs, again, again. He's always considerate, he waits for her. Is this what she wants? All she could think of at the time was: Let's get on with it.

She tries to remember whether she ever loved him and concludes that she did, though in ways that were not sufficient. Nate was a good man and she recognized goodness, though she could not withhold a slight contempt. On their wedding day, what had she felt? Safety, relief: at last she was out of danger. She would become a homemaker, she would make a home. This in itself seemed to her improbable, even at the time. What else had happened, besides the usual erosion, attrition, the death of cells? She'd made the home but she could not quite believe in it, make it solid. And safety was not all she wanted. *Slumming*, Auntie Muriel said when she'd married Nate, but that was wrong. Slumming was dangerous and Nate was not that. Or not in the usual way.

She hasn't heard from Auntie Muriel lately; she expects never

240

to hear from her again. This ought to make her feel victorious. *Happy and glorious.* Auntie Muriel either has to cut her out completely or pretend that last unthinkable scene, hair-breadth escape for her white velour potty hat, never happened. It's quite possible that Elizabeth will receive a call in December, as usual, setting the date of the New Year's visit. She can't imagine going. She also can't imagine not going. She will sit on the slippery pink chesterfield once more, surrounded by polished surfaces, the baby grand piano, the silver tray, Auntie Muriel squatting across from her with her pebble-colored eyes, and the past will yawn around her, a cavern filled with menacing echoes.

"Exactly what sacrifices do you want me to make?" Nate says, still angry. Meaning: *You can't get blood from a stone.*

"Nate," she says, "I know how difficult this is for you. Believe me, it's difficult for me, too. But let's try to be as calm about it as possible. I'm not trying to torture you," she adds. "You have to take that on faith."

This is more or less true. She isn't trying to torture Nate: torture is a by-product. She's merely trying to win. Looking at him, watching him subside back onto his chair, she knows she will win, there's no way she can help winning. She'll win, and she hopes it will make her feel better.

241

LESJE

Lesje is in the living room, in the Upper Jurassic, where she runs along the path worn by the iguanodons. She's wearing her Adidas and a navy-blue sweatshirt that says SMALL IS BEAUTIFUL on it in red. This was once William's idea of a good thing to give her for her birthday; it didn't occur to him that the lettering would run across her chest. She hasn't worn it much. She carries her binoculars in their leather case, slung over her shoulder where they thump unpleasantly against her hip.

There's nothing behind her, nothing in front of her but the muddy path. To either side the undergrowth is unbroken; moisture drips from the fronds, it's hot as a steambath, her flesh simmers. The lake is miles away. She slows to a walk. In the distance ahead, where she knows there will be open space, scrub and hot sunlight, she can hear the raucous cries of the circling pterodactyls, intent on carrion.

There's nowhere else she wants to be, but this time it isn't exploration; she knows the terrain too well. It's merely flight.

She cuts herself off, gets out of her chair, walks back to the kitchen with her empty cup, tracking sawdust. He should sweep up. She turns on the element under the kettle, adds brown powder to her cup.

It's Saturday, and for once she's alone. There's a good reason: Nate is over at Elizabeth's house and at last they're discussing the divorce. She's wanted this to happen for a long time, so it's unfair of her to resent being left out of it. Shut out, like a child whose parents have closed the door on important matters, things they consider too adult for her to hear. She'd like to tiptoe, press her ear to the keyhole. She'd like to spy. She wants to hear what is being said about her. If anything.

But it's none of her business. Now it's started, though, it will

242

continue. Elizabeth has him hooked. She'll demand more and more conferences of this sort, more negotiations. It could go on for years.

She pours boiling water into her cup, adds white from a jar. She doesn't really want to drink this but she has to do something. To pass the time she begins to classify Elizabeth, a familiar exercise by now. If she had Elizabeth on a shelf, nicely ossified, the label would read: CLASS: *Chondrichthyes*; ORDER: *Selachii*; GENUS: *Squalidae*; SPECIES: *Elizabetha*. Today she classifies Elizabeth as a shark; on other days it's a huge Jurassic toad, primitive, squat, venomous; on other days a cephalopod, a giant squid, soft and tentacled, with a hidden beak.

Lesje knows scientific objectivity is a fraud. She's read the stories of plunder and revenge, of evidence stolen from one scientist by another, of the great dinosaur hunters who bribed each other's workmen and attacked each other's reputations. She knows that a passion for science is like any other passion. Nevertheless she wishes scientific objectivity really did exist and that she could have some of it. Then she would be able to apply it to her own life. She would become philosophical and wise, she would be able to cope with Elizabeth in some way more adult, more dignified than this secret game, which is after all little better than juvenile name-calling.

As it is she can't cope. Neither, it seems, can Nate. Although he indulges in private fits of rage, a relief anyway from the earlier phase in which he refused to criticize Elizabeth at all, when he actually has to confront her, haggle over money or the children's visits, he turns to putty. He justifies this by saying he's doing it for Lesje, he doesn't want to jeopardize the divorce. He's perennially short of money, but Elizabeth gets her support check on the dot each month. He's taken to borrowing small sums from Lesje, five dollars, ten dollars. How can she refuse, how can she refuse him cigarettes and the odd case of beer when he's so obviously going quietly mad? She feels sorry for him. She doesn't want to feel sorry for him. He doesn't want it either. So she says nothing and lends him the money.

A week ago Lesje raised again the subject of a child, for herself, for them. She was tentative about it; but maybe, before she gets too old, maybe now is the right time?

Nate was reluctant. He could hardly afford it now, he said.

"But it was your idea in the first place," Lesje said. She felt as if she'd propositioned him and been rejected. Was she unattractive? Genetically deficient?

Nate explained that when he said he wanted to have a child with her he'd been expressing a wish, a desire, not making a practical suggestion that was meant to be acted on right away.

Lesje, who felt she seldom made this distinction, tried to understand it. She supposed he was right. Elizabeth's children were living on Nate's income, what there was of it, and she and Nate were living on hers. She could hardly sabotage this arrangement by having a child. She isn't absolutely positive she wants to have a child, but she resents being denied one by Elizabeth.

Perhaps, Lesje thinks, she should join a discussion group. She's heard about such groups, she reads about them in the family sections of the papers Nate brings home every night. They meet in church basements and offer bandages to those wounded by the shrapnel of exploding families. Maybe she should go and drink cups of tea with such a group and eat cookies and bitch about Elizabeth. But she knows she can't. She's hopeless in groups, she'd be afraid of what she might say. In any gathering of the disabled she will always be the least disabled, or pretend to be. Also, the groups have names like Second Time Round and are aimed at married couples, and she isn't married.

She supposes that if she had independence and strength of character this wouldn't bother her, in fact she would welcome it. Many women no longer use their husbands' names, they object to being called "my this" or "my that," and Nate, when he has to introduce her to anyone, which isn't all that often, doesn't use the possessive. He simply uses her name, without even a Miss, and this pleases him. He's glad, he says, that her name isn't Mrs. Schoenhof. God forbid she should in any way resemble his mother or his wife. But instead of making her feel like an entity in her own right, as Nate claims it's supposed to, this makes her feel like a cipher. Though her own conservatism, unsuspected till now, appalls her, she wants to belong, to be seen to belong; she wants to be classifiable, a member of a group. There is already a group of Mrs. Schoenhofs: one is Nate's mother, the other is the mother of his children. Lesje isn't the mother of anyone; officially she is nothing.

Surely she didn't used to be like this, plugged into this constant inner whine, critical, begrudging. Maybe she's been thinking too much about Elizabeth. *If you make that face too much*, they said at school, *you'll grow up to look like that*. If she isn't careful she'll turn into Elizabeth. Sometimes she thinks Nate is an obscure practical joke being played on her by Elizabeth, for an unfathomable reason of her own. So laugh, she tells herself. But she can't.

It's no good, she should say to him. It's no use. But that isn't true: it is good, it is of use. Some days, some minutes. From time to time.

The fact is that she's addicted to Nate's version of her. Sometimes, when he touches her, she feels not naked but clothed, in some long unspecified garment that spreads around her like a shimmering cloud. She's realized with something close to panic that the picture he's devised of her is untrue. He expects her to be serene, a refuge; he expects her to be kind. He really thinks she is, underneath, and that if he can dig into her far enough this is what he'll unearth. He ought to be able to tell by now that she isn't like this at all. Nevertheless she wants to be; she wants to be this beautiful phantom, this boneless wraith he's conjured up. Sometimes she really does want it.

Lesje paces the kitchen floor, which needs washing. Not that it looks any different clean. White lumps in her coffee, the sink is paved with cups and spoons, similarly lumpy. She should take a bath. Instead she puts her cup into the sink with the other cups and goes out, locking the door.

She walks south on the heated sidewalk, then west along streets of crumbling red insulbrick siding, sagging porches, old houses skewed and crowded. This place is more and more familiar to her; it's almost the land of the grandmothers. Her small grandmother's house was on this street, or possibly not this street but the one next to it; her round grandmother lived a few blocks further west, nearer the gold-domed church, but in the same kind of house.

She hasn't thought much about these streets since the year both grandmothers died and she'd ceased to visit. She could remember the grandmothers themselves, what they looked like, certain rooms in their houses, but not the houses themselves. It was as if this district had been neatly snipped from the map. But now she wants to find the houses again, the actual houses. They will be a kind of evidence, since the grandmothers who are the real evidence are gone.

She stands still. She's in a small street choked with trees, parked cars, with children playing between them and running out onto the pavement. The houses look smaller than she expected; some of them have been painted, bright blue, yellow, the cement between the bricks done carefully in a different color. She doesn't recognize anything; if she wants to find her grandmothers she'll have to look elsewhere. New people are here now, from other countries. They in their turn will make money and shift north. This is not a settled neighborhood, here for eternity as she thought when she was a child, but a way station, a campground. In some distant future archeologists will dig through the rubble and unearth the successive layers. *The black people have it now*, her grandmother said; talking about her store.

If her grandmothers had lived, they too might have moved north. In any case they would have discarded their dark dresses, gone on day excursions to Niagara Falls, had their hair permed as her mother had done, bought crimplene pantsuits. Assimilated. As it is they're fixed, mounted specimens in her head, cut from their own wrecked and shadowy backgrounds and pasted here. Anachronisms, the last of their kind.

A mother's blessing, that's what we had then. That was important. If a young man goes to war he has to get a mother's blessing. I was the first one to work in Eaton's, the rest was all English. They didn't like it. I just didn't say nothing, when they said what kind of a name is that. I kept my mouth shut and I got along good enough that way. What we had back then, we had the flowers on our head, and the dancing. They try to do it now but it's not the same.

At the time Lesje had not been able to think of her grandmother as having ever been thin, much less young. She seemed always to have been what she was, seamy-faced, melancholy, smelling of underarms and furniture polish. The other grandmother had danced too, or so she claimed. She'd mentioned handkerchiefs; Lesje hadn't understood, so finally she'd pulled

246

a crumpled Kleenex from her sleeve and waved it in the air. All Lesje had been able to picture was her grandmother at her present age, hopping about ridiculously in her tiny black boots, waving handfuls of Kleenex.

A man, olive-skinned and short, brushes past and says something Lesje doesn't understand but guesses is not friendly. She doesn't know where she is, she'll have to take bearings. The sun is going down so that must be west, towards the golden church she's seen from the outside but was never allowed to enter. She'd never been in a synagogue either, before the funeral. She turns back, trying to retrace her way.

She didn't listen properly, their stories bored her, she felt them as attempts to convert her, to one side or the other. She was impatient with them and their complaints and bickering, with these stories which were so foreign and which, like their endless stories about wars and suffering and horror, children spitted on swords, had nothing to do with her. The old country, archaic and terrible; not like here. Now she wants these voices back; even the squabbling, even the rage. She wants to dance with flowers on her head, she wants to be endorsed, sanctified, she doesn't care who by. She wants a mother's blessing. Though she can't imagine her own mother doing such a thing.

This is the problem. She knows by now that people do not behave the way she wishes them to. So what should she do, change wishes?

When she was ten she wanted to go to the Museum, not with one grandmother on Saturday mornings as usual but with both of them. One would hold her right hand, one her left. She didn't expect them to speak to each other, she'd heard them say often enough they would sooner die than do that. But there was no rule against walking. The three of them would walk together, slowly because of her fat grandmother, up the stone steps of the Museum, herself in the middle, and in under the golden dome. Unlike the dinosaurs, this was something that might really happen; when she finally saw it never could, she forgot about it.

As for Nate, it's simple. All she wants is for both of them to be different. Not very different, a little would do it. Same molecules, different arrangement. All she wants is a miracle, because anything else is hopeless.

Friday, November 25, 1977

NATE

Nate, slumped in a horseshoe booth in the bar of the Selby Hotel, drinks draft beer and watches television. It's Friday night and voices babble, it's hard to hear the sound. Over the past few months more driblets of dirt concerning the Mounties have been trickling in, and these are now being relentlessly scrutinized by a trio of pundits. The Mounties, pretending to be Separatist terrorists, sent violent letters somewhere. They burnt a barn and stole some mail, and there's some suggestion that an erstwhile head of Intelligence was a double agent for the CIA. The Prime Minister claims he knew nothing about it, and furthermore he doesn't think it's his place to know such things. This is old news which is not being treated with any new wisdom. Nate smokes, watching the ghostly heads frown and smirk, skeptical.

His mother is gathering signatures on a letter of protest, as usual. There will be a lot of talk and nothing will happen. He dislikes the pundits for pretending something will, their earnestness and tired outrage. Right now he'd rather hear about the hockey scores, though the Leafs are fucking up as usual. Around him smoke rises, glasses clank, voices shuffle through their routines, desolation spreads, as far as the eyes can see.

Martha comes in and stands uncertainly at the far end of the bar. Nate lifts his arm to catch her attention. She sees him and strides forward, smiling.

"Long time no see," Martha says. This is heavy irony, as Nate now sees Martha every day at the office. But tonight he's taking her to dinner. He owes her something. As soon as she sits down he realizes he's made a blunder, he shouldn't have suggested the Selby. They used to drink here a lot. He hopes Martha won't become maudlin.

So far she's not showing any signs of it. She plops her elbows onto the table. "Jeez, my feet are sore," she says.

Nate interprets this the way he's always interpreted this

248

bluntness, her insistence on the vernacular: it's a cover-up for other, more delicate things. He thinks she's done something to her hair, though he has trouble remembering what her hair was like before. She's thinner than she used to be. Her breasts rest on her folded arms, she smiles at him, he feels a twitch of desire. Against his will. It can't be the boots, Martha has always had boots.

He orders two more drafts and reminds himself that this dinner is purely routine. Without Martha, or with Martha against him, he would never have been able to get even the menial job he's doing now. Young lawyers, lawyers younger than he is – it suddenly alarms him to see how much younger – are a dime a dozen now, and why should the firm have rehired him after his desertion? He's rusty too, he's forgotten a lot, things he once thought he'd never again have to remember. But he's desperate for money, he didn't know where else to go.

He's grateful to Martha for not laughing, not sneering. She didn't even say, *I knew you'd be back*. She'd listened to him as if she were a nurse or a case worker; then she said she would see what she could do.

What he's got isn't what he would have chosen. He does the legal aid. *Legal Band-Aid*. Because of the firm's radical reputation, it feels it has to take on more than its share of legal aid cases; there's more coming in than Adams and Stein and the juniors can handle. Nate is their Office Overload. He takes part-time pay for what has turned out to be a full-time job, shepherding the unimportant cases, the ones no one else wants to take because they're foredoomed to failure, the thugs, housebreakers and junkies, through the courts, into the pen, through the courts again, into the pen. He knows it's a circular process.

He's resurrected his briefcase and his two suits, wondering as he dug through the trunk at the back of the cupboard in his old room why he had never thrown these things away. He polishes his shoes now and cleans his fingernails; the permanent cuticle of blackened paint has almost vanished. In the mornings, he breathes the antiseptic smell of jails, the smell of co-ops, caged flesh, sour air breathed in and out too many times; the smell of boredom and hatred. He listens to the lies of his clients, watches their eyes twitch momentarily away from his, knows they're scornful of him and his polished shoes and his belief in them.

They don't know he doesn't believe in them. He goes to court with them, does what he can, plea-bargains, makes shoddy little deals with the Crown prosecutors. He listens to the shoptalk, the jocularity of the other lawyers, which he once found offensive; lately he's been joining in. Sometimes he wins a case and his client goes free, but not often. Even so it's no triumph. The pettiness of petty crime, the absurd particularity grates on him. There seems to be no connection between what happens to these men and what they've done: two radios and a stereo, shooting up in an alley, the contents of some old lady's bureau drawers.

His mother would say his clients are products of their environment, which no doubt is true. Culture shock, they suffer from it; the point at which one set of skewed rules collides blindly with another. His mother manages to combine this view with a belief in human dignity and free will, at least as it applies to herself. Nate doesn't feel capable of this logical contradiction. He doesn't judge these people, nor does he feel he's an instrument of justice. He does a job. He might as well be working for the SPCA. He'd like to be in on the Mountie stuff: the firm is acting for a maniac fringe newspaper vandalized at the time. But Stein is taking that, naturally.

The waiter plunks down their two drafts and Martha sprinkles hers with salt. "So how's it going?" she says. She drinks, leaving a suds moustache on her upper lip. He used to love that, the way she swills her beer. Tenderness floats in him, hovers, is gone.

On the screen, which he can see but she can't, it's now René Lévesque, gesturing, shrugging, explaining, sad eyes peering from his creased mime's face. Something about the economy, from what Nate can catch. These days they're saying they never meant separation, not just like that. Nate is disappointed in him; the whole thing so far has been an anticlimax. Missed chances, compromise and hedging, like the rest of the country. It's a world of unfreedom after all. Only a fool could have believed in anything else, and Lévesque is no fool. (Like Nate: not any more.) He looks less and less like a clown. More like a turtle: wisdom has wrinkled him, encased him in a useful shell.

"Hey, dreamer," Martha says. The first sign she's given that they were once lovers: it's her old word. Nate lowers his eyes to her.

"Great," he says. "I guess." He'd like to express as much enthusiasm as possible. Martha wants to believe her action, her good turn, has made him happy. He knows she's gone out of her way for him; he doesn't know why.

Martha gives him no clues. "Down the old rat hole," she says, and empties her glass.

In the dining room of the Selby, less than he would have liked, more than he can afford, they eat liver and homefries and Martha talks about the office: who's left, who's come, whose marriage is splitting up, who's having it on with whom. As usual Martha knows all about these things; she reports them jovially. "Better her than me," she says, or "Good luck to him." Nate settles into familiar comfort with her, as if he's listening to the breathing of some large, warm-flanked animal.

He'd like to nuzzle into her, shove his head under her arm and close his eyes; but Martha is treating him like a friend, an old friend, trustworthy and neutral. She acts as if she can't remember ever having cried, ever having hit him or screamed, and Nate reflects once more upon the shamelessness of women. Their lack of shame. They believe whatever they do is justified at the time, so why be guilty? Nate envies this. He himself knows he did not treat Martha as well as he'd intended, but she seems to have forgotten all about that, as well.

With the canned cherry pie Martha describes her latest interests: she does volunteer fund-raising for Nellie's Halfway House, and on Tuesday and Thursday evenings she goes to yoga class. Nate can't quite imagine Martha, ample but hardly graceful, wearing a black leotard and bent into a pretzel, nor can he picture her identifying to any extent with the battered wives sheltered by Nellie's. She was never much at exercise, and theories, *issues* as she called them, left her cold. He knows: he once tried to get her to buy a bicycle, and when he would talk about what was at stake in Québec, in Israel, in Cambodia, she would say she got enough of that on the television news. But here she is now, improbability materialized, sitting across from him, forking in pie crust and talking about the reform of rape laws.

251

Nate tells himself that it's just like Martha to take up a cause or a hobby after the peak, during the slow descent into that outmoded trough inhabited by people like his mother: Christadelphians, vegetarians of the autointoxication school, Esperanto-speakers, lecturers on spaceships, Unitarians. This was always Elizabeth's view of her, based, as far as Nate could see, on Martha's wardrobe. According to Elizabeth, women's lib is on the wane; and interest in Eastern cults is not what it was. But none of this seems to bother Martha. She comments on Nate's appearance: he looks oxygen-starved, she says. Very few people breathe properly. He should try a little full breathing and a simple version of the Salute to the Sun. Martha personally guarantees it would do wonders for him.

Then she veers back to the law. She has pronounced views on the family court system; in fact, if she can save enough money she would like to go to law school and become a lawyer herself, so she can do some specialized work in this field. As far as school goes, it will be a cinch, since she knows quite a lot of the stuff already; God knows she's typed enough of it. Nate blinks. He sees now that he thinks of Martha as not exactly stupid, but certainly not ultra-bright. Though quite possibly she knows more law at this point than he does himself. She might be all right, she might even be quite good. For family court.

But Nate feels diminished. He's gone for days, weeks, months of his life without thinking once of Martha. His hands retain only a faint memory of the insides of her thighs, her taste has faded from his tongue, he can't even remember her bedroom: what color are the curtains? Yet he's aggrieved that he himself has been so easily, so quickly forgotten. Was he that unimportant? He tells himself that Martha cannot possibly have a new man up her sleeve, someone who holds for her the same significance that he himself once held; otherwise she would not be so interested in law school.

He pays the bill and they walk towards the door, Martha in front. She's carrying her coat over her arm, and he watches her haunches under the gored tweed of her skirt. Will she perhaps invite him back? They could sit in her living room and have a few drinks. Nothing more than that. He deliberates: of course he shouldn't accept. It's Friday ni ght, the children will be there, Lesje's expecting him. He didn't tell her where he was going; he

252

said he had to do some legal work. Taking Martha to dinner was legal work in a way, but this would have been too difficult to explain.

On the street, however, Martha thanks him, dismisses him. "See you Monday," she says. "Back at the old grind." She walks towards the corner, in her boots, waving for a cab. He watches her stop one, open the door, get in. He would like to know where she's going, but she'll go there whether he knows or not. The world exists apart from him. He's rehearsed this often enough in theory; he's just never known it with certainty. It follows that his body is an object in space and that someday he will die.

Now he can remember having had this perception several times before. He stands where she's left him. He doesn't want to go home.

ELIZABETH

Auntie Muriel is in the hospital. That in itself is incredible enough. First, that anything should ever go wrong with her. Elizabeth has never thought of her aunt as compounded of mortal flesh like other people; rather as being, from neck to knees, built of a warty growth, something like gum rubber, impermeable and indestructible. Second, that if something has gone wrong with her, which Elizabeth still doubts, Auntie Muriel could have brought herself to admit it. Nevertheless she's in the hospital, the Princess Margaret to be precise, and Elizabeth has been summoned. Despite her vow never to see Auntie Muriel again she has not dared to refuse.

She sits in the visitor's chair beside the raised bed, while Auntie Muriel, wearing an ice-blue bed jacket, cranked up and propped up, complains. They put extra chlorine in the water here, she can taste it. She can remember when water was water but she doesn't suppose Elizabeth can tell the difference. At first she could not get a private room. Can Elizabeth imagine? She had to share a room, share one, with a terrible old woman who wheezed at night. Auntie Muriel is convinced the woman was dying. She could hardly get any sleep. And now that she's finally here in her private room, no one pays any attention to her. She has to ring and ring, three times even, before the nurse will come. They all read detective novels, she's seen them. The night nurse is from the West Indies. The food is atrocious. She cannot tolerate beets, she always ticks the other vegetables on the menu but they bring beets. Sometimes Auntie Muriel thinks they do things like this to her on purpose. She will speak to Doctor MacFadden, tomorrow. If she has to stay here for a little rest and some tests, which is what he says, the least he can do is make sure she's comfortable. She's never been sick a day in her life, there's nothing really wrong with her now, she isn't used to hospitals.

Elizabeth thinks this may be true. She connects her own stays

254

in hospitals with the births of her children, but of course Auntie Muriel has never undergone that. Elizabeth can't imagine her giving birth, much less engaged in the preliminaries. It's difficult to picture weak-chinned Uncle Teddy storming those elastic-sheathed barricades, uncovering those thighs the hue of potato sprouts; difficult to picture Auntie Muriel allowing it. Though she might have done it out of a sense of duty.

Auntie Muriel has brought her petit-point cushion cover with her to the hospital, the same piece she's been doing for years: pansies in a basket. In times past it has reposed on various chairs and sofas in Auntie Muriel's house, testimony to the fact that she's not a lazy woman. It looks out of place on the hospital coverlet. Auntie Muriel lifts it as she talks, lets it fall.

Elizabeth sits in the visitor's chair. She's brought some flowers, chrysanthemums, in a pot rather than cut; she thought Auntie Muriel might like something that was still growing, but Auntie Muriel immediately pronounced them too smelly. Doesn't Elizabeth remember that she can't stand the smell of chrysanthemums?

Perhaps she does remember; perhaps she conveniently forgot. She'd felt she should bring something, some offering, for Auntie Muriel is going to die; is dying at this very moment. Elizabeth, as the next of kin, was the first to be notified.

"It's all through her," Doctor MacFadden said in his semi-whisper. "It must've started as cancer of the bowel. The colon. I expect she was in considerable pain for some time before she came to see me. She's always said she was strong as a horse. It was the blood that frightened her."

Considerable pain, naturally. She'd grit her teeth for weeks before forcing herself to acknowledge that she had a colon and that this portion of her had turned traitor. And Auntie Muriel must have been as surprised as Elizabeth to find she could actually bleed. But frightened? A word surely alien to Auntie Muriel's vocabulary. Elizabeth stares at her, pitiless, unbelieving. Such malevolent vitality cannot die. Hitler lived on after the discovery of his smoldering teeth, and Auntie Muriel too is one of the immortals.

But she has shriveled. The flesh once compact and stolid is drooping on the bones; the powder Auntie Muriel has continued to apply is caked in small ravines of collapsing skin.

255

Her throat is a cavity above the virginal bow of the bed jacket, her prowlike bosom has withered. Her color, once a confident beige, has faded to the off-white of a dirty tooth. Her eyes, once slightly protruberant like those of a Pekinese, are being sucked into the depths of her head. She's falling in on herself, she's melting, like the witch in *The Wizard of Oz*, and seeing it Elizabeth remembers: Dorothy was not jubilant when the witch turned into a puddle of brown sugar. She was terrified.

Auntie Muriel has not yet been told. Doctor MacFadden doesn't feel she's one of the kind that can benefit from such an early revelation. Elizabeth, as delicately as she could, has pressed for a possible date. How long can Auntie Muriel be expected to, well, hang on? But he was vague. It would depend on many factors. There were sometimes astonishing reversals. They would keep her on analgesics and, if necessary, sedatives, and of course they were hoping that she'd get a certain amount of moral support from her family.

Meaning Elizabeth, who is now questioning her motives for even being here. She should have told the old bitch to kiss off a long time ago and stuck to it. There's not even a practical excuse for her presence: she knows the terms of Auntie Muriel's will, which are unlikely to change. A few thousand to the children when they turn twenty-one, and the rest to Timothy Eaton's bloated warthog of a church. Elizabeth doesn't care. She's practiced not caring.

Has she come to gloat? Possibly. Revenges sweep through her head. She'll tell Auntie Muriel she's going to die. Auntie Muriel won't believe it, but the mere suggestion will cause outrage. Or she'll threaten to bury her somewhere other than her own cemetery plot. She'll cremate her and sprinkle her over Center Island, where the Italians play soccer. She'll put her in a jam jar and plant her in Regent's Park; dark feet will walk over her. That'll fix her.

Elizabeth does not approve of this, this vengefulness she cradles; nevertheless it exists. She stares at Auntie Muriel's hands, which squeeze themselves against the blue bed jacket; which she cannot bear to touch.

* * *

256

The woman who grabbed her arm that day outside Eaton's College Street, when they'd just come out after seeing the Toronto Children's Players Christmas show, a special concession on Auntie Muriel's part, *Toad of Toad Hall*. Beside them, the Sally Ann sextet sang and jingled. A scruffy brown cloth coat and that smell on her breath, sweet and acid. The woman had only one glove; it was the naked hand on Elizabeth's arm. Elizabeth was eleven. Caroline was with her. They were both wearing the blue tweed coats with velveteen collars and matching velveteen hats that Auntie Muriel considered the proper thing for downtown excursions.

The woman was crying. Elizabeth couldn't understand what she was saying; her voice slurred. On her own blue tweed arm the hand convulsed, slackened, like a dead cat twitching. Elizabeth took Caroline's hand and pulled her away. Then she ran. *That was Mother*, Caroline said. *No it wasn't*. Outside Maple Leaf Gardens, out of breath. *Don't say it was*.

That was Mother, Caroline said. Elizabeth punched her in the stomach and Caroline doubled over, crouching on the sidewalk, screaming. *Get up*, Elizabeth said. *You can walk, we're going home*. Caroline squatted on the sidewalk, howling, faithful.

This is what Elizabeth cannot forgive. She can't forgive her own treachery. Auntie Muriel must not be allowed to get away with it. She must, for Elizabeth's benefit, visibly suffer. At last.

"You never listen to me," Auntie Muriel says.

"Pardon?" says Elizabeth. Even Auntie Muriel's voice is different. It's no longer an accusation, it's a whine.

"You never listen to me," Auntie Muriel says. "I gave you all the advantages."

Not all, Elizabeth thinks, but she can't argue.

"I said you didn't know. You think I was hard on her but I gave her money, all those years. It wasn't your Uncle Teddy."

Elizabeth realizes that Auntie Muriel is talking about her mother. She doesn't want to listen, she doesn't want to listen to another genealogy of her own worthlessness.

"I never missed a week. Nobody gave me any credit for that," says Auntie Muriel. "Of course all she ever spent it on was drink. I gave it to her anyway; I wouldn't have her on my conscience. I don't suppose you understand what that means."

Elizabeth can do without this information. She'd prefer to think of her mother as having been entirely destitute, a wronged party, a saint under the street lights. Even when she was older, when she'd known she could find out where her mother was, she had chosen not to. Her mother, like clouds or angels, lived on air, or possibly – when she thought about the more material aspects – on Uncle Teddy. The image of the two sisters meeting, perhaps touching each other, disturbs her.

"Did you see her?" Elizabeth says. "Did you talk to her?"

"I left instructions at my bank," Auntie Muriel says. "She hated me. She wouldn't see me, she used to call me on the phone when she was drunk and say. . . . But I did my duty. It was what Father would have wanted. Your mother was always the favorite."

To Elizabeth's horror, Auntie Muriel is beginning to cry. Tears seep from her puckered eyes; a reversal of nature, a bleeding statue, a miracle. Elizabeth watches, remote. She ought to be rejoicing. Auntie Muriel is finally tasting the ashes of her life. But Elizabeth does not rejoice.

"You think I don't know," Auntie Muriel says. "I know I'm dying. Everyone here is dying." She picks up her embroidery hoop again, stabs at it with the thick needle, shutting out knowledge of her own tears, which she makes no effort to wipe from her face. "You knew," she says, accusing now. "And you didn't tell me. I'm not a baby."

Elizabeth hates Auntie Muriel. She has always hated her and she always will hate her. She will not forgive her. This is an old vow, an axiom. Nevertheless.

Nevertheless, this is not Auntie Muriel. The Auntie Muriel of Elizabeth's childhood has melted, leaving in her place this husk, this old woman who now drops her blockish embroidery and with eyes closed and weeping gropes with her hands across the hospital covers.

Elizabeth wants to get up out of the visitor's chair and walk, run from the room, leaving her there alone. She deserves it.

Nevertheless, she leans forward and takes Auntie Muriel's blinded hands. Desperately the stubby fingers clutch her. Elizabeth is no priest: she cannot give absolution. What can she offer?

Nothing sincerely. Beside her own burning mother she has sat, not saying anything, holding the one good hand. The one good fine-boned hand. The ruined hand, still beautiful, unlike the veined and mottled stumps she now cradles in hers, soothing them with her thumbs as in illness she has soothed the hands of her children.

Sickness grips her. Nevertheless, nevertheless, she whispers: It's all right. It's all right.

NATE

Nate on the subway hurtles eastward through the familiar tunnel, his face cadaverous in the dark window opposite, topped by a poster depicting a brassiere turning into a bird. He's going to his mother's to collect the children. They've been there overnight; he's spent the morning alone with Lesje, who has intimated more than once since he returned to what everyone else calls *work* that they haven't been seeing much of each other lately. She means alone.

This morning they were alone, but nothing out of the ordinary happened. They ate boiled eggs and then he read the Friday night papers, sitting in the front room in the sunlight, among the idle machines and the unfinished rocking horses. He'd thought he would be able to continue with the toys, in the evenings and on weekends, but he's too tired. It isn't only that. He can't put the two things together in his head, assault and battery back of the warehouse on Front Street East, Jerry the Giraffe with its oblivious smile. Reality is one or the other, and day by day the toys fade, lose blood. Already he sees them as museum pieces, quaint, handmade, a hundred years old. Soon they will vanish and this room will fill with paper.

Lesje had wanted the whole weekend, but he could not refuse Elizabeth, who is adamant these days about needing time to herself. Nate wonders idly what she does with it. He hopes she's seeing a man, which would make life easier. For him. In any case it would not have been Elizabeth he'd be refusing, but the children. Put that way it's impossible, which Lesje cannot quite grasp. Her obtuseness, her refusal to see that their predicament is theirs, not his or hers, infuriates him. It's a simple and obvious fact that he's doing much of what he's doing for her, or, to rephrase it, if it wasn't for her he wouldn't have to do it. He's tried to explain this but she seems to think he's accusing her of something. She stares out the window, at the wall, at any available space except the one between his ears.

Luckily there's his mother. Nate feels his mother is always willing to take the children, always waiting in fact for chances just like these. After all, she's their grandmother.

Nate gets off at Woodbine, climbs the stairs, emerges into weak April sunlight. He walks north to the street of jerry-built boxes that contains his childhood. His mother's house is a box like the others, covered with the dingy beige stucco that never ceases to remind him of certain radio programs: *The Green Hornet, Our Miss Brooks*. The woman in the house next door to it has a statue on her lawn, a black boy dressed as a jockey and holding a coach lamp. This statue is a source of perpetual irritation to Nate's mother. Nate sometimes teases her by equating this statue with the soulful painting of the black boy at the front of the Unitarian church. Lower-class Catholics, he says, have plaster Marys and Jesuses on their lawns; maybe the woman next door is a lower-class Unitarian. Nate's mother has never found this particularly funny, but Nate would be disappointed if she did.

He rings the doorbell, lights a cigarette while he waits. His mother, wearing the frazzled turquoise bedroom slippers she's had for at least ten years, finally opens the door. The children are downstairs in the basement playing dress-ups, she says as he takes off his pea jacket. She keeps a cardboard box down there for them. In it are the few garments she hasn't found suitable for giving away to service organizations: evening gowns of the late thirties, a cut-velvet cloak, a long magenta slip. Every time he sees them, Nate is freshly amazed by the fact that his mother once went to parties, danced, was courted.

His mother has tea made and offers Nate some. He wonders if she might have a beer in the house, but she doesn't. She buys beer only for him, he knows, and this was short notice. He doesn't complain or press the point; she seems a little more tired than usual. He sits at the kitchen table with her, drinking tea and trying to avoid looking at her map of world atrocities, on which the stars are multiplying like mice. Soon the children will finalize their costumes and come upstairs to display themselves, which is the point of the whole game.

"Elizabeth tells me you've gone back to Adams, Prewitt and Stein," his mother says.

261

Nate feels conspiracy roping him round. How does Elizabeth know? He hasn't told her, he hasn't wanted to admit that defeat. Is it Martha, is that network still in operation? Elizabeth never used to phone his mother; but perhaps – treachery! – it's his mother who phones Elizabeth. It's the kind of thing she would do on principle. Though they've never been close. She's been slow to accept the fact that he and Elizabeth have separated. She hasn't said so, but he can tell she considers this bad for the children. For instance, she never mentions Lesje. He wishes she would protest, criticize, so he could defend himself; tell her what a termite's life Elizabeth led him.

"I'm so glad," his mother says, her china-blue eyes shining as if he's just won something: not a lottery but a prize. "I always felt that was what you were really suited for. You must be happier now."

Nate's throat is gripped by fearful anger. Can't she tell, couldn't any idiot see that he's compelled, forced, he has no choice? The weight of her ideal son presses on his chest, a plaster mannequin threatening to enter and choke him. Angel of the oppressed. She'll absolve anyone of anything, any crime, any responsibility, except herself, except him.

"I'm not," he says. "I am goddamned well not *suited* for it. I'm doing it because I need the money."

Her smile does not fade. "But it's the right thing," she says brightly. "At least you're doing something with your life."

"I was doing something with my life before," Nate says.

"There's no need to raise your voice, dear," his mother says with wounded complacency. He hates it, this tone, which is supposed to make him feel, does make him feel as if he's jumping up and down like an ape, swinging a club and thumping his chest. Years of her moral smugness, burying him like snow, like layers of wool. Intolerable smugness of all of them, Elizabeth, his mother, even Lesje. She complains but her complaints are smug, hedged bets. He knows that silent equation, he's been well schooled: *I suffer, therefore I am right.* But he suffers too, can't they see that? What does he have to do, blow his head off before they'll take him seriously? He thinks of Chris, lying shattered on the bier of his mattress, mourned by two policemen. *Serious.* Not that he would.

"If you want to know," Nate says, nevertheless lowering his

voice, "I hate every minute of it." Wondering if he actually does, he's good at it, as good as you can be at something like that.

"But you're helping people," his mother says, baffled, as if he's failed to grasp an elementary geometrical axiom. "Isn't it legal aid? Aren't they poor?"

"Mother," he says with renewed patience, "anyone who thinks they can really help people, especially doing what I'm doing, is a horse's ass."

His mother sighs. "You've always been so afraid of being a horse's ass," she says. "Even as a child."

Nate is startled. Has he? He tries to remember manifestations of this.

"I suppose you think I'm a horse's ass, too," his mother says. Implacably she smiles on. "I guess I am one. But I guess I think everyone is."

Nate is unprepared for this degree of cynicism, coming from his mother. She's supposed to believe in the infinite perfectability of man; isn't she? "Then why do you do it all?" he says.

"All what, dear?" she asks, a little absentmindedly, as if she's had this conversation with him several times before.

"The Korean poets, the crippled vets, all that." He sweeps his arm, taking in her red-starred map, her mushroom cloud.

"Well," she says, sipping her tea, "I had to do something to keep myself alive. During the war, you know. Right after you were born."

What does she mean? Surely this is metaphorical, she's only talking about housewifely boredom or something like that. But she leaves him no doubt. "I thought of several ways," she continues, "but then I thought, what if it doesn't work? I could have ended up, you know, damaged. And then you start thinking about whoever might find you. It was right after your father, right after I got the cable, but that wasn't the only thing. I guess I simply didn't want to live on this kind of an earth."

Nate is horrified. He can't, he cannot see his mother as a potential suicide. It's incongruous. Not only that, she hasn't once mentioned him. Could she have abandoned him so easily, just left him in a basket and stepped blithely off into the unknown? His father is unforgivable enough, but at least he died by accident. Irresponsible, a bad mother, she couldn't. Potential orphan, he sways at the lip of the abyss which has suddenly gaped in front of him.

"At first I did knitting," his mother says, with a small laugh. "I knitted socks. You know, for the war effort. But it didn't keep me busy enough. Anyway I guess I felt I would rather do something more useful than just knitting. When you were old enough I started with the veterans, and one thing leads to another."

Nate stares at his mother, who however looks just the same as she has always looked. It's not only the revelation but the unexpected similarity to himself that appalls him. He has thought her incapable of such despair, and he now sees that he's always depended on it, this incapability of hers. What now, what next?

But his children intervene, clumping up the cellar stairs in toeless high heels, wrapped in cut velvet and satin, their mouths reddened with some long-discarded lipstick of his mother's, their eyebrows penciled black. He applauds boisterously, relieved by their presence, their uncomplicated delight.

Nevertheless he thinks: *Soon they will be women,* and that recognition runs through him like a needle. They will demand brassieres and then reject them, blaming both needs on him. They will criticize his clothes, his job, his turn of phrase. They'll leave home to live with surly, scrofulous young men; or they'll marry dentists and go in for white rugs and hanging sculptures made of wool. Either way they will judge him. Motherless, childless, he sits at the kitchen table, the solitary wanderer, under the cold red stars. At the front door he kisses his mother as usual, the obligatory peck. She acts as if nothing has happened, as if they've been talking about something he's known all along.

She starts to close the front door and suddenly he can't handle it, this closing of the door. He vaults the low iron railing of the cement porch, hurdles the short hedge onto the neighbors' lawn. He leapfrogs the black jockey and takes the next hedge and the next, landing on grass yellow from winter, mushy with melted snow; his heels sink, mud splatters his legs. Behind him he hears the chorus, the army of tired female voices: *childish.* To hell with them. He soars, over dog dirt, into soggy beds of someone's crocuses, up again. His children race along the sidewalk, laughing, calling: "*Daddy! Wait for me!*"

He knows he will land soon; already his heart is pounding. But he aims again for it, that nonexistent spot where he longs to be. Mid-air.

LESJE

Lesje is holding a piece of paper. She's tried to read it four or five times, but she can't seem to get it into focus. Which is stupid, since pieces of paper exactly like it arrive in her mail almost every day. It's a letter, printed with a blue ballpoint pen on lined notebook paper, addressed to *Dinosaurs*, care of the Museum.

Dear Sirs:

I am in Grade Six and our Teacher has made us do a Project on Dinosaurs and I was wondering if you can give full answers with examples.
1) What does Dinosaur mean
2) Why is it called the Mesozoic
3) Trace the geological developments that took place in this Era in North America, please include Maps
4) what is a Fossil
5) Why were no Dinosaur fossils been found in Ontario

Please send the answers very soon as my Project is due on June 15.

Yours truely, Lindy Lucas

Everything about this letter is familiar to Lesje. She knows it's been sent by a wily child, bent on shortcuts, who would rather copy out a ready-made answer than condense one from a book. She even recognizes the questions, which have been rephrased slightly, first by the teacher, then, more drastically, by the student, but which are still almost identical to some of those in the Museum pamphlet on dinosaurs which she herself helped to prepare and edit. The teacher takes shortcuts too.

Ordinarily she would simply clip several mimeographed sheets together and attach a form letter. *Thank you for your interest.*

We hope these fact sheets will help you to find the information you require. Today though, looking at the round ingenuous printing, she realizes she's angry. She resents the implications of the letter: that dinosaurs are too boring to be worth much time, that she herself exists to be exploited. She resents the absence of a stamp and a return envelope. DO YOUR OWN HOMEWORK, she wants to scrawl, in red crayon across the neat blue printing. But she can't do that. Answering these letters is part of her job.

She reads the letter again, and the words float. Why is it called the Mesozoic? The correct answer, the one the teacher wants, is on the fact sheet. *Meso*, middle, *zoos*, life. After the Paleozoic, before the Cenozoic. But does the Mesozoic exist? When it did it was called nothing. The dinosaurs didn't know they were in the Mesozoic. They didn't know they were only in the middle. They didn't intend to become extinct; as far as they knew they would live forever. Perhaps she should write the truth: *The Mesozoic isn't real. It's only a word for a place you can't go to any more because it isn't there. It's called the Mesozoic because we call it that.* And risk an outraged letter from some beleaguered teacher: What sort of an answer is that?

Her hands are shaking, she needs a cigarette. She can't deal with this letter at all, right now she's devoid of answers, she knows nothing. She would like to crumple the letter and chuck it into the wastebasket, but instead she folds it neatly in two so she can't see the printing and lays it beside her typewriter. She puts on her raincoat and carefully does up the buttons and the belt.

There's some bread and cheese in her desk drawer which she intended to have for lunch but instead she'll walk up to Murray's. She'll find a single table and watch the office workers bolt their food, and the breathless, soup-spotted waitresses. She needs to get out of the Museum, if only for an hour.

Last night she fought with Nate, all-out for the first time, after the children were asleep upstairs, or possibly not asleep. That was another thing: the children were there, and it was a weeknight. They'd agreed that the children wouldn't come on weeknights, but Nate had a last-minute call from Elizabeth. Recently all her calls have been last-minute.

"Her aunt just died," Nate told her when she came in the door and found the children eating macaroni and cheese and playing Scrabble at the kitchen table. "Elizabeth felt it would be better

266

for the children to spend the night here. She doesn't want them to be upset by her own reaction."

The children did not appear unduly traumatized, and Lesje didn't believe Elizabeth was either. This was just another flank attack. She said nothing until after the children had washed the dishes and Nate had read to them and tucked them in. They were old enough to read to themselves, but Nate said it was a tradition.

When he came downstairs, he announced that he felt he should go to the funeral.

"Why?" Lesje said. The aunt was Elizabeth's, not Nate's; the funeral was none of his business.

Nate said he felt he should give Elizabeth some support. She would be brought down by the funeral, he said.

"From everything you've told me," Lesje said, "she hated that aunt."

Nate said that although this was true, the aunt had been important in Elizabeth's life. In his opinion the importance of something to someone had nothing to do with its positive qualities but only with its impact, its force, and the aunt had been a force.

"I've got news for you," Lesje said. "Elizabeth doesn't need any support. Elizabeth needs support like a nun needs tits. I've never seen anyone who needs less support than Elizabeth."

Nate said appearances were deceptive and he felt that after twelve years of marriage to her he was perhaps in a better position than Lesje to judge how much support Elizabeth needed. Elizabeth, he said, had had an unhappy childhood.

"Who didn't?" Lesje said. "Who didn't have an unhappy childhood? What's so special?" If he wanted unhappy childhoods, she'd tell him about hers. On second thought, she probably wouldn't, since the unhappiness in it had been without event. She could not, she knew, match the almost flamboyant melodrama of Elizabeth's, which Nate had conveyed to her fragment by fragment. In any competition for unhappy childhoods she would lose.

Nate said he thought they ought to keep their voices down, since they had to think of the children.

Lesje thought of the children and saw a blur. The fact was that though the children were in her house almost every weekend she could hardly tell one from the other, she so seldom looked directly at them. She did not dislike them; she was afraid of them. On their part, they had their own oblique methods. They borrowed her belts and shirts without asking, which Nate said meant they had accepted her. They mixed themselves drinks of milk and chocolate powder and ice cream and left the unwashed glasses around the house, brown scum hardening in them, for Lesje to find on Mondays or Tuesdays after they had left. Nate said she should speak to them about anything they did which she objected to, but she wasn't such a fool. If she ever really did that he would hate it. Though they were always scrupulously polite to her, as she knew they'd been told to be. By both parents no doubt. The children were not individuals, they were a collective, a word. *The children*. He thought all he had to do was say *the children* and she would shut up, like magic.

"To hell with the children," she said recklessly.

"I know you feel that way," Nate said, with patronizing resignation.

She ought to have backed down, explained that this wasn't what she meant really. She'd done it often enough before. But this time she said nothing. She was too angry. If she tried to say anything at all, it would come out in the form of her grandmother's curses: *Jesus asshole poop! I hope your bum falls off! I hope you die!*

She ran up to the bathroom, her boots crashing on the uncarpeted stairs, not caring if the children heard, and locked herself in. On the spur of the moment she'd decided to kill herself. She was amazed by this decision; she'd never considered anything remotely like it before. People like Chris had merely puzzled her. But at last she could see why Chris did it: it was this anger and the other thing, much worse, the fear of being nothing. People like Elizabeth could do that to you, blot you out; people like Nate, merely by going about their own concerns. Other people's habits could kill you. Chris hadn't died for love. He'd wanted to be an event, and he'd been one.

She knelt beside the tub, clutching the knife she'd snatched from the counter on her way past. Unfortunately it was a grapefruit knife. She would have to saw rather than slash, which wasn't the effect she'd had in mind. But the end result would be the same. Nate would break down the door, when

268

he got around to it, and find her floating in a sea of pink. Warm water, she knew, made it come out faster. He'd smell the salt, the dead bird smell. What would he do then? With her effigy, waxen and staring.

But this wasn't really what Lesje wanted to do. After a while of thinking about it she stashed the grapefruit knife in the medicine cabinet. Nate hadn't even seen her take it; otherwise he'd be up there pounding at the door. (Wouldn't he?) She was still angry though. With some deliberation, she flushed the remaining pills in her green plastic dial-a-pill dispenser down the toilet. When Nate came to bed she turned to him and put her arms around him, exactly as if she'd forgiven him. If children were the key, if having them was the only way she could stop being invisible, then she would goddamn well have some herself.

In the morning she was unrepentant. She knew she'd committed a wrong and vengeful act, an act so vengeful she could not have imagined herself doing such a thing a year ago. Surely no child conceived in such rage could come to much good. She would have a throwback, a reptile, a mutant of some kind with scales and a little horn on the snout. It's long been her theoretical opinion that Man is a danger to the universe, a mischievous ape, spiteful, destructive, malevolent. But only theoretical. Really she believed that if people could see how they were acting they would act some other way. Now she knows this isn't true.

She would not recant. Nate, ignorant of what was in store for him, ate corn flakes and made conversation. It was raining, he noted. Lesje, gnawing a bran muffin, hair falling over her face, peered out at him like Fate, sullen, gauging. When would her body strike?

"I'd just like you to realize," she said, to let him know she was still at large, had not been caged and propitiated, "that if you die Elizabeth gets your body. I'll have it sent to her in a crate. After all she's still your wife."

Nate treated this as a joke.

Winding down the stairs, hands held quiet in her raincoat pockets, she vacillates. She has a narrow pelvis, she'll die in childbirth, she knows nothing about children, what about her job? Even with Nate working part time they can't afford it. It isn't too late, nothing can have happened so soon. She'll crack open another package, take two pills and a hot bath, and everything will go on as before.

But then she thinks: Not this time. She wants no more encounters, spurious or otherwise, with the grapefruit knife.

Under the golden dome, head down, steering for the door, she feels a touch on her arm: Nate, she hopes, bringing reconciliation, capitulation, a graceful way out. But instead it is William. "I just happened to be in the Museum," he says, "and I thought I'd look you up."

Lesje knows perfectly well that William never just happens to be anywhere, much less the Museum. Wonderful, transparent William, easy to read as a phone book, everything in alphabetical order. He has something to say to her, therefore he's come to say it. He didn't telephone first because he knew she might refuse to see him. Quite right, she would have. But now she smiles, she grins.

"I was just going up to Murray's for some lunch," she says. She will not alter anything for William.

William, although he thinks Murray's is grubby and the food will give you cancer of the colon, says that in that case does she mind if he joins her? Not at all, Lesje says, and it's true, she doesn't mind. William is now safely in the past. She walks beside him, air filling her bones. It's pure joy to be with someone who cannot affect her.

Lesje has a chopped egg sandwich and a cigarette. William has a Western. What he feels, he says, dabbing buttery crumbs, is that enough time has gone by and he would just like her to know that he realizes he didn't behave very well, at the end, if she knows what he means. His blue eyes regard her candidly, his pink cheeks glow.

Lesje does not mistake this verbal construction of William's for true repentance. Rather it's an entry on William's balance sheet, that balance sheet required by London, Ontario, that little page William carries around in his head on which everything must eventually tot up right. One attempted rape, one apology. But

Lesje by now is willing to accept a convention of decency. Once she would have demanded sincerity.

"I guess nobody behaved very well," she says.

William is relieved, and glances at his watch. He will stay another ten minutes, she calculates, doing the thing properly. He has not really wanted to see her. Right now he's thinking about something else and she finds, trying to guess, that she does not know what it is.

She cups her hand across her face, watches him through the smoke. It dismays her that she can no longer judge William as easily, as glibly as she once could. What she wants to ask him is: Have you changed? Have you learned anything? She herself feels she has learned more than she ever intended to, more than she wants. Does he find her different?

She studies his face: perhaps it is thinner. She can't remember. And those sky-blue eyes, they are not the eyes of a Caucasian doll, a hat mannequin, as she'd once thought.

William sits opposite her, drinking water from a Murray's glass with a trace of lipstick on the rim. His fingers hold the glass, his other hand lies on the table, his neck comes out of his shirt collar, which is light green, and on top of that is his head. His eyes are blue and he has two of them. This is the sum total of William in the present tense.

ELIZABETH

Elizabeth, hatless but with gloves, is standing in one of the more desirable districts of the Mount Pleasant Cemetery. Near the old family mausoleums, Eaton's Department Stores, Weston's Biscuits; not, heaven forbid, in the newer parts with their adolescent trees or in the strange surburban areas of square flat stones with Chinese markings or ornate monuments with plastic-encased photos beside the names.

Two men are shoveling earth onto Auntie Muriel, who, although she's incinerated all the members of her immediate family she could get her hands on, has chosen to have herself lowered more or less intact into the earth. A roll of green pseudo-sod stands ready to cover the unpleasantly exposed brown earth once Auntie Muriel is safely tamped down.

Elizabeth's hair blows in the warm breeze. It's a fine spring day, which is too bad; Auntie Muriel, she is sure, would have preferred a heavy drizzle. But even Auntie Muriel cannot arrange the weather from beyond the grave.

Though she's managed to arrange almost every other detail of her own funeral and interment. Full instructions were in her will, composed before her death, when she was finally, irrevocably, dying. Her coffin and plot had been bought and paid for. Her wardrobe, including the underwear, had been meticulously selected and laid aside, Scotch-taped in tissue paper. ("It's an old dress," Elizabeth can imagine her saying. "No sense burying a good one.") She'd vetoed beautification of her corpse as a waste of money and had opted for a closed coffin. She'd even selected the hymns and Bible readings for the service. They'd been enclosed in a separate sealed envelope, addressed to the church. Elizabeth, knowing this, felt she was hearing Auntie Muriel's own voice, intransigent as ever, projecting itself through the mouths of the gathered mourners.

Timothy Eaton had found itself embarrassed by Auntie

Muriel. In death as doubtless in life, Elizabeth thought, listening to the diffident voice of the young man who had phoned her. "It's about the service," he said. "I'm wondering whether you might consider some changes. The selections are a little incongruous."

"Of course," Elizabeth said.

"Good," said the man. "Perhaps we could meet and go over . . ."

"I mean, of course they're incongruous," Elizabeth said. "Didn't you know her? What did you expect? Let the old reptile get what she wants. She always did in life." They were inheriting the loot; the least they could do was go through with it, whatever it was.

She thought the man would be offended – she was intending to be offensive – but she was almost sure she heard a snicker at the other end of the line.

"Very well, Mrs. Schoenhof," the voice said. "We'll charge ahead."

Nevertheless, Elizabeth had been unprepared when the organ burst forth with the opening hymn: " Jesus Christ Is Risen Today." Was it the old beast letting everyone know she considered herself immortal, or was it just something Auntie Muriel had stuck in because she happened to like it? She glanced around at the surprisingly large group of mourners, old fellow-parishioners, distant relatives: they were singing, gamely though uneasily. After the hymn the minister cleared his throat, rotated his shoulders like a diver warming up, then launched into the Bible reading.

" 'How much she hath glorified herself, and lived deliciously, so much torment and sorrow give her: for she saith in her heart, I sit a queen, and am no widow, and shall see no sorrow. And the kings of the earth, who have committed fornication and lived deliciously with her, shall bewail her, and lament for her, when they shall see the smoke of her burning.' "

He was doing his best, rolling the r's and acting as if he knew what was going on, but a puzzled whispering rose from the congregation. Auntie Muriel was verging on bad taste. She should have chosen something more conventional, grass withering and passing away, everlasting mercy. But fornication, at a funeral? Elizabeth remembered the young minister they'd sacked, with his hot-coal eyes and his fondness for blood-hued

273

suns and rending veils. Perhaps they suspected Auntie Muriel of being one of the same kind, hidden all these years in their midst. Possibly not entirely sane: look at the sister, the niece.

Elizabeth had little doubt that this was a personal message aimed directly at her: Auntie Muriel's last word on the subject of her mother, fiery death and all, and probably on herself as well. She could imagine Auntie Muriel poring through the Bible, bifocals on the end of her nose, searching for the right verses: scathing, punitive, self-righteous. The joke was that the congregation didn't realize this. Knowing their habits of mind, Elizabeth felt it was likely they thought Auntie Muriel was repenting, even confessing, in some bizarre way. To a secret life of delicious living.

" 'Therefore shall her plagues come in one day, death, and mourning, and famine; and she shall be utterly burned with fire: for strong is the Lord God who judgeth her." ' The minister shut the Bible and looked up apologetically, and everyone relaxed.

Auntie Muriel had not composed her own eulogy, which laid heavy stress on the words *dedication* and *generosity*. Everyone knew what that meant. Elizabeth let her eyes wander, over to the familiar bronze dead of World War One, then to the other wall. READY TO EVERY GOOD WORK. Some female Eaton or other.

But at the final hymn Elizabeth nearly disgraced herself by laughing out loud. Auntie Muriel had chosen "Away in a Manger," and the faces around Elizabeth shifted rapidly from bewilderment to panic. Voices faltered and stopped, and Elizabeth dropped her face into her cupped hands and snorted. She hoped these snorts would be mistaken for grief.

"Mother, stop laughing," Janet hissed. But though she kept her mouth closed, Elizabeth could not stop. When the hymn ended and she could raise her head again, she was astonished to see that a number of people were crying. She wondered what they were mourning: it could not possibly be Auntie Muriel.

The children are attached to her hands, Janet on the right, Nancy on the left. They're wearing their white knee socks and Mary Janes: Janet's idea, since these were what they wore to visit Auntie Muriel. Janet is weeping decorously; she knows this is what you do at funerals. Nancy is looking around, her head swiveling unabashed. "What's that, Mum? Why is he doing that?"

274

Elizabeth herself is dry-eyed and feels slightly giddy. There is still laughter in her throat. Was the service the result of premature senility, or could it be that Auntie Muriel at last had been making a joke? Perhaps she'd planned it for years, that moment of helpless astonishment; gloated over it, picturing the faces of her old associates as they realized that she might be other than what she seemed. Elizabeth doubts it, but hopes so. Now that Auntie Muriel is actually dead, she is free to restructure her closer to her own requirements; also, she would like to find something in her to approve.

Nate is there, on the other side of the grave. He kept apart from them during the service; perhaps he didn't want to intrude. He looks across at Elizabeth now and she smiles at him. It was sweet of him to think of coming; she didn't ask him to. Sweet but not necessary. It occurs to her that Nate in general is not necessary. He can be there or not. Elizabeth blinks, and Nate vanishes; she blinks again and he reappears. She finds herself able to be grateful for his presence. She knows well enough that her momentary gratitude may not lead to anything and will evaporate the next time he's late picking up the children. Nevertheless, that war is over. *Dismissed.*

"I'm going over to see Dad," Nancy whispers, letting go of Elizabeth's hand. Nancy wants the excuse to walk quite near the grave and get a closer look at the men shoveling; but also she wants to be with her father. Elizabeth smiles and nods.

Hilarity is draining from her, leaving her shaky. She's finding it difficult to believe that Auntie Muriel, now shriveled, boxed, dirted over and done with, actually did all the harmful, even devastating things she remembers her doing. Possibly Elizabeth has exaggerated, invented; but why would she invent Auntie Muriel? Anyway, Auntie Muriel really was like that; Elizabeth should know, she's got the scars.

Why then can she suddenly not bear to see Auntie Muriel being merged, leveled, as if she's a flower plot? Prettied over. "She was awful," Elizabeth wants to say, testify. "She was *awful.*" Auntie Muriel was a phenomenon, like a two-headed calf or Niagara Falls. She would like to bear witness to this fact. She wants it admired; she doesn't want it diminished or glossed over.

275

Auntie Muriel is out of sight now, and the older mourners are beginning to shift, fade away toward their cars. Their scarves and the wreaths flutter.

Elizabeth would like to leave now too, but she can't: Auntie Muriel's death is not yet complete for her. She didn't sing at the funeral or join in the prayers. If she opened her mouth, she felt, something disreputable would come out. But she has to say something, some word of dismissal, before the green rug is finally installed. *Rest in peace* seems inappropriate. Auntie Muriel had nothing to do with rest or peace.

"Ancestral voices prophesying war," she hears herself murmuring.

Janet looks up at her, frowning. Elizabeth smiles absently; she's searching her head for the source. *A stately pleasure dome.* They'd had to memorize the whole thing in Grade Eleven. Where Alph the sacred river ran, something about caverns, down to a sunless sea. She remembers the teacher, a Miss Macleod, who had frizzy white hair and talked about fairies, revolving in a circle with her eyes closed. *Those caves of ice.*

Except for the shovels, it's very quiet. The cloudy green of the trees stretches into the distance, spongy, soft as gauze, there's nothing to push against, hold on to. A black vacuum sucks at her, there's a wind, a slow roar. Still clutching Janet's hand, Elizabeth falls through space. It's Nate who picks her up. "All right now?" he says. He rubs clumsily at the mud on her coat.

"Don't do that," Elizabeth says. "I'll get it dry cleaned."

Now that she's obviously still alive, Nancy decides it's safe to cry. Janet, exasperated, asks Nate if he's got any liquor on him; to revive her, Elizabeth assumes. For once he doesn't, and for Janet this is the last straw. Her parents are graceless, and incompetent as well. She turns her back.

"I'm perfectly all right," Elizabeth says. It maddens her, this need everyone has to be told she's all right. She isn't, she's frightened. She's done other things but she's never blacked out like this before. She foresees a future of sudden power failures, keeling over on the subway, at intersections, with no one to drag her out of the way. Falling down stairs. She decides to have her blood sugar tested. The old ladies, those that are left, regard her with friendly interest. As far as they're concerned this is exactly what she should have done.

The two men are lifting the carpet of green plastic grass, unrolling it. The funeral is over now, she can take the children home.

Instead of riding back in the undertaker's car, to the funeral parlor or the church where coffee and cake will be served, they'll walk to the subway. At home they'll change their clothes and she'll make them something. Peanut butter sandwiches.

It suddenly amazes her that she is able to do this, something this simple. How close has she come, how many times, to doing what Chris did? More important: what stopped her? Was that his power over her, that piece of outer space he'd carried, locked in the pressures of his body until the final explosion? She remembers a high-school game she'd heard about but never played: *chicken*. They would drive to the bluffs, race their cars, heading for the long drop to the lake, trying not to be the first to brake. Standing in the sunlight, she feels the horrified relief of someone who has stopped just in time to watch an opponent topple in slow motion over the edge.

But she's still alive, she wears clothes, she walks around, she holds down a job even. She has two children. Despite the rushing of wind, the summoning voices she can hear from underground, the dissolving trees, the chasms that open at her feet; and will always from time to time open. She has no difficulty seeing the visible world as a transparent veil or a whirlwind. The miracle is to make it solid.

She thinks with anticipation of her house, her quiet living room with its empty bowls, pure grace, her kitchen table. Her house is not perfect; parts of it are in fact crumbling, most noticeably the front porch. But it's a wonder that she has a house at all, that she's managed to accomplish a house. Despite the wreckage. She's built a dwelling over the abyss, but where else was there to build it? So far, it stands.

NATE

Nate sits on a folding wooden chair behind a card table, on the east side of Yonge Street a block south of Shuter Street. The afternoon sun beats down on his head. He shades his eyes with his hand; he should have worn sunglasses. He wishes he could drink beer, just one can anyway of Molson's tucked between his feet, a quick lift to the mouth. But it wouldn't look good.

Across the street the intestinal tubing of the Eaton's Center festoons itself over walls and stairways. Shoppers enter and leave, legs brisk, faces thrust forward, intent on small lusts, small consummations of their own. Those on his side of the street are less hopeful. Old men with the shuffle of the perennially drunk, youths with armless black T-shirts cinched into their jeans by studded belts, their arms tattooed; pasty office workers in summer suits whose pinkish eyes evade his own; disgruntled women with fat ankles and scuffed shoes, their fingers locked on shopping bags. Few smile. Some scowl, but most are blank-faced, keeping their muscular twitches of anger or joy for safer, more private moments.

Nate fixes each approaching pedestrian with what he hopes is a compelling stare: *Your Country Needs* You. Most glance at the sign propped on the table and quicken their pace, trying to get past before he can rope them into anything upsetting, any commitment. RCMP WRONGDOING, the sign says, rapping the Mounties lightly across the knuckles. CORRUPTION or, even better, SIN, would have brought more money.

Some pause and he hands them leaflets. Occasionally he gets a nibble of interest and goes into his spiel. He's collecting signatures on a petition, he says; surely they are opposed to RCMP Wrongdoing? He mentions mail-opening but leaves out barn-burning and office-wrecking in Québec. Most people have no barns or offices and are indifferent or hostile towards Québec, but they do have mail. To show their seriousness, signers of the

278

petition are being asked to contribute a dollar each to a fund which will be used to further the campaign.

Nate speaks quietly, without undue fervor. Anything like fanaticism must be avoided. He's supposed to represent the average decent-minded citizen. But knows he does not. It gives him a wry satisfaction that most of those who have so far responded with any enthusiasm have come from the ranks of the black-shirted youths, obvious dope-pushers, fences and petty thieves. At any moment he expects to see a client or a former client among them.

"Jail the bastards," one says. "Bust into my place last weekend and went through it like a goddamn chainsaw. Didn't find nothing on me though."

He wonders what his mother would make of this phenomenon, concludes she would not be offended or even surprised. "A signature is a signature," she would say. Will say next weekend, when her capable buttocks will rest squarely on this very chair, her feet in their sensible crepe-soled shoes hold down this sidewalk.

It should have been her today, but she twisted her ankle at the hospital. "A twist, not a sprain," she'd said on the phone. "They're very short of volunteers, otherwise I wouldn't ask you. I've never asked you before."

This isn't true, she has asked him before. Pieces for Peace, rescue the Korean poet, ban the bomb. It's just that he's never agreed to do anything before. He wonders why, this time, he has. Not that this enterprise is any more likely to succeed than her other enterprises. But collecting signatures against RCMP Wrongdoing does not at the moment seem any more futile than most other things in his life.

A middle-aged man scans the leaflet, then thrusts it towards Nate as if it's hot, glancing behind him. "I'll give you a dollar," he whispers, "but I can't sign my name." He has an accent, not French, not Italian. Nate thanks him and stashes the dollar in the cash box. More people than he would have imagined seem to think they'll be in deep shit if they sign their names. The Mounties will get hold of them, whip the bottoms of their feet with dog whips, apply electric hair-curling machines to their genital organs; at the very least, open their mail.

Nate doubts it; he doubts that the Mounties even care. Nothing like that will happen here, not yet. Which is probably why he's

279

never done anything like this before. It's too safe. He's held out for some overwhelming choice, danger, his life on the line; a careless laugh, eyes shining, death one false step away. Instead he broils in the August sun, wheedles strangers, lights another cigarette to combat the exhaust fumes from the street.

When he went upstairs to the office to collect his stack of leaflets, they greeted him like the prodigal son. Three women in wrinkled summer dresses shot from their cubbyholes to shake his hand; his mother was a wonder, they said, so much energy, he must be proud. The director invited him into his brownish office, its desk stacked waist-high with grimy papers: letters, forms, old newspaper clippings. Nate explained about the twisted ankle and made it as clear as he could without being rude that he was merely temporary, a substitute. There seemed no need to add that he finds the petition a kind of joke. It's supposed to go to the Prime Minister, who will doubtless make paper airplanes with it. Why not? He's read the letters to the editor, he knows that most people will allow six million Québeckers, Pakistanis, union leaders and transvestites to have their fingernails pulled out rather than admit that the paint is chipped on the bright red musical Mountie of their dreams.

Possibly the director himself knows it's a joke. He was grinning at something. He'd smiled like a clown penny bank, white teeth slightly open and acquisitive, his blandness deceptive. His eyes above his apple cheeks were shrewd and in that gaze Nate had squirmed. They all acted as if he is in truth what he's spent so much effort to avoid becoming: his mother's son. Which maybe he is.

But not only, not only. He refuses to be defined. He's not shut, time carries him on, other things may happen. By his elbow is this morning's *Globe*, which he hopes to scan later when the stream of prospects thins. Perhaps there will finally be some news. A small part of him still waits, still expects, longs for a message, a messenger; as he sits in his booth proclaiming to others a message he suspects is a joke.

At four o'clock his replacement, a German Catholic theologian, he's been told, will arrive and grip his hand earnestly as if he is indeed a kindred spirit. Nate, embarrassed, will leave the booth and join the walkers, those homeward bound, those merely wandering; he will lose himself among the apathetic, the fatalistic, the uncommitted, the cynical; among whom he would like to feel at home.

LESJE

Uniformed in her lab coat Lesje descends, winding around the totem pole on her way to the basement. She isn't doing lab work today but she wears the lab coat anyway. It makes her feel she belongs here. She does belong here.

She remembers the way she once followed with her eyes those others she used to glimpse on her Saturday excursions, men and women but especially the women, walking purposefully along the corridors or whisking through the doors marked STAFF ONLY. Then she'd seen their lab coats as badges, of nationality, membership of some kind. She'd wanted so much to be able to go through those doors: secrets, wonders even, lay beyond. Now she has keys, she can go almost anywhere, she's familiar with the jumble-sale pieces of rock, the fragments, the dust-covered bundles of unsorted papers. Secrets perhaps but no wonders. Still, this is the only place she wants to work. Once there had been nothing equally important to her, but there is still nothing more important. This is the only membership she values.

She will not give it up. Fists jammed into her lab-coat pockets, she paces the basement floor, among the cases of mannequin Indians in their stolen ceremonial clothes, the carved masks, joyous, fearful. She walks briskly, as if she knows where she's going; but in fact she's soothing herself, running the Museum through her head once more, room by familiar room, a litany of objects. How soon will it be before she will never see it again?

Sometimes she thinks of the Museum as a repository of knowledge, the resort of scholars, a palace built in the pursuit of truth, with inadequate air conditioning but still a palace. At other times it's a bandits'cave: the past has been vandalized and this is where the loot is stored. Whole chunks of time lie here, golden and frozen; she is one of the guardians, the only guardian, without her the whole edifice would melt like a jellyfish on the beach, there would be no past. She knows it's really the other way around, that without the past she would not exist. Still, she must hold on somehow to her own importance. She's threatened, she's greedy. If she has to she'll lock herself into one of these cases, hairy mask on her face, she'll stow away, they'll never get her out.

Will they ask her to leave? Resign. She doesn't know. A pregnant paleontologist is surely a contradiction in terms. Her business is the naming of bones, not the creation of flesh. The fact is that she's missed her period twice in a row. Which could be what they call *strain*. She hasn't yet gone for tests, for confirmation, she hasn't thought past the fact. She will be an unwed mother. Of course that is becoming more common, but what will Dr. Van Vleet, a gentleman of the old school who demonstrably does not live in the year 1978, do then?

And what will Nate do, what will she do? It's hard to believe that such a negligible act of hers can have measurable consequences for other people, even such a small number of them. Though the past is the sediment from such acts, billions, trillions of them.

She's not used to being a cause, of anything at all. On her office wall the tree of evolution branches like coral towards the ceiling: Fishes, Amphibians, Therapsids, Thecodonts, Archosaurs, Pterosaurs, Birds, Mammals and Man, a mere dot. And herself another, and within her another. Which will exfoliate in its turn.

Or not; she's thought about that. She could have an abortion, stop time. She knows it's easier than it used to be. She hasn't yet told Nate, she doesn't need to tell him. Everything could go on as before. Which is not what she wants.

She can't tell whether he will be delighted or angry or despairing; possibly, considering his feelings about his two other children, he will be all three. But whatever his reaction is, she knows her final decision will not be based on it. Nate has been displaced, if only slightly, from the center of the universe.

She climbs the back stairs and walks forward through European Costumes, skirting the Chinese Peasant Art Exhibit, which doesn't much interest her. As she rounds the corner towards the main staircase, she glimpses a square dark figure on the floor above. It's Elizabeth. Elizabeth doesn't see her. She's looking over the balustrade, out over the rotunda. Lesje has almost never seen Elizabeth like this, unconscious. It's as if she's seeing her on the last day of her life. Lesje isn't used to this; she's used to thinking of Elizabeth as permanent, like an icon. But Elizabeth standing by herself, unconnected with anyone, is shorter, worn, ordinary; mortal. The lines of her face and body slope down. Even though she knows her own pregnancy will cut no ice with Elizabeth, may even make her delay the divorce as long as possible, to prove something – what? That she's first wife? – Lesje can't remember why she has been afraid of her.

Will they still be doing this in twenty years? Older women, old women, wearing black and not speaking; ill-wishing; never seeing each other, but each keeping the other locked in her head, a secret area of darkness like a tumor or the black vortex at the center of a target. Someday they may be grandmothers. It occurs to her, a new idea, that this tension between the two of them is a difficulty for the children. They ought to stop.

Still, she doesn't feel like going through the charade of nodding and smiling; not right now. She ducks into the open elevator and is carried up.

She enters the Gallery of Vertebrate Evolution the wrong way, past the EXIT sign. She's feeling slightly dizzy, probably because she hasn't eaten all day. Too much coffee. She sits down on the padded ledge that separates the pedestrians from the dinosaurs. She longs to smoke a cigarette in the soothing Cretaceous dusk before walking out into the blast-furnace of the afternoon, but she knows about the fire hazard. Instead she'll just rest. It's warm here also, too warm, but at least it's dark.

Here are her old acquaintances, familiar to her as pet rabbits: Allosaurus, the carnivore, parrot-beaked Chasmosaurus, Parasaurolophus with its deer-antler crest. They're merely bones, bones and wire in a scenery of dusty plastic, and she's an adult; why does she continue to think of them as alive?

When she was much younger she used to believe, or try hard to believe, that at night when the Museum was closed the things inside it carried on a hidden life of their own; if she could only find her way inside she would be able to watch. Later she

283

abandoned this daydream in favor of a less extravagant one: the things were silent and unmoving, true, but somewhere there existed an implement or force (a secret ray, atomic energy) that would bring them back to life. Childish plots, based no doubt on the odd science-fiction comic book or on that Christmas matinée of *The Nutcracker Suite* she'd been dragged to when they'd decided, so disastrously, that she should take ballet.

Now, however, looking up at the immense skulls towering above her in the dim light, the gigantic spines and claws, she almost expects these creatures of hers to reach down their fingers in friendly greeting. Though if they were really alive they'd run away or tear her apart. Bears, however, dance to music; so do snakes. What if she were to press the buttons on the filmstrips and, instead of the usual speeches or the cries of walruses and seals used to simulate the underwater voices of the marine reptiles, some unknown song were to emerge? Indian music, droning, hypnotic. *Try to imagine,* says the brochure she wrote, a guide for parents and teachers, *what it would be like if suddenly the dinosaurs came to life.*

She'd like to; she'd like to sit here for an hour and do nothing else. She'd close her eyes and one after another the fossils would lift their ponderous feet, moving off along the grove of resurrected trees, flesh coalescing like ice or mist around them. They'd dance stumpily down the stairs of the Museum and out the front door. Eight-foot horsetails would sprout in Queen's Park, the sun would turn orange. She'd throw in some giant dragonflies, some white and yellow flowers, a lake. She'd move among the foliage, at home, an expedition of one.

But she can't do it. Either she's lost faith or she's too tired; at any rate she can no longer concentrate. The fragments of new images intrude. She looks down at the pebbles, the bark chips, the dusty cycad trees on the other side of the ledge, a thousand miles away.

In the foreground, pushing in whether she wants it to or not, is what Marianne would call her life. It's possible she's blown it. This is what they mean when they say *maturity*: you get to the point where you think you've blown your life. She should have learned more, in advance, she should have studied more before jumping in; but she isn't sorry.

True, there's a chance she's done a stupid thing. Several,

284

many. Or she may have done a wise thing for a stupid reason. She will tell Nate today, this evening. Will he forgive her?

(Forgiveness is not what she needs; not, anyway, from Nate. She would prefer instead to forgive, someone, somehow, for something; but she isn't sure where to begin.)

NATE

Nate is running. He jogs up University, against the traffic, the sun glinting on the roofs and windshields of the oncoming cars, beating on his head. The blood in his ears is a gong, he heats like metal, the sidewalk thumps relentlessly against the soles of his feet. He tugs at his blue-striped shirt, neat citizen's shirt for the collection of signatures, pulls it loose from the waist of his cords, lets it flap behind him. There's a muggy wind which smells of garages and spilled oil.

At the Parliament Buildings he waits for a gap in traffic, sprints across, continues, under the porte-cochère, along beside the pinkish stone which used to be dingy brown before they sandblasted it. One day he may go into politics, he's thought about it. Provincial, not municipal. Not federal, he has no yen for exile. But not yet, not yet.

His shadow paces him, thin and pinheaded, stretching away to his right, a blackness flickering over the grass. A premonition, always with him; his own eventual death. Which he will think about some other time.

He should pay more attention though, at least try. A regular schedule would do him good. Up at six, run for half an hour in the morning mists before the exhaust fumes get too bad. Then a frugal breakfast, watch the eggs and butter, cut down to a pack a day. With every drink a brain cell dies. Luckily there are billions of them; it will take him a while to go senile. If he could run he'd feel better, he could take hold, he knows it. Same time every day, on and on forever.

Right now he's not going to make it around. Sweat drenches him, his breath rasps in his throat, oxygen sharpens all the edges. There's nothing he will do forever. He heads for the War Memorial, halfway, but throws himself down on the grass before he reaches it, rolling onto his back. Small dots swim in the amniotic blue; rods and cones, black stars in his head. Beneath

286

him grass strains upwards.

He'd like to be able to take Lesje somewhere, out into the country, the country which surely lies all around, though he can't remember the last time he was there. But how would they get there? A bus, a walk along some uncharted and dusty gravel road? Never mind. They could make love, slowly and gently, under some trees or in a field, gold waving over them and the smell of crushed grass. The possible day shimmers ahead of him, an oval of light; in this light Lesje is indistinct, her features shine and blur, her dark hair melts in his hands, her body extended white and lean on the grass shifts itself, glows, fades. It's as if he's too close to her to be able to see her, fix her in his mind. When he's away from her he can barely remember what she looks like.

Though he can see Elizabeth distinctly, every line and shadow. He used to take Elizabeth out into the country, before Janet was born, before he sold the car. But she didn't want to climb fences and crawl under bushes and he'd lacked the trick of persuading her. Instead they went to auctions, farm sales, families giving up or too old who were selling off their belongings. Elizabeth did the bidding, kitchen chairs, bundles of spoons, while he stood at the soft drink and hot-dog stand, hands in his pockets fingering pennies, keys, feeling out of place, a scavenger.

He thinks of Elizabeth, briefly, with detachment. For a moment she's someone he once knew. He wonders what has become of her. It's the walks they never took, the fields he could never convince her to enter he regrets now.

He sits, takes off his damp shirt and wipes his head and chest with it, then spreads it beside him for the sun to dry. He's chilly now despite the heat. In a few minutes, when he gets his breath, he'll light a cigarette and smoke it. Perhaps he'll throw half of it away. Then he'll stand up and put his shirt back on. He'll wait for a gap in the traffic and run across the road, lightly, on the balls of his feet.

He'll walk north, past the Planetarium and its hoarding, which he can see from here. THE PLANETARIUM IS STILL OPEN. They're adding a wing to the Museum; Lesje says it's none too soon. ROM *Wasn't Built In A Day*, says the plywood wall,

287

punning on the Museum's name, pleading for money. Another worthy cause. They'll suck him dry, despite his sawdust heart.

He'll climb the steps and lean in the same spot where he used to do time for Elizabeth, one shoulder against the stone. He'll light another cigarette, watch the museum-goers passing in and out like shoppers, and wait for Lesje. She won't be expecting him. Perhaps she'll be surprised and pleased to see him; once he could count on it. Perhaps she'll only be surprised, and possibly not even that. He anticipates this moment, which he cannot predict, which leaves room for hope and also for disaster. They will either go for a drink or not. In any case, they will go home.

ELIZABETH

Elizabeth stands looking at a picture. The picture is framed and glassed. Behind the glass, bright green leaves spread with the harmonious asymmetry of a Chinese floral rug; purple fruits glow among them. Three women, two with baskets, are picking. Their teeth shine within their smiles, their cheeks are plump and rosy as a doll's. *A Fine Crop of Eggplants*, the caption says, in Chinese, English and French. Elizabeth reminds herself to pick up some hot dogs on the way home, the children's request, and for herself cooked chicken. They'll sit on the front porch, Nancy's idea of a picnic. Perhaps by then it will be cooler.

A man in overalls, pushing a large floor-polishing machine, reaches Elizabeth's corner and tells her to move. She walks along the wall. It's just after closing time and most people have left the Museum. She's been waiting for this comparative emptiness to take a close look at the exhibit, which opened four days ago, but which she's been too busy to see. She's pleased with the press coverage, though. China is news, unlike, for instance, India, which was news several years ago, during that war. And the crowds have been good, though of course not as good as the long lineups they had for *The Art of Ancient China* exhibit a few years ago. People will stand in line for quite a long time to see gold, especially gold unearthed from tombs. Elizabeth still remembers the horses; those fierce-toothed horses from some Emperor's grave. They weren't gold; she can't remember what they were made of, but keeps an impression of darkness. An omen, a catastrophe, rearing up, bearing down.

There is no catastrophe in these paintings, however. *The New Look of Our Piggery*, Elizabeth reads. She's not much interested in pigs. These pigs are like toys, like the plastic pigs from the farm set the children still play with occasionally. They're discreet and neat and evidently they don't root or shit. Squashes and pumpkins grow like decorative borders between the rows of sties.

289

The floor polisher is following her. She crosses over, turns the corner into the second aisle. The paintings are hung on movable screens which divide the gallery. They've done a good job setting up the exhibit, she thinks; the life-size black and white photos of the actual artists add a nice touch. She can remember when this whole section was used to display medieval armour and weapons: crossbows, maces, halberds, inlaid blunderbusses, muskets. Only the parquet floor remains the same.

Do Not Allow Lin Piao and Confucius to Slander Women, she reads, and smiles. *Everyone Helps in Building Each Others' Houses.*

Suddenly Elizabeth feels, not lonely, but single, alone. She can't remember the last time anyone other than her children helped her to do something. She knows it rains in China, even though it does not rain in these pictures. She knows the people there do not invariably smile, do not all have such white teeth and rosy cheeks. Underneath the poster-paint colors, primary as a child's painting, there is malice, greed, despair, hatred, death. How could she not know that? China is not paradise; paradise does not exist. Even the Chinese know it, they must know it, they live there. Like cavemen, they paint not what they see but what they want.

Persimmons Are Ripe at the Foot of Mount Chungman, she reads. Orange-yellow globes crowd the page; among the interwoven branches girls climb, happy faces peer, bright and uniformly patterned as birds. Elizabeth blinks back tears: foolishness, to be moved by this. This is propaganda. She does not want to line up and learn to throw grenades, she doesn't want to work a threshing machine, she has no desire to undergo group criticism and have a lot of other people tell her what to think. This isn't what touches her so that she's fumbling in her purse now for a Kleenex, a scrap of paper, anything she can use to blot her face. It's the turnips in their innocent rows, ordinary, lit from within, the praise lavished on mere tomatoes, the bunches of grapes, painted in all their translucent hues. As if they are worth it.

Elizabeth dabs at her nose. If she wants to see grapes she can go the supermarket. She has to go there anyway, since there's nothing in the house for dinner.

China does not exist. Nevertheless she longs to be there.

CAT'S EYE

MARGARET ATWOOD

This book is for S.

The paintings and other modern works of art in this book do not exist. Nevertheless, they have been influenced by visual artists Joyce Wieland, Jack Chambers, Charles Pachter, Erica Heron, Gail Geltner, Dennis Burton, Louis de Niverville, Heather Cooper, William Kurelek, Greg Curnoe and pop-surreal potter Lenore M. Atwood, among others; and by the Isaacs Gallery, the old original.

The physics and cosmology sideswiped herein are indebted to Paul Davies, Carl Sagan, John Gribbin and Stephen W. Hawking, for their entrancing books on these subjects, and to my nephew, David Atwood, for his enlightening remarks about strings.

Many thanks to Graeme Gibson, for undergoing this novel; to my agent, Phoebe Larmore; to my English agents, Vivienne Schuster and Vanessa Holt; to my editors and publishers, Nan Talese, Nancy Evans, Ellen Seligman, Adrienne Clarkson, Avi Bennett, Liz Calder and Anna Porter; and to my indefatigable assistant, Melanie Dugan; as well as to gnomes and wizards Donya Peroff, Michael Bradley, Alison Parker, Gary Foster, Cathy Gill, Kathy Minialoff, Fanny Silberman, Coleen Quinn, Rosie Abella, C. M. Sanders, Gene Goldberg, John Gallagher and Dorothy Goulbourne.

When the Tukanas cut off her head, the old woman collected her own blood in her hands and blew it towards the sun. "My soul enters you too!" she shouted. Since then anyone who kills receives in his body, without wanting or knowing it, the soul of his victim.

— Eduardo Galeano, *Memory of Fire: Genesis*

Why do we remember the past, and not the future?

— Stephen W. Hawking, *A Brief History of Time*

Contents

I
Iron Lung

1

Time is not a line but a dimension, like the dimensions of space. If you can bend space you can bend time also, and if you knew enough and could move faster than light you could travel backwards in time and exist in two places at once.

It was my brother Stephen who told me that, when he wore his ravelling maroon sweater to study in and spent a lot of time standing on his head so that the blood would run down into his brain and nourish it. I didn't understand what he meant, but maybe he didn't explain it very well. He was already moving away from the imprecision of words.

But I began then to think of time as having a shape, something you could see, like a series of liquid transparencies, one laid on top of another. You don't look back along time but down through it, like water. Sometimes this comes to the surface, sometimes that, sometimes nothing. Nothing goes away.

2

"Stephen says time is not a line," I say. Cordelia rolls her eyes, as I knew she would.

"So?" she says. This answer pleases both of us. It puts the nature of time in its place, and also Stephen, who calls us "the teenagers", as if he himself is not one.

Cordelia and I are riding on the streetcar, going downtown, as we do on winter Saturdays. The streetcar is muggy with twice-breathed air and the smell of wool. Cordelia sits with nonchalance, nudging me with her elbow now and then, staring blankly at the other people with her grey-green eyes, opaque and glinting as metal. She can outstare anyone, and I am almost as good. We're impervious, we scintillate, we are thirteen.

We wear long wool coats with tie belts, the collars turned up to look like those of movie stars, and rubber boots with the tops folded down and men's work socks inside. In our pockets are stuffed the kerchiefs our mothers make us wear but that we take off as soon as we're out of their sight. We scorn head-coverings. Our mouths are tough, crayon-red, shiny as nails. We think we are friends.

On the streetcars there are always old ladies, or we think of them as old. They're of various kinds. Some are respectably dressed, in tailored Harris tweed coats and matching gloves and tidy no-nonsense hats with small brisk feathers jauntily at one side. Others are poorer and foreign-looking and have dark shawls wound over their heads and around their shoulders. Others are bulgy, dumpy, with clamped self-righteous mouths, their arms festooned with shopping bags; these we associate with sales, with bargain basements. Cordelia can tell cheap cloth at a glance. "Gabardine," she says. "Ticky-tack."

Then there are the ones who have not resigned themselves, who still try for an effect of glamour. There aren't many of these, but they stand out. They wear scarlet outfits or purple ones, and dangly earrings, and hats that look like stage props. Their slips show at the bottoms of their skirts, slips of unusual, suggestive colours. Anything other than white is suggestive. They have hair dyed straw-blonde or baby-blue, or, even more startling against their papery skins, a lustreless old-fur-coat black. Their lipstick mouths are too big around their mouths, their rouge blotchy, their eyes drawn screw-jiggy around their real eyes. These are the ones most likely to talk to themselves. There's one who says "mutton, mutton," over and over again like a song, another who pokes at our legs with her umbrella and says "bare naked."

This is the kind we like best. They have a certain gaiety to them, a power of invention, they don't care what people think. They have escaped, though what it is they've escaped from isn't clear to us. We think that their bizarre costumes, their verbal tics, are chosen, and that when the time comes we also will be free to choose.

"That's what I'm going to be like," says Cordelia. "Only I'm going to have a yappy Pekinese, and chase kids off my lawn. I'm going to have a shepherd's crook."

"I'm going to have a pet iguana," I say, "and wear nothing but cerise." It's a word I have recently learned.

Now I think, what if they just couldn't see what they looked like? Maybe it was as simple as that: eye problems. I'm having that trouble myself now: too close to the mirror and I'm a blur, too far back and I can't see the details. Who knows what faces I'm making, what kind of modern art I'm drawing onto myself? Even when I've got the distance adjusted, I vary. I am transitional; some days I look like a worn-out thirty-five, others like a sprightly fifty. So much depends on the light, and the way you squint.

I eat in pink restaurants, which are better for the skin. Yellow ones turn you yellow. I actually spend time thinking about this. Vanity is becoming a nuisance; I can see why women give it up, eventually. But I'm not ready for that yet.

Lately I've caught myself humming out loud, or walking along the street with my mouth slightly open, drooling a little. Only a little; but it may be the thin edge of the wedge, the crack in the wall that will open, later, onto what? What vistas of shining eccentricity, or madness?

There is no one I would ever tell this to, except Cordelia. But which Cordelia? The one I have conjured up, the one with the roll-top boots and the turned-up collar, or the one before, or the one after? There is never only one, of anyone.

If I were to meet Cordelia again, what would I tell her about myself? The truth, or whatever would make me look good?

Probably the latter. I still have that need.

I haven't seen her for a long time. I wasn't expecting to see her. But now that I'm back here I can hardly walk down a street without a glimpse of her, turning a corner, entering a door. It goes without saying that these fragments of her – a shoulder, beige, camel's-hair, the side of a face, the back of a leg – belong to women who, seen whole, are not Cordelia.

I have no idea what she would look like now. Is she fat, have her breasts sagged, does she have little grey hairs at the corners of her mouth? Unlikely: she would pull them out. Does she wear glasses with fashionable frames, has she had her lids lifted, does she streak or tint? All of these things are possible: we've both reached that borderline age, that buffer zone in which it can still be believed such tricks will work if you avoid bright sunlight.

I think of Cordelia examining the growing pouches under her eyes, the skin, up close, loosened and crinkled like elbows. She sighs, pats in cream, which is the right kind. Cordelia would know the right kind. She takes stock of her hands, which are shrinking a little, warping a little, as mine are. Gnarling has set in, the withering of the mouth; the outlines of dewlaps are beginning to be visible, down towards the chin, in the dark glass of subway windows. Nobody else notices these things yet, unless they look closely; but Cordelia and I are in the habit of looking closely.

She drops the bath towel, which is green, a muted sea-green to match her eyes, looks over her shoulder, sees in the mirror the dog's-neck folds of skin above the waist, the buttocks drooping like wattles, and, turning, the dried fern of hair. I think of her in a sweatsuit, sea-green as well, working out in some gym or other, sweating like a pig. I know what she would say about this, about all of this. How we giggled, with repugnance and delight, when we found the wax her older sisters used on their legs, congealed

302

in a little pot, stuck full of bristles. The grotesqueries of the body were always of interest to her.

I think of encountering her without warning. Perhaps in a worn coat and a knitted hat like a tea cosy, sitting on a kerb, with two plastic bags filled with her only possessions, muttering to herself. *Cordelia! Don't you recognize me?* I say. And she does, but pretends not to. She gets up and shambles away on swollen feet, old socks poking through the holes in her rubber boots, glancing back over her shoulder.

There's some satisfaction in that, more in worse things. I watch from a window, or a balcony so I can see better, as some man chases Cordelia along the sidewalk below me, catches up with her, punches her in the ribs – I can't handle the face – throws her down. But I can't go any farther.

Better to switch to an oxygen tent. Cordelia is unconscious.

I have been summoned, too late, to her hospital bedside. There are flowers, sickly-smelling, wilting in a vase, tubes going into her arms and nose, the sound of terminal breathing. I hold her hand. Her face is puffy, white, like an unbaked biscuit, with yellowish circles under the closed eyes. Her eyelids don't flicker but there's a faint twitching of her fingers, or do I imagine it? I sit there wondering whether to pull the tubes out of her arms, the plug out of the wall. No brain activity, the doctors say. Am I crying? And who would have summoned me?

Even better: an iron lung. I've never seen an iron lung, but the newspapers had pictures of children in iron lungs, back when people still got polio. These pictures – the iron lung a cylinder, a gigantic sausage roll of metal, with a head sticking out one end of it, always a girl's head, the hair flowing across the pillow, the eyes large, nocturnal – fascinated me, more than stories about children who went out on thin ice and fell through and were drowned, or children who played on the railroad tracks and had their arms and legs cut off by trains. You could get polio without knowing how or where, end up in an iron lung without knowing why. Something you breathed in or ate, or picked up from the dirty money other people had touched. You never knew.

The iron lungs were used to frighten us, and as reasons why we couldn't do things we wanted to. No public swimming pools, no crowds in summer. *Do you want to spend the rest of your life in an iron lung?* they would say. A stupid question; though for me such a life, with its inertia and pity, had its secret attractions.

Cordelia in an iron lung, then, being breathed, as an accordion is played. A mechanical wheezing sound comes from around her. She is fully conscious, but unable to move or speak. I come into the room, moving, speaking. Our eyes meet.

Cordelia must be living somewhere. She could be within a mile of me, she could be right on the next block. But finally I have no idea what I would do if I bumped into her by accident, on the subway for instance, sitting across from me, or waiting on the platform reading the ads. We would stand side by side, looking at a large red mouth stretching itself around a chocolate bar, and I would turn to her and say: *Cordelia. It's me, it's Elaine.* Would she turn, give a theatrical shriek? Would she ignore me?

Or would I ignore her, given the chance? Or would I go up to her wordlessly, throw my arms around her? Or take her by the shoulders, and shake and shake.

I've been walking for hours it seems, down the hill to the downtown, where the streetcars no longer run. It's evening, one of those grey watercolour washes, like liquid dust, the city comes up with in fall. The weather at any rate is still familiar.

Now I've reached the place where we used to get off the streetcar, stepping into the kerbside mounds of January slush, into the grating wind that cut up from the lake between the flat-roofed dowdy buildings that were for us the closest thing to urbanity. But this part of the city is no longer flat, dowdy, shabby-genteel. Tubular neon in cursive script decorates the restored brick façades, and there's a lot of brass trim, a lot of real estate, a lot of money. Up ahead there are huge oblong towers, all of glass, lit up, like enormous gravestones of cold light. Frozen assets.

I don't look much at the towers though, or the people passing me in their fashionable get-ups, imports, handcrafted leather, suede, whatever. Instead I look down at the sidewalk, like a tracker.

I can feel my throat tightening, a pain along the jawline.
I've started to chew my fingers again. There's blood, a taste
I remember. It tastes of orange popsicles, penny gumballs, red
licorice, gnawed hair, dirty ice.

II
Silver Paper

3

I'm lying on the floor, on a futon, covered by a duvet. *Futon, duvet*: this is how far we've come. I wonder if Stephen ever figured out what futons and duvets were. Most likely not. Most likely if you'd said *futon* to him, he'd have looked at you as if he was deaf or you were brain-damaged. He did not exist in the futon dimension.

When there were no futons and no duvets, the price of an ice-cream cone was five cents. Now it's a dollar if you're lucky, and not as big either. That's the bottom-line difference between then and now: ninety-five cents.

This is the middle of my life. I think of it as a place, like the middle of a river, the middle of a bridge, halfway across, halfway over. I'm supposed to have accumulated things by now: possessions, responsibilities, achievements, experience and wisdom. I'm supposed to be a person of substance.

But since coming back here I don't feel weightier. I feel lighter, as if I'm shedding matter, losing molecules, calcium from my bones, cells from my blood; as if I'm shrinking, as if I'm filling with cold air, or gently falling snow.

With all this lightness I do not rise, I descend. Or rather I am dragged downwards, into the layers of this place as into liquefied mud.

The fact is that I hate this city. I've hated it so long I can hardly remember feeling any other way about it.

Once it was fashionable to say how dull it was. First prize a week in Toronto, second prize two weeks in Toronto, Toronto the Good, Toronto the Blue, where you couldn't get wine on Sundays. Everyone who lived here said those things: provincial, self-satisfied, boring. If you said that, it showed you recognized these qualities but did not partake of them yourself.

Now you're supposed to say how much it's changed. *World-class city* is a phrase they use in magazines these days, a great deal too much. All those ethnic restaurants, and the theatre and the boutiques. New York without the garbage and muggings, it's supposed to be. People from Toronto used to go to Buffalo for the weekends, the men to watch girlie shows and drink after-hours beer, the women to shop; they'd come back jumped-up and pissed and wearing several layers of clothes to smuggle them through Customs. Now the weekend traffic is the other way around.

I've never believed either version, the dull, the world-class. Toronto was never dull, for me. Dull isn't a word you'd use to describe such misery, and enchantment.

And I can't believe it's changed. Driving in from the airport yesterday in the taxi, past the flat neat factories and warehouses that were once flat neat farms, mile after mile of caution and utilitarianism, and then through the centre of the city with the glitz and the European-style awnings and the paving-stones, I could see it's still the same. Underneath the flourish and ostentation is the old city, street after street of thick red brick houses, with their front porch pillars like the off-white stems of toadstools and their watchful, calculating windows. Malicious, grudging, vindictive, implacable.

In my dreams of this city I am always lost.

Apart from all this, I do of course have a real life. I sometimes have trouble believing in it, because it doesn't seem like the kind of life I could ever get away with, or deserve. This goes along with another belief of mine: that everyone else my age is an adult, whereas I am merely in disguise.

I live in a house, with window curtains and a lawn, in British Columbia, which is as far away from Toronto as I could get without drowning. The unreality of the landscape there encourages me: the greeting-card mountains, of the sunset-and-sloppy-message variety, the cottage houses that look as if they were built by the Seven Dwarfs in the thirties, the giant slugs, so much larger than a slug needs to be. Even the rain is overdone, I can't take it seriously. I suppose these things are as real, and as oppressive, to the people who grew up there as this place is to me. But on good days it still feels like a vacation, an evasion. On bad days I don't notice it, or much else.

I have a husband, not my first, whose name is Ben. He is not any sort of an artist, for which I am thankful. He runs a travel agency, specializing in Mexico. Among his other sterling qualities are cheap tickets to the Yucatán. The travel agency is why he hasn't come with me on this trip: the months before Christmas are a hectic time in the travel business.

I also have two daughters, by now grown up. Their names are Sarah and Anne, good sensible names. One of them is almost a doctor, the other an accountant. These are sensible choices. I am a believer in sensible choices, so different from many of my own. Also in sensible names for children, because look what happened to Cordelia.

Alongside my real life I have a career, which may not qualify as exactly real. I am a painter. I even put that on my passport, in a moment of bravado, since the other choice would have been *housewife*. It's an unlikely thing for me to have become; on some days it still makes me cringe. Respectable people do not become painters: only overblown, pretentious, theatrical people. The word *artist* embarrasses me; I prefer *painter*, because it's more like a valid job. An artist is a tawdry, lazy sort of thing to be, as most people in this country will tell you. If you say you are a painter, you will be looked at strangely. Unless you paint wildlife, or make a lot of money at it, of course. But I only make enough to generate envy, among other painters, not enough so I can tell everyone else to stuff it.

Most of the time though I exult, and think I have had a narrow escape.

My career is why I'm here, on this futon, under this duvet. I'm having a retrospective, my first. The name of the gallery is Sub-Versions, one of those puns that used to delight me before they became so fashionable. I ought to be pleased by this retrospective, but my feelings are mixed; I don't like admitting I'm old enough and established enough to have such a thing, even at an alternative gallery run by a bunch of women. I find it improbable, and ominous: first the retrospective, then the morgue. But also I'm cheesed off because the Art Gallery of Ontario wouldn't do it. Their bias is towards dead, foreign men.

*   *   *

The duvet is in a studio that belongs to my first husband Jon. It interests me that he would have a duvet here, although his house is elsewhere. So far I've restrained myself from going through his medicine cabinet, in search of hairpins and female deodorants, as I once would have done. This is none of my business any longer, I can leave the hairpins to his iron-clad wife.

Staying here is possibly a silly thing to do, too retrospective. But we've always kept in touch because of Sarah, who is his daughter also, and after we got through the shouting and the broken glass we settled into being friends of a sort, by long distance, which is always easier than up close. When he heard about the retrospective, he offered. The price of a hotel in Toronto, he said, even a second-rate hotel, is becoming offensive. Sub-Versions would have put me up, but I didn't mention that. I don't like the neatness of hotels, the squeaky-clean bathtubs. I don't like hearing my own voice echo in there, especially at night. I prefer the shedding and disorder and personal dirt of people like myself, people like Jon. Transients and nomads.

Jon's studio is down on King Street, near the waterfront. King Street used to be one of those places you never went, a place of dingy warehouses and rumbling trucks and dubious alleyways. Now it's come up in the world. Artists have infested it; in fact the first wave of artists has almost come and gone, and brass lettering and heating pipes painted fire-engine red and firms of lawyers are taking over. Jon's studio, on the fifth and top floor of one of the warehouses, doesn't have long to live in its present form. Track lighting is spreading over the ceilings, the lower floors are being stripped of their old linoleum, smelling of Pine Sol with an obscure base note of ancient throwup and pee, and the wide boards underneath are being sandblasted. I know all this because I walk up the five floors; they haven't got around to an elevator yet.

Jon left me the key in an envelope under the mat, and a note saying *Blessings*, which is a measure of how much he's softened, or mellowed. *Blessings* was not his former style. He's temporarily in Los Angeles, doing a chain-saw murder, but he'll be back before my opening.

I last saw him at Sarah's college graduation four years ago. He flew out to the coast, luckily without the wife, who is not fond of me. Although we haven't met, I know about her lack of fondness.

312

During the proceedings, the ritual mumbo-jumbo and the tea and cookies afterwards, we acted like responsible, grown-up parents. We took both the girls out to dinner and behaved ourselves. We even dressed the way we knew Sarah wanted us to: I had on an outfit, matching shoes and all, and Jon wore a suit and an actual tie. I told him he looked like an undertaker.

But the next day we snuck out to lunch, alone, and got plastered. That word, *plastered*, on the brink of obsolescence, indicates to me what sort of an event that was. It was a retrospective. And I still think of it as sneaking out, though of course Ben knew all about it. Though he would never go to lunch with his own first wife.

"You've always said it was such a disaster," Ben said to me, puzzled.

"It was," I said. "It was horrible."

"Then why would you want to have lunch with him?"

"That's hard to explain," I said, though it may not be. What we share, Jon and I, may be a lot like a traffic accident, but we do share it. We are survivors, of each other. We have been shark to one another, but also lifeboat. That counts for something.

In the old days Jon did constructions. He made them out of bits of wood and leather he'd pick out of people's trash, or else he'd smash things – violins, glassware – and glue the pieces into the position of the smash; shatter patterns, he called them. At one time he wrapped pieces of coloured tape around tree trunks and took photographs of them, at another he made a replica of a mould-covered loaf of bread that breathed in and out with the aid of a small electric motor. The mould was made from the hair-clippings of himself and friends. I think there's even some of my hair on that loaf of bread; I caught him snitching some out of my hairbrush.

He does special effects for movies now, to support his artist habit. The studio is scattered with his half-finished doings. On the workbench where he keeps his paints, glues, knives, and pliers, there's a hand and arm, done in plastic resin, arteries worming from the cut end, straps to strap it on. There are hollow casts of legs and feet standing around on the floor like elephant-foot umbrella stands; in one of them there's an umbrella. Also there's part of a face, with the skin blackened

313

and withered, made to fit over the actor's real face. A monster, warped by others, bent on revenge.

Jon has told me he isn't sure this hacked-up body-part stuff is the sort of thing he should be doing. It's too violent, it doesn't contribute to human goodness. He's coming to believe in human goodness in his old age, which is certainly a change; I've even found some herbal tea in the cupboard. He claims he'd rather make friendly animals for children's shows. But as he says, you have to eat, and there's just more demand for cut-off limbs.

I wish he were here, or Ben, or any man I know. I'm losing the appetite for strangers. Once I would have focused on the excitement, the hazard; now it's the mess, the bother. Getting your clothes off gracefully, always such an impossibility; thinking up what to say afterwards, without setting the echoes going in your head. Worse, the encounter with another set of particularities: the toenails, the ear-holes, the nosehairs. Perhaps at this age we return to the prudishness we had as children.

I get up off the duvet, feeling as if I haven't slept. I riffle through the herbal tea-bags in the kitchenette, Lemon Mist, Morning Thunder, and bypass them in favour of some thick, jolting, poisonous coffee. I find myself standing in the middle of the main room, not knowing exactly how I got in here from the kitchenette. A little time-jump, a little static on the screen, probably jet-lag: up too late at night, drugged in the morning. Early Alzheimer's.

I sit at the window, drinking my coffee, biting my fingers, looking down the five storeys. From this angle the pedestrians appear squashed from above, like deformed children. All around are flat-roofed, boxy warehouse buildings, and beyond them the flat railroad lands where the trains used to shunt back and forth, once the only entertainment available here on Sundays. Beyond that is flat Lake Ontario, a zero at the beginning and a zero at the end, slate-grey and brimming with venoms. Even the rain from it is carcinogenic.

I wash in Jon's tiny, greasy bathroom, resisting the medicine cabinet. The bathroom is smeared with fingerprints and painted dingy white, not the most flattering light. Jon wouldn't feel like an artist without a certain amount of dinge around. I squint into the mirror, preparing my face: with my contact lenses in I'm too close to the mirror, without them I'm too far away. I've taken to doing these mirror things with one lens in my mouth, glassy and thin like the tag-end of a lemon drop. I could choke on it by mistake, an undignified way to die. I should get bifocals. But then I'd look like an old biddy.

I pull on my powder-blue sweatsuit, my disguise as a non-artist, and go down the four flights of stairs, trying to look brisk and purposeful. I could be a businesswoman out jogging, I could be a bank manager, on her day off. I head north, then east along Queen Street, which is another place we never used to go. It was rumoured to be the haunt of grubby drunks, rubby-dubs we called them; they were said to drink rubbing alcohol and sleep in telephone booths and vomit on your shoes in the streetcar. But now it's art galleries and bookshops, boutiques filled with black clothing and weird footgear, the sawtoothed edge of trend.

I decide I'll go and have a look at the gallery, which I have never seen because all of this has been arranged by phone and mail. I don't intend to go in, make myself known, not yet. I just want to look at it from the outside. I'll walk past, glance casually, pretending to be a housewife, a tourist, someone window-shopping. Galleries are frightening places, places of evaluation, of judgment. I have to work up to them.

But before I reach the gallery I come to a wall of plywood, concealing a demolition. On it is spray-painted, in defiance of squeaky-clean Toronto: *It's Bacon or Me, Babe.* And underneath: *What Is This Bacon and Where Can I Get Some?* Beside this there's a poster. Or not a poster, more like a flyer: a violent shade of purple, with green accents and black lettering. RISLEY IN RETROSPECT, it says; just the last name, like a boy. The name is mine and so is the face, more or less. It's the photo I sent the gallery. Except that now I have a moustache.

Whoever drew this moustache knew what he was doing. Or she: nothing precludes that. It's a curled, flowing moustache, like a cavalier's, with a graceful goatee to match. It goes with my hair.

I suppose I should be worried about this moustache. Is it just doodling, or is it political commentary, an act of aggression?

315

Is it more like *Kilroy Was Here* or more like *Fuck Off?* I can remember drawing such moustaches myself, and the spite that went into them, the desire to ridicule, to deflate, and the feeling of power. It was defacing, it was taking away someone's face. If I were younger I'd resent it.

As it is, I study the moustache and think: *That looks sort of good.* The moustache is like a costume. I examine it from several angles, as if I'm considering buying one for myself. It casts a different light. I think about men and their facial hair, and the opportunities for disguise and concealment they have always at their disposal. I think about moustache-covered men, and about how naked they must feel with the thing shaved off. How diminished. A lot of people would look better in a moustache.

Then, suddenly, I feel wonder. I have achieved, finally, a face that a moustache can be drawn on, a face that attracts moustaches. A public face, a face worth defacing. This is an accomplishment. I have made something of myself, something or other, after all.

I wonder if Cordelia will see this poster. I wonder if she'll recognize me, despite the moustache. Maybe she'll come to the opening. She'll walk in through the door and I will turn, wearing black as a painter should, looking successful, holding a glass of only moderately bad wine. I won't spill a drop.

4

Until we moved to Toronto I was happy.

Before that we didn't really live anywhere; or we lived so many places it was hard to remember them. We spent a lot of the time driving, in our low-slung, boat-sized Studebaker, over back roads or along two-lane highways up north, curving past lake after lake, hill after hill, with the white lines going down the middle of the road and the telephone poles along the sides, tall ones and shorter ones, the wires looking as if they were moving up and down.

I sit by myself in the back of the car, among the suitcases and the cardboard boxes of food and the coats, and the gassy, dry-cleaning smell of the car upholstery. My brother Stephen sits in the front seat, beside the partly open window. He smells of peppermint LifeSavers; underneath that is his ordinary smell, of cedarwood lead pencils and wet sand. Sometimes he throws up into paper bags, or beside the road if my father can stop the car in time. He gets carsick and I do not, which is why he has to sit in the front. It's his only weakness that I know of.

From my cramped vantage point in the back I have a good view of my family's ears. My father's, which stick out from under the brim of the old felt hat he wears to keep twigs and tree sap and caterpillars out of his hair, are large and soft-looking, with long lobes; they're like the ears of gnomes, or those of the flesh-coloured, dog-like minor characters in Mickey Mouse comic books. My mother wears her hair pinned back at the sides with bobby-pins, so her ears are visible from the back. They're narrow, with fragile upper edges, like the handles of china cups, although she herself is not fragile. My brother's ears are round, like dried apricots, or like the ears of the green-tinged, oval-headed aliens from outer space he draws with his coloured pencils. Around and over his round ears and down the back of his neck his hair, dark blond and straight, grows in thick wisps. He resists haircuts.

317

It's difficult for me to whisper into my brother's round ears when we're in the car. In any case he can't whisper back, because he has to look straight ahead at the horizon, or at the white lines of the road that washes towards us, wave after slowly undulating wave.

The roads are mostly empty, because it's the war, though once in a while there's a truck loaded with cut tree trunks or fresh lumber, trailing its perfume of sawdust. At lunchtime we stop by the roadside and spread a groundsheet among the white papery everlasting and the purple fireweed and eat the lunch our mother makes, bread and sardines or bread and cheese, or bread and molasses or bread and jam if we can't get anything else. Meat and cheese are scarce, they are rationed. That means you have a ration book with coloured stamps in it.

Our father makes a small fire to boil water in a billy tin for tea. After lunch we disappear into the bushes, one by one, with pieces of toilet paper in our pockets. Sometimes there are other pieces of toilet paper there already, melting among the bracken and dead leaves, but mostly there are not. I squat, listening behind me for bears, aster leaves rough on the tops of my legs, then bury the toilet paper under sticks and bark and dried bracken. Our father says you should make it look as if you haven't been there at all.

Our father walks into the forest, carrying his axe, a pack-sack, and a large wooden box with a leather shoulder strap. He looks up, from tree to tree to tree, considering. Then he spreads a tarpaulin out on the ground, underneath the chosen tree, wrapping it around the trunk. He opens the wooden box, which is filled with racks of small bottles. He hits the tree trunk with the back of his axe. The tree shakes; leaves and twigs and caterpillars patter down, bouncing off his grey felt hat, hitting the tarpaulin. Stephen and I crouch, picking up the caterpillars, which are blue-striped, and velvety and cool, like the muzzles of dogs. We put them into the collecting bottles filled with pale alcohol. We watch them twist and sink.

My father looks at the harvest of caterpillars as if he's grown them himself. He examines the chewed leaves. "A beautiful infestation," he says. He's joyful, he's younger than I am now.

The alcohol smell is on my fingers, cold and remote, piercing, like a steel pin going in. It smells like white enamel basins. When

I look up at the stars in the night-time, cold and white and sharp, I think they must smell like that.

When it gets to the end of the day we stop again and put up our tent, heavy canvas with wooden poles. Our sleeping bags are khaki and thick and lumpy, and always feel a little damp. Underneath them we put groundsheets, and inflatable mattresses that make you feel dizzy while you blow them up and fill your nose and mouth with the taste of stale rainboots or spare tyres piled in a garage. We eat around the fire, which turns brighter as the shadows grow out from the trees like darker branches. We crawl into the tent and take our clothes off inside our sleeping bags, the flashlight making a circle on the canvas, a light ring enclosing a darker one, like a target. The tent smells of tar and kapok and brown paper with cheese grease on it, and crushed grass. In the mornings the weeds outside are sprinkled with dew.

Sometimes we stay in motels, but only if it's too late at night to find a place to set up the tent. The motels are always far from anything, set against a dark wall of forest, their lights glimmering in the uniform obscuring night like those of ships, or oases. They have gas pumps outside, human-sized, with round discs on top, lit up like pale moons or haloes minus the head. On each disc is a shell or a star, an orange maple leaf, a white rose. The motels and the gas pumps are often empty or closed: gas is rationed, so people don't travel much unless they have to.

Or we stay in cabins belonging to other people or to the government, or we stay in abandoned logging camps, or we pitch two tents, one for sleeping and one for supplies. In the winters we stay in towns or cities up north, the Soo or North Bay or Sudbury, in apartments that are really the top floors of other people's houses, so that we have to be careful about the noise of our shoes on the wooden floors. We have furniture which comes from storage. It's always the same furniture but it always looks unfamiliar.

In these places there are flush toilets, white and alarming, where things vanish in an instant, with a roar. When we first get to cities my brother and I go to the bathroom a lot, and drop things in as well, such as pieces of macaroni, to see them disappear. There are air-raid sirens, and then we pull the curtains and turn off the lights, though our mother says the war will never come here. The war filters in over the radio, remote and crackly, the voices from London fading through the static. Our parents are dubious as they listen, their mouths tighten: it could be that we are losing.

My brother does not think so. He thinks our side is the good side, and therefore it will win. He collects cigarette cards with pictures of airplanes on them, and knows the names of all the planes.

My brother has a hammer and some wood, and his own jackknife. He whittles and hammers: he's making a gun. He nails two pieces of wood at right angles, with another nail for the trigger. He has several of these wooden guns, and daggers and swords also, with blood coloured onto the blades with red pencils. Some of the blood is orange, from when he ran out of red. He sings:

> Coming in on a wing and a prayer,
> Coming in on a wing and a prayer,
> Though there's one motor gone
> We will still carry on,
> Coming in on a wing and a prayer.

He sings this cheerfully, but I think it's a sad song, because although I've seen the pictures of the airplanes on the cigarette cards I don't know how they fly. I think it's like birds, and a bird with one wing can't fly. This is what my father says in the winters, before dinner, lifting his glass when there are other men there at the table: "You can't fly on one wing." So in fact the prayer in the song is useless.

Stephen gives me a gun and a knife and we play war. This is his favourite game. While our parents are putting up the tent or making the fire or cooking, we sneak around behind the trees and bushes, aiming through the leaves. I am the infantry, which means I have to do what he says. He waves me forward, motions me back, tells me to keep my head down so the enemy won't blow it off.

"You're dead," he says.

"No I'm not."

"Yes you are. They got you. Lie down."

320

There is no arguing with him, since he can see the enemy and I can't. I have to lie down on the swampy ground, propped against a stump to avoid getting too wet, until it's time for me to be alive again.

Sometimes, instead of war, we hunt through the forest, turning over logs and rocks to see what's underneath. There are ants, grubs and beetles, frogs and toads, garter snakes, even salamanders if we're lucky. We don't do anything with the things we find. We know they will die if we put them into bottles and leave them by accident in the sun in the back window of the car, as we have done before. So we merely look at them, watching the ants hiding their pill-shaped eggs in panic, the snakes pouring themselves into darkness. Then we put the logs back where they were, unless we need some of these things for fishing.

Once in a while we fight. I don't win these fights: Stephen is bigger and more ruthless than I am, and I want to play with him more than he wants to play with me. We fight in whispers or well out of the way, because if we're caught we will both be punished. For this reason we don't tell on each other. We know from experience that the satisfactions of betrayal are scarcely worth it.

Because they're secret, these fights have an extra attraction. It's the attraction of dirty words we aren't supposed to say, words like *bum*; the attraction of conspiracy, of collusion. We step on each other's feet, pinch each other's arms, careful not to give away the pain, loyal even in outrage.

How long did we live this way, like nomads on the far edges of the war?

Today we've driven a long time, we're late setting up our tent. We're near the road, beside a raggedy anonymous lake. The trees around the shore are doubled in the water, the leaves of the poplars are yellowing towards fall. The sun sets in a long, chilly, lingering sunset, flamingo pink, then salmon, then the improbable vibrant red of Mercurochrome. The pink light rests on the surface, trembling, then fades and is gone. It's a clear night, moonless, filled with antiseptic stars. There is the Milky Way clear as can be, which predicts bad weather.

We pay no attention to any of this, because Stephen is teaching

321

me to see in the dark, as commandos do. You never know when you might need to do this; he says. You can't use a flashlight; you have to stay still, in the darkness, waiting until your eyes become accustomed to no light. Then the shapes of things begin to emerge, greyish and glimmering and insubstantial, as if they're condensing from the air. Stephen tells me to move my feet slowly, balancing on one foot at a time, careful not to step on twigs. He tells me to breathe quietly. "If they hear you they'll get you," he whispers.

He crouches beside me, outlined against the lake, a blacker patch of water. I catch the glint of an eye, then he's gone. This is a trick of his.

I know he's sneaking up on the fire, on my parents, who are flickering, shadowy, their faces indistinct. I'm alone with my heartbeat and my too-loud breathing. But he's right: now I can see in the dark.

Such are my pictures of the dead.

5

I have my eighth birthday in a motel. My present is a Brownie box-camera, black and oblong, with a handle on top and a round hole at the back to look through.

The first picture taken with it is of me. I'm leaning against the doorframe of the motel cabin. The door behind me is white and closed, with the metal number on it showing: 9. I'm wearing pants, baggy at the knees, and a jacket too short in the sleeves. Under the jacket, I know though you can't see it, is a hand-me-down brown and yellow striped jersey of my brother's. Many of my clothes were once his. My skin is ultra-white from over-exposure of the film, my head is tilted to one side, my mittenless wrists dangle. I look like old photos of immigrants. I look as if I've been put there in front of the door and told to stand still.

What was I like, what did I want? It's hard to remember. Did I want a camera for my birthday? Probably not, although I was glad to have it.

I want some more cards from the Nabisco Shredded Wheat boxes, the grey cards with pictures on them that you colour, cut out, and fold to make the houses in a town. Also I want some pipe-cleaners. We have a book called *Rainy Day Hobbies* that shows how to make a walkie-talkie out of two cans and a piece of string, or how to make a boat that will go forward if you drop lubricating oil into a hole in it; also how to make a doll's chest-of-drawers out of miniature matchboxes, and how to make various animals – a dog, a sheep, a camel – out of pipe-cleaners. The boat and the chest-of-drawers don't appeal to me, only the pipe-cleaners. I've never seen a pipe-cleaner.

I want some silver paper out of cigarette packages. I have several pieces already, but I want more. My parents don't smoke cigarettes, so I have to collect this paper where I can find it, on the edges of gas stations, in the weedy grass near motels. I am in the habit of scavenging along the ground this way. When I find some I clean it off and flatten it out and store it between the pages of my school reader. I don't know what I'll do with it when I have enough, but it will be something amazing.

I want a balloon. Balloons are coming back, now that the war is over. When I was sick with the mumps, once in the winter, my mother found one at the bottom of her steamer trunk. She must have tucked it away there before the war, suspecting perhaps that there would not be any more for a while. She blew it up for me. It was blue, translucent, round, like a private moon. The rubber was old and rotting and the balloon burst almost at once, and I was heartbroken. But I want another balloon, one that will not break.

I want some friends, friends who will be girls. Girl friends. I know that these exist, having read about them in books, but I've never had any girl friends because I've never been in one place long enough.

Much of the time it's raw and overcast, the low metallic sky of late autumn; or else it rains and we have to stay inside the motel. The motel is the kind we're used to: a row of cottages, flimsily built, strung together with Christmas tree lights, yellow or blue or green. These are called "housekeeping cottages", which means they have some kind of a stove in them, a pot or two and a tea kettle, and a table covered with oilcloth. The floor of our housekeeping cottage is linoleum, with a faded pattern of floral squares. The towels are skimpy and thin, the sheets have worn places in the middles, rubbed there by other people's bodies. There's a framed print of the woods in winter and another of ducks in flight. Some motels have outhouses, but this one has a real though smelly flush toilet, and a bathtub.

We've been living in this motel for weeks, which is unusual: we never stay in motels for more than a night at a time. We eat cans of Habitant pea soup, heated up on the two-burner stove in a dented pot, and slices of bread spread with molasses, and hunks of cheese. There's more cheese, now that the war is over. We wear our outdoor clothes indoors, and socks at night, because these cottages with their one-layer walls are supposed to be for summer tourists. The hot water is never more than lukewarm, and our mother heats water in the tea kettle and pours it into the tub for our baths. "Just to get the crust off," she says.

In the mornings we wrap blankets around our shoulders while we eat our breakfast. Sometimes we can see our own breath, even inside the cottage. All of this is irregular, and slightly festive. It isn't just that we aren't going to school. We've never gone to school for more than three or four months at a time anyway. I was in school the last time eight months ago and have only dim and temporary ideas of what it was like.

In the mornings we do our schoolwork, in our workbooks. Our mother tells us which pages to do. Then we read our school readers. Mine is about two children who live in a white house with ruffled curtains, a front lawn, and a picket fence. The father goes to work, the mother wears a dress and an apron, and the children play ball on the lawn with their dog and cat. Nothing in these stories is anything like my life. There are no tents, no highways, no peeing in the bushes, no lakes, no motels. There is no war. The children are always clean, and the little girl, whose name is Jane, wears pretty dresses and patent-leather shoes with straps.

These books have an exotic appeal for me. When Stephen and I draw with our coloured pencils, he draws wars, ordinary wars and wars in space. His red and yellow and orange are worn to stubs, from the explosions, and his gold and silver are used up too, on the shining metal carapaces of the tanks and spaceships and on the helmets and the complicated guns. But I draw girls. I draw them in old-fashioned clothing, with long skirts, pinafores and puffed sleeves, or in dresses like Jane's, with big hairbows on their heads. This is the elegant, delicate picture I have in my mind, about other little girls. I don't think about what I might say to them if I actually met some. I haven't got that far.

In the evenings we're supposed to do the dishes – "Rattle them up," our mother calls it. We squabble in whispers and monosyllables about whose turn it is to wash: drying with a clammy tea-towel isn't as good as washing, which warms up your hands. We float the plates and glasses in the dish pan and dive-bomb them with the spoons and knives, whispering "Bombs away." We try to aim as close as possible without actually hitting them. They aren't our dishes. This gets on our mother's nerves. If it gets on her nerves enough, she will do the dishes herself, which is intended to be a rebuke.

At night we lie in the saggy pull-out bed, head to toe, which is supposed to make us go to sleep sooner, and kick each other silently under the covers; or else we try to see how far we can get our sock feet up each other's pyjama legs. Once in a while the headlights of a passing car show through the window, moving first along one wall, then along the next wall, then fading away. There's an engine sound, then the sizzle of tyres on the wet road. Then silence.

6

I don't know who took that picture of me. It must have been my brother, because my mother is inside the cabin, behind the white door, wearing grey slacks and a dark-blue plaid shirt, packing our food into cardboard boxes and our clothes into suitcases. She has a system for packing; she talks to herself while she's doing it, reminding herself of details, and she likes us out of the way.

Right after the picture it begins to snow, small dry flakes falling singly out of the hard northern November sky. There's a kind of hush and lassitude until that first snow, with the light waning and the last moose-maple leaves dangling from the branches like seaweed. We felt sleepy until it began to snow. Now we feel exhilarated.

We're running around outside the motel, wearing nothing but our worn-out summer shoes, with our bare hands outstretched to the falling snowflakes, our heads thrown back, our mouths open, eating snow. If it were thick on the ground we would roll in it, like dogs in dirt. It fills us with the same kind of rapture. But our mother looks out the window and sees us, and the snow, and makes us come inside and dry our feet off with the skimpy towels. We have no winter boots that fit. While we're inside, the snow turns to sleet.

Our father is pacing the floor, jingling his keys in his pocket. He always wants things to happen sooner than they do, and now he wants to leave right away, but my mother says he'll have to hold his horses. We go outside and help him scrape the crust of ice off the car windows and then we carry boxes, and finally we squeeze into the car ourselves and drive south. I know it's south because of the direction of the sunlight, which is coming weakly through the clouds now, touching the icy trees with glitter, glaring off the ice patches at the sides of the road, making it hard to see.

Our parents say we're going to our new house. This time the house will be really ours, not rented. It's in a city called Toronto.

327

This name means nothing to me. I think about the house in my school reader, white, with a picket fence and a lawn, and window curtains. I want to see what my bedroom will be like.

By the time we arrive at the house it's late afternoon. At first I think there must be some mistake; but no, this is the house all right, because my father is already opening the door with a key. The house is hardly on a street at all, more like a field. It's square-shaped, a bungalow, built of yellow brick and surrounded by raw mud. On one side of it is an enormous hole in the ground, with large mud-piles heaped around it. The road in front is muddy too, unpaved, pot-holed. There are some concrete blocks sunk in the mud for stepping stones so we can get to the door.

Inside, things are even more daunting. There are doors and windows, true, and walls, and the furnace works. There's a picture window in the living room, though the view is of a large expanse of rippling mud. The toilet actually flushes, though it has a yellowish-brown ring around the inside of the bowl and several floating cigarette butts; and reddish, warmish water comes from the hot-water tap when I turn it on. But the floors are not polished wood or even linoleum. They're made of wide, rough boards with cracks in between, grey with plaster dust and scattered with white speckles, like bird droppings. Only a few of the rooms have light fixtures; the others have wires dangling out of the middle of the ceiling. There are no counters in the kitchen, only the bare sink; there's no stove. Nothing is painted. Dust is on everything: the windows, the window-ledges, the fixtures, the floor. There are a lot of dead flies around.

"We all have to pitch in," says our mother, which means that we are not to complain. We will have to do the best we can, she says. We will have to finish the house ourselves, because the man who was supposed to do it has gone bankrupt. Flown the coop, is how she puts it. Our father is not so cheerful. He paces around the house, peering and prodding at it, muttering to himself and making small whistling noises. "Son of a gun, son of a gun," is what he says.

From somewhere in the depths of the car our mother unearths a primus stove, which she sets up on the kitchen floor, since there is no table. She begins to heat up some pea soup. My brother goes outside; I know he's climbing up the mountain of dirt next door, or assessing the possibilities of the large hole in the ground, but I don't have the heart to join him.

I wash my hands in the reddish water in the bathroom. There's a crack in the sink, which at this moment seems a disaster, worse than any of the other flaws and absences. I look at my face in the dust-smeared mirror. There's no shade on the light, just a bare bulb overhead, which makes my face look pallid and ill, with circles under the eyes. I rub my eyes; I know it would be wrong to be seen crying. Despite its rawness, the house feels too hot, maybe because I'm still wearing my outside clothes. I feel trapped. I want to be back in the motel, back on the road, in my old rootless life of impermanence and safety.

The first nights we sleep on the floor, in our sleeping bags, on top of our air mattresses. Then some army surplus cots appear, canvas stretched across a metal frame smaller at the base than at the top, so that if you roll over in the night you tip off onto the floor and the cot falls on top of you. Night after night I fall out and wake up lying on the rough dusty floor wondering where I am, and my brother is not there to snicker at me or order me to shut up, because I'm in a room by myself. At first I found the thought of my own room exciting – an empty space to be arranged as I wanted, without regard to Stephen and his strewn clothes and wooden guns – but now I'm lonely. I've never been in a room by myself at night before.

Each day new things appear in the house while we're at school: a stove, a refrigerator, a card-table and four chairs, so that we can eat in the ordinary way, sitting at a table, instead of cross-legged on a groundsheet spread in front of the fireplace. The fireplace actually works; this is one part of the house that has been finished. In it we burn scrap pieces of wood left over from the construction.

In his spare time our father hammers away at the interior of the house. Floor coverings spread across the floors: narrow hardwood boards in the living room, asphalt tiles in our bedrooms, advancing row by row. The house begins to look more like a house. But this takes a lot longer than I would like: we are a far cry from picket fences and white curtains, here in our lagoon of postwar mud.

7

We're used to seeing our father in windbreakers, battered grey
felt hats, flannel shirts with the cuffs tightly buttoned to keep the
blackflies from crawling up his arms, heavy pants tucked into the
tops of woollen work socks. Except for the felt hats, what our
mother wore wasn't all that different.

Now, however, our father wears jackets and ties and white
shirts, and a tweed overcoat and a scarf. He has galoshes that
buckle on over his shoes instead of leather boots waterproofed
with bacon grease. Our mother's legs have appeared, sheathed
in nylons with seams up the backs. She draws on a lipstick mouth
when she goes out. She has a coat with a grey fur collar, and a hat
with a feather in it that makes her nose look too long. Every time
she puts on this hat, she looks into the mirror and says, "I look
like the Witch of Endor."

Our father has changed his job: this explains things. Instead
of being a forest-insect field researcher, he is now a university professor. The smelly jars and collecting bottles that once
were everywhere have diminished in number. Instead, scattered
around the house, there are stacks of drawings made by his
students with coloured pencils. All of them are of insects. There
are grasshoppers, spruce budworms, forest tent caterpillars,
wood-boring beetles, each one the size of a page, their parts
neatly labelled: mandibles, palps, antennae, thorax, abdomen.
Some of them are in section, which means they're cut open so
you can see what's inside them: tunnels, branches, bulbs and
delicate filaments. I like this kind the best.

My father sits in an armchair in the evenings with a board
across the arms of the chair and the drawings on the board,
going through them with a red pencil. Sometimes he laughs to
himself while doing this, or shakes his head, or makes ticking
noises through his teeth. "Idiot," he says, or "blockhead." I stand
behind his chair, watching the drawings, and he points out that
this person has put the mouth at the wrong end, that person has

made no provision for a heart, yet another one cannot tell a male from a female. This is not how I judge the drawings: I find them better or worse depending on the colours.

On Saturdays we get into the car with him and drive down to the place where he works. It is actually the Zoology Building, but we don't call it that. It is just the building.

The building is enormous. Whenever we're there it's almost empty, because it's Saturday; this makes it seem even larger. It's of dark-brown weathered brick, and gives the impression of having turrets, although it has none. Ivy grows on it, leafless now in winter, covering it with skeletal veining. Inside it there are long hallways with hardwood floors, stained and worn from generations of students in slushy winter boots, but still kept polished. There are staircases, also of wood, which creak when we climb them, and banisters we aren't supposed to slide down, and iron radiators that make banging noises and are either stone cold or blazing hot.

On the second floor there are corridors leading into other corridors, lined with shelves that contain jars full of dead lizards or pickled ox eyeballs. In one room there are glass cages with snakes in them, snakes bigger than any we've ever seen before. One is a tame boa constrictor, and if the man in charge of it is there he gets it out and winds it around his arm, so we can see how it crushes things to death in order to eat them. We're allowed to stroke it. Its skin is cool and dry. Other cages have rattlesnakes, and the man shows us how he milks the venom out of their fangs. For this he wears a leather glove. The fangs are curved and hollow, the venom dripping from them is yellow.

In the same room is a cement pool filled with thick-looking greenish water in which large turtles sit and blink or clamber ponderously up onto the rocks provided for them, hissing if we get too close. This room is hotter and steamier than the others because the snakes and turtles need it to be; it smells musky. In yet another room is a cage full of gigantic African cockroaches, white-coloured and so poisonous that their keeper has to gas them to make them unconscious every time he opens the cage to feed them or get one out.

Down in the cellar there are shelves and shelves of white rats and black mice, special ones that aren't wild. They eat food pellets from hoppers in their cages and drink from bottles fitted with eyedroppers. They have chewed-newspaper nests full of pink hairless baby mice. They run over and under one another and sleep in heaps, and sniff one another with their quivering noses. The mouse feeder tells us that if you put a strange mouse into one of their cages, one with the wrong, alien scent, they will bite it to death.

The cellar smells strongly of mouse droppings, a smell which wafts upward through the whole building, getting fainter as you go up, mingling with the smell of the green Dustbane used to clean the floors, and with the other smells, the floor polish and furniture wax and formaldehyde and snakes.

We don't find any of the things in the building repulsive. The general arrangements, though not the details, are familiar to us, though we've never seen so many mice in one place before and are awed by their numbers and stench. We would like to get the turtles out of their pool and play with them, but since they're snapping turtles and bad-tempered and can take your fingers off, we know enough not to. My brother wants an ox eyeball out of one of the jars: it's the sort of thing other boys find impressive.

Some of the upstairs rooms are labs. The labs have vast ceilings and blackboards across the front. They contain rows and rows of large dark desks, more like tables than desks, with high stools to sit on. Each desk has two lamps with green glass shades, and two microscopes, old microscopes, with heavy thin tubing and brass fittings.

We've seen microscopes before, but not at such length; we can spend a lot of time with them before getting tired of them. Sometimes we're given slides to look at: butterfly wings, cross-sections of worms, planaria stained with pink and purple dyes so you can see the different parts. At other times we put our fingers under the lenses and examine our fingernails, the pale parts curved like hills against their dark pink sky, the skin around them grainy and creased like the edge of a desert. Or we pull hairs out of our heads to look at them, hard and shiny like the bristles that grow out of the chitonous skins of insects, with the hair roots at the end like tiny onion bulbs.

We like scabs. We pick them off – there isn't room for a whole arm or leg under the microscope – and turn the magnification up as high as it will go. The scabs look like rocks, bumpy, with a sheen like silica; or else like some kind of fungus. If we can get a scab off a finger we put the finger under and watch the place where the blood oozes out, bright red, in a round button, like a berry. Afterwards we lick off the blood. We look at ear-wax, or snot, or dirt from our toes, checking first to see that there's no one around: we know without asking that such things would not be approved of. Our curiosity is supposed to have limits, though these have never been defined exactly.

This is what we do on Saturday mornings, while our father attends to things in his office and our mother goes grocery shopping. She says it keeps us out of her hair.

The building overlooks University Avenue, which has lawns and some copper-green statues of men on horses. Right across the road is the Ontario Parliament Building, which is also old and dingy. I think it must be another building like the building, filled with long creaky corridors and shelves of pickled lizards and ox eyes.

It's from the building that we watch our first Santa Claus Parade. We've never seen a parade before. You can listen to this parade on the radio, but if you want to actually see it you have to bundle up in your winter clothes and stand on the sidewalk, stomping your feet and rubbing your hands to keep warm. Some people climb up onto the horse statues to get a better view. We don't have to do this, as we can sit on the window-ledge of one of the main labs in the building, separated from the weather by a pane of dusty glass, with blasts of heat from the iron radiator going up our legs.

From there we watch as people dressed like snowflakes, like elves, like rabbits, like sugar plum fairies, march past us, strangely truncated because we're looking down on them. There are bands of bagpipers in kilts, and things like big cakes, with people on them waving, that slide past on wheels. It's begun to drizzle. Everyone down there looks cold.

Santa Claus is at the end, smaller than expected. His voice and his loudspeaker jinglebells are muted by the dusty glass; he rocks back and forth behind his mechanical reindeer, looking soggy, blowing kisses to the crowd.

I know he isn't the real Santa Claus, just someone dressed up like him. Still, my idea of Santa Claus has altered, has acquired a new dimension. After this it becomes hard for me to think of him without thinking also of the snakes and the turtles and

333

the pickled eyes, and the lizards floating in their yellow jars, and of the vast, echoing, spicy, ancient and forlorn but also comforting smell of old wood, furniture polish, formaldehyde and distant mice.

III

Empire
Bloomers

8

There are days when I can hardly make it out of bed. I find it an effort to speak. I measure progress in steps, the next one and the next one, as far as the bathroom. These steps are major accomplishments. I focus on taking the cap off the toothpaste, getting the brush up to my mouth. I have difficulty lifting my arm to do even that. I feel I am without worth, that nothing I can do is of any value, least of all to myself.

What do you have to say for yourself? Cordelia used to ask. *Nothing*, I would say. It was a word I came to connect with myself, as if I was nothing, as if there was nothing there at all.

Last night I felt the approach of nothing. Not too close but on its way, like a wingbeat, like the cooling of the wind, the slight initial tug of an undertow. I wanted to talk to Ben. I phoned the house but he was out, the machine was on. It was my own voice I heard, cheerful and in control. *Hi there. Ben and I can't come to the phone at the moment, but leave a message and we'll get back to you as soon as we can.* Then a beep.

A disembodied voice, an angel voice, wafting through the air. If I died this minute it would go on like that, placid and helpful, like an electronic afterlife. Hearing it made me want to cry.

"Big hugs," I said into the empty space. I closed my eyes, thought about the mountains on the coast. That's home, I told myself. That's where you really live. Among all that stagey scenery, too beautiful, like a cardboard movie backdrop. It's not real, it's not drab, not flat, not grubby enough. They're working on it though. Go a few miles here, a few miles there, out of sight of the picture windows, and you come to the land of stumps.

Vancouver is the suicide capital of the country. You keep going west until you run out. You come to the edge. Then you fall off.

*   *   *

I crawl out from under the duvet. I am a busy person, in theory. There are things to be done, although none of them are things I want to do. I check through the refrigerator in the kitchenette, dig out an egg, boil it, dump it into a teacup, mush it up. I don't even glance at the herbal teas, I go straight for the real, vile coffee. Jitter in a cup. It cheers me up to know I'll soon be so tense.

I pace among the severed arms and hollow feet, drinking blackness. I like this studio, I could work here. There's the right amount of makeshift and dinginess for me. Things that are falling apart encourage me: whatever else, I'm in better shape than they are.

Today we hang. An unfortunate term.

I tuck myself into my clothes, handling my arms and legs as if they're someone else's, someone not very big or not very well. It's the powder-blue sweatsuit again today; I didn't bring very much clothing with me. I don't like to check things, I like to jam it all under the airplane seat. At the back of my mind is the idea that if something goes wrong, up there in the air, I'll be able to grab my bag out from under the seat and jump out the window, gracefully, without leaving any of my possessions behind.

I head out into the open, walk quickly along the street, mouth slightly open, keeping time in my head. *Keep happy with the Happy Gang.* I used to jog but it's bad for the knees. Too much beta carotene turns you orange, too much calcium gives you kidney stones. Health kills.

The old emptiness of Toronto is gone. Now it's chock full: Toronto's bloating itself to death, that much is clear. The traffic is astonishing, there's honking and barging, people drive right out to the middle of the intersections and sit there when the light changes. I'm glad I'm on foot. Every building I pass down here among the warehouses seems to cry *Renovate me! Renovate me!* The first time I saw the word Reno in the real-estate section I thought it meant the gambling resort. Language is leaving me behind.

I hit the corner of King and Spadina, walk north. This used to be where you came to get wholesale clothing, and it still is; but the old Jewish delis are disappearing, replaced by Chinese emporia, wicker furniture, cutwork tablecloths, bamboo wind chimes. Some of the street signs are subtitled in Chinese, multiculturalism on the march, others have *Fashion District* underneath the names. Everything is a district now. There never used to be districts.

It comes over me that I need a new dress for the opening. I've brought one with me, of course; I've already pressed it with my travel iron, clearing a corner of Jon's workbench for the ironing board, folding a towel across it. This dress is black, because black is the best thing for such occasions: a simple, sober black dress, like those of the women who play cellos in symphony orchestras. It doesn't do to outdress the clients.

But the thought of this dress is depressing to me now. Black attracts lint, and I've forgotten my clothes brush. I remember the Scotch tape ads from the forties: mummify your hand in inside-out Scotch tape, defuzz your clothing. I think of myself standing there in the gallery, surrounded by one-of-a-kind boutique-wear and real pearls, widow-coloured and linty where the Scotch tape has missed. There are other colours, pink for instance: pink is supposed to weaken your enemies, make them go soft on you, which must be why it's used for baby girls. It's a wonder the military hasn't got onto this. Pale-pink helmets, with rosettes, a whole battalion, onto the beachhead, over the top in pink. Now is the time for me to make the switch, I could use a little pink right now.

I cruise the cut-rate windows. Each one is like a shrine, lit up from within, its goddess on display, hand on hip or leg thrust out, the faces beige and inaccessible. Party dresses have come back, bows and flamenco ruffles, straplessness and crinolines, puffed sleeves like cloth marshmallows: everything I thought was left behind forever. And mini-skirts too, as bad as ever, but I draw the line at those. I didn't like them the last time around either: too much underpants. I can't wear the ruffled things, I'd look like a cabbage, and not the strapless ones either, not with my collarbone high and dry, my hen's-foot elbows sticking out. What I need is something vertical, maybe a little draped.

A SALE sign lures me in. The name of this store is The Sleek Boutique, though it's not really a boutique: it's crammed full of ends-of-line, low on overhead. It's crowded, which pleases me. Salesladies intimidate me, I don't like to be caught shopping. I riffle furtively through the SALE rack, bypassing sequins, angora roses, gold thread, grubby white leather, looking for something.

What I'd like is to be transformed, which becomes less possible. Disguise is easier when you're young.

I take three things to the fitting room: salmon with dollar-sized white polka dots, electric blue with satin inserts, and, to be on the safe side, something in black that will do if all else fails. The salmon is what I'd really like, but can I handle the dots? I slip it on, zipper and hook it, turn this way and that, in front of the mirror which is as usual badly lit. If I ran a store like this I'd paint all the cubicles pink and put some money into the mirrors: whatever else women want to see, it's not themselves; not in their worst light anyway.

I crane my neck, trying to get the rear view. Maybe with different shoes, or different earrings? The price tag dangles, pointing to my rump. There are the polka dots, rolling across a broad expanse. It's amazing how much bigger you always look from the back. Maybe because there are fewer distracting features to break up the wide monotony of hill and plane.

As I turn back, I see my purse, lying on the floor where I put it, and after all these years I should know better. It's open. The cubicle wall only comes down to a foot above the floor, and back through the gap a noiseless arm is retreating, the hand clutching my wallet. The fingernails are painted Day-Glo green.

I bring my shoeless foot down hard on the wrist. There's a shriek, some loud plural giggling: youth on the fast track, schoolgirls on the prowl. My wallet is dropped, the hand shoots back like a tentacle.

I jerk open the door. *Damn you, Cordelia!* I think.

But Cordelia is long gone.

9

The school we are sent to is some distance away, past a cemetery, across a ravine, along a wide curving street lined with older houses. The name of it is Queen Mary Public School. In the mornings we walk across the freezing mud in our new winter overshoes, carrying our lunches in paper bags, and down through the remains of an orchard to the nearest paved road, where we wait for the school bus to come lurching towards us, up the hill and over the pot-holes. I wear my new snowsuit, my skirt wrapped around my legs and stuffed down into the bulgy legs of the snowpants, which whisk together as I walk. You can't wear pants to school, you have to wear skirts. I'm not used to this, or to sitting still at a desk.

We eat our lunches in the chilly dimly lit cellar of the school-house, where we sit in supervised rows on long scarred wooden benches under a festoon of heating pipes. Most of the children go home for lunch, it's only the school-bus ones that have to stay. We're issued small bottles of milk which we drink through straws stuck in through a hole in the cardboard bottle tops. These are my first drinking-straws, and they amaze me.

The school building itself is old and tall, made of liver-coloured brick, with high ceilings, long ominous wood-floored hallways, and radiators that are either on full blast or not at all, so that we're either shivering with cold or too hot. The windows are high and thin and many-paned, and decorated with cut-outs made of construction paper; right now there are snowflakes, for winter. There's a front door which is never used by children. At the back are two grandiose entranceways with carvings around them and ornate insets above the doors, inscribed in curvy, solemn lettering: GIRLS and BOYS. When the teacher in the yard rings her brass handbell we have to line up in twos by classrooms, girls in one line, boys in another, and file into our separate doors. The girls hold hands; the boys don't. If you go in the wrong door you get the strap, or so everyone says.

I am very curious about the BOYS door. How is going in through a door different if you're a boy? What's in there that merits the strap, just for seeing it? My brother says there's nothing special about the stairs inside, they're plain ordinary stairs. The boys don't have a separate classroom, they're in with us. They go in the BOYS door and end up in the same place we do. I can see the point of the boys' washroom, because they pee differently, and also the boys' yard, because of all the kicking and punching that goes on among them. But the door baffles me. I would like to have a look inside.

Just as there are separate doors for boys and girls, there are also separate parts of the schoolyard. At the front, outside the teachers' entrance, is a dirt field covered with cinders, the boys' playing field. At the side of the school facing away from the street is a hill, with wooden steps going up it and eroded runnels worn down the side, and a few stunted evergreens on top. By custom this is reserved for the girls, and the older ones stand around up there in groups of three or four, their heads bent inwards, whispering, although boys sometimes make charges up the hill, yelling and waving their arms. The cement-paved area outside the BOYS and GIRLS is common territory, since the boys have to cross it in order to go in their door.

Lining up is the only time I see my brother at school. At home we've rigged up a walkie-talkie with two tin cans and a piece of string, which runs between our two bedroom windows and doesn't work very well. We push messages under each other's doors, written in the cryptic language of the aliens, which is filled with x's and z's and must be decoded. We nudge and kick each other under the table, keeping our faces straight above the tablecloth; sometimes we tie our shoe-laces together, for signalling. These are my main communications with my brother now, these raspy tin-can words, sentences without vowels, the Morse of feet.

But in the daytime I lose sight of him as soon as we go out the door. He's up ahead, throwing snowballs; and on the bus he's at the back, in a noisy whirlpool of older boys. After school, after he's gone through the fights that are required of any new boy at any school, he's off helping to wage war on the boys from the Catholic school nearby. It's called Our Lady of Perpetual Help, but the boys from our school have re-named it Our Lady of Perpetual Hell. It's said that the boys from this Catholic school are very tough and that they conceal rocks inside their snowballs.

I know better than to speak to my brother during these times, or to call his or any boy's attention to me. Boys get teased for having younger sisters, or sisters of any kind, or mothers; it's like having new clothes. When he gets anything new my brother dirties it as soon as possible, to avoid having it noticed; and if he has to go anywhere with me and my mother, he walks ahead of us or crosses to the other side of the street. If he's teased about me, he will have to fight some more. For me to contact him, or even to call him by name, would be disloyal. I understand these things, and do my best.

So I am left to the girls, real girls at last, in the flesh. But I'm not used to girls, or familiar with their customs. I feel awkward around them, I don't know what to say. I know the unspoken rules of boys, but with girls I sense that I am always on the verge of some unforeseen, calamitous blunder.

A girl called Carol Campbell makes friends with me. In a way she has to, because she's the only school-bus girl in my grade. The children who come on the school bus, who eat their lunches in the cellar instead of going home, are considered a little foreign, and are in danger of finding themselves without a partner when the bell rings and it's time to line up. So Carol sits beside me on the school bus, holds my hand in line, whispers to me, eats her lunch beside me on the wooden bench in the cellar.

Carol lives in one of the older houses on the other side of the abandoned orchard, closer to the school, a yellow brick house with two storeys and green-painted shutters framing the windows. She's a stubby girl with a frequent laugh. She tells me her hair is honey-blonde, that her haircut is called a pageboy, that she has to go to the hairdresser's every two months to get it done. I haven't known there are such things as pageboys and hairdressers. My mother doesn't go to the hairdresser's. She wears her hair long, pinned up at the sides, like the women in wartime posters, and my own hair has never been cut.

Carol and her younger sister have matching outfits for Sundays: fitted brown tweed coats with velvet collars, round brown velvet hats with an elastic under the chin to hold them on. They have brown gloves and little brown purses. She tells me all this.

343

They are Anglicans. Carol asks me what church I go to, and I say I don't know. In fact we never go to church.

After school Carol and I walk home, not the way the school bus goes in the morning but a different way, along back streets and across a decaying wooden footbridge over the ravine. We've been told not to do this alone, and not to go down into the ravine by ourselves. There might be men down there, is what Carol says. These are not ordinary men but the other kind, the shadowy, nameless kind who do things to you. She smiles and whispers when saying *men*, as if they are a special, thrilling joke. We cross the bridge lightly, avoiding the places where the boards have rotted through, on the lookout for men.

Carol invites me to her house after school, where she shows me her cupboard with all her clothes hanging in it. She has a lot of dresses and skirts; she even has a dressing-gown, with fuzzy slippers to match. I have never seen so many girls' clothes in one place.

She lets me look at her living room from the doorway, although we aren't allowed to go into it. She herself can't go in except to practise the piano. The living room has a sofa and two chairs and matching drapes, all of a flowered rose and beige material Carol says is chintz. She pronounces this word with awe, as if it's the name of something sacred, and I repeat it silently to myself: *chintz*. It sounds like the name of a kind of crayfish, or of one of the aliens on my brother's distant planet.

Carol tells me that her piano teacher hits her fingers with a ruler if she gets a note wrong, and that her mother spanks her with the back of a hairbrush or else a slipper. When she's really in for it she has to wait until her father comes home and whacks her with his belt, right on the bare bum. All of these things are secrets. She says her mother sings on a radio programme, under a different name, and we do overhear her mother practising scales in the living room, in a loud quavery voice. She says her father takes some of his teeth out at night and puts them into a glass of water beside his bed. She shows me the glass, although the teeth aren't in it. There seems to be nothing she won't tell.

She tells me which boys at school are in love with her, making me promise not to tell. She asks me which ones are in love with me. I've never thought about this before, but I can see that some sort of an answer is expected. I say I'm not sure.

344

Carol comes to my house and takes it all in – the unpainted walls, the wires dangling from the ceilings, the unfinished floors, the army cots – with incredulous glee. "This is where you *sleep?*" she says. "This is where you *eat*? These are your *clothes?*" Most of my clothes, which are not many in number, are pants and jersey tops. I have two dresses, one for summer and one for winter, and a tunic and a wool skirt, for school. I begin to suspect that more may be required.

Carol tells everyone at school that our family sleeps on the floor. She gives the impression that we do this on purpose, because we're from outside the city; that it's a belief of ours. She's disappointed when our real beds arrive from storage, four-legged and with mattresses, like everybody else's. She puts it around that I don't know what church I go to, and that we eat off a card-table. She doesn't repeat these items with scorn, but as exotic specialities. I am, after all, her lining-up partner, and she wants me to be marvelled at. More accurate: she wants herself to be marvelled at, for revealing such wonders. It's as if she's reporting on the antics of some primitive tribe: true, but incredible.

345

10

On Saturday we take Carol Campbell to the building. When we walk into it she says, wrinkling up her nose, "Is this where your father *works*?" We show her the snakes and the turtles; she makes a noise that sounds like "Ew," and says she wouldn't want to touch them. I'm surprised by this; I've been discouraged from having such feelings for so long that I no longer have them. Neither does Stephen. There's not much we won't touch, given the chance.

I think Carol Campbell is a sissy. At the same time I find myself being a little proud of her delicacy. My brother looks at her in an odd way: with contempt, true, and if I myself said such a thing he would make fun of me. But there's an undertone, like an invisible nod, as if something he wants to suspect has come true after all.

By rights he should ignore her after this, but he tries her out on the jars of lizards and ox eyeballs. "Ew," she says. "What if they put one down your *back*?" My brother says how would she like some for dinner? He makes chewing and slurping noises.

"Ew," says Carol, screwing up her face and wriggling all over. I can't pretend to be shocked and disgusted too: my brother wouldn't be convinced. Neither can I join in the game of making up revolting foods, such as toadburgers and leech chewing-gum, although if we were alone or with other boys I would do it without a second thought. So I say nothing.

After we get back from the building I go to Carol's house again. She asks me if I want to see her mother's new twin set. I don't know what this is, but it sounds intriguing, so I say yes. She takes me stealthily into her mother's bedroom, saying that she'll really get it if we're caught, and shows me the twin set, folded on a shelf. The twin set is just two sweaters, both the same colour, one with buttons down the front, the other without. I've already seen Mrs. Campbell wearing a different twin set, a beige one, her breasts pronging out, the buttoned sweater draped over her shoulders like a cape. So this is all twin

346

sets are. I'm disappointed, because I was expecting something to do with twins.

Carol's mother and father don't sleep in one big bed, the way mine do. Instead they sleep in two little beds, exactly alike, with matching pink chenille bedspreads and matching night-tables. These beds are called twin beds, which makes more sense to me than the twin set. Still, it's strange to think of Mr. and Mrs. Campbell lying in them at night, with different heads – his with a moustache, hers without – but nevertheless twin-like, identical, under the sheets and blankets. It's the matching bedspreads, the night-tables, the lamps, the bureaus, the doubleness of everything in their room, that gives me this impression. My own parents' room is less symmetrical, and also less neat.

Carol says her mother wears rubber gloves while washing the dishes. She shows me the rubber gloves and a spray thing attached to the water tap. She turns on the tap and sprays the inside of the sink, and part of the floor by accident, until Mrs. Campbell comes in, wearing her beige twin set and frowning, and says hadn't we better go upstairs to play. Possibly she isn't frowning. She has a mouth that turns slightly down even when she's smiling, so it's hard to tell whether she's pleased or not. Her hair is the same colour as Carol's, but done in a cold wave all over her head. It's Carol who points out that this is a cold wave. A cold wave has nothing to do with water. It's like doll's hair, very tidy and arranged, as if sewn into place.

Carol is more and more gratified the more bewildered I am. "You didn't know what a *cold wave* is?" she says, delighted. She's eager to explain things to me, name them, display them. She shows me around her house as if it's a museum, as if she personally has collected everything in it. Standing in the downstairs hall, where there is a coat-tree – "You've never seen a *coat-tree*?" – she says I am her best friend.

Carol has another best friend, who is sometimes her best friend and sometimes not. Her name is Grace Smeath. Carol points her out to me, on the bus, the same way she's pointed out the twin set and the coat-tree: as an object to be admired.

Grace Smeath is a year older and in the next grade up. At school she plays with the other girls in her class. But after school and on Saturdays she plays with Carol. There are no girls in her class on our side of the ravine.

Grace lives in a two-storey shoebox-shaped red brick house with a front porch that has two thick round white pillars holding it up. She's taller than Carol, with dark thick coarse hair done into two braids. Her skin is extremely pale, like a body under a bathing-suit, but covered with freckles. She wears glasses. Usually she wears a grey skirt with two straps over the shoulders, and a red sweater pebbled with little balls of wool. Her clothes smell faintly of the Smeaths' house, a mixture of scouring powder and cooked turnips and slightly rancid laundry, and the earth under porches. I think she is beautiful.

On Saturdays I no longer go to the building. Instead I play with Carol and Grace. Because it's winter, we play mostly inside. Playing with girls is different and at first I feel strange as I do it, self-conscious, as if I'm only doing an imitation of a girl. But I soon get more used to it.

The things we play are mostly Grace's ideas, because if we try to play anything she doesn't like she says she has a headache and goes home, or else tells us to go home. She never raises her voice, gets angry, or cries; she is quietly reproachful, as if her headache is our fault. Because we want to play with her more than she wants to play with us, she gets her way in everything.

We colour in Grace's movie star colouring books, which show the movie stars in different outfits, doing different things: walking their dogs, going sailing in sailor suits, swirling around in evening dresses at parties. Grace's favourite movie star is Esther Williams. I have no favourite movie star – I've never been to a movie – but I say mine is Veronica Lake, because I like the name. The Veronica Lake book is paper-doll cut-outs, with Veronica Lake in her bathing-suit and dozens of outfits you can stick onto her with tabs that fold around her neck. Grace won't let us cut out these outfits, although we can put them on and take them off once she's done it, but we're allowed to work away at her colouring books as long as we stay inside the lines. She likes to get these books all coloured in. She tells us what colours to use, on which parts. I know what my brother would do – green skin for Esther, with beetle antennae, and hairy legs for Veronica, eight of them – but I refrain from doing it. Anyway I like the clothes.

We play School. Grace has a couple of chairs and a wooden

table in her cellar, and a small blackboard and chalk. These are set up underneath the indoors clothesline where the Smeath underwear is hung up to dry when it rains or snows. The cellar isn't a finished cellar: the floor is cement, the pillars holding up the house are brick, the water pipes and wires are showing, and the air smells of coal dust because the coal bin is right beside the blackboard.

Grace is always the teacher, Carol and I the students. We have to do spelling tests and sums in arithmetic; it's like real school, but worse, because we never get to draw pictures. We can't pretend to be bad, because Grace doesn't like disorder.

Or we sit on the floor in Grace's room with piles of old Eaton's Catalogues. I've seen lots of Eaton's Catalogues before: up north they're hung in outhouses for use as toilet paper. Eaton's Catalogues remind me of the stench of such outhouses, the buzzing of the flies down the hole underneath, the box of lime and the wooden paddle for dumping the lime down, onto the piles of old and recent droppings, of all shapes and colours of brown. But here we treat these catalogues with reverence. We cut the small coloured figures out of them and paste them into scrapbooks. Then we cut out other things – cookware, furniture – and paste them around the figures. The figures themselves are always women. We call them "My lady." "My lady's going to have this refrigerator," we say. "My lady's getting this rug." "This is my lady's umbrella."

Grace and Carol look at each other's scrapbook pages and say, "Oh, yours is so good. Mine's no good. Mine's *awful*." They say this every time we play the scrapbook game. Their voices are wheedling and false; I can tell they don't mean it, each one thinks her own lady on her own page is good. But it's the thing you have to say, so I begin to say it too.

I find this game tiring – it's the weight, the accumulation of all these objects, these possessions that would have to be taken care of, packed, stuffed into cars, unpacked. I know a lot about moving house. But Carol and Grace have never moved anywhere. Their ladies live in a single house each and have always lived there. They can add more and more, stuff the pages of their scrapbooks with dining-room suites, beds, stacks of towels, one set of dishes after another, and think nothing of it.

I begin to want things I've never wanted before: braids, a

dressing-gown, a purse of my own. Something is unfolding, being revealed to me. I see that there's a whole world of girls and their doings that has been unknown to me, and that I can be part of it without making any effort at all. I don't have to keep up with anyone, run as fast, aim as well, make loud explosive noises, decode messages, die on cue. I don't have to think about whether I've done these things well, as well as a boy. All I have to do is sit on the floor and cut frying pans out of the Eaton's Catalogue with embroidery scissors, and say I've done it badly. Partly this is a relief.

11

For Christmas, Carol gives me some Friendship's Garden bath-salts and Grace gives me a colouring book of Virginia Mayo. I open their presents before anyone else's.

I also get a photo album, to go with my camera. The pages and covers are black, tied together with something that looks like a big black shoe-lace; there's a package of black triangles with glue on them to stick the photos in with. So far I have taken only one roll of film with my camera. I think about what each picture will look like as I press the button. I don't want to waste any. When the pictures come back from being developed, the negatives come too. I hold them up to the light: everything that's white in the real picture is black in the negative. Snow for instance is black, and people's eyeballs and teeth.

I stick my photos into the album with the black triangles. Some of the pictures are of my brother, making threatening gestures with snowballs. Some are of Carol, some of Grace. There's only that one picture of me, standing in front of the motel door with 9 on it, long ago, a month ago. Already that child seems much younger, poorer, farther away, a shrunken, ignorant version of myself.

Another thing I get for Christmas is a red plastic purse, oval in shape, with a gold-coloured clasp and a handle at the top end. It's soft and pliable inside the house, but hardens outside in the cold, so that things rattle in it. I keep my allowance in it, five cents a week.

By this time we have a living-room floor, hardwood, waxed by my mother down on her knees, polished with a long-handled weighted brush that she pushes back and forth, making a sound like waves. The living room has been painted, the fixtures installed, the baseboards added on. There are even curtains; drapes, they're called. The public, visible parts of the house have been finished first.

Our bedrooms remain in a rawer state. The windows there do

351

not yet have drapes. Lying in bed at night, I can look out of my window at the snow falling, illuminated by the light from my brother's bedroom window beside mine.

It's the darkest time of the year. Even in the daytime it seems dark; and at night, when the lights are on, this darkness pervades everything, like a fog. Outside there are only a few streetlights, and they're far apart and not very bright. The lamps in people's houses cast a yellowish light, not cold and greenish but a buttery dim yellow with a tinge of brown. The colours of things in houses have darkness mixed into them: maroon, mushroom beige, a muted green, a dusty rose. These colours look a little dirty, like the squares in a paint box when you forget to rinse the brush.

We have a maroon chesterfield which has come out of storage, with an oriental-style maroon and purple rug in front of it. We have a tri-light floor lamp. The air in the evening lamplight is coagulated, like a custard thickening; heavier sediments of light collect in the corners of the living room. The drapes are kept closed at night, folds and folds of cloth drawn against the winter, hoarding the dim heavy light, keeping it in.

In this light I spread the evening paper out on the polished hardwood floor and rest on my knees and elbows, reading the comics. In the comics there are people with round holes for eyes, others who can hypnotize you instantly, others with secret identities, others who can stretch their faces into any shape at all. Around me is the scent of newsprint and floor wax, the bureau-drawer smell of my itchy stockings mingled with that of grimy knees, the scratchy hot smell of wool plaid and the cat-box aroma of cotton underpants. Behind me the radio plays square-dance music from the Maritimes, Don Messer and His Islanders, in preparation for the six o'clock news. The radio is of dark varnished wood with a single green eye that moves along the dial as you turn the knob. Between the stations this eye makes eerie noises from outer space. Radio waves, says Stephen.

Often, now, Grace Smeath asks me over to her house after school without asking Carol. She tells Carol there's a reason why she isn't invited: it's because of her mother. Her mother is tired, so Grace can only have one best friend over that day.

Grace's mother has a bad heart. Grace doesn't treat this as a

352

secret, as Carol would. She says it unemotionally, politely, as if requesting you to wipe your feet on the mat; but also smugly, as if she has something, some privilege or moral superiority that the two of us don't share. It's the attitude she takes towards the rubber plant that stands on the landing halfway up her stairs. This is the only plant in Grace's house, and we aren't allowed to touch it. It's very old and has to be wiped off leaf by leaf with milk. Mrs. Smeath's bad heart is like that. It's because of this heart that we have to tiptoe, walk quietly, stifle our laughter, do what Grace says. Bad hearts have their uses; even I can see that.

Every afternoon Mrs. Smeath has to take a rest. She does this, not in her bedroom, but on the chesterfield in the living room, stretched out with her shoes off and a knitted afghan covering her. That is how she is always to be found when we go there to play after school. We come in through the side door, up the steps to the kitchen, trying to be as quiet as possible, and into the dining room as far as the double French doors, where we peer in through the glass panes, trying to see whether her eyes are open or closed. She's never asleep. But there's always the possibility – put into our heads by Grace, in that same factual way – that on any given day she may be dead.

Mrs. Smeath is not like Mrs. Campbell. For instance, she has no twin sets, and views them with contempt. I know this because once, when Carol was bragging about her mother's twin sets, Mrs. Smeath said, "Is that so," not as a question but as a way of making Carol shut up. She doesn't wear lipstick or face-powder, even when she goes out. She has big bones, square teeth with little gaps between them so that you can see each tooth distinctly, skin that looks rubbed raw as if scrubbed with a potato brush. Her face is rounded and bland, with that white skin of Grace's, though without the freckles. She wears glasses like Grace too, but hers have steel rims instead of brown ones. Her hair is parted down the middle and greying at the temples, braided and wound over her head into a flat hair crown crisscrossed with hairpins.

She wears print housedresses, not only in the mornings but most of the time. Over the dresses she wears bibbed aprons that sag at the bosom and make it look as if she doesn't have two breasts but only one, a single breast that goes all the way across her front and continues down until it joins her waist. She wears lisle stockings with seams, which make her legs look stuffed and sewn up the backs. She wears brown Oxfords. Sometimes, instead of the stockings, she has thin cotton socks, above which her legs rise white and sparsely haired, like a woman's moustache. She has a moustache too, though not very much of one, just a sprinkling of hairs around the corners of the mouth. She smiles a lot, with her lips closed over her large teeth; but, like Grace, she does not laugh.

She has big hands, knuckly and red from the wash. There's a lot of wash, because Grace has two younger sisters who get her skirts and blouses and also her underpants passed down to them. I'm used to getting my brother's jerseys, but not his underpants. It's these underpants, thin and grey with use, that hang dripping on the line over our heads as we sit in Grace's cellar pretending to be schoolchildren.

Before Valentine's Day we have to cut out hearts of red construction paper at school and decorate them with pieces of paper doily to stick on the tall thin windows. While I am cutting mine I think about Mrs. Smeath's bad heart. What exactly is wrong with it? I picture it hidden, underneath her woollen afghan and the billow of her apron bib, pumping in the thick fleshy darkness of the inside of her body: something taboo, intimate. It would be red, but with a reddish-black patch on it, like rot in an apple or a bruise. It hurts when I think about it. A little sharp wince of pain goes through me, as it did when I watched my brother cut his finger once on a piece of glass. But the bad heart is also compelling. It's a curiosity, a deformity. A horrible treasure.

Day after day I press my nose against the glass of the French doors, trying to see if Mrs. Smeath is still alive. This is how I will see her forever: lying unmoving, like something in a museum, with her head on the antimacassar pinned to the arm of the chesterfield, a bed pillow under her neck, the rubber plant on the landing visible behind her, turning her head to look at us, her scrubbed face, without her glasses, white and strangely luminous in the dim space, like a phosphorescent mushroom. She is ten years younger than I am now. Why do I hate her so much? Why do I care, in any way, what went on in her head?

12

The snow erodes, leaving the pot-holes in the roads near our house filled with muddy water. Thin bubbles of ice form across these puddles overnight; we shatter them with the heels of our boots. Icicles crash down from the eaves of roofs, and we pick them up and lick them like popsicles. We wear our mittens dangling. On the lawns, as we walk home from school, we can see damp pieces of paper under the hedges, old dog turds, crocuses poking up through the grainy, soot-coloured snow. The gutters run with brownish water; the wooden bridge over the ravine is slippery and soft and has regained its smell of rot.

Our house looks like something left over from the war: all around it spreads rubble, devastation. My parents stand in their backyard, hands on their hips, looking out over the expanse of raw mud, planning their garden. Already clumps of couch-grass are beginning to thrust up. Couch-grass can grow in anything, my father says. He also says that the contractor, the same one that flew the coop, took the dense clay from where our cellar went in and spread it around the house, over what should have been the topsoil. "An idiot as well as a crook," says my father.

My brother watches the water level in the giant hole next door, waiting for the hole to dry up so he can use it for a bunker. He would like to roof it over, with sticks and old planks, but he knows this isn't possible because the hole is too big and also he wouldn't be allowed. Instead he plans to dig a tunnel down there, into the side of the hole, and to get up and down to it by a rope ladder. He has no rope ladder, but he says he'll make one, if he can get some rope.

He and the other boys run around in the mud; large extra feet of clay stick to the soles of their boots, leaving tracks like monsters. They crouch behind the trees in the old orchard, sniping at one another, shouting:

"You're dead!"

"I am not!"

355

"You're dead!"

At other times they crowd into my brother's room, lying on their stomachs on his bed or on the floor, reading his huge piles of comic books. I sometimes do this too, wallowing among the pages of coloured paper, surrounded by the fuggy scent of boys. Boys don't smell the same as girls. They have a pungent, leathery, underneath smell, like old rope, like damp dogs. We keep the door closed because my mother doesn't approve of comics. The reading of comics is done in reverential silence, with now and then a few monosyllables of trade.

Comic books are what my brother is collecting now. He's always collected something. Once it was milk-bottle tops, from dozens of dairies; he carried sheafs of them around in his pockets, held together with rubber bands, and stood them up against walls and threw other milk-bottle tops at them to win more. Then it was pop-bottle tops, then cigarette cards, then sightings of licence plates from different provinces and states. There is no way of winning comic books. Instead you trade them, one good one for three or four of lesser value.

At school we make Easter eggs out of construction paper, pink and purple and blue, and stick them onto the windows. After that it's tulips, and soon there are real tulips. It seems to be a rule that the paper things always appear before the real ones.

Grace produces a long skipping rope, and she and Carol teach me how to turn it. As we turn, we chant, in monotonous minor-key voices:

Salome was a dancer, she did the hoochie kootch;
And when she did the hoochie kootch, she didn't wear
* very mooch.*

Grace puts one hand on her head, the other on her hip, and wiggles her bum. She does this with perfect decorum; she's wearing her pleated skirt with the straps over the shoulders. I know Salome is supposed to be more like the movie stars in our paper-doll books. I think of gauzy skirts, high heels with stars on the toes, hats covered with fruit and feathers, lifted eyebrows, pencil-thin; gaiety and excess. But Grace in her pleats and woollen straps can wipe out all that.

Our other game is ball. We play it against the side wall of Carol's house. We throw our rubber balls up against the wall and catch them as they come down, clapping and twirling in time to the chant:

> *Ordinary, moving, laughing, talking, one hand, the other hand, one foot, the other foot, clap front, clap back, back and front, front and back, tweedle, twydle, curtsy, salute, and roundabout.*

For *roundabout* you throw the ball and twirl all the way around before catching it. This is the hardest thing, harder even than the left hand.

The sun lasts longer and longer and goes down golden-red. The willow trees drop yellow catkins over the bridge; the maple keys fall twirling to the sidewalks and we split the sticky seed part and pinch the keys onto our noses. The air is warm, humid, like invisible mist. We wear cotton dresses to school, and cardigans, which we take off walking home. The old trees in the orchard are in flower, white and pink; we climb up into them, breathing in their hand-lotion smells, or we sit in the grass making chains of dandelions. We unbraid Grace's hair, which falls down her back in coarse brown ripples, and wind the chains around her head like a crown. "You're a princess," says Carol, stroking the hair. I take a picture of Grace and stick it into my photo album. There she sits, smiling primly, festooned with blossoms.

The field across from Carol's house is sprouting new houses, and in the evenings groups of children, boys and girls alike, clamber about inside them, in the fresh wood smell of shavings, walking through walls that don't yet exist, climbing ladders where there will soon be stairs. This is forbidden.

Carol won't climb to the higher floors because she's afraid. Grace won't climb either, but not because of fear: she doesn't want anybody, any boy, to see her underpants. No girl can wear slacks to school, but Grace never wears them at any time. So the two of them stay on the ground floor while I climb, up and along the beams with no ceiling covering them, up again to the attic. I sit on the top floor where there is no floor, among the rafters in this house of air, basking in the red-gold sunset, looking down. I don't think about falling. I am not yet afraid of heights.

* * *

One day someone appears in the schoolyard with a bag of marbles, and the next day everyone has them. The boys desert the boys' playground and throng into the common playground in front of the BOYS and GIRLS doors; they need to come to this side of the playground, because marbles have to be played on a smooth surface and the boys' yard is all cinders.

For marbles you're either the person setting up the target or the person shooting. To shoot you kneel down, sight, and roll your marble at the target marble like a bowling ball. If you hit it you keep it, and your own marble too. If you miss, you lose your marble. If you're setting up, you sit on the cement with your legs spread open and put a marble on a crack in front of you. It can be an ordinary marble, but these don't get many shooters, unless you offer two for one. Usually the targets are more valuable: cat's eyes, clear glass with a bloom of coloured petals in the centre, red or yellow or green or blue; puries, flawless like coloured water or sapphires or rubies; waterbabies, with undersea filaments of colour suspended in them; metal bowlies; aggies, like marbles only bigger. These exotics are passed from winner to winner. It's cheating to buy them; they have to be won.

Those with target marbles call out the names of their wares: *purie, purie, bowlie, bowlie*, the two-syllable words drawn out into a singsong, the voice descending, the way you call dogs, or children when they're lost. These cries are mournful, although they aren't meant to be. I sit that way myself, the cold marbles rolling in between my legs, gathering in my outspread skirt, calling out *cat's eye, cat's eye*, in a regretful tone, feeling nothing but avarice and a pleasurable terror.

The cat's eyes are my favourites. If I win a new one I wait until I'm by myself, then take it out and examine it, turning it over and over in the light. The cat's eyes really are like eyes, but not the eyes of cats. They're the eyes of something that isn't known but exists anyway; like the green eye of the radio; like the eyes of aliens from a distant planet. My favourite one is blue. I put it into my red plastic purse to keep it safe. I risk my other cat's eyes to be shot at, but not this one.

I don't collect many marbles because I'm not a very good shot. My brother is deadly. He takes five common marbles to school with him in a blue Crown Royal Whisky bag and comes back with the bag and his pockets bulging. He keeps his winnings in screw-top Crown preserving jars, donated by my mother, which he lines up on his desk. He never talks about his skill though. He just lines up the jars.

One Saturday afternoon he puts all his best marbles – his puries, his waterbabies and cat's eyes, his gems and wonders – into a single jar. He takes it down into the ravine somewhere, in under the wooden bridge, and buries it. Then he makes an elaborate treasure map of where it's buried, puts it in another jar, and buries that one too. He tells me he's done these things but he doesn't say why, or where the jars are buried.

13

The raw house and its lawn of mud and the mountain of earth beside it recede behind us; I watch them out of the back window of the car, from where I sit jammed in among the boxes of food, the sleeping bags and raincoats. I'm wearing a blue striped jersey of my brother's, a worn pair of corduroy pants. Grace and Carol stand under the apple trees, in their skirts, waving, disappearing. They still have to go to school; I don't. I envy them. Already the tarry, rubbery travel smell is wrapping itself around me, but I don't welcome it. I'm being wrenched away from my new life, the life of girls.

I settle back into the familiar perspective, the backs of heads, the ears, and past them the white line of the highway. We drive up through the meadowy farmlands, with their silos and elms and their smell of cut hay. The broad-leafed trees become smaller, there are more pines, the air cools, the sky turns an icier blue: we're heading away from spring. We hit the first ridges of granite, the first lakes; there's snow in the shadows. I sit forward, leaning my arms on the back of the front seat. I feel like a dog, ears pricked and sniffing.

The north smells different from the city: clearer, thinner. You can see farther. A sawmill, a hill of sawdust, the teepee shape of a sawdust burner; the smokestacks of the copper smelters, the rocks around them bare of trees, burnt-looking, the heaps of blackened slag: I've forgotten about these things all winter, but here they are again, and when I see them I remember them, I know them, I greet them as if they are home.

Men stand on corners, outside general stores, outside small banks, outside beer parlours with grey asphalt shingles on the walls. They have their hands in their windbreaker pockets. Some have dark, Indian-looking faces, others are merely tanned. They walk differently from men in the south, slower, more considering; they say less and their words are farther apart. My father jingles his keys and the change in his pockets while he talks with

360

them. They talk about water levels, the dryness of the forest, how the fish are biting. "Chewing the fat," he calls it. He comes back to the car with a brown paper bag of groceries and packs it in behind my feet.

My brother and I stand at the end of a ramshackle dock beside a long blue craggy lake. It's evening, with a melon-coloured sunset, loons calling in the distance, the drawn-out rising note that sounds like wolves. We're fishing. There are mosquitoes, but I'm used to them, I hardly bother to slap them. The fishing goes on without commentary: a cast, the plop of the lure, the sound of reeling in. We watch the lure to see if anything is following it. If there's a fish, we'll do our best to net it, step on it to hold it down, whack it over the head, stick a knife behind its eyes. I do the stepping, my brother does the whacking, the sticking. Despite his silence he is poised, alert, the corners of his mouth tensed. I wonder if my eyes are gleaming like his, like some animal's, in the pink dusk.

We're living in an abandoned logging camp. We sleep on our air mattresses, in our sleeping bags, in the wooden bunks where the loggers used to sleep. Already the logging camp has a feeling of great age about it, although it's only been empty for two years. Some of the loggers have left inscriptions, their names, their initials, intertwined hearts, short dirty words and crude pictures of women, carved or pencilled in the wood of the two-by-fours of the walls. I find an old tin of maple syrup, the lid rusted shut, but when Stephen and I get it open the syrup is mouldy. I think of this syrup tin as an ancient artefact, like something dug up out of a tomb.

We prowl around among the trees, looking for bones, for hummocks in the earth that could mark diggings, the outlines of buildings, turning over logs and rocks to see what's underneath them. We would like to discover a lost civilization. We find a beetle, many small yellow and white roots, a toad. Nothing human.

Our father has shed his city clothing, turned back into himself. He has on his old jacket again, his baggy pants, his squashed

361

felt hat with the fishing flies stuck into it. He tromps through the woods in his heavy lace-up bacon-greased workboots, with his axe in its leather sheath, us in his wake. There's an outbreak of forest tent caterpillars, the biggest in years: this is what fills him with glee, makes his eyes of a gnome shine in his head like blue-grey buttons. The caterpillars are everywhere in the woods, striped and bristly. They dangle from the branches on threads of silk, forming a hanging curtain you have to brush out of the way; they river along the ground like a rug come to life, they cross roads, turning to greasy mush under the tyres of the logging trucks. The trees around are denuded, as if they've been burnt; webbing sheathes their trunks.

"Remember this," our father says. "This is a classic infestation. You won't see an infestation like this again for a long time." It's the way I've heard people talk about forest fires, or the war: respect and wonderment mixed in with the sense of catastrophe.

My brother stands still and lets the caterpillars wash up over his feet, down on the other side of him, like a wave. "When you were a baby I caught you trying to eat those," says our mother. "You had a whole handful, you were squashing them around. You were just about to pop them into your mouth when I caught you."

"In some respects they're like one animal," our father says. He sits at the table made of planks left over from the loggers, eating fried Spam and potatoes. All during this meal he talks about the caterpillars: their numbers, their ingenuity, the various methods of defeating them. It's wrong to spray them with DDT and other insecticides, he says. That merely poisons the birds which are their natural enemies, whereas they themselves, being insects and therefore resourceful, more resourceful than humans in fact, will merely develop a resistance to the sprays, so all you get is dead birds and more caterpillars later on. He's working on something else: a growth hormone that will throw their systems out of whack and make them pupate before they're supposed to. Premature aging. But in the end, if he were a betting man, he says, he'd put his money on the insects. The insects are older than people, they have more experience at surviving, and there are a lot more of them than there are of us. Anyway, we'll probably blow ourselves sky-high before the end of the century, given the atom bomb and the way things are going. The future belongs to the insects.

"Cockroaches," my father says. "That's all that'll be left, once they get through with it." He says this jovially, skewering a potato.

I sit eating my fried Spam, drinking my milk mixed from powder. What I relish the most are the lumps that float on the top. I'm thinking about Carol and Grace, my two best friends. At the same time I can't remember exactly what they look like. Did I really sit on the floor of Grace's bedroom, on her braided bedside rug, cutting out pictures of frying pans and washing machines from the Eaton's Catalogue and pasting them into a scrapbook? Already it seems implausible, and yet I know I did it.

Out behind the logging camp is a huge cut-over where they've taken off the trees. Only the roots and stumps remain. There's a lot of sand out there. The blueberry bushes have come up, as they do after a fire: first the fireweed, then the blueberries. We pick the berries into tin cups. Our mother pays us a cent a cup. She makes blueberry puddings, blueberry sauce, canned blueberries, boiling the jars in a large canning kettle over the outdoor fire.

The sun beats down, the heat comes wavering up off the sand. I wear a cotton kerchief on my head, folded into a triangle and tied behind my ears, the front of it damp with sweat. Around us is the drone of flies. I try to listen through it, behind it, for the sound of bears. I'm not sure what they would sound like, but I know that bears like blueberries, and they're unpredictable. They may run away. Or they may come after you. If they come you should lie down and pretend to be dead. This is what my brother says. Then they might go away, he says; or they might scoop out your innards. I've seen fish guts, I can picture this. My brother finds a bear turd, blue and speckled and human-looking, and pokes a stick into it to see how fresh it is.

In the afternoons, when it's too hot to pick berries, we swim in the lake, in the same water the fish come out of. I'm not supposed to go out of my depth. The water is gelid, murky; down there, past where the sand drops away and it's deep, there are old rocks covered with slime, sunken logs, crayfish, leeches, huge pike with undershot jaws. Stephen tells me fish can smell. He says they'll smell us, and keep out of the way.

We sit on the shore, on rocks that poke up from the narrow beach, and toss bits of bread into the water, seeing what we can entice: minnows, a few perch. We search for flat stones and skip them, or we practise burping at will, or we put our mouths against the insides of our arms and blow to make farting noises, or we fill our mouths with water and see how far we can spit. In these contests I am not the winner, I am more like an audience; though my brother does not brag, and would probably do the same things, by himself, if I weren't there.

Sometimes he writes in pee, on the thin edge of sand or on the surface of the water. He does this methodically, as if it's important to do it well, the pee arching delicately out from the front of his swimming trunks, from his hand and its extra finger, the writing angular, like his real writing, and ending always with a period. He doesn't write his name, or dirty words, as other boys do, as I know from snowbanks. Instead he writes: MARS. Or, if he's feeling up to it, something longer: JUPITER. By the end of the summer he has done the whole solar system, three times over, in pee.

It's the middle of September; the leaves are already turning, dark red, bright yellow. At night when I walk to the outhouse, in the dark with no flashlight because I can see better that way, the stars are sharp and crystalline and my breath goes before me. I see my parents, in through the window, sitting beside the kerosene lamp, and they are like a far-away picture with a frame of blackness. It's disquieting to look at them, in through the window, and know that they don't know I can see them. It's as if I don't exist; or as if they don't.

When we come back down from the north it's like coming down from a mountain. We descend through layers of clarity, of coolness and uncluttered light, down past the last granite outcrop, the last small raggedy-edged lake, into the thicker air, the dampness and warm heaviness, the cricket noises and weedy meadow smells of the south.

364

We reach our house in the afternoon. It looks strange, different, as if enchanted. Thistles and goldenrod have grown up around it, like a thorny hedge, out of the mud. The huge hole and the mountain of earth next door have vanished, and in their place is a new house. How has this happened? I wasn't expecting such changes.

Grace and Carol are standing among the apple trees, just where I left them. But they don't look the same. They don't look at all like the pictures of them I've carried around in my head for the past four months, shifting pictures in which only a few features stand out. For one thing they're bigger; and they have on different clothes.

They don't come running over, but stop what they're doing and stare, as if we're new people, as if I've never lived here. A third girl is with them. I look at her, empty of premonition. I've never seen her before.

14

Grace waves. After a moment Carol waves too. The third girl doesn't wave. They stand among the asters and goldenrod, waiting as I go towards them. The apple trees are covered with scabby apples, red ones and yellow ones; some of the apples have fallen off and are rotting on the ground. There's a sweet, cidery smell, and the buzz of drunken yellowjackets. The apples mush under my feet.

Grace and Carol are browner, less pasty; their features are farther apart, their hair lighter. The third girl is the tallest. Unlike Grace and Carol, who are in summer skirts, she wears corduroys and a pullover. Both Carol and Grace are stubby-shaped, but this girl is thin without being fragile: lanky, sinewy. She has dark-blonde hair cut in a long pageboy, with bangs falling half into her greenish eyes. Her face is long, her mouth slightly lopsided; something about the top lip is a little skewed, as if it's been cut open and sewn up crooked.

But her mouth evens out when she smiles. She has a smile like a grownup's, as if she's learned it and is doing it out of politeness. She holds out her hand. "Hi, I'm Cordelia. And you must be . . ."

I stare at her. If she were an adult, I would take the hand, shake it, I would know what to say. But children do not shake hands like this.

"Elaine," Grace says.

I feel shy with Cordelia. I've been riding in the back of the car for two days, sleeping in a tent; I'm conscious of my grubbiness, my unbrushed hair. Cordelia is looking past me to where my parents are unloading the car. Her eyes are measuring, amused. I can see, without turning around, my father's old felt hat, his boots, the stubble on his face, my brother's uncut hair and seedy sweater and baggy knees, my mother's grey slacks, her man-like plaid shirt, her face blank of makeup.

"There's dog poop on your shoe," Cordelia says.

366

I look down. "It's only a rotten apple."

"It's the same colour though, isn't it?" Cordelia says. "Not the hard kind, the soft squooshy kind, like peanut butter." This time her voice is confiding, as if she's talking about something intimate that only she and I know about and agree on. She creates a circle of two, takes me in.

Cordelia lives farther east than I do, in a region of houses even newer than ours, with the same surrounding mud. But her house is not a bungalow, it has two storeys. It has a dining room separated by a curtain which you can pull back to make the living room and the dining room into one big room, and a bathroom on the ground floor with no bathtub in it which is called the powder room.

The colours in Cordelia's house are not dark, like those in other houses. They're light greys and light greens and whites. The sofa, for instance, is apple-green. There's nothing flowered or maroon or velvet. There's a picture, framed in light grey, of Cordelia's two older sisters, done in pastels when they were younger, both wearing smocked dresses, their hair feathery, their eyes like mist. There are real flowers, several different kinds at once, in chunky, flowing vases of Swedish glass. It's Cordelia who tells us the glass is Swedish. Swedish glass is the best kind, she says.

Cordelia's mother arranges the flowers herself, wearing gardening gloves. My own mother doesn't arrange flowers. Sometimes she sticks a few into a pot and puts them on the dinner table, but these are flowers she picks herself, during her exercise walks, in her slacks, along the road or in the ravine. Really they are weeds. She would never think of spending money on flowers. It occurs to me for the first time that we are not rich.

Cordelia's mother has a cleaning lady. She is the only one of our mothers who has one. The cleaning lady is not called the cleaning lady, however. She is called the woman. On the days when the woman comes, we have to stay out of her way.

"The woman before this one," Cordelia tells us, in a hushed, scandalized voice, "was caught stealing potatoes. She put her bag down and they rolled out, all over the floor. It was so embarrassing." She means for them, not for the woman. "Of course we had to let her go."

Cordelia's family does not eat boiled eggs mushed up in a bowl but out of egg-cups. Each egg-cup has an initial on it, one for each person in the family. There are napkin-rings too, also with initials. I have never heard of an egg-cup before and I can tell Grace hasn't either, by the way she keeps silent about it. Carol says uncertainly that she has them at home.

"After you eat the egg," Cordelia tells us, "you have to put a hole in the bottom of the shell."

"Why?" we say.

"So the witches can't put out to sea." She says this lightly but scornfully, as if only a fool would need to ask. But there's the possibility she's joking, or teasing. Her two older sisters have this habit also. It's hard to tell when they mean to be taken seriously. They have an extravagant, mocking way of talking, which seems like an imitation of something, only it's unclear what they're imitating.

"I almost *died*," they say. Or, "I look like the wrath of God." Sometimes they say, "I look like an absolute hag," and sometimes, "I look like Haggis McBaggis." This is an ugly old woman they seem to have made up. But they don't really believe they almost died, or that they look ugly. Both of them are beautiful: one dark and intense, the other blonde and kind-eyed and soulful. Cordelia is not beautiful in the same way.

Cordelia's two older sisters are Perdita and Miranda, but nobody calls them that. They're called Perdie and Mirrie. Perdie is the dark one; she takes ballet, and Mirrie plays the viola. The viola is kept in the coat closet, and Cordelia takes it out and shows it to us, lying there mysterious and important in its velvet-lined case. Perdie and Mirrie make drawling, gentle fun of each other and of themselves for doing these things, but Cordelia says they are gifted. This sounds like vaccinated, something that's done to you and leaves a mark. I ask Cordelia if she is gifted, but she puts her tongue in the corner of her mouth and turns away, as if she's concentrating on something else.

Cordelia ought to be Cordie, but she's not. She insists, always, on being called by her full name: Cordelia. All three of these names are peculiar; none of the girls at school have names like that. Cordelia says they're out of Shakespeare. She seems proud of this, as though it's something we should all recognize. "It was Mummie's idea," she says.

All three of them call their mother Mummie, and speak of her with affection and indulgence, as if she's a bright but wilful child who has to be humoured. She's tiny, fragile, absent-minded; she wears glasses on a silver chain around her neck and takes painting classes. Some of her paintings hang in the upstairs hall, greenish paintings of flowers, of lawns, of bottles and vases.

The girls have spun a web of conspiracy around Mummie. They agree not to tell her certain things. "Mummie isn't supposed to know that," they remind one another. But they don't like to disappoint her. Perdie and Mirrie try to do what they like as much as they can, but without disappointing Mummie. Cordelia is less agile at this: less able to do what she likes, more disappointing. This is what Mummie says when she's angry: "I am disappointed in you." If she gets very disappointed, Cordelia's father will be called into it, and that is serious. None of the girls jokes or drawls when mentioning him. He is large, craggy, charming, but we have heard him shouting, upstairs.

We sit in the kitchen, avoiding the dust-mop of the woman, waiting for Cordelia to come down to play. She has been disappointing again, she has to finish tidying her room. Perdie strolls in, her camel's-hair coat thrown loosely, gracefully over one shoulder, her schoolbooks balanced on one hip. "Do you know what Cordelia says she wants to be when she grows up?" she says, in her husky, mock-serious, confiding voice. "A horse!" And we can't tell at all whether or not it's true.

Cordelia has a whole cupboard filled with dress-up costumes: old dresses of Mummie's, old shawls, old sheets you can cut up and drape around yourself. These used to be Perdie's and Mirrie's, but they've outgrown them. Cordelia wants us to act out plays, with her dining room and its curtain for the stage. She has an idea that we'll put these plays on and charge money for them. She turns out the lights, holds a flashlight under her chin, laughs in an eerie manner: this is how such things are done. Cordelia has been to plays, and even the ballet, once: *Giselle*, she says, offhand, as if we know. But somehow these plays never take shape the way she wants them to. Carol giggles and can't remember what she's supposed to say. Grace doesn't like being told what to do, and says she has a headache. Made-up stories don't interest her unless they contain a lot of real things: toasters, ironing boards, the wardrobes of movie stars. Cordelia's melodramas are beyond her.

"Now you kill yourself," says Cordelia.

"Why?" says Grace.

"Because you've been deserted," says Cordelia.

"I don't want to," says Grace. Carol, who is playing the maid, starts to giggle.

So we merely dress up and then trail down the stairs and out across the newly sodded front lawn, our shawls dragging behind us, uncertain what's supposed to happen next. Nobody wants to take boys' parts because there are no good clothes for them, though from time to time Cordelia draws a moustache on herself with Perdie's eyebrow pencil and wraps herself up in an old velvet curtain, in a last-ditch attempt at plot.

We walk home from school together, four now instead of three. There's a little shop on a side street halfway home where we stop and spend our allowances on penny gumballs, red licorice whips, orange popsicles, sharing everything out equally. There are horse chestnuts in the gutters, wet-looking and glossy; we fill the pockets of our cardigans with them, uncertain what to use them for. The boys of our school and the Catholic boys from Our Lady of Perpetual Help throw them at one another, but we would not do that. They could put out your eye.

The dirt path going down to the wooden footbridge is dry, dusty; the leaves of the trees which hang over it are dull green and worn out from the summer. Along the edge of the path is a thicket of weeds: goldenrod, ragweed, asters, burdocks, deadly nightshade, its berries red as valentine candies. Cordelia says that if you want to poison someone this would be a good way. The nightshade smells of earth, damp, loamy, pungent, and of cat piss. Cats prowl around in there, we see them every day, crouching, squatting, scratching up the dirt, staring out at us with their yellow eyes as if we're something they're hunting.

There are empty liquor bottles tossed into this thicket, and pieces of Kleenex. One day we find a safe. Cordelia knows it's

370

called a safe, Perdie told her that once, when she was little and mistook one for a balloon. She knows it's a thing men use, the kind of men we're supposed to watch out for, though she doesn't know why it's called that. We pick it up on the end of a stick and examine it: whitish, limp, rubbery, like something inside a fish. Carol says "Ew." We carry it furtively back up the hill and shove it through a grating in the pavement; it floats down there on the surface of the dark water, pallid and drowned-looking. Even finding such a thing is dirty; even concealing it.

The wooden bridge is more askew, rottener than I remember. There are more places where the boards have fallen away. As a rule we walk down the middle, but today Cordelia goes right to the railing and leans on it, looking over. One by one and gingerly we follow. The stream below is shallow at this time of year; we can see the junk people have dumped into it, the wornout tyres, the broken bottles and rusty pieces of metal.

Cordelia says that because the stream flows right out of the cemetery it's made of dissolved dead people. She says that if you drink it or step into it or even get too close to it, the dead people will come out of the stream, all covered with mist, and take you with them. She says the only reason this hasn't happened to us is that we're on the bridge and the bridge is wooden. Bridges are safe, over dead-people streams like this one.

Carol gets frightened, or acts frightened. Grace says Cordelia is being silly.

"Try it and see," says Cordelia. "Go on down there. I dare you." But we don't.

I know this is a game. My mother goes down there for her walks, my brother goes there with other older boys. They slosh through the culverts in their rubber boots and swing from trees and from the lower beams of the bridge. The reason the ravine is forbidden to us is not the dead people but the men. All the same, I wonder what the dead people would look like. I believe in them and I don't believe in them, both at the same time.

We pick blue and white weed flowers and some of the night-shade berries, and arrange them on burdock leaves by the side of the path, a horse chestnut on each. They are pretend meals, but it isn't clear who they're for. When we're finished we walk up the hill, leaving these arrangements behind us, half wreath, half lunch. Cordelia says we have to wash our hands really well because of the deadly nightshade berries; we have to wash off the poisonous juice. She says one drop could turn you into a zombie.

The next day when we come home from school these flower meals of ours are gone. Probably boys have destroyed them, it's the sort of thing boys destroy; or else the lurking men. But Cordelia makes her eyes wide, lowers her voice, looks over her shoulder.

"It's the dead people," she says. "Who else could it be?"

15

When the handbell rings we line up in front of GIRLS, two by
two, holding hands: Carol and me, then Grace and Cordelia
back behind us because they're a grade ahead. My brother is
over there in front of BOYS. During recess he disappears into
the cinder playground, where last week he had his lip kicked
open during a soccer game and had to have stitches. I've seen the
stitches, up close, black thread surrounded by swollen purple. I
admire them. I know about the status conferred by wounds.

Now that I've changed back from pants to skirts, I have to
remember the moves. You can't sit with your legs spread apart,
or jump too high or hang upside-down, without ridicule. I've had
to re-learn the importance of underwear, which has a liturgy of
its own:

> I see England, I see France,
> I can see your underpants.

Or else:

> Me no know, me no care,
> Me no wear no underwear.

This is said by boys, while making faces like monkeys.

There's a lot of speculation about underwear, especially the
underwear of the teachers; but only that of the female teachers.
Male underwear is of no importance. There aren't very many
male teachers anyway, and the few that do exist are elderly;
there are no young men, because the war has eaten them. The
teachers are mostly women over a certain age, women who
aren't married. Married women don't have jobs; we know this
from our own mothers. There's something strange and laughable
about older, unmarried women.

At recess, Cordelia doles out underwear: lavender frills for
Miss Pigeon, who's fat and saccharine; plaid for Miss Stuart,
lace-edged to go with her hankies; red satin long-johns for Miss

Hatchett, who's over sixty and wears garnet brooches. We don't believe any of this underwear actually exists, but thinking about it is a nasty joy.

My own teacher is Miss Lumley. It's said that every morning before the bell rings, even in late spring when it's warm, she goes to the back of the classroom and takes off her bloomers, which are rumoured to be of heavy navy-blue wool and to smell of mothballs and of other, less definable things. This isn't repeated as speculation or as part of the underwear invention, but as fact. Several girls claim they've seen Miss Lumley putting her bloomers on again when they've had to stay in after school, and several others say they've seen them hanging in the cloakroom. The aura of Miss Lumley's dark, mysterious, repulsive bloomers clings around her and colours the air in which she moves. It makes her more terrifying; but she is terrifying in any case.

My teacher of the year before was kindly but so unmemorable that Cordelia doesn't even mention her in the underwear game. She had a face like a dinner roll and blancmange-coloured skin, and ruled by wheedling. Miss Lumley rules by fear. She's short, and oblong in shape, so that her iron-grey cardigan falls straight from shoulder to hip with no pause in between for a waist. She always wears this cardigan, and a succession of dark skirts, which can't possibly be the same one. She has steel-rimmed glasses, behind which her eyes are hard to see, and black shoes with Cuban heels, and a tiny lipless smile. She does not send children to the Principal for the strap, but does it herself, in front of the class, holding the hand out flat, bringing the black rubber strap down in sharp quick efficient strokes, her face white and quivering, while we watch, wincing, our eyes filling with involuntary tears. Some girls snivel audibly while she does this, even though she isn't doing it to them, but this isn't wise: Miss Lumley hates snivelling, and is likely to say, "I'll give you something to cry about." We learn to sit up straight, eyes front, faces blank, both feet on the floor, listening to the whack of rubber on cringing flesh.

Mostly it's boys who get the strap. They are thought to need it more. Also they fidget, especially during sewing. We are supposed to sew pot-holders, for our mothers. The boys cannot seem to do this right; their stitches are large and clumsy, and they stick one another with the needles. Miss Lumley stalks the aisles, whacking their knuckles with a ruler.

The schoolroom is high-ceilinged, yellowy-brown, with black-boards at the front and along one side and tall many-paned windows above the radiators on the other side. Over the door to the cloakroom, so that you feel you're being watched from behind, there's a large photograph of the King and Queen, the King with medals, the Queen in a white ballgown and diamond tiara. High wooden desks that sit two, with slanted tops and holes for inkwells, are arranged in rows. It's like all the other schoolrooms at Queen Mary, but it seems darker, possibly because there's less decoration. Our old teacher brought paper doilies to school in her many efforts at appeasement, and her windows were always crawling with paper vegetation. But although Miss Lumley observes the seasons in this way too, the plants we bring forth under her glittering steel-rimmed eyes are smaller, shrivelled-looking, so that there are never enough of them to cover the bare spaces of wall and glass. Also, if your fall-foliage leaf or your pumpkin is not symmetrical, Miss Lumley won't put it up. She has standards.

Things are more British than they were last year. We learn to draw the Union Jack, using a ruler and memorizing the various crosses, for St. George of England, St. Patrick of Ireland, St. Andrew of Scotland, St. David of Wales. Our own flag is red and has a Union Jack in one corner, although there's no saint for Canada. We learn to name all the pink parts of the map.

"The sun never sets on the British Empire," says Miss Lumley, tapping the roll-down map with her long wooden pointer. In countries that are not the British Empire, they cut out children's tongues, especially those of boys. Before the British Empire there were no railroads or postal services in India, and Africa was full of tribal warfare, with spears, and had no proper clothing. The Indians in Canada did not have the wheel or telephones, and ate the hearts of their enemies in the heathenish belief that it would give them courage. The British Empire changed all that. It brought in electric lights.

Every morning, after Miss Lumley blows a thin metallic note

on her pitch-pipe, we stand up to sing "God Save the King". We also sing,

> Rule Britannia, Britannia rules the waves;
> Britons never, never, never shall be slaves!

Because we're Britons, we will never be slaves. But we aren't real Britons, because we are also Canadians. This isn't quite as good, although it has its own song:

> In days of yore, from Britain's shore,
> Wolfe, the dauntless hero, came
> And planted firm Britannia's flag
> On Canada's fair domain.
> Here may it wave, our boast, our pride
> And join in love together
> The thistle, shamrock, rose entwine
> The Maple Leaf forever.

Miss Lumley's jaw quivers in a frightening way when we sing this. Wolfe's name sounds like something you'd call a dog, but he conquered the French. This is puzzling, because I've seen French people, there are lots of them up north, so he couldn't have conquered all of them. As for maple leaves, they're the hardest part to draw on our red flag. Nobody ever gets them right.

Miss Lumley brings newspaper clippings about the Royal Family and sticks them to the side blackboard. Some of them are old clippings, and show Princess Elizabeth and Princess Margaret Rose, in Girl Guide uniforms, making radio and other speeches during the Blitz. This is what we should be like, Miss Lumley implies: steadfast, loyal, courageous, heroic.

There are other newspaper pictures too, showing thin-looking children in scruffy clothes, standing in front of piles of rubble. These are to remind us that there are many starving war orphans in Europe, and we should remember that and eat our breadcrusts and potato skins and everything else on our plates, because waste is a sin. Also we should not complain. We are not really entitled to complain, because we are lucky children: English children got their houses bombed and we did not. We bring our used clothing, from home, and Miss Lumley ties it up into brown paper packages and sends it to England. There isn't much I can bring, because my mother tears our worn-out clothing up

376

for dusters, but I manage to salvage a pair of corduroy pants, once my brother's, then mine, now too small, and a Viyella shirt of my father's that got washed wrong by mistake and shrank. It gives me a strange feeling on my skin to think of someone else, someone in England, walking around in my clothes. My clothes seem a part of me, even the ones I've outgrown.

All these things – the flags, the pitch-pipe songs, the British Empire and the princesses, the war orphans, even the strappings – are superimposed against the ominous navy-blue background of Miss Lumley's invisible bloomers. I can't draw the Union Jack or sing "God Save the King" without thinking about them. Do they really exist, or not? Will I ever be in the classroom when she puts them on or – unthinkable – takes them off?

I'm not afraid of snakes or worms but I am afraid of these bloomers. I know it will be the worse for me if I ever actually catch sight of them. They're sacrosanct, at the same time holy and deeply shameful. Whatever is wrong with them may be wrong with me also, because although Miss Lumley is not what anyone thinks of as a girl, she is also not a boy. When the brass handbell clangs and we line up outside our GIRLS door, whatever category we are in also includes her.

IV

Deadly
Nightshade

16

I walk along Queen Street, past used comic book stores, windows full of crystal eggs and seashells, a lot of sulky black clothing. I wish I were back in Vancouver, in front of the fireplace with Ben, looking out over the harbour, while the giant slugs munch away at the greenery in the back garden. Fireplaces, back gardens: I wasn't thinking about them when I used to come down here to visit Jon, over the wholesale luggage store. Around the corner was the Maple Leaf Tavern, where I drank draught beer in the dark, two stoplights away from the art school where I drew naked women and ate my heart out. The streetcars rattled the front windows. There are still streetcars.

"I don't want to go," I said to Ben.

"You don't have to," he said. "Call it off. Come down to Mexico."

"They've gone to all the trouble," I said. "Listen, you know how hard it is to get a retrospective anywhere, if you're female?"

"Why is it important?" he said. "You sell anyway."

"I have to go," I said. "It wouldn't be right." I was brought up to say please and thank you.

"Okay," he said. "You know what you're doing." He gave me a hug.

I wish it were true.

Here is Sub-Versions, between a restaurant-supply store and a tattoo parlour. Both of these will go, in time: once places like Sub-Versions move in, the handwriting's on the wall.

I open the gallery door, walk in with that sinking feeling I always have in galleries. It's the carpets that do it to me, the hush, the sanctimoniousness of it all: galleries are too much like churches, there's too much reverence, you feel there should be some genuflecting going on. Also I don't like it that this is where paintings end up, on these neutral-toned walls with the track lighting, sterilized, rendered safe and acceptable. It's as if somebody's been around spraying the paintings with air freshener, to kill the smell. The smell of blood on the wall.

This gallery is not totally sterilized, there are touches of cutting edge: a heating pipe shows, one wall is black. I don't give a glance to what's still on the walls, I hate those neo-expressionist dirty greens and putrid oranges, post this, post that. Everything is post these days, as if we're all just a footnote to something earlier that was real enough to have a name of its own.

Several of my own paintings have been uncrated and are leaning against the wall. They've been tracked down, requested, gathered in from whoever owns them. Whoever owns them is not me; worse luck, I'd get a better price now. The owners' names will be on little white cards beside the paintings, along with mine, as if mere ownership is on a par with creation. Which they think it is.

If I cut off my ear, would the market value go up? Better still, stick my head in the oven, blow out my brains. What rich art collectors like to buy, among other things, is a little vicarious craziness.

Face out is a piece I painted twenty years ago: Mrs. Smeath, beautifully rendered in egg tempera, with her grey hairpin crown and her potato face and her spectacles, wearing nothing but her flowered one-breast bib apron. She's reclining on her maroon velvet sofa, rising to Heaven, which is full of rubber plants, while a moon shaped like a doily floats in the sky. *Rubber Plant: The Ascension*, it's called. The angels around her are 1940s Christmas stickers, laundered little girls in white, with rag-set curly hair. The word *Heaven* is stencilled at the top of the painting with a child's school stencil set. I thought that was a nifty thing to do, at the time.

I caught some shit for that piece, as I recall. But not because of the stencil.

I don't look at this painting for very long, or at any of them. If I do I'll start finding things wrong with them. I'll want to take an Exacto knife to them, torch them, clear the walls. Begin again.

*　　*　　*

382

A woman strides towards me from the back, in a modified blonde porcupine haircut, a purple jumpsuit and green leather boots. I know immediately that I should not have worn this powder-blue jogging outfit. Powder-blue is lightweight. I should've worn nun black, Dracula black, like all proper female painters. I should have some clotted-neck vampire lipstick, instead of wimping out with Rose Perfection. But that really would make me look like Haggis McBaggis. At this age the complexion can't stand those grape-jelly reds, I'd look all white and wrinkly.

But I will tough out the jogging suit, I'll pretend I meant it. It could be iconoclasm, how do they know? A powder-blue jogging suit lacks pretensions. The good thing about being out of fashion is that you're never in fashion either, so you can never be last year's model. That's my excuse for my painting, too; or it was for years.

"Hi," says the woman. "You must be Elaine! You don't look much like your picture." What does that mean, I think: better or worse? "We've talked a lot on the phone. My name is Charna." Toronto didn't used to have names like Charna. My hand gets crunched, this woman's got about ten heavy silver rings strung onto her fingers like knuckle-dusters. "We were just wondering about the order." There are two more women; each of them looks five times more artistic than I do. They have abstract-art earrings, hair arrangements. I am feeling dowdy.

They've got take-out gourmet sprout-and-avocado sandwiches and coffee with steamed milk, and we eat those and drink that while we discuss the arrangement of the pictures. I say I favour a chronological approach, but Charna has other ideas, she wants things to go together tonally and resonate and make statements that amplify one another. I get more nervous, this kind of talk makes me twitch. I'm putting some energy into silence, resisting the impulse to say I have a headache and want to go home. I should be grateful, these women are on my side, they planned this whole thing for me, they're doing me an honour, they like what I do. But still I feel outnumbered, as if they are a species of which I am not a member.

Jon comes back tomorrow, from Los Angeles and his chain-saw murder. I can hardly wait. We'll circumvent his wife, go out for lunch, both of us feeling sneaky. But it's merely a civilized thing to do, having lunch with an ex-husband in a comradely way: a good coda to all that smashed crockery and mayhem. We've known each other since the year zot; at my age, our age, that's becoming important. And from here he looks like relief.

Someone else comes in, another woman. "Andrea!" says Charna, stalking over to her. "You're late!" She gives Andrea a kiss on the cheek and walks her over to me, holding her arm. "Andrea wants to do a piece on you," she says. "For the opening.'

"I wasn't told about this," I say. I've been ambushed.

"It came up at the last minute," says Charna. "Lucky for us! I'll put you two in the back room, okay? I'll bring you some coffee. Getting the word out, they call it," she adds, to me, with a wry smile. I allow myself to be herded down the corridor; I can still be bossed around by women like Charna.

"I thought you would be different," says Andrea as we settle.

"Different how?" I ask.

"Bigger," she says.

I smile at her. "I am bigger."

Andrea checks out my powder-blue jogging suit. She herself is wearing black, approved, glossy black, not early sixties holdover as mine would be. She has red hair out of a spray can and no apologies, cut into a cap like an acorn. She's upsettingly young; to me she doesn't look more than a teenager, though I know she must be in her twenties. Probably she thinks I'm a weird middle-aged frump, sort of like her high-school teacher. Probably she's out to get me. Probably she'll succeed.

We sit across from each other at Charna's desk and Andrea sets down her camera and fiddles with her tape-recorder. Andrea writes for a newspaper. "This is for the Living section," she says. I know what that means, it used to be the Women's Pages. It's funny that they now call it Living, as if only women are alive and the other things, such as the Sports, are for the dead.

"Living, eh?" I say. "I'm the mother of two. I bake cookies." All true. Andrea gives me a dirty look and flicks on her machine.

"How do you handle fame?" she says.

"This isn't fame," I say. "Fame is Elizabeth Taylor's cleavage. This stuff is just a media pimple."

384

She grins at that. "Well, could you maybe say something about your generation of artists – your generation of woman artists – and their aspirations and goals ?"

"Painters, you mean," I say. "What generation is that?"

"The seventies, I suppose," she says. "That's when the women's – that's when you started getting attention."

"The seventies isn't my generation," I say.

She smiles. "Well," she says, "what is?"

"The forties."

"The forties?" This is archaeology as far as she's concerned. "But you couldn't have been . . ."

"That was when I grew up," I say.

"Oh right," she says. "You mean it was *formative*. Can you talk about the ways, how it reflects in your work?"

"The colours," I say. "A lot of my colours are forties colours." I'm softening up. At least she doesn't say *like* and *you know* all the time. "The war. There are people who remember the war and people who don't. There's a cut-off point, there's a difference."

"You mean the Vietnam War?" she says.

"No," I say coldly. "The Second World War." She looks a bit scared, as if I've just resurrected from the dead, and incompletely at that. She didn't know I was *that* old. "So," she says. "What is the difference?"

"We have long attention spans," I say. "We eat everything on our plates. We save string. We make do."

She looks puzzled. That's all I want to say about the forties. I'm beginning to sweat. I feel as if I'm at the dentist, mouth gracelessly open while some stranger with a light and mirror gazes down my throat at something I can't see.

Brightly and neatly she veers away from the war and back towards women, which was where she wanted to be in the first place. Is it harder for a woman, was I discriminated against, undervalued? What about having children? I give unhelpful replies: all painters feel undervalued. You can do it while they're at school. My husband's been terrific, he gives me a lot of support, some of which has been financial. I don't say which husband.

"So you don't feel it's sort of demeaning to be propped up by a man?" she says.

"Women prop up men all the time," I say. "What's wrong with a little reverse propping?"

What I have to say is not altogether what she wants to hear. She'd prefer stories of outrage, although she'd be unlikely to tell them about herself, she's too young. Still, people my age are supposed to have stories of outrage; at least insult, at least putdown. Male art teachers pinching your bum, calling you *baby*, asking you why there are no great female painters, that sort of thing. She would like me to be furious, and quaint.

"Did you have any female mentors?" she asks.

"Female what?"

"Like, teachers, or other woman painters you admired."

"Shouldn't that be mentresses?" I say nastily. "There weren't any. My teacher was a man."

"Who was that?" she says.

" Josef Hrbik. He was very kind to me," I add quickly. He'd fit the bill for her, but she won't hear that from me. "He taught me to draw naked women."

That startles her. "Well, what about, you know, feminism?" she says. "A lot of people call you a feminist painter."

"What indeed," I say. "I hate party lines, I hate ghettoes. Anyway, I'm too old to have invented it and you're too young to understand it, so what's the point of discussing it at all?"

"So it's not a meaningful classification for you?" she says.

"I like it that women like my work. Why shouldn't I?"

"Do men like your work?" she asks slyly. She's been going through the back files, she's seen some of those witch-and-succubus pieces.

"Which men?" I say. "Not everyone likes my work. It's not because I'm a woman. If they don't like a man's work it's not because he's a man. They just don't like it." I am on dubious ground, and this enrages me. My voice is calm; the coffee seethes within me.

She frowns, diddles with the tape-recorder. "Why do you paint all those women then?"

"What should I paint, men?" I say. "I'm a painter. Painters paint women. Rubens painted women, Renoir painted women, Picasso painted women. Everyone paints women. Is there something wrong with painting women?"

"But not like that," she says.

386

"Like what?" I say. "Anyway, why should my women be the same as everyone else's women?" I catch myself picking at my fingers, and stop. In a minute my teeth will be chattering like those of cornered mice. Her voice is getting farther and farther away, I can hardly hear her. But I see her, very clearly: the ribbing on the neck of her sweater, the fine hairs of her cheek, the shine of a button. What I hear is what she isn't saying. *Your clothes are stupid. Your art is crap. Sit up straight and don't answer back.*

"Why do you paint?" she says, and I can hear her again as clear as anything. I hear her exasperation, with me and my refusals.

"Why does anyone do anything?" I say.

17

The light fades earlier; on the way home from school we walk through the smoke from burning leaves. It rains, and we have to play inside. We sit on the floor of Grace's room, being quiet because of Mrs. Smeath's bad heart, and cut out rolling pins and frying pans and paste them around our paper ladies.

But Cordelia makes short work of this game. She knows, instantly it seems, why Grace's house has so many Eaton's Catalogues in it. It's because the Smeaths get their clothes that way, the whole family – order them out of the Eaton's Catalogue. There in the Girls' Clothing section are the plaid dresses, the skirts with straps, the winter coats worn by Grace and her sisters, three colours of them, in lumpy, serviceable wool, with hoods: Kelly Green, Royal Blue, Maroon. Cordelia manages to convey that she herself would never wear a coat ordered from the Eaton's Catalogue. She doesn't say this out loud though. Like the rest of us, she wants to stay on the good side of Grace.

She bypasses the cookware, flips through the pages. She turns to the brassieres, to the elaborately laced and gusseted corsets – foundation garments, they're called – and draws moustaches on the models, whose flesh looks as if it's been painted over with a thin coat of beige plaster. She pencils hair in, under their arms, and on their chests between the breasts. She reads out the descriptions, snorting with stifled laughter: "'Delightfully trimmed in dainty lace, with extra support for the mature figure.' That means big bazooms. Look at this – *cup* sizes! Like teacups!"

Breasts fascinate Cordelia, and fill her with scorn. Both of her older sisters have them by now. Perdie and Mirrie sit in their room with its twin beds and sprigged-muslin flounces, filing their nails, laughing softly; or they heat brown wax in little pots in the kitchen and take it upstairs to spread on their legs. They look into their mirrors, making sad faces – "I look like Haggis McBaggis! It's the curse!" Their wastebaskets smell of decaying flowers.

They tell Cordelia there are some things she's too young to understand, and then they tell these things to her anyway. Cordelia, her voice lowered, her eyes big, passes on the truth: the curse is when blood comes out between your legs. We don't believe her. She produces evidence: a sanitary pad, filched from Perdie's wastebasket. On it is a brown crust, like dried gravy. "That's not blood," Grace says with disgust, and she's right, it's nothing like when you cut your finger. Cordelia is indignant. But she can prove nothing.

I haven't thought much about grown-up women's bodies before. But now these bodies are revealed in their true, upsetting light: alien and bizarre, hairy, squashy, monstrous. We hang around outside the room where Perdie and Mirrie are peeling the wax off their legs while they utter yelps of pain, trying to see through the keyhole, giggling: they embarrass us, although we don't know why. They know they're being laughed at and come to the door to shoo us away. "Cordelia, why don't you and your little friends bug off!" They smile a little ominously, as if they know already what is in store for us. "Just wait and see," they say.

This frightens us. Whatever has happened to them, bulging them, softening them, causing them to walk rather than run, as if there's some invisible leash around their necks, holding them in check – whatever it is, it may happen to us too. We look surreptitiously at the breasts of women on the street, of our teachers; though not of our mothers, that would be too close for comfort. We examine our legs and underarms for sprouting hairs, our chests for swellings. But nothing is happening: so far we are safe.

Cordelia turns to the back pages of the catalogue, where the pictures are in grey and black and there are crutches and trusses and prosthetic devices. "Breast pumps," she says. "See this? It's for pumping your titties up bigger, like a bicycle pump." And we don't know what to believe.

We can't ask our mothers. It's hard to imagine them without clothes, to think of them as having bodies at all, under their dresses. There's a great deal they don't say. Between us and them is a gulf, an abyss, that goes down and down. It's filled with wordlessness. They wrap up the garbage in several layers of newspaper and tie it with string, and even so it drips

389

onto the freshly waxed floor. Their clotheslines are strung with underpants, nighties, socks, a display of soiled intimacy, which they have washed and rinsed, plunging their hands into the grey curdled water. They know about toilet brushes, about toilet seats, about germs. The world is dirty, no matter how much they clean, and we know they will not welcome our grubby little questions. So instead a long whisper runs among us, from child to child, gathering horror.

Cordelia says that men have carrots, between their legs. They aren't really carrots but something worse. They're covered with hair. Seeds come out the end and get into women's stomachs and grow into babies, whether you want it or not. Some men have their carrots pierced and rings set into them as if they are ears.

Cordelia's unclear about how the seeds get out or what they're like. She says they're invisible, but I think this can't be so. If there are seeds at all they must be more like bird seeds, or carrot seeds, long and fine. Also she can't say how the carrot gets in, to plant the seeds. Belly buttons are the obvious choice, but there would have to be a cut, a tear. The whole story is questionable, and the idea that we ourselves could have been produced by such an act is an outrage. I think of beds, where all of this is supposed to take place: the twin beds at Carol's house, always so tidy, the elegant canopy bed at Cordelia's, the dark mahogany-coloured bed in Grace's house, heavily respectable with its crocheted spread and layers of woollen blankets. Such beds are a denial in themselves, a repudiation. I think of Carol's wry-mouthed mother, of Mrs. Smeath with her hairpinned crown of greying braids. They would purse their lips, draw themselves up in a dignified manner. They would not permit it.

Grace says, "God makes babies," in that final way of hers which means there is nothing more to be discussed. She smiles her buttoned-up disdainful smile, and we are reassured. Better God than us.

But there are doubts. I know, for instance, a lot of things. I know that "carrot" is not the right word. I've seen dragonflies and beetles, flying around, stuck together, one on the back of the other; I know it's called "mating". I know about ovipositors, for laying eggs, on leaves, on caterpillars, on the surface of the water; they're right out on the page, clearly labelled, on the diagrams of insects my father corrects at home. I know about queen ants, and

390

about the female praying mantises eating the males. None of this is much help. I think of Mr. and Mrs. Smeath, stark naked, with Mr. Smeath stuck to the back of Mrs. Smeath. Such an image, even without the addition of flight, will not do.

I could ask my brother. But, although we've examined scabs and toe-jam under the microscope, although we aren't worried by pickled ox eyes and gutted fish and whatever can be found under dead logs, putting this question to him would be indelicate, perhaps hurtful. I think of *JUPITER* scrolled on the sand in his angular script, by his extra, dextrous finger. In Cordelia's version it will end up covered with hair. Maybe he doesn't know.

Cordelia says boys put their tongues in your mouth when they kiss you. Not any boys we know, older ones. She says this the same way my brother says "slug juice" or "snot" when Carol's around, and Carol does the same thing, the same wrinkle of the nose, the same wriggle. Grace says that Cordelia is being disgusting.

I think about the spit you sometimes see, downtown, on the sidewalk; or cow's tongues in butcher's shops. Why would they want to do such a thing, put their tongues in other people's mouths? Just to be repulsive, of course. Just to see what you would do.

18

I go up the cellar stairs, which have black rubber stair-treads nailed onto them. Mrs. Smeath is standing at the kitchen sink in her bib apron. She's finished her nap and now she's upright, getting supper. She's peeling potatoes; she often peels things. The peel falls from her large knuckly hands in a long pale spiral. The paring knife she uses is worn so thin its blade is barely more than a crescent-moon sliver. The kitchen is steamy, and smells of marrow-fat and stewing bones.

Mrs. Smeath turns and looks at me, a skinless potato in her left hand, the knife in her right. She smiles. "Grace says your family don't go to church," she says. "Maybe you'd like to come with us. To our church."

"Yes," says Grace, who has come up the stairs behind me. And the idea is pleasing. I'll have Grace all to myself on Sunday mornings, without Carol or Cordelia. Grace is still the desirable one, the one we all want.

When I tell my parents about this plan they become anxious. "Are you sure you really want to go?" my mother says. When she was young, she says, she had to go to church whether she liked it or not. Her father was very strict. She couldn't whistle on Sundays. "Are you really sure?"

My father says he doesn't believe in brainwashing children. When you're grown up, then you can make up your own mind about religion, which has been responsible for a lot of wars and massacres in his opinion, as well as bigotry and intolerance. "Every educated person should know the Bible," he says. "But she's only eight."

"Almost nine," I say.

"Well," says my father. "Don't believe everything you hear."

On Sunday I put on the clothes my mother and I have picked out, a dress of dark-blue and green wool plaid, white ribbed stockings that attach with garters onto my stiff white cotton waist. I have more dresses than I once had, but I don't go

392

shopping with my mother to help pick them out, the way Carol does. My mother hates shopping, nor does she sew. My girls' clothes are second-hand, donated by a distant friend of my mother's who has a larger daughter. None of these dresses fits me very well; the hems droop, or the sleeves bunch up under my arms. I think this is the norm, for dresses. The white stockings are new though, and even itchier than the brown ones I wear to school.

I take my blue cat's eye marble out of my red plastic purse and leave it in my bureau drawer, and put the nickel my mother's given me for the collection plate into my purse instead. I walk along the rutted streets towards Grace's house, in my shoes; it isn't time for boots yet. Grace opens her front door when I ring. She must have been waiting for me. She has a dress on too and white stockings, and navy-blue bows at the ends of her braids. She looks me over. "She doesn't have a hat," she says.

Mrs. Smeath, standing in the hallway, considers me as if I'm an orphan left on her doorstep. She sends Grace upstairs to search for another hat, and Grace comes back down with an old one of dark-blue velvet with an elastic under the chin. It's too small for me but Mrs. Smeath says it will do for now. "We don't go into our church with our heads uncovered," she says. She emphasizes *our*, as if there are other, inferior, bareheaded churches.

Mrs. Smeath has a sister, who is going with us to church. Her name is Aunt Mildred. She's older and has been a missionary in China. She has the same knuckly red hands, the same metal-rimmed glasses, the same hair crown as Mrs. Smeath, only hers is all grey, and the hairs on her face are grey too and more numerous. Both of them have hats that look like packages of felt carelessly done up, with several ends sticking into the air. I've seen such hats in the Eaton's Catalogues of several years back, worn by models with sleeked-back hair and high cheekbones and dark-red, glossy mouths. On Mrs. Smeath and her sister they don't have the same effect.

When all of the Smeaths have their coats and hats on we climb into their car: Mrs. Smeath and Aunt Mildred in the front, me and Grace and her two little sisters in the back. Although I still worship Grace, this worship is not at all physical, and being squashed into the back seat of her car, so close to her, embarrasses me. Right in front of my face Mr. Smeath is driving.

He is short and bald and hardly ever seen. It's the same with Carol's father, with Cordelia's: in the daily life of houses, fathers are largely invisible.

We drive through the nearly empty Sunday streets, following the streetcar tracks west. The air inside the car fills with the used breath of the Smeaths, a stale smell like dried saliva. The church is large and made of brick; on the top of it, instead of a cross, there's a thing that looks like an onion and goes around. I ask about this onion, which may mean something religious for all I know, but Grace says it's a ventilator.

Mr. Smeath parks the car and we get out of it and go inside. We sit in a row, on a long bench made of dark shiny wood, which Grace says is a pew. This is the first time I've ever been inside a church. There's a high ceiling, with lights shaped like morning glories hanging down on chains, and a plain gold cross up at the front with a vase of white flowers. Behind that there are three stained-glass windows. The biggest, middle one has Jesus in white, with his hands held out sideways and a white bird hovering over his head. Underneath it says in thick black Bible-type letters with dots in between the words: THE·KINGDOM·OF·GOD·IS·WITHIN·YOU. On the left side is Jesus sitting down, sideways in pinky-red, with two children leaning on his knees. It says: SUFFER·THE·LITTLE·CHILDREN. Both of the Jesuses have haloes. On the other side is a woman in blue, with no halo and a white kerchief partly covering her face. She's carrying a basket and reaching down one hand. There's a man sitting down at her feet, with what looks like a bandage wound around his head. It says: THE·GREATEST·OF·THESE·IS·CHARITY. Around all these windows are borders, with vines twining around and bunches of grapes, and different flowers. The windows have light coming in behind them, which illuminates them. I can hardly take my eyes off them.

Then there's organ music and everyone stands up, and I become confused. I watch what Grace does, and stand up when she stands up, sit when she sits. During the songs she holds the hymnbook open and points, but I don't know any of the tunes. After a while it's time for us to go to Sunday School, and so we file out with the other children in a line and go down into the church basement.

At the entrance to the Sunday School place there's a black-board, where someone has printed, in coloured chalk: KILROY WAS HERE. Beside this is a drawing of a man's eyes and nose, looking over a fence.

Sunday School is in classes, like ordinary school. The teachers are younger though; ours is an older teenager with a light-blue hat and a veil. Our class is all girls. The teacher reads us a Bible story about Joseph and his coat of many colours. Then she listens as the girls recite things they're supposed to have memorized. I sit on my chair, dangling my legs. I haven't memorized anything. The teacher smiles at me and says she hopes I will come back every week.

After this all the different classes go into a large room with rows of grey wooden benches in it, like the benches we eat our lunches on at school. We sit on the benches, the lights are turned off, and coloured slides are projected onto the bare wall at the far end of the room. The slides aren't photographs but paintings. They look old-fashioned. The first one shows a knight riding through the forest, gazing upwards to where a shaft of light streams down through the trees. The skin of this knight is very white, his eyes are large like a girl's, and his hand is pressed to where his heart must be, under his armour, which looks like car fenders. Under his large, luminous face I can see the light-switches and the top boards of the wainscoting, and the corner of the small piano, where it juts out.

The next picture has the same knight only smaller, and under-neath him some words, which we sing to the heavy thumping of chords from the unseen piano:

> I would be true, for there are those who trust me,
> I would be pure, for there are those who care,
> I would be strong, for there is much to suffer,
> I would be brave, for there is much to dare.

Beside me, in the dark, I hear Grace's voice going up and up, thin and reedy, like a bird's. She knows all the words; she knew all the words to her memory passage from the Bible too. When we bend our heads to pray I feel suffused with goodness, I feel included, taken in. God loves me, whoever he is.

After Sunday School we go back into the regular church for the last part, and I put my nickel on the collection plate. Then there is something called the Doxology. Then we walk out of the church and stuff back into the Smeaths' car, and Grace says carefully, "Daddy, may we go and see the trains?" and the little girls, with a show of enthusiasm, say, "Yes, yes."

Mr. Smeath says, "Have you been good?" and the little girls say, "Yes, yes" again.

Mrs. Smeath makes an indeterminate sound. "Oh, all right," says Mr. Smeath to the little girls. He drives the car south through the empty streets, along the streetcar tracks, past a single streetcar like a gliding island, until finally we see the flat grey lake in the distance, and below us, over the edge of a sort of low cliff, a flat grey plain covered with train tracks. On this metal-covered plain several trains are shunting slowly back and forth. Because it is Sunday, and because this is evidently a routine after-church Sunday event for the Smeaths, I have the idea that the train tracks and the lethargic, ponderous trains have something to do with God. It is also clear to me that the person who really wants to see the trains is not Grace, or any of the little girls, but Mr. Smeath himself.

We sit there in the parked car watching the trains until Mrs. Smeath says that the dinner will be ruined. After that we drive back to Grace's house.

I am invited for Sunday dinner. It's the first time I've ever stayed for dinner at Grace's. Before dinner Grace takes me upstairs so we can wash our hands, and I learn a new thing about her house: you are only allowed four squares of toilet paper. The soap in the bathroom is black and rough. Grace says it's tar soap.

The dinner is baked ham and baked beans and baked potatoes and mashed squash. Mr. Smeath carves the ham, Mrs. Smeath adds the vegetables, the plates get passed around. Grace's little sisters look at me through their eyeglasses when I start to eat.

"We say grace in this house," says Aunt Mildred, smiling firmly, and I don't know what she's talking about. I look at Grace: why do they want to say her name? But they all bend their heads and put their hands together and Grace says, "For what we are about to receive may the Lord make us truly thankful, Amen," and Mr. Smeath says, "Good food, good drink, good God, let's eat," and winks at me. Mrs. Smeath says, "Lloyd," and Mr. Smeath gives a small, conspiratorial laugh.

After dinner Grace and I sit in the living room, on the velvet chesterfield, the same one Mrs. Smeath takes her naps on. I've never sat on it before and feel I'm sitting on something reserved, like a throne or a coffin. We read our Sunday School paper, which has the story of Joseph in it and a modern story about a boy who steals from the collection plate but repents and collects waste-paper and old bottles for the church, to make reparations. The pictures are black and white pen and ink drawings, but on the front is a coloured picture of Jesus, in pastel robes, surrounded by children, all of different colours, brown, yellow, white, clean and pretty, some holding his hand, others gazing up at him with large worshipful eyes. This Jesus does not have a halo.

Mr. Smeath dozes in the maroon easy chair, his round belly swelling up. From the kitchen comes the clatter of silverware. Mrs. Smeath and Aunt Mildred are doing the dishes.

I reach home in the late afternoon, with my red plastic purse and my Sunday School paper. "Did you like it?" says my mother, still with the same air of anxiety.

"Did you learn anything?" says my father.

"I have to memorize a psalm," I say importantly. The word *psalm* sounds like a secret password. I am a little resentful. There are things my parents have been keeping from me, things I need to know. The hats, for instance: how could my mother have forgotten about the hats? God is not an entirely new idea for me: they have him at school in the morning prayers, and even in "God Save the King". But it seems there is more to it, more things to be memorized, more songs to be sung, more nickels to be donated, before he can be truly appeased. I am worried about Heaven though. What age will I be when I get there? What if I'm old when I die? In Heaven I want to be the age I am.

I have a Bible, on loan from Grace, her second-best. I go to my room and begin to memorize: *The heavens declare the glory of God; and the firmament sheweth his handywork. Day unto day uttereth speech, and night unto night sheweth knowledge.*

I still don't have any bedroom curtains. I look out the window, look up: there are the heavens, there are the stars, where they usually are. They no longer look cold and white and remote, like alcohol and enamel trays. Now they look watchful.

397

19

The girls stand in the schoolyard or up on top of the hill, in small clumps, whispering and whispering and doing spoolwork. It's now the fashion to have a spool with four nails pounded into one end, and a ball of wool. You loop the wool over each nail in turn, twice around, and use a fifth nail to hook the bottom loops over the top ones. Out of the other end of the spool dangles a round thick wool tail, which you're supposed to wind up like a flat snail-shell and sew into a mat to put the teapot on. I have such a spool, and so do Grace and Carol, and even Cordelia, although her wool is a snarl.

These clumps of whispering girls with their spools and coloured wool tails have to do with boys, with the separateness of boys. Each cluster of girls excludes some other girls, but all boys. The boys exclude us too, but their exclusion is active, they make a point of it. We don't need to.

Sometimes I still go into my brother's room and lie around on the floor reading comic books, but I never do this when any other girl is there. Alone I am tolerated, as part of a group of girls I would not be. This goes without saying.

Once I took boys for granted, I was used to them. But now I pay more attention, because boys are not the same. For example, they don't take baths as often as they're expected to. They smell of grubby flesh, of scalp, but also of leather, from the knee-patches on their breeks, and wool, from the breeks themselves, which come down only to below the knee, and lace up there like football pants. On the bottom parts of their legs they wear thick wool socks, which are usually damp and falling down. On their heads, outdoors, they wear leather helmets that strap under the chin. Their clothing is khaki, or navy-blue or grey, or forest green, colours that don't show the dirt as much. All of this has a military feel to it. Boys pride themselves on their drab clothing, their drooping socks, their smeared and inky skin: dirt, for them, is almost as good as wounds. They work at acting like boys. They call each other by their last names, draw attention to any extra departures from cleanliness. "Hey, Robertson! Wipe off the snot!" "Who farted?" They punch one another on the arm, saying, "Got you!" "Got you back!" There always seem to be more of them in the room than there actually are.

My brother punches arms and makes remarks about smells like the rest of them, but he has a secret. He would never tell it to these other boys, because of the way they would laugh.

The secret is that he has a girlfriend. This girlfriend is so secret she doesn't even know about it herself. I'm the only one he's told, and I have been double-sworn not to tell anyone else. Even when we're alone I'm not allowed to refer to her by her name, only by her initials, which are B.W. My brother will sometimes murmur these initials when there are other people around, my parents for instance. When he says them he stares at me, waiting for me to nod or give some sign that I have heard and understood. He writes me notes in code, which he leaves where I'll find them, under my pillow, tucked into my top bureau drawer. When I translate these notes they turn out to be so unlike him, so lacking in invention, so moronic in fact, that I can hardly believe it: "Talked to B.W." "Saw HER today." He writes these notes in coloured pencil, different colours, with exclamation marks. One night there's a freak early snowfall, and in the morning when I wake up and look out my bedroom window there are the supercharged initials, etched in pee on the white ground, already melting.

I can see that this girlfriend is causing him some anguish, as well as excitement, but I can't understand why. I know who she is. Her real name is Bertha Watson. She hangs around with the older girls, up on the hill under the stunted fir trees. She has straight brown hair with bangs and she's of ordinary size. There's no magic about her that I can see, or any abnormality. I'd like to know how she's done it, this trick with my brother that's turned him into a stupider, more nervous identical twin of himself.

Knowing this secret, being the only one chosen to know, makes me feel important in a way. But it's a negative importance, it's the importance of a blank sheet of paper. I can know because I don't count. I feel singled out, but also bereft. Also protective of him, because for the first time in my life I feel responsible for him. He is at risk, and I have power over him. It occurs to me that I could tell on him, lay him open to derision; I have that choice. He is at my mercy and I don't want it. I want him back the way he was, unchanged, invincible.

The girlfriend doesn't last long. After a while nothing more is heard of her. My brother makes fun of me again, or ignores me; he's back in charge. He gets a chemistry set and does experiments down in the basement. As an obsession I prefer the chemistry set to the girlfriend. There are things stewing, horrible stinks, little sulphurous explosions, amazing illusions. There's invisible writing that comes out when you hold the paper over a candle. You can make a hard-boiled egg rubbery so it will go into a milk bottle, although getting it out again is more difficult. *Turn Water to Blood*, the instructions say, *and Astound Your Friends*.

He still trades comic books, but effortlessly, absent-mindedly. Because he cares less about them he makes better trades. The comic books pile up under his bed, stacks and stacks of them, but he seldom reads them any more when the other boys aren't around.

My brother exhausts the chemistry set. Now he has a star map, pinned to the wall of his room, and at night he turns out the lights and sits beside the darkened, open window, in the cold, with his maroon sweater pulled on over his pyjamas, gazing skyward. He has a pair of my father's binoculars, which he's allowed to use as long as he keeps the strap around his neck so he won't drop them. What he really wants next is a telescope.

When he allows me to join him, and when he feels like talking, he teaches me new names, charts the reference points: Orion, the Bear, the Dragon, the Swan. These are constellations. Every one of them is made up of a huge number of stars, hundreds of times bigger and hotter than our own sun. These stars are light-years away, he says. We aren't really seeing them at all, we're just seeing the light they sent out years, hundreds of years, thousands of years ago. The stars are like echoes. I sit there in my flannelette pyjamas, shivering, the back of my neck hurting from the upward tilt, squinting into the cold and the infinitely receding darkness, into the black cauldron where the fiery stars

400

boil and boil. His stars are different from the ones in the Bible: they're wordless, they flame in an obliterating silence. I feel as if my body is dissolving and I am being drawn up and up, like thinning mist, into a vast emptying space.

"Arcturus," my brother says. It's a foreign word, one I don't know, but I know the tone of his voice: recognition, completion, something added to a set. I think of his jars of marbles in the spring, the way he dropped the marbles into the jar, one by one, counting. My brother is collecting again; he's collecting stars.

20

Black cats and paper pumpkins gather on the school windows. On Hallowe'en Grace wears an ordinary lady's dress, Carol a fairy outfit, Cordelia a clown suit. I wear a sheet, because that's what there is. We walk from door to door, our brown paper grocery bags filling with candy apples, popcorn balls, peanut brittle, chanting at each door: *Shell out! Shell out! The witches are out!* In the front windows, on the porches, the large orange heads of the pumpkins float, glowing, unbodied. The next day we take our pumpkins to the wooden bridge and throw them over the edge, watching them smash open on the ground below. Now it's November.

Cordelia is digging a hole, in her back garden where there's no sod. She has started several holes before, but they have been unsuccessful, they struck rock. This one is more promising. She digs with a pointed shovel; sometimes we help her. It isn't a small hole but a large, square hole; it gets deeper and deeper as the dirt piles up around it. She says we can use it for a clubhouse, we can put chairs down in the hole and sit on them. When it's deep enough she wants to cover it over with boards, for a roof. She's already collected the boards, scrap boards from the two new houses they're building near her house. She's very wrapped up in this hole, it's hard to get her to play anything else.

On the darkening streets the poppies blossom, for Remembrance Day. They're made of fuzzy cloth, red like valentine hearts, with a black spot and a pin through the centre. We wear them on our coats. We memorize a poem about them:

> *In Flanders fields the poppies' blow,*
> *Between the crosses row on row*
> *That mark our place.*

At eleven o'clock we stand beside our desks in the dustmotes of the weak November sunshine for the three minutes of silence, Miss Lumley grim at the front of the room, heads bowed, eyes closed, listening to the hush and the rustle of our own bodies and the booming of the guns in the distance. *We are the Dead.* I keep my eyes closed, trying to feel pious and sorry for the dead soldiers, who died for us, whose faces I can't imagine. I have never known any dead people.

Cordelia and Grace and Carol take me to the deep hole in Cordelia's backyard. I'm wearing a black dress and a cloak, from the dress-up cupboard. I'm supposed to be Mary Queen of Scots, headless already. They pick me up by the underarms and the feet and lower me into the hole. Then they arrange the boards over the top. The daylight air disappears, and there's the sound of dirt hitting the boards, shovelful after shovelful. Inside the hole it's dim and cold and damp and smells like toad burrows.

Up above, outside, I can hear their voices, and then I can't hear them. I lie there wondering when it will be time to come out. Nothing happens. When I was put into the hole I knew it was a game; now I know it is not one. I feel sadness, a sense of betrayal. Then I feel the darkness pressing down on me; then terror.

When I remember back to this time in the hole, I can't really remember what happened to me while I was in it. I can't remember what I really felt. Maybe nothing happened, maybe these emotions I remember are not the right emotions. I know the others came and got me out after a while, and the game or some other game continued. I have no image of myself in the hole; only a black square filled with nothing, a square like a door. Perhaps the square is empty; perhaps it's only a marker, a time marker that separates the time before it from the time after. The point at which I lost power. Was I crying when they took me out of the hole? It seems likely. On the other hand I doubt it. But I can't remember.

Shortly after this I became nine. I can remember my other birthdays, later and earlier ones, but not this one. There must have been a party, my first real one, because who would have come to the others? There must have been a cake, with candles and wishes and a quarter and a dime wrapped in wax paper hidden between the layers for someone to chip a tooth on, and presents. Cordelia would have been there, and Grace and Carol. These things must have occurred, but the only trace they've left on me has been a vague horror of birthday parties, not other people's, my own. I think of pastel icing, pink candles burning in the pale November afternoon light, and there is a sense of shame and failure.

I close my eyes, wait for pictures. I need to fill in the black square of time, go back to see what's in it. It's as if I vanish at that moment and reappear later, but different, not knowing why I have been changed. If I could even see the undersides of the boards above my head it might help. I close my eyes, wait for pictures.

At first there's nothing; just a receding darkness, like a tunnel. But after a while something begins to form: a thicket of dark-green leaves with purple blossoms, dark purple, a sad rich colour, and clusters of red berries, translucent as water. The vines are intergrown, so tangled over the other plants they're like a hedge. A smell of loam and another, pungent scent rises from among the leaves, a smell of old things, dense and heavy, forgotten. There's no wind but the leaves are in motion, there's a ripple, as of unseen cats, or as if the leaves are moving by themselves.

Nightshade, I think. It's a dark word. There is no nightshade in November. The nightshade is a common weed. You pull it out of the garden and throw it away. The nightshade plant is related to the potato, which accounts for the similar shape of the flowers. Potatoes too can be poisonous, if left in the sun to turn green. This is the sort of thing it's my habit to know.

I can tell it's the wrong memory. But the flowers, the smell, the movement of the leaves persist, rich, mesmerizing, desolating, infused with grief.

404

V
Wringer

21

I leave the gallery, walk east. I need to go shopping, get some decent food, organize. When I'm by myself I revert to the times when I would forget about eating, stay up all night working, go until I felt an odd sensation I'd identify after some thought as hunger. Then I'd go through the refrigerator like a vacuum cleaner, sucking in whatever there was. Leftovers.

This morning there were eggs, but there are no more eggs. There's no more bread, there's no more milk. Why were there eggs and bread and milk in the first place? It must have been a stash of Jon's, he must eat there sometimes. Or could it have been that he got this stuff for me? It's hardly believable.

I will buy oranges, yogurt without the jam. I will have a positive attitude, take care of myself, I'll feed myself enzymes, and friendly bacteria. These good thoughts carry me until I'm right downtown.

This is where Eaton's used to be, here on this corner, yellow and four-square. Now there's a huge building in its place, what they call a shopping complex, as if shopping were a psychic disease. It's glassy and be-tiled, green as an iceberg.

Across the street from it is known territory: Simpsons department store. I know it has a food hall somewhere. In the plate-glass windows there are heaps of bath towels, overstuffed sofas and chairs, sheets in modern prints. I wonder where all this cloth ends up. People cart it away, stuff it into their houses: the nesting instinct. A less attractive concept if you've ever seen a nest up close. There must be a limit to how much cloth you can cram into any one house, but of course it's disposable. You used to buy for quality, things that would last. You kept your clothes until they were part of you, you checked the hemlines, the way the buttons were sewed on, you rubbed the cloth between your finger and thumb.

The next windows contain disgruntled mannequins, their pelvises thrust out, their shoulders flung this way and that, making them look like hunchbacked axe-murderers. I guess this is the look now: surly aggression. On the sidewalks there are a lot of androgynes, in the flesh, the girls in the black leather jackets and tough boots of boys, crewcuts, ducktails, the boys with the sullen pouty look of those women on the front covers of fashion magazines, their hair gelled into quills. At a distance I can't tell the difference, though they themselves probably can. They make me feel outmoded.

What are they aiming for? Is each an imitation of the other? Or does it only seem that way to me because they're all so alarmingly young? Despite their cool poses they wear their cravings on the outside, like the suckers on a squid. They want it all.

But I suppose that's what Cordelia and I looked like then, to older people, crossing the street right here with our collars turned up and our eyebrows plucked into sceptical arches, swaggering in our rubber boots and straining for nonchalance, on our way down to Union Station where the trains came in, to put our quarters into the photo machine, four shots in monochrome, wallet-sized. Cordelia with a cigarette in the corner of her mouth, her eyelids half closed, trying for sultry. Ultra-sharp.

I revolve through the revolving doors into Simpsons, where I become lost immediately. They've changed the whole thing over. It used to be sedate wood-rimmed glass counters, with gloves in standard models, appropriate wristwatches, accent scarves in floral prints. Serious-minded good taste. Now it's a cosmetic fairground: silver trim, gold pillars, marquee lights, brand-name letters the size of a human head. The air is saturated with the stink of perfumes at war. There are video screens on which flawless complexions turn, preen, sigh through their parted lips, are caressed. On other screens are closeups of skin pores, before and after, details of regimes for everything, your hands, your neck, your thighs. Your elbows, especially your elbows: aging begins at the elbows and metastasizes.

This is religion. Voodoo and spells. I want to believe in it, the creams, the rejuvenating lotions, the transparent unguents in vials that slick on like roll-top glue. "Don't you know what that

408

junk is made of?" Ben said once. "Ground-up cock's combs." But this doesn't deter me, I'd use anything if it worked – slug juice, toad spit, eye of newt, anything at all to mummify myself, stop the drip drip of time, stay more or less the way I am.

But I own enough of this slop already to embalm all of the girls in my high-school graduating class, who must need it by now as much as I do. I stop only long enough to allow myself to be sprayed by a girl giving away free squirts of some venomous new perfume. The femme fatale must be back, Veronica Lake slinks again. The stuff smells like grape Kool-Aid. I can't imagine it seducing anything but a fruit fly.

"You like this?" I say to the girl. They must get lonely, standing here all day in their high heels, spraying strangers.

"It's been very popular," she says evasively. Briefly I glimpse myself through her eyes: bloom off the rose, teetering on the brink of matronhood, hoping for the best. I am the market.

I ask her where the Food Hall is, and she tells me. It's down. I get on the escalator, but suddenly I'm going up. This is bad, confusing directions like that, or am I jumping time, did I go down already? I get off, and find myself wading through rack after rack of children's party dresses. They have the lace collars, the puffed sleeves, the sashes I remember; many of them are in plaid, the authentic sombre blood-lit colours, dark greens with a stripe of red, dark blues, black. Black Watch. Have these people forgotten history, don't they know anything about the Scots, don't they know any better than to clothe small girls in the colours of despair, slaughter, treachery and murder? *My way of life*, new line, *Is fall'n into the sere and yellow leaf*. Once we had to memorize things. Still, plaid was the fashion in my day too. The white socks, the Mary Janes, the always-inadequate birthday present swathed in tissue paper, and the little girls with their assessing eyes, their slippery deceitful smiles, tartaned up like Lady Macbeth.

In the endless time when Cordelia had such power over me, I peeled the skin off my feet. I did it at night, when I was supposed to be sleeping. My feet would be cool and slightly damp, smooth, like the skin of mushrooms. I would begin with the big toes. I would bend my foot up and bite a small opening

409

in the thickest part of the skin, on the bottom, along the outside edge. Then, with my fingernails, which I never bit because why bite something that didn't hurt, I would pull the skin off in narrow strips. I would do the same to the other big toe, then to the ball of each foot, the heel of each. I would go down as far as the blood. Nobody but me ever looked at my feet, so nobody knew I was doing it. In the mornings I would pull my socks on, over my peeled feet. It was painful to walk, but not impossible. The pain gave me something definite to think about, something immediate. It was something to hold onto.

I chewed the ends of my hair, so that there was always one lock of hair that was pointed and wet. I gnawed the cuticles off from around my fingernails, leaving welts of exposed, oozing flesh which would harden into rinds and scale off. In the bathtub or in dishwater my fingers looked nibbled, as if by mice. I did these things constantly, without thinking about them. But the feet were more deliberate.

I remember thinking when the girls were born, first one and then the other, that I should have had sons and not daughters. I didn't feel up to daughters, I didn't know how they worked. I must have been afraid of hating them. With sons I would have known what to do: frog-catching, fishing, war strategies, running around in the mud. I would have been able to teach them how to defend themselves, and what from. But the world of sons has changed; it's more likely to be the boys now with that baffled look, like a night-dweller gone blind in sunlight. "Stand up for yourself like a man," I would have said. I would have been on shifty ground.

As for the girls, my girls at any rate, they seem to have been born with some kind of protective coating, some immunity I lacked. They look you in the eye, level and measuring, they sit at the kitchen table and the air around lights up with their lucidity. They are sane, or so I like to think. My saving graces.

They amaze me, they always have. When they were little I felt I had to protect them from certain things about myself, the fear, the messier parts of the marriages, the days of nothing. I didn't want to pass anything on to them, anything of mine they would be better off without. At those times I would lie on the floor in the dark, with the curtains drawn and the door closed. I would say, *Mummy has a headache. Mummy's working.* But they didn't seem to need that protection, they seemed to take everything in, look at it straight, accept everything. "Mummy's in there lying on the floor. She'll be fine tomorow," I heard Sarah tell Anne when one was ten and the other was four. And so I was fine. Such faith, like the faith in sunrise or the phases of the moon, sustained me. It must be this sort of thing that keeps God going.

Who knows what they'll make of me later on, who knows what they've already made of me? I would like them to be the happy end, of my story. But of course they are not the end of their own.

Someone comes up behind me, a sudden voice out of thin air. She startles me. "May I help you?" It's a saleslady, an older woman this time. Middle-aged. My age, I then think, discouraged. Mine and Cordelia's.

I'm standing among the plaid dresses, fingering a sleeve. God knows how long I've been doing it. Have I been talking out loud? My throat feels tight and my feet hurt. But whatever else may be in store for me, I do not intend to slide off my trolley tracks in the middle of Simpsons Girlswear.

"The food hall," I say.

She smiles gently. She is tired, and I am a disappointment to her, I don't want any plaid. "Oh, you need to be right downstairs," she says, "in the cellar." Kindly, she directs me.

22

The black door opens. I'm sitting in the mouse-dropping and formaldehyde smell of the building, on the window-ledge, with the heat from the radiator going up my legs, watching out the window as the fairies and gnomes and snowballs below me slog through the drizzle to the tune of "Jingle Bells" played by a brass band. The fairies look foreshortened, damaged, streaked by the dust and rain on the window glass; my breath makes a foggy circle. My brother isn't here, he's too old for it. This is what he said. I have the whole window-ledge to myself.

On the window-ledge beside mine, Cordelia and Grace and Carol are sitting, jammed in together, whispering and giggling. I have to sit on a window-ledge by myself because they aren't speaking to me. It's something I said wrong, but I don't know what it is because they won't tell me. Cordelia says it will be better for me to think back over everything I've said today and try to pick out the wrong thing. That way I will learn not to say such a thing again. When I've guessed the right answer, then they will speak to me again. All of this is for my own good, because they are my best friends and they want to help me improve. So this is what I'm thinking about as the pipe band goes past in sodden fur hats, and the drum majorettes with their bare wet legs and red smiles and dripping hair: what did I say wrong? I can't remember having said anything different from what I would ordinarily say.

My father walks into the room, wearing his white lab coat. He's working in another part of the building, but he's come to check on us. "Enjoying the parade, girls?" he says.

"Oh yes, thank you," Carol says, and giggles. Grace says, "Yes, thank you." I say nothing. Cordelia gets down off her windowsill and slides up onto mine, sitting close beside me.

"We're enjoying it extremely, thank you very much," she says in her voice for adults. My parents think she has beautiful manners. She puts an arm around me, gives me a little squeeze, a

412

squeeze of complicity, of instruction. Everything will be all right as long as I sit still, say nothing, reveal nothing. I will be saved then, I will be acceptable once more. I smile, tremulous with relief, with gratitude.

But as soon as my father is out of the room Cordelia turns to face me. Her expression is sad rather than angry. She shakes her head. "How could you?" she says. "How could you be so impolite? You didn't even answer him. You know what this means, don't you? I'm afraid you'll have to be punished. What do you have to say for yourself?" And I have nothing to say.

I'm standing outside the closed door of Cordelia's room. Cordelia, Grace, and Carol are inside. They're having a meeting. The meeting is about me. I am just not measuring up, although they are giving me every chance. I will have to do better. But better at what?

Perdie and Mirrie come up the stairs, along the hall, in their armour of being older. I long to be as old as they are. They're the only people who have any real power over Cordelia, that I can see. I think of them as my allies; or I think they would be my allies if they only knew. Knew what? Even to myself I am mute.

"Hello, Elaine," they say. Now they say, "What's the little game today? Hide and Seek?"

"I can't tell," I answer. They smile at me, condescending and kind, and head towards their room, to do their toenails and talk about older things.

I lean against the wall. From behind the door comes the indistinct murmur of voices, of laughter, exclusive and luxurious. Cordelia's Mummie drifts by, humming to herself. She's wearing her painting smock. There's a smudge of apple-green on her cheek. She smiles at me, the smile of an angel, benign but remote. "Hello, dear," she says. "You tell Cordelia there's a cookie for you girls, in the tin."

"You can come in now," says the voice of Cordelia from inside the room. I look at the closed door, at the doorknob, at my own hand moving up, as if it's no longer a part of me.

This is how it goes. It's the kind of thing girls of this age do to one another, or did then, but I'd had no practice in it. As

413

my daughters approached this age, the age of nine, I watched them anxiously. I scrutinized their fingers for bites, their feet, the ends of their hair. I asked them leading questions: "Is everything all right, are your friends all right?" And they looked at me as if they had no idea what I was talking about, why I was so anxious. I thought they'd give themselves away somehow: nightmares, moping. But there was nothing I could see, which may only have meant they were good at deception, as good as I was. When their friends arrived at our house to play, I scanned their faces for signs of hypocrisy. Standing in the kitchen, I listened to their voices in the other room. I thought I would be able to tell. Or maybe it was worse. Maybe my daughters were doing this sort of thing themselves, to someone else. That would account for their blandness, the absence of bitten fingers, their level blue-eyed gaze.

Most mothers worry when their daughters reach adolescence, but I was the opposite. I relaxed, I sighed with relief. Little girls are cute and small only to adults. To one another they are not cute. They are life-sized.

It turns colder and colder. I lie with my knees up, as close to my body as I can get them. I'm peeling the skin off my feet; I can do it without looking, by touch. I worry about what I've said today, the expression on my face, how I walk, what I wear, because all of these things need improvement. I am not normal, I am not like other girls. Cordelia tells me so, but she will help me. Grace and Carol will help me too. It will take hard work and a long time.

In the mornings I get out of bed, put on my clothes, the stiff cotton waist with the garters, the ribbed stockings, the nubbled wool pullover, the plaid skirt. I remember these clothes as cold. Probably they were cold.

I put my shoes on, over my stockings and my peeled feet.

I go out to the kitchen, where my mother is cooking breakfast. There's a pot with porridge in it, Red River cereal or oatmeal or Cream of Wheat, and a glass coffee percolator. I rest my arms on the edge of the white stove and watch the porridge, simmering and thickening, the flaccid bubbles coming up out of it one at a time and releasing their small puffs of steam. The porridge is like

414

boiling mud. I know that when it comes time to eat the porridge I will have trouble: my stomach will contract, my hands will get cold, it will be difficult to swallow. Something tight sits under my breastbone. But I will get the porridge down somehow, because it's required.

Or I watch the coffee percolator, which is better because I can see everything, the pinpoint bubbles gathering under the upside-down glass umbrella, then hesitating, then the column of water shooting upwards through the stem, falling down over the coffee in its metal basket, the drops of coffee dripping down into the clear water, inking it brown.

Or I make toast, sitting at the table where the toaster is. Each of our spoons has a dark-yellow halibut liver oil capsule in it, shaped like a small football. There are the plates, gleaming whitely, and the glasses of juice. The toaster is on a silver heat pad. It has two doors, with a knob at the bottom of each, and a grid up the centre that glows red-hot. When the toast is done on one side I turn the knobs and the doors open and the toast slides down and turns over, all by itself. I think about putting my finger in there, onto the red-hot grid.

All of these are ways of delaying time, slowing it down, so I won't have to go out through the kitchen door. But no matter what I do, and despite myself, I am pulling on my snowpants, wadding my skirt in between my legs, tugging thick woollen socks on over my shoes, stuffing my feet into boots. Coat, scarf, mittens, knitted hat, I am encased, I am kissed, the door opens, then closes behind me, frozen air shoots up my nose. I waddle through the orchard of leafless apple trees, the legs of my snowpants whisking against each other, down to the bus stop.

Grace is waiting there and Carol, and especially Cordelia. Once I'm outside the house there is no getting away from them. They are on the school bus, where Cordelia stands close beside me and whispers into my ear: "Stand up straight! People are looking!" Carol is in my classroom, and it's her job to report to Cordelia what I do and say all day. They're there at recess, and in the cellar at lunchtime. They comment on the kind of lunch I have, how I hold my sandwich, how I chew. On the way home from school I have to walk in front of them, or behind. In front is worse because they talk about how I'm walking, how I look

415

from behind. "Don't hunch over," says Cordelia. "Don't move your arms like that."

They don't say any of the things they say to me in front of others, even other children: whatever is going on is going on in secret, among the four of us only. Secrecy is important, I know that: to violate it would be the greatest, the irreparable sin. If I tell I will be cast out forever.

But Cordelia doesn't do these things or have this power over me because she's my enemy. Far from it. I know about enemies. There are enemies in the schoolyard, they yell things at one another and if they're boys they fight. In the war there were enemies. Our boys and the boys from Our Lady of Perpetual Help are enemies. You throw snowballs at enemies and rejoice if they get hit. With enemies you can feel hatred, and anger. But Cordelia is my friend. She likes me, she wants to help me, they all do. They are my friends, my girlfriends, my best friends. I have never had any before and I'm terrified of losing them. I want to please.

Hatred would have been easier. With hatred, I would have known what to do. Hatred is clear, metallic, one-handed, un-wavering; unlike love.

23

None of this is unrelenting.

On some days Cordelia decides that it's Carol's turn to be improved. I am invited to join Grace and Cordelia as they walk ahead on the way home from school, with Carol trailing behind, and to think of things Carol has done wrong. "Carol is a smarty-pants," Cordelia says. At these times I don't pity Carol. She deserves what's happening to her, because of all the times she's done the same things to me. I rejoice that it's her turn instead of mine.

But these times don't last long. Carol cries too easily and noisily, she gets carried away with her own crying. She draws attention, she can't be depended on not to tell. There's a recklessness in her, she can be pushed just so far, she has a weak sense of honour, she's reliable only as an informer. If this is obvious to me, it must be even more obvious to Cordelia.

Other days appear normal. Cordelia seems to forget about improving anybody, and I think she may have given up on it. I'm expected to behave as if nothing has ever happened. But it's hard for me to do this, because I feel I'm always being watched. At any time I may step over some line I don't even know is there.

Last year I was hardly ever home, by myself, after school or on weekends. Now I want to be. I make excuses so I won't have to go out and play. I still call it playing.

"I have to help my mother," I say. This has a ring of truth to it. Girls do have to help their mothers, sometimes; Grace in particular has to help her mother. But it's less true than I would like it to be. My mother doesn't linger over housework, she'd rather be outside raking up leaves in the fall, shovelling snow in the winter, pulling weeds in the spring. When I help her I slow her down. But I dangle around the kitchen, saying, "Can I help?" until she gives me a duster and has me dust the scrolled legs of the dining table, or the edges of the bookcases; or I cut up dates, chop nuts, grease the muffin-cups with a corner of waxed paper torn from the inside wrapper of the Crisco box; or I rinse the wash.

I like rinsing the wash. The laundry room is small and enclosed, secret, underground. On the shelves there are packages of odd, power-filled substances: laundry starch in white twisted shapes like bird droppings, bluing to make the whites look whiter, Sunlight soap in bars, Javex bleach with a skull and crossbones on it, reeking of sanitation and death.

The washing machine itself is tubular white enamel, a hulk on four spindly legs. It dances slowly across the floor, *chug-lug, chug-lug*, the clothes and the soapy water moving as if boiling sluggishly, like cloth porridge. I watch it, hands on the edge of the tub, chin on hands, my body dragging downwards from this ledge, not thinking about anything. The water turns grey and I feel virtuous because of all the dirt that's coming out. It's as if I myself am doing this just by looking.

My job is to run the washed clothes through the wringer into the laundry sink full of clean water and then into the second laundry sink for the second rinse, and after that into the creaky laundry basket. After that my mother takes the clothes outside and hangs them on the clothesline with wooden clothespins. Sometimes I do this too. In the cold the clothes freeze stiff, like plywood. One day a small neighbourhood boy collects horse buns, from the milk-wagon horse, and puts them along the bottom folds of the freshly washed double-hung white sheets. All sheets are white, all milk comes from horses.

The wringer is two rubber rollers, the colour of pale flesh, that revolve around and around, the clothes squeezing in between them, water and suds squooshing out like juice. I roll up my sleeves, stand on tiptoe, rummage in the tub and haul up the sopping underpants and slips and pyjamas, which feel like something you might touch just before you know it's a drowned person. I poke the corners of the clothes in between the wringers and they are grabbed and dragged through, the arms of the shirts ballooning with trapped air, suds dripping from the cuffs. I've been told to be very careful when doing this: women can get their hands caught in wringers, and other parts of their bodies, such as hair. I think about what would happen to my hand if it did get caught: the blood and flesh squeezing up my arm like a travelling bulge, the hand coming out the other side flat as a glove, white as paper. This would hurt a lot at first, I know that. But there's something compelling about it. A whole person could go through the wringer and come out flat, neat, completed, like a flower pressed in a book.

"You coming out to play?" says Cordelia, on our way home from school.

"I have to help my mother," I say.

"Again?" says Grace. "How come she does that so much? She never used to do it." Grace has begun talking about me in the third person, like one grownup to another, when Cordelia is there.

I think of saying my mother is sick, but my mother is so obviously healthy I know I won't get away with this.

"She thinks she's too good for us," says Cordelia. Then, to me: "Do you think you're too good for us?"

"No," I say. Thinking you are too good is bad.

"We'll come and ask your mother if you can play," says Cordelia, switching back to her concerned, friendly voice. "She won't make you work all the time. It isn't fair."

And my mother smiles and says yes, as if she's pleased that I'm so much in demand, and I am pried away from the muffin-cups and the washing machine wringer, expelled into the outside air.

On Sundays I go to the church with the onion on top of it, crammed into the Smeaths' car with all the Smeaths, Mr. Smeath, Mrs. Smeath, Aunt Mildred, Grace's younger sisters, whose nostrils in the winter season are forever plugged with yellowy-green snot. Mrs. Smeath seems pleased about this arrangement, but she is pleased with herself, for going out of her way, for displaying charity. She's not especially pleased with me. I can tell this by the line between her eyebrows when she looks at me, although she smiles with her closed lips, and by the way she keeps asking whether I wouldn't like to bring my brother next time, or my parents? I focus on her chest, on

419

her single breast that goes all the way down to her waist, with her dark-red, black-spotted heart beating within it, gasping in out, in out, out of breath like a fish on shore, and shake my head, ashamed. My failure to produce these other members of my family tells against me.

I have memorized the names of all the books of the Bible, in order, and the Ten Commandments and the Lord's Prayer, and most of the Beatitudes. I've been getting ten out of ten on my Bible quizzes and my memory-work, but I'm beginning to falter. In Sunday School we have to stand up and recite, out loud, in front of the others, and Grace watches me. She watches everything I do on Sundays, and reports on me, matter-of-factly, to Cordelia.

"She didn't stand up straight in Sunday School yesterday." Or: "She was a goody-goody." I believe each of these comments: my shoulders sag, my spine crumples, I exude the wrong kind of goodness; I see myself shambling crookedly, I make an effort to stand straighter, my body rigid with anxiety. And it's true that I got ten out of ten, again, and Grace only got nine. Is it wrong to be right? How right should I be, to be perfect? The next week I put five wrong answers, deliberately.

"She only got five out of ten on Bible," Grace says on Monday.

"She's getting stupider," Cordelia says. "You aren't really that stupid. You'll have to try harder than that!"

Today is White Gift Sunday. We have all brought cans of food from home for the poor, wrapped up in white tissue paper. Mine are Habitant pea soup and Spam. I suspect they are the wrong things, but they're what my mother had in the cupboard. The idea of White Gifts bothers me: such hard gifts, made uniform, bleached of their identity and colours. They look dead. Inside those blank, sinister bundles of tissue paper piled up at the front of the church there could be anything.

Grace and I sit on the wooden benches in the church basement, watching the illuminated slides on the wall, singing the words to the songs, while the piano plods onwards in the darkness.

420

Jesus bids us shine
With a pure, clear light,
Like a little candle
Burning in the night:
In this world is darkness;
So let us shine,
You in your small corner,
And I in mine.

I want to shine like a candle. I want to be good, to follow instructions, to do what Jesus bids. I want to believe you should love your neighbours as yourself and the Kingdom of God is within you. But all of this seems less and less possible.

In the darkness I can see a gleam of light, to the side. It's not a candle: it's light reflected back off Grace's glasses, from the light on the wall. She knows the words by heart, she doesn't have to look at the screen. She's watching me.

After church I go with the Smeaths through the vacant Sunday streets to watch the trains shunting monotonously back and forth along their tracks, on the grey plain beside the flat lake. Then I go back to their house for Sunday dinner. This happens every Sunday now, it's part of going to church; it would be very bad if I said no, to either thing.

I've learned the way things are done here. I climb the stairs past the rubber plant, not touching it, and go into the Smeaths' bathroom and count off four squares of toilet paper and wash my hands afterwards with the gritty black Smeath soap. I no longer have to be admonished, I bow my head automatically when Grace says, "For what we are about to receive may the Lord make us truly thankful, Amen."

"Pork and beans the musical fruit, the more you eat, the more you toot," says Mr. Smeath, grinning round the table. Mrs. Smeath and Aunt Mildred do not think this is funny. The little girls regard him solemnly. They both have glasses and white freckled skin and Sunday bows on the ends of their brown wiry braids, like Grace.

"Lloyd," says Mrs. Smeath.

"Come on, it's harmless," Mr. Smeath says. He looks me in the eye. "Elaine thinks it's funny. Don't you, Elaine?"

I am trapped. What can I say? If I say no, it could be rudeness.

If I say yes, I have sided with him, against Mrs. Smeath and Aunt Mildred and all three of the Smeath girls, including Grace. I feel myself turn hot, then cold. Mr. Smeath is grinning at me, a conspirator's grin.

"I don't know," I say. The real answer is no, because I don't in fact know what this joke means. But I can't abandon Mr. Smeath, not entirely. He is a squat, balding, flabby man, but still a man. He does not judge me.

Grace repeats this incident to Cordelia, next morning, in the school bus, her voice a near whisper. "She said she didn't know."

"What sort of an answer was that?" Cordelia asks me sharply. "Either you think it's funny or you don't. Why did you say 'I don't know'?"

I tell the truth. "I don't know what it means."

"You don't know what *what* means?"

"Musical fruit," I say. "The more you toot." I am now deeply embarrassed, because I don't know. Not knowing is the worst thing I could have done.

Cordelia gives a hoot of contemptuous laughter. "You don't know what *that* means?" she says. "What a stupe! It means *fart*. Beans make you fart. Everyone knows that."

I am doubly mortified, because I didn't know, and because Mr. Smeath said *fart* at the Sunday dinner table and enlisted me on his side, and I did not say no. It isn't the word itself that makes me ashamed. I'm used to it, my brother and his friends say it all the time, when there are no adults listening. It's the word at the Smeath dinner table, stronghold of righteousness.

But inwardly I do not recant. My loyalty to Mr. Smeath is similar to my loyalty to my brother: both are on the side of ox eyeballs, toe-jam under the microscope, the outrageous, the subversive. Outrageous to whom, subversive of what? Of Grace and Mrs. Smeath, of tidy paper ladies pasted into scrapbooks. Cordelia ought to be on this side too. Sometimes she is, sometimes she isn't. It's hard to tell.

24

In the mornings the milk is frozen, the cream risen in icy, granular columns out of the bottle necks. Miss Lumley bends over my desk, her invisible navy-blue bloomers casting their desolating aura around her. On either side of her nose the skin hangs down, like the jowls of a bulldog; there's a trace of dried spit in the corner of her mouth. "Your handwriting is deteriorating," she says. I look at my page in dismay. She's right: the letters are no longer round and beautiful, but spidery, frantic, and disfigured with blots of black rusty ink where I've pressed down too hard on the steel nib. "You must try harder." I curl my fingers under. I think she's looking at the ragged edges of skin. Everything she says, everything I do, is heard and seen by Carol and will be reported later.

Cordelia is in a play and we go to watch her. This is my first play and I ought to be excited. Instead I am filled with dread, because I know nothing of the etiquette of play-going and I'm sure I'll do something wrong. The play is at the Eaton's Auditorium; the stage has blue curtains with black velvet horizontal stripes on them. The curtains part to reveal *The Wind in the Willows*. All the actors are children. Cordelia is a weasel, but since she's in a weasel costume with a weasel head, it's impossible to tell her apart from all the other weasels. I sit in the plush theatre seat, biting my fingers, craning my neck, looking for her. Knowing she's there but not knowing where is the worst thing. She could be anywhere.

The radio fills with sugary music: "I'm Dreaming of a White Christmas", "Rudolph the Red-Nosed Reindeer", which we have to sing in school, standing beside our desks with Miss Lumley tooting on her pitch-pipe to give the note and keeping time with her wooden ruler, the same one she whacks the boys' hands with when they fidget. Rudolph bothers me, because there's something wrong with him; but at the same time he gives me hope, because he ended up beloved. My father says he is a nauseating commercial neologism. "A fool and his money are soon parted," he says.

We make red bells out of construction paper, folding the paper in half before cutting out the shape. We make snowmen the same way. It's Miss Lumley's recipe for symmetry: everything has to be folded, everything has two halves, a left and a right, identical.

I go through these festive tasks like a sleepwalker. I take no interest in bells or snowmen or for that matter in Santa Claus, in whom I've ceased to believe, since Cordelia has told me it's really just your parents. There's a class Christmas party, which consists of cookies brought from home and eaten silently at our desks, and different-coloured jelly beans provided by Miss Lumley, five for each child. Miss Lumley knows what the conventions are and pays her own rigid tributes to them.

For Christmas I get a Barbara Ann Scott doll, which I've said I wanted. I had to say I wanted something and I did in a way want this doll. I haven't had any girl-shaped dolls before. Barbara Ann Scott is a famous figure-skater, a very famous one. She has won prizes. I've studied the pictures of her in the newspaper.

The doll of her has little leatherette skates and a fur-trimmed costume, pink with white fur, and fringed eyes that open and close, but it looks nothing at all like the real Barbara Ann Scott. According to the pictures she's muscular, with big thighs, but the doll is a slender stick. Barbara is a woman, the doll is a girl. It has the worrying power of effigies, a lifeless life that fills me with creeping horror. I put it back into its cardboard box and tuck the tissue paper around it, over the face. I say I'm doing this to keep it safe, but in fact I don't want it watching me.

Over our chesterfield there's a badminton net, festooned across the wall. In the squares of this net my parents have hung their Christmas cards. No one else I know has a badminton net like this on their wall. Cordelia's Christmas tree is not like others: it's covered in gauzy angel hair, and all the lights and decorations on it are blue. But she can get away with such differences, I can't. I know I'll be made to pay for the badminton net, sooner or later.

*　　*　　*

We sit around the table, eating our Christmas dinner. There's a student of my father's, a young man from India who's here to study insects and who's never seen snow before. We're having him to Christmas dinner because he's foreign, he's far from home, he will be lonely, and they don't even have Christmas in his country. This has been explained to us in advance by our mother. He's polite and ill at ease and he giggles frequently, looking with what I sense is terror at the array of food spread out before him, the mashed potatoes, the gravy, the lurid green and red Jello salad, the enormous turkey: my mother has said that the food is different there. I know he's miserable, underneath his smiles and politeness. I'm developing a knack for this, I can sniff out hidden misery in others now with hardly any effort at all.

My father sits at the head of the table, beaming like the Jolly Green Giant. He lifts his glass, his gnome's eyes twinkling. "Mr. Banerji, sir," he says. He always calls his students Mr. and Miss. "You can't fly on one wing."

Mr. Banerji giggles and says, "Very true, sir," in his voice that sounds like the BBC News. He lifts his own glass and sips. What is in the glass is wine. My brother and I have cranberry juice in our wineglasses. Last year or the year before we might have tied our shoe-laces together, under the table, so we could signal each other with secret jerks and tugs, but we're both beyond this now for different reasons.

My father ladles out the stuffing, deals the slices of dark and light; my mother adds the mashed potatoes and cranberry sauce and asks Mr. Banerji, enunciating carefully, whether they have turkeys in his country. He says he doesn't believe so. I sit across the table from him, my feet dangling, staring at him, enthralled. His spindly wrists extend from his over-large cuffs, his hands are long and thin, ragged around the nails, like mine. I think he is very beautiful, with his brown skin and brilliant white teeth and his dark appalled eyes. There's a child these colours in the ring of children on the front of the Sunday School missionary paper, yellow children, brown children, all in different costumes, dancing around Jesus. Mr. Banerji doesn't have a costume, only a jacket and tie like other men. Nevertheless I can hardly believe he's a man, he seems so unlike one. He's a creature more like myself: alien and apprehensive. He's afraid of us. He has no idea what we will do next, what impossibilities we will expect

425

of him, what we will make him eat. No wonder he bites his fingers.

"A little off the sternum, sir?" my father asks him, and Mr. Banerji brightens at the word.

"Ah, the sternum," he says, and I know they have entered together the shared world of biology, which offers refuge from the real, awkward world of manners and silences we're sitting in at the moment. As he slices away with the carving knife my father indicates to all of us, but especially to Mr. Banerji, the areas where the flight muscles attach, using the carving fork as a pointer. Of course, he says, the domestic turkey has lost the ability to fly.

"*Meleagris gallopavo*," he says, and Mr. Banerji leans forward; the Latin perks him up. "A pea-brained animal, or bird-brained you might say, bred for its ability to put on weight, especially on the drumsticks" – he points these out – "certainly not for intelligence. It was originally domesticated by the Mayans." He tells a story of a turkey farm where the turkeys all died because they were too stupid to go into their shed during a thunderstorm. Instead they stood around outside, looking up at the sky with their beaks wide open and the rain ran down their throats and drowned them. He says this is a story told by farmers and probably not true, although the stupidity of the bird is legendary. He says that the wild turkey, once abundant in the deciduous forests in these regions, is far more intelligent and can elude even practised hunters. Also it can fly.

I sit picking at my Christmas dinner, as Mr. Banerji is picking at his. Both of us have messed the mashed potatoes around on our plates without actually eating much. Wild things are smarter than tame ones, that much is clear. Wild things are elusive and wily and look out for themselves. I divide the people I know into tame and wild. My mother, wild. My father and brother, also wild; Mr. Banerji, wild also, but in a more skittish way. Carol, tame. Grace, tame as well, though with sneaky vestiges of wild. Cordelia, wild, pure and simple.

"There are no limits to human greed," says my father.

"Indeed, sir?" says Mr. Banerji, as my father goes on to say that he's heard some son of a gun is working on an experiment to breed a turkey with four drumsticks, instead of two drumsticks and two wings, because there's more meat on a drumstick.

426

"How would such a creature walk, sir?" asks Mr. Banerji, and my father, approving, says, "Well may you ask." He tells Mr. Banerji that some darn fool scientists are working on a square tomato, which will supposedly pack more easily into crates than the round variety.

"All the flavour will be sacrificed, of course," he says. "They care nothing for flavour. They bred a naked chicken, thinking they'd get more eggs by utilizing the energy saved from feather production, but the thing shivered so much they had to double-heat the coop, so it cost more in the end."

"Fooling with Nature, sir," says Mr. Banerji. I know already that this is the right response. Investigating Nature is one thing and so is defending yourself against it, within limits, but fooling with it is quite another.

Mr. Banerji says he hears there is now a naked cat available, he's read about it in a magazine, though he himself does not see the point of it at all. This is the most he has said so far.

My brother asks if there are any poisonous snakes in India, and Mr. Banerji, now much more at ease, begins to enumerate them. My mother smiles, because this is going better than she thought it would. Poisonous snakes are fine with her, even at the dinner table, as long as they make people happy.

My father has eaten everything on his plate and is digging for more stuffing in the cavity of the turkey, which resembles a trussed, headless baby. It has thrown off its disguise as a meal and has revealed itself to me for what it is, a large dead bird. I'm eating a wing. It's the wing of a tame turkey, the stupidest bird in the world, so stupid it can't even fly any more. I am eating lost flight.

25

After Christmas I'm offered a job. The job is wheeling Brian
Finestein around the block in his baby carriage after school, for
an hour or a little longer if it isn't too cold, one day a week. For
this I get twenty-five cents, which is a lot of money.

The Finesteins live in the house beside ours, the big house
that was built suddenly where the mud-mountain used to be.
Mrs. Finestein is short for a woman, plump, with dark curly
hair and lovely white teeth. These show often, as she laughs a
lot, wrinkling up her nose like a puppy as she does it, shaking
her head, which makes her gold earrings twinkle. I'm not sure,
but I think these earrings actually go through little holes in her
ears, unlike any earrings I have ever seen.

I ring the doorbell and Mrs. Finestein opens the door. "My
little life-saver," she says. I wait in the vestibule, my winter boots
dripping onto the spread newspapers. Mrs. Finestein, wearing
a flowered pink housecoat and slippers with high heels and
real fur, bustles upstairs to get Brian. The vestibule smells of
Brian's ammonia-soaked diapers, which are in a pail waiting
to be collected by the diaper company. I'm intrigued by the
idea that someone else can come and take away your laundry.
Mrs. Finestein always has a bowl of oranges out, on a table up
a few steps from the vestibule; no one else leaves oranges lying
around like that when it isn't Christmas. There's a gold-coloured
candlestick like a tree behind the bowl. These things – the
sickly sweet baby-shit smell of the festering diapers, the bowl
of oranges and the gold tree – blend in my mind into an image
of ultra-sophistication.

Mrs. Finestein clops down the stairs carrying Brian, who is
zipped into a blue bunny suit with ears. She gives him a big
kiss on his cheek, joggles him up and down, tucks him into
the carriage, snaps up the waterproof carriage-cover. "There,
Bry-Bry," she says. "Now Mummy can hear herself think." She
laughs, wrinkles her nose, shakes her gold earrings. Her skin

is rounded out, milky-smelling. She's not like any mother I've ever seen.

I wheel Brian out into the cold air and we start off around the block, over the crunchy snow which is spread with cinders from people's furnaces and dotted here and there with frozen horse buns. I can't figure out how Brian would ever be able to interfere with Mrs. Finestein thinking, because he never cries. Also he never laughs. He never makes any noises at all, nor does he go to sleep. He just lies there in his carriage, gazing solemnly up at me with his round blue eyes as his button of a nose gets redder and redder. I make no attempt to entertain him. But I like him: he's silent, but also uncritical.

When I think it's time I wheel him back, and Mrs. Finestein says, "Don't tell me it's five o'clock already!" I ask her to give me nickels instead of a quarter, because it looks like more. She laughs a lot at that, but she does it. I keep all my money in an old tin tea-caddy with a picture of the desert on it, palm trees and camels. I like taking it out and spreading it over my bed. Instead of counting it, I arrange it by the year that's stamped on each piece of money: 1935, 1942, 1945. Every coin has a King's head on it, cut off neatly at the neck, but the Kings are different. The ones from before I was born have beards, but the ones now don't, because it's King George, the one at the back of the classroom. It gives me an odd comfort to sort this money into piles of cut-off heads.

Brian and I wheel around the block, around the block again. It's hard for me to tell when it's an hour because I don't have a watch. Cordelia and Grace come around the corner up ahead, with Carol trailing. They see me, walk over.

"What rhymes with Elaine?" Cordelia asks me. She doesn't wait for an answer. "Elaine is a pain."

Carol peers into the baby carriage. "Look at the bunny ears," she says. "What's his name?" Her voice is wistful. I see Brian in a new light. It isn't everyone who's allowed to wheel a baby.

"Brian," I say. "Brian Finestein."

"Finestein is a Jewish name," says Grace.

I don't know what Jewish is. I've seen the word Jew, the Bible is full of that word, but I didn't know there were any live, real ones, especially next door to me.

"Jews are kikes," says Carol, glancing at Cordelia for approval.

"Don't be vulgar," says Cordelia, in her adult voice. "Kike is not a word we use."

I ask my mother what Jewish is. She says it's a different kind of religion. Mr. Banerji is a different kind of religion as well, though not Jewish. There are many different kinds. As for the Jews, Hitler killed a great many of them, during the war.

"Why?" I say.

"He was demented," says my father. "A megalomaniac." Neither of these words is much help.

"A bad person," says my mother.

I wheel Brian over the cindery snow, easing him around the pot-holes. He goggles up at me, his nose red, his tiny mouth unsmiling. Brian has a new dimension: he is a Jew. There is something extra and a little heroic about him; not even the blue ears of his bunny suit can detract from that. *Jewish* goes with the diapers, the oranges in the bowl, Mrs. Finestein's gold earrings and her possibly real ear-holes, but also with ancient, important matters. You wouldn't expect to see a Jew every day.

Cordelia and Grace and Carol are beside me. "How's the little baby today?" asks Cordelia.

"He's fine," I say guardedly.

"I didn't mean him, I meant you," says Cordelia.

"Can I have a turn?" asks Carol.

"I can't," I tell her. If she does it wrong, if she upsets Brian Finestein into a snowbank, it will be my fault.

"Who wants an old Jew-baby anyway," she says.

"The Jews killed Christ," says Grace primly. "It's in the Bible."

But Jews don't interest Cordelia much. She has other things on her mind. "If a man who catches fish is a fisher, what's a man who catches bugs?" she says.

"I don't know," I say.

"You are so stupid," says Cordelia. "That's what your father is, right? Go on. Figure it out. It's really simple."

"A bugger," I say.

"Is that what you think of your own father?" Cordelia says. "He's an *entomologist*, stupid. You should be ashamed. You should have your mouth washed out with soap."

I know that *bugger* is a dirty word, but I don't know why. Nevertheless I have betrayed, I have been betrayed. "I have to go," I say. Wheeling Brian back to Mrs. Finestein's, I cry silently, while Brian watches me, expressionless. "Goodbye, Brian," I whisper to him.

I tell Mrs. Finestein that I can't do the job any more because I have too much schoolwork. I can't tell her the real reason: that in some obscure way Brian is not safe with me. I have images of Brian head-first in a snowbank; Brian hurtling in his carriage down the icy hill by the side of the bridge, straight towards the creek full of dead people; Brian tossed into the air, his bunny ears flung upwards in terror. I have only a limited ability to say no.

"Honey, that's all right," she says, looking into my raw, watery eyes. She puts her arm around me and gives me a hug and an extra nickel. No one has ever called me *honey* before this.

I go home, knowing I have failed her, and also myself. *Bugger*, I think to myself. I say it over and over until it disappears into its own syllables. *Erbug, erbug*. It's a word with no meaning, like *kike*, but it reeks of ill will, it has power. What have I done to my father?

I take all of Mrs. Finestein's King's-head nickels and spend them at the store on the way home from school. I buy licorice whips, jelly beans, many-layered blackballs with the seed in the middle, packages of fizzy sherbet you suck up through a straw. I dole them out equally, these offerings, these atonements, into the waiting hands of my friends. In the moment just before giving, I am loved.

26

It's Saturday. Nothing has happened all morning. Icicles form on the eavestrough above the south window, dripping in the sunlight with a steady sound like a leak. My mother is baking in the kitchen, my father and brother are elsewhere. I eat my lunch alone, watching the icicles.

The lunch is crackers and orange cheese and a glass of milk, and a bowl of alphabet soup. My mother thinks of alphabet soup as a cheerful treat for children. The alphabet soup has letters floating in it, white letters: capital A's and O's and S's and R's, the occasional X or Z. When I was younger I would fish the letters out and spell things with them on the edge of the plate, or eat my name, letter by letter. Now I just eat the soup, taking no particular interest. The soup is orangey-red and has a flavour, but the letters themselves taste like nothing.

The telephone rings. It's Grace. "You want to come out and play?" she says, in her neutral voice that is at the same time blank and unsoft, like glazed paper. I know Cordelia is standing beside her. If I say no, I will be accused of something. If I say yes, I will have to do it. I say yes.

"We'll come and get you," Grace says.

My stomach feels dull and heavy, as if it's full of earth. I put on my snowsuit and boots, my knitted hat and mittens. I tell my mother I'm going out to play. "Don't get chilled," she says.

The sun on the snow is blinding. There's a crust of ice over the drifts, where the top layer of snow has melted and then refrozen. My boots make clean-edged footprints through the crust. There's no one around. I walk through the white glare, towards Grace's house. The air is wavery, filled with light, overfilled; I can hear the pressure of it against my eyes. I feel translucent, like a hand held over a flashlight or the pictures of jellyfish I've seen in magazines, floating in the sea like watery flesh balloons.

At the end of the street I can see the three of them, very dark, walking towards me. Their coats look almost black. Even their faces when they come closer look too dark, as if they're in shadow.

Cordelia says, "We said we would come and get you. We didn't say you could come here."

I say nothing.

Grace says, "She should answer when we talk to her."

Cordelia says, "What's the matter, are you deaf?"

Their voices sound far away. I turn aside and throw up onto a snowbank. I didn't mean to do it and didn't know I was going to. I feel sick to my stomach every morning, I'm used to that, but this is the real thing, alphabet soup mixed with shards of chewed-up cheese, amazingly red and orange against the white of the snow, with here and there a ruined letter.

Cordelia doesn't say anything. Grace says, "You better go home." Carol, behind them, sounds as if she's going to cry. She says, "It's on her face." I walk back towards my house, smelling the vomit on the front of my snowsuit, tasting it in my nose and throat. It feels like bits of carrot.

I lie in bed with the scrub-pail beside me, floating lightly on waves of fever. I throw up several times, until nothing but a little green juice comes out. My mother says, "I suppose we'll all get it," and she's right. During the night I can hear hurrying footsteps and retching and the toilet flushing. I feel safe, small, wrapped in my illness as if in cotton wool.

I begin to be sick more often. Sometimes my mother looks into my mouth with a flashlight and feels my forehead and takes my temperature and sends me to school, but sometimes I'm allowed to stay home. On these days I feel relief, as if I've been running for a long time and have reached a place where I can rest, not forever but for a while. Having a fever is pleasant, vacant. I enjoy the coolness of things, the flat ginger ale I'm given to drink, the delicacy of taste, afterwards.

I lie in bed, propped up on pillows, a glass of water on a chair beside me, listening to the far-away sounds coming from my mother: the eggbeater, the vacuum cleaner, music from the radio, the lakeshore sound of the floor polisher. Winter sunlight slants in through the window, between the half-drawn curtains. I now have curtains. I look at the ceiling light fixture, opaque yellowish glass with the shadows of two or three dead flies caught inside it showing through as if through cloudy jelly. Or I look at the doorknob.

Sometimes I cut things out of magazines and paste them into a scrapbook with LePage's mucilage, from the bottle that looks like a chess bishop. I cut out pictures of women, from *Good Housekeeping, The Ladies' Home Journal, Chatelaine.* If I don't like their faces I cut off the heads and glue other heads on. These women have dresses with puffed sleeves and full skirts, and white aprons that tie very tightly around their waists. They put germ-killers onto germs, in toilet bowls; they polish windows, or clean their spotty complexions with bars of soap, or shampoo their oily hair; they get rid of their unwanted odours, rub hand lotion onto their rough wrinkly hands, hug rolls of toilet paper against their cheeks.

Other pictures show women doing things they aren't supposed to do. Some of them gossip too much, some are sloppy, others bossy. Some of them knit too much. "Walking, riding, standing, sitting, Where she goes, there goes her knitting," says one. The picture shows a woman knitting on a streetcar, with the ends of her knitting needles poking into the people beside her and her ball of wool unrolling down the aisle. Some of the women have a Watchbird beside them, a red and black bird like a child's drawing, with big eyes and stick feet. "This is a Watchbird watching a Busybody," it says. "This is a Watchbird watching YOU."

I see that there will be no end to imperfection, or to doing things the wrong way. Even if you grow up, no matter how hard you scrub, whatever you do, there will always be some other stain or spot on your face or stupid act, somebody frowning. But it pleases me somehow to cut out all these imperfect women, with their forehead wrinkles that show how worried they are, and fix them into my scrapbook.

At noon there's the Happy Gang, on the radio, knocking at the door.

> *Knock knock knock.*
> *Who's there?*
> *It's the Happy Gang!*
> *Well, come ON IN!*

434

Keep happy in the Happy Gang way,
Keep healthy, hope you're feeling okay,
'Cause if you're happy, and healthy,
The heck with being wealthy,
So be happy with the Happy Gang!

The Happy Gang fills me with anxiety. What happens to you if you aren't happy and healthy? They don't say. They themselves are always happy, or say they are; but I can't believe anyone can be always happy. So they must be lying some of the time. But when? How much of their fake-sounding laughter is really fake?

A little later there's the Dominion Observatory Official Time Signal: first a series of outer-space beeps, then silence, then a long dash. The long dash means one o'clock. Time is passing; in the silence before the long dash the future is taking shape. I turn my head into the pillow. I don't want to hear it.

27

The winter melts, leaving a grubby scum of cinders, wet paper, soggy old leaves. A huge pile of topsoil appears in our backyard, then a pile of rolled-up squares of grass. My parents, in muddy boots and earth-stained pants, lay them over our mud like bathroom tiles. They pull out couch-grass and dandelions, plant green onions and a row of lettuce. Cats appear from nowhere, scratching and squatting in the soft, newly planted earth, and my father throws clumps of dug-up dandelions at them. "Dad-ratted cats," he says.

The buds turn yellow, the skipping ropes come out. We stand in Grace's driveway, beside her dark pink crabapple tree. I turn the rope, Carol turns the other end, Grace and Cordelia skip. We look like girls playing.

We chant:

> *Not last night but the night before*
> *Twenty-four robbers come to my back door*
> *And this is what they said . . . to . . . me!*
> *Lady turn around, turn around, turn around,*
> *Lady touch the ground, touch the ground, touch the*
>   *ground;*
> *Lady show your shoe, show your shoe, show your*
>   *shoe,*
> *Lady, lady, twenty-four skiddoo!*

Grace, skipping in the middle, turns around, touches the driveway, kicks up one foot sedately, smiling her little smile. She rarely trips.

This chant is menacing to me. It hints at an obscure dirtiness. Something is not understood: the robbers and their strange commands, the lady and her gyrations, the tricks she's compelled to perform, like a trained dog. And what does "twenty-four skiddoo" mean, at the end of it? Is she scooted out the door of her house while the robbers remain inside, free to take anything they like, break anything, do whatever they want? Or is it the end of her altogether? I see her dangling from the crabapple tree, the skipping rope noosed around her neck. I am not sorry for her.

The sun shines, the marbles return, from wherever they've been all winter. The voices of the children rise in the schoolyard: *purie, purie, bowlie, bowlie, two for one.* They sound to me like ghosts, or like animals caught in a trap: thin wails of exhausted pain.

We cross the wooden bridge on the way home from school. I am walking behind the others. Through the broken boards I can see the ground below. I remember my brother burying his jar full of puries, of waterbabies and cat's eyes, a long time ago, down there somewhere under the bridge. The jar is still there in the earth, shining in the dark, in secret. I think about myself going down there alone despite the sinister unseen men, digging up the treasure, having all that mystery in my hands. I could never find the jar, because I don't have the map. But I like to think about things the others know nothing about.

I retrieve my blue cat's eye from where it's been lying all winter in the corner of my bureau drawer. I examine it, holding it up so the sunlight burns through it. The eye part of it, inside its crystal sphere, is so blue, so pure. It's like something frozen in the ice. I take it to school with me, in my pocket, but I don't set it up to be shot at. I hold onto it, rolling it between my fingers.

"What's that in your pocket?" says Cordelia.

"Nothing," I say. "It's only a marble."

It's marble season; everyone has marbles in their pockets. Cordelia lets it pass. She doesn't know what power this cat's eye has, to protect me. Sometimes when I have it with me I can see the way it sees. I can see people moving like bright animated dolls, their mouths opening and closing but no real words coming out. I can look at their shapes and sizes, their colours, without feeling anything else about them. I am alive in my eyes only.

We stay in the city later than we've ever stayed before. We stay until school ends for the summer and the daylight lasts past bedtime and wet heat descends over the streets like a steaming blanket. I drink grape Freshie, which does not taste like grapes but like something you might use to kill insects, and wonder when we're going to leave for the north. I tell myself it will be never, so I won't be disappointed. But despite my cat's eye I know I can't stand to be here in this place much longer. I will burst inwards. I've read in the *National Geographic* about deep-sea diving and why you have to wear a thick metal suit or the invisible pressure of the heavy undersea water will crush you like mud in a fist, until you implode. This is the word: *implode*. It has a dull final sound to it, like a lead door closing.

I sit in the car, packed into the back seat like a parcel. Grace and Cordelia and Carol are standing among the apple trees, watching. I hunch down, avoiding them. I don't want to pretend, to undergo goodbyes. As the car moves away they wave.

We drive north. Toronto is behind us, a smear of brownish air on the horizon, like smoke from a distant burning. Only now do I turn and look.

The leaves get smaller and yellower, folding back towards the bud, and the air crisps. I see a raven by the side of the road, picking at a porcupine that's been run over by a car, its quills like a huge burr, its guts pink and scrambled like eggs. I see the northern granite rock rising straight up out of the ground with the road cut through it. I see a raggedy lake with dead trees stuck into the marsh around the edges. A sawdust burner, a fire tower.

Three Indians stand beside the road. They aren't selling anything, no baskets and it's too early for blueberries. They just stand there as if they've been doing it for a long time. They're familiar to me but only as scenery. Do they see me as I stare at them out of the car window? Probably not. I'm a blur to them, one more face in a car that doesn't stop. I have no claim on them, or on any of this.

I sit in the back seat of the car that smells of gasoline and cheese, waiting for my parents, who are buying groceries. The car is beside a wooden general store, saggy and weathered grey, stuck together by the signs nailed all over the outside of it: BLACK CAT CIGARETTES, PLAYERS, COCA-COLA. This isn't even a village, just a wide place in the highway, beside a bridge beside a river.

438

Once I would have wanted to know the river's name. Stephen stands on the bridge, dropping pieces of wood upstream, timing how long it takes them to come out the other side, calculating the rate of flow. The blackflies are out. Some of them are in the car, crawling up the window, jumping, crawling up again. I watch them do this: I can see their hunched backs, their abdomens like little black-red bulbs. I squash them against the glass, leaving red smears of my own blood.

I've begun to feel not gladness, but relief. My throat is no longer tight, I've stopped clenching my teeth, the skin on my feet has begun to grow back, my fingers have healed partially. I can walk without seeing how I look from the back, talk without hearing the way I sound. I go for long periods without saying anything at all. I can be free of words now, I can lapse back into wordlessness, I can sink back into the rhythms of transience as if into bed.

This summer we're in a rented cabin on the north shore of Lake Superior. There are a few other cottages around, most of them empty; there are no other children. The lake is huge and cold and blue and treacherous. It can sink freighters, drown people. In a wind the waves roll in with the crash of oceans. Swimming in it doesn't frighten me at all. I wade into the freezing water, watching my feet and then my legs go down into it, long and white and thinner than on land.

There's a wide beach, and to one end of it a colony of boulders. I spend time among them. They're rounded, like seals, only hard; they heat up in the sun, and stay warm in the evening when the air cools. I take pictures of them with my Brownie camera. I give them the names of cows.

Above the beach, on the dunes, there are beach plants, fuzzy mulleins and vetch with its purple flowers and tiny bitter peapods, and grasses that will cut your legs; and behind that the forest, oak and moose-maple and birch and poplar, with balsam and spruce among them. There's poison ivy sometimes. It's a secretive, watchful forest, though hard to get lost in, so close to the shore.

Walking in the forest I find a dead raven. It's bigger than they look alive. I poke it with a stick, turning it over, and see the maggots. It smells like rot, like rust, and, more strangely, like some sort of food I've eaten once but can't remember. It's black, but not like a colour; more like a hole. Its beak is dingy, horn-coloured, like old toenails. Its eyes are shrivelled up.

I've seen dead animals before, dead frogs, dead rabbits, but this raven is deader. It looks at me with its shrivelled-up eye. I could poke this stick right through it. No matter what I do to it, it won't feel a thing. No one can get at it.

It's hard to fish from the shore of this lake. There's nowhere to stand, no dock. We aren't allowed out in a boat by ourselves because of the currents; anyway we have no boat. Stephen is doing other things. He makes a collection of the boat funnels from the lake freighters, checking them through binoculars. He sets up chess problems and works them out, or splits kindling, or goes for long walks by himself with a butterfly book. He isn't interested in catching the butterflies and mounting them on a board with pins; he just wants to see them, identify them, count them. He writes them down in a list at the back of the book.

I like looking at the pictures of butterflies in his book. My favourite is the luna moth, huge and pale green, with crescents on the wings. My brother finds one of these, and shows it to me. "Don't touch it," he says. "Or the dust will come off its wings, and then it can't fly."

But I don't play chess with him. I don't start my own list of boat funnels or butterflies. I'm ceasing to be interested in games I can't win.

Along the edges of the forest, where there's open sunlight, there are chokecherry trees. The red chokecherries ripen and turn translucent. They're so sour they dry up the inside of your mouth. I pick them into a lard pail, then sort out the dead twigs and leaves, and my mother makes jelly from them, boiling them up, straining the pits out through a cloth jelly bag, adding sugar. She pours the jelly into hot jars, capping them with paraffin wax. I count the beautiful red jars. I helped make them. They look poisonous.

* * *

As if I've been given permission I begin to dream. My dreams are brightly coloured and without sound.

I dream that the dead raven is alive, only it looks the same, it still looks dead. It hops around and flaps its decaying wings and I wake up, my heart beating fast.

I dream I'm putting on my winter clothes, in Toronto, but my dress doesn't fit. I pull it on over my head and struggle to get my arms into the sleeves. I'm walking along the street and parts of my body are sticking out through the dress, parts of my bare skin. I am ashamed.

I dream that my blue cat's eye is shining in the sky like the sun, or like the pictures of planets in our book on the solar system. But instead of being warm, it's cold. It starts to move nearer, but it doesn't get any bigger. It's falling down out of the sky, straight towards my head, brilliant and glassy. It hits me, passes right into me, but without hurting, except that it's cold. The cold wakes me up. My blankets are on the floor.

I dream that the wooden bridge over the ravine is falling apart. I'm standing on it, the boards crack and separate, the bridge sways. I walk along what's left, clinging to the railing, but I can't get onto the hill where the other people are standing because the bridge isn't attached to anything. My mother is on the hill, but she's talking to the other people.

I dream I'm picking the chokecherries off the chokecherry tree and putting them into the lard pail. Only they aren't choke-cherries. They're deadly nightshade berries, translucent, brilliantly red. They're filled with blood, like the bodies of blackflies. As I touch them they burst, and the blood runs over my hands.

None of my dreams is about Cordelia.

Our father plays touch-tag with us on the beach in the evenings, running lumberingly like a bear, laughing at the same time, *wuff wuff wuff*. Pennies and dimes fall out of his pockets into the sand. The lake boats go slowly by in the distance, their smoke trailing behind them, the sun sets to the left, pink and tranquil. I look in the mirror over the washbasin: my face is brown and rounder. My mother smiles at me, in the little kitchen with the woodstove, and hugs me with one arm. She thinks I am happy. Some nights we have marshmallows, for a treat.

VI

Cat's Eye

28

Simpsons Basement used to be bargain clothes and wrenches. Now it's resplendent. There are pyramids of imported chocolates, an ice-cream counter, aisles and aisles of fancy cookies and canned gourmet food, ticking away like little clocks towards the obsolescence dates stamped on their packages. There's even an espresso counter. It's all very world-class down here, where I used to buy cheap nighties in high school with my tiny clothes allowance, on sale at that and a size too large, I'm overwhelmed by all the chocolates. Just looking at them reminds me of Christmas and the sticky feeling after eating too many, the surfeit and glut.

I sit at the espresso counter and have a cappuccino, to deal with the inertia that's come over me at the sight of so much sugar-coated self-indulgence. The espresso counter is either fake or real dark-green marble; it has a cute canopy over it, someone's idea of Italy, and little swivel stools. The view from here is the shoe-repair counter, which is not very world-class but is reassuring to me. People still get their shoes repaired, despite all this chocolate, they don't just toss them out at the first hint of wear.

I think about the shoes of my childhood, the brown Oxfords scuffed at the toes, half-soled, new-heeled, the falling-apart grubby white running shoes, the brown sandals with two buckles that you wore with socks. Most shoes were brown. They went with the pot-roast done in the pressure-cooker along with the limp carrots and the flaccid potatoes and the onions with their slippery layers. The pressure-cooker had a whistle-shaped thing on the top. If you forgot to pay attention to it the lid would blow off like a bomb, and the carrots and potatoes would be hurled to the ceiling, where they'd stick like mush. This happened to my mother once. Luckily she was not in the kitchen at the time and was not scalded. When she saw what had happened she did not swear. She laughed; and said, "Wouldn't that take the gold-plated gingerbread."

My mother did most of the cooking but it was not her favourite thing. She was not fond of housework generally. In the steamer trunk in the cellar, along with a cut-velvet evening gown from the twenties and a pair of riding jodhpurs, there were several things made of real silver, ornate salt and pepper shakers, sugar tongs in the shape of chickens' feet, rose bowls lavish with silver flowers. They were down there, wrapped in tissue paper and turning black, because otherwise they would have to be polished. Our knives and forks and spoons had to be polished, with an old toothbrush for the decorations. The scrolled legs under the dining table were dust-catchers, and so were the kinds of objects – doodads, my mother called them – other people kept on their mantelpieces. But she liked making cakes, though this may only be something I prefer to think.

What would I have done if I had been my mother? She must have realized what was happening to me, or that something was. Even towards the beginning she must have noted my silences, my bitten fingers, the dark scabs on my lips where I'd pulled off patches of the skin. If it were happening now, to a child of my own, I would know what to do. But then? There were fewer choices, and a great deal less was said.

I once did a series about my mother. It was six images, six panels, like a double triptych or a comic book, arranged in two groups, three on top, three underneath. The first was my mother in coloured pencil, in her city-house kitchen and her late-forties dress. Even she had a bib apron, blue flowers with navy piping, even she wore it, from time to time. The second image was the same figure in collage, made from the illustrations from old *Ladies' Home Journals* and *Chatelaines*, not the photos but the artwork, with those rancid greens and faded blues and dirty-looking pinks. The third was the same figure, white on white, the raised parts pipe-cleaners contoured side by side and glued onto a white cloth-covered backing. Reading across from left to right it looked as if my mother was slowly dissolving, from real life into a Babylonian bas-relief shadow.

The bottom set of images went the other way: first the pipe-cleaners, then the same image in collage, then the final one in full-coloured realistic detail. But this time my mother was in her slacks and boots and her man's jacket, making chokecherry jam over the outdoor fire. You could read it as a materialization, out of the white pipe-cleaner mist into the solid light of day.

I called the whole series *Pressure Cooker*. Because of when it was done and what was going on in those years, some people thought it was about the Earth Goddess, which I found hilarious in view of my mother's dislike of housework. Other people thought it was about female slavery, others that it was a stereotyping of women in negative and trivial domestic roles. But it was only my mother cooking, in the ways and places she used to cook, in the late forties.

I made this right after she died. I suppose I wanted to bring her back to life. I suppose I wanted her timeless, though there is no such thing on earth. These pictures of her, like everything else, are drenched in time.

I finish my cappuccino, pay for it, leave a tip for the imitation Italian waiter who served it to me. I know I won't buy any food in the Food Hall, I'm too intimidated by it. Ordinarily, or in some other city, I would not be: I am a grownup and used to shopping. But how could I find, down here, anything I want right now? I'll stop in at some corner store on the way back, some place where they sell milk till midnight and slightly stale sliced white bread. Such stores are run, now, by people the colour of Mr. Banerji, or by Chinese people. They aren't necessarily any friendlier than the pasty-white people who used to run such stores, but the general content of their disapproval is more easily guessed; though not the details.

I head back up the escalator, into the perfumed fug of the ground floor. The air is bad here, there's too much musk, the overpowering scent of money. I make it into the open air and walk west, past the murderous mannequins in the windows, past the bivalvular City Hall.

Ahead of me there's a body lying on the sidewalk. People walk around it, look down, look away, keep going. I see their faces coming towards me bearing that careful rearrangement of the features that's meant to say, *This is none of my business*.

447

When I get up even, I see that this person is a woman. She's lying on her back, staring straight at me. "Lady," she says. "Lady. Lady."

That word has been through a lot. Noble lady, Dark Lady, she's a real lady, old-lady lace, Listen lady, Hey lady watch where you're going, Ladies' Room, run through with lipstick and replaced with Women. But still the final word of appeal. If you want something very badly you do not say *Woman, Woman*, you say *Lady, Lady*. As she is saying now.

I think, *What if she's had a heart attack?* I look: there's blood on her forehead, not much, but a cut. She must have hit her head falling. And no one's stopping, and she's lying there on her back, a bulky fifty-odd woman in a poor-person green coat, gabardine, and lamentable shoes all cracked, her arms outflung. The tanned-looking skin around her brown eyes is red and puffy, her long black and grey hair is splayed across the sidewalk.

"Lady," she says, or something, it's a mumble, but she's got me now.

I look over my shoulder to see if anyone else will do this, but there are no takers. I kneel, say to her, "Are you all right?" What a stupid question, she so obviously isn't. Vomit and alcohol are around here somewhere. I have visions of myself taking her for coffee, and then where? I won't be able to get rid of her, she'll follow me back to the studio, throw up in the bathtub, sleep on the futon. They get me every time, they can spot me coming, pick me out of the crowd no matter how hard I frown. Sidewalk rap artists, Moonies, guitar-playing young men who ask me for subway tokens. In the clutch of the helpless I am helpless.

"She's only drunk," a man says in passing. What does he mean, *only*? It's hell enough.

"Here," I say, "I'll help you up." Wimp, I tell myself. She'll ask you for money and you'll give it to her, and she'll spend it on cheap sweet wine. But I have her on her feet now, she's slumped against me. If I can lug her over to the nearest wall I can prop her up, dust her off a little, think how to get away.

"There," I say. But she won't lean against the wall, she's leaning against me instead. Her breath smells like a bad accident. She's crying now, the shameless abandoned weeping of a child; her fingers clutch my sleeve.

"Don't leave me," she says. "Oh God. Don't leave me all

alone." Her eyes are closed, her voice is pure neediness, pure woe. It hits the weakest, most sorrowing part of me; but I am only a surrogate, for who knows what lack, what loss. There's nothing I can do.

"Here," I say. I fumble in my purse, find a ten, crumple it into her hand, paying her off. I'm a sucker, I'm a bleeding heart. There's a cut in my heart, it bleeds money.

"Bless you," she says. Her head rolls from side to side, back against the wall. "God bless you, lady, Our Lady bless you." It's a slurred blessing, but who's to say I don't need it? She must be a Catholic. I could find a church, slide her in through the door like a packet. She's theirs, let them deal with her.

"I have to go now," I say. "You'll be all right." Lying through my teeth. She opens her eyes wide, trying to focus. Her face goes quiet.

"I know about you," she says. "You're Our Lady and you don't love me."

Fullblown booze madness, and absolutely the wrong person. I draw my hand back from her as if she's a live socket. "No," I say. She's right, I don't love her. Her eyes are not brown but green. Cordelia's.

I walk away from her, guilt on my hands, absolving myself: I'm a good person. She could have been dying. Nobody else stopped.

I'm a fool, to confuse this with goodness. I am not good.

I know too much to be good. I know myself.

I know myself to be vengeful, greedy, secretive and sly.

29

We come back in September. In the north the nights are cold and the leaves are beginning to turn, but the city is still hot, still damp. It's astonishingly noisy and stinks of gasoline and the tar of melting roads. The air inside our house is stale and flat, air that's been locked up in the heat all summer. The water's rusty at first, coming out of the taps. I take a bath in the reddish lukewarm water. Already my body is stiffening, emptying itself of feeling. The future is closing on me like a door.

Cordelia has been waiting for me. I know this as soon as I see her standing at the school-bus stop. Before the summer she would alternate between kindness and malice, with periods of indifference; but now she's harsher, more relentless. It's as if she's driven by the urge to see how far she can go. She's backing me towards an edge, like the edge of a cliff: one step back, another step, and I'll be over and falling.

Carol and I are in Grade Five now. We have a new teacher, Miss Stuart. She's Scottish and has an accent. "Now gerruls," she says. She has a little bunch of dried heather stuck into a jelly jar on her desk, and a miniature of Bonnie Prince Charlie who was ruined by the English and whose last name is the same as her own, and a bottle of hand lotion in her desk drawer. She cooks this hand lotion herself.

In the afternoons she makes herself a cup of tea, which does not smell entirely like tea but of something else she puts into it, out of a small silver bottle. She has bluish-white hair, beautifully waved, and wears rustling, silky mauve dresses with a lace-edged handkerchief tucked into the sleeve. She often has a nurse's white gauze mask over her nose and mouth because she's allergic to chalk dust. This doesn't stop her from throwing the blackboard brushes at boys who aren't paying attention. Although she throws underhand and not hard, she never misses. After she hits the boy he has to bring the blackboard brush back to her. The boys don't seem to resent this habit of hers; they take it as a mark of distinction to get hit.

Everyone loves Miss Stuart. Carol says we are lucky to be in her class. I would love her too, if I had the energy. But I am too numb, too enthralled.

I keep my cat's eye in my pocket, where I can hold onto it. It rests in my hand, valuable as a jewel, looking out through bone and cloth with its impartial gaze. With the help of its power I retreat back into my eyes. Up ahead of me are Cordelia, Grace and Carol. I look at their shapes as they walk, the way shadow moves from one leg to another, the blocks of colour, a red square of cardigan, a blue triangle of skirt. They're like puppets up ahead, small and clear. I could see them or not, at will.

I reach the path to the bridge, start down, past the nightshade vines with their red berries, past the undulating leaves, the lurking cats. The three of them are already on the bridge but they've stopped, they're waiting for me. I look at the ovals of their faces, the outline of hair around each one. Their faces are like mouldy eggs. My feet move down the hill.

I think about becoming invisible. I think about eating the deadly nightshade berries from the bushes beside the path. I think about drinking the Javex out of the skull-and-crossbones bottle in the laundry room, about jumping off the bridge, smashing down there like a pumpkin, half of an eye, half of a grin. I would come apart like that, I would be dead, like the dead people.

I don't want to do these things, I'm afraid of them. But I think about Cordelia telling me to do them, not in her scornful voice, in her kind one. I hear her kind voice inside my head. *Do it. Come on.* I would be doing these things to please her.

I consider telling my brother, asking him for help. But tell him what exactly? I have no black eyes, no bloody noses to report: Cordelia does nothing physical. If it was boys, chasing or teasing, he would know what to do, but I don't suffer from boys in this way. Against girls and their indirectness, their whisperings, he would be helpless.

Also I'm ashamed. I'm afraid he'll laugh at me, he'll despise

451

me for being a sissy about a bunch of girls, for making a fuss about nothing.

I'm in the kitchen, greasing muffin-tins for my mother. I see the patterns the grease leaves on the metal, I see the moons of my nails, the raggedy flesh. My fingers go around and around.

My mother makes the batter for the muffins, measuring the salt, sifting the flour. The sifter sounds dry, like sandpaper. "You don't have to play with them," my mother says. "There must be other little girls you can play with instead."

I look at her. Misery washes over me like a slow wind. What has she noticed, what has she guessed, what is she about to do? She might tell their mothers. This would be the worst thing she could do. Also I can't imagine it. My mother is not like the other mothers, she doesn't fit in with the idea of them. She does not inhabit the house, the way the other mothers do; she's airy and hard to pin down. The others don't go skating on the neighbourhood rink, or walk in the ravine by themselves. They seem to me grown up in a way that my own mother is not. I think of Carol's mother in her twin set, her sceptical smile, Cordelia's with her glasses on a chain and her vagueness, Grace's and her hairpins and drooping apron. My mother will turn up on their doorsteps, wearing slacks, carrying a bouquet of weeds, incongruous. They won't believe her.

"When I was little and the kids called names, we used to say, 'Sticks and stones will break my bones but names will never hurt me,'" she says. Her arm goes vigorously around, mixing, efficient and strong.

"They don't call me names," I say. "They're my friends." I believe this.

"You have to learn to stand up for yourself," says my mother. "Don't let them push you around. Don't be spineless. You have to have more backbone." She dollops the batter into the tins.

I think of sardines and their backbones. You can eat their backbones. The bones crumble between your teeth; one touch and they fall apart. This must be what my own backbone is like: hardly there at all. What is happening to me is my own fault, for not having more backbone.

My mother sets down the bowl and puts her arms around me.

452

"I wish I knew what to do," she says. This is a confession. Now I know what I've been suspecting: as far as this thing is concerned, she is powerless.

I know that muffins have to be baked right away, right after they've been ladled out, or they'll be flat and ruined. I can't afford the distraction of comfort. If I give in to it, what little backbone I have left will crumble away to nothing.

I pull away from her. "They need to go into the oven," I say.

30

Cordelia brings a mirror to school. It's a pocket-mirror, the small plain oblong kind without any rim. She takes it out of her pocket and holds the mirror up in front of me and says, "Look at yourself! Just look!" Her voice is disgusted, fed up, as if my face, all by itself, has been up to something, has gone too far. I look into the mirror but I don't see anything out of the ordinary. It's just my face, with the dark blotches on the lips where I've bitten off the skin.

My parents have bridge parties. They push the furniture in the living room to the walls and unfold two metal bridge-tables and eight bridge-chairs. In the middle of each table there are two china dishes, one with salted nuts, the other with mixed candies. These candies are called "bridge mixture". There are also two ashtrays on each table.

Then the doorbell begins to ring and the people come in. The house fills with the alien scent of cigarettes, which will still be there in the morning along with a few uneaten candies and salted nuts, and with bursts of laughter that get louder as time passes. I lie in my bed listening to the bursts of laughter. I feel isolated, left out. Also I don't understand why this activity, these noises and smells, is called "bridge". It is not like a bridge.

Sometimes Mr. Banerji comes to these bridge parties. I lurk in the corner of the hallway in my flannelette pyjamas, hoping to catch a glimpse of him. I don't have a crush on him or anything like that. My wish to see him is anxiety, and fellow-feeling. I want to see how he is managing, how he is coping with his life, with having to eat turkeys, and with other things. Not very well, judging from his dark, haunted-looking eyes and slightly hysterical laughter. But if he can deal with whatever

454

it is that's after him, and something is, then so can I. Or this is what I think.

Princess Elizabeth is coming to Toronto. She's visiting Canada with her husband, who is a Duke. It's a Royal Visit. On the radio there are cheering crowds, and solemn voices describing what colour she's wearing, a different colour every day. I crouch on the living room floor with the Maritimes fiddle music going on in the background, the *Toronto Star* spread out underneath my elbows, studying the picture of her on the front page. She's older than she should be and more ordinary: no longer in a Girl Guide uniform as in the days of the Blitz, but not in an evening gown and a tiara either, like the Queen at the back of the classroom. She's wearing a plain suit and gloves and carrying a handbag, like anyone, and she has on a ladies' hat. But still she's a Princess. On the inside of the paper there's a full page of her, with women curtsying to her, little girls presenting bouquets of flowers. She smiles down upon them, always the same benevolent smile, and is described as radiant.

Day after day, crouching on the floor, turning the pages of the newspapers, I watch her make her way across the map, by plane, by train, by car, from city to city. I memorize the diagrams of her proposed route through Toronto. I'll get a good chance to see her, because she's supposed to drive right by our house, along the raw, pot-holed road that runs between the cemetery, with its spindly new trees and heaps of bulldozed earth, and the line of five new mud-mountains.

The mud-mountains are on our side of the road. They have recently appeared, replacing the strip of weedy field that used to be there before. Each mountain stands beside its own hole, roughly cellar-shaped, with a slop of muddy water at the bottom. My brother has claimed one of them for his own; he plans to excavate it, tunnelling down from the top, then in from the side to make a side entrance. What he wishes to do in there is unknown.

I don't know why the Princess is going to be driven past these mud-mountains. I don't think of them as anything she would necessarily want to see, but I'm not sure, because she's seeing a lot of other things that don't seem to be of more interest.

455

There's a picture of her outside a city hall, another beside a fish-canning factory. But whether she wants to see them or not, the mud-mountains will be a good place to stand.

I am looking forward to this visit. I expect something from it, although I'm not sure what. This is the same Princess that defied the bombs in London, the one that is brave and heroic. I think something will happen for me on that day. Something will change.

The Royal Visit finally reaches Toronto. The day is overcast, with pinpoints of rain; spitting, they call it. I go out early and stand on the top of the middle mud-mountain. There's a straggly line of people, adults and children, along the roadside among the draggled weeds. Some of the children have small Union Jacks. I have one as well: they were handed out at school. There's not much of a crowd, because not that many people live around here and some of them have probably gone further downtown, to where there are sidewalks. I can see Grace and Carol and Cordelia, along the road towards Grace's house. I hope they will not see me.

I stand on the mud-mountain with my Union Jack hanging slack from its stick. It gets later and nothing happens. I think maybe I should go back to our house and listen to the radio, to see how far away the Princess is, but suddenly there's a police car, to the left, coming along by the cemetery. It begins to drizzle. In the distance there's cheering.

There are some motorcycles, then some cars. I can see the arms of the people along the road going up into the air, hear scattered hoorays. The cars are going too fast, despite the pot-holes. I can't see which car is the right one.

Then I do see. It's the car with the pale glove coming out the window, waving back and forth. Already it's opposite me, already it's passing. I don't wave my Union Jack or cheer, because I see that it's too late, I won't have time for what I've been waiting for, which has only now become clear to me. What I must do is run down the mountain with my arms stretched out to either side, for balance, and throw myself in front of the Princess's car. In front of it, or onto it, or into it. Then the Princess will tell them to stop the car. She'll have to, in order to avoid running over me. I don't picture myself being driven away in the royal car, I'm more realistic than that. Anyway I don't want to leave my parents. But things will change, they will be different, something will be done.

The car with the glove is moving away, it's turned the corner, it's gone, and I haven't moved.

31

Miss Stuart likes art. She has us bring old shirts of our fathers from home so we can do messier art without getting our clothes dirty. While we scissor and paint and paste she walks the aisles in her nurse's mask, looking over our shoulders. But if anyone, a boy, draws a silly picture on purpose, she holds the page up in mocking outrage. "This lad here thinks he's being smarrut. You've got more between the ears than that!" And she flicks him on the ear with her thumb and fingernail.

For her we make the familiar paper objects, the pumpkins, the Christmas bells, but she has us do other things too. We make complicated floral patterns with a compass, we glue odd substances to cardboard backings: feathers, sequins, pieces of macaroni garishly dyed, lengths of drinking-straw. We do group murals on the blackboards or on large rolls of brown paper. We draw pictures about foreign countries: Mexico with cactuses and men in enormous hats, China with cones on the heads and seeing-eye boats, India with what we intend to be graceful, silk-draped women balancing copper urns, and jewels on their foreheads.

I like these foreign pictures because I can believe in them. I desperately need to believe that somewhere else these other, foreign people exist. No matter that at Sunday School I've been told such people are either starving or heathens or both. No matter that my weekly collection goes to convert them, feed them, smarten them up. Miss Lumley saw them as crafty, given to the eating of outlandish or disgusting foods and to acts of treachery against the British, but I prefer Miss Stuart's versions, in which the sun above their heads is a cheerful yellow, the palm trees a clear green, the clothing they wear is floral, their folksongs gay. The women chatter together in quick incomprehensible languages, they laugh, showing perfect, pure-white teeth. If these people exist I can go there sometime. I don't have to stay here.

* * *

Today, says Miss Stuart, we are going to draw what we do after school.

The others hunch over their desks. I know what they will draw: skipping ropes, jolly snowmen, listening to the radio, playing with a dog. I stare at my own paper, which remains blank. Finally I draw my bed, with myself in it. My bed has a dark wooden headboard with curlicues on it. I draw the window, the chest-of-drawers. I colour in the night. My hand holding the black crayon presses down, harder and harder, until the picture is almost entirely black, until only a faint shadow of my bed and my head on the pillow remains to be seen.

I look at this picture with dismay. It isn't what I meant to draw. It's unlike everyone else's picture, it's the wrong thing. Miss Stuart will be disappointed in me, she'll tell me I have more between the ears than that. I can feel her standing behind me now, looking over my shoulder; I can smell her smell of hand lotion, and the other smell that is not tea. She moves around so I can see her, her bright blue wrinkly eyes looking at me over the top of her nurse's mask.

For a moment she says nothing. Then she says, not harshly, "Why is your picture so darruk, my dear?"

"Because it's night," I say. This is an idiotic answer, I know that as soon as it's out of my mouth. My voice is almost inaudible, even to me.

"I see," she says. She doesn't say I've drawn the wrong thing, or that surely there's something else I do after school besides going to bed. She touches me on the shoulder, briefly, before continuing down the aisle. Her touch glows briefly, like a blown-out match.

In the schoolroom windows the paper hearts are blossoming. We make a huge Valentine's Day post-box out of a cardboard box covered with pink crêpe paper and red hearts with paper-doily edging. Into the slot at the top we slip our valentines, cut from books of them you can buy at Woolworth's, with special, single ones for the people we especially like.

On the day itself the whole afternoon is a party. Miss Stuart loves parties. She's brought dozens of heart-shaped shortbread cookies she's made herself, with pink icing and silver balls on

459

them, and there are tiny cinnamon hearts and pastel hearts with messages on them, messages from some earlier era which is not ours. "Hubba Hubba," they say. "She's My Baby." "Oh You Kid!"

Miss Stuart sits at her desk, supervising, while several girls open the box and deliver the valentines. On my desk the cards pile up. Most of them are from boys. I can tell this because of the sloppy writing, and because a lot of them aren't signed. Others have only initials or Guess Who? Some have x's and o's. The cards from girls are all neatly signed, with their full names, so there will be no mistake about who gave what.

On the way home from school Carol giggles and shows off her cards from boys. I have more cards from boys than Carol has, more than Cordelia and Grace have collected in their Grade Six classroom. Only I know this. I've hidden the cards in my desk so they won't be seen on the way home. When questioned I say I didn't get many. I hug my knowledge, which is new but doesn't surprise me: boys are my secret allies.

Carol is only ten and three quarters but she's growing breasts. They aren't very big, but the nipples are no longer flat, they're pointed, and there's a swelling behind them. It's easy to see this because she sticks out her chest, she wears sweaters, pulling them down tightly so the breasts poke out. She complains about these breasts at recess: they hurt, she says. She says she will have to get a bra. Cordelia says, "Oh shut up about your stupid tits." She's older, but she doesn't have any yet.

Carol pinches her lips and cheeks to make them red. She finds a worn-down tube of lipstick in her mother's waste-paper basket and hides it away, and takes it to school in her pocket. Using the tip of her little finger, she rubs some of it on her lips after school. She wipes it off with a Kleenex before we get to her house but she doesn't do a good enough job.

We play upstairs in her room. When we go down to the kitchen for a glass of milk, her mother says, "What's that on your face, young lady?" Right in front of us she scrubs Carol's face with the dirty dishcloth. "Don't let me catch you doing such a cheap thing again! At your age, the idea!" Carol wriggles, cries and screams, abandoning herself. We watch, horrified and

460

thrilled. "Just wait till your father gets home!" her mother says in a cold, furious voice. "Making a spectacle of yourself," as if there's something wrong in the mere act of being looked at. Then she remembers we're still here. "Off you go!"

Two days later Carol says her father has given it to her good, with his belt, buckle end, right across the bare bum. She says she can hardly sit down. She sounds proud of this. She shows us, after school, up in her room: she pulls up her skirt, pulls down her underpants, and sure enough there are the marks, almost like scratch marks, not very red but there.

It's difficult to match this evidence with Carol's father, nice Mr. Campbell, who has a soft moustache and calls Grace Beautiful Brown Eyes and Cordelia Miss Lobelia. It's strange to imagine him hitting anyone with a belt. But fathers and their ways are enigmatic. I know without being told, for instance, that Mr. Smeath lives a secret life of trains and escapes in his head. Cordelia's father is charming to us on the rare occasions when he is seen, he makes wry jokes, his smile is like a billboard, but why is she afraid of him? Because she is. All fathers except mine are invisible in daytime; daytime is ruled by mothers. But fathers come out at night. Darkness brings home the fathers, with their real, unspeakable power. There is more to them than meets the eye. And so we believe the belt.

Carol says she's seen a wet spot on the sheet of her mother's twin bed, in the morning, before the bed was made. We tiptoe into her parents' room. The bed with its tufty chenille bedspread is so neatly made up we're afraid to turn down the covers to look. Carol opens the drawer of her mother's bedside table and we peer in. There's a rubber thing like the top of a mushroom, and a tube of toothpaste that isn't toothpaste. Carol says these things are to keep you from having babies. Nobody giggles, nobody scoffs. Instead we read the label. Somehow the red marks on Carol's bum have given her a credibility she lacked before.

Carol lies on top of her own bed, which has a white ruffled spread that matches the curtains. She's pretending to be sick, with an unspecified illness. We've dampened a washcloth, draped it over her forehead, brought her a glass of water. Illness is now a game we play.

461

"Oh, I'm so sick, oh, I'm so sick," Carol moans, twisting her body on the bed. "Nurse, do something!"

"We have to listen to her heart," says Cordelia. She pulls up Carol's sweater, then her undershirt. We've all been to the doctor, we know about the brusque humiliations involved. "This won't hurt." There are the breasts, puffy-looking, their nipples bluish, like veins on a forehead. "Feel her heart," Cordelia says to me.

I don't want to. I don't want to touch that swollen, unnatural flesh. "Go on," says Cordelia. "Do as you're told."

"She's being disobedient," says Grace.

I reach out my hand, place it on the left breast. It feels like a balloon half filled with water, or like lukewarm oatmeal porridge. Carol giggles. "Oh, your hand's so cold!" Nausea grips me.

"Her heart, stupid," says Cordelia. "I didn't say her tit. Don't you know the difference?"

An ambulance comes and my mother is carried out to it on a stretcher. I don't see this, Stephen tells me about it. It was in the middle of the night when I was asleep, but Stephen has taken to getting up secretly and looking out of his bedroom window at the stars. He says you can see the stars much better when most of the lights in the city are off. He says that the way to wake up at night without using an alarm clock is to drink two glasses of water before you go to bed. Then you have to concentrate on the hour you want to wake up. This is what the Indians used to do.

So he was awake, and listened, and snuck across to the other side of the house to look out the window there, where he could see what was going on out on the street. He says there were flashing lights but no siren, so it's no wonder I didn't hear anything.

When I get up in the morning my father is in the kitchen frying bacon. He knows how to do this, though he never does it in the city, only over campfires. In my parents' bedroom there's a pile of crumpled sheets on the floor, and the blankets are folded up on a chair; on the mattress there's a huge oval splotch of blood. But when I come home from school the sheets are gone and the bed is made up, and there is nothing more to be seen.

My father says there has been an accident. But how can you have an accident lying in bed asleep? Stephen says it was a baby, a baby that came out too soon. I don't believe him: women who are going to have babies have big fat stomachs, and my mother didn't have one.

My mother comes back from the hospital and is weaker. She has to rest. No one is used to this, she isn't used to it herself. She resists it, getting up as usual, putting her hand on the wall or on the edges of the furniture as she walks, standing hunched over at the kitchen sink, a cardigan over her shoulders. In the middle of something she's doing she has to go and lie down. Her skin is pale and dry. She looks as if she's listening to a sound, outside the house perhaps, but there is no sound. Sometimes I have to repeat things twice before she hears me. It's as if she's gone off somewhere else, leaving me behind; or forgotten I am there.

All of this is more frightening, even, than the splotch of blood. Our father tells us to help out more, which means that he's frightened as well.

After she gets better I find a small knitted sock, pastel green, in my mother's sewing basket. I wonder why she would have knitted only one sock. She doesn't like knitting, so maybe she knitted one and then got tired of it.

I dream that Mrs. Finestein from next door and Mr. Banerji are my real parents.

I dream that my mother has had a baby, one of a set of twins. The baby is grey. I don't know where the other twin is.

I dream that our house has burned down. Nothing of it remains; blackened stumps dot the place where it's been, as if there has been a forest fire. A huge mountain of mud rises beside it.

My parents are dead but also alive. They're lying side by side, in their summer clothes, and sinking down through the earth, which is hard but transparent, like ice. They look up at me sorrowfully as they recede.

463

32

It's Saturday afternoon. We're going down to the building, to something called a Conversat. I don't know what a Conversat is but I'm relieved to be going to the building, where there are mice and snakes and experiments and no girls. My father asked if I wanted to bring a friend. I said no. My brother is bringing Danny, whose nose runs all the time, who wears knitted vests in diamond patterns, who has a stamp collection. They sit in the back seat – my brother no longer gets carsick – and talk in pig Latin.

"Or-yay ose-nay is-say unning-ray."

"O-say ut-whey? Awnt-way oo-tay eat-ay ome-say?"

"Um-yay um-yay."

I know that some of this, at least on Danny's part, is for my benefit. He has confused me with other girls, girls who wriggle and shriek. Once I would have replied with something equally disgusting, but I have lost interest in such things as eating snot. I look out the car window, pretending not to hear.

The Conversat turns out to be sort of like a museum. The Zoology Department is throwing itself open to the public, to give people a crack at Science and improve their minds. This is what my father said, grinning the way he does when he's partly joking. He said people's minds could use some improving. My mother said she doesn't think her mind is capable of further improvement, so she's going grocery shopping instead.

There are a lot of people at the Conversat. There isn't that much to do for entertainment on the weekends in Toronto. The building has a festive air: its usual smells of Dustbane and furniture polish and mouse droppings and snakes mingle with other smells, of winter clothing, cigarette smoke and women's perfume. Streamers of coloured paper are taped to the walls, with arrows of construction paper at intervals, along the halls and up and down the stairs and into the different rooms, to show the way. Each room has its own displays, grouped according to what you are supposed to learn.

In the first room there are chicken embryos at various stages of development, from a red dot to a big-headed, bulgy-eyed, pin-feathered chick, looking not fluffy and cute the way they do on Easter cards, but slimy, its claws curled under, its eyelids a slit open, showing a crescent of agate-blue eye. The embryos have been pickled; the scent of formaldehyde is very strong. In another display there's a jar of twins, real dead identical human twins with their placenta attached, grey-skinned, floating in something that looks like dishwater. Their veins and arteries have been injected with coloured rubber, blue for the veins, purple for the arteries, so we can see that their blood systems are connected. There's a human brain in a bottle, like a giant flabby grey walnut. I can't believe there is such a thing inside my head.

In another room there's a table where you can get your finger-prints taken, so you can see they aren't the same as anyone else's. There's a large piece of Bristol board with enlarged photographs of people's fingerprints pinned up on it. My brother and Danny and I all get our fingerprints taken. Danny and my brother have made light of the chickens and the twins – "Awnt-way any-nay icken-chay or-fay upper-say?" "Ow-hay about-way ome-say ewed-stay in-tway?" – but they weren't in any hurry to stay in that room. Their enthusiasm for the fingerprints is boisterous. They make fingerprints in the centres of each other's foreheads with their inky fingers, saying, "The Mark of the Black Hand!" in loud, ominous voices, until our father passes nearby and tells them to pipe down. Beautiful Mr. Banerji from India is with him. He smiles nervously at me and says, "How are you, Miss?" He always calls me Miss. Among all these winter-white faces he looks darker than usual; his teeth shine and shine.

In the same room with the fingerprints they're handing out pieces of paper; you're supposed to taste them and say whether they taste bitter, like peach pits, or sour, like lemons. This proves that some things are inherited. There's also a mirror where you can do tongue exercises, to see if you can roll your tongue up at the sides or into a cloverleaf shape. Some people can't do either. Danny and my brother hog the mirror and make gruesome faces by sticking their thumbs into the sides of their mouths and pulling the edges of their eyelids down so that the red shows.

Some of the Conversat is less interesting, with too much writing, and some of it is only charts on the wall or looking through microscopes, which we can do whenever we want to anyway.

It's crowded as we shuffle along the halls, following the paper streamers, baby-blue and yellow, in our winter overshoes. We haven't taken our coats off. It's very warm. The clanking radiators are going full blast, and the air is filling with other people's breath.

We come to a room where there's a cut-open turtle. It's in a white enamel tray, like the ones in butcher shops. The turtle is alive; or it's dead, but its heart is alive. This turtle is an experiment to show how the heart of a reptile can keep on going after the rest of it is dead.

The turtle's bottom shell has a hole sawed into it. The turtle is on its back so you can see down into it, right to the heart, which is beating away slowly, glistening dark red down there in its cave, wincing like the end of a touched worm, lengthening again, wincing. It's like a hand, clenching and unclenching. It's like an eye.

They've attached a wire to the heart, which runs to a loudspeaker, so you can hear the heart beating throughout the entire room, agonizingly slow, like an old man walking up stairs. I can't tell if the heart is going to make it to the next beat, or not. There's a footstep, a pause, then a crackling like the kind of static on the radio that my brother says comes from outer space, then another pulse, a gasp of air sucked in. Life is flowing out of the turtle, I can hear it over the loudspeaker. Soon the turtle will be empty of life.

I don't want to stay in this room but there's a lineup, in front of me and behind. All of the people are grownups; I've lost sight of Danny and my brother. I'm hemmed in by tweed coats, my eyes as high as their second buttons. I hear another sound, coming over the sound of the heart like an approaching wind: a rustling, like poplar leaves, only smaller, drier. There's black around the edges of my eyes and it closes in. What I see is like the entrance to a tunnel, rushing away from me; or I am rushing away from it, away from that spot of daylight. After that I'm looking at a lot of overshoes, and

466

the floorboards, stretching into the distance, at eye level. My head hurts.

"She fainted," somebody says, and then I know what I have done.

"It must have been the heat."

I am carried out into the cold grey air; it's Mr. Banerji who carries me, making sounds of distress. My father hurries out and tells me to sit with my head down between my knees. I do this, looking at the tops of my overshoes. He asks if I'm going to be sick and I say no. My brother and Danny come out and stare at me, not saying anything. Finally my brother says, "Eee-shay ainted-fay," and they go back in.

I stay outside until my father brings the car around and we drive home. I'm beginning to feel that I've discovered something worth knowing. There's a way out of places you want to leave, but can't. Fainting is like stepping sideways, out of your own body, out of time or into another time. When you wake up it's later. Time has gone on without you.

Cordelia says, "Think of ten stacks of plates. Those are your ten chances." Every time I do something wrong, a stack of plates comes crashing down. I can see these plates. Cordelia can see them too, because she's the one who says *Crash!* Grace can see them a little, but her crashes are tentative, she looks to Cordelia for confirmation. Carol tries a crash once or twice but is scoffed at: "*That* wasn't a crash!"

"Only four left," says Cordelia. "You better watch yourself. Well?"

I say nothing.

"Wipe that smirk off your face," says Cordelia.

I say nothing.

"Crash!" says Cordelia. "Only three left."

Nobody ever says what will happen if all of the stacks of plates fall down.

I'm standing against the wall, near the GIRLS door, the cold creeping up my legs and in under the edges of my sleeves. I'm not supposed to move. Already I've forgotten why. I've

467

discovered that I can fill my head up with music, *Coming in on a wing and a prayer, Keep happy with the Happy Gang,* and forget almost anything.

It's recess. Miss Lumley patrols the playground with her brass bell, her face clamped against the cold, minding her own business. I'm still just as afraid of her, although she's no longer my teacher. Chains of girls career past, chanting *We don't stop for anybody.* Other girls promenade more sedately, arms linked two by two. They look at me curiously, then away. It's like the people in cars, on the highway, who slow down and look out the window when there's a car accident by the side of the road. They slow down but they don't stop. They know when there's trouble, they know when to keep out of it.

I'm standing a little out from the wall. I put my head back and stare up into the grey sky and hold my breath. I'm making myself dizzy. I can see a stack of plates as it sways, begin to topple over, into a silent explosion of china shards. The sky closes to a pinpoint and a wave of dry leaves sweeps over my head. Then I can see my own body lying on the ground, just lying there. I can see the girls pointing and gathering, I can see Miss Lumley stalking over, bending with difficulty to look at me. But I'm seeing all this from above, as if I'm in the air, somewhere near the GIRLS sign over the door, looking down like a bird.

I come to with Miss Lumley's face looming inches away from me, scowling more than ever, as if I've made a mess, with a ring of girls around her jostling for a better look.

There's blood, I've cut my forehead. I am taken off to the nurse's office. The nurse wipes off the blood and sticks a wad of gauze onto me with a Band-Aid. The sight of my own blood on the wet white washcloth is deeply satisfying to me.

Cordelia is subdued: blood is impressive, even more impressive than vomit. She and Grace are solicitous on the way home, linking their arms through mine, asking me how I feel. This kind of attention from them makes me tremulous. I'm afraid I will cry, great sopping tears of reconciliation. But I'm far too wary for that by now.

The next time Cordelia tells me to stand against the wall I faint again. Now I can do it almost whenever I want to. I hold my breath and hear the rustling noise and see the blackness and then I slip sideways, out of my body, and I'm somewhere else. But I

468

can't always watch from above, like the first time. Sometimes there's just black.

I begin to be known as the girl who faints.

"She's doing it on purpose," Cordelia says. "Go ahead, let's see you faint. Come on. Faint." But now, when she tells me to, I can't.

I begin to spend time outside my body without falling over. At these times I feel blurred, as if there are two of me, one superimposed on the other, but imperfectly. There's an edge of transparency, and beside it a rim of solid flesh that's without feeling, like a scar. I can see what's happening, I can hear what's being said to me, but I don't have to pay any attention. My eyes are open but I'm not there. I'm off to the side.

VII

Our Lady of
Perpetual Help

33

I walk west from Simpsons, still looking for something to eat. Finally I buy a slice of take-out pizza and devour it en route, with my fingers, folding it in two and gnawing. When I'm with Ben I eat at regular times because he does, I eat regular things, but when I'm alone I indulge in junk food and scavenging, my old, singular ways. It's bad for me, but I need to remember what bad for me is like. I could begin to take Ben for granted, with his ties and haircuts and grapefruits for breakfast. It makes me appreciate him more.

Back at the studio I call him, counting the hours backwards to the coast. But there's only my own voice on the message, followed by the beep, the Dominion Observatory Official Time Signal, ushering in the future. *Love you*, I say, so he can hear it later. Then I remember: by now he's in Mexico, he won't be back till I am.

By now it's dark outside. I could go out for something more like dinner, or try for a movie. Instead I crawl onto the futon, under the duvet, with a cup of coffee and the Toronto phone book, and start looking up names. There are no more Smeaths, they must have moved or died off, or got married. There are more Campbells than you can shake a stick at. I look up Jon, whose name was once my own. No Josef Hrbik, though there are Hrbeks, Hrens, Hrastniks, Hriczus.

There are no more Risleys.

There is no Cordelia.

It's strange to be lying in Jon's bed again. I haven't thought of this as Jon's bed because I've never seen him in it, but of course it is. It's a lot neater than his beds used to be, and a great deal cleaner. His first bed was a mattress on the floor, with an old sleeping bag on top of it. I didn't mind this, in fact I liked it; it was like camping out. Usually there would be

473

a tide-line of empty cups and glasses and plates with scraps of food surrounding it, which I didn't like as much. There was an etiquette about such messes, in those days: there was a line you crossed, from ignoring them to cleaning them up. Whether the man would think you were moving in on him, trying to take him over.

We were lying on that bed one time, right at the beginning, before I'd started to pick up the plates, when the bedroom door opened and a woman I'd never seen before appeared in the doorway. She was wearing dirty jeans and a wan pink T-shirt; her face thin and bleached-looking, with huge pupils. It looked as if she was on some sort of drug, which was beginning to be a possibility, then. She stood there saying nothing, one hand behind her back, her face tight and blank, while I pulled the sleeping bag up over me.

"Hey," said Jon.

She drew her hand out from behind her back then and threw something at us. It was a paper bag full of warm spaghetti, sauce included. It burst when it hit, festooning us. She went out, still without saying anything, and slammed the door.

I was frightened, but Jon started laughing. "What was that?" I said. "How the hell did she get in?"

"Through the door," said Jon, still laughing. He untangled a piece of spaghetti from my hair and leaned over to kiss me. I knew this woman must have been a girfriend, or an ex-girlfriend, and I was furious with her. It didn't occur to me that she might have reason. I hadn't yet encountered the foreign hairpins left in the bathroom like territorial dog pee on snowy hydrants, the lipstick marks placed strategically on pillows. Jon knew how to cover his tracks, and when he didn't cover them it was for a reason. It didn't occur to me either that she must have had a key.

"She's crazy," I said. "She should be in a bin."

I did not pity her at all. In a way I admired her. I admired her lack of compunction, the courage of her bad manners, the energy of simple rage. Throwing a bag of spaghetti had a simplicity to it, a recklessness, a careless grandeur. It got things over with. I was a long way, then, from being able to do anything like it myself.

474

34

Grace says grace. Mr. Smeath says, "Praise the Lord and pass the ammunition," and reaches for the baked beans. Mrs. Smeath says, "Lloyd." Mr. Smeath says, "It's harmless," and shoots me a sideways grin. Aunt Mildred contracts her whiskery mouth. I chew away at the rubber-plant Smeath food. Under cover of the tablecloth, I tear at my fingers. Sunday goes on.

After the stewed pineapple Grace wants me to come down into the cellar with her to play School. I do this, but I have to come up the stairs again to go to the bathroom. Grace has given me permission, the same way the teachers in school give you permission. As I come up the cellar stairs I can hear Aunt Mildred and Mrs. Smeath, who are in the kitchen doing the dishes.

"She's exactly like a heathen," says Aunt Mildred. Because she's been a missionary in China, she's an authority. "Nothing you've done has made a scrap of difference."

"She's learning her Bible, Grace tells me," Mrs. Smeath says, and then I know it's me they're discussing. I stop on the top step, where I can see into the kitchen: the kitchen table where the dirty dishes are piled, the back edges of Mrs. Smeath and Aunt Mildred.

"They'll learn all that," says Aunt Mildred. "Till you're blue in the face. But it's all rote learning, it doesn't sink in. The minute your back is turned they'll go right back the way they were."

The unfairness of this hits me like a kick. How can they say that, when I've won a special mention for my essay on Temperance, about drunken men having car accidents and freezing to death in snowstorms because the alcohol dilates their capillaries? I even know what capillaries are, I even spelled it right. I can recite whole psalms, whole chapters, I can sing all the coloured-slide white-knight Sunday School songs without looking.

"What can you expect, with that family?" says Mrs. Smeath.

She doesn't go on to say what's wrong with my family. "The other children sense it. They know."

"You don't think they're being too hard on her?" says Aunt Mildred. Her voice is relishing. She wants to know how hard.

"It's God's punishment," says Mrs. Smeath. "It serves her right."

A hot wave moves through my body. This wave is shame, which I have felt before, but it is also hatred, which I have not, not in this pure form. It's hatred with a particular shape, the shape of Mrs. Smeath's one breast and no waist. It's like a fleshy weed in my chest, white-stemmed and fat; like the stalk of a burdock, with its rank leaves and little green burrs, growing in the cat-piss earth beside the path down to the bridge. A heavy, thick hatred.

I stand there on the top step, frozen with hate. What I hate is not Grace or even Cordelia. I can't go as far as that. I hate Mrs. Smeath, because what I thought was a secret, something going on among girls, among children, is not one. It has been discussed before, and tolerated. Mrs. Smeath has known and approved. She has done nothing to stop it. She thinks it serves me right.

She moves away from the sink and walks to the kitchen table for another stack of dirty plates, into my line of vision. I have a brief, intense image of Mrs. Smeath going through the flesh-coloured wringer of my mother's washing machine, legs first, bones cracking and flattening, skin and flesh squeezing up towards her head, which will pop in a minute like a huge balloon of blood. If my eyes could shoot out fatal rays like the ones in comic books I would incinerate her on the spot. She is right, I am a heathen. I cannot forgive.

As if she can feel my stare she turns and sees me. Our eyes meet: she knows I've heard. But she doesn't flinch, she isn't embarrassed or apologetic. She gives me that smug smile, with the lips closed over the teeth. What she says is not to me but to Aunt Mildred. "Little pitchers have big ears."

Her bad heart floats in her body like an eye, an evil eye, it sees me.

*　　*　　*

476

We sit on the wooden bench in the church basement, in the dark, watching the wall. Light glints from Grace's glassy eyes as she watches me sideways.

> God sees the little sparrow fall,
> It meets His tender view;
> If God so loves the little bird,
> I know He loves me too.

The picture is of a dead bird in an enormous hand, with a shaft of light coming down onto it.

I am moving my lips, but I'm not singing. I am losing confidence in God. Mrs. Smeath has God all sewed up, she knows what things are his punishments. He's on her side, and it's a side from which I'm excluded.

I consider Jesus, who is supposed to love me. But he isn't showing any sign of it, and I don't think he can be of much help. Against Mrs. Smeath and God he can do nothing, because God is bigger. God is not Our Father at all. My image of him now is of something huge, hard, inexorable, faceless and moving forward as if on tracks. God is a sort of engine.

I decide not to pray to God any more. When it's time for the Lord's Prayer I stand in silence, moving my lips only.

Forgive us our trespasses, as we forgive those who trespass against us.

I refuse to say this. If it means I will have to forgive Mrs. Smeath or else go to Hell when I die, I'm ready to go. Jesus must have known how hard it is to forgive, that was why he put this in. He was always putting in things that were impossible to do really, such as giving away all your money.

"You weren't praying," Grace says to me in a whisper.

My stomach goes cold. Which is worse, to contradict her or to admit? Either way there will be penalties.

"Yes I was," I say.

"You weren't. I heard you."

I say nothing.

"You lied," says Grace, pleased, forgetting to whisper.

I still say nothing.

"You should ask God to forgive you," Grace says. "That's what I do, every night."

I sit in the dark, attacking my fingers. I think about Grace

477

asking God to forgive her. But for what? God only forgives you if you're sorry, and she never gives a sign of being sorry. She never thinks she's done anything wrong.

Grace and Cordelia and Carol are up ahead, I am a block behind. They aren't letting me walk with them today because I have been insolent, but they don't want me too far behind either. I am walking along, in time to the music, *Keep happy with the Happy Gang*, my head empty except for these words. I walk head down, scanning the sidewalk, the gutters, for silver cigarette papers, although I no longer collect them as I did long ago. I know that nothing I could make with them would be worthwhile.

I see a piece of paper with a coloured picture on it. I pick it up. I know what the picture is: it's the Virgin Mary. The paper is from Our Lady of Perpetual Help, Our Lady of Perpetual Hell. The Virgin Mary is wearing a long blue robe, no feet at all visible below the hem, a white cloth over her head and a crown on top of that, and a yellow halo with light rays coming out of it like nails. She's smiling sadly in a disappointed way; her hands are outstretched as if in welcome, and her heart is on the outside of her chest, with seven swords stuck into it. Or they look like swords. The heart is large, red and tidy, like a satin heart pin-cushion, or a valentine. Under the picture is printed: *The Seven Sorrows*.

The Virgin Mary is in some of our Sunday School papers, but never with a crown, never with a pin-cushion heart, never all by herself. She is always more or less in the background. Not much fuss is made over her except at Christmas, and even then Baby Jesus is a lot more important. When Mrs. Smeath and Aunt Mildred speak of Catholics, as they have been known to do at the Sunday dinner table, it's always with contempt. Catholics pray to statues and drink real wine at Communion, instead of grape juice. "They worship the Pope," is what the Smeaths say; or else, "They worship the Virgin Mary," as if this is a scandalous thing to do.

I look at the picture up close. But I know it would be dangerous to keep it, so I throw it away. This is the right impulse, because now the three of them have stopped, they're

478

waiting for me to catch up to them. Anything I do, other than standing, other than walking, attracts their attention.

"What was that thing we saw you pick up?" says Cordelia.

"A paper."

"What sort of a paper?"

"Just a paper. A Sunday School paper."

"Why did you pick it up?"

Once I would have thought about this question, tried to answer it truthfully. Now I say, "I don't know." This is the only answer I can give, to anything, that will not be ridiculed or questioned.

"What did you do with it?"

"I threw it away."

"Don't pick things up off the street," says Cordelia. "They have germs." She lets it go at that.

I decide to do something dangerous, rebellious, perhaps even blasphemous. I can no longer pray to God so I will pray to the Virgin Mary instead. This decision makes me nervous, as if I'm about to steal. My heart beats harder, my hands feel cold. I feel I'm about to get caught.

Kneeling seems called for. In the onion church we don't kneel, but the Catholics are known for it. I kneel down beside my bed and put my hands together, like the children in Christmas cards, except that I'm wearing blue-striped flannelette pyjamas and they always have white nightgowns on. I close my eyes and try to think about the Virgin Mary. I want her to help me or at least show me that she can hear me, but I don't know what to say. I haven't learned the words for her.

I try to picture what she would look like, if I met her on the street for instance: would she be wearing clothes like my mother's, or that blue dress and crown, and if it was the blue dress would a crowd gather? Maybe they would think she was just someone out of a Christmas play; but not if she had her heart on the outside like that, stuck full of swords. I try to think what I would tell her. But she knows already: she knows how unhappy I am.

I pray harder and harder. My prayers are wordless, defiant, dry-eyed, desperate, without hope. Nothing happens. I squeeze my fists into my eyes until they hurt. For an instant I think I see a face, then a splash of blue, but now all I can see is the heart. There it is, bright red, rounded, with a dark light around it, a blackness like luminous velvet. Gold comes out from the centre, then fades. It's the heart all right. It looks like my red plastic purse.

35

It's the middle of March. In the schoolroom windows the Easter tulips are beginning to bloom. There's still snow on the ground, a dirty filigree, though the winter is losing its hardness and glitter. The sky thickens, sinks lower.

We walk home under the low thick sky that is grey and bulging with dampness. Moist soft flakes are falling out of it, piling up on roofs and branches, sliding off now and then to hit with a wet cottony thunk. There's no wind and the sound is muffled by the snow.

It isn't cold. I undo the ties on my blue knitted wool hat, let it flap loose on my head. Cordelia takes off her mittens and scoops up snowballs, throwing them at trees, at telephone poles, at random. It's one of her friendly days; she puts her arm through my arm, her other arm through Grace's, and we march along the street, singing *We don't stop for anybody*. I sing this too. Together we hop and slide.

Some of the euphoria I once felt in falling snow comes back to me; I want to open my mouth and let the snow fall into it. I allow myself to laugh, like the others, trying it out. My laughter is a performance, a grab at the ordinary.

Cordelia throws herself backwards onto a blank front lawn, spreads her arms out in the snow, raises them above her head, draws them down to her sides, making a snow angel. The flakes fall onto her face, into her laughing mouth, melting, clinging to her eyebrows. She blinks, closing her eyes against the snow. For a moment she looks like someone I don't know, a stranger, shining with unknown, good possibilities. Or else a victim of a traffic accident, flung onto the snow.

She opens her eyes and reaches up her hands, which are damp and reddened, and we pull her upwards so she won't disturb the image she's made. The snow angel has feathery wings and a tiny pin-head. Where her hands stopped, down near her sides, are the imprints of her fingers, like little claws.

481

We've forgotten the time; it's getting dark. We run along the street that leads to the wooden footbridge. Even Grace runs, lumpily, calling "Wait up!" For once she is the one left behind.

Cordelia reaches the hill first and runs down it. She tries to slide but the snow is too soft, not icy enough, and there are cinders and pieces of gravel in it. She falls down and rolls. We think she's done it on purpose, the way she made the snow angel. We rush down upon her, exhilarated, breathless, laughing, just as she's picking herself up.

We stop laughing, because now we can see that her fall was an accident, she didn't do it on purpose. She likes everything she does to be done on purpose.

Carol says, "Did you hurt yourself?" Her voice is quavery, she's frightened, already she can tell that this is serious. Cordelia doesn't answer. Her face is hard again, her eyes baleful.

Grace moves so that she's beside Cordelia, slightly behind her. From there she smiles at me, her tight smile.

Cordelia says, to me, "Were you laughing?" I think she means, was I laughing at her because she fell down.

"No," I say.

"She was," says Grace neutrally. Carol shifts to the side of the path, away from me.

"I'm going to give you one more chance," says Cordelia. "Were you laughing?"

"Yes," I say, "but . . ."

" Just yes or no," says Cordelia.

I say nothing. Cordelia glances over at Grace, as if looking for approval. She sighs, an exaggerated sigh, like a grownup's. "Lying again," she says. "What are we going to do with you?"

We seem to have been standing there for a long time. It's colder now. Cordelia reaches out and pulls off my knitted hat. She marches the rest of the way down the hill and onto the bridge and hesitates for a moment. Then she walks over to the railing and throws my hat down into the ravine. Then the white oval of her face turns up towards me. "Come here," she says.

Nothing has changed, then. Time will go on, in the same way, endlessly. My laughter was unreal after all, merely a gasp for air.

I walk down to where Cordelia stands by the railing, the snow

482

not crunching but giving way under my feet like cotton-wool packing. It sounds like a cavity being filled, in a tooth, inside my head. Usually I'm afraid to go so near the edge of the bridge, but this time I'm not. I don't feel anything as positive as fear.

"There's your stupid hat," says Cordelia; and there it is, far down, still blue against the white snow, even in the dimming light. "Why don't you go down and get it?"

I look at her. She wants me to go down into the ravine where the bad men are, where we're never supposed to go. It occurs to me that I may not. What will she do then?

I can see this idea gathering in Cordelia as well. Maybe she's gone too far, hit, finally, some core of resistance in me. If I refuse to do what she says this time, who knows where my defiance will end? The two others have come down the hill and are watching, safely in the middle of the bridge.

"Go on then," she says, more gently, as if she's encouraging me, not ordering. "Then you'll be forgiven."

I don't want to go down there. It's forbidden and dangerous; also it's dark and the hillside will be slippery, I might have trouble climbing up again. But there is my hat. If I go home without it, I'll have to explain, I'll have to tell. And if I refuse to go, what will Cordelia do next? She might get angry, she might never speak to me again. She might push me off the bridge. She's never done anything like that before, never hit or pinched, but now that she's thrown my hat over there's no telling what she might do.

I walk along to the end of the bridge. "When you've got it, count to a hundred," says Cordelia. "Before coming up." She doesn't sound angry any more. She sounds like someone giving instructions for a game.

I start down the steep hillside, holding onto branches and tree trunks. The path isn't even a real path, it's just a place worn by whoever goes up and down here: boys, men. Not girls.

When I'm among the bare trees at the bottom I look up. The bridge railings are silhouetted against the sky. I can see the dark outlines of three heads, watching me.

My blue hat is out on the ice of the creek. I stand in the snow, looking at it. Cordelia is right, it's a stupid hat. I look at it and feel resentment, because this stupid-looking hat is mine, and deserving of ridicule. I don't want to wear it ever again.

I can hear water running somewhere, down under the ice. I step out onto the creek, reach for the hat, pick it up, go through. I'm up to my waist in the creek, slabs of broken ice up-ended around me.

Cold shoots through me. My overshoes are filling, and the shoes inside them; water drenches my snowpants. Probably I've screamed, or some noise has come out of me, but I can't remember hearing anything. I clutch the hat and look up at the bridge. Nobody is there. They must have walked away, run away. That's why the counting to a hundred: so they could run away.

I try to move my feet. They're very heavy, because of the water inside my boots. If I wanted to I could just keep standing here. It's true dusk now and the snow on the ground is bluish-white. The old tyres and pieces of rusted junk in the creek are covered over; all around me are blue arches, blue caves, pure and silent. The water of the creek is cold and peaceful, it comes straight from the cemetery, from the graves and their bones. It's water made from the dead people, dissolved and clear, and I am standing in it. If I don't move soon I will be frozen in the creek. I will be a dead person, peaceful and clear, like them.

I flounder through the water, the edges of the ice breaking off as I step. Walking with waterlogged overshoes is hard; I could slip, and fall all the way in. I grab a tree branch and haul myself up onto the bank and sit down in the blue snow and take off my overshoes and pour out the water. The arms of my jacket are wet to the elbows, my mittens are soaked. Now there are knives going through my legs and hands, and tears running down my face from the pain.

I can see lights along the edges of the ravine, from the houses there, impossibly high up. I don't know how I'm going to climb up the hill with my hands and feet hurting like this; I don't know how I'm going to get home.

My head is filling with black sawdust; little specks of the darkness are getting in through my eyes. It's as if the snow-flakes are black, the way white is black on a negative. The snow has changed to tiny pellets, more like sleet. It makes a rustling noise coming down through the branches, like the shifting and whispering of people in a crowded room who know they must be quiet. It's the dead people, coming up

484

invisible out of the water, gathering around me. *Hush*, is what they say.

I'm lying on my back beside the creek, looking up at the sky. Nothing hurts any more. The sky has a reddish undercolour. The bridge is different-looking; it seems higher above me, more solid, as if the railings have disappeared or been filled in. And it's glowing, there are pools of light along it, greenish-yellow, not like any light I've ever seen before. I sit up to get a better look. My body feels weightless, as it does in water.

There's someone on the bridge, I can see the dark outline. At first I think it's Cordelia, come back for me. Then I see that it's not a child, it's too tall for a child. I can't see the face, there's just a shape. One of the yellowish-green lights is behind it, coming out in rays from around the head.

I know I should get up and walk home, but it seems easier to stay here, in the snow, with the little pellets of ice caressing my face gently. Also I'm very sleepy. I close my eyes.

I hear someone talking to me. It's like a voice calling, only very soft, as if muffled. I'm not sure I've heard it at all. I open my eyes with an effort. The person who was standing on the bridge is moving through the railing, or melting into it. It's a woman, I can see the long skirt now, or is it a long cloak? She isn't falling, she's coming down towards me as if walking, but there's nothing for her to walk on. I don't have the energy to be frightened. I lie in the snow, watching her with lethargy, and with a sluggish curiosity. I would like to be able to walk on air like that.

Now she's quite close. I can see the white glimmer of her face, the dark scarf or hood around her head, or is it hair? She holds out her arms to me and I feel a surge of happiness. Inside her half-open cloak there's a glimpse of red. It's her heart, I think. It must be her heart, on the outside of her body, glowing like neon, like a coal.

Then I can't see her any more. But I feel her around me, not like arms but like a small wind of warmer air. She's telling me something.

You can go home now, she says. *It will be all right. Go home.*
I don't hear the words out loud, but this is what she says.

485

36

The lights on the top of the bridge are gone. I make my way in the dark, up the hill, sleet rustling around me, hauling myself up by branches and tree trunks, my shoes slipping on the packed icy snow. Nothing hurts, not even my feet, not even my hands. It's like flying. The small wind moves with me, a warm touch against my face.

I know who it is that I've seen. It's the Virgin Mary, there can be no doubt. Even when I was praying I wasn't sure she was real, but now I know she is. Who else could walk on air like that, who else would have a glowing heart? True, there was no blue dress, no crown; her dress looked black. But it was dark. Maybe the crown was there and I couldn't see it. Anyway she could have different clothes, different dresses. None of that matters, because she came to get me. She didn't want me freezing in the snow. She is still with me, invisible, wrapping me in warmth and painlessness, she has heard me after all.

I am up on the main path now; the lights from the houses are nearer, above me, on either side of me. I can hardly keep my eyes open. I'm not even walking straight. But my feet keep on moving, one in front of the other.

Up ahead is the street. As I reach it I see my mother, walking very fast. Her coat isn't done up, she has no scarf on her head, her overshoes flap, half fastened. When she sees me she begins to run. I stop still, watching her running figure with the coat flying out on either side and the unwieldy overshoes, as if she's just some other person I'm watching, someone in a race. She comes up to me under a streetlamp and I see her eyes, large and gleaming with wet, and her hair dusted with sleet. She has no mittens on. She throws her arms around me, and as she does this the Virgin Mary is suddenly gone. Pain and cold shoot back into me. I start to shiver violently.

"I fell in," I say. "I was getting my hat." My voice sounds thick, the words mumbled. Something is wrong with my tongue.

486

My mother does not say, *Where have you been?* or *Why are you so late?* She says, "Where are your overshoes?" They are down in the ravine, covering over with snow. I have forgotten them, and my hat as well.

"It fell over the bridge," I say. I need to get this lie over with as soon as possible. Telling the truth about Cordelia is still unthinkable for me.

My mother takes off her coat and wraps it around me. Her mouth is tight, her face is frightened and angry at the same time. It's the look she used to have when we would cut ourselves, a long time ago, up north. She puts her arm under my armpit and hurries me along. My feet hurt at every step. I wonder if I will be punished for going down into the ravine.

When we reach the house my mother peels off my soggy half-frozen clothes and puts me into a lukewarm bath. She looks carefully at my fingers and toes, my nose, my ear-lobes. "Where were Grace and Cordelia?" she asks me. "Did they see you fall in?"

"No," I say. "They weren't there."

I can tell she's thinking about phoning their mothers no matter what I do, but I am too tired to care. "A lady helped me," I say.

"What lady?" says my mother, but I know better than to tell her. If I say who it really was I won't be believed. "Just a lady," I say.

My mother says I'm lucky I don't have severe frostbite. I know about frostbite: your fingers and toes fall off, as punishment for drink. She feeds me a cup of milky tea and puts me into bed with a hot-water bottle and flannelette sheets, and spreads two extra blankets on top. I am still shivering. My father has come home and I hear them talking in low, anxious voices out in the hallway. Then my father comes in and puts his hand on my forehead, and fades to a shadow.

I dream I'm running along the street outside the school. I've done something wrong. It's autumn, the leaves are burning. A lot of people are chasing after me. They're shouting.

An invisible hand takes mine, pulls upwards. There are steps into the air and I go up them. No one else can see where the steps are. Now I'm standing in the air, out of reach above the upturned faces. They're still shouting but I can no longer hear them. Their mouths close and open silently, like the mouths of fish.

I am kept home from school for two days. The first day I lie in bed, floating in the glassy delicate clarity of fever. By the second day I am thinking about what happened. I can remember Cordelia throwing my blue knitted hat over the bridge, I remember falling through the ice and then my mother running towards me with her sleety hair. All these things are certain, but in between them there's a hazy space. The dead people and the woman in the cloak are there, but in the same way dreams are. I'm not sure, now, that it really was the Virgin Mary. I believe it but I no longer know it.

I'm given a Get Well card with violets on it from Carol, shoved through the letter slot. On the weekend Cordelia calls me on the telephone. "We didn't know you fell in," she says. "We're sorry we didn't wait. We thought you were right behind us." Her voice is careful, precise, rehearsed, unrepentant.

I know she's told some story that conceals what really happened, as I have. I know that this apology has been exacted from her, and that I will be made to pay for it later. But she has never apologized to me before. This apology, however fake, makes me feel not stronger but weaker. I don't know what to say. "It's okay," is what I manage. I think I mean it.

When I go back to school, Cordelia and Grace are polite but distant. Carol is more obviously frightened, or interested. "My mother says you almost froze to death," she whispers as we stand in line, two by two, waiting for the bell. "I got a spanking, with the hairbrush. I really *got* it."

The snow is melting from the lawns; mud reappears on the floors, at school, in the kitchen at home. Cordelia circles me warily. I catch her eyes on me, considering, as we walk home from school. Conversation is artificially normal. We stop at the store for licorice whips, which Carol buys. As we stroll along, sucking in licorice, Cordelia says, "I think Elaine should be punished for telling on us, don't you?"

488

"I didn't tell," I say. I no longer feel the sinking in my gut, the held-back tearfulness that such a false accusation would once have produced. My voice is flat, calm, reasonable.

"Don't contradict me," Cordelia says. "Then how come your mother phoned our mothers?"

"Yeah, how come?" says Carol.

"I don't know and I don't care," I say. I'm amazed at myself.

"You're being insolent," says Cordelia. "Wipe that smirk off your face."

I am still a coward, still fearful; none of that has changed. But I turn and walk away from her. It's like stepping off a cliff, believing the air will hold you up. And it does. I see that I don't have to do what she says, and, worse and better, I've never had to do what she says. I can do what I like.

"Don't you dare walk away on us," Cordelia says behind me. "You get back here right now!" I can hear this for what it is. It's an imitation, it's acting. It's an impersonation, of someone much older. It's a game. There was never anything about me that needed to be improved. It was always a game, and I have been fooled. I have been stupid. My anger is as much at myself as at them.

"Ten stacks of plates," says Grace. This would once have reduced me. Now I find it silly.

I keep walking. I feel daring, light-headed. They are not my best friends or even my friends. Nothing binds me to them. I am free.

They follow along behind me, making comments on the way I walk, on how I look from behind. If I were to turn I would see them imitating me. "Stuck up! Stuck up!" they cry. I can hear the hatred, but also the need. They need me for this, and I no longer need them. I am indifferent to them. There's something hard in me, crystalline, a kernel of glass. I cross the street and continue along, eating my licorice.

I stop going to Sunday School. I refuse to play with Grace or Cordelia or even Carol after school. I no longer walk home over the bridge, but the long way around, past the cemetery. When they come in a group to the back door to collect me I tell them

489

I'm busy. They try kindness, to lure me back, but I am no longer susceptible to it. I can see the greed in their eyes. It's as if I can see right into them. Why was I unable to do this before ?

I spend a lot of time reading comic books in my brother's room when he isn't there. I would like to climb up skyscrapers, fly with a cape, burn holes in metal with my fingertips, wear a mask, see through walls. I would like to hit people, criminals, each fist making a red or yellow lightburst. *Kapow. Krac. Kaboom.* I know that I have the will to do these things. I intend to do them somehow.

At school I make friends with a different girl, whose name is Jill. She is interested in other kinds of games, games of paper and wood. We go to her house and play Old Maid, Snap, Pick Up Sticks. Grace and Cordelia and Carol hang around the edges of my life, enticing, jeering, growing paler and paler every day, less and less substantial. I hardly hear them any more because I hardly listen.

490

VIII
Half a Face

37

For a long time, I would go into churches. I told myself I wanted to see the art; I didn't know I was looking for something. I wouldn't seek these churches out, even if they were in a guidebook and of historic significance, and I would never go into them during services, in fact I disliked the idea: it was what was in them, not what went on in them, that interested me. Mostly I would just see them by accident and go into them on impulse.

Once in, I paid little attention to the architecture, although I knew the terms: clerestories and naves were things I'd written papers about. I would look at the stained-glass windows, if any. I preferred Catholic churches to Protestant ones, the more ornate the better, because there was more to look at. I liked the shameless extravaganza: gold leaf and baroque excesses did not put me off.

I would read the inscriptions on walls, and carved into floors, a special foible of rich Anglicans who thought they'd get more points with God by being engraved. Anglicans too went in for tattered military flags, and war memorials of other kinds.

But especially I sought out statues. Statues of saints, and of crusaders on their biers, or those pretending to be crusaders; effigies of all kinds. Statues of the Virgin Mary I would save for last. I would approach them with hope, but I was always disappointed. The statues were of no one I recognized. They were dolls dressed up, insipid in blue and white, pious and lifeless. Then I would not know why I'd been expecting to see something else.

I went to Mexico the first time with Ben. It was also our first trip together, our first time together; I thought it might be only an interlude. I wasn't even sure I wanted a man in my life again; by that time I'd exhausted the notion that the answer to a man

493

is another man, and I was out of breath. But it was a relief to be with someone who was so uncomplicated, and easily pleased.

We were by ourselves, on a two-week excursion that turned out to have something to do with Ben's business. Sarah was staying with her best friend. We began in Veracruz, checking out shrimp and the hotels and cockroaches, then took a car up into the hills, looking as always for something picturesque and under-visited.

There was a small town beside a lake. The place was subdued, for Mexico, which had struck me as visceral, like a body turned inside out so the blood was on the outside. Perhaps it was the coolness, the lake.

While Ben was inspecting the market, searching for things to take pictures of, I went into the church. It wasn't large, and looked poor. There was nobody in it; it smelled of old stone, old neglect, mustiness. I wandered around the outside aisles, looking at the awkward Stations of the Cross, done in grubby oils, almost a paint-by-numbers. They were bad, but genuine: someone had meant them.

Then I saw the Virgin Mary. I didn't know it was her at first, because she was dressed not in the usual blue or white and gold, but in black. She didn't have a crown. Her head was bowed, her face in shadow, her hands held out open at the sides. Around her feet were the stubs of candles, and all over her black dress were pinned what I thought at first were stars, but which were instead little brass or tin arms, legs, hands, sheep, donkeys, chickens, and hearts.

I could see what these were for: she was a Virgin of lost things, one who restored what was lost. She was the only one of these wood or marble or plaster Virgins who had ever seemed at all real to me. There could be some point in praying to her, kneeling down, lighting a candle. But I didn't do it, because I didn't know what to pray for. What was lost, what I could pin on her dress.

Ben came after a while and found me. "What's the matter?" he said. "What're you doing down on the floor? Are you all right?"

"Yes," I said. "Nothing. Just resting."

I was chilled through from the stone, my muscles were cramped and stiff. I'd forgotten how I got down there. My daughters, both of them, went through a phase when they would say *So?* Meaning *So what.* It was when the first one hit twelve or thirteen. They'd fold their arms and stare at me, or at their friends, or at each other. *So?*

"Don't do that," I'd say. "It's driving me crazy."

"So?"

Cordelia did the same thing, at the same age. The same folded arms, the same immobile face, the blank-eyed stare. Cordelia! Put on your gloves, it's cold out. *So?* I can't come over, I have to finish my homework. *So?*

Cordelia, I think. You made me believe I was nothing.
So?

To which there is no answer.

38

The summer comes and goes and then it's fall and then winter, and the King dies. I hear it on the news at lunchtime. I walk back to school along the snowy street, thinking, *The King is dead.* Now all the things that happened when he was alive are over and done with: the war, the planes with only one wing, the mud outside our house, a lot of things. I think of those heads of his, thousands of them, on the money, which are now the heads of a dead person instead of a living one. The money will have to be changed, and the postage stamps; they will have the Queen on them instead. The Queen used to be Princess Elizabeth. I remember seeing her in photos, when she was much younger. I have some other memory of her, but it's indistinct and makes me faintly uneasy.

Cordelia and Grace have both skipped a grade. They're now in Grade Eight, even though they're only eleven and the other ones in Grade Eight are thirteen. Carol Campbell and I are merely in Grade Six. All of us are at a different school now, one that's finally been built on our side of the ravine, so we don't have to take the school bus in the mornings or eat our lunches in the cellar or walk home over the collapsing footbridge after school. Our new school is a modern one-storey yellow brick building that looks like a post office. It has soft-textured, eye-saving green blackboards instead of screechy black ones, and tiled pastel floors instead of the old creaky wooden ones in Queen Mary. There are no BOYS and GIRLS doors, there are no separate playgrounds. Even the teachers are different: younger, more casual. Some of them are young men.

I've forgotten things, I've forgotten that I've forgotten them. I remember my old school, but only dimly, as if I was last there five years ago instead of five months. I remember going to Sunday School, but not the details. I know I don't like the thought of Mrs. Smeath, but I've forgotten why. I've forgotten about fainting and about the stacks of plates, and about falling into the creek and also about seeing the Virgin Mary. I've forgotten all of the bad things that happened. Although I see Cordelia and Grace and Carol every day, I remember none of those things; only that they used to be my friends, when I was younger, before I had other friends. There's something to do with them, something like a sentence in tiny dry print on a page, flattened out, like the dates of ancient battles. Their names are like names in a footnote, or names written in spidery brown ink in the fronts of Bibles. There is no emotion attached to these names. They're like the names of distant cousins, people who live far away, people I hardly know. Time is missing.

Nobody mentions anything about this missing time, except my mother. Once in a while she says, "That bad time you had," and I am puzzled. What is she talking about? I find these references to bad times vaguely threatening, vaguely insulting: I am not the sort of girl who has bad times, I have good times only. There I am, in the Grade Six class picture, smiling broadly. *Happy as a clam*, is what my mother says for happy. I am happy as a clam: hard-shelled, firmly closed.

My parents labour away at our house. Rooms are being con-structed in the cellar, gradually and with a lot of hammering and sawing, in my father's spare time: a darkroom, a storeroom for jars and jellies and jams. The lawn is a lawn now. In the garden they've planted a peach tree, a pear tree, an asparagus bed, rows and rows of vegetables. The borders are lush with flowers: tulips and daffodils, irises, peonies, pinks, chrysanthemums, something for every season. Occasionally I have to help, but mostly I watch with detachment as they up-end themselves in the mud, digging and weeding, clay stains on the knees of their pants. They're like kids in a sandpile. I like the flowers, but know I would not go to such lengths, make such efforts, get myself so dirty to produce them.

The wooden footbridge over the ravine is torn down. Everyone says it's about time, it was getting so unsafe. They're going to

497

replace it with a bridge made of concrete. I go one day and stand at the top of the hill on our side of the ravine, watching the bridge come down. There's a pile of rotten boards down by the creek. The vertical piles are still standing, like the trunks of dead trees, and part of the cross-planking is attached to them, but the railings are gone. I have an uneasy feeling, as if something's buried down there, a nameless, crucial thing, or as if there's someone still on the bridge, left by mistake, up in the air, unable to get to the land. But it's obvious there's no one.

Cordelia and Grace graduate and go elsewhere; Cordelia, it's rumoured, to St. Sebastian's, a private school for girls, Grace to a high school farther north which emphasizes math. She's good at adding things up in neat little rows. She still has her long braids when she graduates. Carol hangs around near the boys at recess, and is often chased by two or three of them. They like to throw her into snowbanks and rub snow into her face, or, when snow is lacking, to tie her up with skipping ropes. When she runs away from them she flings her arms around a lot. She runs in a funny wiggling way, slow enough to be caught, and screams loudly when she is. She wears a training bra. She isn't much liked by the other girls.

For Social Studies I do a project on Tibet, where there are prayer wheels and reincarnation and women have two husbands, and for Science I do different kinds of seeds. I have a boyfriend, as is the fashion. Occasionally he sends me a note across the aisle, written in very black pencil. Sometimes there are parties, with awkward dancing and clumsy guffaws and horseplay by the boys, and wet, inexpert, toothy kisses. My boyfriend carves my initials into the top of his new school desk and gets the strap for it. He gets the strap for other things too. This is admired. I see my first television set, which is like a small black and white puppet show of no great interest.

Carol Campbell moves away and I hardly notice. I skip Grade Seven and go straight into Grade Eight, missing the Kings of England in chronological order, missing the circulatory system, leaving my boyfriend behind. I get my hair cut. I want to do this.

I'm tired of having long wavy hair that has to be held back by barrettes or hairbands, I'm tired of being a child. I watch with satisfaction as my hair falls away from me like fog and my head emerges, sharper-featured, more clearly defined. I'm ready for high school, I want to go there right away.

I reorganize my room in preparation. I clear old toys out of my cupboard, I empty out all the drawers in my bureau. I find a solitary cat's eye marble rolling around at the back of the drawer, and some old dried-up chestnuts. Also a red plastic purse, which I remember getting for Christmas once. It's a babyish purse. It rattles when I pick it up; inside there's a nickel. I take the nickel out to spend, and put the marble inside the purse. I throw out the chestnuts.

I find my photo album with the black pages. I haven't taken any pictures with my Brownie camera for a long time, so this album has slipped from view. Stuck into it with the black triangles there are pictures I can't recall taking. For instance, there are several pictures of what look like large boulders, beside a lake. Underneath is printed, in white pencil: *Daisy. Elsie.* It's my writing, but I don't remember printing this.

I take these things down to the cellar and put them into the trunk, where old things go that are not thrown out. My mother's wedding dress is in there, several pieces of ornate silver, some sepia-toned portraits of people I don't know, a packet of bridge tallies with silk tassels on them, left over from before the war. Some of our old drawings are in there, my brother's spaceships and red and gold explosions, my delicate, old-fashioned little girls. I look at their pinafores and hairbows and their rudimentary faces and hands with distaste. I don't like looking at things connected so closely with my life as a child. I think these drawings are inept: I can do much better now.

The day before the first day of high school the telephone rings. It's Cordelia's Mummie; she wants to speak to my mother. I assume it's boring grownups' business and go back to reading the newspaper on the living-room floor. But after she puts the phone down, my mother comes into the room.

"Elaine," she says. This is unusual, as she doesn't often use my name. She sounds solemn.

I look up from Mandrake the Magician. She looks down. "That was Cordelia's mother," she says. "Cordelia will be going to your high school. Cordelia's mother wonders whether you girls would like to walk to school together."

"Cordelia?" I say. I haven't seen or spoken to Cordelia for a whole year. She has vanished completely. I've chosen that school because I can walk to it, instead of going on a bus; so why not walk with Cordelia? "Okay," I say.

"Are you sure you want to?" my mother says, a little anxiously. She doesn't say why Cordelia will be coming to my school now and I don't ask.

"Why wouldn't I?" I say. I'm already sliding into flippancy, which goes with high school, but also I can't see what she's getting at. I'm being asked to do Cordelia, or Cordelia's mother, some kind of a minor favour. My mother's usual line is that you should do these favours when asked, so why is she hedging on this one?

She doesn't answer this. Instead she hovers. I go back to reading the comics. "Shall I call her mother back, then, or would you like to speak with Cordelia yourself?" she says.

"You can call her," I say. I add, "Please." I have no particular wish to speak to Cordelia right now.

The next morning I go to Cordelia's house, which is on the way to school, to pick her up. The door opens and Cordelia is there, but she is no longer the same. She's no longer angular and rangy; she's grown full breasts and is heavier in the hips and face. Her hair is longer now, not a pageboy. She wears it in a ponytail with small white cloth lilies-of-the-valley wired around the elastic band. She's bleached a peroxide streak into the bangs. She has orange lipstick, and orange nail polish to match. My own lipstick is pale pink. Seeing Cordelia, I realize that I don't look like a teenager, I look like a kid dressed up as one. I am still thin, still flat. I have a ferocious desire to be older.

We walk to school together, not saying much at first, past a gas station, a funeral parlour, then a mile along a strip of shops, a Woolworth's, an I.D.A. drugstore, a fruit and vegetable shop, a hardware store, all of them side by side in two-storey flat-roofed yellow brick buildings. We hold our schoolbooks up against our

500

chests, our full cotton skirts brushing against our bare legs. Right now it's the end of summer, when all the lawns are dull green or yellow and used up.

I've assumed Cordelia would be a grade ahead of me. But she isn't, she's in the same grade now. She's been expelled from St. Sebastian's for drawing a penis on a bat. Or this is what she says. She says there was a large drawing of a bat on the blackboard, with its wings outspread and just a tiny bump between its legs. So she went up to the blackboard when the teacher was out of the room and rubbed out the little bump and made a bigger, longer one – "Not that much bigger" – and the teacher came into the room and caught her doing it.

"Is that all?" I say.

Not exactly. She also printed "Mr. Malder," neatly, underneath the bump. Mr. Malder was the teacher's name.

Probably this wasn't all she did, but it's all she's telling about. As an afterthought she mentions that she failed her year. "I was too young for it," she says. This sounds like something she's been told by other people, her mother most likely. "I was only twelve. They shouldn't have skipped me."

Now she's thirteen. I am twelve. I too have been skipped. I begin to wonder if I'll end up the same way she has, drawing penises on bats, failing my year.

39

The school we go to is called Burnham High School. It's recently built, oblong in shape, flat-roofed, undecorated, unrevealing, sort of like a factory. It's the latest thing in modern architecture. Inside, it has long corridors with mottled floors of something that looks like granite but is not. The yellowish walls are lined with dark-green lockers, and there's an auditorium and a P.A. system.

Every morning we have announcements over the P.A. system. First we have a Bible reading and prayers. I bow my head during the prayers but I refuse to pray, though I don't know why I do this. After the prayers the Principal tells us of coming events, and he also warns us to pick up our chewing-gum wrappers and not to moon around in the halls like old married couples. His name is Mr. MacLeod, although everyone calls him Chrome Dome behind his back because he's bald on top; and he's a Scot by affiliation. Burnham High has a school plaid, a school crest with a thistle and a couple of those Scottish knives they stick in their socks, and a Gaelic motto. The plaid, the crest, the motto, and the school colours all belong to Mr. MacLeod's personal clan.

In the front hall, alongside the Queen, hangs a portrait of Dame Flora MacLeod with her two bagpipe-playing grandsons, posed outside Dunvegan Castle. We are encouraged to think of this castle as our ancestral home, and of Dame Flora as our spiritual leader. In choir we learn "The Skye Boat Song", about Bonnie Prince Charlie escaping the genocidal English. We learn "Scots Wha' Hae", and a poem about a mouse, which causes some snickering as it contains the word "breast". I think all this Scottishness is normal for high schools, never having gone to one before; and even the several Armenians, Greeks, and Chinese in our school lose the edges of their differences, immersed as we all are in a mist of plaid.

I don't know many people at this school and neither does Cordelia. In my graduating class from public school there were only eight people, and in Cordelia's there were four. So it's a school full of strangers. In addition to that, we're in different home-rooms, so we don't even have each other to rely on.

Everyone in my home-room is bigger than I am. This is to be expected, because everyone is also older. The girls have breasts and a drowsy, powdery, hot-day smell; the skin of their faces is slippery-looking, slick with oily juice. I'm wary of them and dislike the changing-room where we have to put on the blue cotton bloomer-bottomed gym suits with our names embroidered on the pockets. In there I feel skinnier than ever; when I catch sight of myself in the mirror I can see the ribs below my collarbone. During volleyball games, these other girls lollop and thunder around me, their voices outsized and raucous, their new, extra flesh wobbling. I take care to keep out of their way, simply because they are bigger and might knock me over. But I'm not really afraid of them. In a way I despise them, because they are so much like Carol Campbell, squealing and flinging themselves around.

Among the boys there are a few pipsqueaks whose voices have not yet changed, but many of the boys are gigantic. Some are fifteen, almost sixteen. They have hair that's long at the sides and greased back into ducktails, and they shave. Some of them look as if they shave a lot. They sit at the back of the room and stick their long legs out into the aisle. They've already failed a grade, at least once; they've given up and been given up on, and they're doing time until they can leave. Although they call remarks at other girls in the halls and make kissing sounds at them, or dangle around their lockers, they pay no attention at all to me. To them I'm just a child.

But I don't feel younger than these people. In some ways I feel older. In our Health book there's a chapter on teenage emotions. According to this book, I'm supposed to be caught in a whirlwind of teenage emotions, laughing one minute, crying the next, zooming around on a rollercoaster, which is their term. However, this description does not apply to me. I am calm; I regard the antics of my fellow students, who act like the textbook, with a combination of scientific curiosity and almost matronly indulgence. When Cordelia says, "Don't you think he's a dreamboat?" I have a hard time understanding what she means. Occasionally I do cry for no reason, as it says you're

503

supposed to. But I can't believe in my own sadness, I can't take it seriously. I watch myself crying in the mirror, intrigued by the sight of tears.

At lunchtime I sit with Cordelia in the cafeteria, which is pale-coloured, with long whitish tables. We eat the lunches that have been sweltering in our school lockers all morning and which taste faintly of gym shoes, and drink chocolate milk through straws, and make what we consider to be witty, sarcastic remarks to each other, about the other kids at the school, about the teachers. Cordelia has been to high school for a year already and knows how to do this. She wears the collar of her blouse turned up and affects a derisive laugh. "He's a pill," she says; or, "What a creep." These are words that apply only to boys. Girls can be tough, stuck up or cheap, mousy or boy-crazy; or they can be brains and sucks and brown-nosers, like boys, if they are thought to study too much. But they can't be pills and creeps. I like the word "pill". I think it refers to the little balls of wool that form on sweaters. Boys who are pills have sweaters like that. I take care to pick all such woollen balls off my own sweaters.

Cordelia collects glossy photos of movie stars and singers, which she sends away for, finding the addresses of the fan clubs in movie magazines that advertise Frederick's of Hollywood peekaboo lingerie at the back, and chocolate-flavoured tablets you chew to lose weight. She thumbtacks the photos to the bulletin board over her desk and Scotch-tapes them to the walls of her room. Whenever I'm in there I feel as if there's a crowd watching me, their glossy black and white eyes following me around the room. Some of these pictures have signatures on them, and we examine them under the light to see if the pen has dented the paper. If not, they're only printed on. Cordelia likes June Allyson, but she also likes Frank Sinatra and Betty Hutton. Burt Lancaster is the sexiest, according to Cordelia.

On the way home from school we go to the record store and try out 78 records in the tiny cork-lined booth. Sometimes Cordelia will buy a record with her allowance, which is larger than mine, but most of the time she just tries them out. She expects me to roll my eyes in ecstasy, the way she does; she expects me to groan. She knows the rituals, she knows how we're supposed to be behaving, now that we're in high school.

But I think these things are impenetrable and fraudulent, and I can't do them without feeling I'm acting.

We take the records back to Cordelia's house and put them on the record-player in the living room, and turn up the sound. Frank Sinatra appears, a disembodied voice, sliding around on the tune like someone slipping on a muddy sidewalk. He slithers up to a note, hits it, flails, recovers, oozes in the direction of another note.

"Don't you just love the way he does that?" says Cordelia. She flings herself onto the chesterfield, legs across the arm, head hanging upside-down. She's eating a doughnut covered with powdered sugar; the sugar has come off on her nose. "I feel as if he's right here, running his hand up and down my spine."

"Yeah," I say.

Perdie and Mirrie come in, and Perdie says, "Not mooning over *him* again," and Mirrie says, "Cordelia dear, would you mind turning down the sound?" These days she speaks to Cordelia in tones of extra sweetness and calls her *dear* a lot.

Perdie is in university now. She goes to frat parties. Mirrie's in the last year of high school, though not our high school. They are both more charming and beautiful and sophisticated than ever. They wear cashmere sweaters and pearl button earrings, and smoke cigarettes. They call them ciggie-poos. They call eggs eggie-poos, and breakfast brekkers. If someone is pregnant they say preggers. They call their mother Mummie, still. They sit and smoke their cigarettes and talk casually and with amused, semi-contemptuous irony about their friends, who have names like Mickie and Bobbie and Poochie and Robin. It's hard to figure out from the names whether these people are boys or girls.

"Are you sufficiently sophonsified?" Perdie asks Cordelia. This is a new thing they've taken to saying. It means, have you had enough to eat. "Those were supposed to be for dinner." She means the doughnuts.

"There's a lot left," says Cordelia, still upside-down, wiping her nose.

"Cordelia," says Perdie. "Don't turn your collar up like that. It's cheap."

"It's not cheap," says Cordelia. "It's sharp."

"Sharp," says Perdie, rolling her eyes, blowing smoke from

her nose. Her mouth is little and plump and curly at the edges. "That sounds like a hair-oil ad."

Cordelia sits around right side up and sticks her tongue in the corner of her mouth and looks at Perdie. "So?" she says at last. "What do you know? You're already over the hill."

Perdie, who's old enough to drink cocktails with the grown-ups before dinner although she's not supposed to do it in bars, curls up her mouth. "I think high school's bad for her," she says to Mirrie. "She's turning into a hardrock." She pronounces this word in a mocking drawl, to show that it's the sort of word she herself has outgrown. "Pull up your socks, Cordelia, or you'll flunk your year again. You know what Daddy said last time."

Cordelia flushes, and can't think what to say back.

Cordelia begins to pinch things from stores. She doesn't call it stealing, she calls it pinching. She pinches tubes of lipstick from Woolworth's, packets of licorice Nibs from the drugstore. She goes in and buys some small item, such as bobby-pins, and when the salesgirl has her back turned getting the change out of the till she slips something off the counter and hides it under her coat or in her coat pocket. By this time it's autumn, and we have long coats which flap against the backs of our legs, coats with baggy, outsize patch pockets, good for pinching. Outside the store she shows me what she's gotten away with. She seems to think there's nothing wrong in what she's doing; she laughs with delight, her eyes sparkle, her cheeks are flushed. It's as if she's won a prize.

The Woolworth's has old wooden floors, stained from years of winter slush on people's boots, and dim overhead lights that hang down from the ceiling on metal stems. Nothing in it is anything we would really want, except maybe the lipsticks. There are photo frames with strangely tinted pictures of movie stars in them to show what the frame would look like with a photo in it; these stars have names like Ramon Novarro and Linda Darnell, stars from some remote period several years ago. There are cheesy hats, old-lady hats with veiling around them, and hair-combs stuck with imitation rhinestones. Just about everything in here is imitation something else. We walk up and down the aisles, spraying ourselves from the cologne testers, rubbing the sample lipsticks on the backs of our hands, fingering the merchandise and disparaging it in loud voices, while the middle-aged salesladies glare at us.

Cordelia pinches a pink nylon scarf and thinks she's been seen by one of the glaring salesladies, so we don't go back there for a while. We go into the drugstore and buy Creamsicles, and while I'm paying for them Cordelia pinches two horror comics. As we walk the rest of the way home from school we take turns reading them out loud, dramatizing the parts like radio plays, pausing to shriek with laughter. We sit on the low stone wall in front of the funeral parlour so we can both see the pictures, reading and laughing.

The comic books are drawn in great detail and garishly coloured, with green and purple and sulphur-yellow prevailing. Cordelia reads a story about two sisters, a pretty one and one who has a burn covering half her face. The burn is maroon-coloured and wrinkled like a dead apple. The pretty one has a boyfriend and goes to dances, the burned one hates her and loves the boyfriend. The burned one hangs herself in front of a mirror, out of jealousy. But her spirit goes into the mirror, and the next time the pretty one is brushing her hair in front of that mirror, she looks up and there's the burned one looking back at her. This is a shock and she faints, and the burned one gets out of the mirror and into the pretty one's body. She takes over the body and fools the boyfriend, she even gets him to kiss her, but although her face is now perfect, her reflection in that one mirror still shows her real, ruined face. The boyfriend sees it. Luckily he knows what to do. He breaks the mirror.

"Sob, sob," says Cordelia. "Oh Bob . . . it was . . . horrible. Never mind, my darling, it's all over now. She's gone . . . back . . . to where she came from . . . forever. Now we can truly be together, without fear. Clinch. The End. Oh, puke!"

I read one about a man and a woman who drown at sea but find they aren't dead exactly. Instead they are enormously bloated and fat, and living on a desert island. They don't love each other any more because of being so fat. Along comes a ship and they wave to it. "They don't see us! They're passing right through us! Oh no . . . that must mean . . . we're condemned to be this way *forever*! Is there no way out?"

In the next picture they've hanged themselves. The fat bodies are dangling from one of the palm trees, and their previous thin bodies, wispy-looking and dressed in falling-apart bathing-suits, are holding hands and walking into the ocean. "Clinch. The End."

"Oh, double puke," says Cordelia.

Cordelia reads one about a dead man coming back out of a swamp, covered with dripping, peeling-off flesh, to strangle the brother who pushed him into the swamp in the first place, and I read one about a man picking up a beautiful girl hitchhiker who turns out to have been dead for ten years. Cordelia reads one about a man who gets cursed by a voodoo witch-doctor and grows a big red lobster claw on his hand, which turns on him and attacks him.

When we get to Cordelia's house, Cordelia doesn't want to take the horror comics inside with her. She says someone might find them and wonder where she got them. Even if they think she bought them, she'll be in trouble. So I end up taking them home with me. It doesn't occur to either of us to throw them out.

Once I get them home, I realize I don't want them in the same room with me at night. It's one thing to laugh at them in the daylight, but I don't like the idea of them lying there, right in my bedroom, while I'm asleep. I think of them glowing in the dark, with a lurid sulphur-yellow light; I think of curling wisps of mist coming out of them and materializing on top of my bureau. I'm afraid I'll find out that there's someone else trapped inside my body; I'll look into the bathroom mirror and see the face of another girl, someone who looks like me but has half of her face darkened, the skin burned away.

I know these things won't really happen, but I don't like the thought. Nor do I want to throw the comics away: that would be letting them loose, they might go out of control. So I take them into Stephen's room and slide them in among his own old comic books, which are still there, stacked up under his bed. He never reads them any more, so he won't find these ones. Whatever emanations may seep from them at night, he will be impervious to them. In my opinion he is up to things, which includes things of this kind.

40

It's Sunday evening. There's a fire in the fireplace; the drapes are drawn against the heavy November darkness. My father sits in the easy chair marking drawings of spruce budworms cut open to show their digestive systems, my mother has made grilled cheese squares with bacon on them. We're listening to "The Jack Benny Show" on the radio, which is punctuated by singing commercials for Lucky Strike cigarettes. On this show there is a man who talks in a raspy voice and another one who says "Pickle in the middle and the mustard on top." I have no idea that the first one is supposed to be black and the second one Jewish; I think they just have funny voices.

Our old radio with the green eye has vanished, and a new, blond one has appeared, in a smooth unornamented cabinet that holds a long-playing record-player as well. We have little wooden nesting tables for our plates with the cheese squares; these tables are blond also, with legs that are wide at the top and taper down without a bump or curlicue, no dust-catchers. They look like the legs of fat women as they appear in comic books: no knees, no ankles. All this blond wood is from Scandinavia. Our silverware has descended to the steamer trunk. In its place there is new silverware, which is not silver but stainless steel.

These items have been chosen, not by my mother, but by my father. He picks out my mother's dressing-up clothes as well; my mother, laughing, says that all her taste is in her mouth. As far as she is concerned a chair is there to sit down on, and she couldn't care less whether it has pink petunias on it or purple polka dots, as long as it doesn't collapse. It's as if, like a cat, she cannot see things unless they are moving. She is becoming even more indifferent to fashion, and strides around in improvised get-ups, a ski-jacket, an old scarf, mitts that don't match. She says she doesn't care what it looks like as long as it keeps out the wind.

Worse, she's taken up ice-dancing; she goes to classes at the local indoor rink, and tangoes and waltzes in time to tinny music, holding hands with other women. This is mortifying but at least she does it indoors, where no one can see her. I can only hope she won't take to practising, later when it's really winter, on the outdoor rink, where somebody I might know could see her. But she isn't even aware of the chagrin this could cause. She never says *What will people think?* the way other mothers do, or are supposed to. She says she doesn't give a hoot.

I think this is irresponsible of her. At the same time, the word *hoot* pleases me. It makes my mother into a non-mother, a sort of mutant owl. I have become picky about my own clothes, and given to looking at myself from behind with the aid of a hand-mirror: although I may appear all right from the front, treachery could sneak up on me: a loose thread, a dropped hem. *Not giving a hoot* would be a luxury. It describes the fine, irreverent carelessness I myself would like to cultivate, in these and other matters.

My brother sits in one of the taper-legged blond chairs that go with the tables. He has become bigger and older, all of a sudden, when I wasn't looking. He has a razor now. Because it's the weekend and he hasn't shaved, he has a line of fine bristles poking out of the skin around his mouth. He's got on his moccasins, old ones he wears around the house, with holes worn under the big toes, and his V-neck maroon sweater with the ravels coming off the elbows. He resists my mother's efforts to mend this sweater or replace it. My mother says frequently that she doesn't give a hoot about clothes, but this indifference does not extend to holes, frayed edges, or dirt.

My brother's ragged sweater and sieve-like moccasins are the clothes he studies in. On weekdays he has to wear a jacket and tie and grey flannels, all of which are required at his school. He can't have a ducktail, like the boys at my school, or even a crewcut: his hair is shaved up the back of the neck and parted at one side, like the hair of English choirboys. This too is a school requirement. With his hair cut this way he looks like an illustration from an adventure book of the 1920s or earlier, of which there are a number in our cellar, or like an Allied air officer from a comic book. He has that kind of nose, that kind of chin, although thinner: clean-cut, good-looking, old-fashioned. His eyes are like that too, a piercing, slightly fanatical blue. His scorn for boys who give a hoot about how they look is devastating. He calls them fruity clothes-horses.

His school is a private school for brainy boys, though not an expensive one: you get in by passing tough exams. My parents asked me, a little anxiously, if I wanted to go to a private school for girls; they thought I'd feel left out if they didn't make the effort for me too. I know about these schools, where you have to wear kilts and play field hockey. I said they were for snobs and had low academic standards, which was true. But in fact I wouldn't be caught dead in a girls' school. The idea fills me with claustrophobic panic: a school with nothing in it but girls would be like a trap.

My brother is listening to Jack Benny too. As he listens, he stuffs the cheese squares into his mouth with his left hand, but his right hand holds a pencil, and this hand is never still. He hardly looks at the scrap pad on which he's doodling, but once in a while he tears off a sheet and crumples it up. These crumpled notes land on the floor. When I gather them up to put them into the wastebasket after the show, I see that they're covered with numbers, long lines of numbers and symbols that go on and on, like writing, like a letter in code.

My brother sometimes has friends over. They sit in his room with the chess table between them, not moving except for their hands, which lift, hover over the board, plunge down. Sometimes they grunt or say "Aha" or "Trade you" or "Got you back"; or they exchange new, obscure good-natured insults: "You surd!" "You square root!" "You throwback!" The captured chess pieces, knights and pawns and bishops, line up on the outskirts of the board. Once in a while, to see how the game is going, I bring in glasses of milk and vanilla-chocolate pinwheel cookies which I've made out of the *Betty Crocker Picture Cookbook*. This is a form of showing-off on my part, but it doesn't get much response. They grunt, drink the milk with their left hands, stuff in the cookies, their eyes never leaving the board. The bishops topple, the queen falls, the king is encircled. "Mate in two," they say. A finger comes down, knocks over the king. "Best of five." And they start again.

In the evenings my brother studies. Sometimes he does this in a curious way. He stands on his head, to improve the circulation to his brain, or he throws spitballs at the ceiling. The area around his ceiling light fixture is pimply with little wads of once-chewed paper. At other times he indulges in manic bouts of physical activity: he splits huge piles of kindling, much more than is needed, or goes running down in the ravine, wearing disgraceful baggy pants and a forest-green sweater even more unravelled than his maroon one, and frayed grey running shoes that look like the kind you see one of in vacant lots. He says he's training for the marathon.

A lot of the time my brother doesn't seem aware of me. He's thinking about other things, solemn things that are important. He sits at the dinner table, his right hand moving, pinching a breadcrust into pellets, staring at the wall behind my mother's head, on which there is a picture of three milkweed pods in a vase, while my father explains why the human race is doomed. This time it's because we've discovered insulin. All the diabetics aren't dying the way they used to, they're living long enough so that they're passing the diabetes on to their children. Soon, by the law of geometric progression, we'll all be diabetics, and since insulin is made from cows' stomachs the whole world will be covered with insulin-producing cows, the parts that aren't covered with human beings, who are reproducing much too rapidly for their own good anyway. The cows burp methane gas. Far too much methane gas is entering the atmosphere already, it will choke out the oxygen and perhaps cause the entire earth to become a giant greenhouse. The polar seas will melt and New York will be under six feet of water, not to mention many another coastal city. Also we have to worry about deserts, and erosion. If we don't get burped to death by the cows we'll end up like the Sahara Desert, says my father cheerfully, finishing up the meatloaf.

My father has nothing against diabetics, or cows either. He just likes following chains of thought to their logical conclusions. My mother says it's coffee soufflé for dessert.

Once my brother would have been more interested in the fate of the human race. Now he says that if the sun went supernova it would be eight minutes before we'd see it. He's taking the long-range view. Sooner or later we're going to be a cinder anyway, he implies, so why worry about a few cows more or less? Although he still collects butterfly sightings, he's moving farther and farther away from biology. In the larger picture, we're just a little green scuzz on the surface, says my brother.

My father eats his coffee soufflé, frowning a little. My mother tactfully pours him a cup of tea. I see that the future of the human race is a battleground, that Stephen has won a point and my father has lost one. Whoever cares the most will lose.

I know more about my father than I used to know: I know he wanted to be a pilot in the war but could not, because the work he did was considered essential to the war effort. How spruce budworms could be essential to the war effort I have not yet figured out, but apparently they were. Maybe this is why he always drives so fast, maybe he's heading for takeoff.

I know he grew up on a farm in the backwoods of Nova Scotia, where they didn't have running water or electricity. This is why he can build things and chop things: everyone there could use an axe and a saw. He did his high school courses by correspondence, sitting at the kitchen table and studying by the light of a kerosene lamp; he put himself through university by working in lumber camps and cleaning out rabbit hutches, and was so poor that he lived in a tent in the summers to save money. He used to play country fiddle at square dances and was twenty-two before he heard an orchestra. All this is known, but unimaginable. Also I wish I did not know it. I want my father to be just my father, the way he has always been, not a separate person with an earlier, mythological life of his own. Knowing too much about other people puts you in their power, they have a claim on you, you are forced to understand their reasons for doing things and then you are weakened.

I harden my heart towards the fate of the human race, and calculate in my head how much money I'll need to save to buy a new lambswool sweater. In Home Economics, which really means cooking and sewing, I've learned how to install a zipper and make a flat-fell seam, and now I make a lot of my clothes myself because it's cheaper, although they don't always turn out exactly like the picture on the front of the pattern. I get very little help from my mother on the fashion front, because whatever I wear she says it looks lovely, as long as it has no visible rents.

For advice I turn to Mrs. Finestein next door, for whom I baby-sit on weekends. "Blue is your colour, honey," she says.

513

"Very gorgeous. And cerise. You'd look stunning in cerise."
Then she goes out for the evening with Mr. Finestein, her hair
upswept, her mouth vivid, teetering in her tiny shoes with high
heels, jingling with bracelets and dangly gold earrings, and I read
The Little Engine That Could to Brian Finestein and tuck him
into bed.

Sometimes Stephen and I still get stuck doing the dishes together,
and then he remembers he's my brother. I wash, he dries, and
he asks me benign, avuncular, maddening questions, such as
how do I like Grade Nine. He is in Grade Eleven, stairways
and stairways above me; he doesn't have to rub it in.

But on some of these dish-drying nights he reverts to what
I consider to be his true self. He tells me the nicknames of
the teachers at his school, all of which are rude, such as The
Armpit or The Human Stool. Or we invent new swear-words
together, words that suggest an unspecific dirtiness. "Frut," he
says. I counter with "pronk," which I tell him is a verb. We
lean against the kitchen counter, doubled over with laughter,
until our mother comes into the kitchen and says, "What are
you two kids up to?"

Sometimes he decides that it's his duty to educate me. He
has a low opinion of most girls, it seems, and doesn't want me
turning into one of the ordinary kind. He doesn't want me to
be a pin-headed fuzzbrain. He thinks I'm in danger of becoming
vain. In the mornings he stands outside the bathroom door and
asks if I can bear to unstick myself from the mirror.

He thinks I should develop my mind. In order to help me do
this, he makes a Möbius strip for me by cutting out a long slip
of paper, twisting it once and gluing the ends together. This
Möbius strip has only one side, you can prove it by running
your finger along the surface. According to Stephen, this is a
way of visualizing infinity. He draws me a Klein bottle, which
has no outside and no inside, or rather the outside and the inside
are the same. I have more trouble with the Klein bottle than the
Möbius strip, probably because it's a bottle, and I can't think
of a bottle that isn't intended to contain something. I can't see
the point of it.

Stephen says he's interested in the problems of two-dimensional universes. He wants me to imagine what a three-dimensional universe would look like to someone who was perfectly flat. If you stood in a two-dimensional universe you would only be perceived at the point of intersection, you'd be perceived as two oblong discs, two two-dimensional cross-sections of your own feet. Then there are five-dimensional universes, seven-dimensional ones. I try very hard to picture these but I can't seem to get past three.

"Why three?" says Stephen. This is a favourite technique of his, asking me questions to which he knows the answers, or other answers.

"Because that's how many there are," I say.

"That's how many we *perceive*, you mean," he says. "We're limited by our own sensory equipment. How do you think a fly sees the world?" I know how a fly perceives the world, I've seen many flies' eyes, through microscopes. "In facets," I say. "But each facet would still have only three dimensions."

"Point taken," he says, which makes me feel grown up, worthy of this conversation. "But actually we perceive four."

"Four?" I say.

"Time is a dimension," he says. "You can't separate it from space. Space-time is what we live in." He says there are no such things as discrete objects which remain unchanged, set apart from the flow of time. He says space-time is curved and that in curved space-time the shortest distance between two points is not a straight line but a line following the curve. He says that time can be stretched or shrunk, and that it runs faster in some places than in others. He says that if you put one identical twin in a high-speed rocket for a week, he'd come back to find his brother ten years older than he is himself. I say I think that would be sad.

My brother smiles. He says the universe is like a dot-covered balloon that's being blown up. The dots are the stars; they're moving farther and farther away from one another all the time. He says that one of the really interesting questions is whether the universe is infinite and unbounded, or infinite but bounded, like the balloon idea. All I can think of in connection with a balloon is the explosion when it breaks.

He says that space is mostly empty and that matter is not really solid. It's just a bunch of widely spaced atoms moving at greater

515

or lesser speeds. Anyway, matter and energy are aspects of each other. It's as if everything is made of solid light. He says that if we knew enough we could walk through walls as if they were air, if we knew enough we could go faster than light, and at that point space would become time and time would become space and we would be able to travel through time, back into the past.

This is the first of these ideas of his that has really interested me. I'd like to see dinosaurs and a good many other things, such as the Ancient Egyptians. On the other hand there's something menacing about this notion. I'm not so sure I want to travel back into the past. I'm not so sure I want to be that impressed, either, by everything he says. It gives him too much of an advantage. Anyway it isn't a sensible way to talk. A lot of it sounds like comic books, the kind with ray-guns.

So I say, "What good would that be?"

He smiles. "If you could do it, you'd know you could do it," is what he says.

I tell Cordelia that Stephen says we could walk through walls if we knew enough. This is the only one of his latest ideas I can trust myself to expound, at the moment. The rest are too complicated, or bizarre.

Cordelia laughs. She says that Stephen is a brain and that if he weren't so cute he'd be a pill.

Stephen has a summer job this summer, teaching canoeing at a boys' camp, but I don't, because I'm only thirteen. I go with my parents up to the north, near Sault Ste. Marie, where my father is overseeing an experimental colony of tent caterpillars in screened-in cages.

Stephen writes me letters, in pencil, on pages torn from lined workbooks, in which he ridicules everything he can get his hands on, including his fellow camp instructors and the girls they go drooling around after on their days off. He describes these instructors with pimples popping from their skins, fangs sprouting in their mouths, their tongues hanging out like those of dogs, their eyes crossed in permanent, girl-inspired imbecility. This makes me think I have power, of a sort. Or will have it: I too am a girl. I go fishing by myself, mostly so I'll have something to put in my letters to him. Other than that I don't have much to tell.

Cordelia's letters are in real ink, black in colour. They are full of superlatives and exclamation marks. She dots her i's with little round circles, like Orphan Annie eyes, or bubbles. She signs them with things like, "Yours till Niagara Falls," "Yours till the cookie crumbles," or "Yours till the sea wears rubber pants to keep its bottom dry."

"I am *so bored*!!!" she writes, with triple underlining. She sounds enthusiastic even about boredom. And yet her burbly style does not ring true. I have seen her, sometimes, when she thinks I'm not looking: her face goes still, remote, unreflecting. It's as if she's not inside it. But then she'll turn and laugh. "Don't you just *love* it when they roll up their sleeves and tuck the cigarette pack inside?" she'll say. "That takes biceps!" And she will be back to normal.

I feel as if I'm marking time. I swim in the lake provided, and eat raisins and crackers spread thickly with peanut butter and honey while reading detective stories, and sulk because there's no one my age around. My parents' relentless cheer is no comfort. It would almost be better if they could be as surly as I am, or surlier; this would make me feel more ordinary.

IX
Leprosy

41

In late morning the phone wakes me. It's Charna. "Hey," she says. "We made the front page of Entertainment, and three, count them, three pictures! It's a real rave!"

I shudder at her idea of a rave; and what does she mean, *we*? But she's pleased: I've graduated from Living to Entertainment, this is a good sign. I remember when I had ideas about eternal greatness, when I wanted to be Leonardo da Vinci. Now I'm in with the rock groups and the latest movie. Art is what you can get away with, said somebody or other, which makes it sound like shoplifting or some other minor crime. And maybe that's all it ever was, or is: a kind of stealing. A hijacking of the visual.

I know it will be bad news. Still, I can't resist. I pull on my clothes, go down in search of the nearest paper-box. I do have the decency to wait until I get upstairs before I open the paper.

The bold print says, CROTCHETY ARTIST STILL HAS POWER TO DISTURB. I take note: *artist* instead of *painter*, the foreboding *still*, signpointing the way to senility. Andrea the acorn-headed ingénue getting her own back. I'm surprised she'd use an old-fashioned word like *crotchety*. It manages to suggest both crotches and crocheting, both of which seem appropriate. But probably she didn't write the headline.

There are indeed three photos. One is of my head, shot a little from beneath so it looks as if I have a double chin. The other two are of paintings. One is of Mrs. Smeath, bare naked, flying heavily through the air. The church spire with the onion on it is in the distance. Mr. Smeath is stuck to her back like an asparagus beetle, grinning like a maniac; both of them have shiny brown insect wings, done to scale and meticulously painted. *Erbug, The Annunciation*, it's called. The other is of Mrs. Smeath by herself, with a sickle-moon paring knife and a skinless potato, unclad from the waist up and the thighs down. This is from the *Empire Bloomers* series. The newspaper photos don't do these paintings justice, because there's no colour. They look too much

521

like snapshots. I know that in real life the bloomers on Mrs. Smeath are an intense indigo blue that took me weeks to get right, a blue that appears to radiate a dark and stifling light.

I scan the first paragraph: "Eminent artist Elaine Risley returns to hometown Toronto this week for a long overdue retrospective." *Eminent*, the mausoleum word. I might as well climb onto the marble slab right now and pull the bedsheet over my head. There are the usual misquotations, nor does my blue jogging suit escape comment. "Elaine Risley, looking anything but formidable in a powder-blue jogging suit that's seen better days, nevertheless can come out with a few pungent and deliberately provocative comments on women today."

I suck in some coffee, skip to the last paragraph: the inevitable *eclectic*, the obligatory *post-feminist*, a *however* and a *despite*. Good old Toronto bet-hedging and qualification. A blistering attack would be preferable, some flying fur, a little fire and brimstone. That way I would know I'm still alive.

I think savagely of the opening. Perhaps I should be deliberately provocative, perhaps I should confirm their deepest suspicions. I could strap on some of Jon's axe-murder special effects, the burnt face with its one peeled bloodshot eye, the plastic blood-squirting arm. Or slip my feet into the hollow casts of feet and lurch in like something from a mad-scientist movie.

I won't do these things, but thinking about them is soothing. It distances the entire thing, reduces it to a farce or prank, in which I have no involvement aside from mockery.

Cordelia will see this piece in the paper, and maybe she will laugh. Even though she's not in the phone book, she must still be around here somewhere. It would be like her to have changed her name. Or maybe she's married; maybe she's married more than once. Women are hard to keep track of, most of them. They slip into other names, and sink without a trace.

At any rate she'll see this. She'll know it's Mrs. Smeath, she'll get a kick out of that. She'll know it's me, and she'll come. She'll come in the door and she'll see herself, titled, framed, and dated, hanging on the wall. She will be unmistakable: the long line of jaw, the slightly crooked lip. She appears to be in a room, alone; a room with walls of a pastel green.

522

This is the only picture I ever did of Cordelia, Cordelia by herself. *Half a Face*, it's called: an odd title, because Cordelia's entire face is visible. But behind her, hanging on the wall, like emblems in the Renaissance, or those heads of animals, moose or bear, you used to find in northern bars, is another face, covered with a white cloth. The effect is of a theatrical mask. Perhaps.

I had trouble with this picture. It was hard for me to fix Cordelia in one time, at one age. I wanted her about thirteen, looking out with that defiant, almost belligerent stare of hers. *So?*

But the eyes sabotaged me. They aren't strong eyes; the look they give the face is tentative, hesitant, reproachful. Frightened.

Cordelia is afraid of me, in this picture.

I am afraid of Cordelia.

I'm not afraid of seeing Cordelia. I'm afraid of being Cordelia. Because in some way we changed places, and I've forgotten when.

42

After the summer I'm in Grade Ten. Although I'm still shorter, still younger, I have grown. Specifically, I've grown breasts. I have periods now, like normal girls; I too am among the knowing, I too can sit out volleyball games and go to the nurse's for aspirin and waddle along the halls with a pad like a flattened rabbit tail wadded between my legs, sopping with liver-coloured blood. There are satisfactions in this. I shave my legs, not because there's much to shave but because it makes me feel good. I sit in the bathtub, scraping away at my calves, which I wish were thicker, bulgier, like the calves of cheerleaders, while my brother mutters outside.

"Mirror, mirror on the wall, who is the most beautiful of all?" he says.

"Go away," I say tranquilly. I now have that privilege.

In school I am silent and watchful. I do my homework. Cordelia plucks her eyebrows into two thin lines, thinner than mine, and paints her nails Fire and Ice. She loses things, such as combs and also her French homework. She laughs raucously in the halls. She comes up with new, complicated swear-words: *excrement of the ungulate*, she says, meaning *bullshit*, and *great flaming blue-eyed bald-headed Jesus*. She takes up smoking and gets caught doing it in the girls' washroom. It must be hard for the teachers, looking, to figure out why we are friends, what we're doing together.

Today on the way home it snows. Big soft caressing flakes fall onto our skin like cold moths; the air fills with feathers. Cordelia and I are elated, we racket along the sidewalk through the twilight while the cars drift past us, hushed and slowed by the snow. We sing:

Remember the name
Of Lydia Pinkham,
Whose remedies for women brought her FAME!

This is a singing commercial from the radio. We don't know what Lydia Pinkham's remedies are, but anything that says "for women" on it has to do with monthly blood or some equally unspeakable female thing, and so we think it's funny. Also we sing:

Leprosy,
Night and day you torture me,
There goes my eyeball
Into my highball . . . .

Or else:

Part of your heart,
That's what I'm eating now,
Too bad we had to part. . . .

We sing these, and other parodies of popular songs, all of which we think are very witty. We run and slide, in our rubber boots with the tops turned down, and make snowballs which we throw at lampposts, at fire hydrants, bravely at passing cars, and as close as we dare at people walking on the sidewalk, women most of them, with shopping bags or dogs. We have to set our schoolbooks down to make the snowballs. Our aim is poor and we don't hit much of anything, though we hit a woman in a fur coat, from behind, by mistake. She turns and scowls at us and we run away, around a corner and up a side street, laughing so much with terror and embarrassment we can hardly stand up. Cordelia throws herself backwards onto a snow-covered lawn. "The evil eye!" she shrieks. For some reason I don't like the sight of her lying there in the snow, arms spread out.

"Get up," I say. "You'll catch pneumonia."

"So?" says Cordelia. But she gets up.

The streetlights come on, though it isn't yet dark. We reach the place where the cemetery begins, on the other side of the street.

"Remember Grace Smeath?" Cordelia says.

I say yes. I do remember her, but not clearly, not continuously.

525

I remember her from the time I first knew her, and later, sitting in the apple orchard with a crown of flowers on her head; and much later, when she was in Grade Eight and about to go off to high school. I don't even know what high school she went to. I remember her freckles, her little smile, her coarse horsehair braids.

"They rationed their toilet paper," Cordelia says. "Four squares a time, even for Number Two. Did you know that?"

"No," I say. But it seems to me that I did know it, once.

"Remember that black soap they had?" says Cordelia. "Remember? It smelled like tar."

I know what we're doing now: we're making fun of the Smeath family. Cordelia remembers all kinds of things: the greying underwear dripping on the clothesline in the cellar, the kitchen paring knife that was worn right down to a sliver, the winter coats from the Eaton's Catalogue. Simpsons is the right place to shop, according to Cordelia. That's where we go now on Saturday mornings, bareheaded, jerking downtown stop by stop on the streetcar. And shopping from the Eaton's Catalogue is much worse than shopping at Eaton's.

"The Lump-lump Family!" Cordelia shouts into the snowy air. It's cruel and appropriate; we snort with laughter. "What does the Lump-lump Family have for dinner? Plates of gristle!"

Now it's a fullblown game. What colour is their underwear? Grunt colour. Why did Mrs. Lump-lump have a Band-Aid on her face? Cut herself shaving. Anything can be said about them, invented about them. They're defenceless, they're at our mercy. We picture the two adult Lump-lumps making love, but this is too much for us, it can't be done, it's too vomit-making. Vomit-making is a new word, from Perdie.

"What does Grace Lump-lump do for fun? Pops her pimples!" Cordelia laughs so hard she doubles over and almost falls down. "Stop, stop, you'll make me pee," she says. She says that Grace started to grow pimples in Grade Eight: by now they must have increased in number. This is not made up but true. We relish the thought.

The Smeaths in our rendition of them are charmless, miserly, heavy as dough, boring as white margarine, which we claim they eat for dessert. We ridicule their piety, their small economies, the size of their feet, their rubber plant, which sums them

526

up. We speak of them in the present tense, as if we still know them.

This for me is a deeply satisfying game. I can't account for my own savagery; I don't question why I'm enjoying it so much, or why Cordelia is playing it, insists on playing it, whips it to life again when it seems to be flagging. She looks at me sideways, as if estimating how far, how much farther I'll go in what we both know, surely, is base treachery. I have a fleeting image of Grace once more, disappearing into her house through the front door, in her skirt with the straps, her pilly sweater. She was adored, by all of us. But she is not any more. And in Cordelia's version, now, she never was.

We run across the street in the falling snow, open the small wrought-iron gate in the cemetery fence, go in. We've never done this before.

This is the raw end of the cemetery. The trees are only saplings; they look even more temporary without their leaves. Much of the ground is untouched, but there are scars like giant claw marks, diggings, earthworks going on. The gravestones are few and recent: blockish oblongs of granite polished to a Presbyterian gloss, the letters cut plainly and without any attempt at prettiness. They remind me of men's overcoats.

We walk among these gravestones, pointing out which ones – particularly grey, particularly oafish – the Lump-lump Family would choose to bury one another beneath. From here we can look through the chain-link fence and see the houses on the other side of the street. Grace Smeath's is one of them. It's strange and oddly pleasant to think that she might be inside it at this very moment, inside that ordinary-looking brick box with the white porch pillars, not knowing a thing about what we've just been saying about her. Mrs. Smeath might be in there, lying on the velvet chesterfield, the afghan spread over her; I remember this much. The rubber plant will be on the landing, not much bigger. Rubber plants grow slowly. We are bigger though, and the house looks small.

The cemetery stretches out before us, acres and acres. Now the ravine is on our left, with the new concrete bridge just visible. I have a quick memory of the old bridge, of the creek beneath it: under our feet the dead people must be dissolving, turning to water, cold and clear, flowing downhill. But I forget about this immediately. Nothing about the cemetery is frightening, I tell myself. It's too pragmatic, too ugly, too neat. It's only like a kitchen shelf, where you put things away.

We walk for a while without speaking, not knowing where we're going, or why. The trees are taller, the tombstones older. There are Celtic crosses now, and the occasional angel.

"How do we get out of here?" says Cordelia, laughing a little.

"If we keep going we'll hit a road," I say. "Isn't that the traffic?"

"I need a ciggie-poo," Cordelia says. We find a bench and sit down so Cordelia can free her hands for the cigarette, cupping it against the air, lighting it. She isn't wearing gloves, or a scarf on her head. She has a tiny black and gold lighter.

"Look at all the little dead-people houses," she says.

"Mausoleums," I say knowingly.

"The Lump-lump Family Mausoleum," she says, giving the joke one last push.

"They wouldn't have one," I say. "Too ritzy."

"Eaton," Cordelia reads. "That must be the store, it's the same lettering. The Eaton's Catalogues are buried in there."

"Mr. and Mrs. Catalogue," I say.

"I wonder if they're wearing foundation garments," says Cordelia, inhaling. We're trying for a return to our hilarity, but it isn't working. I think of the Eatons, both of them or maybe more, tucked away for storage as if they're fur coats or gold watches, in their private tomb, which is all the stranger for being shaped like a Greek temple. Where exactly are they, inside there? On biers? In cobwebby stone-lidded coffins, as in the horror comics? I think of their jewels, glinting in the dark – of course they would have jewels – and of their long dry hair. Your hair grows after you're dead, also your fingernails. I don't know how I know this.

"Mrs. Eaton is really a vampire, you know," I say slowly. "She comes out at night. She's dressed in a long white ballgown. That door creaks open and she comes out."

"To drink the blood of Lump-lumps out too late," says Cordelia hopefully, stubbing out her cigarette.

528

I refuse to laugh. "No, seriously," I say. "She does. I happen to know."

Cordelia looks at me nervously. The snow is falling, it's twilight, there's nobody here but us. "Yeah?" she says, waiting for the joke.

"Yes," I say. "We sometimes go together. Because I'm a vampire too."

"You're not," says Cordelia, standing up, brushing off the snow. She's smiling uncertainly.

"How do you know?" I say. "How do you *know*?"

"You walk around in the daytime," Cordelia says.

"That's not me," I say. "That's my twin. You've never known, but I'm one of a twins. Identical ones, you can't tell us apart by looking. Anyway it's just the sun I have to avoid. On days like this it's perfectly safe. I have a coffin full of earth where I sleep; it's down in, down in" – I search for a likely place – "the cellar."

"You're being silly," Cordelia says.

I stand up too. "Silly?" I say. I lower my voice. "I'm just telling you the truth. You're my friend, I thought it was time you knew. I'm really dead. I've been dead for years."

"You can stop playing that," says Cordelia sharply. I'm surprised at how much pleasure this gives me, to know she's so uneasy, to know I have this much power over her.

"Playing what?" I say. "I'm not playing. But *you* don't have to worry. I won't suck any of your blood. You're my friend."

"Don't be a brat," says Cordelia.

"In a minute," I say, "we're going to be locked in." It strikes both of us that this may be the truth. We run along the roadway, gasping and laughing, and find a large gateway, which is luckily still open. Beyond it is Yonge Street, lined with rush-hour traffic.

Cordelia wants to point out Lump-lump Family cars, but I'm tired of this. I have a denser, more malevolent little triumph to finger: energy has passed between us, and I am stronger.

43

Now I'm in Grade Eleven, and as tall as many other girls, which is not very tall. I have a charcoal-grey pencil skirt that's hard to walk in despite the kick-pleat, and a bat-wing sweater, a red one with modulated grey horizontal stripes across it. I have a wide black elastic cinch belt with an imitation gold clasp buckle, and flat ballerina shoes of velveteen that scuff as I walk and bulge out at the sides. I have a shortie coat to go with the pencil skirt. This is the look: boxy and flared at the top, with a long skinny stem of thighs and legs coming out the bottom. I have a mean mouth.

I have such a mean mouth that I become known for it. I don't use it unless provoked, but then I open my mean mouth and short, devastating comments come out of it. I hardly have to think them up, they're just there suddenly, like thought balloons with light bulbs in them. "Don't be a pain" and "Takes one to know one" are standard repartee among girls, but I go much farther than that. I'm willing to say *pain in the ass*, which skirts good taste, and to go in for crushing inventions, such as The Walking Pimple and The Before Part of an Arrid Armpit Ad. If any girl calls me a brain, I say, "Better a brain than a pin-headed moron like you." "Use much hair grease?" I will say, or "Suck much?" I know where the weak spots are. "Suck" is an especially satisfying word, especially annihilating. Boys say it mostly, to one another; it suggests thumbs and babies. I haven't yet considered what else might be sucked, or under what circumstances.

Girls at school learn to look out for my mean mouth and avoid it. I walk the halls surrounded by an aura of potential verbal danger, and am treated with caution, which suits me fine. Strangely enough, my mean behaviour doesn't result in fewer friends, but, on the surface, more. The girls are afraid of me but they know where it's safest: beside me, half a step behind. "Elaine is a riot," they say, without conviction. Some

530

of them are already collecting china and housewares, and have Hope Chests. For this kind of thing I feel amused disdain. And yet it disturbs me to learn I have hurt someone unintentionally. I want all my hurts to be intentional.

I don't have occasion to use my mean mouth on boys, since they don't say provoking things to me. Except for Stephen, of course. These days we trade verbal meannesses as a kind of game, like badminton. *Got you. Got you back.* I can usually silence him with, "Where'd you get that haircut? Lawnmowerville?" He's sensitive about the haircut. Or, when he's all spiffed up in his private-school grey flannels and jacket: "Hey, you look like a Simpsons Rep." Simpsons Reps are sucky kids who appear in high school yearbooks wearing blazers with crests on the pockets, looking clean-cut, and advertising Simpsons.

My father says, "Your sharp tongue will get you in trouble some day, young lady." *Young lady* is a sign that I've gone too daringly close to some edge or other, but although it silences me for the moment it doesn't tone me down. I've come to enjoy the risk, the sensation of vertigo when I realize that I've shot right over the border of the socially acceptable, that I'm walking on thin ice, on empty air.

The person I use my mean mouth on the most is Cordelia. She doesn't even have to provoke me, I use her as target practice. We sit on the hill overlooking the football field, wearing our jeans, which are only allowed at school on the days of football games. We have our over-long pant cuffs pinned up with blanket pins, the latest thing. The cheerleaders leap around in their mid-thigh skirts, waving their paper pom-poms; they don't look long-legged and golden, like the cheerleaders at the back of *Life* magazine, but ill-assorted, dumpy and dark. However I still envy their calves. The football team jogs on. Cordelia says, "That Gregory! What a hunk," and I say, "Of cheese." Cordelia gives me a hurt look. "I think he's a doll." "If you like them covered with corn oil," I say. When she says it's a bad idea to sit down on the high school toilet seats without wiping them off first because you might get a disease, I say, "Who told you that? Your Mummie?"

I make fun of her favourite singers. "Love, love, love," I say. "They're always moaning." I have developed a searing contempt for gushiness and schmaltz. Frank Sinatra is The Singing Marshmallow, Betty Hutton is The Human Grindstone. Anyway, these people are out of date, they are sentimental mushballs. The real truth is to be found in rock and roll: "Hearts Made of Stone" is more like it.

Sometimes Cordelia can think of things to say back, but sometimes she can't. She says, "That's cruel." Or she sticks her tongue in the side of her mouth and changes the subject. Or she lights a cigarette.

I sit in History class, doodling on the side of the page. We are taking the Second World War. The teacher is an enthusiast, he's hopping around at the front of the room, waving his arms and his pointer. He's a short man with an unruly strand of hair and a limp, who may have been in the war himself, or so rumour goes. On the board he's drawn a large map of Europe, in white, with yellow dotted lines for the borders between countries. Hitler's armies invade, by means of pink chalk arrows. Now it's the Anschluss, and now Poland falls, and now France. I draw tulips and trees, putting a line for the ground and including the root systems in every case. Submarines appear in the English Channel, in green. I draw the face of the girl sitting across the aisle from me. The Blitz is on, bombs drift down through the air like sinister silver angels, London is disintegrating block by block, house by house, mantelpieces, chimneys, double beds hand-carved and passed down through the generations blasted into burning splinters, history reduced to shards. "It was the end of an era," says the teacher. It's hard for us to understand, he says, but nothing will ever be the same again. He is deeply moved by this, you can tell, it's embarrassing. The same as what? I think.

It's incredible to me that I myself was alive when all those chalk things were going on, all those statistical deaths. I was alive when women wore those ridiculous clothes with the big shoulder pads and the nipped-in waists, with peplums over their bums like backwards aprons. I draw a woman with wide shoulders and a picture hat. I draw my own hand. Hands are the hardest. It's difficult to keep them from looking like clumps of sausages.

*   *   *

I go out with boys. This is not part of a conscious plan, it just happens. My relationships with boys are effortless, which means that I put very little effort into them. It's girls I feel awkward with, it's girls I feel I have to defend myself against; not boys. I sit in my bedroom picking the pilly fuzzballs off my lambswool sweaters and the phone will ring. It will be a boy. I take the sweater into the hall, where the phone is, and sit on the hall chair with the receiver cradled between my ear and shoulder and continue to pick off the fuzzballs, while a long conversation goes on that is mostly silence.

Boys by nature require these silences; they must not be startled by too many words, spoken too quickly. What they actually say is not that important. The important parts exist in the silences between the words. I know what we're both looking for, which is escape. They want to escape from adults and other boys, I want to escape from adults and other girls. We're looking for desert islands, momentary, unreal, but there.

My father paces the living room, jingling his keys and small change in his pockets. He's impatient, he can't help hearing these monosyllables, these murmurs, these silences. He walks into the hall and makes snipping motions with his fingers, meaning I'm to cut it short. "I have to go now," I say. The boy makes a sound like air coming out of an inner tube. I understand it.

I know things about boys. I know what goes on in their heads, about girls and women, things they can't admit to other boys, or to anyone. They're fearful about their own bodies, shy about what they say, afraid of being laughed at. I know what kind of talk goes on among them as they horse around in the locker-room, sneak cigarettes behind the field house. *Stunned broad*, *dog*, *bag* and *bitch* are words they apply to girls, as well as worse words. I don't hold these words against them. I know these words are another version of pickled ox eyes and snot-eating, they're prove-it words boys need to exchange, to show they are strong and not to be taken in. The words don't necessarily mean they don't like real girls, or one real girl. Sometimes real girls are an alternative to these words and sometimes they're an incarnation of them, and sometimes they're just background noise.

I don't think any of these words apply to me. They apply to other girls, girls who walk along the high school halls in

533

ignorance of them, swinging their hair; swaying their little hips as if they think they're seductive, talking too loudly and carelessly to one another, fooling nobody; or else acting pastel, blank, daisy-fresh. And all the time these clouds of silent words surround them, *stunned broad, dog, bag* and *bitch*, pointing at them, reducing them, cutting them down to size so they can be handled. The trick with these silent words is to walk in the spaces between them, turn sideways in your head, evade. Like walking through walls.

This is what I know about boys in general. None of it has to do with individual boys by themselves, the boys I go out with. These boys are usually older than I am, although they aren't the kind with greasy ducktails and a lot of leather, they're nicer than that. When I go out with them I'm supposed to be home on time. If I'm not, my father has long conversations with me in which he explains that being home on time is like being on time for a train. If I were to be late for a train, I would miss the train, wouldn't I? "But this house isn't a train," I say. "It's not going anywhere." My father is exasperated; he jingles his keys in his pocket. "That's not the point," he says.

What my mother says is, "We worry." "What about?" I say. There's nothing to worry about, as far as I can see.

My parents are a liability in this as in other matters. They won't buy a television, like everyone else, because my father says it turns you into a cretin and emits harmful radiation and subliminal messages as well. When the boys come to pick me up, my father emerges from the cellar wearing his old grey felt hat and carrying a hammer or a saw, and grips their hands in his bearpaw handshake. He assesses them with his shrewd, twinkly, ironic little eyes and calls them "Sir," as if they're his graduate students. My mother goes into her nice-lady act and says almost nothing. Or else she tells me I look sweet, right in front of the boys.

In the spring they appear around the corner of the house in their baggy gardening pants, smudged with mud, to see me off. They drag the boys out to the backyard, where there is now a large pile of cement blocks accumulated by my father for some future contingency. They want the boys to see their display of

534

irises, as if these boys are old ladies; and the boys have to say something about the irises, although irises are the last thing on their minds. Or else my father attempts to engage them in improving conversation about current topics, or asks them if they've read this book or that one, pulling books from the bookshelves while the boys shift on their feet. "Your father's a card," the boys say uneasily, later.

My parents are like younger, urchin-like brothers and sisters whose faces are dirty and who blurt out humiliating things that can neither be anticipated nor controlled. I sigh and make the best of it. I feel I'm older than they are, much older. I feel ancient.

What I do with the boys is nothing to worry about. It's normal. We go to movies, where we sit in the smoking section and neck, or we go to drive-ins and eat popcorn and neck there as well. There are rules for necking, which we observe: approach, push away, approach, push away. Garter-belts are going too far and so are brassieres. No zippers. The boys' mouths taste of cigarettes and salt, their skin smells like Old Spice aftershave. We go to dances and twirl around during the rock numbers, or shuffle in the blue light, surrounded by the shuffling of the other couples. After formal dances we go to someone's house or to the St. Charles Restaurant, and after that we neck, though not for long because the time has usually run out. For formal dances I have dresses which I sew myself because I can't afford to buy them. They have layers of tulle and are propped up underneath with crinolines, and I worry about the hooks coming unfastened. I have shoes in matching satin or silver straps, I have earrings which pinch like hell. For these dances the boys send corsages, which I press afterwards and keep in my bureau drawer: squashed carnations and brown-edged rosebuds, wads of dead vegetation, like a collection of floral shrunken heads.

My brother Stephen treats these boys with scorn. As far as he's concerned they are dimwits and unworthy of my serious consideration. He laughs at them behind their backs and makes fun of their names. They are not George but Georgie-Porgie, not Roger but Rover. He makes bets as to how long each one will last. "Three months for him," he'll say, after seeing the boy for the first time; or, "When are you going to throw him over?"

I don't dislike my brother for this. I expect it of him, because he's partly right. I don't feel about these boys the way girls do in true-romance comic books. I don't sit around wondering when they'll call. I like them but I don't fall in love with them. None of the teenage-magazine descriptions of girls moping, one tear on each cheek like pearl earrings, applies to me. So partly the boys are not a serious matter. But at the same time they are.

The serious part is their bodies. I sit in the hall with the cradled telephone, and what I hear is their bodies. I don't listen much to the words but to the silences, and in the silences these bodies re-create themselves, are created by me, take form. When I am lonely for boys it's their bodies I miss. I study their hands lifting the cigarettes in the darkness of the movie theatres, the slope of a shoulder, the angle of a hip. Looking at them sideways, I examine them in different lights. My love for them is visual: that is the part of them I would like to possess. *Don't move*, I think. *Stay like that. Let me have that.* What power they have over me is held through the eyes, and when I'm tired of them it's an exhaustion partly physical, but also partly visual.

Only some of this has to do with sex; although some of it does. Some of the boys have cars, but others do not, and with them I go on buses, on streetcars, on the newly opened Toronto subway that is clean and uneventful and looks like a long pastel-tiled bathroom. These boys walk me home, we walk the long way around. The air smells of lilac or mown grass or burning leaves, depending on the season. We walk over the new cement footbridge, with the willow trees arching overhead, the sound of running water from the creek beneath. We stand in the dim light coming from the lampposts on the bridge and lean back against the railing, their arms around me and mine around them. We lift each other's clothing, run our hands over each other's backbones, and I feel the backbone tensed and strung to breaking. I feel the length of the whole body, I touch the face, amazed. The faces of the boys change so much, they soften, open up, they ache. The body is pure energy, solidified light.

536

44

A girl is found murdered, down in the ravine. Not the ravine near our house, but a larger branch of it, farther south, past the brick-works, where the Don River, willow-bordered, junk-strewn and dingy, winds sluggishly towards the lake. Such things are not supposed to happen in Toronto, where people leave their back doors unlocked, their windows unlatched at night; but they do happen, it seems. It's on the front pages of all the papers.

This girl is our age. Her bicycle has been found near her. She has been strangled, and also molested. We know what "molested" means. There are photos of her when alive, which already have that haunted look such photos usually take years to acquire, the look of vanished time, unrecoverable, unredeemed. There are extensive descriptions of her clothing. She was wearing an angora sweater, and a little fur collar with pom-poms, of the sort that is currently fashionable. I don't have a collar like this, but would like one. Hers was white but you can get them in mink. She was wearing a pin on the sweater, in the shape of two birds with red glass jewels for eyes. It's what anyone would wear to school. All these details about her clothing strike me as unfair, although I devour them. It doesn't seem right that you can just walk out one day, wearing ordinary clothes, and be murdered without warning, and then have all those people looking at you, examining you. Murder ought to be a more ceremonial occasion.

I have long since dismissed the idea of bad men in the ravine. I've considered them a scarecrow story, put up by mothers. But it appears they exist, despite me.

This murdered girl troubles me. After the first shock, nobody at school says much about her. Even Cordelia does not want to talk about her. It's as if this girl has done something shameful, herself, by being murdered. So she goes to that place where all things go that are not mentionable, taking her blonde hair, her angora sweater, her ordinariness with her. She stirs up something, like dead leaves. I think of a doll I had once, with

537

white fur on the border of her skirt. I remember being afraid of this doll. I haven't thought about that in years.

Cordelia and I sit at the dining table doing our homework. I am helping Cordelia, I'm trying to explain the atom to her, but she's refusing to take it seriously. The diagram of the atom has a nucleus, with electrons circling it. The nucleus looks like a raspberry, the electrons and their rings look like the planet Saturn. Cordelia sticks her tongue in the side of her mouth and frowns at the nucleus. "This looks like a raspberry," she says.

"Cordelia," I say. "The exam is tomorrow." Molecules do not interest her, she doesn't seem able to grasp the Periodic Table. She refuses to understand mass, she refuses to understand why atom bombs blow up. There's a picture of one blowing up in the Physics book, mushroom cloud and all. To her it's just another bomb. "Mass and energy are different aspects," I tell her. "That's *why* E = mc²."

"It would be easier if Percy the Prude weren't such a creep," she says. Percy the Prude is the Physics teacher. He has red hair that stands up at the top like Woody Woodpecker's, and he lisps.

Stephen walks through the room, looks over our shoulders. "So they're still teaching you kiddie physics," he says indulgently. "They've still got the atom looking like a raspberry."

"See?" says Cordelia.

I feel subverted. "This is the atom that's going to be on the exam, so you'd better learn it," I say to Cordelia. To Stephen I say, "So what does it really look like?"

"A lot of empty space," Stephen says. "It's hardly there at all. It's just a few specks held in place by forces. At the subatomic level, you can't even say that matter exists. You can only say that it has a tendency to exist."

"You're confusing Cordelia," I say. Cordelia has lit a cigarette and is looking out the window, where several squirrels are chasing one another around the lawn. She is paying no attention to any of this.

Stephen considers Cordelia. "Cordelia has a tendency to exist," is what he says.

*   *   *

538

Cordelia doesn't go out with boys the way I do, although she does go out with them. Once in a while I arrange double dates, through whatever boy I'm going out with. Cordelia's date is always a boy of lesser value, and she knows this and refuses to approve of him.

Cordelia can't seem to decide what kind of boy she really does approve of. The ones with haircuts like my brother's are drips and pills, but the ones with ducktails are sleazy greaseballs, although sexy. She thinks the boys I go out with, who go no further than crewcuts, are too juvenile for her. She's abandoned her ultra-red lipstick and nail polish and her turned-up collars and has taken up moderate pinks and going on diets, and grooming. This is what magazines call it: Good Grooming, as in horses. Her hair is shorter, her wardrobe more subdued.

But something about her makes boys uneasy. It's as if she's too attentive to them, too polite, studied and overdone. She laughs when she thinks they've made a joke and says, "That's very witty, Stan." She will say this even when they haven't intended to be funny, and then they aren't sure whether or not she's making fun of them. Sometimes she is, sometimes she isn't. Inappropriate words slip out of her. After we've finished our hamburgers and fries she turns to the boys and says brightly, "Are you sufficiently sophonsified?" and they gape at her. They are not the kind of boys who would have napkin-rings.

She asks them leading questions, tries to draw them into conversations, as a grownup would do, not appearing to know that the best thing, with them, is to let them exist in their own silences, to look at them only out of the corners of the eyes. Cordelia tries to look at them sincerely, head-on; they are blinded by the glare, and freeze like rabbits in a headlight. When she's in the back seat with them I can tell, from the breathing and gasps, that she's going too far in that direction as well. "She's kind of strange, your friend," the boys say to me, but they can't say why. I decide it's because she has no brother, only sisters. She thinks that what matters with boys is what you say; she's never learned the intricacies, the nuances of male silence.

But I know Cordelia isn't really interested in anything the boys themselves have to say, because she tells me so. Mostly she thinks they're dim. Her attempts at conversation with them are a performance, an imitation. Her laugh, when she's with them, is refined and low, like a woman's laugh on the radio, except when she forgets herself. Then it's too loud. She's mimicking something, something in her head, some role or image that only she can see.

The Earle Grey Players come to our high school, as they do every year. They go from high school to high school, they are well known for this. Every year they do one play by Shakespeare; it's always the play that's on the province-wide Grade Thirteen Examinations, the ones you have to pass in order to get into university. There aren't many theatres in Toronto, in fact there are only two, so many people go to these plays. The kids go to them because it's on the exam and the parents go because they don't often get a chance to see plays.

The Earle Grey Players are Mr. Earle Grey, who always plays the leads, Mrs. Earle Grey who plays the lead woman, and two or three other actors who are thought to be Earle Grey cousins and who are likely to double up and do two or more parts. The rest of the parts are played by students in whatever high school they're performing at that week. Last year the play was *Julius Caesar*, and Cordelia got to be part of the crowd. She had to smear burnt cork on her face for dirt and wrap herself up in a bedsheet from home, and say *rabble rabble* during the crowd scene when Mark Antony was making his Ears speech.

This year the play is *Macbeth*. Cordelia is a serving woman, and also a soldier in the final battle scene. This time she has to bring a plaid car-rug from home. She's lucky because she also has a kilt, an old one of Perdie's from when she went to her girls' private school. In addition to her parts, Cordelia is the Props Assistant. She's in charge of tidying up the props after each performance, setting them in order, always the same order, so that the actors can grab them backstage and run on without a moment's thought.

During the three days of rehearsal Cordelia is very excited. I can tell by the way she chain-smokes on the way home and acts bored and nonchalant, referring, every once in a while, to the real, professional actors by their first names. The younger ones make such an effort to be funny, she says. They call the Witches

The Three Wired Sisters; they call Cordelia a cream-faced loon, and they threaten to put eye of newt and toe of frog into her coffee. They say that when Lady Macbeth says, "Out, damned spot," during the mad scene, she's referring to her dog Spot, who has poo'ed on the carpet. She says real actors will never say the name *Macbeth* out loud, because it's bad luck. They call it "The Tartans" instead.

"You just said it," I say.

"What?"

"Macbeth," I say.

Cordelia stops short in the middle of the sidewalk. "Oh God," she says. "I did, didn't I?" She pretends to laugh it off, but it bothers her.

At the end of the play Macbeth's head gets cut off and Macduff has to bring it onto the stage. The head is a cabbage wrapped up in a white tea-towel; Macduff throws it onto the stage, where it hits with an impressive, flesh-and-bone thud. Or this is what has happened in rehearsal. But the night before the first performance – there are to be three – Cordelia notices that the cabbage is going bad, it's getting soft and squooshy and smells like sauerkraut. She replaces it with a brand-new cabbage.

The play is put on in the school auditorium, where the school assemblies are, and the choir practice. Opening night is packed. Things go without much mishap, apart from the sniggers in the wrong places and the anonymous voice that says, "Go on, do it!" when Macbeth is hesitating outside Duncan's chamber, and the catcalls and whistles from the back of the auditorium when Lady Macbeth appears in her nightgown. I watch for Cordelia in the battle scene, and there she is, running across backstage in her kilt with a wooden sword, her car-rug thrown over her shoulder. But when Macduff comes in at the end and tosses down the cabbage in the tea-towel, it doesn't hit once and lie still. It bounces, bumpity-bump, right across the stage like a rubber ball, and falls off the edge. This dampens the tragic effect, and the curtain comes down on laughter.

It's Cordelia's fault, for replacing the cabbage. She is mortified. "It was *supposed* to be rotten," she wails backstage, where I have gone to congratulate her. "So now they tell me!" The actors have made light of it; they tell her it's a novel effect. But although Cordelia laughs and blushes and tries to pass it off lightly, I can see she is almost in tears.

I ought to feel pity, but I do not. Instead, on the way home from school the next day, I say, "Bumpity bumpity bump, plop," and Cordelia says, "Oh, don't." Her voice is toneless, leaden. This is not a joke. I wonder, for an instant, how I can be so mean to my best friend. For this is what she is.

Time passes and we are older, we are the oldest, we are in Grade Thirteen. We can look down on the incoming students, those who are still mere children as we were once. We can smile at them. We're old enough to take Biology, which is taught in the Chemistry lab. For this we leave our home-room group and meet with students from other home-rooms. This is why Cordelia is my Biology lab partner, at the Chemistry lab table, which is black and has a sink. Cordelia doesn't like Biology any more than she liked Physics, which she barely squeaked through, but she has to take something in the sciences and it's easier, to her mind, than a number of the things she might have to take otherwise.

We are given dissecting kits with scalpel-like knives that could be sharper, and trays with a coating of wax at the bottom, and a package of pins, as in sewing classes. First we have to dissect a worm. Each of us is given one of these. We look at the diagram of the inside of the worm, in the Zoology textbook: this is what we're supposed to see once we get the worm open. The worms wriggle and twine in the wax-bottomed trays, and snout their way along the sides, trying to get out. They smell like holes in the ground.

I pin my worm at either end and make a slick vertical cut; the worm twists as they do on fish-hooks. I pin the worm's skin out to the sides. I can see its worm heart, which isn't the shape of a heart, its central artery pumping worm blood, its digestive system, which is full of mud. "Oh," says Cordelia. "How can you." Cordelia is becoming mushier and mushier, I think. She is becoming a drip. I do her worm for her, when the teacher isn't looking. Then I draw a diagram of the worm, cut open, beautifully labelled.

542

After that comes the frog. The frog kicks and is more difficult than the worm, it looks a little too much like a person swimming. I conk the frog out with chloroform as directed and dissect it with flair, sticking in the pins. I make a drawing of the inside of the frog, with all its curlicues and bulbs, its tiny lungs, its cold-blooded amphibian heart.

Cordelia can't do the frog either. She says she feels sick to her stomach just thinking about putting her dissecting knife through its skin. She looks at me, pale, her eyes big. The frog smell is getting to her. I do her frog for her. I'm good at this.

I memorize the statocysts of the crayfish, its gills and mouthparts. I memorize the circulatory system of the cat. The teacher, who is usually the boys' football coach but who has recently taken a summer course in Zoology so he can teach us this, orders a dead cat for us, with its veins and arteries pumped full of blue and pink latex. He's disappointed when it arrives, because the cat is definitely rancid, you can smell it even through the formaldehyde. So we don't have to dissect it, we can just use the diagram in the book.

But worms, frogs, and cats aren't enough for me. I want more. I go down to the Zoology Building on Saturday afternoons to use the microscopes in the empty labs. I look at slides, planaria worms in section with their triangular heads and cross-eyes, bacteria coloured with vivid dyes, hot pinks, violent purples, radiant blues. These are lit up from beneath, they're breathtaking, like stained-glass windows. I draw them, delineating the structures with different coloured pencils; though I can never get the same luminous brilliance.

Mr. Banerji, who is now Dr. Banerji, discovers what I'm doing. He brings me slides he thinks I would like to see and offers them to me shyly and eagerly, with a conspiratorial giggle, as if we are sharing a delicious, esoteric secret, or something religious. "Parasite of the tent caterpillar," he says, depositing the slide with reverence on a clean piece of paper at my table. "Egg of the budworm."

"Thank you," I say, and he looks at my drawings, picking them up by the corners with his deft, bitten fingers. "Very good, very good, Miss," he says. "Soon you will take over my job."

He has a wife now, who has come from India, and a little boy. I see them sometimes, looking in through the doorway of the lab, the child gentle and dubious, the wife anxious. She wears gold earrings and a scarf with spangles on it. Her red sari shows beneath her brown Canadian winter coat, her overshoes poking out beneath it.

Cordelia comes to my house and I help her with her Zoology homework, and she stays to dinner. My father, dishing out the beef stew, says that a species a day is becoming extinct. He says we are poisoning the rivers and ruining the gene pools of the planet. He says that when a species becomes extinct, some other species moves in to fill up the ecological niche, because Nature abhors a vacuum. He says that the things that move in are common weeds, and cockroaches and rats: soon all flowers will be dandelions. He says, waving his fork, that if we continue to overbreed as a species, a new epidemic will arise to redress the balance. All this will happen because people have neglected the basic lessons of science, they have gone in for politics and religion and wars instead, and sought out passionate excuses for killing one another. Science on the other hand is dispassionate and without bias, it is the only universal language. The language is numbers. When at last we are up to our ears in death and garbage, we will look to science to clean up our mess.

Cordelia listens to all of this, smirking a little. She thinks my father is quaint. I hear him the way she must: this is not what people are supposed to talk about at the dinner table.

I go to dinner at Cordelia's house. Dinners at Cordelia's house are of two kinds: those when her father is there and those when he isn't. When he isn't there, things are slapdash. Mummie comes to the table absent-mindedly still in her painting smock, Perdie and Mirrie and also Cordelia appear in blue jeans with a man's shirt over the top and their hair in pin-curls. They jump up from the table, saunter into the kitchen for more butter, or the salt, which has been forgotten. They talk all at once, in a languid, amused way, and groan when it's their turn to clear the table, while Mummie says "Now girls," but without conviction. She is losing the energy for disappointment.

But when Cordelia's father is there, everything is different. There are flowers on the table, and candles. Mummie has on her pearls, the napkins are neatly rolled in the napkin-rings instead of crumpled in under the edges of the plates. Nothing is forgotten. There are no pin-curls, no elbows on the table, even the spines are straighter.

Today is one of the candle days. Cordelia's father sits at the head of the table, with his craggy eyebrows, his wolvish look, and bends upon me the full force of his ponderous, ironic, terrifying charm. He can make you feel that what he thinks of you matters, because it will be accurate, but that what you think of him is of no importance.

"I'm hag-ridden," he says, pretending to be mournful. "The only man in a houseful of women. They won't let me into the bathroom in the morning to shave." Mockingly, he invites my sympathy and collusion. But I can think of nothing to say.

Perdie says, "He should consider himself lucky that we put up with him." She can get away with a little impertinence, with coltish liberties. She has the haircut for it. Mirrie, when hard-pressed, looks reproachful. Cordelia is not good at either of these things. But they all play up to him.

"What are you studying these days?" he says to me. It's a usual question of his. Whatever I say amuses him.

"The atom," I say.

"Ah, the atom," he says. "I remember the atom. And what does the atom have to say for itself these days?"

"Which one?" I say, and he laughs.

"Which one, indeed," he says. "That's very good." This may be what he wants: a give and take, of sorts. But Cordelia can never come up with it, because she's too frightened of him. She's frightened of not pleasing him. And yet he is not pleased. I've seen it many times, her dithering, fumble-footed efforts to appease him. But nothing she can do or say will ever be enough, because she is somehow the wrong person.

I watch this, and it makes me angry. It makes me want to kick her. How can she be so abject? When will she learn?

Cordelia fails the mid-year Zoology test. She doesn't seem to care. She has spent half the exam time drawing surreptitious cartoons of various teachers in the school, which she shows to me on the way home, laughing her exaggerated laugh.

*   *   *

545

Sometimes I dream about boys. These are wordless dreams, dreams of the body. They stay with me for minutes after I wake up and I luxuriate in them, but I forget them soon.

I have other dreams as well.

I dream that I can't move. I can't talk, I can't even breathe. I'm in an iron lung. The iron is clenched around my body like a hard cylindrical skin. It's this iron skin that is doing my breathing for me, in and out. I'm dense and heavy, I feel nothing other than this heaviness. My head sticks out the end of the iron lung. I'm looking up at the ceiling, on which there is a light fixture like yellowish cloudy ice.

I dream that I'm trying on a fur collar, in front of the mirror on my bureau. There's someone standing behind me. If I move so that I can see into the mirror, I'll be able to look over my own shoulder without turning around. I'll be able to see who it is.

I dream that I've found a red plastic purse, hidden in a drawer or trunk. I know there is treasure inside it, but I can't get it open. I try and try and finally it bursts, like a balloon. It's full of dead frogs.

I dream that I've been given a head wrapped up in a white tea-towel. I can see the outlines of the nose, the chin, the lips through the white cloth. I could unwrap the cloth to see whose head it is, but I don't want to, because I know that if I do the head will come alive.

45

Cordelia tells me that when she was younger she broke a thermometer and ate some of the mercury in it to make herself sick so she wouldn't have to go to school. Or she'd stick her finger down her throat and throw up, or she'd hold the thermometer near a light bulb to make it look as if she had a temperature. Her mother caught her doing that because she left it near the light bulb too long and the mercury shot up to a hundred and ten. After that her other deceptions were harder to pull off.

"How old were you then?" I ask her.

"Oh, I don't know. Before high school," she tells me. "You know, the age when you do those things."

It's Tuesday, in the middle of May. We're sitting in a booth at Sunnysides. Sunnysides has a soda fountain counter, which is speckled bloodstone red with chrome trim and has a row of round swivel-seat stools screwed to the floor along beside it. The black tops of the seats, which may not be leather, make a gentle farting sound when you sit down on them, so Cordelia and I and all girls prefer the booths. They're dark wood, and the table-top between the two facing benches is red like the soda fountain counter. This is where the Burnham students go after school to smoke and to drink glasses of Coca-Cola with maraschino cherries in them. If you drink a Coke and mix two aspirins in with it, it's supposed to make you drunk. Cordelia says she has tried this; she says it's nothing like being really drunk.

Instead of Cokes, we're drinking vanilla milkshakes, with two straws each. We ease the paper covers off the straws so that they pleat up into short caterpillars of paper. Then we drop water onto them out of our water glasses, and the paper caterpillars expand and look as if they're crawling. The tables at Sunnysides are littered with strips of soggy paper.

"What did the chickens say when the hen laid an orange?" Cordelia says, because there is a wave of corny chicken jokes sweeping the school. Chicken jokes, and moron jokes. *Why*

547

did the moron throw the clock out the window? To see time fly.

"Look at the orange marmalade," I say in a bored voice. "What did the moron say when he saw the three holes in the ground?"

"What?" says Cordelia, who has trouble remembering jokes even when she's heard them.

"Well, well, well," I say.

"Ha ha," says Cordelia. Part of this ritual is mild derision, of other people's jokes.

Cordelia doodles on the table, using our spilled water. "Remember those holes I used to dig?" she says.

"What holes?" I say. I don't remember any holes.

"Those holes in my backyard. Boy, did I want a hole out there. I started one, but the ground was too hard, it was full of rocks. So I dug another one. I used to work away at it after school, day after day. I got blisters on my hands from the shovel." She smiles a pensive, reminiscent smile.

"What did you want it for?" I ask.

"I wanted to put a chair in it and sit down there. By myself." I laugh. "What for?"

"I don't know. I guess I wanted some place that was all mine, where nobody could bug me. When I was little, I used to sit on a chair in the front hall. I used to think that if I kept very still and out of the way and didn't say anything, I would be safe."

"Safe from what?" I say.

"Just safe," she says. "When I was really little, I guess I used to get into trouble a lot, with Daddy. When he would lose his temper. You never knew when he was going to do it. 'Wipe that smirk off your face,' he would say. I used to stand up to him." She squashes out her cigarette, which has been smouldering in the ashtray. "You know, I hated moving to that house. I hated the kids at Queen Mary's, and those boring things like skipping. I didn't really have any good friends there, except for you."

Cordelia's face dissolves, re-forms: I can see her nine-year-old face taking shape beneath it. This happens in an eyeblink. It's as if I've been standing outside in the dark and a shade has snapped up, over a lighted window, revealing the life that's been going on inside in all its clarity and detail. There is that glimpse, during which I can see. And then not.

A wave of blood goes up to my head, my stomach shrinks together, as if something dangerous has just missed hitting me. It's as if I've been caught stealing, or telling a lie; or as if I've heard other people talking about me, saying bad things about me, behind my back. There's the same flush of shame, of guilt and terror, and of cold disgust with myself. But I don't know where these feelings have come from, what I've done.

I don't want to know. Whatever it is, it's nothing I need or want. I want to be here, on Tuesday, in May, sitting in the red-topped booth at Sunnysides, watching Cordelia as she delicately slurps the last of her milkshake up through the straws. She's noticed nothing.

"I've got one," I say. "Why did the unwashed chicken cross the road twice?"

"Why?" says Cordelia.

"Because it was a dirty double-crosser," I say.

Cordelia rolls her eyes, like Perdie. "Very funny," she says.

I close my eyes. In my head there's a square of darkness, and of purple flowers.

46

I begin to avoid Cordelia. I don't know why.

I no longer arrange double dates with her. I tell her that the boy I'm going out with doesn't have any suitable friends. I say I have to stay after school, which is true: I'm painting the decorations for the next dance, palm trees and girls in hula skirts.

Some days Cordelia waits for me, so I have to walk home with her anyway. She talks and talks as if there's nothing wrong, and I say little; but then I've never said a lot anyway. After a while she'll say, overly brightly, "But here I've been going on and on about me. What's doing with you?" and I smile and say, "Nothing much." Sometimes she makes a joke of it and says, "But that's enough about me. What do *you* think of me?" and I add to the joke by saying, "Nothing much."

Cordelia is failing more and more tests. It doesn't seem to bother her, or at any rate she doesn't want to talk about it. I no longer help her with her homework, because I know she won't pay attention even if I do. She has trouble concentrating on anything. Even when she's just talking, on the way home, she changes the subject in the middle of a sentence so it's hard to follow what she's saying. She's slipping up on the grooming, too, reverting to her old sloppy ways of years ago. She's let her bleached strip grow out, so it's disconcertingly two-toned. There are runs in her nylons, buttons popped off her blouses. Her lipstick doesn't seem to fit her mouth.

It is decided that it would be best for Cordelia to change schools again, so she does. After this she phones me frequently, but then less frequently. She says we should get together soon. I never deny this, but I never set a time either. After a while I say, "I have to go now."

Cordelia's family moves to a different, larger house, in a

550

ritzier neighbourhood farther north. Some Dutch people move into her old house. They plant a lot of tulips. That seems to be the end of her.

I write the final Grade Thirteen exams, subject after subject, day after day, sitting at a desk in the gymnasium. The leaves are fully out, the irises are in bloom, there's a heat wave; the gymnasium heats up like an oven and we all sit in there, superheated, writing away, while the gymnasium exudes its smell of bygone athletes. The teachers police the aisles. Several girls faint. One boy keels over and is found afterwards to have drunk a pitcher of tomato juice out of the refrigerator which was really Bloody Marys for his mother's bridge club. As the bodies are carried out I scarcely look up from the page.

I know I'll do well in the two Biology exams. I can draw anything: the insides of crayfish ears, the human eye, frogs' genitalia, the blossom of the snapdragon (*Antirrhinum majus*) in cross-section. I know the difference between a raceme and a rhizome, I explicate photosynthesis, I can spell *Scrofulariaciae*. But in the middle of the Botany examination it comes to me, like a sudden epileptic fit, that I'm not going to be a biologist, as I have thought. I am going to be a painter. I look at the page, where the life cycle of the mushroom from spore to fruiting body is taking shape, and I know this with absolute certainty. My life has been changed, soundlessly, instantaneously. I continue my explication of tubers, bulbs, and legumes, as if nothing has happened.

One night, just after the exams have finished, the phone rings. It's Cordelia. I realize I've been expecting this.

"I'd like to see you," she says. I don't want to see her, but I know I will. What I hear is not *like* but *need*.

The next afternoon I take the subway and then the bus, northwards through the heated city, to where Cordelia now lives. I've never been up here before. The streets wind in and around, the houses are large, ponderous, Georgian, set off with weighty shrubbery. I see or think I see Cordelia's face, pale and

551

indistinct, behind the front window as I come up the walk. She opens the door before I have time to ring.

"Well, hi there," she says. "Long time no see." This is false heartiness and we both know it, because Cordelia is a wreck. Her hair is lustreless, the flesh of her face pasty. She's gained a lot of weight, not solid muscled weight, but limp weight, bloated and watery. She's gone back to the too-vivid orange-red lipstick, which turns her yellowish. "I know," she says. "I look like Haggis McBaggis."

The house is cool inside. The front hall floor is white and black squares; there's a graceful central staircase. A flower arrangement with gladioli sits on a polished table beside it. The house is silent, except for a clock chiming in the living room. Nobody else seems to be home.

We don't go into the living room but back past the stairs and through a door into the kitchen, where Cordelia makes me a cup of instant coffee. The kitchen is beautiful, perfectly arranged, pale-coloured and peaceful. The refrigerator and stove are white. Some people now have coloured refrigerators, pale-green or pink, but I don't like these colours and I'm pleased that Cordelia's mother doesn't either. There's a lined school notebook open on the kitchen table, which I recognize as the dining table from their other house with the two middle leaves taken out. That means they must have a new dining table. It appals me to discover that I want to see this new dining table more than I want to see Cordelia.

Cordelia rummages in the fridge and brings out an opened package of store doughnuts. "I've been waiting for an excuse to eat the rest of these," she says. But as soon as she's taken her first bite she lights a cigarette.

"So," she says. "What are you up to these days?" It's her too-bright voice, the one she used to use on boys. Right now it frightens me.

"Oh, just the usual," I say. "You know. Finishing exams." We look at each other. Things are bad for her, that much is clear. I don't know whether she wants me to ignore this or not. "What about you?" I say.

"I have a tutor," she says. "I'm supposed to be studying. For summer courses." We both know without mentioning it that she must have failed her year, despite the new school. She must have

552

failed badly. Unless she passes whatever subjects she failed, at the next set of exams or sometime or other, she'll be locked out of university forever.

"Is the tutor nice?" I say, as if I'm asking about a new dress.

"I guess so," says Cordelia. "Her name is Miss Dingle. It really is. She blinks all the time, she has watery eyes. She lives in this squalid apartment. She has salmon-coloured lingerie, I see it hanging over the shower-curtain rod in her squalid bathroom. I can always get her off the subject by asking about her health."

"Off what subject?" I ask.

"Oh, any subject," says Cordelia. "Physics, Latin. Any of it." She sounds a little ashamed of herself, but proud and excited too. It's like the time when she used to pinch things. This is her accomplishment these days: deluding the tutor. "I don't know why they all think I spend the days studying," she says. "I sleep a lot. Or else I drink coffee and smoke and listen to records. Sometimes I have a little nip out of Daddy's whisky decanter. I fill it up with water. He hasn't found out!"

"But Cordelia," I say. "You have to do *something*!"

"Why?" she says, with a little of her old belligerence. She isn't only joking.

And I have no reason to give her. I can't say, "Because everyone does." I can't even say, "You have to earn a living," because she obviously doesn't, she's here in this large house and she isn't earning a living at all. She could just go on like this, like a woman from old-fashioned times, a maiden aunt, some aging perennial girl who never leaves home. It isn't likely that her parents would kick her out.

So I say, "You'll get bored."

Cordelia laughs, too loudly. "So what if I study?" she says. "I pass my exams. I go to university. I learn it all. I turn into Miss Dingle. No thanks."

"Don't be a cretin," I say. "Who says you have to be Miss Dingle?"

"Maybe I am a cretin," she says. "I can't concentrate on that stuff, I can hardly look at the page, it all turns into little black dots."

"Maybe you could go to secretarial school," I say. I feel like a traitor as soon as I've said it. She knows what we both think of girls who would go to secretarial school, with their spidery plucked eyebrows and pink nylon blouses.

"Thanks a bundle." There's a pause. "But let's not talk about all that," she says, returning to her ultra-bright voice. "Let's talk about fun things. Remember that cabbage? The bouncy one?"

"Yes," I say. It occurs to me that she could be pregnant, or that she might have been. It's natural to wonder that about girls who drop out of school. But I decide this is unlikely.

"I was so mortified," she says. "Remember when we used to go downtown and take our pictures at Union Station? We thought we were so sharp!"

"Right before the subway was built," I say.

"We used to throw snowballs at old ladies. We used to sing those silly songs."

"Leprosy," I say.

"Part of your heart," she says. "We thought we were the cat's ass. I see kids that age now and I think: *brats!*"

She's looking back on that time as if it was her golden age; or maybe it seems that way to her because it's better than now. But I don't want her to remember any more. I want to protect myself from any further, darker memories of hers, get myself out of here gracefully before something embarrassing happens. She's balanced on the edge of an artificial hilarity that could topple over at any moment into its opposite, into tears and desperation. I don't want to see her crumple up like that, because I have nothing to offer her in the way of solace.

I harden towards her. She's acting like a jerk. She doesn't have to stay locked into place, into this mournful, drawn-out, low-grade misery. She has all kinds of choices and possibilities, and the only thing that's keeping her away from them is lack of will-power. *Smarten up*, I want to tell her. *Pull up your socks.*

I say I have to get back, that I'm going out later. This isn't true and she suspects it. Although she's a mess, her instinct for social fraud has sharpened. "Of course," she says. "That's entirely understandable." It's her distant, grown-up voice.

Now that I'm hurrying, making a show of bustle, it strikes me that one of my reasons for escape is that I don't want to meet her mother coming back, from wherever she's been. Her mother would look at me with reproach, as if I am responsible for Cordelia in her present shape, as if she's disappointed, not in

554

Cordelia, but in me. Why should I have to undergo such a look, for something that is not my fault?

"Goodbye, Cordelia," I say in the front hall. I squeeze her arm briefly, move back before she can kiss me on the cheek. Kissing on the cheek is what they do in her family. I know she has expected something from me, some connection to her old life, or to herself. I know I have failed to provide it. I am dismayed by myself, by my cruelty and indifference, my lack of kindness. But also I feel relief.

"Call you soon," I say. I'm lying, but she chooses not to acknowledge this.

"That would be nice," she says, shielding us both with politeness.

I go down the walk towards the street, turn to look back. There's her face again, a blurred reflection of a moon, behind the front window.

X

Life Drawing

47

There are several diseases of the memory. Forgetfulness of nouns, for instance, or of numbers. Or there are more complex amnesias. With one, you can lose your entire past; you start afresh, learning how to tie your shoe-laces, how to eat with a fork, how to read and sing. You are introduced to your relatives, your oldest friends, as if you've never met them before; you get a second chance with them, better than forgiveness because you can begin innocent. With another form, you keep the distant past but lose the present. You can't remember what happened five minutes ago. When someone you've known all your life goes out of the room and then comes back in, you greet them as if they've been gone for twenty years; you weep and weep, with joy and relief, as if at a reunion with the dead.

I sometimes wonder which of these will afflict me, later; because I know one of them will.

For years I wanted to be older, and now I am.

I sit in the harsh ultra-black of the Quasi, drinking red wine, staring out the window. On the other side of the glass, Cordelia drifts past; then melts and reassembles, changing into someone else. Another mistaken identity.

Why did they name her that? Hang that weight around her neck. Heart of the moon, jewel of the sea, depending on which foreign language you're using. The third sister, the only honest one. The stubborn one, the rejected one, the one who was not heard. If she'd been called Jane, would things have been different?

My own mother named me after her best friend, as women did in those days. Elaine, which I once found too plaintive. I wanted something more definite, a monosyllable: Dot or Pat, like a foot set down. Nothing you could make a mistake about; nothing watery. But my name has solidified around me, with time. I think of it as tough but pliable now, like a well-worn glove.

There's a lot of neo-black in here, some of it leather, some shiny vinyl. I've come prepared this time, I have my black cotton turtleneck and my black trenchcoat with the button-on hood, but I'm not the right texture. Also not the right age: everyone in here is twelve. This place was Jon's suggestion. Trust him to cling to the surfboard as it up-ends in the froth of the latest wave.

He always made a fetish of lateness, to indicate that his life was crammed with many things, all of them more important than I was, and today is no exception. Thirty minutes later than agreed he breezes in. This time however he apologizes. Has he learned something, or does his new wife run a tighter ship? Funny I still think of her as new.

"That's all right, I programmed for it," I say. "I'm glad you could come out to play." A small preliminary kick at the wife.

"Having lunch with you hardly qualifies as play," he says, grinning.

He's still up to it. We look each other over. In four years he's achieved more wrinkles, and the sideburns and moustache are greying further. "Don't mention the bald spot," he says.

"What bald spot?" I say, meaning I'll overlook his physical degeneration if he'll overlook mine. He's up to that one, too.

"You're looking better than ever," he says. "Selling out must agree with you."

"Oh, it does," I say. "It's so much better than licking bums and hacking up women's bodies in screw-and-spew movies." Once this would have drawn blood, but he must have accepted his lot in life by now. He shrugs, making the best of it; but he looks tired.

"Live long enough and the licker becomes the lickee," he says. "Ever since the exploding eyeball I can do no wrong. Right now I'm head-to-toe saliva."

The possibility for crude sexual innuendo is there, but I duck it. Instead I think, he's right: we are the establishment now, such as it is. Or that's what we must look like. Once the people I knew died of suicide and motorcycle crashes and other forms of violence. Now it's diseases: heart attacks, cancer, the betrayals of the body. The world is being run by people my age, men my age, with falling-out hair and health worries, and it frightens

560

me. When the leaders were older than me I could believe in their wisdom, I could believe they had transcended rage and malice and the need to be loved. Now I know better. I look at the faces in newspapers, in magazines, and wonder: what greeds, what furies drive them on?

"How's your real work going?" I say, relenting, letting him know I still take him seriously.

This bothers him. "All right," he says. "I haven't been able to get to it much lately."

We are silent, considering shortfalls. There's not much time left, for us to become what we once intended. Jon had potential, but it's not a word that can be used comfortably any more. Potential has a shelf-life.

We talk about Sarah, easily and without competing, as if we are her aunt and uncle. We talk about my show.

"I guess you saw that hatchet job in the paper," I say.

"Was that a hatchet job?" he says.

"It's my fault. I was rude to the interviewer," I say, with what I try to pass off as penitence. "I'm well on my way to becoming a cantankerous old witch."

"I'd be disappointed in you if you weren't," he says. "Make 'em sweat, it's what they're paid for." We both laugh. He knows me. He knows what a shit I can be.

I look at him with the nostalgic affection men are said to feel for their wars, their fellow veterans. I think, I once threw things at this man. I threw a glass ashtray, a fairly cheap one which didn't break. I threw a shoe (his) and a handbag (mine), not even snapping the handbag shut first, so that he was showered with a metal rain of keys and small change. The worst thing I threw was a small portable television set, standing on the bed and heaving it at him with the aid of the bouncy springs, although the instant I let fly I thought, *Oh God, let him duck!* I once thought I was capable of murdering him. Today I feel only a mild regret that we were not more civilized with each other at the time. Still, it was amazing, all those explosions, that recklessness, that technicolour wreckage. Amazing and agonizing and almost lethal.

Now that I'm more or less safe from him, and him from me,

I can recall him with fondness and even in some detail, which is more than I can say for several others. Old lovers go the way of old photographs, bleaching out gradually as in a slow bath of acid: first the moles and pimples, then the shadings, then the faces themselves, until nothing remains but the general outlines. What will be left of them when I'm seventy? None of the baroque ecstasy, none of the grotesque compulsion. A word or two, hovering in the inner emptiness. Maybe a toe here, a nostril there, or a moustache, floating like a little curl of seaweed among the other flotsam.

Across from me at the night-black table, Jon, though diminishing, still moves and breathes. There's a sliver of pain, of longing in me: *Don't go yet! It's not time! Don't go!* It would be stupid, as always, to reveal my own sentimentality, my weakness to him.

What we eat is vaguely Thai: chicken, spicy and succulent, a salad of exotic foliage, red leaves, tiny splinters of purple. Gaudy food. This is the kind of thing people eat now, people who eat in places like this: Toronto is no longer the land of chicken pot pie, beef stew, overboiled vegetables. I recall my first avocado, when I was twenty-two. It was like my father's first symphony orchestra. Perversely I long for the desserts of my childhood, the desserts of war, simple and inexpensive and bland: tapioca pudding, with its gelatinous fish-eyes, Jello caramel pudding, junket. Junket was made with white tablets that came out of a tube, and served with a dollop of grape jelly on the top. Probably it's vanished by now.

Jon has ordered a bottle, no glass-by-glass for him. It's a hint of the old bombast, the old peacock tail, and reassuring.

"How's your wife?" I ask him.

"Oh," he says, looking down, "Mary Jean and I have decided to try it apart for a while."

This may explain the herbal tea: some younger, more vegetarian influence, in the studio, on the sly. "I suppose you've got some little number," I say. "They say 'he goes' instead of 'he says,' have you noticed?"

"As a matter of fact," he says, "Mary Jean was the one who left."

"I'm sorry," I say. And immediately I am, I'm indignant, how could she do that to him, the cold unfeeling bitch. I side with him, despite the fact that I did the same thing to him myself, years ago.

"I guess I'm partly to blame," he says. This is not something he ever would have admitted before. "She said she couldn't get through to me."

I bet that isn't all she said. He's lost something, some illusion I used to think was necessary to him. He's come to realize he too is human. Or is this a performance, for my benefit, to show me he's up to date? Maybe men shouldn't have been told about their own humanity. It's only made them uncomfortable. It's only made them trickier, slyer, more evasive, harder to read.

"If you hadn't been so crazy," I say, "it could have worked out. With us, I mean."

That perks him up. "Who was crazy?" he says, grinning again. "Who drove who to the hospital?"

"If it hadn't been for you," I say, "I wouldn't have needed to be driven to the hospital."

"That's not fair and you know it," he says.

"You're right," I say. "It's not fair. I'm glad you drove me to the hospital."

Forgiving men is so much easier than forgiving women.

"I'll walk you where you're going," he says when we're out on the sidewalk. I would like that. We're getting along so well, now there's nothing at stake. I can see why I fell in love with him. But I don't have the energy for it now.

"That's okay," I say. I don't want to admit that I don't know where I'm going. "Thanks for the studio. Let me know if you need anything out of it." Though I know he won't come over while I'm there, it's still too awkward, and hazardous, for us to be together behind a door that locks.

"Maybe we could have a drink, later," he says.

I say, "Maybe we could."

After leaving Jon I walk east along Queen, past the street dealers selling risqué T-shirts, past the garter-belts and satin underpants

563

in the windows. What I'm thinking about is a picture I painted, years ago now. *Falling Women*, it was called. A lot of my paintings then began in my confusion about words.

There were no men in this painting, but it was about men, the kind who caused women to fall. I did not ascribe any intentions to these men. They were like the weather, they didn't have a mind. They merely drenched you or struck you like lightning and moved on, mindless as blizzards. Or they were like rocks, a line of sharp slippery rocks with jagged edges. You could walk with care along between the rocks, picking your steps, and if you slipped you'd fall and cut yourself, but it was no use blaming the rocks.

That must be what was meant by fallen women. Fallen women were women who had fallen onto men and hurt themselves. There was some suggestion of downward motion, against one's will and not with the will of anyone else. Fallen women were not pulled-down women or pushed women, merely fallen. Of course there was Eve and the Fall; but there was nothing about falling in that story, which was only about eating, like most children's stories.

Falling Women showed the women, three of them, falling as if by accident off a bridge, their skirts opened into bells by the wind, their hair streaming upwards. Down they fell, onto the men who were lying unseen, jagged and dark and without volition, far below.

48

I'm staring at a naked woman. In a picture she would be a nude, but she is not in a picture. This is the first live naked woman I've ever seen, apart from myself in the mirror. The girls in the high-school locker-room always had their underwear on, which is not the same thing, and neither are the women in stretch Lycra one-piece bathing-suits with modesty panels, in magazine ads.

Even this woman is not entirely naked, as she has a sheet draped over her left thigh and tucked in between her legs: no hair shows. She's sitting on a stool, her buttocks squashing out sideways; her stocky back is curved, her right leg is crossed over her left at the knee, her right elbow rests on her right knee, her left arm is placed behind her with the hand on the stool. Her eyes are bored, her head droops forward, the way it has been put. She looks cramped and uncomfortable, and also cold: I can see the goose-bumps on her upper arms. She has a thick neck. Her hair is frizzly and short, red with darker roots, and I suspect she is chewing gum: every once in a while there is a slow, furtive, sideways motion of her jaw. She is not supposed to move.

I am trying to draw this woman, with a piece of charcoal. I am trying for fluidity of line. This is how the teacher has arranged her: for fluidity of line. I would rather be using a hard pencil; the charcoal gets on my fingers and smears, and is no good for hair. Also this woman frightens me. There is a lot of flesh to her, especially below the waist; there are folds across her stomach, her breasts are saggy and have enormous dark nipples. The harsh fluorescent light, falling straight down on her, turns her eye sockets to caverns, emphasizes the descending lines from nose to chin; but the massiveness of her body makes her head look like an afterthought. She is not beautiful, and I am afraid of turning into that.

This is a night class. It's called Life Drawing, and is held on Tuesdays at the Toronto College of Art, in a large bare room, beyond which is a utilitarian stairway, then McCaul Street,

565

then Queen with its drunks and streetcar tracks, and beyond that square, boxy Toronto. There are a dozen of us in the room, with our hopeful, almost-new Bristol drawing-boards and our black-tipped fingers; two older women, eight young men, another girl my own age, and me. I am not a student here, but even those who aren't students can sign up for this class, under certain circumstances. The circumstances are that you have to convince the teacher you are serious. It's not clear however how long I will last.

The teacher is Mr. Hrbik. He is in his mid-thirties, with dark thickly curled hair, a moustache, an eagle nose, and eyes that look almost purple, like mulberries. He has a habit of staring at you without saying anything, and, it seems, without blinking.

It was the eyes I noticed first, when I went for my interview with him. He was sitting in his tiny paper-covered office at the College, leaning back in his chair and chewing the end of a pencil. When he saw me he put the pencil down.

"How old are you?" he said.

"Seventeen," I said. "Almost eighteen."

"Ah," he said, and sighed as if this was bad news. "What have you done?"

This made it sound as if he was accusing me of something. Then I saw what he meant: I was supposed to bring something called "a portfolio of recent work", which meant pictures, so he could judge me. But I didn't have much work to bring. About the only contact I'd had with art was in high school, in the Art Appreciation class we had to take in Grade Nine, where we listened to the *Moonlight Sonata* and interpreted it with wavy crayon lines, or drew a tulip in a vase. I'd never been to an art gallery, though I'd read an article on Picasso, in *Life* magazine.

Over the past summer, when I'd had a job making beds and cleaning toilets at a resort in Muskoka to earn extra money, I'd bought a small oil-painting set in one of the tourist shops. The names on the little tubes were like passwords: Cobalt Blue, Burnt Umber, Crimson Lake. On my time off I'd take this set out along the shore, and sit with my back against a tree with the pine needles digging into me from underneath, and mosquitoes collecting around me, looking out across the flat sheet-metal water, the varnished mahogany inboards moving

566

across it, little flags at their sterns. In these boats were sometimes other chambermaids, the kind who went to illegal parties in people's rooms to drink rye and ginger ale out of paper cups, and were rumoured to go all the way. There had been tearful confrontations in the laundry room, over the folded sheets.

I did not know how to paint or even what to paint, but I knew I had to begin. After a while I'd painted a picture of a beer bottle minus the label, and a tree shaped like a damaged whisk, and several uncertain, sludge-coloured pictures of rocks, with a violently blue lake in the background. Also a sunset, which came out looking like something you might spill on yourself.

I produced these from the black file folder in which I'd been carrying them. Mr. Hrbik frowned and twiddled his pencil and said nothing. I was discouraged, and also in awe of him, because he had power over me, the power to shut me out. I could see he thought my paintings were bad. They were bad.

"Any more?" he said. "Any drawings?"

Out of desperation I'd included some of my old Biology drawings, in hard lead pencil with coloured shadings. I knew I could draw better than I could paint, I'd been doing it longer. I had nothing to lose and so I brought them out.

"What is it you call this?" he said, holding the top one upside-down.

"It's the inside of a worm," I said.

He did not show surprise. "This?"

"It's a planaria. In stained section."

"And this?"

"It's the reproductive system of a frog. A male frog," I added.

Mr. Hrbik stared up at me with his shining purple eyes. "Why do you want to take this class?" he said.

"It's the only one I can get into," I said. Then I realized how bad that sounded. "It's my only hope. I don't know anyone else who can teach me."

"Why do you want to learn?"

"I don't know," I said.

Mr. Hrbik picked up his pencil and stuck the end of it into the side of his mouth, like a cigarette. Then he took it out again. He twirled his fingers in his hair. "You are a complete amateur," he said. "But sometimes this is better. We can begin from nothing."

He smiled at me, the first time. He had uneven teeth. "We will see what we can make of you," he said.

Mr. Hrbik paces the room. He despairs of us, all of us, including the model, whose surreptitious gum-chewing maddens him. "Keep still," he says to her, tugging at his hair. "Enough gum." The model shoots him a malevolent look and clenches her jaw. He takes her arms and her sulky-faced head and rearranges them, as if she is a mannequin. "We will try again."

He strides up and down among us, looking over our shoulders and grunting to himself, as the room fills with the sandy rasping noise of charcoal on paper. "No, no," he says to a young man. "This is a *body*." He pronounces it "bowdy". "This is not an automobile. You must think of the fingers, touching this flesh, or the running of the hand over. This must be tactile." I try to think the way he wants me to, but recoil. I have no wish to run my fingers over this woman's goose-pimply flesh.

To one of the older women he says, "We do not want pretty. The bowdy is not pretty like a flower. Draw what is there." He stops behind me, and I cringe, waiting. "We are not making a medical textbook," he says to me. "What you have made is a corpse, not a woman." He pronounces it "voman".

I look at what I have drawn, and he is right. I am careful and accurate, but I have drawn a person-shaped bottle, inert and without life. Courage, which has brought me here, flows out of me. I have no talent.

But at the end of the class, when the model has risen stiffly to her feet and has clutched her sheet around her and padded off to dress, when I am putting away my charcoal, Mr. Hrbik comes to stand beside me. I rip out the drawings I have made, intending to crumple them up, but he puts his hand quickly on mine. "Save these," he says.

"Why?" I say. "They're no good."

"You will look at them later," he says, "and you will see how far you have come. You can draw objects very well. But as yet you cannot draw life. God first made the bowdy out of dirt, and after he breathed in the soul. Both are necessary. Dirt and soul." He gives me a brief smile, squeezes my upper arm. "There must be passion."

568

I look at him uncertainly. What he says is a trespass: people don't talk about bodies unless they're discussing illnesses, or about souls except in church, or about passion unless they mean sex. But Mr. Hrbik is a stranger, and can't be expected to know this.

"You are an unfinished voman," he adds in a lower voice, "but here you will be finished." He doesn't know that *finished* means over and done with. He intends to be encouraging.

49

I sit in the darkened auditorium, downstairs at the Royal Ontario Museum, leaning back in the hard seat covered with scratchy plush and breathing in the smell of dust and airlessness and stale upholstery and the sweetish face-powder of the other students. I feel my eyes getting rounder and rounder, the pupils enlarging like an owl's: for an hour I've been looking at slides, yellowy, sometimes unfocused slides of white marble women with flat-topped heads. These heads are holding up stone entablatures, which look very heavy; no wonder the tops of their heads are flat. These marble women are called caryatids, which originally referred to the priestesses of Artemis at Caryae. But they are no longer priestesses; they are now ornamental devices doubling as supporting columns.

There are many slides of columns as well, various kinds of columns from various periods: Doric, Ionic, Corinthian. Doric columns are the strongest and simplest, Corinthian ones are the lightest and most ornate, adorned with rows of acanthus leaves giving rise to graceful volutes and helices. A long pointer, emerging from the area of no light beside the screen, rests on the volutes and helices, indicating which is which. I will need these words later, when I have to regurgitate them for exams, so I attempt to write them in my notebook, bending my head down close to the paper in order to see. I spend a lot of time now writing obscure words in the dark.

I expect things to be better next month, when we'll get away from the Greeks and Romans and into Mediaeval and Renaissance. *Classical* has come to mean, for me, bleached-out and broken. Most of the Greek and Roman things have body parts missing, and the general armlessness, leglessness and noselessness is getting to me, not to mention the snapped-off penises. Also the greyness and whiteness, although I have learned to my surprise that all these marble statues used to be painted, in bright colours, with yellow hair and blue eyes and flesh tones, and sometimes dressed up in real clothing, like dolls.

This class is a survey course. It's supposed to orient us in time, in preparation for later, more specialized courses. It's part of Art and Archaeology at the University of Toronto, which is the only sanctioned pathway that leads anywhere close to art. Also the only thing I can afford: I have won a scholarship to university, which was no more than expected. "You should use the brains God gave you," my father is in the habit of saying, though we both know he thinks this gift was really bestowed by him. If I left university, threw over my scholarship, he would not see his way clear to putting up the cash for anything else.

When I first told my parents I was not going into Biology after all but was going to be an artist, they reacted with alarm. My mother said that was fine if it was what I really wanted to do, but they were worried about how I would make a living. Art was not something that could be depended on, though all right for a hobby, like shellwork or wood carving. But Art and Archaeology was reassuring to them: I could veer off in the archaeology direction and take to digging things up, which was more serious.

At the very least I will come out of it with a degree, and with a degree you can always teach. I have private reservations about this: I think of Miss Creighton, the Art Appreciation teacher at Burnham High, pudgy and beleaguered, who got routinely locked into the supply closet where the paper and paints were kept by some of the greasier and more leathery boys.

One of my mother's friends tells her that art is something you can always do at home, in your spare time.

The other students in Art and Archaeology are all girls but one, just as the professors are all men but one. The student who is not a girl and the professor who is not a man are considered strange; the first has an unfortunate skin condition, the second a nervous stammer. None of the girl students wants to be an artist; instead they want to be teachers of art in high schools, or, in one case, a curator in a gallery. Or else they are vague about their wants, which means they intend to get married before any of these other things becomes necessary.

What they wear is cashmere twin sets, camel's-hair coats, good tweed skirts, pearl button earrings. They wear tidy medium-heel pumps and tailored blouses, or jumpers, or little weskits with matching skirts and buttons. I wear these things too, I try to blend in. Between classes I drink cups of coffee with them and eat doughnuts, sitting in various common rooms and butteries and coffee shops. They discuss clothes, or talk about the boys they are going out with, licking the doughnut sugar off their fingers. Two of them are already pinned. Their eyes during these conversations look dewy, blurred, pulpy, easily hurt, like the eyes of blind baby kittens; but also sly and speculative, and filled with greed and deceit.

I feel ill at ease with them, as if I am here under false pretences. Mr. Hrbik and the tactility of the body do not fit into Art and Archaeology; my botched attempts at drawing naked women would be seen as a waste of time. Art has been accomplished, elsewhere. All that remains to be done with it is the memory-work. The entire Life Drawing class would be viewed as pretentious, and also ludicrous.

But it is my lifeline, my real life. Increasingly I begin to eliminate whatever does not fit in with it, paring myself down. To the first class I made the mistake of wearing a plaid jumper and a white blouse with a Peter Pan collar, but I learn quickly. I switch to what the boys wear, and the other girl: black turtle-necks and jeans. This clothing is not a disguise, like other clothing, but an allegiance, and in time I work up the courage to wear these things even in the daytime, to Art and Archaeology; all except the jeans, which nobody wears. Instead I wear black skirts. I grow out my high school bangs and pin my hair back off my face, hoping to look austere. The girls at university, in their cashmere and pearls, make jokes about arty beatniks and talk to me less.

The two older women in Life Drawing notice my transformation as well. "So who died?" they ask me. Their names are Babs and Marjorie, and they are professionals. They both do portraits, Babs of children, Marjorie of dog owners and their dogs; they are doing Life Drawing as a refresher course, they say. They themselves do not wear black turtlenecks, but smocks, like pregnant women. They call each other "kid" and make raucous comments about their work, and smoke in the washroom, as if

572

it's naughty. Because they are my mother's age, it embarrasses me to be in the same room with them and the naked model both together. At the same time I find them undignified. They remind me less of my mother, however, than of Mrs. Finestein from next door.

Mrs. Finestein has taken to wearing fitted red suits and jaunty pillbox hats trimmed with matching cherries. She catches sight of me in my new get-up and is disappointed. "She looks like an Italian widow," she tells my mother. "She's letting herself go. Such a shame. With a good haircut and a little makeup, she could be stunning." My mother reports this to me, smiling as if it's funny, but I know it's her way of expressing concern. I am verging on grubbiness. *Letting yourself* go is an alarming notion; it is said of older women who become frowzy and fat, and of things that are sold cheap.

Of course there is something to it. I am letting myself go.

50

I'm in a beer parlour, drinking ten-cent draught beer, with the other students from Life Drawing. The grumpy waiter comes, balancing a circular tray on one hand, and plonks down the glasses, which are like ordinary water glasses only full of beer. Froth slops over. I don't like the taste of beer much, but by now I know how to drink it. I even know enough to sprinkle salt on the top, to cut down the foam.

This beer parlour has a dingy-red carpet and cheesy black tables and plastic-upholstered chairs and scant lighting, and reeks of car ashtray; the other beer parlours we drink in are similar. They are called things like Lundy's Lane and The Maple Leaf Tavern, and they're all dark, even in daytime, because they aren't allowed to have windows you can see in through from the street. This is to avoid corrupting minors. I am a minor myself – the legal drinking age is twenty-one – but none of the waiters ever asks for my I.D. Jon says I look so young they think I'd never have the nerve to try it unless I was really over-age.

The beer parlours are divided into two sections. The Men Only sections are where the rowdy drunks and rubby-dubs hang out; they're floored with sawdust, and the smell of spilled beer and old urine and sickness wafts out from them. Sometimes you can hear shouts and the crash of glass from within, and see a man being ejected by two wrestler-sized waiters, his nose bleeding, his arms flailing.

The Ladies and Escorts sections are cleaner and quieter and more genteel, and smell better. If you're a man you can't go into them without a woman, and if you're a woman you can't go into the Men Onlys. This is supposed to keep prostitutes from bothering men, and to keep the male hard-drinkers from bothering women. Colin, who is from England, tells us about pubs, where there are fireplaces and you can play darts and stroll around and even sing, but none of that is allowed in beer parlours. They are for drinking beer, period. If you laugh too much you can be asked to leave.

The Life Drawing students prefer Ladies and Escorts, but they need a woman to get in. This is why they invite me: they even buy me free beers. I am their passport. Sometimes I'm the only one available after class, because Susie, the girl my age, frequently begs off, and Marjorie and Babs go home. They have husbands, and are not taken seriously. The boys call them "lady painters".

"If they're lady painters, what does that make me?" I say.

"A girl painter," Jon says, joking.

Colin, who has manners of a sort, explains: "If you're bad, you're a lady painter. Otherwise you're just a painter." They don't say "artist". Any painter who would call himself an artist is an asshole, as far as they're concerned.

I've given up on going out on dates in the old way: somehow it's no longer a serious thing to do. Also I haven't been asked that often since the advent of the black turtlenecks: boys of the blazer-and-white-shirt variety know what's good for them. In any case they are boys, not men. Their pink cheeks and group sniggering, their good-girl and bad-girl categories, their avid, fumbling attempts to push back the frontiers of garter-belt and brassiere no longer hold my attention. Moustaches of long standing do, and nicotine-stained fingers; experienced wrinkles, heavy eyelids, a world-weary tolerance; men who can blow cigarette smoke out through their mouths and breathe it in through their nostrils without a second thought. I'm not sure where this picture has come from. It seems to have arrived fully formed, out of nowhere.

The Life Drawing students aren't like this, though they don't wear blazers either. With their deliberately shoddy and paint-stained clothing, their newly sprouted facial hair, they are a transitional form. Although they talk, they distrust words; one of them, Reg from Saskatchewan, is so inarticulate he's practically mute, and this wordlessness of his gives him a special status, as if the visual has eaten up part of his brain and left him an idiot saint. Colin the Englishman is distrusted because he talks not too much but too well. Real painters grunt, like Marlon Brando.

But they can make their feelings known. There are shrugs,

mutterings, half-finished sentences, hand movements: jabs, fists, openings of the fingers, jerky sculptings of the air. Sometimes this sign-language is about other people's painting: "It sucks," they say, or very occasionally, "fan-fuckin'-tastic." They don't approve of much. Also they think Toronto is a dump. "Nothing's happening here," is what they say, and many of their conversations revolve around their plans for escape. Paris is finished, and even Colin the Englishman doesn't want to go back to England. "They all paint yellowy-green there," he says. "Yellowy-green, like goose turds. Bloody depressing." Nothing but New York will do. That's where everything is happening, that's where the action is.

When they've had several beers they might talk about women. They refer to their girlfriends, some of whom live with them; these are called "my old lady". Or they make jokes about the models in Life Drawing, who change from night to night. They speak of going to bed with them, as if this depends only on their inclination or lack of it. There are two possible attitudes to this: lip-smacking or nauseated revulsion. "A cow," they say. "A bag." "What a discard." Sometimes they do this with an eye towards me, looking to see how I will take it. When the descriptions of body parts get too detailed – "Cunt like an elephant's arse," "How would you know, eh, screw elephants much?" – they shush one another, as if in front of mothers; as if they haven't decided who I am.

I don't resent any of this. Instead I think I am privileged: I am an exception, to some rule I haven't even identified.

I sit in the dankness and beer fug and cigarette smoke, getting a little dizzy, keeping my mouth shut, my eyes open. I think I can see them clearly because I expect nothing from them. In truth I expect a lot. I expect to be accepted.

There's one thing they do that I don't like: they make fun of Mr. Hrbik. His first name is Josef and they call him Uncle Joe, because he has a moustache and an Eastern European accent and is authoritarian in his opinions. This is unfair, since I know – all of us know by now – that he was shunted around in four different countries, because of the upheavals of the war, and got trapped behind the Iron Curtain and lived on garbage and almost starved, and escaped during the Hungarian Revolution, probably with danger to his life. He has never mentioned the exact circumstances. In fact he has mentioned none of this, in class. Nevertheless it is known.

But it cuts no ice with the boys. Drawing sucks and Mr. Hrbik is a throwback. They call him a D.P., which means *displaced person*, an old insult I remember from high school. It was what you called refugees from Europe, and those who were stupid and uncouth and did not fit in. They mimic his accent, and the way he talks about the body. They only take Life Drawing because it's a requirement. Life Drawing is not what's happening, Action Painting is, and for that you sure as hell don't need to know how to draw. In particular you don't need to know how to draw a cow with no clothes on. Nevertheless they sit in Life Drawing, scratching away with the charcoal and turning out rendering after rendering of breasts and buttocks, thighs and necks, and some nights nothing but feet, as I do, while Mr. Hrbik strides up and down, tugging at his hair and despairing.

The faces of the boys are impassive. To me their contempt is obvious, but Mr. Hrbik doesn't notice. I feel sorry for him, and grateful to him, for letting me into the class. Also I admire him. The war is far enough away now to be romantic, and he has been through it. I wonder if he has any bullet holes in him, or other marks of grace.

Tonight, in the Ladies and Escorts of the Maple Leaf Tavern, it isn't just the boys and me. Susie is here too.

Susie has yellow hair, which I can tell she rolls and sets and then dishevels, and tips ash-blonde at the ends. She wears jeans and black turtlenecks too, but her jeans are skin-tight and she's usually got something around her neck, a silver chain or a medallion. She does her eyes with a heavy black line over the lid like Cleopatra, and black mascara and smoky dark-blue eye-shadow, so her eyes are blue-rimmed, bruise-coloured, as if someone's punched her; and she uses white face-powder and pale pink lipstick, which makes her look ill, or as if she's been up very late every night for weeks. She has full hips, and breasts that are too large for her height, like a rubber squeaky toy that's been pushed down on the top of the head and has bulged out in these places. She has a little breathless voice and a startled little laugh; even her name is like a powder-puff. I think of her as a silly girl who's just fooling around at art school, too dumb to get into university, although I don't make judgments like this about the boys.

"Uncle Joe was raving tonight," says Jon. Jon is tall, with sideburns and big hands. He has a denim jacket with a lot of snap fasteners on it. Besides Colin the Englishman, he's the most articulate one. He uses words like "purity" and "the picture plane", but only among two or three, never with the whole group.

"Oh," says Susie, with a tiny, gaspy laugh, as if the air is going into her instead of out, "that's mean! You shouldn't call him that!"

This irritates me: because she's said something I should have said myself and didn't have the guts to, but also because she's made even this defence come out like a cat rubbing against a leg, an admiring hand on a bicep.

"Pompous old fart," says Colin, to get some of her attention for himself.

Susie turns her big blue-rimmed eyes on him. "He's not old," she says solemnly. "He's only thirty-five." Everyone laughs.

But how does she know? I look at her and wonder. I remember the time I went early to class. The model wasn't there yet, I was in the room by myself, and then Susie walked in with her coat already off, and right after that Mr. Hrbik.

Susie came over to where I was sitting and said, "Don't you just hate the snow!" Ordinarily she didn't talk to me. And I was the one who'd been out in the snow: she looked warm as toast.

51

In the daytime it's February. The grey museum auditorium steams with wet coats and the slush melting from winter boots. There's a lot of coughing.

We've finished the Mediaeval period, with its reliquaries and elongated saints, and are speeding through the Renaissance, hitting the high points. Virgin Marys abound. It's as if one enormous Virgin Mary has had a whole bunch of daughters, most of which look something like her but not entirely. They've shed their gold-leaf haloes, they've lost the elongated, flat-chested look they had in stone and wood, they've filled out more. They ascend to Heaven less frequently. Some are dough-faced and solemn, sitting by fireplaces or in chairs of the period, or by open windows, with roof-work going on in the background; some are anxious-looking, others are milk-fed and pinky-white, with wire-thin haloes and fine gold tendrils of hair escaping from their veils and clear Italian skies in the distance. They bend over the cradle of the Nativity, or they hold Jesus on their laps.

Jesus has trouble looking like a real baby because his arms and legs are too long and spindly. Even when he does look like a baby, he's never newborn. I've seen newborn babies, with their wizened dried-apricot look, and these Jesuses are nothing like them. It's as if they've been born at the age of one year, or else are shrivelled men. There's a lot of red and blue in these pictures, and a lot of breast-feeding.

The dry voice from the darkness concentrates on the formal properties of the compositions, the arrangement of cloth in folds to accentuate circularity, the rendering of textures, the uses of perspective in archways and in the tiles underfoot. We skim over the breast-feeding: the pointer emerging from nowhere never alights on these bared breasts, some of which are an unpleasant pinky-green or veiny, or have a hand pressing the nipple and even real milk. There is some shifting in the seats at this: nobody wants to think about breast-feeding, not the professor and certainly not the girls. Over coffee they shiver: they themselves are fastidious, they will bottle-feed, which is anyway more sanitary.

"The point of the breast-feeding," I say, "is that the Virgin is humble enough to do it. Most women then got their kids wet-nursed by somebody else, if they could afford it." I have read this in a book, dug up from the depths of the stacks, in the library.

"Oh Elaine," they say. "You're such a brain."

"The other point is that Christ came to earth as a mammal," I say. "I wonder what Mary did for diapers? Now that would be a relic: the Sacred Diaper. How come there are no pictures of Christ on the potty? I know there's a piece of the Holy Foreskin around, but what about the Holy Shit?"

"You're awful!"

I grin, I cross my ankle over my knee, I put my elbows on the table. I enjoy pestering the girls in this minor, trivial way: it shows I am not like them.

This is one life, my life of daytimes. My other, my real life, takes place at night.

I've been watching Susie closely, and paying attention to what she does. Susie is not in fact my age, she is two years older and more, she's almost twenty-one. She doesn't live at home with her parents, but in a bachelorette apartment in one of the new high-rise buildings on Avenue Road, north of St. Clair. It is thought her parents pay for this. How else could she afford it? These buildings have elevators in them, and wide foyers with plants, and are called things like "The Monte Carlo". Living in them is a daring and sophisticated thing to do, though scoffed at by the painters: trios of nurses live there. The painters themselves live on Bloor Street or Queen, above hardware stores and places that sell suitcases wholesale, or on side streets where there are immigrants.

Susie stays after class, she turns up early, she hangs around; during the class itself she looks at Mr. Hrbik only sideways, furtively. I meet her coming out of his office and she jumps and smiles at me, then turns and calls, artificially and too loudly, "Thank you, Mr. Hrbik! See you next week!" She gives a little wave, although the door is partly closed and he can't possibly see her: the wave is for me. I now guess what I should have spotted right away: she is having a love affair with Mr. Hrbik. Also, she thinks nobody has figured this out.

In this she is wrong. I overhear Marjorie and Babs discussing it in an oblique way: "Listen, kid, it's one way to pass the course," is what they say. "Wish I could do it just by flipping on my back." "Don't you wish! Those days are long gone, eh?" And they laugh in a comfortable way, as if what is going on is nothing at all, or funny.

I don't think this love affair is at all funny. Love affair is how I think of it; I can't detach the word *affair* from the word *love*, although which of them loves the other is not clear. I decide that it's Mr. Hrbik who loves Susie. Or he doesn't really love her: he's besotted by her. I like this word *besotted*, suggestive as it is of sogginess, soppiness, flies drunk on syrup. Susie herself is incapable of love, she's too shallow. I think of her as the conscious one, the one in control: she's toying with him, in a hard, lacquered way straight out of forties movie posters. Hard as nails, and I even know what colour of nails: Fire and Ice. This, despite her easily hurt look, her ingratiating ways. She throws off guilt like a sweet aroma, and Mr. Hrbik staggers besotted towards his fate.

After she realizes the people in the class know – Babs and Marjorie have a way of conveying their knowledge – Susie becomes bolder. She starts referring to Mr. Hrbik by his first name, and popping him into sentences: Josef thinks, Josef says. She always knows where he is. Sometimes he is in Montreal for the weekend, where they have much better restaurants and decent wines. She's definite about this, although she's never been there. She throws out inside tidbits of information about him: he was married in Hungary, but his wife didn't come with him and now he's divorced. He has two daughters whose pictures he keeps in his wallet. It kills him to be separated from them – "It just *kills* him," she says softly, her eyes misting.

Marjorie and Babs gobble this up. Already she's losing her floozie status with them, she's entering the outskirts of domesticity. They egg her on: "Listen, I don't blame you! I think he's just cute as a button!" "I could eat him up! But that would be robbing the cradle, eh?" In the washroom the two of them sit side by side in separate cubicles, talking over the noise of gushing pee, while I stand in front of the mirror, listening in. "I just hope he knows what he's doing. A nice kid like her." What they mean is that he should marry her. Or perhaps they mean that he should marry her if she gets pregnant. That would be the decent thing.

The painters, on the other hand, turn rough on her. "Jeez, will you shut up about Josef! You'd think the sun shines out of his ass!" But she can't shut up. She resorts to craven, apologetic giggling, which annoys them further, and me also. I've seen that saturated, brimming look before.

I feel that Mr. Hrbik needs protecting, or even rescuing. I don't yet know that a man can be admirable in many ways but a jerk in others. Also I haven't yet learned that chivalry in men is idiocy in women: men can get out of a rescue a lot more easily, once they get into it.

52

I am still living at home, which is humiliating; but why should I pay extra to live in a dormitory, when the university is in the same city? This is my father's view, and the reasonable one. Little does he know it isn't a dormitory I have in mind, but a crumbling walkup above a bakery or cigar store, with streetcars rumbling by outside and the ceilings covered with egg cartons painted black.

But I no longer sleep in my childhood room with the vanilla-coloured light fixture and the window curtains. I've retreated to the cellar, claiming I can study better. Down there in a dim storage room adjacent to the furnace I've set up a realm of ersatz squalor. From the cupboardful of old camping equipment I've excavated one of the army-surplus cots and a lumpy khaki sleeping bag, short-circuiting my mother's plans to move my bed down to the cellar so I can have a proper mattress. On the walls I've taped theatre posters, from local productions – Beckett's *Waiting for Godot*, Sartre's *No Exit* – with deliberate fingerprints and inkstain-black lettering on them, and shadowy figures that look as if they've run in the wash; also several of my careful drawings of feet. My mother thinks the theatre posters are gloomy, and doesn't understand the feet at all: feet should have a body. I narrow my eyes at her, knowing better.

As for my father, he thinks my talent for drawing is impressive, but wasted. It would have been better applied to cross-sections of stems and the cells of algae. For him I am a botanist manqué.

His view of life has darkened since Mr. Banerji returned to India. There is some obscurity around this: it is not talked of much. My mother says he was homesick, and hints at a nervous breakdown, but there was more to it than that. "They wouldn't promote him," says my father. There's a lot behind *they* (not *we*), and *wouldn't* (not *didn't*). "He wasn't properly appreciated." I think I know what this means. My father's view of human nature has always been bleak, but scientists were excluded from it, and now they aren't. He feels betrayed.

My parents' footsteps pace back and forth above my head; the sounds of the household, the Mixmaster and the telephone and the distant news, filter down to me as if in illness. I emerge, blinking, for meals and sit in stupor and demi-silence, picking at my chicken fricassee and mashed potatoes, while my mother comments on my lack of appetite and pallor and my father tells me useful and interesting things as if I am still young. Do I realize that nitrogen fertilizers are destroying fish life by fostering an overgrowth of algae? Have I heard of the new disease which will turn us all into deformed cretins unless the paper companies are forced to stop dumping mercury into the rivers? I do not realize, I have not heard.

"Are you getting enough sleep, dear?" says my mother.

"Yes," I say untruthfully.

My father has noticed an ad in the paper, for an atomic radiation monster-insect movie. "As you know," he says, "those giant grasshoppers could never actually exist. At that size their respiratory systems would collapse."

I do not know.

In April, while I'm studying for exams and before the buds come out, my brother Stephen gets arrested. This happens the way it would.

Stephen has not been here as he should have been to help me out at the dinner table, he hasn't been home all year. Instead he's running around loose in the world. He's studying Astrophysics at a university in California, having finished his undergraduate degree in two years instead of four. Now he is doing graduate work.

I have no clear picture of California, having never been there, but I think of it as sunny, and warm all the time. The sky is a vibrant aniline blue, the trees a preternatural green. I populate it with tanned, handsome men in sunglasses and sports shirts with palm trees on them, and with real palm trees, and with blonde, long-legged women, also tanned, with white convertibles.

Among these sunglassed, fashionable people my brother is an anomaly. After he left his boys' school he reverted to his old, unkempt ways, and goes around in his moccasins and his sweaters with the worn-through elbows. He doesn't get a haircut unless reminded, and who is there to remind him? He walks among the palm trees, oblivious, whistling, his head sheathed in a halo of invisible numbers. What do the Californians make of him? They think he is a kind of tramp.

On this particular day he takes his binoculars and his butterfly book and heads out into the countryside on his second-hand bicycle, to look for Californian butterflies. He comes to a promising field, descends, locks up the bike: he is prudent enough within limits. He heads into the field, which must have tall grass in it and some smallish bushes. He sees two exotic Californian butterflies and starts in pursuit of them, pausing to scan them with his binoculars; but at this distance he can't identify them, and every time he moves forward they take off.

He follows them to the end of the field, where there is a chain-link fence. They fly through it, he climbs over. On the other side there's another field, a flatter one with less vegetation. There's a dirt road crossing it, but he disregards this and follows the butterflies, red and white and black in colour, with an hourglass pattern, something he's never seen before. At the other side of this field there's another fence, a higher one, and he scales this too. Then, when the butterflies have finally stopped, on a low tropical bush with pink flowers, and he's down on one knee focusing his binoculars, three uniformed men in a jeep drive up.

"What're you doing in here?" they say.

"In where?" says my brother. He's impatient with them, they've disturbed the butterflies, which have flown off again.

"Didn't you see the signs?" they say. "The ones that said, *Danger, Keep Out?*"

"No," says my brother. "I was chasing those butterflies."

"Butterflies?" says one. The second one makes a twirling motion beside his ear, with his finger, denoting craziness. "Wacko," he says. The third one says, "You expect us to believe that?"

"What you believe is your own concern," says my brother. Or something of the sort.

"Wise guy," they say, because this is what Americans say in comic books. I add some cigarettes, in the sides of their mouths, a few pistols and other hardware, and boots.

585

It turns out they are the military and this is a military testing zone. They take my brother back to their headquarters and lock him up. Also they confiscate his binoculars. They don't believe he's a graduate student in Astrophysics out chasing butterflies, they think he's a spy, although they can't figure out why he would have been so open about it. Spy novels, as I and the military know but my brother does not, are crawling with spies who pretend to be harmless butterfly fanciers.

Finally they allow him to make a phone call, and his graduate supervisor from the university has to come and bail him out. When he goes back to retrieve his bike, it's been pinched.

I get the bare bones of this from my parents over the beef stew. They don't know whether to be amused or alarmed. From my brother, however, I hear nothing of the sort. Instead I get a letter, written in pencil on a page torn from a loose-leaf notebook. His letters always begin without greeting and end without signature, as if they're part of one single letter, unrolling through time like an endless paper towel.

He's writing this letter, he says, from the top of a tree, where he's watching the football game over the stadium wall – cheaper than buying a ticket – and eating a peanut butter sandwich, cheaper than eating in a restaurant: he doesn't like monetary transactions. There are in fact several grease spots on the paper. He says he can see a bunch of pom-pom-covered capons jumping up and down. These must be the cheerleaders. He's living in a student dormitory with a lot of mucous membranes who do nothing but drool over girls and get pissed on American beer. In his opinion this takes some doing, as the stuff is weaker than shampoo and tastes like it into the bargain. In the mornings he eats pre-frozen re-heated fried eggs, which are square in shape and have ice crystals in the yolks. A triumph of modern technology, he says.

Apart from that he's enjoying himself, as he is hard at work on The Nature Of The Universe. The burning question is: is the universe more like a giant ever-enlarging blimp, or does it pulsate, does it expand and contract? Probably the suspense is killing me, but I will just have to wait a few years till he works out the final answer. TUNE IN FOR

THE NEXT THRILLING INSTALMENT, he writes, in block letters.

I hear you've gone into the picture business, he continues in normal-sized writing. *I used to do that sort of thing when I was younger. I hope you're taking your cod-liver-oil pills and keeping out of trouble.* And that is the end of the letter.

I think of my brother sitting at the top of a tree, in California. He no longer knows who he's writing to, because I have surely changed beyond all recognition. And I no longer know who's writing. I think of him as staying always the same, but of course this can't be true. He must know things by now that he didn't know before, as I do.

Also: if he's eating a sandwich and writing a letter both at the same time, how is he holding on? He seems happy enough, up there in his perch of a sniper. But he should be more careful. What I have always assumed in him to be bravery may be merely an ignorance of consequences. He thinks he is safe, because he is what he says he is. But he's out in the open, and surrounded by strangers.

53

I sit in a French restaurant with Josef, drinking white wine and eating snails. They're the first snails I have ever eaten, this is the first French restaurant I have ever been in. It's the only French restaurant in Toronto, according to Josef. It's called La Chaumière, which Josef says means "thatched cottage". La Chaumière is not however a thatched cottage, but a prosaic, dowdy building like other Toronto buildings. The snails themselves look like large dark pieces of snot; you eat them with a two-pronged fork. I think they are quite good, though rubbery.

Josef says they aren't fresh snails but have come out of a tin. He says this sadly, with resignation, as if it means the end, though the end of what is not clear; this is how he says many things.

It was the way he first said my name, for instance. That was back in May, in the last week of Life Drawing. Each of us was supposed to meet with Mr. Hrbik for an individual evaluation, to discuss our progress during the year. Marjorie and Babs were ahead of me, standing in the hall with take-out coffees. "Hi, kid," they said. Marjorie was telling a story about how a man exposed himself to her in Union Station, where she had gone to meet her daughter on the train from Kingston. Her daughter was my age, and going to Queen's.

"He had on a raincoat, would you believe," said Marjorie.

"Oh God," said Babs.

"So I looked him in the eye – the *eye* – and I said, 'Can't you do any better than that?' I mean, talk about weenies. No wonder the poor boob runs around in train stations trying to get somebody to look at it!"

"And?"

"Listen, what goes up must come down, eh?"

They snorted, spewing droplets of coffee, coughing out smoke.

As usual I found them slightly disreputable: making jokes about things that were no joking matter.

Susie came out of Mr. Hrbik's office. "Hi, you guys," she said, trying for cheer. Her eyeshadow was smudged, her eyes pinkish. I'd been reading modern French novels, and William Faulkner as well. I knew what love was supposed to be: obsession, with undertones of nausea. Susie was the sort of girl who would go in for this kind of love. She would be abject, she would cling and grovel. She would lie on the floor, moaning, hanging onto Mr. Hrbik's legs, her hair falling like blonde seaweed over the black leather of his shoes (he would have his shoes on, being about to stalk out of the door). From this angle, Mr. Hrbik was cut off at the knees and Susie's face was invisible. She would be squashed by passion, obliterated.

I was not sorry for her, however. I was a little envious.

"Poor bunny rabbit," Babs said behind her retreating back.

"Europeans," said Marjorie. "I don't believe for a minute he was ever divorced."

"Listen, maybe he was never even *married*."

"What about those kids of his?"

"Most likely his nieces or something."

I scowled at them. Their voices were way too loud; Mr. Hrbik would hear them.

After they had gone it was my turn. I went in, and stood while Mr. Hrbik sat, going through my portfolio, which was spread out on his desk. I thought it was this that was making me nervous.

He flipped through the pages, hands, heads, bottoms, in silence, chewing his pencil. "This is nice," he said at last. "You have made progress. This is more relaxed, this line here."

"Where?" I said, leaning my hand on the desk, bending forward. He turned his head to the side, towards me, and there were his eyes. They were not purple after all but dark brown.

"Elaine, Elaine," he said sadly. He put his hand over mine. Cold shot up my arm, into my stomach; I stood there frozen, revealed to myself. Is this what I'd been angling for, with my notions of rescue?

He shook his head, as if he'd given up or had no choice, then drew me down, between his knees. He didn't even stand up. So I was on the floor, on my knees, with my head tilted back, his hands caressing the back of my neck. I'd never been kissed that way before. It was like a perfume ad: foreign and dangerous and potentially degrading. I could get up and run for it, but if I stayed put, even for one more minute, there would be no more groping in car seats or movie theatres, no skirmishes over brassiere hooks. No nonsense, no fooling around.

We went to Josef's apartment in a taxi. In the taxi Josef sat quite far apart from me, although he kept his hand on my knee. I was not used to taxis then, and thought the driver was looking at us in the rear-view mirror.

Josef's apartment was on Hazelton Avenue, which was not quite a slum although close to it. The houses there are old, close together, with frumpy little front gardens and pointed roofs and mouldering wooden scrollwork around the porches. There were cars parked bumper to bumper along the sidewalk. Most of the houses were in pairs, attached together down one side. It was in one of these crumbling, pointy-roofed twin houses that Josef lived. He had the second floor.

A fat older man in shirtsleeves and suspenders was rocking on the porch of the house next to Josef's. He stared as Josef paid the taxi, then as we came up the front walk. "Nice day," he said.

"Isn't it?" I said. Josef paid no attention. He put his hand lightly on the back of my neck as we went up the narrow inner stairs. Everywhere he touched me felt heavy.

His apartment was three rooms, a front room, a middle room with a kitchenette, and a back room. The rooms were small, and there was little furniture. It was as if he'd just moved in, or was moving out. His bedroom was painted mauve. On the walls were several prints, which were of elongated figures, murkily coloured. There was nothing else in this room but a mattress on the floor, covered with a Mexican blanket. I looked at it, and thought I was seeing adult life.

Josef kissed me, standing up this time, but I felt awkward. I was afraid someone would see in through the window. I was afraid he would ask me to take off my own clothes, that he would then turn me this way and that, looking at me from a distance. I didn't like being looked at from behind: it was a view over which I had no control. But if he asked this I would have to do it, because any hesitation on my part would place me beneath consideration.

He lay down on the mattress, and looked up as if waiting. After a moment I lay down beside him and he kissed me again, gently undoing my buttons. The buttons were on an outsize cotton shirt, which was what had replaced the turtlenecks now that it was warm. I put my arms around him, and thought: he was in the war.

"What about Susie?" I said. As soon as I said it I realized it was a high-school question.

"Susie?" Josef asked, as if trying to remember her name. His mouth was against my ear; the name was like a regretful sigh.

The Mexican blanket was scratchy, which did not bother me: sex was supposed to be unpleasant the first time. I expected the smell of rubber too, and the pain; but there was not as much pain, and not nearly as much blood as everyone said.

Josef was not expecting the pain. "This is hurting you?" he said at one point. "No," I said, flinching, and he did not stop. He was not expecting the blood either. He would have to get his blanket cleaned, but he didn't mention this. He was considerate, and stroked my thigh.

Josef has gone on all summer. Sometimes he takes me to restaurants, with checked tablecloths and candles stuck in Chianti bottles; sometimes to foreign films about Swedes and Japanese, in small uncrowded theatres. But we always end up back at his apartment, under or on top of the Mexican blanket. His lovemaking is unpredictable; sometimes he is avid, sometimes routine, sometimes absent-minded, as if doodling. It's partly the unpredictability that keeps me hooked. This and his need, which seems to me at times helpless and beyond his control.

"Don't leave me," he says, running his hands over me; always before, not after. "I couldn't bear it." This is an old-fashioned thing to say, and in another man I would find it comical, but not in Josef. I am in love with his need. Only to think of it makes me feel suffused, inert, like the flesh of a watermelon. For this reason I've cancelled my plans to return to the Muskoka resort, to work as I did last summer. Instead I've taken a job at the Swiss Chalet on Bloor Street. This is a place that serves nothing but chicken,

591

"broasted", as it says on the sign. Chicken and dipping sauce, and coleslaw and white buns, and one flavour of ice cream: Burgundy Cherry, which is a striking shade of purple. I wear a uniform with my name stitched on the pocket, as in high-school gym class.

Josef sometimes picks me up there, after work. "You smell of chicken," he murmurs in the taxi, his face against my neck. I've lost all modesty in taxis; I lean against him, his hand around me, under my arm, on my breast, or I lie down along the seat, head in his lap.

Also I have moved out of home. On the nights when I'm with him, Josef wants me to stay all night. He wants to wake up with me asleep beside him, start to make love to me without waking me up. I've told my parents it's only for the summer, so I can be closer to the Swiss Chalet. They think it's a waste of money. They are racketing around up north somewhere and I would have the house to myself; but my idea of myself and my parents' idea of me no longer belong in the same place.

If I'd gone to Muskoka I wouldn't be living at home this summer either, but not living at home in the same city is different. Now I live with two of the other Swiss Chalet girls, student workers like myself, in a corridor-shaped apartment on Harbord Street. The bathroom is festooned with stockings and underpants; hair-rollers perch on the kitchen counter like bristly caterpillars, dishes cake in the sink.

I see Josef twice a week, and know enough not to try calling him or seeing him at other times. Either he won't be there or he will be with Susie, because he hasn't stopped seeing her, not at all. But we are not to tell her about me; we are to keep it secret. "She would be so terribly hurt," he says. It's the last one in line who must bear the burden of knowing: if anyone is to be hurt it will have to be me. But I feel entrusted by him: we are in this together, this protecting of Susie. It's for her good. In this there is the satisfaction of all secrets: I know something she doesn't.

She's found out somehow that I'm working at the Swiss Chalet – probably it's Josef who's told her, casually, skirting discovery, probably he finds it exciting to think of us together – and once in a while she comes in for a cup of coffee, late in the afternoon when there's nobody much around. She's gained a little weight, and the flesh of her cheeks is puffy. I can see what she'll look like in fifteen years, if she isn't careful.

I am nicer to her than I ever have been. Also I'm a little wary of her. If she finds out, will she lose whatever grip on herself is left and go for me with a steak knife?

She wants to talk. She wants us to get together sometime. She still says "Josef and me." She looks forlorn.

Josef talks to me about Susie as if discussing a problem child. "She wants to get married," he says. He implies she is being unreasonable, but that to deny her this thing, this too-expensive toy, wounds him deeply just the same. I have no wish to put myself in the same category: irrational, petulant. I don't want to marry Josef, or anyone else. I have come to think of marriage as dishonourable, a crass tradeoff rather than a free gift. And even the idea of marriage would diminish Josef, spoil him; this is not his place in the scheme of things. His place is to be a lover, with his secrecy and his almost-empty rooms, and his baleful memories and bad dreams. Anyway, I've put myself beyond marriage. I can see it back there, innocent and beribboned, like a child's doll: irretrievable. Instead of marriage I will be dedicated to my painting. I will end up with my hair dyed, wearing outlandish clothes and heavy, foreign silver jewellery. I will travel a lot. Possibly I will drink.

(There is of course the spectre of pregnancy. You can't get a diaphragm unless you're married, rubbers are sold under the counter and only to men. There are those girls who went too far in back seats and got knocked up and dropped out of high school, or had strange, never-explained accidents. There are jocular terms for it: up the spout, bun in the oven. But such washroom notions have nothing to do with Josef and his experienced mauve bedroom. They also have nothing to do with me, wrapped as I am in dense minor-key enchantment. But I make little checkmarks on my pocket calendar, all the same.)

On the days when I have time off, when I'm not seeing Josef, I try to paint. Sometimes I draw with coloured pencils. What I draw is the furniture in the apartment: the overstuffed sofa from the Sally Ann strewn with shed clothing, the bulbous lamp lent by a roommate's mother, the kitchen stool. More often I don't have the energy, and end up reading murder mysteries in the bathtub.

Josef won't tell me about the war, or about how he got out of Hungary during the revolution. He says these things are too disturbing for him and he wants only to forget them. He says there are many ways to die and some are less pleasant than others. He says I am lucky I will never have to know things like this. "This country has no heroes," he says. "You should keep it that way." He tells me I am untouched. This is the way he wants me, he says. When he says these things he runs his hands over my skin as if he's erasing me, rubbing me smooth.

But he tells me his dreams. He's very interested in these dreams, and they are in fact like no dreams I can remember hearing about. There are red velvet curtains in them, red velvet sofas, red velvet rooms. There are white silk ropes in them, with tassels on the ends; there's a lot of attention to fabrics. There are decaying teacups.

He dreams of a woman wrapped up in cellophane, even over her face, and of another walking along the railing of a balcony dressed in a white shroud, and of another lying face down in the bathtub. When he tells me these dreams, he doesn't look at me exactly; it's as if he's looking at a point several inches inside my head. I don't know how to respond, so I smile weakly. I'm a little jealous of these women in his dreams: none of them are me. Josef sighs and pats my hand. "You are so young," he says.

There is nothing that can be said in reply to this, although I don't feel young. Right now I feel ancient, and overworked and too warm. The constant odour of broasting chicken is taking away my appetite. It's late July, the Toronto humidity hangs like swamp gas over the city, and the air-conditioning at the Swiss Chalet broke down today. There were complaints. Someone upset a platter of quarters with buns and dipping sauce onto the kitchen floor, causing skids. The chef called me a stupid bitch.

"I have no country," says Josef mournfully. He touches my cheek tenderly, gazing into my eyes. "You are my country now."

I eat another tinned, inauthentic snail. It strikes me with no warning that I am miserable.

54

Cordelia has run away from home. This is not how she puts it.

She's tracked me down through my mother. I meet her for coffee, during my afternoon break, not at the Swiss Chalet. I could get the coffee free, but by now I want to be out of there as much as possible, away from the sickly back-room odour of raw poultry, the rows of naked chickens like dead babies, the mushed-up, lukewarm, dog-dish debris of customers' meals. So instead we are in Murray's, down the street in the Park Plaza Hotel. It's medium clean, and although there's no air-conditioning there are ceiling fans. At least here I don't know what goes on in the kitchen.

Cordelia is thinner now, almost gaunt. The cheekbones of her long face are visible, her grey-green eyes are big in her face. Around each one of them is drawn a green line. She is tanned, her lips an understated orangey-pink. Her arms are angular, her neck elegant; her hair is pulled back like a ballerina's. She's wearing black stockings although it's summer, and sandals, although the sandals are not dainty women's summer sandals, but thick-soled and artistic, with primitive peasant buckles. Also a scoop-neck short-sleeved black jersey top that shows off her breasts, a full cotton skirt of a dull blue-green with abstract black swirls and squares on it, a wide black belt. She has on two heavy rings, one with a turquoise, and chunky square earrings, and a silver bracelet: Mexican silver. You would not say beautiful about her, but you would stare, as I am doing: for the first time in her life she looks distinguished.

We greeted each other on sight with the outstretched hands, the demi-hugs, the cries of surprise and delight that women are supposed to make who haven't seen each other for a while. Now I slump in Murray's, drinking wishy-washy coffee, while Cordelia talks and I wonder why I have agreed to this. I am at a disadvantage: I'm in my crumpled, gravy-spotted Swiss Chalet uniform, my armpits are sweaty, my feet hurt, my hair in this humidity is unruly and dank and curling like singed wool. There are dark circles under my eyes, because last night was one of Josef's nights.

Cordelia on the other hand is showing herself off to me. She wants me to see what has become of her, since her days of sloth and overeating and failure. She has reinvented herself. She's cool as a cucumber, and brimming with casual news.

What she is doing is working at the Stratford Shakespearean Festival. She is a bit-part player. "*Very* minor things," she says, waving her bracelet and rings dismissively, which means less minor than she says. "You know. Spear-carrying, though of course I don't carry spears." She laughs, and lights a cigarette. I wonder if Cordelia has ever eaten snails, decide she is most likely on familiar terms with them; a depressing thought.

The Stratford Shakespearean Festival is quite famous by now. It was started several years ago in the town of Stratford, which has an Avon River running through it, and swans of both colours. I have read all this in magazines. People go there on the train, in buses, or in cars with picnic baskets; sometimes they stay all weekend and see three or four Shakespeare plays, one after the other. At first this festival was held in a big tent, like a circus. But now there is a real building, a strange, modern building, circular in shape. "So you have to project to three sides. It's such a strain on the voice," Cordelia says with a deprecating smile, as if she is projecting and straining her voice all in the line of work. She is like someone making herself up as she goes along. She's improvising.

"What do your parents think?" I say. This has been on my own mind lately: what parents think.

Her face closes down for a moment. "They're pleased I'm doing something," she says.

"What about Perdie and Mirrie?"

"You know Perdie," she says tightly. "Always the little putdowns. But that's enough about me. What do *you* think of me?" This is an old joke of hers, and I laugh. "Seriously, what are you up to these days?" It's the tone I remember: polite but not too interested. "Since the last time I saw you."

I remember this last time with guilt. "Oh, nothing much," I say. "Going to school. You know." Right now it does look like nothing much. What have I really done all year? A smattering of art history, messing around with charcoal. There's nothing to show. There's Josef, but he's not exactly an accomplishment and I decide not to mention him.

"School!" says Cordelia. "Was I glad to see the end of *school*. God, what boredom." Stratford is only on in the summers, though. She will have to think of something else for the winter. Maybe the Earle Grey Players, going around to high schools. Maybe she will be ready for that.

She got the job at Stratford with the help of one of the Earle Grey cousins, who remembered her from her bedsheet days at Burnham. "People who know people," she says. She is one of Prospero's attendant spirits in *The Tempest*, and has to wear a body stocking, with a gauzy costume over the top, sprinkled with dried leaves and spangles. "Obscene," she says. She's also a mariner in the first scene; she can get away with this because of her height. She's a court lady in *Richard III*, and she's the chief nun in *Measure for Measure*. In this one she actually speaks some lines. She recites for me, in a honey-coloured Englishy voice:

> Then, if you speak, you must not show your face,
> Or, if you show your face, you must not speak.

"At rehearsal I kept getting mixed up," she says. She counts on her fingers. "Speak, hide face, show face, shut up." She puts her hands together in an attitude of prayer, bows forward, lowering her head. Then she gets up and does a full court curtsy out of *Richard III*, with the women shoppers having tea in Murray's gawking at her. "What I'd like to do next year is the First Witch in 'The Tartans.' 'When shall we three meet again, in thunder, lightning, or in rain?' The Old Man says I might be ready for it. He thinks it would be brilliant to have a *young* First Witch."

The Old Man, it turns out, is Tyrone Guthrie the director, from England and so famous I can't pretend not to have heard of him. "That's great," I say.

"Remember 'The Tartans' at Burnham? Remember that cabbage?" she says. "I was so humiliated."

I don't want to remember. The past has become discontinuous, like stones skipped across water, like postcards: I catch an image of myself, a dark blank, an image, a blank. Did I ever wear bat-wing sleeves and velveteen slippers, did I wear dresses like tinted marshmallows to formal dances, shuffle around the floor with some stranger's groin digging into mine? The dried corsages were thrown out long ago, the diplomas and class pins and photos must be down in my mother's cellar, in the steamer trunk along with the tarnishing silver. I glimpse those photos, rows and rows of lipsticked, spit-curled children. I would never smile, for those pictures. I would gaze stony-faced into the distance, beyond such adolescent diversions.

I remember my mean mouth, I remember how wise I thought I was. But I was not wise then. Now I am wise.

"Remember how we used to pinch things?" says Cordelia. "That was the only thing I really liked about that whole time."

"Why?" I say. I had not liked it much. I was always afraid of getting caught.

"It was something I could have," she says, and I'm not sure what she means.

Cordelia takes her sunglasses out of her shoulder bag and puts them on. There I am in her mirror eyes, in duplicate and monochrome, and a great deal smaller than life-size.

Cordelia gets me a free ticket to Stratford, so I can see her in action. I go on the bus. It's a matinee: I can get there, see the show, then take the bus back in time for my evening shift at the Swiss Chalet. The play is *The Tempest*. I watch for Cordelia, and when Prospero's attendants come on, with music and jittery lighting effects, I peer hard, trying to see which one she is, behind the disguise of costume. But I can't tell.

55

Josef is rearranging me. "You should wear your hair loose," he says, unpinning it from its ramshackle bun, running his hands through it to make it fluff out. "You look like a marvellous gypsy." He presses his mouth to my collarbone, untucks the bedsheet he's draped me in.

I stand still and let him do this. I let him do what he likes. It's August and too hot to move. Haze hangs over the city like wet smoke; it covers my skin with an oily film, seeps into my flesh. I move through the days like a zombie, going from one hour to the next without direction. I've stopped drawing the furniture at the apartment; I fill the bathtub with cool water and get into it, but I no longer read in there. Soon it will be time to go back to school. I can hardly think about it.

"You should wear purple dresses," says Josef. "It would be an improvement." He places me against the twilight of the window, turns me, stands back a little, running his hand up and down my side. I no longer care whether anyone can see in. I feel my knees begin to give, my mouth loosen. In our time together he does not pace or tug his hair, he moves slowly, gently, with great deliberation.

Josef takes me to the Park Plaza Hotel Roof Garden, in my new purple dress. It has a tight bodice, a low neck, a full skirt; it brushes against my bare legs as I walk. My hair is loose, and damp. I think it looks like a mop. But I catch a glimpse of myself, without expecting it, in the smoked-mirror wall of the elevator as we go up, and I see for an instant what Josef sees: a slim woman with cloudy hair, pensive eyes in a thin white face. I recognize the style: late nineteenth century. Pre-Raphaelite. I should be holding a poppy.

We sit on the outside patio, drinking Manhattans and looking over the stone balustrade. Josef has recently discovered a taste for Manhattans. This is one of the tallest buildings around. Below us Toronto festers in the evening heat, the trees spreading like worn moss, the lake zinc in the distance.

Josef tells me he once shot a man in the head; what disturbed him was how easy it was to do it. He says he hates the Life Drawing class, he will not go on with it for ever, cooped up in this provincial deadwater teaching the rudiments to morons. "I come from a country that no longer exists," he says, "and you come from a country that does not yet exist." Once I would have found this profound. Now I wonder what he means.

As for Toronto, he says, it has no gaiety or soul. In any case, painting itself is a hangover from the European past. "It is no longer important," he says, waving it away with one hand. He wants to be in films, he wants to direct, in the United States. He will go there as soon as it can be arranged. He has good connections. There's a whole network of Hungarians, for instance. Hungarians, Poles, Czechoslovakians. There is more opportunity in films down there, to say the least, since the only films made in this country are short ones that come on before real movies, about leaves spiralling downwards into pools or flowers opening in time-lapse photography, to flute music. The other people he knows are doing well in the United States. They will get him in.

I hold Josef's hand. His lovemaking these days is ruminative, as if he is thinking of something else. I discover I am somewhat drunk; also that I am afraid of heights. I have never been this high up in the air before. I think of standing close to the stone balustrade, toppling slowly over. From here you can see the United States, a thin fuzz on the horizon. Josef says nothing about me going there with him. I ask nothing.

Instead he says, "You are very silent." He touches my cheek. "Mysterious." I do not feel mysterious, but vacant.

"Would you do anything for me?" he says, gazing into my eyes. I sway towards him, far away from the earth. *Yes* would be so easy.

"No," I say. This is a surprise to me. I don't know where it has come from, this unexpected and stubborn truthfulness. It sounds rude.

"I did not think so," he says sadly.

*   *   *

600

Jon appears one afternoon in the Swiss Chalet. I don't recognize him at first because I don't look at him. I'm wiping off the table with a dish-rag, every movement an effort, my arm heavy with lethargy. Last night I was with Josef, but tonight I won't be because it's not my night, it's Susie's night.

These days Josef rarely mentions Susie. When he does, it's with nostalgia, as if she's already a thing of the past, or beautifully dead, like someone in a poem. But this may be only his way of speaking. They may spend prosaic domestic evenings together, him reading the paper while she serves up a casserole. Despite his claim that I am a secret, they may discuss me the way Josef and I used to discuss Susie. This is not a comfortable thought.

I prefer to think of Susie as a woman shut inside a tower, up there in The Monte Carlo on Avenue Road, gazing out the window over the top of her painted sheet-metal balcony, weeping feebly, waiting for Josef to appear. I can't imagine her having any other life apart from that. I can't see her washing out her underpants, for instance, and wringing them in a towel, hanging them on the bathroom towel-rack, as I do. I can't imagine her eating. She is limp, without will, made spineless by love; as I am.

"Long time no see," says Jon. He leaps into focus beyond my wiping arm, grinning at me, his teeth white in a face more tanned than I remember. He's leaning on the table I'm wiping, wearing a grey T-shirt, old jeans cut off above the knees, running shoes with no socks. He looks healthier than he did in the winter. I've never seen him in the daytime before.

I'm conscious of my stained uniform: do I smell of underarm sweat, of chicken fat? "How did you get in here?" I say.

"Walked," he says. "How about a coffee?"

He has a summer job, with the Works Department, filling in pot-holes in the roads, tarring over the cracks made by frost-heave; he does have a faint tarry smell about him. He's not what you would call clean. "How about a beer, later?" he says. This is a thing he's said often before: he wants a passport to the Ladies and Escorts, as usual. I'm not doing anything, so I say, "Why not? But I'll have to change."

After work I take the precaution of a shower and put on my purple dress. I meet him at the Maple Leaf and we go into the

Ladies and Escorts. We sit there in the gloom, which is at least cool, and drink draught beer. It's awkward with just him: before there was always a group of them. Jon asks me what I've been up to and I say nothing much. He asks me if I've seen Uncle Joe around anywhere, and I say no.

"Probably he's disappeared into Susie's knickers," he says. "The lucky shit." He's still treating me like an honorary boy, still saying crude things about women. I'm surprised at the word "knickers". He must have picked it up from Colin the Englishman. I wonder if he knows about me as well, whether he's making remarks about my knickers behind my back. But how could he?

He says the Works Department is good money, but he doesn't let on to the other guys that he's a painter, especially not to the old regulars. "They might think I'm a fruit or something," he says.

I drink more draught beer than I should, and then the lights flicker on and off and it's closing time. We walk out onto the hot night summer street, and I don't want to go home by myself.

"Can you get back all right?" says Jon. I say nothing. "Come on, I'll walk you," he says. He puts his hand on my shoulder and I smell his smell of tar and outdoors dust and sunny skin, and I begin to cry. I stand in the street, with the drunks staggering out of the Men Only, my hands pressed to my mouth, crying and feeling stupid.

Jon is startled. "Hey, pal," he says, patting me awkwardly. "What's wrong?"

"Nothing," I say. Being called *pal* makes me cry even more. I feel like a wet sock; I feel ugly. I hope he will think I've had too much to drink.

He puts an arm around me, gives a squeeze. "Come on," he says. "We'll go for coffee."

I stop crying as we walk along the street. We walk to a door beside a wholesale suitcase store, he takes out a key, and we go up the stairs in the dark. Inside the upstairs door he kisses me, with his tarry, beery mouth. There are no lights on. I put my arms around his waist and hold on as if I'm sinking into mud, and he lifts me like that and carries me through the dark room, bumping into the walls and furniture, and we fall together onto the floor.

XI
Falling Women

56

I continue east along Queen Street, still a little dizzy from the wine at lunch. Tipsy was once the word. Alcohol's a depressant, it will let me down later, but right now I'm jaunty, I hum to myself, mouth slightly open.

Right here there's a group of statues, coppery-green, with black smears running down them like metal blood: a seated woman, holding a sceptre, with three young soldiers marching forward grouped around her, their legs wound with bandage-like puttees, defending the Empire, their faces earnest, doomed, frozen into time. Above them on a stone tablet stands another woman, this time with angel wings: Victory or Death, or maybe both. This monument is in honour of the South African War, ninety years ago, more or less. I wonder if anyone remembers that war, or if anyone in all these cars barging forward ever even looks.

I head north on University Avenue, past the sterility of hospitals, along the old route of the Santa Claus Parade. The Zoology Building has been torn down, it must have been years ago. The window-ledge where I once watched the soggy fairies and chilblained snowflakes, breathing in the smell of snakes and antiseptic and mice, is now empty air. Who else remembers where it used to be?

There are fountains up and down this roadway now, and squared-off beds of flowers, and new, peculiar statues. I follow the curve around the Parliament Building with its form of a squatting Victorian dowager, darkish pink, skirts huffed out, stolid. The flag I could never draw, demoted to the flag of a province, flies before it, bright scarlet, with the Union Jack in the top corner and all those impossible beavers and leaves encrested lower down. The new national flag flutters there as well, two red bands and a red maple leaf rampant on white, looking like a trademark for margarine of the cheaper variety, or an owl-kill in snow. I still think of this flag as new, although they changed it long ago.

*   *   *

I cross the street, cut in behind a small church, left stranded here when they redeveloped. Sunday's sermon is announced on a billboard identical to the kind for supermarket specials: *Believing Is Seeing*. A vertical wave of plate glass breaks against it. Behind the polished façades, bouquets of teased cloth, buffed leather, cunning silver trinkets. Pasta to die for. Theology has changed, over the years: *just deserts* used to be what everyone could expect to get, in the end. Now it's a restaurant specializing in cakes. All they had to do was abolish guilt, and add an s.

I turn a corner, onto a side street, a double row of expensive boutiques: hand-knits and French maternity outfits and ribbon-covered soaps, imported tobaccos, opulent restaurants where the wineglasses are thin-stemmed and they sell you location and overhead. The designer jeans emporium, the Venetian paper knick-knack shop, the stocking boutique with its kicking neon leg.

These houses used to be semi-hovels; Josef's old territory, where beer-saturated fat men sat on the front porches, sweating in the August heat, while their children screamed and their dogs lay panting with frayed ropes tethering them to the fence, and paint peeled from their woodwork and the dispirited cat-pee marigolds wilted along their cracked walkways. A few thousand dollars in the right place then and you'd be a millionaire today, but who could have guessed? Not me, going up the narrow stairs to Josef's second floor, with my breath quickening and his hand weighing on the small of my back, in the dying light of summer evenings: slow-paced, forbidden, sadly delicious.

I know more things about Josef now than I did then. I know them because I'm older. I know about his melancholy, his ambition, his desperation, the corners of emptiness in him that needed to be filled. I know the dangers.

What for instance was he doing with two women fifteen years younger than himself? If one of my daughters fell in love with such a man, I'd be frantic. It would be like the time Sarah and her best friend came rushing home from school, to tell me they'd seen their first flasher in the park. "Mummy, mummy, a man had his pants down!"

To me it meant fear, and a ferocious anger. *Touch them*

606

and I'll kill you. But to them it was merely noteworthy, and hilarious.

Or the first time I saw my own kitchen, after I had Sarah. I brought her home from the hospital and thought: *All those knives, All those sharp things and hot things.* All I could see was what might hurt her.

Maybe one of my daughters has a man like Josef, or a man like Jon, hidden away in her life, in secret. Who knows what grubby or elderly boys they are bending to their own uses, or to counterpoint me? All the while protecting me from themselves, because they know I would be horrified.

I see words on the front pages of newspapers that never used to be said out loud, much less printed – *sexual intercourse, abortion, incest* – and I want to hide their eyes, even though they are grown up, or what passes for it. Because I am a mother, I am capable of being shocked; as I never was when I was not one.

I should get a little present for each of them, as I always did when they were younger and I went away. Once I knew by instinct what they would like. I don't any more. It's hard for me to remember exactly what age they've reached. I used to resent it when my mother would forget I was an adult, but I'm approaching the maundering phase myself, digging out the yellowing baby pictures, mooning over locks of hair.

I'm squinting into a window at some Italian silk scarves, wonderful indeterminate colours, grey-blue, sea-green, when I feel a touch on my arm, a chilly jump of the heart.

"Cordelia," I say, turning.

But it's not Cordelia. It's nobody I know. It's a woman, a girl really, middle-eastern of some kind: a long full skirt to above the ankles, printed cotton, Canadian gum-soled boots incongruous beneath; a short jacket buttoned up, a kerchief folded straight across the forehead with a pleat at either side, like a wimple. The hand that touches me is lumpy in its northern mitten, the skin of the wrist between mitten and jacket cuff brownish, like coffee with double cream. The eyes are large, as in painted waifs.

"Please," she says. "They are killing many people." She doesn't say where. It could be a lot of places, or in between places; homelessness is a nationality now. Somehow the war never ended after all, it just broke up into pieces and got scattered, it gets in everywhere, you can't shut it out. Killing is endless now, it's an industry, there's money in it, and the good side and the bad side are pretty hard to tell apart.

"Yes," I say. This is the war that killed Stephen.

"Some are here. They have no, they have nothing. They would be killed . . ."

"Yes," I say. "I see." This is what I get for walking. In a car you're more insulated. And how do I know she is what she purports to be? She could be a dope addict. In the soft-touch market, scams abound.

"I have with me a family of four. Two children. They are with me, it is my, it is my own responsibility." She stumbles a little on "responsibility", but she gets it out. She's shy, she doesn't like what she's doing, this grabbing people on the street.

"Yes?"

"I am doing it." We look at each other. She is doing it. "Twenty-five dollars can feed a family of four for a month."

What can they be eating? Stale bread, cast-off doughnuts? Does she mean a week? If she can believe this, she deserves my money. I take off my glove, raid my purse, rustle bills, pink ones, blue ones, purple. It's obscene to have such power; also to feel so powerless. Probably she hates me.

"Here," I say.

She nods. She's not grateful, merely confirmed, in her opinion of me, or of herself. She takes off her bulky-knit mitten to receive the cash. I look at our hands, her smooth one, the nails pale moons, mine with its tattered cuticles, its skin of incipient toad. She tucks the bills in between the buttons of her jacket. She must have a purse in there, out of the reach of snatching. Then she slips on the mitt, dark red with a pink wool embroidered leaf.

"God will bless you," she says. She doesn't say Allah. Allah I might believe.

I walk away from her, pulling on my glove. Every day there's more of it, more of that silent wailing, those starving outstretched hands, *need need, help help*, there's no end.

608

57

In September I leave the Swiss Chalet and return to school. I also return to the cellar of my parents' house, because I can't afford not to. Both of these locations are hazardous: my life is now multiple, and I am in fragments. But I'm no longer lethargic. On the contrary I am alert, I crackle with adrenalin, despite the late-summer heat. It's treachery that does this for me, keeping on top of my own deceptions: I need to hide Josef from my parents, and Jon from all of them. I sneak around, heart in my mouth, dreading revelations; I avoid late nights, I evade and tiptoe. Strangely enough, this does not make me feel more insecure, but safer.

Two men are better than one, or at least they make me feel better. I am in love with both, I tell myself, and having two means that I don't have to make up my mind about either of them.

Josef offers me what he has always offered, plus fear. He tells me, casually, in the same way he told me about shooting a man in the head, that in most countries except this one a woman belongs to a man: if a man finds his woman with another man, he kills both of them and everyone excuses him. He says nothing about what a woman does, in the case of another woman. He tells me this while running his hand up my arm, over my shoulder, lightly across the neck, and I wonder what he suspects. He has taken to demanding speech from me; or else he puts his hand over my mouth. I close my eyes and feel him as a source of power, nebulous and shifting. I suspect there would be something silly about him, if I could see him objectively. But I can't.

As for Jon, I know what he offers. He offers escape, running away from the grownups. He offers fun, and mess. He offers mischief.

I consider telling him about Josef, to see what would happen.

609

But the danger in this would be of a different order. He would laugh at me for sleeping with Josef, whom he considers ridiculous as well as old. He would not understand how I could take such a man seriously, he would not understand the compulsion. He would think less of me.

Jon's apartment over the luggage store is long and narrow and smells of acrylic and used socks, and has only two rooms plus the bathroom. The bathroom is purple, with red footprints painted up the wall, across the ceiling and down the opposite wall. The front room is painted stark white, the other one – the bedroom – is glossy black. Jon says this is to get back at the landlord, who is a prick. "When I move out, it'll take him fifteen coats to cover that up," he says.

Sometimes Jon lives in this apartment by himself; sometimes another person will be there, sometimes two, camping out on the floor in sleeping bags. These are other painters, on the lam from irate landlords or between odd jobs. When I ring the downstairs doorbell I never know who will open the door or what will be going on: the morning remains of an all-night party, a multiple argument, someone tossing their cookies in the toilet. "Tossing their cookies" is what Jon calls it. He thinks it's funny.

Different women pass me on the stairs, going up or down; or they are found hovering around the far end of the white room, where there's an improvised kitchen consisting of a hotplate and an electric kettle. It's never clear who these women are paired with; occasionally they are other art students, dropping in to talk. They don't talk much to one another though. They talk to the men, or are silent.

Jon's pictures hang in the white room or are stacked against the walls. They change almost weekly: Jon is productive. He paints very swiftly, in violent eye-burning acrylics, reds and pinks and purples, in frenzied loops and swirls. I feel I should admire these paintings, because I'm incapable of painting that way myself, and I do admire them, in monosyllables. But secretly I don't like them very much: I've seen things like this beside the highway, when something's been run over.

However, the pictures are not supposed to be pictures of anything you would recognize. They are a moment of process, trapped on the canvas. They are pure painting.

Jon is big on purity, but only in art: it doesn't apply to his housekeeping, which is an exuberant protest against all mothers and especially his own. He washes the dishes, when he washes them, in the bathtub, where scraps of crust and kernels of canned corn are to be seen caught in the drain. His living-room floor is like a beach after the weekend. His bedsheets are a moment of process in themselves, but a moment that has gone on for some time. I prefer the top of his sleeping bag, which is less septic. The bathroom is like the bathrooms of service stations, on out-of-the-way roads, up north: a brown ring around the toilet bowl, which is likely to contain floating cigarette butts, handprints on the towels, if any, nondescript pieces of paper here and there on the floor.

At the moment I make no moves towards cleanliness. To do so would be to overstep the bounds, and to display a bourgeois lack of cool. "What are you, my mom?" I've heard him say, to one of the hovering women who was making feeble attempts to corral some of the mouldier clutter. I don't want to be his mom, but rather a fellow conspirator.

Making love with Jon is not the leisurely, agonizing trance it is with Josef, but rambunctious, like puppies in mud. It's dirty, as in street-fighting, as in jokes. Afterwards we lie on top of his sleeping bag, eating potato chips out of the bag and giggling about nothing. Jon doesn't think women are helpless flowers, or shapes to be arranged and contemplated, as Josef does. He thinks they are smart or stupid. These are his categories. "Listen pal," he says to me. "You've got more brains than most." This pleases me, but also dismisses me. I can take care of myself.

Josef begins asking me where I've been, what I've been doing. I am casual and sly. I hold Jon against him like an ace: if he can be duplicitous, then so can I. But he does not talk about Susie any more.

The last time I saw her was in late August, before I left the Swiss Chalet. She came in and had dinner by herself, a half-chicken and some Burgundy Cherry ice cream. She'd been neglecting her hair, which was darker and straighter; her body had grown stubby, her face round. She ate in a mechanical way, as if eating was a chore, but she finished everything. It could be that she was eating for consolation, because of Josef: whatever else might happen, he would never marry her, and she must have known that. I assumed she was there to talk to me about him and I evaded her, brushing her away with a neutral smile. Her table wasn't one of mine.

But before she left she walked right up to me. "Have you seen Josef?" she asked. Her voice was plaintive, which annoyed me.

I lied, not well. "Josef?" I said, flushing. "No. Why would I?"

"I just thought you might know where he is," she said. She wasn't reproachful, but hopeless. She walked out, slumping like a middle-aged woman. With such an ass-end, I thought, no wonder Josef's keeping away. He didn't like scrawny women but there was a limit in the other direction too. Susie was letting herself go.

Now, however, she calls me. It's late afternoon and I'm studying in the cellar when my mother summons me to the phone.

Susie's voice on the line is a soft, desperate wail. "Elaine," she says. "Please come over."

"What's the matter?" I say.

"I can't tell you. Just come over."

Sleeping pills, I think. That would be her style. And why me, why hasn't she phoned Josef? I feel like slapping her.

"Are you all right?" I say.

"No," she says, her voice rising. "I'm not all right. Something's gone wrong."

It doesn't occur to me to call a taxi. Taxis are for Josef; I'm used to going everywhere on buses and streetcars, and the subway. It takes me nearly an hour to get over to The Monte Carlo. Susie didn't tell me her apartment number and I didn't think to ask, so I have to locate the superintendent. When I knock on the door, nobody answers, and I resort to the superintendent again.

"I know she's in there," I say, when he's reluctant to unlock the door for me. "She called me. It's an emergency."

When I finally get in, the apartment is dark; the drapes are drawn, the windows are closed, and there's an odd smell. Clothes are scattered here and there, jeans, winter boots, a black shawl I've seen Susie wearing. The furniture looks as if it's been picked out by her parents: a square-armed off-green sofa, a wheat-coloured carpet, a coffee table, two lamps with the cellophane still on the shades. None of it goes with Susie as I've imagined her.

On the carpet there's a dark footprint.

Susie is behind the curtain that closes off the sleeping area. She's lying on the bed in her pink nylon shortie nightie, white as an uncooked chicken, eyes closed. The top covers of the bed and the pink tufted spread are on the floor. Underneath her, across the sheet, is a great splotch of fresh blood, spreading out like bright red wings to either side of her.

Desolation sweeps through me: I feel, for no good reason, that I have been abandoned.

Then I feel sick. I run into the bathroom and throw up. It's worse because the toilet bowl is dark red with blood. There are footprints of blood on the white and black tiled floor, fingerprints on the sink. The wastebasket is crammed with sopping sanitary pads.

I wipe my mouth on Susie's baby-blue towel, wash my hands in the blood-spattered sink. I don't know what to do next; whatever this is, I don't want to be involved. I have the fleeting, absurd idea that if she's dead I will be accused of murder. I think of sneaking out of the apartment, closing the door behind me, covering my tracks.

Instead I go back to the bed and feel Susie's pulse. I know that this is what you're supposed to do. Susie is still alive.

I find the superintendent, who calls an ambulance. I also call Josef, who is not there.

I ride to the hospital with Susie, in the back of the ambulance. She is now semi-conscious, and I hold her hand, which is cold and small. "Don't tell Josef," she whispers to me. The pink nightie brings it home to me: she is none of the things I've thought about her, she never has been. She's just a nice girl playing dress-ups.

But what she's done has set her apart. It belongs to the submerged landscape of the things that are never said, which lies beneath ordinary speech like hills under water. Everyone my age knows about it. Nobody discusses it. Rumours are down there, kitchen tables, money exchanged in secret; evil old women, illegal doctors, disgrace and butchery. Down there is terror.

The two attendants are casual, and scornful. They have seen this before.

"What'd she use, a knitting needle?" one says. His tone is accusing: he may think I was helping her.

"I have no idea," I say. "I hardly even know her." I don't want to be implicated.

"That's what it usually is," he says. "Stupid kids. You'd think they'd have more sense."

I agree with him that she's been stupid. At the same time I know that in her place I would have been just as stupid. I would have done what she has done, moment by moment, step by step. Like her I would have panicked, like her I would not have told Josef, like her I would not have known where to go. Everything that's happened to her could well have happened to me.

But there is also another voice; a small, mean voice, ancient and smug, that comes from somewhere deep inside my head: *It serves her right.*

Josef, when he is finally located, is devastated. "The poor child, the poor child," he says. "Why didn't she tell me?"

"She thought you'd get mad at her," I say coldly. "Like her parents. She thought you'd kick her out, for getting pregnant."

Both of us know this is a possibility. "No, no," Josef says uncertainly. "I would have taken care of her." This could mean several things.

He calls the hospital, but Susie refuses to see him. Something has changed in her, hardened. She tells him she might never be able to have babies. She doesn't love him. She doesn't want to see him ever again.

Now Josef wallows. "What have I done to her?" he moans, tugging his hair.

He becomes more melancholy than ever; he doesn't want to go out for dinner, he doesn't want to make love. He stays in his apartment, which is no longer neat and empty but is filling up with disorganized parts of his life: take-out Chinese-food containers, unwashed sheets.

He says he will never get over it, what he has done to Susie.

This is how he thinks of it: something he's done, to Susie, to her inert and innocent flesh. At the same time he has been wounded by her: how can she treat him like this, cut him out of her life?

He expects me to console him, for his own guilt and the damage that's been done to him. But I am not good at this. I am beginning to dislike him.

"It was my child," he says.

"Would you have married her?" I ask. The spectacle of his suffering does not make me compassionate, but ruthless.

"You are cruel to me," says Josef. This was something he used to say before, in a sexual context, teasing. Now he means it. Now he is right.

Without Susie, whatever has been keeping us in equilibrium is gone. The full weight of Josef rests on me, and he is too heavy for me. I can't make him happy, and I resent my failure: I am not enough for him, I am inadequate. I see him as weak now, clinging, gutted like a fish. I can't respect a man who can allow himself to be reduced to such rubble by women. I look at his doleful eyes and feel contempt.

I make excuses, over the phone. I tell him I am very busy. One evening I stand him up. This is so deeply gratifying that I do it again. He tracks me down at the university, rumpled and unshaven and suddenly too old, and pleads with me as I walk between classes. I'm angered by this overlap of worlds.

"Who was that?" say the girls in the cashmere twin sets.

"Just someone I used to know," I say lightly.

Josef waylays me outside the museum and announces I have driven him to despair: because of the way I've treated him, he is leaving Toronto forever. He does not fool me: he was planning to do this anyway. My mean mouth takes over.

"Good," I say.

He gives me a pained, reproachful stare, drawing himself up into the proud, theatrical, poker-up-the-bum stance of a matador.

615

I walk away from him. It's enormously pleasing to me, this act of walking away. It's like being able to make people appear and vanish, at will.

I do not dream about Josef. Instead I dream about Susie, in her black turtleneck and jeans but shorter than she really is, her hair cut into a pageboy. She's standing on a street I know but do not recognize, among piles of smouldering autumn leaves, holding a coiled skipping rope, licking one half of an orange popsicle.

She is not drained and boneless, as I've last seen her. Instead she is sly-eyed, calculating. "Don't you know what a twin set is?" she says spitefully.

She continues to lick her popsicle. I know I have done something wrong.

58

Time passes, and Susie fades. Josef does not reappear.

This leaves me with Jon. I have the sense that, like one of a pair of bookends, he is incomplete by himself. But I feel virtuous, because I'm no longer hiding anything from him. This makes no difference to him, however, since he didn't know I was hiding anything in the first place. He doesn't know why I am less casual about what he does with the rest of his time.

I decide I'm in love with him. Though I am too cagey to say it: he might object to the vocabulary, or think he's being pinned down.

I still go over to his long white and black apartment, still end up on top of his sleeping bag, although haphazardly: Jon isn't big on planning in advance, or on remembering. Sometimes when I arrive at his downstairs door there's no answer. Or else his phone gets cut off because he hasn't paid the bill. We are a couple, in a way, though nothing is explicit between us. When he's with me he's with me: that's about as far as he'll go in his definition of what is not yet called our relationship.

There are murky, smoky parties, with the lights turned out and candles flickering in bottles. The other painters are there, and assorted turtlenecked women, who have begun to appear in long, straight hair, parted in the middle. They sit in clumps, on the floor, in the dark, listening to folksongs about women being stabbed with daggers, and smoking marijuana cigarettes, which is what people do in New York. They refer to these as "dope" or "pot", and claim they loosen up your art.

Cigarettes of any kind make me choke, so I don't smoke them. Some nights I wind up in the back hall with one or another of the painters, because I would rather not see what Jon may be getting up to with the straight-haired girls. Whatever it is, I wish he would do it in secret. But he doesn't feel the need to hide anything: sexual possessiveness is bourgeois, and just a

617

hangover from notions about the sanctity of private property. Nobody owns anybody.

He doesn't say all this. All he says is, "Hey, you don't own me."

Sometimes the other painters are merely stoned, or drunk, but sometimes they want to tell me their problems. They do this fumblingly, in starts and stops, in short words. Their problems are mostly about their girlfriends. Soon they will be bringing me their socks to darn, their buttons to sew on. They make me feel like an aunt. This is what I do instead of jealousy, in which there is no future. Or so I think.

Jon has given up on his paintings of swirls and innards. He says they are too romantic, too emotional, too sloppy, too sentimental. Now he's doing pictures in which all the shapes are either straight lines or perfect circles. He uses masking tape to get the lines straight. He works in blocks of flat colour, no impasto showing.

He calls these paintings things like *Enigma: Blue and Red*, or *Variation: Black and White*, or *Opus 36*. They make your eyes hurt when you look at them. Jon says this is the point.

In the daytime I go to school.

Art and Archaeology is murkier and more velvety than last year, and filled with impasto and chiaroscuro. There are still Madonnas, but their bodies have lost their previous quality of suffused light and are more likely to be seen at night. There are still saints, though they no longer sit in quiet rooms or deserts, with their memento mori skulls and their dog-like lions resting at their feet; instead they writhe in contorted poses, stuck full of arrows or tied to stakes. Biblical subjects tilt towards violence: Judith cutting off the head of Holofernes is now popular. There are a lot more classical gods and goddesses. There are wars, fights and slaughters, as before, but more confused and with intertwined arms and legs. There are still portraits of rich people, although in darker clothing.

As we run through the centuries, new things appear: ships by themselves, animals by themselves, such as dogs and horses.

Peasants by themselves. Landscapes, with or without houses. Flowers by themselves, plates of fruit and cuts of meat, with or without lobsters. Lobsters are a favourite, because of the colour.

Naked women.

There is considerable overlap: a naked goddess wreathed in flowers, with a couple of dogs standing by; biblical people with or without clothes, plus or minus animals, trees, and ships. Rich people pretending to be gods and goddesses. Fruit and slaughters are not usually combined, nor are gods and peasants. The naked women are presented in the same manner as the plates of meat and dead lobsters, with the same attention to the play of candlelight on skin, the same lusciousness, the same sensuous and richly rendered detail, the same painterly delight in tactility. (*Richly rendered*, I write. *Painterly delight in tactility.*) They appear served up.

I don't like these shadowy, viscous pictures. I prefer the earlier ones, with their daytime clarity, their calm arrested gestures. I have given up, too, on oil paints; I have come to dislike their thickness, their obliteration of line, their look of licked lips, the way they call attention to the brushstrokes of the painter. I can make nothing of them. What I want instead is pictures that seem to exist of their own accord. I want objects that breathe out light; a luminous flatness.

I draw with coloured pencils. Or I paint in egg tempera, the technique of monks. Nobody teaches this any more, so I hunt through the library, searching for instructions. Egg tempera is difficult and messy, painstaking and, at first, heartbreaking. I muck up my mother's kitchen floor and pots, cooking the gesso, and ruin panel after panel before I can work out how to paint it on for a smooth working surface. Or I forget about my bottles of egg yolk and water, which go bad and stink up the cellar with a smell like sulphur. I use up a lot of egg yolks. The whites I separate carefully, and take upstairs to my mother, who makes them into meringue cookies.

I draw beside the picture window in the living room upstairs, when there is nobody home, or in the daylight from the cellar window. At night I use two goose-neck lamps, each of which takes three bulbs. None of this is adequate, but it's all I can manage. Later, I think, I will have a large studio, with skylights;

though what I will paint in it is far from clear. Whatever it is will appear, even later, in coloured plates, in books; like the work of Leonardo da Vinci, whose studies of hands and feet and hair and dead people I pore over.

I become fascinated with the effects of glass, and of other light-reflecting surfaces. I study paintings in which there are pearls, crystals, mirrors, shiny details of brass. I spend a long time over Van Eyck's *The Arnolfini Marriage*, going over the inadequate colour print of it in my textbook with a magnifying glass; what fascinates me is not the two delicate, pallid, shoulderless hand-holding figures, but the pier-glass on the wall behind them, which reflects in its convex surface not only their backs but two other people who aren't in the main picture at all. These figures reflected in the mirror are slightly askew, as if a different law of gravity, a different arrangement of space, exists inside, locked in, sealed up in the glass as if in a paperweight. This round mirror is like an eye, a single eye that sees more than anyone else looking: over this mirror is written, "Johannes de Eyck fuit hic. 1434." It's disconcertingly like a washroom scribble, something you'd write with spray paint on a wall.

There is no pier-glass in our house for me to practise on. So instead I paint gingerale bottles, wineglasses, ice cubes from the refrigerator, the glazed teapot, my mother's fake pearl earrings. I paint polished wood, and metal: a copper-bottomed frying pan, as seen from the bottom, an aluminium double-boiler. I fiddle over details, hunch over my pictures, dabbing at the highlights with tiny brushes.

I'm aware that my tastes are not fashionable, and so I pursue them in secret. Jon, for instance, would call this illustration. Any picture that's a picture of something recognizable is illustration, as far as he's concerned. There is no spontaneous energy in this kind of work, he would say. No process. I might as well be a photographer, or Norman Rockwell. Some days I agree with him, because what have I done so far? Nothing that doesn't look like a random sampling from the Housewares Department of the Eaton's Catalogue. But I keep on.

On Wednesday evenings I take another night course: not Life Drawing, which is taught this year by an excitable Yugoslavian, but Advertising Art. The students are quite different from the Life Drawing bunch. They're mostly from the Commercial division of the Art College, not the Fine Arts one. Again they're mostly boys. Some of them have serious artistic ambitions, but they don't drink as much beer. They're cleaner and more earnest, and they want paying jobs when they graduate. So do I.

The teacher is an elderly man, thin and defeated-looking. He thinks he has failed in the real world, although he once created a famous illustration for canned pork and beans that I can remember from childhood. We ate a lot of canned pork and beans, during the war. His speciality is the rendering of smiles: the trick is to be able to do teeth, nice white even teeth, without putting in the separation between each tooth, which makes the smile appear too canine or too much like false teeth (which he himself has). He tells me I show ability in smiles, and that I could go far.

Jon teases me a little about this night course, but not as much as I thought he would. He refers to the teacher as Mr. Beanie Weenie, and lets it go at that.

59

I graduate from university, and discover that there's nothing much I can do with my degree. Or nothing I want to do at any rate. I don't want to go on to graduate work, I don't want to teach high school or be a curator's flunkey in a museum.

By this time I've accumulated five night courses from the Art College, four of them in the Commercial area, and I trot them and my portfolio of smiles and dishes of caramel pudding and canned peach halves around to various ad agencies. For these purposes I buy a beige wool suit (on sale), medium-heel pumps to match, some pearl button earrings and a tasteful silk scarf (on sale) at Simpsons; this on the recommendation of my last night-course instructor, in Layout and Design, who was a woman. She also recommended a haircut, but I would only go so far as a French roll, engineered with the help of some big rollers and hair-setting gel and a lot of bobby-pins. Eventually I get a menial job doing mock-ups, and a small furnished two-bedroom apartment with kitchenette and separate entrance in a large crumbling house in the Annex, north of Bloor. I use the second bedroom for painting, and keep the door to it closed.

This place has a real bed, and a real kitchen sink. Jon comes for dinner and teases me about the towels I've bought (on sale), the ovenproof dishes I've acquired, my shower curtain. "*Better Homes and Gardens*, eh?" he says. He teases me about the bed, but he likes sleeping in it. He comes to my place, now, more often than I go to his.

My parents sell their house and move up north. My father has left the university and has gone back to research; he's now head of the Forest Insect Laboratory at Sault Ste. Marie. He says Toronto is getting overpopulated, and also polluted. He says the lower Great Lakes are the world's largest sewer and that if we knew what was going into the drinking water we would

622

all become alcoholics. As for the air, it's so full of chemicals we should be wearing gas masks. Up north you can still breathe.

My mother was not too happy to leave her garden, but made the best of it: "At least it's a chance to throw out a lot of that junk in the cellar," she said. They've started another garden in the Soo, although the growing season is shorter. In the summers though they're mostly on the road, driving from infestation to infestation. There is no shortage of insect life.

I don't miss my parents. Not yet. Or rather I don't want to be living with them. I am happy to be left to my own devices, my own messes. I can eat haphazardly now, snack on junk food and take-outs without worrying about balanced meals, go to bed when I like, let my dirty laundry rot, neglect the dishes.

I get a promotion. After a time I move to the art department of a publishing company, where I design book covers. At night, when Jon is not there, I paint. Sometimes I forget to go to bed, and find that it has become dawn and I have to change into my work clothes and go to work. I am groggy on those days, and have trouble hearing what is said to me; but nobody seems to notice.

I get postcards and the occasional short letter from my mother, sent from places like Duluth and Kapuskasing. She says the roads are getting too crowded. "Too many trailers," she says. I reply with news about my job, my apartment, and the weather. I don't mention Jon, because there is no news. News would be something definite and respectable, such as an engagement.

My brother Stephen is here and there. He has become more taciturn: he too now communicates by postcard. One comes from Germany, with a man in short leather pants on it and the message: *Great particle accelerator*; one from Nevada, with a cactus and the note, *Interesting life forms*. He goes to Bolivia on what I suppose to be a holiday, and sends a cigar-smoking woman in a high-crowned hat: *Excellent butterflies. Hope you are well.* At one point he gets married, which is announced by a postcard from San Francisco, with the Golden Gate Bridge and a sunset on it, and, *Got married. Annette sends regards.* This is all I hear about it until several years later, when he sends a postcard of the Statue of Liberty from New York, which says:

Got divorced. I assume he has been puzzled by both events, as if they're not something he's done himself, on purpose, but things that have happened to him accidentally, like stubbing your toe. I think of him as walking into marriage as into a park, in a foreign country, at night, unaware of the possibilities for damage.

He turns up in Toronto to give a lecture, at a conference, notifying me in advance with a postcard of a statue of Paul Revere, from Boston: *Arrive Sun. 12th. My paper is on Mon. See you.*

I attend the lecture, not because I have high hopes for it on my own account – the title of it is "The First Picoseconds and the Quest for a Unified Field Theory: Some Minor Speculations" – but because he is my brother. I sit nibbling my fingers as the university auditorium fills with the audience, which is composed largely of men. Most of them look like people I wouldn't have gone out with in high school.

Then my brother comes in, with the man who will introduce him. I haven't seen my brother for years; he's thinner, and his hair is beginning to recede. He needs glasses to read his text; I can see them poking out of his breast pocket. Someone has upgraded his wardrobe for him and he's wearing a suit and tie. These alterations don't make him appear more normal, however, but more anomalous, like a creature from an alien planet disguised in human clothing. He has a look of amazing brilliance, as if at any minute his head will light up and become transparent, disclosing a huge brightly coloured brain inside. At the same time he looks rumpled and bewildered, as if he's just wakened from a pleasant dream to find himself surrounded by Munchkins.

The man introducing my brother says he needs no introduction, then goes on to list the papers he has written, the awards he has won, the contributions he has made. There is clapping, and my brother goes to the podium. He stands in front of a white projection screen, clears his throat, shifts from one foot to the other, puts on his glasses. Now he looks like someone who will turn up, later, on a stamp. He is ill at ease and I am nervous for him. I think he will mumble. But once he begins he is fine.

"When we gaze at the night sky," he says, "we are looking at fragments of the past. Not only in the sense that the stars as we see them are echoes of events that occurred light-years distant

624

in time and space: everything up there and indeed everything down here is a fossil, a leftover from the first picoseconds of creation, when the universe crystallized out from the primal homogeneous plasma. In the first picosecond, conditions were scarcely imaginable. If we could travel in a time machine back towards this explosive moment, we would find ourselves in a universe replete with energies we do not understand and strangely behaving forces distorted beyond recognition. The farther back we probe, the more extreme these conditions become. Current experimental facilities can take us only a short way along this path. Beyond that point, theory is our only guide." After this he continues, in a language that sounds like English but is not, because I can't understand one word of it.

Luckily there is something to look at. The room darkens and the screen lights up, and there is the universe, or parts of it: the black void punctuated by galaxies and stars, white-hot, blue-hot, red. An arrow moves among them on the screen, searching and finding. Then there are diagrams and strings of numbers, and references to things that everyone here seems to recognize except me. There are, apparently, a great many more dimensions than four.

Murmurs of interest ripple through the room; there are whisperings, the rustling of paper. At the end, when the lights have come on again, my brother returns to language. "But what of the moment beyond the first moment?" he says. "Or does it even make sense to use the word *before*, since time cannot exist without space and space-time without events and events without matter-energy? But there is something that must have existed before. That something is the theoretical framework, the parameters within which the laws of energy must operate. Judging from the scanty but mounting evidence now available to us, if the universe was created with a *fiat lux*, that fiat must have been expressed, not in Latin, but in the one truly universal language: mathematics." This sounds a lot like metaphysics to me, but the men in the audience don't seem to take it amiss. There is applause.

I go to the reception afterwards, which offers the usual university fare: bad sherry, thick tea, cookies out of a package. The numbers men murmur in groups, shake one another's hands. Among them I feel overly visible, and out of place.

I locate my brother. "That was great," I say to him.

"Glad you got something out of it," he says with irony.

"Well, math was never my totally strong point," I say. He smiles benignly.

We exchange news of our parents, who when last I heard from them were in Kenora, and heading west. "Still counting the old budworms, I guess," says my brother.

I remember how he used to throw up by the side of the road, and his smell of cedar pencils. I remember our life in tents and logging camps, the scent of cut lumber and gasoline and crushed grass and rancid cheese, the way we used to sneak around in the dark. I remember his wooden swords with the orange blood, his comic book collection. I see him crouching on the swampy ground, calling *Lie down, you're dead*. I see him dive-bombing the dishes with forks. All my early images of him are clear and sharp and technicolour: his baggy-legged shorts, his striped T-shirt, his raggedy hair bleached by the sun, his winter breeks and leather helmet. Then there is a gap, and he appears again on the other side of it, unaccountably two years older.

"Remember that song you used to sing?" I say. "During the war. Sometimes you whistled it. 'Coming in on a Wing and a Prayer'?"

He looks perplexed, frowns a little. "I can't say I do," he says.

"You used to draw all those explosions. You borrowed my red pencil, because yours was used up."

He looks at me, not as if he doesn't remember these things himself, but as if he's puzzled that I do. "You can't have been very old then," he says.

I wonder what it was like for him, having a little sister tagging along. For me, he was a given: there was never a time when he didn't exist. But I was not a given, for him. Once he was singular, and I was an intrusion. I wonder if he resented me when I was born. Maybe he thought I was a pain in the bum; there's no doubt that he thought this sometimes. Considering everything and on the whole though, he made the best of me.

"Remember that jar of marbles you buried, under the bridge?" I say. "You would never tell me why you did it." The best ones, the red and blue puries, the waterbabies and cat's eyes, put into

626

the ground, out of reach. He would have stamped the dirt down on top of the jar, and scattered leaves.

"I think I recall that," he says, as if not entirely willing to be reminded of his former, younger self. It disturbs me that he can remember some of these things about himself, but not others; that the things he's lost or misplaced exist now only for me. If he's forgotten so much, what have I forgotten?

"Maybe they're still down there," I say. "I wonder if anyone ever found them, when they built that new bridge. You buried the map, too."

"So I did," he says, smiling in his old, secret, maddening way. He still isn't telling, and I am reassured: despite his changed façade, his thinning hair and provisional suit, he is still the same person underneath.

After he has gone back, to wherever he's going next, I think of getting him a star named after himself, for his birthday. I have seen an advertisement for these: you send in your money, and you get a certificate with a star map, your own star marked on it. Possibly he would find this amusing. But I'm not sure that the word "birthday", for him, would still have meaning.

60

Jon has given up his eye-damaging geometrical shapes and is painting pictures that look like commercial illustrations: huge popsicles, giant salt and pepper shakers, peach halves in syrup, paper dishes overflowing with French fries. He does not talk about purity any more but of the necessity of using common cultural sign systems to reflect the iconic banality of our times. I think I could give him a few tips from my own professional experience: his peach halves could be glossier, for instance. But I don't say this.

Increasingly, Jon paints these things in my living room. He's been gradually moving in his things, beginning with the paints and canvas. He says he can't paint at his place because there are too many people in it, which is true: the front room is silting up with American draft-dodgers, a shifting population, all of whom seem to be friends of friends. Jon has to step over them to get to the walls, because they lie around on their sleeping bags, forlorn and smoking dope, wondering what to do next. They are depressed because Toronto isn't the United States without a war on, as they thought it would be, but some limbo they have strayed into by accident and can't get out of. Toronto is nowhere, and nothing happens in it.

Jon stays over three or four nights a week. I don't ask what he does on the other nights.

He thinks he is making a large concession, to something he assumes I want. And maybe I do want it. When I'm alone, I let the dishes accumulate in the sink, I allow coloured fur to grow in jars of leftovers, I use up all my underpants before washing any of them. But Jon turns me into a model of tidiness and efficiency. I get up in the morning and make coffee for him, I set two places at the table, with my newly acquired ovenproof earthenware in off-white, with speckles. I don't even mind doing his laundry at the laundromat, along with my own.

Jon is not used to having all these clean clothes. "You're the sort of girl who should get married," he says one day, when I appear with a pile of folded shirts and jeans. I think this may be an insult, but I'm not sure.

"Do your own laundry then," I say.

"Hey," he says, "don't be like that."

On Sundays we sleep late, make love, go for walks, holding hands.

One day, when nothing has changed, nothing has been done or happened that is any different from usual, I discover I am pregnant. My first reaction is unbelief. I count and recount, wait another day, then another, listening to the inside of my body as if for a footfall. Finally I slink off to the drugstore with some pee in a bottle, feeling like a criminal. Married women go to their doctors. Unmarried women do this.

The man in the drugstore tells me the results are positive. "Congratulations," he says, with disapproving irony. He can see right through me.

I'm afraid to tell Jon. He will expect me to go and have it out, like a tooth. He will say "it". Or he will want me to sit in the bathtub while he pours boiling water into it; he will want me to drink gin. Or else he will vanish. He's said, often enough, that artists can't live like other people, tied down to demanding families and expensive material possessions.

I think about things I've heard: drinking a lot of gin, knitting needles, coat-hangers; but what do you do with them? I think about Susie and her wings of red blood. Whatever it was she did, I will not do it. I am too frightened. I refuse to end up like her.

I go back to my apartment, lie down on the floor. My body is numb, inert, without sensation. I can hardly move, I can hardly breathe. I feel as if I'm at the centre of nothingness, of a black square that is totally empty; that I'm exploding slowly outwards, into the cold burning void of space.

When I wake up it's the middle of the night. I don't know where I am. I think I'm back in my old room with the cloudy light fixture, in my parents' house, lying on the floor because I've fallen out of bed, as I used to do when we had the army cots. But I know that the house has been sold, that my parents are no longer there. I have somehow been overlooked, left behind.

This is only the end of a dream. I get up, turn on the lights, make myself some hot milk, sit at the kitchen table, shivering with cold.

Until now I've always painted things that were actually there, in front of me. Now I begin to paint things that aren't there.

I paint a silver toaster, the old kind, with knobs and doors. One of the doors is partly open, revealing the red-hot grill within. I paint a glass coffee percolator, with bubbles gathering in the clear water; one drop of dark coffee has fallen, and is beginning to spread.

I paint a wringer washing machine. The washing machine is a squat cylinder of white enamel. The wringer itself is a disturbing fleshtone pink.

I know that these things must be memories, but they do not have the quality of memories. They are not hazy around the edges, but sharp and clear. They arrive detached from any context; they are simply there, in isolation, as an object glimpsed on the street is there.

I have no image of myself in relation to them. They are suffused with anxiety, but it's not my own anxiety. The anxiety is in the things themselves.

I paint three sofas. One of them is chintz, in dirty rose; one is maroon velvet, with doilies. The one in the middle is apple-green. On the middle cushion of the middle sofa is an egg-cup, five times life-size, with a broken eggshell in it.

I paint a glass jar, with a bouquet of nightshade rising out of it like smoke, like the darkness from a genie's bottle. The stems twist and intertwine, the branches cluster with red berries, purple flowers. Scarcely visible, far back in the dense tangle of the glossy leaves, are the eyes of cats.

In the daytime I go to work, come back, talk, and eat. Jon comes over, eats, sleeps, and goes away. I watch him with detachment; he notices nothing. Every move I make is sodden with unreality.

630

When no one is around, I bite my fingers. I need to feel physical pain, to attach myself to daily life. My body is a separate thing. It ticks like a clock; time is inside it. It has betrayed me, and I am disgusted with it.

I paint Mrs. Smeath. She floats up without warning, like a dead fish, materializing on a sofa I am drawing: first her white, sparsely haired legs without ankles, then her thick waist and potato face, her eyes in their steel rims. The afghan is draped across her thighs, the rubber plant rises behind her like a fan. On her head is the felt hat like a badly done-up package that she used to wear on Sundays.

She looks out at me from the flat surface of paint, three-dimensional now, smiling her closed half-smile, smug and accusing. Whatever has happened to me is my own fault, the fault of what is wrong with me.

Mrs. Smeath knows what it is. She isn't telling.

One picture of Mrs. Smeath leads to another. She multiplies on the walls like bacteria, standing, sitting, flying, with clothes, without clothes, following me around with her many eyes like those 3-D postcards of Jesus you can get in the cheesier corner stores. Sometimes I turn her faces to the wall.

61

I wheel Sarah along the street in her stroller, avoiding the mounds of melting slush. Although she is over two, she still can't walk fast enough in her red rubber boots to keep up when we go shopping. Also this way I can hang the grocery bags from the stroller handle, or tuck them in around her. I know a great many such minor tricks now, involving objects and gadgets and the rearrangement of space, that I didn't need to know before.

We're living in a larger place now, the three of us: the upper two storeys of a red brick semi-detached house with a sagging wooden square-pillared porch, on a side street west along Bloor. There are a lot of Italians around here. The older women, the married ones and the widows, wear black clothes and no makeup, as I used to do. When I was in the later months of pregnancy, they would smile at me, as if I was almost one of them. Now they smile at Sarah first.

I myself wear mini-skirts in primary colours, with tights underneath and boots, and an ankle-length coat over the top. I am not entirely satisfied with this clothing. It's hard to sit down in. Also I've put on some weight, since having Sarah. These skimpy skirts and tiny bodices were designed for women a lot skinnier than I am, of which there now seem to be dozens, hundreds: weasel-faced girls with long hair hanging to the place where their bums ought to be, their chests flat as plywood, making me feel bulbous by comparison.

A new vocabulary has come with them. *Far out*, they say. *Cosmic. Blew my mind. Uptight. Let it all hang out.* I consider myself too old for such words: they are for young people, and I am no longer young. I have found a grey hair behind my left ear. In a couple of years I will be thirty. Over the hill.

I wheel Sarah up the walk, unbuckle her, set her at the foot of the porch steps, unhook and lift out the grocery bags, fold up the stroller. I walk Sarah up the steps to the front door: these steps can be slippery. I go back for the bags and the stroller, lug them up the steps, fumble in my purse for the key, open the door, lift Sarah inside, then the bags and stroller, close and lock the door. I walk Sarah up the inside stairs, open the inside door, put her inside, close the baby gate, go back down for the bags, carry them up, open the gate, go in, close the gate, go into the kitchen, set the bags on the table and begin to unpack: eggs, toilet paper, cheese, apples, bananas, carrots, hotdogs and buns. I worry about serving too many hotdogs: when I was young they were carnival food, and supposed to be bad for you. You might get polio from them.

Sarah is hungry, so I stop unpacking the groceries to get her a glass of milk. I love her ferociously, and am frequently irritated by her.

For the first year I was tired all the time, and fogged by hormones. But I'm coming out of it now. I'm looking around me.

Jon comes in scoops Sarah up, gives her a kiss, tickles her face with his beard, carries her squealing off into the living room. "Let's hide on Mummy," he says. He has a way of putting the two of them into the same camp, in pretended league against me that annoys me more than it should. Also I don't like it when he calls me Mummy. I am not his mummy, but hers. But he too loves her. This was a surprise, and I'm not finished being grateful for it. I don't yet see Sarah as a gift I have given him, but one he has allowed me. It's because of her that we got married, at City Hall, for the oldest of reasons. One that was nearly obsolete. But we didn't know that.

Jon, who is a lapsed Lutheran from Niagara Falls, thought we should go there for our honeymoon. He broke up over the word "honeymoon". He thought it would be a sort of joke: self-conscious corniness, like a painting of a giant Coke bottle. "Amazing visuals," he said. He wanted to take me to the waxworks, the flower clock, the *Maid of the Mist*. He wanted us to get satin shirts with our names embroidered on the pockets and NIAGARA FALLS across the back. But I was silently offended by this approach to our marriage. Whatever else we were getting into as the weeks passed one another and my body swelled like a slow flesh balloon, it was not a joke. So we ended by not going.

Right after we were married, I lapsed into a voluptuous sloth. My body was like a feather bed, warm, boneless, deeply comforting, in which I lay cocooned. It may have been the pregnancy, sponging up my adrenalin. Or it may have been relief. Jon glowed for me then like a plum in sunlight, richly coloured, perfect in form. I would lie in bed beside him or sit at the kitchen table, running my eyes over him like hands. My adoration was physical, and wordless. I would think *Ah*, nothing more. Like a breath breathed out. Or I would think, like a child, *Mine*. Knowing it wasn't true. *Stay that way*, I would think. But he could not.

Jon and I have begun to have fights. Our fights are secret fights, conducted at night, when Sarah is asleep: a squabbling in undertones. We keep them from her, because if they are frightening to us – as they are – how much more frightening will they be to her?

We thought we were running away from the grownups, and now we are the grownups: this is the crux of it. Neither of us wants to take it on, not the whole thing. We compete, for instance, over which of us is in worse shape. If I get a headache, he gets a migraine. If his back hurts, my neck is killing me. Neither one of us wants to be in charge of the Band-Aids. We fight over our right to remain children.

At first I do not win these fights, because of love. Or so I say to myself. If I were to win them, the order of the world would be changed, and I am not ready for that. So instead I lose the fights, and master different arts. I shrug, tighten my mouth in silent rebuke, turn my back in bed, leave questions unanswered. I say, "Do it however you like," provoking sullen fury from Jon. He does not want just capitulation, but admiration, enthusiasm, for himself and his ideas, and when he doesn't get it he feels cheated.

Jon has a job now, supervising part-time at a co-op graphics studio. I am part-time as well. Between the two of us, we can manage to cover the rent.

Jon is no longer painting on canvas, or on anything flat. In fact he is no longer painting. Flat surfaces with paint on them he calls "art-on-the-wall". There is no reason for art to be on the wall, there's no reason for it to have a frame around it or paint on it. Instead he is making constructions, out of things he gathers from junk-heaps or finds here and there. He makes wooden boxes with compartments, each containing a different item: three pairs of outsize ladies' panties in fluorescent colours, a plaster hand with long false nails glued onto it, an enema bag, a toupee. He makes a motorized furry bedroom-slipper that runs around on the floor by itself, and a family of diaphragms fitted up with monster-movie eyes and mouths and jumping legs underneath that hop around on the table like radiation-damaged oysters. He's decorated our bathroom in red and orange, with purple mermaids swimming on the walls, and hooked up the toilet seat so that it plays "Jingle Bells" when it's raised. This is for Sarah's benefit. He makes toys for her as well, and lets her play with ends of wood and leftover pieces of cloth and some of his less dangerous tools, while he's working.

That's when he's here. Which is by no means most of the time.

For the first year after Sarah was born I didn't paint at all. I was freelancing then, working at home, and just keeping up with the few book-cover assignments I'd taken on was a major effort. I felt clogged, as if swimming with my clothes on. Now that I'm half a day at work, it's better.

I've done some of what I call my own work as well, although hesitantly: my hands are out of practice, my eyes disused. Most of what I do is drawing, because the preparation of the surface, the laborious underpainting and detailed concentration of egg tempera are too much for me. I have lost confidence: perhaps all I will ever be is what I am now.

I'm sitting on a wooden folding chair, on a stage. The curtains are open and I can see the auditorium, which is small, battered, and empty. Also on the stage is a stage set, not yet dismantled, for a play which has just closed. The set consists of the future, which will be sparsely furnished, but will contain a

635

good many cylindrical black columns and several austere flights of stairs.

Arranged around the columns on other wooden chairs, and sitting here and there on the stairs, are seventeen women. Every one of them is an artist, or something like it. There are several actresses, two dancers, three painters besides me. There's one magazine writer, and an editor from my own publishing company. One woman is a radio announcer (daytime classical music), one does puppet shows for children, one is a professional clown. One is a set designer, which is why we're here: she got us the space for this meeting. The reason I know all of this is that we had to say our names, going around the circle, and what we do. Not for a living: for a living is different, especially for the actresses. Also for me.

This is a meeting. It's not the first such meeting I've been to, but I still find it startling. For one thing, it's all women. That in itself is unusual, and has an air of secrecy about it, and an unfocused, attractive dirtiness: the last all-women gathering I was at was Health Class in high school, where the girls were separated off from the boys so they could be told about the curse. Not that the word was used. "Those days" was the accepted, official phrase. It was explained that tampons, although not recommended for young girls, which we knew meant virgins, could not get lost inside you and end up in your lung. There was considerable giggling, and when the teacher spelled *blood* – "B-L-O-O-D" – one girl fainted.

Today there is no giggling or fainting. This meeting is about anger.

Things are being said that I have never consciously thought about before. Things are being overthrown. Why, for instance, do we shave our legs? Wear lipstick? Dress up in slinky clothing? Alter our shapes? What is wrong with us the way we are?

It's Jody asking these questions, one of the other painters. She does not dress up or alter her shape. She wears workboots, and striped coveralls, one leg of which she hauls up to show us the real leg underneath, which is defiantly, resplendently hairy. I think of my own cowardly, naked legs, and feel brainwashed, because I know I cannot go all the way. I draw the line at armpits.

What is wrong with us the way we are is men.

Many things are said about men. Two of these women have been raped, for instance. One has been beaten up. Others have been discriminated against at work, passed over or ignored; or their art has been ridiculed, dismissed as too feminine. Others have begun to compare their salaries with those of men, and have found them to be less.

I have no doubt that all of these things are true. Rapists exist, and those who molest children and strangle girls. They exist in the shadows, like the sinister men who lurk in ravines, not one of whom I have ever seen. They are violent, wage wars, commit murders. They do less work and make more money. They shove the housework off on women.

They are insensitive and refuse to confront their own emotions. They are easily fooled, and wish to be: for instance, with a few gasps and wheezes they can be conned into thinking they are sexual supermen. There are giggles of recognition over this. I begin to wonder if I've been faking orgasm without knowing it.

But I am on shaky ground, in this testifying against men, because I live with one. Women like me, with a husband, a child, have been referred to with some scorn as "nukes", for *nuclear family*. *Pronatalist* is suddenly a bad word. There are some other nukes in this group, but they are not in the majority and say nothing in their own defence. It seems to be worthier to be a woman with a child but no man. That way you've paid your dues. If you stay with the man, whatever problems you are having are your own fault.

None of this is actually said.

These meetings are supposed to make me feel more powerful, and in some ways they do. Rage can move mountains. In addition, they amaze me: it's shocking, and exciting, to hear such things emerging from the mouths of women. I begin to think that women I have thought were stupid, or wimps, may simply have been hiding things, as I was.

But these meetings also make me nervous, and I don't understand why. I don't say much, I am awkward and uncertain, because whatever I do say might be the wrong thing. I have not suffered enough, I haven't paid my dues, I have no right to speak. I feel as if I'm standing outside a closed door while decisions are being made, disapproving judgments are being pronounced, inside, about me. At the same time I want to please.

Sisterhood is a difficult concept for me, I tell myself, because I never had a sister. Brotherhood is not.

I work at night, when Sarah is asleep, or in the early morning. Right now I am painting the Virgin Mary. I paint her in blue, with the usual white veil, but with the head of a lioness. Christ lies in her lap in the form of a cub. If Christ is a lion, as he is in traditional iconography, why wouldn't the Virgin Mary be a lioness? Anyway it seems to me more accurate about motherhood than the old bloodless milk-and-water Virgins of art history. My Virgin Mary is fierce, alert to danger, wild. She stares levelly out at the viewer with her yellow lion's eyes. A gnawed bone lies at her feet.

I paint the Virgin Mary descending to the earth, which is covered with snow and slush. She is wearing a winter coat over her blue robe, and has a purse slung over her shoulder. She's carrying two brown paper bags full of groceries. Several things have fallen from the bags: an egg, an onion, an apple. She looks tired.

Our Lady of Perpetual Help, I call her.

Jon does not like me painting at night. "When else can I do it?" I say. "You tell me." There is only one answer, one that would not involve the loss of his own time: *Don't do it at all.* But he doesn't say this.

He doesn't say what he thinks of my paintings, but I know anyway. He thinks they are irrelevant. In his mind, what I paint is lumped in with the women who paint flowers. Lumped is the word. The present tense is moving forward, discarding concept after concept, and I am off to the side somewhere, fiddling with egg tempera and flat surfaces, as if the twentieth century has never happened.

There is freedom in this: because it doesn't matter what I do, I can do what I like.

*   *   *

We have begun to slam doors, and to throw things. I throw my purse, an ashtray, a package of chocolate chips, which breaks on impact. We are picking up chocolate chips for days. Jon throws a glass of milk, the milk, not the glass: he knows his own strength, as I do not. He throws a box of Cheerios, unopened.

The things I throw miss, although they are worse things. The things he throws hit, but are harmless.

I begin to see how the line is crossed, between histrionics and murder.

Jon smashes things, and glues the shards into place in the pattern of breakage. I can see the appeal.

Jon sits in the living room, having a beer with one of the painters. I am in the kitchen, slamming around the pots.

"What's with her?" says the painter.

"She's mad because she's a woman," Jon says. This is something I haven't heard for years, not since high school. Once it was a shaming thing to say, and crushing to have it said about you, by a man. It implied oddness, deformity, sexual malfunction.

I go to the living-room doorway. "I'm not mad because I'm a woman," I say. "I'm mad because you're an asshole."

62

Some of us from the meetings are having a group show, of women only. This is risky business, and we know it. Jody says we could get trashed by the male art establishment. Their line these days is that great art transcends gender. Jody's line is that art so far has been mostly men admiring one another. A woman artist can get admired by them only as a sideline, a sort of freaky exception. "Titless wonders," says Jody.

We could get trashed by women as well, for singling ourselves out, putting ourselves forward. We could be called elitist. There are many pitfalls.

There are four of us in on the show. Carolyn, who has an angelic moon-face framed in a Dutch cut with dark bangs, calls herself a fabric artist. Some of her pieces are patchwork quilts, in inventive designs. One has condoms stuffed with tampons (unused), glued onto it in the shapes of letters, spelling out WHAT IS LUV? Another is done in florals, with an appliquéd message:

UP YOUR

MAN

IFESTO!

Or else she makes wall-hangings out of toilet paper twisted like rope, braided and woven with reels of outdated girlie movies, the kind that used to be called "art films". "Used porn," she says cheerfully. "Why not recycle it, eh?"

Jody does store mannequins, sawn apart, the pieces glued back together in disturbing poses. She fixes them up with paint and collage and steel wool stuck on at appropriate places. One hangs from a meat-hook, stuck through the solar plexus, another has trees and flowers painted all over her face like fine tattooing, with a delicacy I wouldn't have suspected from Jody. Another has the heads of six or seven old dolls attached to her stomach.

I recognize some of them: Sparkle Plenty, Betsy Wetsy, Barbara Ann Scott.

Zillah is blonde and skimpy, like the frail flower-girls of a few years back. She calls her pieces *Lintscapes*. They are made from the wads of felt-like fuzz that accumulate on dryer filters and can be peeled off in sheets. I have admired these myself as I stuffed them into the wastebasket: their texture, their soft colours. Zillah has bought a number of towels in different shades and run them repeatedly through the dryer, to get shades of pink, of grey-green, of off-white, as well as the standard underneath-the-bed grey. These she has cut and shaped and glued carefully to a backing, to form multi-layered compositions that resemble cloudscapes. I am entranced by them, and wish I had thought of this first. "It's like making a soufflé," Zillah says. "One breath of cold air and you're dead in the water."

Jody, who is more in charge than anyone, has gone through my paintings and chosen the ones for the show. She's taken some of the still lifes, *Wringer, Toaster, Deadly Nightshade*, and *Three Witches*. *Three Witches* is the one of the three different sofas.

Apart from the still lifes, what I'm showing is mostly figurative, although there are a couple of constructions made from drinking-straws and uncooked macaroni, and one called *Silver Paper*. I didn't want to include these, but Jody liked them. "Domestic materials," she said.

The Virgin Mary pieces are in the show, and all of the Mrs. Smeaths. I thought there were too many of her, but Jody wanted them. "It's woman as anti-cheesecake," she said. "Why should it always be young, beautiful women? It's good to see the aging female body treated with compassion, for a change." This, only in more high-flown language, is what she's written in the catalogue.

The show is held in a small defunct supermarket, west on Bloor Street. It is to be converted to a hamburger heaven, shortly; but meanwhile it's empty, and one of the women who knows a cousin of the wife of the developer who owns it has managed to persuade him to let us use it for two weeks. She told him that in the Renaissance the most famous dukes were known

641

for their aesthetic taste and patronage of the arts, and this idea appealed to him. He doesn't know it's an all-woman show; just some artists, is what she told him. He says it's okay with him as long as we don't get the place dirty.

"What's to get dirty?" says Carolyn, as we look around. She's right, it's dirty enough already. The produce counters and shelves have been torn up, there are patches ripped off the erstwhile linoleum-tile flooring where the wide bare boards show through, lights dangle in wire cages; only some of them work. The checkout counters are still in place, though, and there are a few tattered signs drooping on the walls: SPECIAL 3/95c. FRESH FROM CALIFORNIA. MEAT LIKE YOU LIKE IT.

"We can make this space work for us," says Jody, striding around with her hands in her coverall pockets.

"How?" says Zillah.

"I didn't take judo for nothing," says Jody. "Let the momentum of the enemy carry him off balance."

In practice this means that she appropriates the MEAT LIKE YOU LIKE IT sign and incorporates it into one of her constructions, an especially violent dismemberment in which the mannequin, dressed only in ropes and leather straps, has ended up with her head tucked upside-down under her arm.

"If you were a man you'd get stomped for that," Carolyn tells her.

Jody smiles sweetly. "But I'm not one."

We work for three days, arranging and rearranging. After we have the stuff in place, there are the rented trestle-tables to be assembled for the bar, the hooch and eats to be bought. "Hooch" and "eats" are Jody's words. We get Canadian wine in gallon jugs, styrofoam cups to serve it in, pretzels and potato chips, hunks of cheddar cheese wrapped in plastic film, Ritz crackers. This is what we can afford; but also there's an unspoken rule that the food has to be unwaveringly plebeian.

Our catalogue is a couple of mimeographed sheets stapled together at the top corner. This catalogue is supposed to be a collective effort, but in fact Jody has written most of it, because she has the knack. Carolyn makes a banner, out of bedsheets dyed to look as if someone's bled on them, to hang above the outside door:

F(OUR) FOR ALL.

"What's that supposed to mean?" says Jon, who has dropped by, supposedly to pick me up, really to see. He is suspicious of my doings with women, although he will not demean himself by saying so. He does however refer to them as "the girls".

"It's a pun on *free for all*," I tell him, although I know he knows this. "Plus it encapsulates the word *our*." *Encapsulate* is also one of Jody's words.

He does not comment.

It's the banner that attracts the newspapers: this kind of thing is new, it's an event, and it promises disruption. One newspaper sends a photographer, in advance, who says, jokingly, "Come on, girls, burn a few bras for me," while he's taking our pictures.

"Pig," says Carolyn in a low voice.

"Cool it," says Jody. "They love it when you freak."

Before the opening, I come to the gallery early. I pace around the show, up and down the former aisles, around the checkout counters where Jody's sculptures pose like models on a runway, past the wall where Carolyn's quilts yell defiance. This is strong work, I think. Stronger than mine. Even Zillah's gauzy constructions appear to me to have a confidence and subtlety, an assurance, that my own paintings lack: in this context my pictures are too highly finished, too decorative, too merely pretty.

I have strayed off course, I have failed to make a statement. I am peripheral.

I drink some of the awful wine and then some more, and feel better; although I know that later I will feel worse. The stuff tastes like something you'd use to tenderize pot-roast.

*　　*　　*

643

I stand against the wall, beside the door, hanging onto my styrofoam cup. I'm standing here because it's the exit. Also the entrance: people arrive, and then more people.

Many, most of these people are women. There are all kinds of them. They have long hair, long skirts, jeans and overalls, earrings, caps like construction workers', lavender shawls. Some of them are other painters, some just look like it. Carolyn and Jody and Zillah are here by now; and there are greetings called, squeezes of the arm, kisses on cheeks, shrieks of delight. They all seem to have more friends than I do, more close women friends. I've never really considered it before, this absence; I've assumed that other women were like me. They were, once. And now they are not.

There is Cordelia, of course. But I haven't seen her for years.

Jon is not here yet, although he said he would come. We even got a baby-sitter so he could. I think maybe I will flirt with someone, someone inappropriate, just to see what could happen; but there aren't many possibilities, because there aren't many men. I make my way through the crowd with another styrofoam cup of the dreadful red marinade, trying not to feel left out.

Right behind me a woman's voice says, "Well, they certainly are *different*." It's the quintessential Toronto middle-class-matron putdown, the ultimate disapproval. It's what they say about slums. It would not look good over the sofa, is what she means. I turn and look at her: a well-cut silver-grey suit, pearls, a suave scarf, expensive suede shoes. She's convinced of her own legitimacy, her right to pronounce: I and my kind are here on sufferance.

"Elaine, I'd like you to meet my mother," says Jody. The idea of this woman being Jody's mother is breathtaking. "Mum, Elaine did the flower painting. The one you like?"

She means *Deadly Nightshade*. "Oh yes," says Jody's mother, smiling warmly. "You girls are all so gifted. I did like that one, the colours are lovely. But what are all those eyes doing in it?"

This is so much what my own mother would say that I

am swept with longing. I want my mother to be here. She would dislike most of this, the cut-up mannequins especially; she wouldn't understand it at all. But she would smile, and dredge up something nice to say. Very recently I would have derided such talents. Now I have need of them.

I get myself another cup of wine and a Ritz cracker with some cheese on it, and peer through the crowd for Jon, for anyone. What I see, over the heads, is Mrs. Smeath.

Mrs. Smeath is watching me. She lies on the sofa with her turban-like Sunday hat on, the afghan wrapped around her. I have named this one *Torontodalisque*: *Homage to Ingres*, because of the pose, and the rubber plant like a fan behind her. She sits in front of a mirror with half of her face peeling off, like the villain in a horror comic I once read; this one is called *Leprosy*. She stands in front of her sink, her wicked paring knife in one hand, a half-peeled potato in the other. This one is called AN·EYE·FOR·AN·EYE.

Next to this is *White Gift*, which is in four panels. In the first one, Mrs. Smeath is wrapped up in white tissue paper like a can of Spam or a mummy, with just her head sticking out, her face wearing its closed half-smile. In the next three she's progressively unwrapped: in her print dress and bib apron, in her back-of-the-catalogue Eaton's flesh-coloured foundation garment – although I don't expect she possessed one – and finally in her saggy-legged cotton underpants, her one large breast sectioned to show her heart. Her heart is the heart of a dying turtle: reptilian, dark red, diseased. Across the bottom of this panel is stencilled: THE·KINGDOM·OF·GOD·IS·WITHIN·YOU.

It's still a mystery to me, why I hate her so much.

I look away from Mrs. Smeath, and there is another Mrs. Smeath, only this one is moving. She's just inside the door and heading towards me. She's the same age as she was. It's as if she's stepped down off the wall, the walls: the same round raw-potato face, the hulky big-boned frame, the glittering spectacles and hairpin crown. My gut clenches in fear; then there's that rancid hate, flashing up in an instant.

But of course this can't be Mrs. Smeath, who must be much older by now. And it isn't. The hairpin crown was an optical

645

illusion: it's just hair, greying and cropped short. It's Grace Smeath, charmless and righteous, in shapeless, ageless clothing, dun in colour; she is ringless and without ornament. By the way she stalks, rigid and quivering, lips pinched, the freckles standing out on her root-white skin like bug bites, I can see that this will not be transformed into a light social occasion by any weak-chinned smiling of mine.

I try anyway. "Is it Grace?" I say. Several nearby people have stopped in mid-word. This is not the sort of woman who usually frequents gallery openings, of any kind.

Grace clumps relentlessly forward. Her face is fatter than it used to be. I think of orthopaedic shoes, lisle stockings, underwear laundered thin and grey, coal cellars. I am afraid of her. Not of anything she could do to me, but of her judgment. And here it comes.

"You are disgusting," she says. "You are taking the Lord's name in vain. Why do you want to hurt people?"

What is there to be said? I could claim that Mrs. Smeath is not Grace's mother but a composition. I could mention the formal values, the careful use of colour. But *White Gift* is not a composition, it's pictures of Mrs. Smeath, and indecent pictures at that. It's washroom graffiti raised to a higher order.

Grace is staring past me at the wall: there are not just one or two foul pictures to be appalled by, there are many. Mrs. Smeath in metamorphosis, from frame to frame, naked, exposed and desecrated, along with the maroon velvet chesterfield, the sacred rubber plant, the angels of God. I have gone way too far.

Grace's hands are fists, her fatted chin is trembling, her eyes are pink and watery, like a laboratory rabbit's. Is that a tear? I am aghast, and deeply satisfied. She is making a spectacle of herself, at last, and I am in control.

But I look again, more closely: this woman is not Grace. She doesn't even look like Grace. Grace is my age, she would not be this old. There's a generic resemblance, that's all. This woman is a stranger.

"You ought to be ashamed of yourself," says the woman who is not Grace. Her eyes narrow behind her glasses. She raises her fist, and I drop my glass of wine. Red splashes the wall and floor.

What she has in her clenched hand is a bottle of ink. With a shaky twist she unscrews the top, and I hold my breath, with fright but also curiosity: is it me she'll throw it at? For throwing is clearly her intention. There are gasps around us, this is happening fast, Carolyn and Jody are pushing forward.

The woman who is not Grace hurls the ink, bottle and all, straight at *White Gift*. The bottle careens and thuds to the carpet, ink pours down over the skyscape, veiling Mrs. Smeath in Parker's Washable Blue. The woman gives me a triumphant smile and turns, not stalking now but scurrying, heading for the door.

I have my hands over my mouth, as if to scream. Carolyn envelops me, hugging. She smells like a mother. "I'll call the police," she says.

"No," I say. "It will come off." And it probably will, because *White Gift* is varnished, and painted on wood. Maybe there won't even be a dent.

There are women gathering around me, the rustle of their feathers, a cooing. I am soothed and consoled, patted, cherished as if in shock. Maybe they mean it, maybe they like me after all. It's so hard for me to tell, with women.

"Who was that?" they ask.

"Some religious nut-case," says Jody. "Some reactionary."

I will be looked at, now, with respect: paintings that can get bottles of ink thrown at them, that can inspire such outraged violence, such uproar and display, must have an odd revolutionary power. I will seem audacious, and brave. Some dimension of heroism has been added to me.

FEATHERS FLY AT FEMINIST FRACAS, says the paper. The picture is of me cringing, hands over my mouth, Mrs. Smeath bare naked and dripping with ink in the background. This is how I learn that women fighting is news. There's something titillating about it, up-ended and comic, like men in evening gowns and high heels. *Henfighting*, it's called.

The show itself attracts bad adjectives: "abrasive", "aggressive" and "shrill". It's mostly Jody's statues and Carolyn's quilts that are called these things. Zillah's lintscapes are termed "subjective", "introverted" and "flimsy". Compared with the rest of them, I get off easy: "naïve surrealism with a twist of feminist lemon".

Carolyn makes a bright yellow banner with the words "abrasive", "aggressive" and "shrill" on it in red, and hangs it outside the door. A great many people come.

63

I'm waiting, in a waiting-room. The waiting-room has several nondescript blond-wood chairs in it, with seats upholstered in olive green, and three end tables. This furniture is a clunky imitation of the early Scandinavian furniture of ten or fifteen years ago, now drastically out of style. On one of the tables there are some thumbed *Reader's Digest* and *Maclean's* magazines, and on another an ashtray, white with a rosebud trim. The carpet is an orangey-green, the walls an off-yellow. There is one picture, a lithoprint of two coy, grisly children in pseudo-peasant costume, vaguely Austrian, using a mushroom for an umbrella.

The room smells of old cigarette smoke, old rubber, the worn intimacy of cloth too long against flesh. On top of that, an overlay of floor-wash antiseptic, seeping in from the corridors beyond. There are no windows. This room sets me on edge, like fingernails on a blackboard. Or like a dentist's waiting-room, or the room where you'd wait before a job interview, for a job you didn't want to get.

This is a discreet private loony bin. A rest home, it's called: The Dorothy Lyndwick Rest Home. The sort of place well-off people use for stowing away those members of their families who are not considered fit to run around in public, in order to keep them from being carted off to 999 Queen, which is neither discreet nor private.

999 Queen is both a real place and high-school shorthand for all funny-farms, booby-hatches, and nut-houses that could possibly be imagined. We had to imagine them, then, never having seen one. "999 Queen," we would say, sticking our tongues out the sides of our mouths, crossing our eyes, making circles near our ears with our forefingers. Craziness was considered funny, like all other things that were in reality frightening and profoundly shameful.

I am waiting for Cordelia. Or I think it will be Cordelia:

her voice on the phone did not sound like her, but slower and somehow damaged. "I saw you," is what she said, as if we had been talking together only five minutes before. But in fact it had been seven years, or eight, or nine: the summer she worked at the Stratford Shakespearean Festival, the summer of Josef. "In the paper," she added. And then a pause, as if this was a question.

"Right," I said. Then, because I knew I should, "Why don't we get together?"

"I can't go out," Cordelia said, in the same slowed-down voice. "You'll have to come here."

And so I am here.

Cordelia comes through a door at the far end of the room, walking carefully, as if balancing, or lame. But she is not lame. Behind her is another woman, with the optimistic, false, toothy smile of a paid attendant.

It takes me a moment to recognize Cordelia, because she doesn't look at all the same. Or rather she doesn't look the way she did when I last saw her, in her wide cotton skirt and barbaric bracelet, elegant and confident. She is in an earlier phase, or a later one: the soft green tweeds and tailored blouses of her good-taste background, which now appear matronly on her, because she has put on weight. Or has she? Flesh has been added, but it has slid down, towards the middle of her body, like mud sliding down a hill. The long bones have risen to the surface of her face, the skin tugged downwards on them as if by irresistible gravitational pull. I can see how she'll be when she's old.

Someone has done her hair. Not her. She would never make it in tight little waves like that.

Cordelia stands uncertainly, squinting a little, head poking forward and swinging imperceptibly from side to side, the way an elephant's does, or some slow, bewildered animal. "Cordelia," I say, standing up.

"There's your friend," says the woman, smiling relentlessly. She takes Cordelia by the arm and gives a small tug, to start her in the right direction. "There you are," I say, falling already into the trap of addressing her like a child. I come forward,

650

give her an awkward kiss. I find to my surprise that I'm glad to see her.

"Better late than never," Cordelia says, with the same hesitation, the thickness in her voice I've heard over the phone. The woman steers her to the chair across from mine, settles her down into it with a little push, as if she's elderly, and stubborn.

Suddenly I'm outraged. No one has a right to treat Cordelia this way. I scowl at the woman, who says, "How nice of you to come! Cordelia enjoys a visit, don't you, Cordelia?"

"You can take me out," Cordelia says. She looks up at the woman, for approval.

"Yes, that's right," says the woman. "For tea or something. If you promise to bring her back, that is!" She gives a cheery laugh, as if this is a joke.

I take Cordelia out. The Dorothy Lyndwick Rest Home is in High Park, a suburb where I've never been before and don't know my way around, but there's a corner café a few blocks along. Cordelia knows it, and her way there. I don't know whether I should take her arm or not, and so I don't; I walk along beside her, watchful at crossings as if she's blind, slowing my pace to hers.

"I don't have any money," says Cordelia. "They won't let me have any. They even get my cigarettes for me."

"That's all right," I say.

We ease into a booth, order coffee and two toasted Danishes. I give the order: I don't want the waitress staring. Cordelia fumbles, produces a cigarette. Her hand, lighting it, is shaky. "Great flaming blue-headed balls of Jesus," she says, making an effort with the syllables. "It's good to be out of there." She tries a laugh, and I laugh with her, feeling culpable and accused.

I should ask her things: what has she been doing, for these years we've skipped? What about her acting, what became of that? Did she get married, have children? What exactly has been going on, to bring her where she is? But all of this is beside the point. It's detachable, it's been added on. The main thing is Cordelia, the fact of her now.

"What the shit have they got you on?" I say.

"Some sort of tranquillizers," she says. "I hate them. They make me drool."

"What for?" I say. "How did you end up in that nut-hatch anyway? You aren't any crazier than I am."

Cordelia looks at me, blowing out smoke. "Things weren't working out very well," she says after a while.

"So?" I say.

"So. I tried pills."

"Oh, Cordelia." Something goes through me with a slice, like watching a child fall, mouth down on rock. "Why?"

"I don't know. It just came over me. I was tired," she says.

There is no point telling her she shouldn't have done such a thing. I do what I'd do in high school: I ask for the details. "So did you conk out?"

"Yes," she said. "I checked into a hotel, to do it. But they figured it out – the manager or someone. I had to get my stomach pumped. That was revolting. Vomit-making, you could say."

She does what would be a laugh, except that her face is so rigid. I think I may cry. At the same time I'm angry with her, though I don't know why. It's as if Cordelia has placed herself beyond me, out of my reach, where I can't get at her. She has let go of her idea of herself. She is lost.

"Elaine," she says, "get me out."

"What?" I say, brought up short.

"Help me get out of there. You don't know what it's like. You have no privacy." This is the closest to pleading she's ever come.

A phrase comes to me, a remnant left over from boys, from Saturday afternoons, reading the comics: *Pick on somebody your own size*. "How could I do that?" I say.

"Visit me tomorrow and we'll go in a taxi." She sees me hesitate. "Or just lend me the money. That's all you have to do. I can hide the pills in the morning, I won't take them. Then I'll be all right. I know it's those pills that're keeping me like this. Just twenty-five dollars is all I need."

"I don't have a lot of money with me," I say, which is true enough, but an evasion. "They'd catch you. They'd know you were off the pills. They could tell."

"I can fool them any day," Cordelia says, with a flicker of her old cunning. Of course, I think, she's an actress. Or was.

652

She can counterfeit anything. "Anyway, those doctors are so dumb. They ask all these questions, they believe anything I tell them, they write it all down."

There are doctors, then. More than one. "Cordelia, how can I take the responsibility? I haven't even talked, I haven't talked to anyone."

"They're all assholes," she says. "There's nothing wrong with me. You know, you said yourself." There's a frantic child in there, behind that locked, sagging face.

I have an image of spiriting Cordelia away, rescuing her. I could do it, or something like it; but then where would she end up? Hiding out in our apartment, sleeping on an improvised bed like the draft-dodgers, a refugee, a displaced person, smoking up the kitchen with Jon wondering who the hell she is and why she's there. Things are uneven between us as it is; I'm not sure I can afford Cordelia. She'd be one more sin of mine, to be chalked up to the account he's keeping in his head. Also I am not feeling totally glued together myself.

And there's Sarah to think of. Would she take to this Auntie Cordelia? How is Cordelia with small children? And exactly how sick in the head is she, anyway? How long before I'd come back and find her out cold on the bathroom floor, or worse? In the middle of a bright red sunset. Jon's work-table is an arsenal, there are little saws lying around, little chisels. Maybe it would just be melodrama, a skin-deep slash or two, her old theatricality; though perhaps theatrical people are not less risky, but more. In the interests of the role they'll sacrifice anything.

"I can't, Cordelia," I say gently. But I don't feel gentle towards her. I am seething, with a fury I can neither explain nor express. *How dare you ask me?* I want to twist her arm, rub her face in the snow.

The waitress brings the bill. "Are you sufficiently sophonsified?" I say to Cordelia, trying for lightness, and a change of subject. But Cordelia has never been stupid.

"So you won't," she says. And then, forlornly: "I guess you've always hated me."

"No," I say. "Why would I? No!" I am shocked. Why would she say such a thing? I can't remember ever hating Cordelia.

"I'll get out anyway," she says. Her voice is not thick now, or hesitant. She has that stubborn, defiant look, the one I remember from years ago. *So?*

I walk her back, deposit her. "I'll come to visit you," I say. I intend to, but know at the same time that the chances are slim. She'll be all right, I tell myself. She was like this at the end of high school, and then things got better. They could again.

On the subway going back, I read the advertisements: a beer, a chocolate bar, a brassiere turning into a bird. I imitate relief. I feel free, and weightless.

But I am not free, of Cordelia.

I dream Cordelia falling, from a cliff or bridge, against a background of twilight, her arms outspread, her skirt open like a bell, making a snow angel in the empty air. She never hits or lands; she falls and falls, and I wake with my heart pounding and gravity cut from under me, as in an elevator plummeting out of control.

I dream her standing in the old Queen Mary schoolyard. The school is gone, there is nothing but a field, and the hill behind with the scrawny evergreen trees. She is wearing her snowsuit jacket, but she is not a child, she's the age she is now. She knows I have deserted her, and she is angry.

After a month, two months, three, I write Cordelia a note, on flowered notepaper of the sort that doesn't leave much space for words. I purchase this notepaper specially. My note is written with such false cheerfulness I can barely stand to lick the flap of the envelope. In it I propose another visit.

But my note comes back in the mail, with *address unknown* scrawled across it. I examine this writing from every angle, trying to figure out if it could be Cordelia's, disguised. If it isn't, if she's no longer at the rest home, where has she gone? She could ring the doorbell at any minute, call on the phone. She could be anywhere.

* * *

654

I dream a mannequin statue, like one of Jody's in the show, hacked apart and glued back together. It's wearing nothing but a gauze costume, covered with spangles. It ends at the neck. Underneath its arm, wrapped in a white cloth, is Cordelia's head.

XII
One Wing

64

In the corner of a parking lot, among the sumptuous boutiques, they've reconstructed a forties diner. 4-D's Diner, it's called. Not a renovation, brand new.

They couldn't tear this stuff down fast enough, once.

Inside it's pretty authentic, except that it looks too clean; and it's less forties than early fifties. They have a soda-fountain countertop, with stools along it topped in acid lime-green, and vinyl-padded booths in a shade of shiny purple that looks like the skin of an early shark-finned convertible. A jukebox, chrome coat-trees, grainy black and white photos on the walls, of real forties diners. The waitresses have white uniforms with black tab trim, although the shade of their red lipstick isn't quite right and they should have run it around the edges of their mouths. The waiters have those soda-jerk caps set at an angle, and the right haircuts, a close shave up the back of the neck. They're doing a roaring business. Kids in their twenties, mostly.

Really it's like Sunnysides, done over as a museum. They could have Cordelia and me in here, in our bat-wing sleeves and cinch belts, stuffed and mounted or made of wax, drinking our milk-shakes, looking as bored as we could.

The last time I saw Cordelia, she was going through the door of the rest home. That was the last time I talked to her. Although it wasn't the last time she talked to me.

There are no avocado-and-sprout sandwiches, the coffee is not espresso, the pie is coconut cream and no worse than it was then. This is what I have, coffee and pie, sitting in one of the purple booths, watching young people exclaim over what they think is the quaintness of the past.

The past isn't quaint while you're in it. Only at a safe distance, later, when you can see it as décor, not as the shape your life's been squeezed into.

They have Elvis Presley zucchini moulds now: you clamp them around your zucchini while it's young, and as it grows it's deformed into the shape of Elvis Presley's head. Is this why he sang? To become a zucchini? Vegetarianism and reincarnation are in the air, but that's taking it too far. I'd rather come back as a sow-bug, myself; or a stir-fried shrimp. Though I suppose the whole idea's more lenient than Hell.

"You've done it well," I say to the waitress. "Of course the prices are wrong. It was ten cents for a coffee, then."

"Really," she says, not as a question. She gives me a dutiful smile: *Boring old frump*. She is half my age, living, already, a life I can't imagine. Whatever her guilts are, her hates and terrors, they are not the same. What do they do about AIDS, these girls? They can't just roll around in the hay, the way we did. Is there a courtship ritual that involves, perhaps, an exchange of doctors' telephone numbers? For us it was pregnancy that was the scary item, the sexual booby-trap, the thing that could finish you off. Not any more.

I pay the bill, overtip, gather up my packages, an Italian scarf for each of my daughters, a fountain-pen for Ben. Fountain-pens are coming back. Somewhere in Limbo, all the old devices and appliances and costumes are lined up, waiting their turn for re-entry.

I walk up the street, along to the corner. The next street is Josef's. I count houses: this one must be his. The front's been ripped out and glassed over, the lawn is paving-stone. There's an antique child's rocking horse in the window, a threadbare quilt, a wooden-headed doll with a battered face. One-time throwouts, recycled as money. Nothing so indiscreet as a price tag, which means outrageous.

I wonder what became of Josef, eventually. If he's still alive he must be sixty-five, or more. If he was a dirty old man then, how dirty is he now?

He did make a film. I think it was him; in any case, the director's name was the same. I saw it by accident, at a film festival. This was a lot later, when I was already living in Vancouver.

It was about two women with nebulous personalities and

660

cloudy hair. They wandered through fields with the wind blowing their thin dresses against their thighs, and gazed inscrutably. One of them took apart a radio and dropped the pieces into a stream, ate a butterfly, and cut the throat of a cat, because she was deranged. These things wouldn't have been as appealing if she had been ugly, instead of blonde and ethereal. The other one made little slashes on the skin of her thigh, using an old-fashioned straight-razor that had belonged to her grandfather. Towards the end she jumped off a railway overpass, into a river, her dress fluttering like a window curtain. Except for the colours of their hair, it was hard to tell the two of them apart.

The man in this film was in love with both of them and couldn't make up his mind. Hence their craziness. This is what convinced me that it must have been Josef: it wouldn't have occurred to him that they might have had reasons of their own for being crazy, apart from men.

None of the blood in this film was real blood. Women were not real to Josef, any more than he was real to me. This was why I could treat his sufferings with such scorn and unconcern: he wasn't real. The reason I've never dreamed about him was that he belonged already to the world of dreams: discontinuous, irrational, obsessive.

I was unfair to him, of course, but where would I have been without unfairness? In thrall, in harness. Young women need unfairness, it's one of their few defences. They need their callousness, they need their ignorance. They walk in the dark, along the edges of high cliffs, humming to themselves, thinking themselves invulnerable.

I can't blame Josef for his film. He was entitled to his own versions, his own conjurings; as I am. I may have served his ends, but he served mine as well.

There is *Life Drawing*, for instance, hanging right now on the gallery wall, Josef preserved in aspic and good enough to eat. He is on the left side of the picture, stark naked but turned with a twist half away from the viewer, so what you get is the ass end, then the torso in profile. On the right side is Jon, in the same position. Their bodies are somewhat idealized: less hairy than they really were, the muscle groups in higher definition, the skin luminous. I thought about putting jockey shorts on them, in deference to Toronto, but decided against it. Both of them have wonderful bums.

Each of them is painting a picture, each picture is on an easel. Josef's is of a voluptuous but not overweight woman, sitting on a stool with a sheet draped between her legs, her breasts exposed; her face is Pre-Raphaelite, brooding, consciously mysterious. Jon's painting is a series of intestinal swirls, in hot pink, raspberry-ripple red and Burgundy Cherry purple.

The model is seated on a chair between them, face front, bare feet flat on the floor. She's clothed in a white bedsheet, wrapped around her below the breasts. Her hands are folded neatly in her lap. Her head is a sphere of bluish glass.

I sit with Jon at a table in the roof bar of the Park Plaza Hotel, drinking white wine spritzers. My suggestion: I wanted to see it again. Outside, the skyline has changed: the Park Plaza is no longer the tallest building around, but a squat leftover, dwarfed by the svelte glassy towers that rise around it. Due south is the CN Tower, lifting up like a huge inverted icicle. This is the sort of architecture you used to see only in science fiction comic books, and seeing it pasted flat against the monotone lake-sky I feel I've stepped not forward in time but sideways, into a universe of two dimensions.

But inside the bar not a lot has changed. The place still looks like a high-class Regency bordello. Even the waiters, with their good-grooming hair and air of harried discretion, look the same, and probably are. The management used to keep ties in the coat check, for gentlemen who'd forgotten them. *Forgotten* was the word, because surely no gentleman would deliberately choose to go tieless. It was a big thing when this place was cracked by women in pant-suits. A chic black model did it: they couldn't refuse to let her in, she could have hit them with racism. Even this memory dates me, and the little thrill of triumph that goes with it: what woman, now, would think of a pant-suit as liberation?

I didn't use to come here with Jon. He would have sneered, then, at the upholstered period chairs, the looped drapes, the men and women cut from a glossy whisky ad. It was Josef I came

662

with, Josef whose hand I touched, across the surface of the table. Not Jon's, as now.

It's only the ends of the fingers, only lightly. This time we don't say much: there's none of the verbal prodding there was at lunch. There's a shared vocabulary, of monosyllable and silence; we know why we're here. Going down in the elevator, I look into the smoked-mirror wall and see my face in the dark glass obscured by time, as a stone overgrown. I could be any age.

We take a taxi back to the warehouse, our hands resting side by side on the seat. We go up the stairs to the studio, slowly, so we won't get out of breath: neither one of us wants to be caught out by the other in a middle-aged wheeze. Jon's hand is on my waist. It's familiar there; it's like knowing where the light-switch is, in a house you once lived in but haven't been back to for years. When we reach the door, before we go in, he pats me on the shoulder, a gesture of encouragement, and of wistful resignation.

"Don't turn on the light," I say.

Jon puts his arms around me, his face in the angle of my neck. It's a gesture less of desire than of fatigue.

The studio is the purplish grey of autumn twilight. The plaster casts of arms and legs glimmer whitely, like broken statues in a ruin. There's a scatter of my clothes in the corner, empty cups dotted here and there, on the work counter, by the window, marking my daily trails, claiming space. This room seems like mine now, as if I've been living here all along, no matter where else I've been or what else been I've been doing. It's Jon who has been away, and has returned at last.

We undress each other, as we used to do at first; but more shyly. I don't want to be awkward. I'm glad it's dusk; I'm nervous about the backs of my thighs, the wrinkling above my knees, the soft fold across my stomach, not fatness exactly but a pleat. The hair on his chest is grey, a shock. I avoid looking at the small beer-belly that's grown on him, though I'm aware of it, of the changes in his body, as he must be of mine.

When we kiss, it's with a gravity we lacked before. Before we were avid, and selfish.

We make love for the comfort of it. I recognize him, I could recognize him in total darkness. Every man has his own rhythm, which remains the same. In this there is the relief of greeting.

I don't feel I'm being disloyal to Ben, only loyal to something else; which pre-dates him, which has nothing to do with him. An old score.

Also I know it's something I'll never do again. It's the last look, before turning away, at some once-visited, once-extravagant place you know you won't go back to. An evening view, of Niagara Falls.

We lie together under the duvet, arms around each other. It's hard to remember what we used to fight about. The former anger is gone, and with it that edgy, jealous lust we used to have for each other. What's left is fondness, and regret. A diminuendo.

"Come to the opening?" I say. "I'd like you to."

"No," he says. "I don't want to."

"Why not?"

"I'd feel bad," he says. "I wouldn't want to see you that way."

"What way?" I say.

"With all those people, slobbering over you."

What he means is that he doesn't want to be merely an onlooker, that there's no room for him in all that, and he's right. He doesn't want to be just my ex-husband. He would be dispossessed, of me and of himself. I realize I don't want it either, I don't really want him to be there. I need him to be, but I don't want it.

I turn, lean on my elbow, kiss him again, on the cheek this time. The hair down low, behind his ears, is already turning white. I think, we did that just in time. It was almost too late.

65

With Jon it's like falling downstairs. Up until now there have been preliminary stumblings, recoveries, a clutching for hand-holds. But now all balance is lost and we plunge down headlong, both of us, noisily and without grace, gathering momentum and abrasions as we go.

I enter sleep angry and dread waking up, and when I do wake I lie beside the sleeping body of Jon, in our bed, listening to the rhythm of his breathing and resenting him for the oblivion he still controls.

For weeks he has been more silent than usual, and home less. Home less, that is, when I am home. When I'm away at work he is there all right, even when Sarah's in pre-school. I've begun to find signs, tiny clues left in my way like breadcrumbs dropped on a trail: a cigarette with a pink mouthmark on it, two used glasses in the sink, a hairpin that is not mine, beneath a pillow that is. I clean up and say nothing, hoarding these things for times of greater need.

"Someone named Monica called you," I tell him.

It's morning, and there's a whole day to get through. A day of evasion, suppressed anger, false calm. We are well beyond throwing things, by now.

He's reading the paper. "Oh?" he says. "What did she want?"

"She said to tell you Monica called," I say.

He comes back late at night and I'm in bed, feigning sleep, my head churning. I think of subterfuges: examining his shirts for perfume, tailing him along the street, hiding in the closet and jumping out, red-hot with discovery. I think of other things I could do. I could leave, go somewhere unspecified, with Sarah. Or I could demand that we talk things through. Or I could pretend nothing is happening, continue on with our lives as usual. This would have been the advice offered in women's magazines, of a decade ago: wait it out.

I see these things as scenarios, to be played through and discarded, perhaps simultaneously. None of them precludes the others.

In real life, the days go on as usual, darkening to winter and heavy with the unspoken.

"You had a thing with Uncle Joe, didn't you?" Jon says casually. It's a Saturday, and we're making a stab at normality by taking Sarah to Grange Park, to play in the snow.

"Who?" I say.

"You know. Josef what's-his-name. The old stick man."

"Oh, him," I say. Sarah is over by the swings with some other kids. We're sitting on a bench, having cleared the snow. I think I should be making a snowman, or doing some other thing good mothers are supposed to do. But I'm too tired.

"But you did, didn't you?" Jon says. "At the same time as me."

"Where did you get that idea?" I say. I know when I'm being accused. I run over my own ammunition: the hairpins, the lipstick, the phone calls, the glasses in the sink.

"I'm not a moron, you know. I figured it out."

He has jealousies of his own then, wounds of his own to lick. Things I have inflicted. I should lie, deny everything. But I don't want to. Josef, at the moment, gives me a little pride.

"That was years ago," I say. "Thousands of years ago. It wasn't important."

"Like shit," he says. I once thought he would ridicule me, if he found out about Josef. The surprise is that he takes him seriously.

That night we make love, if that is any longer the term for it. It's not shaped like love, not coloured like it, but harsh, war-coloured, metallic. Things are being proved. Or repudiated.

666

In the morning he says, "Who else has there been?" Out of nowhere. "How do I know you weren't hopping into the sack with every old fart around?"

I sigh. "Jon," I say. "Grow up."

"How about Mr. Beanie Weenie?" he keeps on.

"Oh, come on," I say. "You were hardly the angel. Your place was crawling with all those skinny girls. You didn't want strings, remember?"

Sarah is still in her crib asleep. We are safe, we can get down to it, this telling of bad truths which are not entirely true. Once you start, it's difficult to stop. There is even a certain relish in it.

"At least I was open about it," he says. "I didn't sneak around. I didn't pretend to be so goddamn pure and faithful, the way you did."

"Maybe I loved you," I say. I notice the past tense. So does he.

"You wouldn't know love if you fell over it," he says.

"Not like Monica?" I say. "You're not being very open right now. I've found those hairpins, in my own bed. You could at least have the decency to do it somewhere else."

"How about you?" he says. "You're always going out, you get around."

"Me?" I say. "I don't have the time. I don't have time to think, I don't have time to paint, I barely have time to shit. I'm too busy paying the goddamn rent."

I've said the worst thing, I've gone too far. "That's it," says Jon. "It's always you, what you contribute, what you put up with. It's never me." He hunts for his jacket, heads for the door.

"Going to see Monica?" I say, with as much venom as I can dredge up. I hate it, this schoolyard bickering. I want embraces, tears, forgiveness. I want them to arrive by themselves, with no effort on my part, like rainbows.

"Trisha," he says. "Monica is just a friend."

It's winter. The heat goes off, comes on again, goes off, at random. Sarah has a cold. She coughs at night and I get up for her, feeding her spoonfuls of cough syrup, bringing her drinks of water. In the daytime we are both exhausted.

667

I am sick a lot myself this winter. I get her colds. I lie in bed on weekend mornings, looking up at the ceiling, my head clogged and cottony. I want glasses of ginger ale, squeezed orange juice, the sound of distant radios. But these things are gone forever, nothing arrives on a tray. If I want ginger ale I'll have to go to the store or the kitchen, buy it or pour it myself. In the main room Sarah watches cartoons.

I don't paint at all any more. I can't think about painting. Although I've received a junior grant from a government arts programme, I can't organize myself enough to lift a brush. I push myself through time, to work, to the bank to get money, to the supermarket to buy food. Sometimes I watch daytime soaps on television, where there are more crises and better clothes than in real life. I tend to Sarah.

I don't do anything else. I no longer go to the meetings of women, because they make me feel worse. Jody phones and says we should get together, but I put her off. She would jolly me along, make bracing and positive suggestions I know I can't live up to. Then I would only feel more like a failure.

I don't want to see anyone. I lie in the bedroom with the curtains drawn and nothingness washing over me like a sluggish wave. Whatever is happening to me is my own fault. I have done something wrong, something so huge I can't even see it, something that's drowning me. I am inadequate and stupid, without worth. I might as well be dead.

One night Jon does not come back. This is not usual, it isn't our silent agreement: even when he stays out late he is always in by midnight. We haven't had a fight this day; we've hardly spoken. He hasn't phoned to say where he is. His intention is clear: he has left me behind, in the cold.

I crouch in the bedroom, in the dark, wrapped in Jon's old sleeping bag, listening to the wheezing sound of Sarah breathing and the whisper of sleet against the window. Love blurs your vision; but after it recedes, you can see more clearly than ever. It's like the tide going out, revealing whatever's been thrown away and sunk: broken bottles, old gloves, rusting pop cans, nibbled fishbodies, bones. This is the kind of thing you see if you sit in

668

the darkness with open eyes, not knowing the future. The ruin you've made.

My body is inert, without will. I think I should keep moving, to circulate my blood, as you are supposed to do in a snowstorm so you won't freeze to death. I force myself to stand up. I will go to the kitchen and make tea.

Outside the house a car slides by, through the mushy snow, a muffled rushing. The main room is dark, except for the light coming in from the lampposts on the street, through the window. The things on Jon's work-table glint in this half-light: the flat blade of a chisel, the head of a hammer. I can feel the pull of the earth on me, the dragging of its dark curve of gravity, the spaces between the atoms you could fall so easily through.

This is when I hear the voice, not inside my head at all but in the room, clearly: *Do it. Come on. Do it.* This voice doesn't offer a choice; it has the force of an order. It's the difference between jumping and being pushed.

The Exacto knife is what I use, to make a slash. It doesn't even hurt, because right after that there's a whispering sound and space closes in and I'm on the floor. This is how Jon finds me. Blood is black in the darkness, it does not reflect, so he doesn't see until he turns on the light.

I tell the people at Emergency that it was an accident. I am a painter, I say. I was cutting canvas and my hand slipped. It's my left wrist, so this is plausible. I'm frightened, I want to hide the truth: I have no intention of being stuffed into 999 Queen Street, now or ever.

"In the middle of the night?" the doctor says.

"I often work at night," I say.

Jon backs me up. He's just as scared as I am. He tied my wrist up in a tea-towel and drove me to the hospital. I leaked through the towel, onto the front seat.

"Sarah," I said, remembering her.

"She's downstairs," Jon said. Downstairs is the landlady, a middle-aged Italian widow.

"What did you tell her?" I asked.

"I said it was your appendix," Jon said. I laughed, a little. "What the hell got into you?"

669

"I don't know," I said. "You'll have to get this car cleaned." I felt white, drained of blood, cared for, purified. Peaceful.

"Are you sure you don't want to talk to someone?" the doctor in Emergency says.

"I'm fine now," I say. The last thing I want to do is talk. I know what he means by *someone*: a shrink. Someone who will tell me I'm nuts. I know what kind of people hear voices: people who drink too much, who fry their brains with drugs, who slip off the rails. I feel entirely steady, I'm not even anxious any more. I've already decided what I will do, afterwards, tomorrow. I'll wear my arm in a sling and say I broke my wrist. So I don't have to tell him, or Jon, or anyone else, about the voice.

I know it wasn't really there. Also I know I heard it.

It wasn't a frightening voice, in itself. Not menacing but excited, as if proposing an escapade, a prank, a treat. Something treasured, and secret. The voice of a nine-year-old child.

66

The snow has melted, leaving a dirty filigree, the wind is blowing around the grit left over from winter, the crocuses are pushing up through the mud of the desolate smashed-down lawns. If I stay here I will die.

It's the city I need to leave as much as Jon, I think. It's the city that's killing me.

It will kill me suddenly. I'll be walking along the street, thinking of nothing in particular, and all at once I will turn sideways and dive off the kerb, to be smashed by a speeding car. I will topple in front of a subway train without warning, I'll plunge from a bridge without intention. All I will hear will be that small voice, inviting and conspiratorial, gleeful, urging me over. I know I'm capable of such a thing.

(Worse: although I'm afraid of this idea and ashamed of it, and although in the daytime I find it melodramatic and ludicrous and refuse to believe in it, I also cherish it. It's like the secret bottle stashed away by alcoholics: I may have no desire to use it, right now, but I feel more secure knowing it's there. It's a fallback, it's a vice, it's an exit. It's a weapon.)

At night I sit beside Sarah's crib, watching the flutter of her eyelids as she dreams, listening to her breathe. She will be left alone. Or not alone, because she will have Jon. Motherless. This is unthinkable.

I turn on the lights in the living room. I know I must start packing, but I don't know what to take. Clothes, toys for Sarah, her furry rabbit. It seems too difficult, so I go to bed. Jon is already in there, turned towards the wall. We have gone through a pretence of truce and reformation, straight into deadlock. I don't wake him up.

In the morning, after he leaves, I bundle Sarah into the stroller and take some of my grant money out of the bank. I don't know where to go. All I can think of is away. I buy us tickets to Vancouver, which has the advantage of being warm, or so I suppose. I stuff our things into duffle bags, which I've bought at Army Surplus.

I want Jon to come back and stop me, because now that I'm in motion I can't believe I'm actually doing this. But he doesn't come.

I leave a note, I make a sandwich: peanut butter. I cut it in two and give half to Sarah, and a glass of milk. I call a taxi. We sit at the kitchen table with our coats on, eating our sandwiches and drinking our milk, and waiting.

This is when Jon comes back. I keep eating.

"Where the hell do you think you're going?" he says.

"Vancouver," I say.

He sits down at the table, stares at me. He looks as if he hasn't slept for weeks, although he's been sleeping a lot, over-sleeping. "I can't stop you," he says. It's a statement of fact, not a manoeuvre: he will let us go without a fight. He too is exhausted.

"I think that's the taxi," I say. "I'll write."

I'm good at leaving. The trick is to close yourself off. Don't hear, don't see. Don't look back.

We don't have a sleeper, because I need to save the money. I sit up all night, Sarah sprawled and snuffling in my lap. She's done some crying, but she's too young to realize what I've done, what we're doing. The other passengers extend themselves into the aisles; baggage expands, smoke drifts in the stale air, food wrappings clog the washrooms. There's a card game going on up at the front of the car, with beer.

The train runs northwest, through hundreds of miles of scraggy forests and granite outcrops, hundreds of small blue anonymous lakes edged with swamp and bulrushes and dead spruce, old snow in the shadows. I peer out through the glass of the train window, which is streaked with rain and dust, and there is the landscape of my early childhood, smudged and scentless and untouchable and moving backwards.

At long intervals the train crosses a road, gravel or thin and paved, with a white line down the middle. This looks like

672

emptiness and silence, but to me it is not empty, not silent. Instead it's filled with echoes.

Home, I think. But it's nowhere I can go back to.

It's worse than I thought it would be, and also better.

Some days I think I'm crazy to have done this; other times that it's the sanest move I've made in years.

It's cheaper in Vancouver. After a short spell in a Holiday Inn, I find a house I can rent, on the rise behind Kitsilano Beach, one of those toytown houses that are bigger inside than they look. It has a view of the bay, and the mountains across it, and, in the summer, endless light. I find a co-op pre-school for Sarah. For a time I live on grant money. I freelance a little, then get a part-time job refinishing furniture for an antique dealer. I like this, because it's mindless and the furniture can't talk. I am thirsty for silence.

I lie on the floor, washed by nothing and hanging on. I cry at night. I am afraid of hearing voices, or a voice. I have come to the edge, of the land. I could get pushed over.

I think maybe I should go to see a shrink, because that is the accepted thing, now, for people who are not in balance, and I am not. Finally I do go. The shrink is a man, a nice man. He wants me to talk about everything that happened to me before I was six, nothing after. Once you are six, he implies, you are cast in bronze. What comes after is not important.

I have a good memory. I tell him about the war.

I tell him about the Exacto knife and the wrist, but not about the voice. I don't want him to think I'm a loony. I want him to think well of me.

I tell him about nothing.

He asks if I have orgasms. I say that isn't the problem.

He thinks I am hiding things.

After a while I stop going.

Gradually I grow back, into my hands. I take to getting up early in the morning, before Sarah is awake, to paint. I find I have a

673

minor, ambiguous reputation, from the show in Toronto, and I am invited to parties. At first there is a resentful edge, because I am from what is known as *back east*, which is supposed to confer unfair advantages; but after a time I've been here long enough so I can pass, and after that I can do the resentful act myself, to easterners, and get away with it.

I'm also invited to take part in several group showings, mostly by women: they've heard about the ink-throwing, read the snotty reviews, all of which render me legitimate, although from the east. Women artists of many kinds, women of many kinds are in ferment here, they are boiling with the pressured energy of explosive forces confined in a small space, and with the fervour of all religious movements in their early, purist stages. It is not enough to give lip-service and to believe in equal pay: there has to be a conversion, from the heart. Or so they imply.

Confession is popular, not of your flaws but of your sufferings, at the hands of men. Pain is important, but only certain kinds of it: the pain of women, but not the pain of men. Telling about your pain is called sharing. I don't want to share in this way; also I am insufficient in scars. I have lived a privileged life, I've never been beaten up, raped, gone hungry. There is the issue of money, of course, but Jon was as poor as me.

There is Jon. But I don't feel overmatched by him. Whatever he did to me, I did back, and maybe worse. He's twisting now, because he misses Sarah. He calls long distance, his voice on the phone fading in and out like a wartime broadcast, plaintive with defeat, with an archaic sadness that seems, more and more, to be that of men in general.

No mercy for him, the women would say. I am not merciful, but I am sorry.

A number of these women are lesbians, newly declared or changing over. This is at the same time courageous and demanded. According to some, it's the only equal relationship possible, for women. You are not genuine otherwise.

I am ashamed of my own reluctance, my lack of desire; but the truth is that I would be terrified to get into bed with a woman. Women collect grievances, hold grudges and change shape. They pass hard, legitimate judgments, unlike the purblind

674

guesses of men, fogged with romanticism and ignorance and bias and wish. Women know too much, they can neither be deceived nor trusted. I can understand why men are afraid of them, as they are frequently accused of being.

At parties they start to ask leading questions that have the ring of inquisition; they are interested in my positions, my dogmas. I am guilty about having so few of these: I know I am unorthodox, hopelessly heterosexual, a mother, quisling and secret wimp. My heart is a dubious object at best, blotchy and treacherous. I still shave my legs.

I avoid gatherings of these women, walking as I do in fear of being sanctified, or else burned at the stake. I think they are talking about me, behind my back. They make me more nervous than ever, because they have a certain way they want me to be, and I am not that way. They want to improve me. At times I feel defiant: what right have they to tell me what to think? I am not Woman, and I'm damned if I'll be shoved into it. *Bitch*, I think silently. *Don't boss me around.*

But also I envy their conviction, their optimism, their care-lessness, their fearlessness about men, their camaraderie. I am like someone watching from the sidelines, waving a cowardly handkerchief, as the troops go boyishly off to war, singing brave songs.

I have several women friends, not very close ones. Single mothers, as I am. I meet them at pre-school. We trade kids for nights out and grumble harmlessly together. We avoid each other's deeper wounds. We're like Babs and Marjorie from my old Life Drawing class, with the same sense of rueful comedy. It's an older pattern, for women; but by now we are older.

Jon comes to visit, a tentative move towards reconciliation, which I think I want as well. It doesn't work, and we divorce, finally, by long distance.

My parents come as well. They miss Sarah, I think, more than they miss me. I have made excuses not to go east for Christmas. Against the backdrop of the mountains, they seem out of place, a little shrunken. They are more themselves in their letters. They are saddened by me and what they probably think of as my broken home, and don't know what to, say about it. "Well,

675

dear," says my mother, talking about Jon. "I always thought he was very intense." A bad word that spells trouble.

I take them to Stanley Park, where there are big trees. I show them the ocean, sloshing around in seaweed. I show them a giant slug.

My brother Stephen sends postcards. He sends a stuffed dinosaur for Sarah. He sends a water pistol. He sends a counting book, about an ant and a bee. He sends the solar system, in the form of a plastic mobile, and stars you can stick on the ceiling that light up at night.

After a time I find that, in the tiny world of art (tiny, because who knows about it really? It's not on television), swirls, squares, and giant hamburgers are out and other things are in, and I am suddenly at the front of a smallish wave. There's a flurry, as such things go. More of my pictures sell, for higher prices. I'm represented by two regular galleries now, one east, one west. I go to New York, briefly, leaving Sarah with one of my single-mother friends, for a group show organized by the Canadian government which is attended by many people who work with the Trade Commission. I wear black. I walk on the streets, feeling sane in comparison with the other people there, who all seem to be talking to themselves. I come back.

I have men, at long intervals and in some desperation. These affairs are rushed and unsatisfactory: I don't have time for the finer points. Even these brief interludes are almost too strenuous for me.

None of these men rejects me. I don't give them the chance. I know what is dangerous for me, and keep away from the edges of things. From anything too bright, too sharp. From lack of sleep. When I start feeling shaky I lie down, expecting nothing, and it arrives, washing over me in a wave of black vacancy. I know I can wait it out.

*   *   *

676

After more time I meet Ben, who picks me up in the most ordinary way, in the supermarket. Actually he asks if he can carry my shopping bags, which look heavy and are, and I let him, feeling silly and archaic and looking first to make sure no women I know are watching.

Years before, I would have considered him too obvious, too dull, practically simple-minded. And for years after that, a chauvinist of the more amiable sort. He is all these things; but he is also like an apple, after a prolonged and gluttonous binge.

He comes over and fixes my back porch with his own saw and hammer, as in the women's magazines of long ago, and has a beer afterwards, on the lawn, as in ads. He tells me jokes I haven't heard since high school. My gratitude for these mundane enjoyments amazes me. But I don't require him, he's no transfusion. Instead he pleases me. It's a happiness, to be so simply pleased.

He takes me to Mexico, as in drugstore romances. He's just bought his small travel business, more as a hobby than anything: he made his money earlier, in real estate. But he likes to take photographs and sit in the sun. To do what he likes and make money at the same time is what he's wanted all his life.

He is shy in bed, easily surprised, quickly delighted.

We combine households, in a third, larger house. After a while we get married. There is nothing dramatic about it. To him it seems appropriate, to me eccentric: it's a defiance of convention, but of a convention he's never heard of. He doesn't know how outlandish I think I'm being.

He's ten years older than I am. He has a divorce of his own, and a grown son. My daughter Sarah becomes the daughter he wanted, and soon we have Anne. I think of her as a second chance. She is less pensive than Sarah, more stubborn. Sarah knows, already, that you can't always have everything you want.

Ben considers me good, and I don't disturb this faith: he doesn't need my more unsavoury truths. He considers me also a little fragile, because artistic: I need to be cared for, like a potted plant. A little pruning, a little watering, a little weeding and straightening up, to bring out the best in me. He makes up a set of books, for the business end of my painting: what has sold, and for how much. He tells me what I can deduct on my

677

income tax return. He fills out the return. He arranges the spices in alphabetical order, on a special shelf in the kitchen. He builds the shelf.

I could live without this. I have before. But I like it, all the same.

My paintings themselves he regards with wonder, and also apprehension, like a small child looking at a candle. What he focuses on is how well I do hands. He knows these are hard. He once wanted to take up something like that himself, he says, but never got around to it because of having to earn a living. This is a lot like the kinds of things people have said to me at gallery openings, but in him I forgive it.

He goes away at judicious intervals, on business, giving me a chance to miss him.

I sit in front of the fireplace, with his arm around me solid as the back of a chair. I walk along the breakwater in the soothing Vancouver drizzle, the half-tones of the seashore, the stroking of the small waves. In front of me is the Pacific, which sends up sunset after sunset, for nothing; at my back are the improbable mountains, and beyond them an enormous barricade of land.

Toronto lies behind it, at a great distance, burning in thought like Gomorrah. At which I dare not look.

XIII

Picoseconds

67

I wake late. I eat an orange, some toast, an egg, mushing it up in a teacup. The hole poked in the bottom of the eggshell was not to keep the witches from going to sea, as Cordelia said. It's to break the vacuum between shell and egg-cup, so the shell can be extracted. Why did it take me forty years to figure that out?

I put on my other jogging suit, the cerise one, and do some desultory stretching exercises on Jon's floor. It's Jon's floor again, not mine. I feel I've returned it to him, along with whatever fragments of his own life, or of our life together, I've been keeping back till now. I remember all those Mediaeval paintings, the hand raised, open to show there is no weapon: *Go in peace*. Dismissal, and blessing. My way of doing this was not exactly the way of the saints, but seems to have worked just as well. The peace was for the bestower of it, also.

I go down to get the morning paper. I leaf through it, without reading much. I know I'm killing time. I've almost forgotten what I'm supposed to be doing here, and I'm impatient to be gone, back to the west coast, back to the time zone where I live my life now. But I can't do that yet. I'm suspended, as in airports or dentists' waiting-rooms, expecting yet another interlude that will be textureless and without desire, like painkiller or the interiors of planes. This is how I think of the coming evening, the opening of the show: something to get through without disaster.

I should go to the gallery, check to see that everything's in order. I should perform at least that minimal courtesy. But instead I take the subway, get off near the main gate of the cemetery, wander south and east, scuffing through the fallen leaves, scanning the gutters; looking down at the sidewalk, for silver paper, nickels, windfalls. I still believe such things exist, and that I could find them.

With a slight push, a slip over some ill-defined edge, I could turn into a bag lady. It's the same instinct: rummaging in junkheaps, pawing through discards. Looking for something that's been thrown away as useless, but could still be dredged up and reclaimed. The collection of shreds, of space in her case, time in mine.

This is my old route home from school. I used to walk along this sidewalk, behind or in front of the others. Between these lampposts my shadow on the winter snow would stretch ahead of me, double, shrink again and disappear, the lamps casting their haloes around them like the moon in fog. Here is the lawn where Cordelia fell down backwards, making a snow angel. Here is where she ran.

The houses are the same houses, though no longer trimmed in peeling white winter-greyed paint, no longer down-at-heel, postwar. The sandblasters have been here, the skylight people; inside, the benjamina trees and tropical climbers have taken over, ousting the mangy African violets once nurtured on kitchen windowsills. I can see through these houses, to what they used to be; I can see the colours that used to cover the walls, dusty rose, muddy green, mushroom, and the chintz curtains no longer there. What time do they really belong in, their own or mine?

I walk along the street, slightly uphill, against a scattered traffic of small children going home for lunch. Although the girls wear jeans, denoting freedom, they aren't as noisy as they used to be; there are no chants, no catcalls. They trudge along doggedly, or so it seems to me. Maybe that's because I'm not at their level any more: I'm higher, so the sound comes up to me filtered. Or maybe it's me, the presence among them of someone they think is an adult, and has power.

A few of them stare, many don't. What's to see? A middle-aged woman, hands in her coat pockets, the legs of her jogging suit bunching above her boot-tops, no more bizarre than most and easily forgotten.

Some of the porches have pumpkins on them, carved with faces, happy or sad or threatening, waiting for tonight. All Souls' Eve, when the spirits of the dead will come back to the living, dressed as ballerinas and Coke bottles and spacemen and Mickey Mice, and the living will give them candy to keep them from turning vicious. I can still taste that festival: the tart air, caramel in the mouth, the hope at the door, the belief in something for nothing all children take for granted. They won't get home-made popcorn balls any more though, or apples: rumours of razor blades abound, and the possibility of poison. Even by the time of my own children, we worried about the apples. There's too much loose malice blowing around.

In Mexico they do this festival the right way, with no disguises. Bright candy skulls, family picnics on the graves, a plate set for each individual guest, a candle for the soul. Everyone goes away happy, including the dead. We've rejected that easy flow between dimensions: we want the dead unmentionable, we refuse to name them, we refuse to feed them. Our dead as a result are thinner, greyer, harder to hear, and hungrier.

68

My brother Stephen died five years ago. I shouldn't say died: was killed. I try not to think of it as murder, although it was, but as some kind of accident, like an exploding train. Or else a natural catastrophe, like a landslide. What they call for insurance purposes an act of God.

He died of an eye for an eye, or someone's idea of it. He died of too much justice.

He was sitting on a plane. He had a window seat. This much is known.

In the nylon-webbing pocket in front of him was an in-flight magazine with an article in it about camels, which he'd read, and another about upgrading your business wardrobe, which he hadn't. There was also a set of earphones and a vomit bag.

Under the seat in front, beyond his bare feet – he's taken off his shoes and socks – is his briefcase, with a paper in it written by himself, on the subject of the probable composition of the universe. The universe, he once thought, may well be made up of infinitesimal pieces of string, in thirty-two different colours. The pieces of string are so small that "colours" is only a manner of speaking. But he is having doubts: there are other theoretical possibilities, two of which he has outlined in his paper. The universe is hard to pin down; it changes when you look at it, as if it resists being known.

He was supposed to deliver his paper the day before yesterday, in Frankfurt. He would have heard other papers. He would have learned.

Stuffed under the seat along with the briefcase is his suit jacket, one of the three he now owns. His shirtsleeves are rolled up, which doesn't solve much: the air-conditioning is on the fritz and the air on the plane is overheated. Also it smells bad: at least one washroom toilet is out of order, and people fart more on planes, as my brother has had occasion to observe before, having taken a lot of plane trips. This is now compounded by panic, which is bad for the digestion. Two seats over, a fat bald-headed man is snoring with his mouth open, releasing an invisible cloud of halitosis.

The shades on the windows are pulled down. My brother knows that if he were to raise his he would see a runway, shimmering with heat, and beyond that a dun landscape alien as the moon, with a blinding sea in the background; and some oblong brown buildings with flat roofs, from which reprieve will come, or not. He saw all this before the shades came down. He doesn't know what country the buildings are in.

He hasn't had anything to eat since this morning. Sandwiches arrived from outside, strange granular bread, the butter on it liquid, some sort of beige meat paste that hinted of ptomaine. Also a piece of pale sweaty cheese in plastic wrap. He ate this cheese and the sandwich, and now his hands smell of old picnics, the roadside lunches of wartime.

The last drink of water was doled out four hours ago. He has a roll of peppermint LifeSavers: he always takes them on trips, in case of bumpy rides. He gave one to the middle-aged woman in oversized glasses and a plaid pant-suit who was sitting beside him. He is somewhat relieved she's gone: her voiceless, colourless weeping, snuffly and monotonous, was beginning to get to him. The women and the children have all been allowed off, but he is not a woman or a child. Everyone left on the plane is a man.

They have been spaced, two by two, with an empty seat between each pair. Their passports have been collected. Those who have done the collecting are standing at intervals in the aisles of the plane, six of them, three with small machine-guns, three with visible grenades. They are all wearing airplane pillowcases over their heads, with holes cut for the eyes and for the mouths, which show in the dim light as white glints, pink glistenings. Below these pillowcases, which are red, their clothes are ordinary: a leisure outfit, a pair of grey flannel slacks with a white shirt tucked in, the bottom of a conservative navy-blue suit.

Naturally they came on board in the guise of passengers; though how they got the weapons past Security is anyone's guess. They must have had help, someone at the airport, so that they could jump up, the way they did, somewhere over the English Channel, and start shouting orders and waving around the firearms. Either that or the things were already on the plane, in pre-arranged hiding places, because nothing metal gets through the X-rays these days.

There are two or possibly three other men up in the cockpit, negotiating with the control tower over the radio. They haven't yet told the passengers who they are or what they want; all they've said, in heavily accented but understandable English, is that everyone on the plane will live together or else die together. The rest has been monosyllables and pointing: *You, here*. It's hard to tell how many of them there are altogether, because of the identical pillowcases. They're like those characters in old comic books, the ones with two identities. These men have been caught halfway through their transformation: ordinary bodies but with powerful, supernatural heads, deformed in the direction of heroism, or villainy.

I don't know whether or not this is what my brother thought. But it's what I think for him, now.

Unlike the open-mouthed man beside him, my brother can't sleep. So he occupies himself with theoretical stratagems: what would he do if he were in their place, the place of the men with pillowcase heads? It's their tension, their hair-trigger excitement and blocked adrenalin that fills the plane, despite the lax bodies of the passengers, their fatigue and resignation.

If he were them, he would of course be ready to die. Without that as a given, such an operation would be pointless and unthinkable. But die for what? There's probably a religious motif, though in the foreground something more immediate: money, the release of others jailed in some sinkhole for doing more or less the same thing these men are doing. Blowing something up, or threatening to. Or shooting someone.

In a way this is all familiar. It's as if he's lived through it before, a long time ago; and despite the unpleasantness, the irritation of it, the combination of boredom and fear, he has a certain fellow-feeling. He hopes these men can keep their heads and carry it off, whatever it is. He hopes there will be no snivelling and pants-wetting among the passengers, that no one will go berserk and start screaming; and trigger a jittery massacre. A cool hand and a steady eye is what he wishes for them.

A man has entered from the front of the plane and is talking with two of the others. It seems to be an argument: there are gestures of the hands, a raised word. The other standing men tense, their square red heads scanning the passengers like odd radars. My brother knows he should avoid eye contact, keep his head down. He looks at the nylon-webbing pocket in front of him, furtively peels off a LifeSaver.

The new man starts to walk down the aisle of the plane, his oblong, three-holed head turning from side to side. A second man walks behind him. Eerily, the taped music comes on over the intercom, saccharine, soporific. The man pauses; his oversized head moves ponderously left, like the head of some short-sighted, dull-witted monster. He extends an arm, gestures with the hand: *Up*. It's my brother he points to.

Here I stop inventing. I've spoken with the witnesses, the survivors, so I know that my brother stands up, eases himself past the man in the aisle seat, saying "Excuse me." The expression on his face is one of bemused curiosity: these people are unfathomable, but then so are most. Perhaps they have mistaken him for someone else. Or they may want him to help negotiate, because they're walking towards the front of the plane, where another pillowhead stands waiting.

It's this one who swings open the door for him, like a polite hotel doorman, letting in the full glare of day. After the semi-darkness it's ferociously bright, and my brother stands blinking as the image clears to sand and sea, a happy vacation postcard. Then he is falling, faster than the speed of light.

This is how my brother enters the past.

I was on planes and in airports for fifteen hours, getting there. I saw the buildings after that, the sea, the stretch of runway; the plane itself was gone. All they got in the end was safe conduct.

I didn't want to identify the body, or see it at all. If you don't see the body, it's easier to believe nobody's dead. But I did want to know whether they shot him before throwing him out, or after. I wanted it to be after, so he could have had that brief moment of escape, of sunlight, of pretended flight.

I did not stay up at night, on that trip. I did not want to look at the stars.

The body has its own defences, its way of blocking things out. The government people said I was wonderful, by which they meant not a nuisance. I didn't collapse or make a spectacle of myself; I spoke with reporters, signed the forms, made the decisions. There was a great deal I didn't see or think about until much later.

What I thought about then was the space twin, the one who went on an interplanetary journey and returned in a week to find his brother ten years older.

Now I will get older, I thought. And he will not.

69

My parents never understood Stephen's death, because it had no reason; or no reason that had anything to do with him. Nor did they get over it. Before it, they were active, alert, vigorous; after it they faded.

"It doesn't matter how old they are," my mother said. "They're always your children." She tells me this as something I will need to know, later on.

My father became shorter and thinner, visibly shrivelled; he sat for long periods, without doing anything. Unlike himself. This is what my mother told me, over the telephone, long distance.

Sons should not die before their fathers. It's not natural, it's the wrong order. Because who will carry on?

My parents themselves died in the usual way, of the things elderly people die of, that I myself will die of sooner than I think: my father instantly, my mother a year later, of a slower and more painful disease. "It's a good thing your father went the way he did," she said. "He would have hated this." She didn't say anything about hating it herself.

The girls came for a week, early on, at the end of summer, when my mother was still in her house in the Soo and we could all pretend this was just another visit. I stayed on after them, digging weeds out of the garden, helping with the dishes because my mother had never got a dishwasher, doing the laundry downstairs in the automatic washer but hanging it out on the line because she thought dryers used up too much electricity. Greasing the muffin-tins. Impersonating a child.

My mother is tired, but restless. She won't take naps in the afternoon, insists on walking to the corner store. "I can manage," she says. She doesn't want me to cook for her. "You'll never find

689

anything in this kitchen," she says, meaning she thinks she'll never find anything herself if I start messing around in there. I smuggle frozen TV dinners into the refrigerator and con her into eating them by saying they'll go to waste if she doesn't. Waste is still a bugaboo for her. I take her to a movie, checking it first for violence, sex and death, and to a Chinese restaurant. In the north, in the old days, the Chinese restaurants were the only ones that could be depended on. The others went in for white bread and gravy-mix sandwiches, lukewarm baked beans, pies made from cardboard and glue.

She is on painkillers, then stronger painkillers. She lies down more. "I'm glad I don't have to have an operation, in a hospital," she says. "The only time I was ever in a hospital was with you kids. With Stephen they gave me ether. I went out like a light, and when I woke up, there he was."

A lot of what she says is about Stephen. "Remember those smells he used to make, with that chemistry set of his? That was the day I was having a bridge party! We had to open the doors, and it was the middle of winter." Or else: "Remember all those comic books he had stowed away under his bed? There were too many to save. I chucked them out, after he went away. I didn't think there was any use for them. But people collect them, I read about it; now they'd be worth a fortune. We always thought they were just trash." She tells this like a joke on herself.

When she talks about Stephen, he is never more than twelve years old. After that he got beyond her. I come to realize that she was, or is, in awe of him, slightly afraid of him. She didn't intend to give birth to such a person.

"Those girls gave you a bad time," she says one day. I've made both of us a cup of tea – she's permitted this – and we sit at the kitchen table, drinking it. She's still surprised to catch me drinking tea, and has asked several times whether I wouldn't prefer milk.

"What girls?" I say. My fingers are a wreck; I shred them quietly, out of sight beneath the tabletop, as I do in times of stress; an old bad habit I cannot seem to break.

"Those girls. Cordelia and Grace, and the other one. Carol Campbell." She looks at me, a little slyly, as if testing.

"Carol?" I say. I remember a stubby girl, turning a skipping rope.

"Of course, Cordelia was your best friend, in high school," she says. "I never thought she was behind it. It was that Grace, not Cordelia. Grace put her up to it, I always thought. What became of her?"

"I have no idea," I say. I don't want to talk about Cordelia. I still feel guilty, about walking away from her and not helping.

"I didn't know what to do," she says. "They came to me that day and said you'd been kept in at school, for being rude to the teacher. It was that Carol who said it. I didn't think they were telling the truth." She avoids the word *lie*, if possible.

"What day?" I say carefully. I don't know what day she means. She's begun to get things mixed up, because of the drugs.

"That day you almost froze. If I'd believed them I wouldn't have gone to look for you. I went down the road, along by the cemetery, but you weren't there." She regards me anxiously, as if wondering what I will say.

"Oh yes," I say, pretending I know what she's talking about. I don't want to confuse her. But I am growing confused myself. My memory is tremulous, like water breathed on. For an instant I see Cordelia and Grace, and Carol, walking towards me through the astonishing whiteness of the snow, their faces in shadow.

"I was so worried," she says. What she wants from me is forgiveness, but for what?

On some days she is stronger, and gives the illusion of improvement. Today she wants me to help her sort through the things in the cellar. "So you won't have to go through a lot of that old junk, later on," she says delicately. She won't say *death*; she wants to spare my feelings.

I don't like cellars. This one is unfinished: grey cement, rafters above. I make sure the upstairs door is left open. "You should have a railing put on these stairs," I say. They are narrow, undependable.

"I can manage," says my mother. From the days when managing was enough.

We sort through the old magazines, the stash of different-sized cardboard boxes, the shelves of clean jars. She threw out a lot less than she could have, when they moved; or else she's accumulated more. I carry things up the stairs and stow them in the garage. In there they seem disposed of.

There's a whole shelf of my father's shoes and boots, lined-up pairs: city shoes with perforated toecaps, overshoes, rubber boots, wading boots for fishing, heavy-soled boots for walking in the woods, with a bacon-grease patina and leather laces. Some of them must be fifty years old, or more. My mother will not throw them out, I know; but neither does she mention them. I can sense what she expects of me, in the way of control. I did my mourning at the funeral. She doesn't need to deal with a tearful child, not now.

I remember the old Zoology Building where we used to go on Saturdays, the creaking, overheated corridors, the bottles of eyeballs, the comforting smells of formaldehyde and mice. I remember sitting at the dinner table, with Cordelia, his warnings washing over our heads, the ruined water, the poisoned trees, species after species snuffed out like stepped-on ants. We did not think such things were prophecies. We thought they were boring then, a form of adult gossip that did not concern us. Now it's all come true, except worse. I live in his nightmare, no less real for being invisible. You can still breathe the air, but for how long?

Against his bleak forecasting is set my mother's cheerfulness, in retrospect profoundly willed.

We start on the steamer trunk. It's the one I remember from our Toronto house; I still think of it as mysterious, the repository of treasure. My mother too views this as an adventure: she says she hasn't looked into that trunk for years, she has no idea what's in there. She is no less alive because dying.

I open the trunk, and the smell of mothballs blossoms upward. Out come the baby clothes folded in tissue paper, the pieces of flowery silver, yellowy-black. "Keep these for the girls," she says. "You have this one." The wedding dress, the wedding pictures, the sepia-coloured relatives. A packet of feathers. Some bridge tallies with tassels on them, two pairs of white kid gloves. "Your father was a wonderful dancer," she says. "Before we were married." I have never known this.

We go down through the layers, unearthing discoveries: my

692

high-school pictures, my lipsticked mouth unsmiling, some-body's hair in an envelope, a single knitted baby sock. Old mittens, old neckties. An apron. Some things are to be kept, others thrown out or given away. Some things I will take back with me. We have several piles.

My mother is excited, and I catch some of this excitement from her: it's like a Christmas stocking. Although not pure joy.

Stephen's packets of airplane trading-cards, held together with rotting elastic bands. His scrapbooks, his drawings of explosions, his old report cards. These she sets aside.

My own drawings and scrapbooks. There are the pictures of little girls I now remember, with their puffed sleeves and pink skirts and hairbows. Then, in the scrapbooks, some unfamiliar pictures cut from magazines: women's bodies, in clothes of the forties, with other women's heads glued onto them. *This is a Watchbird watching* YOU.

"You loved those magazines," says my mother. "You used to pore over them for hours, when you were sick in bed."

Underneath the scrapbooks is my old photo album, the black pages held together with the tie like a shoe-lace. Now I can remember putting it into the trunk, before I went to high school.

"We gave you that," says my mother. "For Christmas, to go with your camera." Inside is my brother, poised with a snowball, and Grace Smeath crowned with flowers. A couple of large boulders, with names printed underneath them in white pencil. Myself, in a jacket with the sleeves too short, standing against a motel cabin door. The number 9.

"I wonder what happened to that camera?" says my mother. "I must've given it away. You lost interest in it, after a while."

I'm aware of a barrier between us. It's been there for a long time. Something I have resented. I want to put my arms around her. But I am held back.

"What's that?" she says.

"My old purse," I say. "I used to take it to church." I did. I can see the church now, the onion on the spire, the pews, the stained-glass windows. THE.KINGDOM.OF.GOD.IS.WITHIN.YOU.

"Well, what do you know. I don't know why I saved that," says my mother, with a little laugh. "Put it on the throwout pile." It's squashed flat; the red plastic is split at the sides, where the sewing is. I pick it up, push at it to make it go back into shape. Something rattles. I open it up and take out my blue cat's eye.

"A marble!" says my mother, with a child's delight. "Remember all those marbles Stephen used to collect?"

"Yes," I say. But this one was mine.

I look into it, and see my life entire.

70

Down this street is where the store was. We bought red licorice whips, bubble-gum, orange popsicles, black jawbreakers that faded to a seed. Things you could buy for a penny, with the King's head on it. *Georgius VI Dei Gratia.*

I've never got used to the Queen being grown up. Whenever I see her cut-off head on the money, I think of her as fourteen years old, in her Girl Guide uniform, her back as straight as ours were supposed to be, looking down at me from the yellowing newspaper clippings on Miss Lumley's Grade Four blackboard; standing in front of the clumsy diamond of a radio microphone, frowning with earnestness and well-concealed fear, rallying the forces as the bombs fell on London, as we sang "There'll Always Be an England" to the waving of Miss Lumley's life-threatening wooden pointer, in a time-warp eight years later.

The Queen has had grandchildren since, discarded thousands of hats, grown a bosom and (heresy to think it) the beginning of a double chin. None of this fools me. She's in there somewhere, that other one.

I walk the next blocks, turn the corner, expecting to see the familiar dingy oblong of the school, in weathered red brick the colour of dried liver. The cindered schoolyard, the tall thin windows with orange paper pumpkins and black cats stuck onto them for Hallowe'en, the graven lettering over the doors, BOYS and GIRLS, like the inscriptions on mausoleums of the late nineteenth century.

But the school has disappeared. In its place a new school has risen instantly, like a mirage: light-coloured, block-shaped, glossy and modern.

I feel hit, in the pit of the stomach. The old school has been erased, wiped from space. It's as if it was never there at all. I lean against a telephone pole, bewildered, as if something has

695

been cut out of my brain. Suddenly I'm bone tired. I would like to go to sleep.

After a while I approach the new school, go towards it through the gate, walk slowly around it. BOYS and GIRLS have been abolished, that much is clear; though there's still a chain-link fence. The schoolyard is dotted with swings, with climbing-bars and slides, in bright primary colours; a few children have come back early from lunch and are clambering about.

It's all so clean-cut, so open. Surely behind those glassy, candid doors there are no more long wooden pointers, no black rubber strap, no hard wooden desks in rows; no King and Queen in their stiff regalia, no inkwells; no sniggering about underpants; no bitter, whiskery old women. No cruel secrets. Everything like that is gone.

I come around the back corner, and there is the eroded hill, with its few sparse trees. That much is still the same, then.

No one's up there.

I climb up the wooden steps, stand where I used to stand. Where I am still standing, never having been away. The voices of the children from the playground below could be any children's voices, from any time, the light under the trees thickens, turns malevolent. Ill will surrounds me. It's hard to breathe. I feel as if I'm pushing against something, a pressure on me, like opening the door against a snowstorm.

Get me out of this, Cordelia. I'm locked in.

I don't want to be nine years old forever.

The air is soft, autumnal, the sun shines. I am standing still. And yet I walk head down, into the unmoving wind.

XIV

Unified Field
Theory

71

I put on my new dress, cutting off the price tag with Jon's wire-cutters. I ended up with black, after all. Then I go into the bathroom to squint at myself in the inadequate, greasy mirror: now that I've got the thing on, it looks much the same as all the other black dresses I've ever owned. I check it for lint, apply my pink lipstick, and end up looking nice, as far as I can tell. Nice, and negligible.

I could jazz myself up somehow. I ought to have some dangly earrings, some bangles, a silver bow-tie on a little chain, an outsize Isadora Duncan strangle-yourself-by-mistake scarf, a rhinestone brooch of the thirties, in sly bad taste. But I don't have any of these things, and it's too late to go out and buy any. I will have to do. Come-as-you-are parties, they used to have. I will come as I am.

I'm at the gallery an hour early. Charna is not here, or the others; they may have gone out to eat, or more likely to change. Everything is set up though, the rented thick-stemmed wineglasses, the bottles of mediocre hooch, the mineral water for teetotallers, because who would serve unadulterated chlorine from the tap? The cheeses hardening at the edges, the sulphur-drenched grapes, luscious and shiny as wax, plumped with blood from the dying field-workers of California. It doesn't pay to know too many of these things; eventually there's nothing you can put into your mouth without tasting the death in it.

The bartender, a severe-eyed young woman in gelled hair and unstructured black, is polishing glasses behind the long table that serves as the bar. I extract a glass of wine from her. She's doing the bartending for money, her nonchalance implies: her true ambitions lie elsewhere. She tightens her lips while doling out my drink: she doesn't approve of me. Possibly she wants to be a painter, and thinks I have compromised my principles, knuckled under to success. How I used to revel in such bitter little snobberies myself; how easy they were, once.

I walk slowly around the gallery, sipping at my glass of wine, permitting myself to look at the show, for the first time really. What is here, and what is not. There's a catalogue, put together by Charna, a professional-looking computer-and-laser-printer affair. I remember the catalogue from the first show, done on a mimeo machine, smeared and illegible, its poverty a badge of authenticity. I remember the sound of the roller turning, the tang of the ink, the pain in my arm.

Chronology won out after all: the early things are on the east wall, what Charna calls the middle period on the end wall, and on the west wall are five recent pictures which I've never shown before. They're all I've been able to do in the past year. I work more slowly, these days.

Here are the still lifes. "Early forays by Risley into the realm of female symbolism and the charismatic nature of domestic objects," says Charna. In other words, the toaster, the coffee percolator, my mother's wringer washer. The three sofas. The silver paper.

Further along are Jon and Josef. I look at them with some fondness, them and their muscles and their cloudy-headed notions about women. Their youngness is terrifying. How could I have put myself into the hands of such inexperience?

Next to them is Mrs. Smeath; many of her. Mrs. Smeath sitting, standing, lying down with her holy rubber plant, flying, with Mr. Smeath stuck to her back, being screwed like a beetle; Mrs. Smeath in the dark-blue bloomers of Miss Lumley, who somehow combines with her in a frightening symbiosis. Mrs. Smeath unwrapped from white tissue paper, layer by layer. Mrs. Smeath bigger than life, bigger than she ever was. Blotting out God.

I put a lot of work into that imagined body, white as a burdock root, flabby as pork-fat. Hairy as the inside of an ear. I laboured on it, with, I now see, considerable malice. But these pictures are not only mockery, not only desecration. I put light into them too. Each pallid leg, each steel-rimmed eye, is there as it was, as plain as bread. I have said, *Look*. I have said, *I see*.

700

It's the eyes I look at now. I used to think these were self-righteous eyes, piggy and smug inside their wire frames; and they are. But they are also defeated eyes, uncertain and melancholy, heavy with unloved duty. The eyes of someone for whom God was a sadistic old man; the eyes of a small-town threadbare decency. Mrs. Smeath was a transplant to the city, from somewhere a lot smaller. A displaced person; as I was.

Now I can see myself, through these painted eyes of Mrs. Smeath: a frazzle-headed ragamuffin from heaven knows where, a gypsy practically, with a heathen father and a feckless mother who traipsed around in slacks and gathered weeds. I was unbaptized, a nest for demons: how could she know what germs of blasphemy and unfaith were breeding in me? And yet she took me in.

Some of this must be true. I have not done it justice, or rather mercy. Instead I went for vengeance.

An eye for an eye leads only to more blindness.

I move to the west wall, where the new paintings are. They are larger than my usual format, and space out the wall nicely.

The first one is called *Picoseconds*. "A *jeu d'esprit*," says Charna, "which takes on the Group of Seven and reconstructs their vision of landscape in the light of contemporary experiment and postmodern pastiche."

It is in fact a landscape, done in oils, with the blue water, the purple underpainting, the craggy rocks and windswept raggedy trees and heavy impasto of the twenties and thirties. This landscape takes up much of the painting. In the lower right-hand corner, in much the same out-of-the-way position as the disappearing legs of Icarus in the painting by Bruegel, my parents are making lunch. They have their fire going, the billy tin suspended over it. My mother in her plaid jacket bends over, stirring, my father adds a stick of wood to the fire. Our Studebaker is parked in the background.

They are painted in another style: smooth, finely modulated, realistic as a snapshot. It's as if a different light falls on them; as if they are being seen through a window which has opened in the landscape itself, to show what lies behind or within it.

Underneath them, like a subterranean platform, holding them

701

up, is a row of iconic-looking symbols painted in the flat style of Egyptian tomb frescoes, each one enclosed in a white sphere: a red rose, an orange maple leaf, a shell. They are in fact the logos from old gas pumps of the forties. By their obvious artificiality, they call into question the reality of landscape and figures alike.

The second painting is called *Three Muses*. Charna has had some trouble with this one. "Risley continues her disconcerting deconstruction of perceived gender and its relationship to perceived power, especially in respect to numinous imagery," she says. If I hold my breath and squint, I can see where she gets that: all Muses are supposed to be female, and one of these is not. Maybe I should have called it *Dancers*, and put her out of her misery. But they are not dancers.

To the right is a short woman, dressed in a flowered housecoat and mules with real fur. On her head is a red pillbox hat with cherries. She has black hair and large golden earrings, and is carrying a round object the size of a beach-ball, which is in fact an orange.

To the left is an older woman with blue-grey hair, wearing a waltz-length lavender silk gown. In her sleeve is tucked a lace handkerchief, over her nose and mouth is a gauze nurse's mask. Above the mask her bright blue eyes look out, crinkly at the edges and sharp as tacks. In her hands she holds a globe of the world.

In the middle is a thin man with medium-brown skin and white teeth, smiling an uncertain smile. He is wearing a richly worked gold and red oriental costume reminiscent of Balthazar's in Jan Gossaert's *Adoration* of the Magi, but without the crown and scarf. He too holds out a round object: it's flat like a disc and appears to be made of purple stained glass. On its surface are arranged, seemingly at random, several bright pink objects not unlike those to be found in abstract paintings. They are in fact spruce budworm eggs, in section; though I would not expect anyone but a biologist to recognize them.

The arrangement of the figures recalls that of classical Graces, or else of the different-coloured children wreathed around Jesus on the front of my old Sunday School paper. But those were facing in, and these are facing out. They hold their gifts forward, as if presenting them to someone who sits or stands outside the painting.

Mrs. Finestein, Miss Stuart from school, Mr. Banerji. Not as they were, to themselves: God knows what they really saw in their own lives, or thought about. Who knows what death-camp ashes blew daily through the head of Mrs. Finestein, in those years right after the war? Mr. Banerji probably could not walk down a street here without dread, of a shove or some word whispered or shouted. Miss Stuart was in exile, from plundered Scotland still declining, three thousand miles away. To them I was incidental, their kindness to me casual and minor; I'm sure they didn't give it a second thought, or have any idea of what it meant. But why shouldn't I reward them, if I feel like it? Play God, translate them into glory, in the afterlife of paint. Not that they'll ever know. They must be dead by now, or elderly. Elsewhere.

The third picture is called *One Wing*. I painted it for my brother, after his death.

It's a triptych. There are two smaller, flanking side panels. In one is a World War Two airplane, in the style of a cigarette card; in the other is a large pale-green luna moth.

In the larger, central panel, a man is falling from the sky. That he is falling and not flying is clear from his position, which is almost upside-down, slantwise to the few clouds; nevertheless he appears calm. He is wearing a World War Two RCAF uniform. He has no parachute. In his hand is a child's wooden sword.

This is the kind of thing we do, to assuage pain.

Charna thinks it's a statement about men, and the juvenile nature of war.

The fourth painting is called *Cat's Eye*. It's a self-portrait, of sorts. My head is in the right foreground, though it's shown only from the middle of the nose up: just the upper half of the nose, the eyes looking outwards, the forehead and the topping of hair. I've put in the incipient wrinkles, the little chicken-feet

703

at the corners of the lids. A few grey hairs. This is cheating, as in reality I pull them out.

Behind my half-head, in the centre of the picture, in the empty sky, a pier-glass is hanging, convex and encircled by an ornate frame. In it, a section of the back of my head is visible; but the hair is different, younger.

At a distance, and condensed by the curved space of the mirror, there are three small figures, dressed in the winter clothing of the girls of forty years ago. They walk forward, their faces shadowed, against a field of snow.

The last painting is *Unified Field Theory*. It's a vertical oblong, larger than the other paintings. Cutting across it a little over a third up is a wooden bridge. To either side of the bridge are the tops of trees, bare of leaves, with a covering of snow on them, as after a heavy moist snowfall. This snow is also on the railing and struts of the bridge.

Positioned above the top railing of the bridge, but so her feet are not quite touching it, is a woman dressed in black, with a black hood or veil covering her hair. Here and there on the black of her dress or cloak there are pinpoints of light. The sky behind her is the sky after sunset; at the top of it is the lower half of the moon. Her face is partly in shadow.

She is the Virgin of Lost Things. Between her hands, at the level of her heart, she holds a glass object: an oversized cat's eye marble, with a blue centre.

Underneath the bridge is the night sky, as seen through a telescope. Star upon star, red, blue, yellow, and white, swirling nebulae, galaxy upon galaxy: the universe, in its incandescence and darkness. Or so you think. But there are also stones down there, beetles and small roots, because this is the underside of the ground.

At the lower edge of the painting the darkness pales and merges to a lighter tone, the clear blue of water, because the creek flows there, underneath the earth, underneath the bridge, down from the cemetery. The land of the dead people.

I go to the bar, ask for another glass of wine. It's better quality than the rotgut we used to buy for such affairs.

I walk the room, surrounded by the time I've made; which is not a place, which is only a blur, the moving edge we live in; which is fluid, which turns back upon itself, like a wave. I may have thought I was preserving something from time, salvaging something; like all those painters, centuries ago, who thought they were bringing Heaven to earth, the revelations of God, the eternal stars, only to have their slabs of wood and plaster stolen, mislaid, burnt, hacked to pieces, destroyed by rot and mildew.

A leaky ceiling, a match and some kerosene would finish all this off. Why does this thought present itself to me, not as a fear but as a temptation?

Because I can no longer control these paintings, or tell them what to mean. Whatever energy they have came out of me. I'm what's left over.

72

Now Charna hustles towards me in mauve leather, clanking with ersatz gold. She whisks me into the back office: she doesn't want me dangling around in the empty gallery, at loose ends while the first revellers trickle in, she doesn't want me looking unsuccessful and too eager. She will make an entrance with me, later, when the noise level is high enough.

"You can relax here," she says; which is unlikely. In her office I drink my second drink, pacing the empty space. This is like birthday parties, with streamers and balloons at the ready and the hotdogs waiting in the kitchen, but what if nobody comes? Which will be worse: if they don't come, or if they do? Soon the door will open, and in will crowd a horde of snide and treacherous little girls, whispering and pointing, and I will be servile, grateful.

My hands begin to sweat. I think another drink will calm me down, which is a bad sign. I will go out there and flirt, just for the hell of it, to see if I can still interest anyone. But there may not be anyone to flirt with. In which case I will get drunk. Maybe I will throw up in the toilet, with or without the excess alcohol.

I'm not like this in other places, not this bad. I shouldn't have come back here, to this city that has it in for me. I thought I could stare it down. But it still has power; like a mirror that shows you only the ruined half of your face.

I think about escaping, out the back way. I could send a telegram later, claiming illness. That would start a good rumour: a lingering, invisible illness, which would get me out of such things forever.

But Charna reappears through the door in time, flushed with excitement. "There's lots of people here already," she says. "They're dying to meet you. We're all very proud of you." This is so much like what a family would say, a mother or an aunt, that I'm thrown off guard. Who is this family, and whose family is it? I've been framed: the recalcitrant child before the piano recital, or, more like it, the bullet-scarred war-horse, veteran of

706

early, barely remembered battles, about to be presented with a gold watch and a handshake and a heartfelt vote of thanks. A fading halo of blue ink clings round me.

Suddenly Charna reaches over to me, gives me a quick metallic hug. Maybe that warmth is genuine, maybe I should be ashamed of my dour, cynical thoughts. Maybe she really does like me, wish me well. I can almost believe it.

I stand in the main gallery, black from neck to toes, with my third glass of red wine. Charna is off now, rummaging in the crowd for people who are dying to meet me. I am at her disposal. I crane my neck, peering through the crowd, which has blotted out the paintings; only a few tops of heads are visible, a few skies, a few backgrounds and clouds. I keep expecting, or fearing, that people I should know, have known, will appear, and I will only half recognize them. They will stride forward, hands outstretched, girls from high school bloated or diminished, skins crinkled, frowns permanent, smooth-fleshed boyfriends of thirty years ago who've gone bald or grown moustaches or shrunk. *Elaine! What the heck! Good to see you!* They will have the advantage of me, it's my face on the poster. My smile will be welcoming, my mind frantic as I scramble through the past, trying to locate their names.

Really it's Cordelia I expect, Cordelia I want to see. There are things I need to ask her. Not what happened, back then in the time I lost, because now I know that. I need to ask her why.

If she remembers. Perhaps she's forgotten the bad things, what she said to me, what she did. Or she does remember them, but in a minor way, as if remembering a game, or a single prank, a single trivial secret, of the kind girls tell and then forget.

She will have her own version. I am not the centre of her story, because she herself is that. But I could give her something you can never have, except from another person: what you look like from outside. A reflection. This is the part of herself I could give back to her.

We are like the twins in old fables, each of whom has been given half a key.

*   *   *

Cordelia will walk towards me through the opening crowd, a woman of wavering age, dressed in Irish tweed of a muted green, mother-of-pearl earrings circled with gold, beautiful shoes; well-groomed, soignée as they used to say. Taking care of herself, as I am. Her hair will be gently frosted, her smile quizzical. I won't know who she is.

There are a lot of women in this room, several other painters, some rich people. Mostly it's the rich people Charna drags over. I shake their hands, watch their mouths move. Elsewhere I have more stamina for these things, these acts of self-exposure; I could brazen them out. But here I feel scraped naked.

In the gap between rich people, a young girl pushes her way through. She's a painter, it goes without saying, but she says it anyway. She's in a mini-skirt and tight leggings and flat clumpy black shoes with laces, her hair is shaved up the back the way my brother's used to be, a late forties square-boy's cut. She is post everything, she is what will come after *post*. She is what will come after me.

"I loved your early work," she says. "*Falling Women*, I loved that. I mean, it sort of summed up an era, didn't it?" She doesn't mean to be cruel, she doesn't know she's just relegated me to the dust-heap along with crank telephones and whalebone stays. In former days I would have said something annihilating to her, some scabby, scalding remark, but I can't think of anything right off the bat. I'm out of training, I'm losing my nerve. In any case, what purpose would it serve? Her past-tense admiration is sincere. I should be gracious. I stand there, my grin turning to stone, institutionalized. Eminence creeps like gangrene up my legs.

"I'm glad," I manage. When in doubt, lie through your teeth. I'm lucky I still have teeth to lie through.

I'm standing back to the wall, with a new, full glass of wine. I crane my neck, peering through the crowd, over the well-arranged heads: it's time for Cordelia to appear, but she has not appeared. Disappointment is building in me, and impatience; and then anxiety. She must have set out, in this direction. Something must have happened to her on the way here.

This goes on while I shake more hands and say more things, and the room gradually clears.

"That went off very well," says Charna, with a sigh, of relief I think. "You were wonderful." She's happy because I haven't bitten anyone or spilled my drink down their legs, or otherwise acted like an artist. "How about dinner, with all of us?"

"No," I say. "No thank you. I'm bone tired. I think I'll just go back." I look around once more: Cordelia is not here.

Bone tired, an old phrase, of my mother's. Though bones as such do not get tired. They're strong, they have a lot of stamina; they can go on for years and years, after the rest of the body has quit.

I'm headed for a future in which I sprawl propped in a wheelchair, shedding hair and drooling, while some young stranger spoons mushed food into my mouth and I stand in the snow under the bridge, and stand and stand. While Cordelia vanishes and vanishes.

I go out, into the sidewalk twilight, outside the gallery. I want to take a taxi, but I can barely lift my hand.

I've been prepared for almost anything; except absence, except silence.

73

I take a taxi back to the studio, climb the four flights of stairs, dimly lit as they are at night, resting on the landings. I listen to my heart, going dull and fast in there under the layers of cloth. A flawed heart, in decline. I shouldn't have drunk all that wine. It's cold here, they've been skimping on the heat. The sound of my breath comes to me, a disembodied gasping, as if it's someone else breathing.

Cordelia has a tendency to exist.

I fumble the key into the keyhole, grope for the light-switch. I could do without all the fake body parts around here. I make my way to the kitchenette, shambling a little, keeping my coat on because of the cold.

Coffee is what I need. I make some, wrap my hands around the warm cup, carry it to the workbench, clearing a space for my elbows among the wire and sharp-edged tools. Tomorrow I'm out of this city, and not a moment too soon. There's too much old time here.

So, Cordelia. Got you back.

Never pray for justice, because you might get some.

I drink my coffee, holding the shaking cup, hot liquid slopping down my chin. It's a good thing I'm not in a restaurant. It isn't chic for women to be drunk. Men drunks are more excusable, more easily absolved, but why? It must be thought they have better reasons.

I wipe my arm with the coat-sleeve across my face, which is wet because I'm crying. This is the kind of thing I should look out for: crying without reason, making a spectacle of myself. I feel it's a spectacle, even though no one's watching.

You're dead, Cordelia.

No I'm not.

Yes you are. You're dead.

Lie down.

710

XV
Bridge

74

I'm light-headed, as if convalescing. I slept rolled up in the duvet, still in my black dress, which I did not have the energy to take off. I woke at noon, with a large, cottony skull, pulsing with hangover, to discover I'd missed my plane. It's a long time since I've drunk that much of anything. As with many things, I should know better.

Now it's late afternoon. The sky is soft and grey, low, damp and blurred like wet blotting paper. The day feels vacant, as if everyone has moved out of it; as if there's nothing more to come.

I pace along the sidewalk, away from the demolished school. My old direction, I could still do it blindfold. As always on these streets I feel disliked.

Down below me is the bridge. From here it looks neutral. I stand at the top of the hill, take a breath. Then I start down.

It's surprising how little has changed. The houses on either side are the same, although the muddy path is gone: in its place is a neat little hand-railing, a trim cement walk. The smell of the fallen leaves is still here, the burning smell of their slow decay, but the nightshade vines with their purple flowers and red blood-drop berries and the weeds and random debris have been cleared away, and everything is pruned and civic.

Nevertheless there's a rustling, a rank undertone of cats and their huntings and furtive scratchings, still going on behind the deceptive tidiness. Another, wilder and more tangled landscape rising up, from beneath the surface of this one.

We remember through smells, as dogs do.

The willow trees overhanging the path are the same. Although they've grown, I've grown also, so the distance between us remains constant. The bridge itself is different, of course; it's made of concrete and lighted up at night, not wooden and falling apart and rotten-smelling. Nevertheless it's the same bridge.

Stephen's jar of light is buried down there somewhere.

At this time of year the day darkens early. It's silent, no voices of children; only the monotonous cawing of a crow, and behind it the sea-sound of distant traffic. I rest my arms on the concrete wall and look down through the bare branches that are like dry coral. I used to think that if I jumped over, it would not be like falling, it would be more like diving; that if I died that way it would be soft, like drowning. Though far below, on the ground, there's a pumpkin, tossed over and smashed open, looking unpleasantly like a head.

The ravine is more filled in with bushes and trees than it used to be. In among them is the creek, running with clear water unsafe to drink. They've cleaned up the junk, the rusted car parts and discarded tyres; this is no longer an unofficial garbage dump but a joggers' route. The neatly gravelled runners' path beneath me leads uphill to the distant road and to the cemetery, where the dead people wait, forgetting themselves atom by atom, melting away like icicles, flowing downhill into the river.

That was where I fell into the water, there is the bank where I scrambled up. That's where I stood, with the snow falling on me, unable to summon the will to move. That's where I heard the voice.

There was no voice. No one came walking on air down from the bridge, there was no lady in a dark cloak bending over me. Although she has come back to me now in absolute clarity, acute in every detail, the outline of her hooded shape against the lights from the bridge, the red of her heart from within the cloak, I know this didn't happen. There was only darkness and silence. Nobody and nothing.

There's a sound: a shoe against loose rock.

It's time to go back. I push away from the cement wall, and the sky moves sideways.

I know that if I turn, right now, and look ahead of me along the path, someone will be standing there. At first I think it will be myself, in my old jacket, my blue knitted hat. But then I see that it's Cordelia. She's standing halfway up the hill, gazing back

714

over her shoulder. She's wearing her grey snowsuit jacket but the hood is back, her head is bare. She has the same green wool kneesocks, sloppily down around her ankles, the brown school brogues scuffed at the toes, one lace broken and knotted, the yellowish-brown hair with the bangs falling into her eyes, the eyes grey-green.

It's cold, colder. I can hear the rustle of the sleet, the water moving under the ice.

I know she's looking at me, the lopsided mouth smiling a little, the face closed and defiant. There is the same shame, the sick feeling in my body, the same knowledge of my own wrongness, awkwardness, weakness; the same wish to be loved; the same loneliness; the same fear. But these are not my own emotions any more. They are Cordelia's; as they always were.

I am the older one now, I'm the stronger. If she stays here any longer she will freeze to death; she will be left behind, in the wrong time. It's almost too late.

I reach out my arms to her, bend down, hands open to show I have no weapon. *It's all right*, I say to her. *You can go home now.*

The snow in my eyes withdraws like smoke.

When I turn, finally, Cordelia is no longer there. Only a middle-aged woman, pink-cheeked and bareheaded, coming down the hill towards me, in jeans and a heavy white pullover, with a dog on a green leash, a terrier. She passes me smiling, a civil, neutral smile.

There's nothing more for me to see. The bridge is only a bridge, the river a river, the sky is a sky. This landscape is empty now, a place for Sunday runners. Or not empty: filled with whatever it is by itself, when I'm not looking.

715

75

I'm on the plane, flying or being flown, westward towards the watery coast, the postcard mountains. Ahead of me, out the window, the sun sinks in a murderous, vulgar, unpaintable and glorious display of red and purple and orange; behind me the ordinary night rolls forward. Down on the ground the prairies unscroll, vast and mundane and plausible as hallucinations, dusted already with snow and scrawled with sinuous rivers.

I have the window seat. In the two seats beside me are two old ladies, old women, each with a knitted cardigan, each with yellowy-white hair and thick-lensed glasses with a chain for around the neck, each with a desiccated mouth lipsticked bright red with bravado. They have their trays lowered and are drinking tea and playing Snap, fumbling the slippery cards, laughing like cars on gravel when they cheat or make mistakes. From time to time they get up, unbuckling themselves laboriously, and hobble to the back of the plane, to smoke cigarettes and line up for the washroom. When they return they make bathroom jokes, quips about wetting your pants and running out of toilet paper, eyeing me cunningly while they do so. I wonder how old they think they are, underneath the disguise of their bodies; or how old they think I am. Perhaps, to them, I look like their mother.

They seem to me amazingly carefree. They have saved up for this trip and they are damn well going to enjoy it, despite the arthritis of one, the swollen legs of the other. They're rambunctious, they're full of beans; they're tough as thirteen, they're innocent and dirty, they don't give a hoot. Responsibilities have fallen away from them, obligations, old hates and grievances; now for a short while they can play again like children, but this time without the pain.

This is what I miss, Cordelia: not something that's gone, but something that will never happen. Two old women giggling over their tea.

*   *   *

716

Now it's full night, clear, moonless and filled with stars, which are not eternal as was once thought, which are not where we think they are. If they were sounds, they would be echoes, of something that happened millions of years ago: a word made of numbers. Echoes of light, shining out of the midst of nothing.

It's old light, and there's not much of it. But it's enough to see by.